May 1895

Lizzie's confident ⋯⋯ that she would find out what had happened to Ann cou⋯ ⋯t reassure Amy, much as she longed to believe it. She told Lizzie the little she could about Mrs Crossley, but she returned to Charlie's house low-spirited and dejected.

There was no use giving into morbid thoughts, and her life had no room for the luxury of self-pity. But her mind kept returning to the fate of that tiny baby. Where was she? What had become of her? The nagging fears troubled her sleep each night, making the days seem long and weary.

It was difficult enough to do her work and keep Charlie in the best temper he was capable of; protecting Malcolm from the consequences of his own foolishness was an added burden, and one that was becoming heavier. More and more often David came home from school by himself, with Malcolm arriving some time later usually grubby and breathless. 'With my mates' was all the reply she could get out of him when she asked where he had been, and with his next school examination many months away any attempt at frightening him into going to school more regularly was useless.

'Your father's going to find out one of these days,' was the worst threat Amy could muster, but Malcolm brushed her warnings aside.

'No, he won't,' he said, with a confidence Amy was sure was misplaced. 'He doesn't know if I'm at school or not.'

The day she had dreaded came not long after the revelation of the baby farming scandal. David arrived home on his own again.

'Where's Mal?' Amy asked, more out of habit than in the hope of a useful answer.

'He'll be home soon,' David said, and Amy let it rest at that. She devoted a few minutes to helping David go over the words he had been given for spelling practice, and he soon had them off pat.

'That's good, Dave,' she told him. 'You're getting on really well at school, aren't you?'

'Am I?' David beamed at her praise, then grimaced. 'I don't like Miss Metcalf. She just growls all the time. Even when you do good she doesn't say anything, just doesn't growl as much.'

'Well, I bet she doesn't find much to growl a clever boy like you about.' Out of habit, Amy glanced over her shoulder for any sight of Charlie before drawing David close for a forbidden hug. 'You make me

3

very proud, the way you're such a good boy.'

David put his arms around her neck and gave her a wet kiss. 'I like being with you, Ma. You never growl. Not like Pa—he's always grumpy. I'm scared of him sometimes.'

'Your father's only hard on you when he thinks you need it,' Amy said. 'You mustn't be frightened of him. He loves you, really.'

'Does he?' David sounded dubious. 'I wish I could go out with Mal. He says he has fun with his mates.'

Amy held him more tightly. 'Please don't, Davie. Don't get in trouble with your father.'

'But Mal says it's *fun*. School's not fun.'

'Please, Davie,' Amy pleaded. 'Please don't.' She felt tears starting from her eyes.

'Don't cry, Ma,' David said, distressed. 'I don't want you to cry.'

Amy forced herself to smile. 'I'm not crying, see? Not with my good boy to keep me company.' She gave David a last kiss before returning to her baking.

The time went quickly with David prattling away about his day. As she worked, Amy listened for the sound of hooves that would mean Malcolm had come home, but the hands of the clock turned inexorably with no sign of his return. He had never been this late before. Today he might not get home before Charlie came in for his afternoon tea.

She heard steps too heavy to be Malcolm's coming up to the porch, and knew her disquiet had been justified. 'That's your father. You'd better go outside or he'll ask where Mal is. Get Biff off the chain and take him for a walk.'

Amy hurried David through into the parlour, from where he could get out the front door unnoticed by his father, then made an effort to appear calm as Charlie came into the kitchen. She needed all her wits about her to try and protect Malcolm; instead she felt dull with the heaviness of spirit that had hung over her ever since she had been caught by the fear her daughter might be dead.

Charlie looked tired. He had been moving the cows to another paddock across ground made soft by the wintry weather, and their hooves had churned the pasture into a boggy mess. His trousers and boots were caked with mud. He slumped into his chair and took hold of the cup of hot tea Amy placed in front of him, grabbing at a scone with his free hand. Weariness made Charlie more taciturn than usual, but did not normally improve his temper.

She refilled his cup when he finished it, and buttered more scones as the plate grew empty, all the time listening for Malcolm's return. When she caught the sound of hoof beats she was momentarily relieved; then she heard wheels. It was not Malcolm, but someone driving a single-horse carriage.

Amy got to the door before a loud rap sounded, and opened it to reveal a grim-faced Miss Metcalf. The teacher all but pushed past her before Amy had the chance to invite her in. She stood in front of Charlie and glared down at him.

'Mr Stewart, it's not good enough,' she announced to a dumbfounded Charlie. 'I've turned a blind eye to this for quite long enough. It's to stop.'

Charlie turned to Amy. 'What's she on about?'

'What's wrong, Miss Metcalf?' Amy asked. 'Is it something to do with the boys?' Or, more precisely, something to do with Malcolm. It must be Malcolm.

'Now, I know you farmers need your sons' help from time to time,' Miss Metcalf said, ignoring Amy. 'As I say, I've turned a blind eye. An odd day here and there when you're particularly busy, that's easily overlooked. But not the way you're carrying on with that son of yours. Mr Stewart, do you know how many days Malcolm has come to school in the last two weeks?'

She answered her own question without giving him time to reply. 'Three,' she announced. 'Three days in two weeks! I have to warn you, I'm not putting up with it any longer. There are laws in this country, Mr Stewart—laws that say you have to send your children to school, farm work or no farm work. If you continue flouting the law, I shall have to report it to the authorities.'

Charlie gazed at her, open-mouthed, then turned back to Amy. 'Is she saying the boy hasn't been going to school? Where the hell's he been, then?'

'Oh, don't try pretending ignorance, Mr Stewart,' Miss Metcalf said. 'That won't cut any ice with me. I expect to see that boy at school regularly from now on.' She swept out of the house, her skirts swishing as she went.

Charlie sat in stunned silence for a few moments. 'What's he been up to?' he demanded of Amy when he had recovered his voice. 'Where's he been going?'

'Charlie, don't get upset—Miss Metcalf's probably making it sound worse than it is. I don't think she likes Mal.'

'I'll teach that boy to go making a fool of me. I'll not have that woman coming into my house lecturing me. Sneak off behind my back, will he? I'll give him a lesson he'll remember.'

'Don't, Charlie,' Amy said, trying desperately to think of excuses for Malcolm. If only Charlie did not make such a fuss over the merest trifles, and if only Malcolm did not give him so many occasions for wrath. She vaguely remembered a few occasions when her own father had found that Harry had played truant; a few strokes of his belt and a stern warning not to do it again, along with ill-concealed amusement at Harry's cheek in thinking he could get away with it, and the matter was over. It was never like that with Charlie.

Charlie crossed the room and flung open the back door. 'Where is he?' While Amy was still trying to think how to tell him that she had no idea just where Malcolm was, a sudden bark betrayed the whereabouts of David and Biff.

'Dave! Get in here,' Charlie shouted. Amy stood behind him and peered around his arm to see David dragging his feet towards the house, Biff prancing excitedly at his heels. 'Hurry up,' Charlie called. 'You can leave that mongrel outside, too.'

David tied Biff up, taking much longer over the task than he needed to, and walked up to the back door.

'Where's your brother?' Charlie asked, looking back in the direction David had come from.

'He'll be back soon,' David said, his eyes darting around as if looking for an escape route.

'Back? What are you talking about? You mean he's not here? Where is he, then?'

'He'll be back soon,' David repeated like one reciting a well-learned lesson.

'Don't keep saying the same thing like a bloody parrot,' Charlie growled. He snatched David by the lower arm and yanked the boy up the steps and into the kitchen, then leaned his face close. 'Where's your brother?'

David looked dangerously close to tears, but Amy resisted the urge to intervene, knowing she would only make Charlie angrier. 'I-I don't know. He didn't tell me where he was going.'

With his penchant for getting into strife, Malcolm chose that moment to rush in the door, breathless from having run up from the horse paddock and with his clothes far grubbier than a day at school could have made them. His eyes widened in alarm at finding his father in the house. For a moment he seemed undecided whether to make a run for it or to try and brazen it out, but Charlie soon took the choice out of his hands.

He let go of David, leaving the boy to rub his sore arm where Charlie

6

had held it in a vice-like grip, and took hold of Malcolm by both shoulders. 'Where the hell have you been?'

'At s-school,' Malcolm said, his eyes darting over to meet David's, obviously trying to guess how much his brother might have told their father.

The back of Charlie's hand lashed against Malcolm's face. 'Lie to me, will you?' Charlie snarled. 'Think you can make a fool of me and get away with it?'

'He only told a lie because he's scared, Charlie,' Amy said. 'Let him say he's sorry. You're sorry, aren't you, Mal?'

'I'll make him sorry, all right,' Charlie said before Malcolm had the chance to say a word. 'You needn't think you can go sneaking off behind my back. You little bugger!'

He gave Malcolm a shove that sent the boy staggering backwards, then grabbed him by the arm and pulled him upright just in time to stop him falling to the floor. 'I'll teach you a lesson you'll not be forgetting in a hurry, boy,' Charlie growled. 'I'll have the skin off your backside before I'm finished with you.'

'Don't, Charlie,' Amy pleaded. 'He won't do it again, will you, Mal? Let him tell you he's sorry.'

'You keep out of it, woman,' said Charlie. 'He'll be sorry enough in a minute.' He turned towards the door, about to drag Malcolm outside, when the boy wrenched his arm out of Charlie's grip.

'I'm *not* sorry,' Malcolm said, his face screwed up in a mixture of anger and threatened tears. 'Why should I have to go that school? Why can't I do what I want?'

A tide of scarlet engulfed Charlie's face. 'You'll do as I tell you, boy.'

Malcolm stamped his foot. 'I *won't*,' he screamed. 'I'm sick of doing what you say. I'm sick of the way you hit me all the time.'

'Mal, don't talk to your father like that,' Amy said, but Charlie and Malcolm had eyes and ears only for each other. Amy had never seen them looking more alike, both red-faced and panting with fury, despite the twelve inches of height and more than forty years of age between them. David crept over to her, fear written in his face. Amy slipped an arm around him and drew him close.

'You never let me do what I want,' Malcolm half-shouted, half-sobbed. 'You never want me to have any fun. You just make me work all the time. You never say I'm any good at anything. And you give me hidings for just nothing.'

'I'll give you a hiding, all right, boy.' Charlie made a grab for Malcolm, but the boy stepped backwards out of his reach.

'I'm sick of milking stupid cows and digging stupid potatoes and all that stuff.' He flung the words at his father. 'I'm sick of your stupid farm.'

Charlie took a long stride forward, snaked his arm around Malcolm's neck and grabbed him by the scruff. He dragged the boy a step towards the door, then stopped in his tracks when Malcolm swung his fist with all his might and planted it in his father's midriff.

Malcolm might be only nine years old, but he was big and strong for his age. He put his whole weight behind the punch, and it winded Charlie long enough for Malcolm to twist once again out of his grasp.

'I hate this place!' he screamed at his father. 'I hate you! I hate you!'

It took Charlie only seconds to recover. He let out a snarl and lunged at Malcolm, this time grabbing a fistful of cloth at his throat. He gave the boy a shove, keeping his tight grip, and Malcolm staggered backwards. He shoved again, giving the boy no time to regain his balance; then again, slamming Malcolm's back against the wall. 'You'll not raise a hand to me, boy.' He yanked Malcolm forward, then pushed him back so that his head hit the wall with a thump, while Charlie's free hand made a fist and slammed into Malcolm's face.

Malcolm screamed in mingled pain and rage. He swung out wildly with his own fists, but his father's long reach defeated him and his blows fell well short of their target. Again and again Charlie slammed the boy's head against the wall, punctuating the rhythmic back-and-forward motion with his well-aimed punches, shouting incoherently above Malcolm's screams.

David clutched at Amy, howling in terror. She freed herself from his grip to snatch at Charlie's sleeve. 'Stop it,' she cried. 'He's only a little boy! You'll kill him!' But Charlie was oblivious to her. When she hauled on his arm he stopped hitting Malcolm just long enough to shake her off, hardly seeming to notice the interruption.

Amy knew she did not have the strength to pull him away from Malcolm. She ran to the bench where she had a saucepan of carrots sitting in cold water ready to be put on the range, snatched up the pan, crossed the room again and flung the contents at Charlie.

He let out a yell as the cold water hit him full in the face. The shock had the desired effect. He loosed his hold long enough for Malcolm to free himself, stagger a few steps away out of his father's reach, then sink to the floor and lean against the wall, clutching at his head. Charlie coughed and spluttered, spat out water and a slice of carrot, then turned on Amy.

'What the hell did you do that for, you silly bitch? I'm covered in this muck!'

In other circumstances Amy might have found the sight laughable: Charlie with bits of carrot stuck in his hair and beard and festooned over his sodden jacket, water dripping down his face. But right now, concern for Malcolm filled her thoughts.

'To stop you from killing your son,' she flung at him over her shoulder as she knelt down to check Malcolm's injuries.

'That'll teach him.' Two steps brought Charlie close enough to stand over Malcolm and glower down at him. 'You won't try that again, will you, boy?' But a glance told Amy that the heat had gone out of his rage, cooled abruptly by the icy shower she had given him.

Malcolm's face showed the beginnings of a black eye, one lip was split, and blood was running freely from his nose, but rather than looking chastened he matched his father's glare with one of his own. Amy put her handkerchief under his nose and made Malcolm hold it in place while she checked the back of his head for wounds.

'The skin's not broken,' she said. 'There's a big lump coming up, though. You'd better lie down for the rest of the afternoon.'

'No, he's not,' said Charlie. 'He'll not be getting out of his work that way.'

'But Charlie, he should lie down in the dark after a knock on the head like that,' Amy protested. 'He's going to have an awful headache.'

'Serves him right. That'll help him remember what'll happen if he ever tries that again.' He took his seat at the table. 'Stop fussing over him, woman, and brew up a fresh pot of tea. This lot's stone cold now.' He picked a piece of carrot out of his beard. 'And you can get me a cloth to wipe this lot off.'

'Can I just clean Mal up a bit first?'

'No, you can't. That can wait until you've fetched my tea. I'll have another of those scones, too.' He stared at Malcolm, who still sat slumped against the wall. 'Get up off the floor, boy. You can sit at the table and wait till I've had a bite. You too—and you can stop that bawling,' he told David. 'Don't stand there like a ninny,' he grumbled when the younger boy stood frozen, too frightened to move. 'Sit down and shut up, or you'll get a taste of the same as your brother.' David scrambled to sit down, staring at his father in wide-eyed fear.

Malcolm stood up gingerly, brushing aside Amy's arm when she tried to help him. He made his way safely, if a little unsteadily, to the table and sat down opposite David, dragging his chair as far away as he could from his father. The three of them sat in silence while Amy passed a clean dishcloth to Charlie, poured hot water into the teapot and buttered some scones, then carried the pot and plate to the table and took her own seat.

Charlie took a large bite out of a scone. 'Your ma thinks I would have killed you if she hadn't butted in,' he told Malcolm. 'She's maybe right—I might have.' He leaned forward to fix his son with a baleful stare. 'I'll tell you this, boy—you ever dare raise a hand to me again and I bloody will.'

Amy closed her eyes for a moment against the wave of nausea Charlie's words roused in her. *Don't talk like that. I've lost enough of my children. He's only a little boy.*

She looked over at Malcolm and thought about the punch he had managed to plant in Charlie's belly. That had not been the wild swing of a little boy; it had had strength and skill behind it. He might be only nine years old, but Malcolm's fighting had clearly got beyond minor schoolyard scuffles. Charlie's strength was that of a grown man, and his long reach gave him an advantage Malcolm could not hope to overcome. Not yet.

She watched as Malcolm stared back at his father, managing a look of naked hostility despite one eye's being half-closed by swelling. A trail of blood escaped through the handkerchief he held under his nose, and dripped onto his shirt. Malcolm wouldn't be nine years old for ever. He wouldn't always be smaller than his father. Amy studied Malcolm's expression more closely, and a cold knot formed in the pit of her stomach as she realised that Malcolm was thinking exactly the same thing.

'Are you sure, Frank?' Lizzie asked yet again, still doubtful after all Frank's assurances. 'Are you really sure it's no use just addressing a letter "Mrs Crossley, Auckland"?'

'Quite sure, Lizzie. It's not worth trying.'

'But if someone sent a letter to "Mrs Kelly, Ruatane" I'd get it all right. And look how many Leiths there are around here, but say if someone wrote just to "Mrs Leith, Ruatane" the right one'd get it sooner or later, even though it'd have to go around Ma and Aunt Susannah and Lily and all them. There can't be as many people as all that in Auckland, surely?'

'Lizzie,' Frank said patiently, 'you know how many houses there are in Ruatane?'

'Quite a lot, really, especially if you count all the farms. And there's two houses on Uncle Jack's farm, remember.'

Frank smiled fondly at her as she defended the status of the only town she had ever seen. 'All right, now try and imagine a hundred—no, maybe two hundred—towns like Ruatane all joined together. All those streets running into one another. Can you do that?'

'Not really.'

'No, it's not easy till you've seen it. That's what Auckland's like. I've been there twice now, and it still just about scared me silly trying to find my way around. If you sent a letter with no address but "Auckland", I think the people at the Post and Telegraph would just throw it in the rubbish.'

'Oh.' Lizzie was crestfallen, but only for a moment. 'Well, I'll just have to find out what her address is.'

'How are you going to do that?'

'Ask the only person around here who knows, of course. Amy said Mrs Crossley told her Aunt Susannah had been to visit her, so she must know the address. I'll go up to Uncle Jack's this afternoon when the girls are home from school to look after the little fellows.'

'Hey, hang on, Lizzie. Didn't you say Amy told you not to talk to your Aunt Susannah about it? You said she made a bit of a fuss when you suggested it.'

'Yes, she did. She got in quite a state over it—said she didn't want Aunt Susannah snooping into her affairs. I think she's worried Uncle Jack might find out about her getting so upset over this baby farming thing, too.'

'Then how can you ask Susannah?'

'I'm not going to tell Amy I've asked her! I'm not stupid, you know.'

'Do you think you should, Lizzie? After Amy telling you not to?'

'Of course I should. I have to get this woman's address, and Amy won't know how I found it out so she won't worry about it. It's all settled.'

Frank knew only too well the futility of trying to shift Lizzie from her chosen course of action. 'Well, just try not to get Susannah's back up too much. She might be a bit funny about it.'

'Oh, I'll be all meek and mild like butter wouldn't melt in my mouth. And there's no need for you to grin like an idiot, Frank Kelly!'

As soon as the three older children arrived home that afternoon Lizzie, who was a firm believer in the doctrine that the devil makes work for idle hands, marshalled them into their tasks.

'Now, you girls, there's a pile of spuds there for you to peel—I'll have them done properly, too, with all the eyes cut out, or there'll be trouble. And you can pull up a load of carrots and get them scraped and sliced. I'll do the meat and pudding when I get home. I want all the scraps cleared away—take them out to the pigs—the bench wiped down and the table set by the time I'm back. Are you pulling faces at me, Maudie?'

'No, Ma,' Maudie said, the scowl instantly wiped from her face.

'Good. Joey, you'll be out helping your pa, so that'll keep you out of mischief. You're not to come inside till I'm back, I don't want you getting in your sisters' way and helping yourself to biscuits. You girls see you keep a good eye on Mickey and Danny.'

'Want to go with Papa,' Mickey protested.

'What do you think, Frank?' Lizzie asked. 'Will he get in your way?'

'No, he'll be all right,' said Frank. 'He's a good little fellow, aren't you, Mickey?' Mickey beamed at him.

'Couldn't you take Danny with you, Ma?' Beth asked.

'No, I couldn't,' Lizzie said briskly. 'He's got too big now, and he wriggles. It's too awkward when I'm riding.'

'*Ma*,' Maudie complained. 'He'll be a little pest.'

'Don't talk about your baby brother like that. You should be pleased to look after him.'

'It's not fair,' Maudie grumbled. 'The boys get to go out with Pa, and we have to look after the pest—and do all the work, too.'

'Now, where's that belt?' Lizzie mused aloud. 'The one I use on girls who complain all the time.'

Maudie made a show of hurrying over to the bench and picking a potato from the mountain Lizzie had ready for her. 'I'm not complaining, Ma.'

'I'm pleased to hear it. Right, I'll be back as soon as I can.' Lizzie delivered kisses all round, with Frank giving her a pat on the bottom that he naively imagined none of the children noticed. He followed her out the back door to help her mount the horse and waved as she rode away.

'You boys ready to come and give me a hand?' he asked when he went back inside. 'We'd better get on with it.'

'Hurry up, Beth,' said Maudie. 'You have to help with these vegies, you know. Pull a chair over so you can reach the bench. Get a move on,' she said, tapping one foot impatiently as Beth dragged at a stool.

'Hey, don't give your sister a hard time, eh, love?' Frank said. 'She's going as fast as she can.' He took the stool from Beth and carried it for her, then lifted her onto it.

'I *have* to hurry her up, Pa,' said Maudie. 'She forgets what she's meant to be doing otherwise. She gets daydreaming—Miss Metcalf's always going on at her for it.'

Beth looked guilty. 'I don't mean to.'

'Well, there's nothing wrong with a bit of dreaming,' Frank said, and Beth turned her soft gaze on him in a smile. The little girl's eyes were a shade somewhere between brown and green, and it could not be denied that they tended to have a dreamy expression. Frank was not in the habit of staring at himself in mirrors; if he was, he might have recognised Beth's eyes as the image of his own.

'It doesn't get the work done, does it?' Maudie said. 'And Ma'll be wild if we don't get it all finished. You know what she's like. She's *so* bossy,' she added in a long-suffering tone.

'Now, Maudie, don't talk about your ma like that,' Frank chided. 'You couldn't ask for a better mother than you've got.' He chose not to hear Maudie's muttered response, though he had to hide a smile at her wounded expression. She was so very like her mother, but Frank suspected she would never become quite as adept at getting her own way. Unlike Lizzie, she did not have a vague, easy-going mother to hone her skills on.

It did not enter Lizzie's head to knock on the door of the house that had been her second home all through childhood. In the kitchen Sophie was lifting a tray of scones from the range while two-year-old Andrew helped himself to raisins from a jar on the table. She looked up at Lizzie's entry and regarded her in mild surprise.

'Keeping well, are you, Sophie?' Lizzie asked.

'Mmm.'

Making conversation with Sophie was always something of a challenge; even Lizzie, who was not usually worried by one-sided conversations, found her heavy going.

'You're looking well,' she remarked. Sophie patted the bulge of her latest pregnancy and smiled at Lizzie, but said nothing.

'Andrew's growing, isn't he?' Lizzie tried.

'Yes,' Sophie agreed, eyeing her son proudly.

'And Boy will be starting school this year, won't he?'

'That's right.'

'Good.' Having exhausted the range of polite conversation, Lizzie turned her attention to her real object. 'Where's Aunt Susannah?'

Sophie frowned in thought. 'In the parlour. Doing fancy-work.' She looked doubtfully at Lizzie. 'Jane's home.'

Lizzie gave a short laugh. 'Yes, I know Jane'd be better company. But it's Madam I want to see, believe it or not. Thanks, Sophie, I know the way.'

Susannah looked up from her needlework and raised her eyebrows on seeing who her visitor was.

'Well, Mrs Kelly! What an unexpected pleasure. Sophie's in the kitchen,' she said, returning her attention to her embroidery.

'It's you I've come to see, not Sophie.'

'Really? I suppose I should be flattered.' Susannah craned her neck to peer past Lizzie. 'You haven't brought any of your children, have you?'

'No, they're all at home, so you needn't look so worried.' Without waiting to be asked, Lizzie took a seat.

Susannah made to rise. 'I'll tell Sophie to make us a pot of tea, then.'

'Don't worry about me. Sophie's up to her elbows in baking, I don't want to put her out.'

'Sophie seems to enjoy that sort of thing,' Susannah said. 'Baking and scrubbing and looking after children. Of course, she was brought up to that style of life. Well, what do you want?'

'It's Amy. I'm worried about her.'

Susannah looked startled. 'What's wrong with her? Is she sick?'

'Sick in the heart, maybe,' said Lizzie. 'It's about that trouble she had before she got married.'

Susannah's expression tightened, and she gripped her embroidery hoop more firmly. 'Whatever do you mean, bringing all that up again? It's all behind Amy now, you've no business stirring it up when she's nicely settled.'

'Oh, yes, very nicely,' Lizzie retorted. 'A nice way to be settled, stuck with a grumpy old so-and-so like him. And we all know whose idea *that* was, don't we?'

Susannah fixed her with a steely gaze. 'I don't intend debating the matter with you, Miss Lizzie. I don't see that it's any of your business, anyway. He was the best she could get, and she jumped at the chance.'

'Jumped at it! Crawled into it, more likely,' Lizzie shot back. 'Because you made her. Oh, she's never said it in so many words, but I know you twisted her arm to make her do it. Just because you wanted her out of the way so Uncle Jack would forget about what your brother did.'

'Be quiet!' Susannah hissed at her. Both hands jerked outwards to grip the arms of her chair, and her embroidery tumbled from her lap to the floor. 'I'm not going to listen to an interfering little madam like you telling me what you think of me. Why is it your concern who Amy married, anyway?'

'Because I love her! I'd have done anything to make Amy happy. Not like you—you didn't care what happened to her as long as she was out of the way. You didn't care how he'd treat her.'

'And what would you have had me do? Keep her at home for ever with a bastard child? Having her know everyone in town was calling her a whore behind her back? At least I found her a husband. He mightn't be much, but he put a ring on her finger. It's easy for you to spout a lot of fine words about loving her—I didn't notice you offering to give her your precious Frank.'

'What?' Lizzie gaped at her, anger driven out by astonishment. 'I-I couldn't have done that!'

'Why not?' Susannah pounced. 'I thought you said you'd have done anything for her. That didn't include finding her a husband, did it? You left that job to me, and then you've the impertinence to tell me you don't like my choice. Why didn't you do it for her, then? I'm sure your wonderful Frank would have treated Amy as nicely as you claim you wanted for her.'

Lizzie was not used to being on the back foot. 'How could I have done that?' she asked, an uncharacteristic quaver in her voice. 'I couldn't have made Frank marry her, even if I'd...' She broke off without completing the sentence. She hadn't wanted to. The thought had never entered her head. It was a ridiculous idea... or was it?

'Couldn't you? Really? I must say, from the way people speak about Frank I'd got the impression you could make him do anything you liked. I don't see that it would have been so hard to talk him into marrying Amy instead of you, not an easy-going fellow like your Frank. It was no use my even thinking of trying to win him around at the time, not when you had him well and truly in your clutches, but I'm sure you could have done it if you'd wanted. He might even have taken in her child as well. After all, men always seemed to think Amy was terribly pretty—much prettier than you, certainly. She and Frank would have made a rather nice-looking couple, don't you think?'

Lizzie's mouth hung open as she tried to absorb the notion that she should have given up Frank to Amy. She stared down at the square of carpet, then turned back to meet Susannah's eyes.

It was the look of satisfaction on Susannah's face that brought Lizzie back to her usual good sense with a bump. 'What a load of rubbish!' she said in disgust. 'You've never even thought of Frank marrying Amy till just this minute—you just said it to upset me.'

'Oh, yes, you would say that, wouldn't you? Much easier to pretend it's all my fault.'

'I know what you said to Amy when you made her marry Charlie—some of the things you said, anyway. You went on and on about how no one else would want her, only a grumpy old man like Charlie. And now you're making out Frank would've married her if I'd just said the word. You can't have it both ways, you know. You're just a nasty old… old battleaxe,' she said, swallowing the riper abuse that hovered on her tongue. 'You can't stand seeing anyone else happy, can you? Just because you're such an old misery, you want everyone else to be miserable too.'

'How dare you speak to me in that fashion? You can leave my house this minute.' Susannah stood up, drawing herself to her full, impressive height, and pointed to the door in a dramatic gesture.

Lizzie stood to face her, unaware of the contrast between Susannah's tall, angular form and her own well-rounded one. She had to tilt her head up to meet Susannah's eyes. 'I'm not going until you tell me what I need to know. I want—'

'Do you think I'm going to listen to a little baggage like you abusing me? Get out of my house.'

'No!' Lizzie shouted. 'Just shut up a minute and let me say—'

'I won't listen for another—' Susannah stopped speaking, and turned to face the door. 'What do you want?'

Lizzie followed her gaze and saw Sophie standing in the doorway, a frightened expression on her face. Little Andrew clutched his mother's skirts and peered nervously around her, his mouth wreathed in jam.

'You all right?' Sophie asked, her eyes flicking from Susannah to Lizzie. 'I heard a bit of a fuss.'

'Yes, yes, we're quite all right,' Susannah said with an impatient wave of her hand. 'You can go away, Sophie.' Sophie hoisted Andrew on to one hip and went obediently, casting an anxious glance over her shoulder.

Susannah followed their retreating forms with a disapproving gaze. 'Such a grubby child,' she murmured. 'He seems to attract dirt like a magnet. I'm sure neither of my boys ever got into the state he does.'

She turned back to Lizzie, but the fire had gone out of her mood. She managed no more than a look that combined languor and hostility. 'Go away,' she said, resuming her chair and retrieving her embroidery from the floor.

'Not just yet.' Lizzie sat down once again opposite Susannah, and stared back undaunted when Susannah glared at her. 'All I want is for you to tell me something about what happened to Amy.'

'Oh, for Heaven's sake! Are you going to sit there all day going on about that? I've the most frightful headache coming on, too. I told you, that's all behind Amy. It's high time you forgot about it—I'm sure she must have by now.'

'I thought it was all behind her, too,' Lizzie admitted. 'But it isn't. And she hasn't forgotten anything. And now with this business in the papers—'

'What on earth are you going on about?' Susannah interrupted. 'What have the newspapers got to do with Amy?'

'This baby farming thing, of course. Amy's got it into her head that the woman she gave her baby to was like that one down south. She's going on about giving her baby away to be buried in the garden, and all that. I need to—'

She stopped abruptly at the expression on Susannah's face. She had thought the older woman was angry before; now she saw her white-faced with cold rage.

'Is that what you think of me?' Susannah said, her voice so quiet it was barely audible, but far more full of fury than her earlier shouts had been. 'You hate me so much that you think I'd do something like that? You actually think I gave Amy's baby to a murderess? A helpless child—my husband's grandchild—and you accuse me of that?'

Up till this moment Lizzie had not thought beyond Amy. It had simply not occurred to her to muse on Susannah's guilt or lack of it. Now she studied the question for a few moments and came to a rapid conclusion: Susannah might be selfish and ill-natured, but she was not capable of that atrocity.

'No, I don't think you did,' Lizzie said. 'I think you probably thought you were doing it for the best—to tell you the truth, back then *I* thought it was best for Amy to give the baby away.'

Susannah looked somewhat mollified. 'When I think of the trouble I went to over that business,' she said in a hurt voice. 'Getting Constance to find a suitable woman, going to see the woman myself to check that she seemed satisfactory—and the *money* your Uncle Jack had to pay for her to look after the baby. And all that time having to keep it secret from Mother and Father—I was never quite sure that Constance wouldn't go telling Mother, just to cause trouble.' She looked at Lizzie with a small gleam of triumph in her eyes. 'I told Constance it was you. I said it was my husband's niece who'd got in trouble, and I was doing them a favour by getting you sorted out. "Poor Elizabeth, she's rather a simple sort of girl."'

If Susannah was hoping for a bite from Lizzie, she was disappointed. The notion that people she had never met, and almost certainly never would meet, might think badly of her was not likely to trouble Lizzie. She shrugged and turned back to the real issue.

'Anyway, what matters is how Amy feels about all this. Like I said, she's got it into her head that this Mrs Crossley woman's done away with the baby—now, you know and I know that it hasn't happened,' she said quickly to forestall a fresh outburst, 'and if she was feeling herself Amy would know it too. But she's got into a state over it, and the only way she's going to come right is if I can convince her some way or other that the baby's all right.'

'And how do you propose to do that?' Susannah asked.

'I figured it out.' There seemed no need to explain that it had been Frank's idea to try and contact Mrs Crossley; Lizzie thought it for the best that no one in the family found out just how much she had told Frank about Amy's 'bit of trouble'. 'I thought if I wrote to the woman who took the baby and got a decent sort of reply from her, that'd put Amy's mind at rest. I mean, the woman wouldn't answer if she was a baby farmer, would she? She'd have run off somewhere by now with all the money.'

Susannah stood and began pacing restively about the room. 'I think you should leave well enough alone. It seems ridiculous, bringing up all that old trouble. Tell Amy she should pull herself together—making such a fuss over it all! Goodness me, hasn't she enough to keep her busy without dwelling on the past? She's got a house and a husband, and two children—that's all you farm girls want, isn't it? What's wrong with her, brooding like that?'

With an effort, Lizzie spoke in a restrained voice. 'Do you know what Amy's had to put up with from him over the years?'

Susannah gave her a look of distaste. 'Of course I do. I'm a married woman myself, you know. I rather think that sort of thing worries you farm girls less than it does someone of… more refined sensibilities, shall we say?'

'I'm not talking about the bedroom business—though I know Amy's never been very keen on that with him, either. Don't you know how he treats her?'

'I've seen bruises once or twice,' Susannah said. 'I told her she should be more careful not to annoy him. She should have sense enough to do that.'

'Bruises!' Lizzie echoed in disgust. 'I'm not talking about the odd slap or something. Didn't Uncle Jack tell you about that time Charlie just about killed her?'

'What?' Susannah stopped pacing and turned a shocked face to her. 'What are you talking about?'

'He punched her face so that you wouldn't have known it was her any more. It was all black and swollen, with a great big split in her lip and one eye so swelled up she couldn't see out of it. She could hardly walk for days, either. *I* think that's why she's never had any more babies—I think he messed up her insides with knocking her around like that so she can't carry them to term any more.'

'I… I never knew,' Susannah said faintly. 'There was one time… when did this happen?'

'Years ago now. Beth was only a little thing. It must have been four years back.'

'Yes,' Susannah said thoughtfully. 'There was a time… Jack got terribly sour for a while—he kept giving me the most dreadful looks and muttering away about fixing that… well, he used some shocking language. So that was it.'

'She's been living with a man like that for ten years now. Do you think it's any wonder if she broods? She hasn't got a lot to be cheerful about, has she? Amy's got enough on her plate, what with *him* and then Mal being such a little devil. All I want to do is take her mind off this latest trouble. Is that such a lot to ask?'

Susannah sat down heavily. 'Well… I don't know if I… oh, what is it you want me to do, then?'

Lizzie gave a sigh of relief. 'Tell me the woman's address,' she said, anxious to extract the information while Susannah's mood remained relatively soft. 'That's all I need you to do.'

'It's so long ago…' Susannah's brow creased in thought. 'I remember the place well enough. There were several children playing in the garden—rather grubby, I thought, but they looked well-fed. Such a noise they were making, laughing and jumping around. It was all I could do to keep Thomas and George from rushing out of the house to play with them. I could hardly let my sons mix with children like that.'

Lizzie nodded in agreement, and was abruptly horrified with herself. 'Children like that' meant children whose fathers did not acknowledge them. Children like Amy's baby.

'Hideous curtains the woman had in her parlour,' Susannah said. 'I remember them quite clearly.'

'What was the name of the street?' Lizzie prompted.

'Something to do with… with hair, I think. It wasn't a long way from town, as I recall. What was the name?' Susannah tapped one finger against the arm of the chair as she mused. 'Auburn!' she said triumphantly. 'That was the name of it! Auburn Street. It's no use asking me the number—I've no chance of remembering that after all this time. But I'm sure it wasn't a very long street.'

Lizzie was used to a town of barely a dozen small streets. 'Oh, that'll be enough of an address, I'm sure. Frank says it's a terrible big place,

Auckland—that's why I had to get the name of the street—but there can't be more than one Auburn Street.'

She shook her head at the memory of Frank's description of the city's vastness. 'It must be awful up there, all those people living on top of one another. You're lucky you got out of it, eh?'

'Lucky!' Susannah gave a bitter little laugh. 'If you call it lucky to be deprived of refined company—of any sort of society—of civilisation, you might as well say. Mud and dust and animals. Coming to live among animals. If only I'd known what I was doing,' she said, her voice heavy with loss.

Lizzie was feeling unusually mellow towards Susannah, and decided to do her the kindness of offering some good advice. 'You know, you want to get out of yourself a bit. Sitting about moping! No wonder you're so down in the mouth all the time. You ought to try keeping busy, that'd cheer you up.'

'I've quite enough to do trying to keep some measure of order in this house, thank you very much,' Susannah said coldly. 'I certainly don't need your opinion on how I should spend my time.'

Lizzie went on, not in the least daunted. 'You should visit a bit more, too. You could come and see me if you like—have a play with the little ones.'

'How kind,' Susannah murmured distantly. 'I'm afraid it's much too far to walk, and your uncle wouldn't trouble himself to drive me down.'

'You should have a go at learning to ride.'

'My father always kept a carriage, so I had no need to learn. I don't really consider it very dignified in a lady—not on these rough farm hacks, anyway. And I've no proper riding habit.'

Lizzie studied Susannah in perplexity, trying to fathom what dignity had to do with riding horses. 'It doesn't matter to the horse what sort of clothes you wear, you know.'

'It matters to me. I have to keep my self-respect, or I'd be dragged down to... to a level I'd find unacceptable. I don't expect you to understand.' Susannah looked with disdain at the area around Lizzie's middle where only Frank's valiant efforts to pull her laces tight each morning gave any semblance of a waist. 'Unlike some women, appearances matter to me. *I've* no intention of letting myself go.'

Lizzie only half understood the jibe, but she knew it was at her expense. 'Letting yourself go?' she said, rising to her full height and giving a toss of her head. 'Why don't you try it sometime? You might find you enjoy it. Now wouldn't *that* be a nasty shock?' she flung over her shoulder as she stalked from the room.

2

May – June 1895

At dinnertime, Frank came into the kitchen and took his place at the table. 'How'd you get on up there?' he asked.

'I got it out of her—it wasn't easy, mind you.'

'What did you get, Ma?' Maudie asked. 'Did Aunt Susannah give you something?'

'Never you mind, nosy. Frank, you'll have to help me write the letter tonight. You're good at that.'

Frank laughed. 'Letters to do with cows, maybe. I've got no more idea than you how to write a letter like that. I'll have a go, though.'

Maudie's eyes darted from one to the other, trying to fathom their conversation, but she soon lost interest in favour of her own news.

'Mal's got a huge black eye,' she announced importantly.

'Yes, it's a beauty,' said Joey. 'His face is all bruised, too.'

'Been fighting at school, has he?' Lizzie said, pursing her lips. 'You see that you don't go getting into fights, Joey, or your father will have something to say about it.'

'He didn't get it at school,' Joey told her.

'No,' said Maudie. 'Uncle Charlie did it.'

Lizzie stopped piling vegetables onto plates and sent Maudie a startled look. 'What, gave him a black eye and all that?'

'Yes,' Maudie said, clearly delighted at the effect she was having. 'Uncle Charlie thumped him against the wall and hit him really hard.'

'He's got a lump on the back of his head like a duck's egg,' Joey put in.

'Dave said Aunt Amy thought Uncle Charlie was going to kill Mal,' Beth added when there was a long enough pause for her quiet voice to be heard. 'She threw a pot of carrots at him. He got all wet.'

'Wish I'd seen that,' Joey said in the tone of one who has missed a rare treat.

'So he's starting on his children now, eh?' Lizzie murmured. 'Beth, did Dave say Aunt Amy was all right?'

Beth looked confused by the question. 'She didn't like it when Uncle Charlie hit Mal,' she offered.

'I don't suppose she did, but was she… oh, never mind, I'll pop up tomorrow and see how she is. Dave probably would have said something about it if she'd had any trouble.'

'Uncle Charlie's horrible, eh?' said Maudie.

'Don't you go talking about your elders like that, my girl,' Lizzie said. 'Little girls should keep their opinions to themselves.' She finished loading the plates and sat down in front of her own. 'Mal probably deserved it, anyway—he's always playing up for poor Aunt Amy.' But there was a lack of conviction in her voice, and Frank saw a troubled look flit over her face. It was hard to imagine what a boy of nine could have done to deserve the sort of beating the children described.

'He got it for wagging school,' Maudie told them, unabashed by Lizzie's admonition. 'He's hardly ever been coming to school lately, and Uncle Charlie found out.'

'Uncle Charlie hit him like that for wagging school?' Lizzie asked. All three children nodded emphatically.

'That's what Mal said—Dave did, too,' said Maudie.

'Well!' With an effort that was clearly visible to Frank, Lizzie resisted making any comment on Charlie's harshness. 'Well, it's naughty to wag school, and if I ever catch any of you lot doing it there'll be trouble. Now, shut up for a minute so your father can say Grace.'

Maudie was silent long enough for Frank to say a quick prayer before the family started on their meal, but she had only had a few mouthfuls before she spoke up again.

'Ma, why do you and Pa sleep in the same bed?'

'Eh?' Lizzie shot a glance at Frank, her eyebrows raised in amusement. 'Because there's seven of us in this house and only three bedrooms. None of us get a bed to ourselves, you know—you and Beth share, and Joey and Mickey. It's going to be a bit of a crowd when Danny gets too big for a cradle.'

Maudie mused on this for a few moments as she chewed another mouthful, then she mustered up a fresh argument.

'But why do you and Pa share? Why don't say you and me and Beth share, and Pa and Joey, and Mickey and Danny? Then it'd be girls together and boys together, wouldn't it?'

'No, that wouldn't be any good,' Lizzie said, managing to keep her expression serious with obvious difficulty. 'I have to sleep with your father. He gets very restless in the night, see, and I'm the only one who can put up with it. You children need your sleep more than I do, it doesn't matter if he keeps me awake half the night.'

'Oh.' Maudie gazed at her father with interest. 'You must be really restless, Pa.'

'No, it's not that, love,' Frank said, careful to hide his own amusement. 'Your ma doesn't like to say, but it's because of her. She snores something terrible.'

'I do not!' Lizzie said. 'Don't you go telling the children such stories!'

'How would you know?' Frank teased. 'You're asleep when you do it. It's me who lies awake wondering if you're going to blow the roof off or not.'

'Gosh!' Maudie said, wide-eyed at the magnitude of Frank's claim. 'It must be really loud.'

'It is,' Frank said, barely straight-faced. 'It's a bit like that earthquake we had the night you were born, Maudie.'

'You stop that, Frank,' Lizzie scolded. 'They're little enough to believe you.'

'Well,' Frank relented, 'maybe it's not as loud as all that. It's more like... leaves rustling in the breeze, say. Or birds singing.' He grinned down the length of the table at Lizzie, who pulled a face back at him.

'Oh,' Maudie said, disappointed at the anticlimax. She spent a few seconds attacking her meal, then looked up with renewed enthusiasm.

'Aunt Amy and Uncle Charlie don't sleep in the same bed,' she announced.

Lizzie's fork dropped onto her plate with a clatter. 'What did you say?'

'Aunt Amy and Uncle Charlie don't sleep in the same bed,' Maudie repeated willingly. 'I know they don't, because Dave said.'

Lizzie placed her knife and fork neatly on her plate and fixed Maudie with an intent stare. 'What did Dave say? Tell me exactly what he told you.'

Maudie launched into her narrative. 'He said they don't sleep in the same room, not like you and Pa. He said they used to, but they don't any more. He knows, because one night he felt sick, and he got out of bed to be sick, but he did it on the floor because he couldn't get outside in time. Beth did that once, remember? Only she was sick right in the bed, and she got it all over her nightie and mine too, and—'

'All right, I remember that,' Lizzie interrupted. 'We don't need to hear all that business about being sick, either, not when we're trying to have our dinner. I just want to hear what Dave told you.'

'Well, I have to tell you about the being sick, because that's what Dave said,' Maudie said with some asperity. 'Anyway, he felt bad, and the sick smelled horrible, and Mal was going crook at him, so he went looking for Aunt Amy. He went into Uncle Charlie's room, but she wasn't there. Uncle Charlie shouted at him to go away, and he was scared, so he went off into the kitchen. *I* think he was bawling, but he said he wasn't. Then Aunt Amy came in from the other bedroom and looked after him and cleaned the floor and all that. And she took him into bed with her for a bit, till he stopped feeling awful. So that's how he knows.'

Lizzie's eyes met Frank's across the table. 'That explains a few things, doesn't it?' she said.

'How do you mean?' Maudie asked, eyes bright.

'Never you mind,' Lizzie said, then she appeared to decide it was safer to give Maudie some sort of answer than leave her to speculate. 'I just meant Aunt Amy doesn't seem as tired as she used to. She's probably sleeping better. Now listen, Maudie,' Lizzie said seriously, 'it's all right for you to tell me and your pa things like that, but you're not to go telling anyone else.'

'Why not?' Maudie asked, clearly indignant at being deprived of the opportunity to spread more widely news that had caused such interest at home.

'Because that's private, all that stuff about who sleeps in what room. People don't like to think that everyone else knows their private business. If Uncle Charlie found out you'd been telling people he'd go really crook.'

'I don't care about him,' Maudie said. 'I'm not scared of him.'

'Maybe not, but it's not you he'd go crook at. It's Aunt Amy, and probably Dave for telling you. You wouldn't want that, would you?'

Maudie considered the question. 'No, I wouldn't,' she said. 'He's so grumpy! I don't want to get Aunt Amy and Dave in trouble.'

'That's a good girl. And don't you go telling anyone else all our business, either. Now, get on and finish your dinner! It'll be getting cold with all your chattering.'

The kitchen was briefly full of the sound of utensils scraping against plates, then Maudie looked up from her food once again.

'Do you know,' she said through a mouthful, 'at Uncle Charlie's place they're not allowed to talk at the table? Children, I mean. Only grown-ups can talk.'

'Yes, I *do* know, and sometimes I think it's not such a bad idea,' Lizzie said. 'I might start it here if you don't get on with your dinner.' She pointed a finger warningly as Maudie opened her mouth to protest. 'Not one more word out of you till your plate's clean, Edith Maud, or you'll go to bed with a sore backside and no pudding.' Thus cowed, Maudie ate in aggrieved silence.

When all the children were safely tucked up in bed, Lizzie brought Frank's pen and inkstand out to the kitchen, along with some of his writing paper, and raised the subject of Maudie's revelation.

'So Amy doesn't sleep with the old so-and-so any more' she said. 'I wonder how long *that's* been going on.'

'Mmm. No wonder he's so grumpy all the time.'

'Humph! He's always been grumpy—even back when she was having the children, and she must have been sharing his bed then.'

'That's true,' said Frank. 'He didn't know when he was well off, eh? Sounds like he's missed out now.'

'He's brought it on himself,' Lizzie said. 'The way he's treated her over the years! I wish I knew how she's managed to get away with it, though.'

Frank dragged his chair close to hers and slipped an arm around her. 'Why?' he asked, trying to sound stern but failing badly. 'You think you might like to try the same trick with your old man?'

'No, I'd sooner put up with you than bunk in with Maudie and Beth. At least you don't wet the bed like Beth, or talk half the night like Maudie. Even if you are restless,' she added, smiling. 'Amy's got enough bedrooms to have one of her own. I just can't figure out how she's managed to keep him out of it.'

'Ask her,' said Frank.

Lizzie frowned in thought. 'No, I don't think I'd better. I think she'd rather no one knew about it, so I'll pretend I don't. And you make sure you don't let it slip to Charlie that you know, either—I bet he'd be really wild if he found out anyone else knows what's going on.'

'Mmm, he'd feel a real idiot. Don't worry, I won't let on about it—not that I wouldn't like to see the old so-and-so squirm. It'd only make trouble for Amy, though.' He traced a hand over the smooth curve of Lizzie's cheek. 'You know, it must be driving him up the wall, having her there in the house and not being able to touch her. I'd be round the bend if it was me and you.'

'You've forgotten something,' Lizzie said. Her meaning expression reminded him at once.

'That's right. He's got the whores. And he was already going there when Amy was still having babies, wasn't he? Well, I suppose he'll just have to make do with whores now—must be costing him a fortune. Anyway, what about this letter you want me to help you with?'

Lizzie spread a sheet of paper in front of her and dipped the pen in the inkstand. 'I'll write it because your writing's too messy, but you can help me think out how to put it.'

'So you got the address all right?'

'Yes, it's a place called Auburn Street. It wasn't easy getting it out of her, I can tell you. We had a bit of a row.'

'What happened to my meek and mild Lizzie, then?'

'I just couldn't do it, not with her! Honestly, the things she comes out with.' Lizzie frowned at the memory. 'It's funny talking to her. It's sort of like you're talking to someone in a story, or… well, I suppose it must be like watching someone in a play. She sort of acts a part about how life's so hard on her and all that rubbish, and you don't know when you're talking to the real her and when it's someone else. Do you know what I mean?'

'No,' Frank admitted. 'She always seems about the same. Always sour about things, anyway.'

'She is! And the way she talks to Sophie—you'd think Sophie was just her servant. Sophie's silly enough to take it, of course, so they get on all right.' She shook her head. 'I don't know, I think Aunt Susannah enjoys being miserable. It lets her feel hard done by. I told her she should let herself go a bit. I said she might enjoy herself if she did.'

'I bet your Uncle Jack would enjoy it, too,' Frank said with a wicked grin. 'I don't think he gets much fun out of her. How much age is there between him and your pa?'

Lizzie shrugged. 'Two years, I think. Maybe a bit less.'

'You wouldn't think it, would you? Your pa looks years and years younger than Jack. That's the difference a good wife makes, eh?'

'Maybe.' Lizzie gave a sidelong glance that struck Frank as oddly shy. 'Frank, do you think I've let myself go? The way I look, I mean?'

Frank suppressed the urge to laugh, seeing that the question was important to Lizzie. 'Well, you've spread out around the middle a bit. That's better than being like Susannah, though. She looks as if she's got too many bones in her. A man'd have to watch himself cuddling her, or the bony bits would be digging in everywhere.' He put both arms around Lizzie and squeezed. 'I like a good armful myself. As long as I can still get my arms around you, you won't hear me complaining.'

Lizzie yielded to his embrace, but she still seemed distracted. 'What would you have said if I'd asked you to marry Amy?'

'I'd have told you there's a law in this country that says a man can only have one wife, and you're trouble enough by yourself,' Frank said. 'What are you going on about?'

'Don't be stupid, Frank. I meant before we got married—before Amy married Charlie. Would you have done it if I'd asked you to?'

'Of course I wouldn't! What's put that idea in your head? Why would I have wanted to do that?'

'Amy's a lot prettier than I am. She hasn't got fat, either.'

Frank took Lizzie's chin in his hand and gently forced her face around till he could look in her eyes. 'Lizzie, for a sensible woman you're being pretty silly. I don't know what your Aunt Susannah's been saying, but you should have enough sense to take no notice. You know what my idea of a pretty woman is? One with yellow hair and plenty of this to grab hold of.' He took a soft handful of breast to illustrate his point. 'You're the only woman around here like that—well, apart from your ma, and she was already taken—so you're the only one I ever thought of marrying. And *I* won't think you're too hefty till I can't lift you up any more.'

'But you can pull cows out of ditches, and haul great fat sheep around and things,' Lizzie protested.

'That's right,' said Frank. 'So you're not likely to get too heavy for me, are you?'

'You great fool.' Lizzie rested against his encircling arms for a few moments. 'Now, let's get this letter written or we'll be up all night,' she said briskly, sitting upright once again.

'All right,' said Frank. 'Then you can help me figure out how to get a few more people interested in this co-operative factory.'

'Oh, I don't know anything about that stuff,' said Lizzie.

'You know how to get your own way. How about giving me a few clues?'

'All you need to do is explain it to them, how a co-operative's better than the sort of factory we've got now. It sounds good sense when you tell me about it. I don't know why you don't just get on and tell them all you're going to have a co-operative and that's that.'

'I've got to get them to agree, Lizzie, that's what a co-operative means. Well, maybe I'll have another try over the winter.'

'You'd better, or I'll never hear the end of it. Never mind about your cows, let's do this letter. I'm going to tell the woman I'm Amy's sister, that sounds better than just her cousin.'

Frank refrained from pointing out that, while it might sound better, it was nevertheless untrue, knowing that this argument would hold little weight with Lizzie. He helped her produce a letter that tactfully referred to the baby-farming scandal and how this had distressed Lizzie's 'sister'; while making it quite plain that the writer did not believe Mrs Crossley to be in any way a baby farmer, the letter explained that Amy needed more detailed reassurance that only Mrs Crossley could offer.

'There,' Lizzie said with satisfaction as she laid down the pen. 'That's just right. We can post it when we go into town on Thursday.'

'I hope the woman writes back.'

'She'd better,' Lizzie said, a firm set to her mouth. 'If she doesn't… well, I'll just have to think of something else.'

*

Any change to the normal routine of life in a small town like Ruatane was likely to be greeted with interest by its populace, and the arrival of a new vicar was no exception. Reverend Hill had been in charge of the parish for as long as the younger inhabitants could remember, and for weeks before the new minister arrived speculation was rife on what he would be like, how old he might be, his marital status and whether he would preach more interesting sermons than his predecessor. Amy joined in the speculations in a half-hearted way, glad of anything that might distract her from the constant, nagging worry over what sort of reply Lizzie would get to her letter.

Reverend Simons, it emerged, was a tall, thin Englishman in his middle fifties, with a burning gaze in his dark eyes and black hair that seemed to need constant smoothing as an accompaniment to speaking, whenever the hand was not busy illustrating his point with emphatic gestures. Within days of his arrival the boys of the town had begun following him around, doing their best to imitate the long-legged stride conducted at great speed that seemed to be his invariable style of walking; at the same time keeping a safe distance from the serious-looking walking stick that Reverend Simons was apt to swing about him on these solitary walks. The people of the town watched the minister closely all during the first week of his residence, and on his first Sunday the church was a good deal fuller than normal.

Those who were hoping for a change in the usual placid pace of life were not disappointed. Reverend Simons ascended the pulpit, smoothed back his hair, swept his gaze over the congregation until several of those present began shifting their feet uncomfortably and regretting their presence, then he began preaching the most fiery sermon Ruatane had ever heard.

His subject was one they would all grow increasingly familiar with over the ensuing weeks: the evils of the demon drink, and the solemn duty each of them had to see that the noxious substance had no place in their own homes. He illustrated his point with descriptions of the consequences of alcohol so lurid that several mothers felt the need to cover the ears of their younger offspring; after the service these women agreed among themselves what a pity it was that the minister had no wife to instruct him in the need to temper his discourse according to his audience. The congregation sat agog during the tirade, and at the end of the service the owner of Ruatane's small brewery, who was also the proprietor and editor of the *Ruatane Herald*, stormed out of the church red-faced and scowling.

Charlie sat dumbfounded through the sermon. After the service he brushed past the new minister, ignoring the hand outstretched for him to shake.

Amy hung back for long enough to say quietly to Reverend Simons, 'I enjoyed your sermon.' 'Enjoyed' was not a strong enough word; she had silently applauded every sentence, but it was all she felt able to risk with Charlie's disapproving back only a few feet ahead.

'Thank you, my dear,' the minister said. Amy found to her surprise that when not denouncing evil he had manners that were almost courtly. 'Perhaps you'd be interested in joining the Temperance Society I intend setting up? It will be aimed at the mutual improvement of all the members, and I'm sure you would be a great asset to it.'

Amy glanced at Charlie and gave Reverend Simons a rueful smile. 'I don't think I'll be able to do that. I'd like to, but... well, I'm a bit too busy at home.' At that point Charlie turned and gestured impatiently to her, and Amy had no choice but to hurry after him.

'What a load of crap,' Charlie grumbled as they drove home. 'Carrying on as if it's a crime for a man to have a drop to quench his thirst. Bloody Englishman!'

Aside from such mutterings, Charlie seemed inclined to give the new minister his version of the benefit of the doubt after that first service. 'He's only coming out with all that rot to impress the women and the other simple folk, what with him being new to the place. He'll stop his nonsense when he sees no one with any sense is taking notice of him.'

But Charlie soon found that he was wrong. The weeks went by and Reverend Simons' sermons became ever more eloquent in their denunciation of drink and its consequences. Charlie sat and listened in stony silence, but he made up for his taciturnity on the drives home.

'A man needs a drink when he's working in the fields,' he pronounced on the third Sunday of Reverend Simons' tenure. 'Drink lemonade instead, he says!' He spat into the dust of the track. 'Lemonade won't quench a man's thirst—not the thirst you get from real work. Ministers! Book-learning! He's not done a decent day's work in his life, that one—he doesn't know what it is to work up a thirst.'

Amy let him rant uninterrupted, though it troubled her to see Malcolm nodding agreement. The single seat of the gig had become too much of a crush now that the boys were growing big, and Malcolm was allowed to ride his pony when they went out as a family. He usually contrived to ride on ahead, or to lag behind so that he could make a show of passing them at a gallop, but he clearly found his father's flow of invective too entertaining to miss.

'Ma?' David tugged on her sleeve. He, too, had become an avid listener to the sermons, though with only the vaguest comprehension of much of their substance. 'What did the minister mean about knocking down houses?'

'What do you mean, Dave?' Amy asked. 'I don't remember him saying anything like that.'

'Yes he did! He said when men drink they knock down their houses… something like that, anyway.'

Amy hid a smile. 'Breaking up homes, he said.'

'And do they knock them right down? The roof and the chimney and everything?'

'He didn't mean it like that, Davie.' She shot a quick glance at Charlie to see if David's prattle was annoying him, but he was concentrating on guiding the horse over a rough part of the track. 'He meant… well, sometimes when men drink too much and go on and on drinking they lose all their money and they go away from their wives and children. And then they're not a family any more, see? So it's like they've broken up the family, and that means it's not a real home any more.'

'Oh.' David looked disappointed at the mundanity of her explanation. 'I thought it might mean like when Uncle Harry broke the door.'

'Uncle Harry doesn't drink!' Amy said, shocked at the suggestion. 'Well, he might have a bit of beer when he's working in the heat, but he doesn't go getting drunk. Not so that he gets grumpy or knocks things down.' She was careful not to look at Charlie as she spoke, but she could feel his eyes turned in her direction. 'Broke what door, anyway?'

'Dolly told me about it one time. She said Uncle Harry and Aunt Jane had a big fight, and Uncle Harry didn't come back for dinner till real late. So they all had their dinner and Aunt Jane put Uncle Harry's out in the porch and said he could eat it there when he came. And she put the bolt across the door so he wouldn't be able to get in.'

'Did she really, Dave?' Amy asked, amused despite herself.

'Yes, and then she put Dolly and Esther to bed. Robbie and Don were just little then, they were already in bed. But Dolly could hear through the bedroom door when Uncle Harry came home. He was wild! He bashed and bashed at the door, and said Aunt Jane had to open it. She just wouldn't, though. So Uncle Harry kicked it real hard, and he knocked the bolt right off. There's a hole in the wall where it used to join on, Dolly showed it to me.'

That was true, Amy reflected. She had noticed the hole ripped in the door surround, and she remembered now that when she had idly asked Jane about the damage Jane had looked flustered and had given her the vaguest of answers.

'Dolly didn't say Uncle Harry was drunk, though,' David said thoughtfully. 'Just wild.'

'Hope he taught the uppish bitch a good, hard lesson, making a fool of him like that,' Charlie said in disgust. 'Serves him right for not getting her sorted out early on.'

'Dolly said they shouted and threw things for a bit,' David volunteered. 'Then they sort of started laughing, then they went quiet. But Uncle Harry must have been really tired from knocking the bolt off the door, because he slept in next morning and Uncle John had to come down and wake him up for the milking. Why are you laughing, Ma?'

'I'm not really, Dave. Just smiling a bit because your Uncle Harry's so funny. See, he yells and makes a fuss, but he doesn't get really grumpy. That's because he doesn't get drunk,' she added daringly.

'Lets his wife make a fool of him,' Charlie said. 'They've no idea in your family.'

'Dolly said they're getting another baby in November,' David blurted out.

'Shh, Dave!' Amy said, shocked that he should have heard such a thing. 'Who told Dolly that?'

'Maudie did. She heard Aunt Lizzie telling Uncle Frank, and she told Dolly. Where are they getting the baby from, Ma?'

'Shut up, boy,' Charlie growled, giving David a scowl that silenced him instantly. Amy met Charlie's eyes and saw resentment there. 'How old's their last one?' he asked.

'Just gone one year old. This one's coming a bit soon after Donny, but… well, it's just the way it's worked out.' She saw thoughts passing transparently across his face: Harry might not follow Charlie's ideas on how to run his home, but he had a wife still willing to share his bed and give him more children.

'Ma, what does "degaration" mean?' David asked, bringing a welcome distraction.

'Do you mean "degradation", Dave?' Amy hazarded.

'Yes! That's what the minister said, de-grad-a-tion,' he enunciated carefully. 'He said when ladies drink it leads them into degradation.'

While Amy struggled to find suitable words to explain the concept, Charlie added his own contribution. 'Now, there's some sense in that,' he said with the air of one being scrupulously just. 'There's no use letting women drink. They haven't strong enough minds for it.'

'What does that word mean, Ma?' David persisted.

'It means… well, getting in trouble. It's when you do things that are wrong so no one likes you any more, and you have to go and live with other bad people. Do you know what it means now, Dave?'

'I think so,' David said, frowning in concentration.

'Now, take you,' Charlie said, enlarging on his earlier speech. 'That just goes to show what happens when you let women have their heads. Aye, when women take to drink they're sure to turn bad.'

'Look, is that a boat out on the horizon?' Amy said to David, hoping to distract him.

'I've no argument with the man there,' Charlie went on. 'If ministers would keep to telling women how to behave, they might do some good instead of trying to interfere with a man's bit of honest pleasure. It might have done you good if someone had taken notice of what you were up to.'

'Charlie, I don't think it's right to talk about such things in front of the children,' Amy said in a low voice.

He gave her a look that showed how much he was enjoying the feeling of power. 'Why shouldn't they hear what their mother is? They've got to know one of these days.'

'You don't drink, do you, Ma?' David asked, looking alarmed. 'You shouldn't! You'll get into degaration.'

'No, I don't!' Amy turned to face Charlie. 'I had a little glass of wine the day we got married, and that was the first time I ever tasted drink. I didn't like it much, either. You might be right about women drinking, for all I know, but it's nothing to do with me.'

'You're just bad by nature, eh?' Charlie said maliciously.

'No, I don't think I am. I've never tasted gin, anyway,' she added, remembering the smell he brought home from the whorehouse.

'Who'd waste good drink on you, you little bitch? You were quick enough to open your legs without it.'

'Charlie!' She put a warning hand on David's arm and gripped it firmly, feeling the child tense with anger at the abuse of which he understood nothing but the tone. 'It's the Sabbath, remember.'

'Don't tell me what day it is,' he said, but the venom had gone out of his voice. 'Bloody fool of a minister,' he grumbled, returning to his original target. 'Getting everyone stirred up. The newspaper man's sworn never to darken the door of the church again while Simons' there.'

'He didn't go all that often before,' Amy remarked, remembering the erratic church attendance of Mr Bateson, Ruatane's brewer-cum-editor.

'Everyone hates old Simons already,' Malcolm put in. Charlie's invective against Amy had left him unmoved, but the minister was still something of a novelty.

'I've heard a few things lately,' Charlie mused. 'There's some talk that people won't put up with the minister if he keeps on with this crap. I've heard a few of the young fellows might be thinking of running the mad bugger out of town.'

'I've heard that, too,' Malcolm said, and at first Amy was inclined to take the remark as one of his persistent attempts to seem part of the adult world.

But a glance at his face brought her up short. It held a knowing expression; a glimmer of secret knowledge. She could be sure of one thing: if there was any mischief being plotted, Malcolm was determined to be part of it. It was no use clinging to the hope that he was far too young to get into such a scrape; his age had never kept him out of trouble before.

3

Amy no longer had to ask Lizzie out loud whether she had heard from Mrs Crossley yet; whenever they saw one another she would shoot a questioning glance at Lizzie that was invariably answered with a brief shake of the head.

'She'll answer soon. She's probably been busy,' Lizzie kept saying. Amy tried to absorb some of Lizzie's determined optimism, but it became more difficult as the weeks passed.

She was fighting an increasingly unequal struggle against despair when at last came the Sunday that Lizzie caught her eye as she and Frank guided their flock into church and gave her a quick nod. The light in Lizzie's face told Amy there was news at last.

'Come around when you can,' Lizzie said to her in a low voice after the service. 'I've got something to show you. Something good.'

Monday was the one day of the week when the women of the valley never considered visiting each other, but the lure of Lizzie's news was too much for Amy to resist. She was up before dawn to boil up her copper and fill her tubs, but that afternoon as soon as she had the last of the clothes off the line and safely inside she set off down the road, ignoring the bone-aching weariness a day spent hauling water and carrying sodden clothes had left her with.

'I didn't expect to see you today!' Lizzie said when Amy found her at the clothesline. 'It's washing day!'

'I know, but I couldn't wait.' Amy began unpegging clothes and placing them in the basket as she spoke. 'What's happened, Lizzie? You've got a letter, haven't you? What does it say? What's happened to Ann?'

'Shut up a minute and let me get a word in,' said Lizzie. 'Yes, I've heard from that woman, and everything's all right. Help me in with this lot and I'll show it to you.' Amy willingly took up one side of the large wicker clothes basket and helped carry it back to the house, holding her pace to Lizzie's stolid trudge with difficulty.

'Such a pile of washing my lot make,' Lizzie grumbled, more out of habit than from any real sense of grievance. 'Why do boys get their clothes twice as dirty as girls, anyway?'

'I think they must roll in the mud sometimes. What does the letter say?'

'I'll show you when we're inside. Four loads I've carried in just now!

This basket's heavy enough with everything dry, I had to make a dozen trips with it this morning when the things were wet or I couldn't lift it at all.'

'I know. What did she say about Ann?'

'I'll be glad when Maudie finishes school, then she'll be able to give me a hand with all this. Frank usually carries the wet stuff for me when he's home, but he's been off on this co-operative thing all day.'

'Lizzie! Tell me what the letter says!'

'You'll just have to wait.' Lizzie trudged on at the same maddeningly slow pace. 'There,' she said as they walked up the porch steps and into the kitchen. 'That didn't take long, did it?'

'Yes, it did.' Amy dropped her side of the basket, forcing Lizzie to let go of the other handle. 'Show me the letter.'

'Come on, then.' Lizzie led the way up the passage and into the front bedroom. 'I put it away safely, I know you won't want anyone nosing into it.'

She opened a drawer and delved into a pile of clothes. Her hand emerged holding a folded piece of paper. 'Here it is. Sit down on the bed and we can look at it together.'

Amy practically snatched the letter from Lizzie's outstretched hand. She hastily unfolded it, sat down beside Lizzie and began reading aloud.

' "Dear Mrs Kelley," '

'She's spelled my name wrong,' Lizzie remarked idly.

' "I now take the opportunity to write these few lines, hoping it finds you in good health as it leaves me"—oh, never mind all that, where's the part about Ann?' Amy quickly scanned several lines spent in apologising for the lateness of the reply, until she found something of more interest.

'Look, here's a bit about the Infant Life Protection Act.'

'What's that, anyway? I've never heard of it.'

'You should read the newspapers. It's what the government brought in to deal with these baby farmers. The women have to register, and they've got inspectors who go around seeing that they look after the babies. Look! She says she registered when the act came in and she's got a proper licence. She must be all right then, mustn't she? She must look after the babies properly. Don't you think so?'

She turned a pleading expression in Lizzie's direction, and Lizzie nodded. 'Of course she does. She wouldn't get a licence if she didn't. That's good, isn't it?'

'But where's the part about Ann?' Amy ran her finger down a few more lines. 'Here it is! "Now, the matter of your sister—" Lizzie, did you say I was your sister?'

35

'I thought it sounded better,' Lizzie said with a slight shrug.

'Trust you!' But Amy was too engrossed in what she was reading to bother exhorting Lizzie to truthfulness. ' "I remember Miss Leith well, as it was quite the saddest case I ever had to deal with. I'm convinced she had been very wronged. So young, and so fond of the little girl. I've wondered many times what became of Miss Leith, as I could see that she was going to take parting with the baby very hard." '

The page began to blur so badly that Amy could barely make out the words. Lizzie reached across and gently pulled it from her hands. 'Shall I read it?' she asked, and Amy nodded, unable to speak through the lump in her throat.

' "As for the child, I am pleased to be able to inform you that I found her a very good home indeed. I hope you will understand that I am not free to give you the name and address of the couple who took the baby, but I can tell you some things about them that may be of interest to your sister.

' "They were an older couple—not elderly, you understand, but of a mature age. They had come to the Colony some years before, I believe they originated in the West Country region of Home. The gentleman was most well set up in his business interests, and was certainly in a position to provide a child with everything a mother could wish. They had only one child, a boy, and the lady was not of an age where she could hope for any more. She was overjoyed at getting the little girl, and eager to shower the child with affection. I passed the baby over to them with no qualms at all, and Miss Leith can rest assured that she did the right thing." '

Lizzie folded the letter and placed it on Amy's lap. 'And that's it, except for "Best wishes" and "I remain" and all that business.' She slipped an arm around Amy's shoulders and gave her a squeeze. 'It's good, isn't it? I mean, it's all right now. You don't need to worry about it any more.'

'Ann's alive,' Amy said quietly. 'She's alive.' She blinked away the tears and gave Lizzie a watery smile. 'Thank you.'

'That's all right.' Lizzie patted Amy's shoulder and stood up. 'I'll put the kettle on and we can have a nice cup of tea.'

'I should be getting home, really.'

'Oh, you can spare another ten minutes,' said Lizzie. 'I could do with a bit of company, with Frank out. And I'll have the little fellows waking up before long, there won't be a moment's peace after that till I've got the whole lot of them in bed tonight. Stay for a cup of tea.'

It was not difficult to let herself be persuaded. Amy carefully tucked the letter away in her dress and went out to the kitchen with Lizzie.

'They sound nice people, don't you think?' she asked, still seeking reassurance. 'Mature, she said, not elderly—I wouldn't want her to be with old people.'

'They're just right, I'm sure.'

'And they must have wanted a little girl a lot, to go to all that trouble. You know, it's silly,' Amy mused, 'whenever I think about Ann, I think of her as a tiny little baby. But she's not at all. She's growing up now.'

'How old is she?'

'Ten,' Amy answered without hesitation. 'She'll be eleven in November. Just twelve months older than Mal.'

'A year and a half older than Maudie, then.'

'Mmm. I wonder what she's like. Is she little like me? She's got dark hair like me, I know that. And her eyes were the bluest blue you could think of—but babies' eyes change sometimes. She's pretty, I just know she is, because she was such a pretty baby. And clever, too, I'm sure.'

'She's sure to be a lovely girl,' said Lizzie. She put the teapot on the table and sat down in the chair next to Amy's. 'Probably more of a thinker like Beth instead of a chatterbox like Maudie.'

'I bet she's got lots of pretty clothes and things. All those lovely frilly dresses you can buy in the big shops. And fancy dolls, and... oh, I don't know, all sorts of things. And books—I hope they buy her lots of books.'

'They sounded pretty rich. She's probably got everything a child could want.'

'But they sounded nice, too, and that's the most important thing. They really wanted Ann. They really love her.'

'Of course they do.'

'So she's happy. I want her to be happy, Lizzie, really I do.'

'I know you do,' Lizzie said, looking puzzled by her insistence.

Amy stared into the distance, but her eyes did not see the walls of Lizzie's cosy kitchen. Instead they saw a tiny baby, drawing its life from her and seeking no existence beyond the circle of her arms.

'She won't ever think about me,' she said quietly. 'She's so busy and happy, she won't ever wonder what I was like. She won't wish I hadn't given her away.'

'That's for the best.'

'I know. I know it is. I just wish... no, I don't really. I'm glad she's happy. But... but she won't want me.'

'Amy, I think you should stop talking about this stuff,' Lizzie said, a note of uncertainty in her voice. 'Your little girl's safe and happy, and that's all you need to worry about.'

'I know. That doesn't stop me thinking about her. It doesn't stop me wanting her.' Amy blinked her eyes rapidly to clear them.

'Well, just try and stop it, then. You won't do yourself any good like that.'

'I didn't want to give her away. I thought it was for the best. I couldn't have given her all the things she deserves like they can. I would have loved her, though. I would have loved her just as much as they do.'

'Stop it, Amy,' said Lizzie. 'You're being silly now. Of course you couldn't keep her. You weren't even married—how could you have brought up a child with no husband? It wouldn't have been right.'

The note of censure that Lizzie did not quite manage to keep out of her voice jarred on Amy. She looked at Lizzie, a picture of matronly dignity and secure in the knowledge that she had never done anything remotely improper in her life; never even been tempted towards any man but her husband. Instead of the warmth she usually felt at being near Lizzie, a surge of resentment went through her.

'I know,' she snapped. 'I know I wasn't good enough to keep her. I don't need you telling me right from wrong. Why don't you just call me a whore to my face like Charlie does?'

'Amy!' Lizzie said, visibly shocked. 'I didn't mean anything like that! I was just trying to tell you that you did the right thing by the baby.' She put her hand on Amy's arm. 'You know I've never thought badly of you because of what happened. How could anyone with any sense blame you? But it would have been wrong for you to keep the baby, you know that really. It wouldn't have been fair on her. You know what people are like for talking.'

Lizzie meant it, Amy knew; and yet she could see that her cousin was embarrassed by the subject. There was an innocence about Lizzie that marriage and bearing five children had done nothing to taint.

'You're right, Lizzie. I'm sorry I bit your head off. I suppose it's because I've been worrying about Ann so much lately, I'm not being very sensible. I appreciate all the trouble you've gone to over this, really I do.'

She rubbed her hand over her dress until she could feel the stiffness of the folded letter through the cloth. 'It's hard to take it in, finding out so much about Ann after just wondering and wondering all these years. I've no right to want more, I know. I should be grateful just to know she's safe and happy.'

'That's right,' Lizzie said. 'You just think about that, and you'll be all right.'

'But I can't help wondering about her,' Amy said dreamily. 'Especially now—I won't keep thinking about her as a little baby now. I can't help wondering what it would be like to meet her.'

'Amy, you know you can't do that,' Lizzie said, the sharpness in her voice snapping Amy's attention back to her. 'You mustn't even think of such a thing.' She studied Amy anxiously. 'Maybe I did the wrong thing, writing to that woman. I didn't think you'd go getting ideas like that in your head.'

Amy took her hand and gave it a grateful squeeze. 'Don't worry, I know I can't meet her. It's just something to dream about.' She pulled out the folded sheet and studied it. 'I shouldn't take this home with me. If Charlie ever found it... well, it wouldn't bear thinking about. He'd take it off me, too.' She held the letter out to Lizzie. 'Will you look after it for me?'

'If that's what you want.' Lizzie tucked it into her apron pocket. 'I'll put it away somewhere safe, don't you worry.'

'And I'll be able to read it sometimes, when I come and see you. It's almost like having a little bit of Ann, see? Something to hold when I want to dream about her.' She gave herself a little shake. 'Dreams don't really come true, do they? I'm old enough to know that.'

'Frank thinks they do,' said Lizzie. 'Of course, Frank can be pretty silly sometimes,' she added with a fond smile. 'Him and his handsome princes, and fancy dresses and jewellery! As if I need anything more than I've already got.' She pressed Amy's hand. 'I want to see you happy, though. That's the one thing that still worries me.'

'Well, you mustn't let it,' Amy said. 'I've got two healthy boys, that's enough for any woman to be grateful for. Don't take any notice when I say silly things, for goodness sake. As long as I can talk about Ann sometimes, that's all I need. I'm not really meant to—I promised Charlie I wouldn't—but talking doesn't do any harm, does it? I don't talk about her to him, anyway—that's an easy enough promise to keep,' she added with a rueful smile.

Lizzie studied her with what struck Amy as a strange expression. 'I didn't know you were so keen on keeping promises to him.'

'Well, that's the only one I've ever made him. It's not much to ask me to keep that one, is it?'

'But you make promises when you get married. What about those?'

Amy shook her head. 'I didn't make any. I got married in the courthouse, remember? All I had to say was that I took him as my husband. Nothing about loving or obeying. Not like you,' she added cheekily. 'I bet you find that one about obeying pretty hard to keep.'

'Frank doesn't complain,' Lizzie said loftily. She glanced at the clock. 'He's been out for ages! He'd better not be late for dinner or I'll give him a piece of my mind.'

'What's he up to, anyway?'

'It's this business about the co-operative. He's been going around seeing different men, trying to get them interested. Harry's quite keen, Frank says, and John's easy-going enough to go along with it.'

'Jane said Frank had been to see Harry a few times, I wondered what that was about.'

'Oh, he's been all over the place. I think he must have been to every farm in Ruatane, especially now he's talking to the older men who haven't got sons for Frank to start on.'

'I don't think he's said anything to Charlie.'

'Well, no, he hasn't,' Lizzie admitted. 'He didn't think Charlie would be very keen.'

'He's right,' said Amy. 'Charlie doesn't like anyone telling him what he should do.' *Especially not Frank*, she added silently; not with the jealous grudge Charlie bore towards Frank for the size and success of his farm, and even more for the rate at which his family was growing.

'Anyway, the idea is he gets the younger men keen on starting up this factory, then he gets them to soften up their fathers. He said Harry and John have talked Uncle Jack around all right. He didn't leave Bill to have a go at Pa by himself, though—Frank said it wouldn't be fair to do that. You know what a know-it-all Pa is. But he listens to Frank sometimes,' she added with a complacent smile. 'He throws off when Frank tries to tell him about what he's doing, but Pa takes more notice than he lets on. He knows Frank's no fool.'

'No, he's not,' Amy agreed. 'He never used to have much to say for himself—you couldn't say that about him now, could you?'

'Not when it's something that really matters to him. He's been to see the bank manager, too, because all the farmers who go in for this co-operative are going to have to borrow money to set up the factory. He said Mr Callaghan seemed pretty keen on it, so Frank doesn't think there'll be any trouble about getting the money. Mr Callaghan says anything Frank's involved in, he's happy to support,' Lizzie said proudly. 'I'm not meant to tell anyone the manager said that, either, so don't you go telling Charlie. Frank doesn't like making a fuss about himself.'

'I won't do that, Lizzie,' Amy said, smiling at the notion that she would boast of Frank's successes to such an unwilling audience. 'Mr Callaghan must think a lot of Frank to say something like that.'

'He does. He says Frank thinks things out better than other people.

And Frank always does those piles of sums before he spends any money—well, we do them together, but Frank's a lot better at them than he used to be. A lot better than I am, not that that's saying much. I never thought Frank'd turn out to be the sort of husband who'd make me do sums! I used to tell him he should get you to help with them.'

'I'd quite like that,' Amy admitted. 'I used to enjoy helping Pa with the accounts. Not that Pa did anything complicated like Frank does, but it was nice to feel I could do something. I don't seem to use my head hardly at all, really. I don't even know if Charlie keeps accounts, but he wouldn't want me anywhere near them if he does. That's not women's work. Anyway, Charlie thinks I'm too stupid to do anything like that.'

'Humph! *I* know who the stupid one is,' said Lizzie. 'Frank doesn't really need the help now, except I write things out tidy for him. He says he likes us to do things like that together—things that really matter, he calls them. He can be soft sometimes, can Frank,' she added fondly.

'He says he needs about a dozen farmers to be able to make a go of it, and he thinks he's got just about enough now,' she went on. 'Then they're going to have a big meeting and thrash it all out. Mr Callaghan's meant to be going to the meeting, too. It'll still take ages after that, I expect—you know what men are like for just talking on and on instead of getting on with things.'

'If Frank's as keen as all that he won't let them muck about too much.'

'No, he won't—and they'll take notice of him, too. I still have to give him a shove sometimes, Frank still thinks people might say he's being stupid if he pushes himself forward. But they all know Frank knows what he's talking about, even if they do try and throw off at him. Everyone knows Frank's got the best herd in Ruatane. And even if the men around here are too stupid to want to buy any Jersey calves off him, they're all pretty keen on hiring Duke William. *And* they all want to buy any of the half-breed calves he's got to sell, and for a good price, too.' A triumphant smile lit up her face. 'And it's fair enough—Frank's worked darned hard to build up this herd.'

'You must be awfully proud of Frank,' Amy said, trying in vain not to sound wistful. 'He's doing so well. And he's a good father, too. And a good husband,' she added quietly.

'Oh, he's a great fool sometimes—and I tell him so, too, I don't want him getting too big for his boots.' Lizzie's face softened. 'He's all right, is my Frank. He knows what he's doing.'

*

Lizzie gave Frank's collar a final twitch, then stood back to inspect the result.

'That's just right,' she announced. 'You'll look the smartest of any of them.'

'No one's going to care what I look like, Lizzie,' Frank protested with a laugh. 'I feel a bit of a fool in this fancy suit.'

The new suit had been Lizzie's idea. After Frank's first visit to Auckland he had mentioned to her how well-dressed the city men seemed to be compared to the standards of Ruatane, and had confessed that this had made him feel rather awkward when mixing with them.

Lizzie had said little on the subject beyond exhorting him not to let anyone think they were better than him, but as soon as Frank had begun planning a second visit Lizzie had suggested, at first casually then in more and more persuasive terms, that Frank have a new suit made for himself while he was in Auckland.

It had seemed a foolish extravagance to Frank, and even more so when he had asked the price of a suit at the smartest tailor's shop he could find in Queen Street. He had eventually gone to a much smaller tailor's off the less fashionable Symonds Street and had had a suit made that, while it might not have met the standards of the smarter Auckland drawing rooms, would stand out on the main street of Ruatane for the quality of its cloth and cut.

As far as Lizzie was concerned, it was quite the smartest suit any man had ever owned. 'Good enough for the Prince of Wales' was one of her more extravagant claims. The suit had yet to see the light of day in Ruatane, since it was being carefully saved for 'special occasions'. Both Frank and Lizzie agreed that the long-awaited public meeting to discuss a new co-operative factory ranked as just such a special occasion.

'Well, you shouldn't feel a fool. Just because you're looking smarter than the rest of them! That should make you feel proud, not silly. *I'm* proud of you.' She beamed at Frank, then took a step back out of range of his outstretched arms.

'No, you don't—you'll crease your suit. Don't you dare, Frank,' she said, taking another step.

'Just let me have a kiss, then. If you don't struggle I won't crease anything.'

'As if I ever struggle.' Lizzie delivered up her face for a chaste kiss. 'There, are you satisfied?' she said when her mouth was free again.

'Not really. But that's the best I can do without getting in trouble.' Frank took advantage of Lizzie's lowered guard to slip an arm around her waist for a quick squeeze. 'I wish you could come with me.'

Lizzie pulled a face. 'Why would I want to go into a public hotel and listen to a lot of men talking?'

'Well, I wouldn't really want to take you into a place like that. But I always feel a bit more sure of myself when you're around. I mean, what say they want me to say something at this meeting?'

'Of course they'll want you to say something! You're the one who knows all about this stuff, they'll expect you to tell them all what to do.'

'I don't think I can do that, Lizzie. Not in front of all those people.'

'Don't talk rot. You haven't been nervous all this time you've been going around talking to everyone about the factory, have you? I can remember a time when you wouldn't say boo to a goose, let alone march all over Ruatane telling people what they should do. Well, it's going to be all the same men there today, with maybe a few more that you didn't get around to seeing. Where's the need to be nervous?'

'It's not the same, talking to a great crowd of them all at once. It was easy just one or two at a time.' Frank pictured a sea of faces staring at him. His face felt hot at the thought of standing up and speaking out in such company. 'What say they all just laugh?'

'Then they're bigger fools than most of them look, and that's saying something.' Lizzie took hold of his hand and held his gaze with hers. 'Now listen, Frank. You needn't think I'm going to let you get out of finishing this after you've gone to all that trouble setting it up, not to mention plaguing me talking about co-operatives day and night. When you stand up there today, don't go thinking about how many men are there. You've only got two eyes, haven't you? So you can only look at a couple of people at once without whizzing your head around all over the place like a dopey chook. Look them in the eye, and just pretend you're still talking to them one or two at a time. Then look at someone else for a minute and do the same. That's not hard, is it?'

'I don't know. I've never tried it.'

'Well, try it today. Then you can tell me if it works. And if you even think someone's having a laugh at you, just look straight back at him and say to yourself, who's got the best herd around here? Who brings ribbons home from the big Show in Auckland? Who gets farmers writing to him from all over the place wanting to buy his cows? Who gets more money for his milk than anyone else in Ruatane? If there's any laughing to be done, I know who should be doing it.'

The nervous fluttering inside Frank had been replaced by a warm glow. 'Gee, you make me feel good, Lizzie.'

'I'm meant to. It's my job.' She let herself be kissed again, then fetched Frank's smartest hat from the wardrobe shelf and passed it to him. 'Now, get a move on or you'll be late.'

Frank cast a longing look at his ancient felt hat, hanging from its peg in the porch, as he walked out the back door. Today he felt more need than usual of the anonymity its broad, floppy brim gave. 'I still wish you could come,' he told Lizzie. 'It'd be good to see you giving people those filthy looks of yours if you didn't think they were taking enough notice of me.'

'No need for that,' Lizzie said. 'Pa's going to be there.'

'Is that supposed to make me feel better? Do you mean he'll tell me if I'm being stupid, save you doing the job?'

'I'll hear no more talk about being stupid,' Lizzie said, raising a warning finger. 'You should know Pa better than that by now. He bosses you around and tells you off, but if he hears anyone else throwing off at you he'll go crook as anything at them.'

'Just like you, eh?' Ignoring Lizzie's protests about creases, Frank drew her into his arms and savoured the feel of her body for all too brief a moment before he set off to where his tethered horse was contentedly cropping grass.

The Masonic Hotel had been chosen for the meeting over its rival, the Royal, for the simple reason that it had a larger main bar. Even so, by the time all the interested parties plus those who had wandered in off the street to see what was going on had assembled, the room was almost full.

The main factor that had enabled Frank to rouse his neighbours and acquaintances beyond mild interest was one he could take little personal credit for. After years of barely surviving depressed prices and indifferent quality of supply, the owners of Ruatane's proprietary dairy factory were ready to give up the struggle. If they were given the opportunity to dispose of their assets at anything like a worthwhile price, they would grasp at it eagerly.

Once this had become common knowledge in the district, even the slowest thinkers had realised that without a factory they would be forced to return to the days of unloading what butter they could on to the storekeeper in exchange for supplies, and the store could not possibly absorb the level of production that the farmers had built up during the years the factory had been in existence.

This raised Frank's talk of a co-operative from the status of 'Frank Kelly's mad idea' to something well worth considering. At the same time, Frank's initial probing of the factory owners had told him that taking it over would give the farmers the chance to have their co-operative running well in time for the new season and for substantially less than they would have to pay if setting up a plant from scratch.

Those present took the opportunity to exchange news and pleasantries with neighbours they had not seen recently, downing several jugs of beer in the process, and it was some time before the talk died down and faces began turning expectantly in Frank's direction.

'What about this factory then?' someone asked. 'What are you going to do about it, Frank?'

'And what's the story with this "co-operative" talk, anyway?' came a voice Frank did not recognise; it must belong to one of the men he had not managed to visit. 'Sounds to me like we've all got to come up with a pile of money for young Kelly to spend.'

'Yes, what are you going to do with it, Frank? Buy more fancy cows? Think the ones you've got are going to peg out soon?' This raised a laugh, and Frank felt one of the hated blushes that he thought he had conquered years ago mounting over his face. For the briefest of moments he considered making a dash for the door; then a glance at the black look that Arthur was directing at the last speaker made Frank think of Lizzie, and he smiled at the thought.

The would-be wit was Mr Carr, Frank saw. Forestalling any remark Arthur might have been about to utter, Frank spoke up. 'Anything wrong with those half-breeds I sold you last year?' he asked, affecting concern. 'Gee, and you said you wished I had twice as many to sell, too, and you'd be first in the queue for this season.' Mr Carr had the good grace to join in the laughter that was now at his expense.

When the room was quiet again, Mr Callaghan came in smoothly. 'Perhaps if Frank just gave us all a run-down on the idea of the co-operative?' he suggested. 'He seems to be the expert on it.'

'Yes, let's hear what you've got to say, Kelly.'

'Stand up, boy, we can't see you at the back,' someone called, raising a laugh over Frank's modest stature.

The bank manager smiled encouragingly, but it took all Frank's courage to stand up in front of the sea of faces that seemed even larger in reality than it had in imagination. When he pushed his chair back from the table, the scraping wood sounded harsh in the quiet room. He swallowed nervously, and even that small action seemed unreasonably loud.

'Look them in the eye, and just pretend you're still talking to them one or two at a time.' Lizzie's words floated into his awareness, and he clung to the vision of her unshakable confidence. When he made the effort to resolve the sea of faces into individuals, it was not hard to find friendly ones. He had known John and Harry Leith, as well as Matt Aitken, all his life; and Bill was far more a brother to him than Ben had ever been. Many of the others were people he saw regularly and exchanged friendly greetings with at church or at the store. These were not people to be frightened of. Frank cleared his throat and spoke.

'Well, I think you all know about how the co-operative's going to work,' he began, astonished at how confident he sounded. 'We'll all put in a bit of money, and we'll all own it together. The way it is now, it's like we're working for the blokes who own the factory. With the co-operative, we'll be working for ourselves.'

He heard murmurs of approval, and thus encouraged went on. 'I've talked to a lot of fellows in Auckland, when I've gone to the Shows up there. They all reckon a co-operative's much better than the old way. Some of them said they were getting nearly twice as much money for the cream since they'd got a co-op.' There were a few gasps at that; he could almost hear their minds figuring the sums.

'The factory gets run how we say it's to be run. There'll be a factory manager, and he'll have men working for him, but we keep an eye on the manager and see that he's doing his job properly. And the more money the factory makes, the more we get. That's about it.' He sat down quickly.

The murmur of conversation sounded positive, he thought. 'Where's the money to set this up going to come from?' someone called.

'Can I say a few words, Frank?' Mr Callaghan asked.

'Um, yes—yes, please,' Frank said.

'Frank asked me to come along today to talk about how the Bank can help with all this,' Mr Callaghan explained. 'As far as the Bank's concerned, these co-operative factories are the way farming should be going. And the government is encouraging the Bank to lend money for them at a very favourable rate of interest. The idea is that the Bank puts up the money to set up the factory, then we take a small part of each month's payout—a very small part,' he emphasised, noting the slight stiffening of the men around him, 'towards the loan. There should be no trouble at all with advancing the money for the factory you men want to set up.'

The men talked animatedly in small groups for several minutes, until Matt Aitken summed up the general feeling. 'Well, I reckon it all sounds pretty good. What do we do now, Frank?'

'I think we're meant to decide who's going to do what, and all that,' Frank began vaguely, trying to think of the right words.

'May I, Frank?' Mr Callaghan asked, and Frank nodded eagerly. 'I'm the first to admit I know nothing about running farms—except for what I've picked up from you men over the years,' the manager said with a smile. 'But I do know something about setting up businesses such as this co-operative. The first thing you need to do is set up a committee to run the factory.'

'I'll be on that,' Harry volunteered.

'And me,' Arthur put in. 'You young fellows needn't think you're going to have it all your own way.'

'Well, the procedure is to have each person who wants to serve on the committee nominated and seconded, then if there are more names put forward than places on the committee you have a vote,' Mr Callaghan explained carefully.

'Bill, nominate me,' Arthur ordered. Bill was about to stand up to do so, when Mr Callaghan intervened.

'Could I just go over one or two other things? Just to save time later. As I said, you'll want to set up a committee. It's up to you men to decide what number you want on it, but I'd suggest between six and twelve. It rather depends how many of you want the extra work of being on a committee, of course. You'll need to decide who'll be secretary and treasurer, too—the Bank will be happy to help you out with the accounts if you wish. And of course you'll need to choose a chairman.'

'That's pretty obvious, isn't it?' Again it was Matt Aitken who chose to speak for many. 'I reckon the Chairman's got to be Frank.'

Frank gave a yelp of surprise. 'Me?' Trying to picture himself telling everyone what to do defeated the best efforts of his imagination. 'Heck, I couldn't do that!'

'Why not? You know more about this business than any of the rest of us.'

'That's right,' other voices chimed in.

'Frank should be Chairman.'

'Yes, good old Frank.'

'But I... um... I'd like to be on the committee and all that, but I couldn't be Chairman,' Frank protested.

'Why not?'

'Well, I...' His eyes wandered the room wildly until his gaze met Arthur's. 'I think it should be someone older,' he said desperately. 'Someone who's been farming a lot longer than I have. What about you, Pa?'

To his amazement, Arthur shook his head. 'No, I'm not interested in being Chairman. I'll be on this committee, all right, but that'll do me. You're the one with all the ideas, Frank, you can have the job of showing us it's not all talk.'

Frank shook his head in disbelief. The notion of his telling Arthur what to do was too ridiculous for words; it was the silliest thing he had ever heard. It was…

It was almost as ridiculous as the idea that Frank Kelly, the quiet fellow without much going on in his head, the one everyone had a laugh at behind his back, might one day have the best herd in the district. Almost as ridiculous as the idea of farmers writing to Frank from up and down the country wanting Kelly Jerseys.

'Frank?' Mr Callaghan prompted. 'Will you accept nomination?'

For foolishness, it ranked with the idea of buying Lizzie a pearl necklace. That particular dream would have to wait a few more years, he knew, but he was certain that one day he was going to fasten those pearls around her neck.

He looked around the room, seeing approving smiles on every face. He beamed back at them, then turned to Mr Callaghan. 'All right,' he said. 'I'll have a go at it.'

4

March – May 1897

Now that George Leith had gone through all the education the valley school could offer, he joined Thomas working with their father. Jack took as much pleasure in having the young sons of his second family around him all the time as the boys did in what they saw as their new-found freedom. Jack was not a hard taskmaster, especially compared to Miss Metcalf; and to the boys, working full-time on the farm meant they had gained adult status. As far as they were concerned, one of the advantages of their new station was that they had now left their mother's realm of authority for ever. If they had known their mother better they would not have been quite so confident.

Susannah's father's failing health had been worrying his family for several years, but in the autumn of 1897 he took a turn for the worse. Susannah had appeared increasingly anxious for her father over the last few months, so it was no surprise to Jack one day in March when she read the latest letter from her mother and announced,

'Father's sinking. Mother says he may only have a few weeks left.'

'I'm sorry to hear it.' He meant it sincerely; Jack felt no resentment towards Susannah's father for his son's misdeeds.

'You do realise I'll have to go up there?' She spoke as if she expected a dispute over it.

'Of course you will.' He recalled that other trip Susannah had made to Auckland. He had felt the need then to warn her that he expected her to return, and that he would have to fetch her if she did not come voluntarily. He felt no such concern this time; for all her complaints, he no longer believed she had any real desire to leave him. It occurred to him to wonder just how distressed he would be if she did, now that the years had taught him to value peace and quiet above the more elusive concept of self-respect. 'We'll go into town tomorrow and see how soon we can get you a passage.'

'If there's a funeral people will expect you to come up, you know.'

'They'll be disappointed, then. I won't be coming.'

Susannah glared at him. 'I was silly enough to hope you might. I don't know why I expected you to put yourself out for me. I should know better than that.'

'Susannah,' he said, 'you don't want me to go up there.'

'I certainly don't want to have to tell everyone that my husband won't even bother coming to my father's funeral. I don't think it's so much to ask.'

Jack closed his eyes for a moment, resisting the urge to shout at her. 'You don't want me to go up there,' he repeated. 'And I'll tell you why, since you seem to have forgotten. Your brother's going to be there, isn't he?'

The resentful look was abruptly wiped from Susannah's face, to be replaced by a wary one. 'Oh. Yes, of course he will.'

'I thought as much. They'll be fetching him home from Australia, with your father being poorly.'

Susannah studied the opposite wall rather than meet Jack's eyes. 'He's already home. He came back years ago, when Father first started ailing.'

'I see. Well, I don't blame you for not telling me—it was too late for him to put right what he'd done. I'm not going anywhere that brother of yours is likely to be. I'm sorry for your ma that she's going to be losing her husband—if I went up to Auckland, she might find herself mourning a son as well.'

'Don't talk like that,' Susannah flung at him. 'Is that how you show respect for the dying? Fighting and brawling and… and… being *disgusting*—that's all you farm men ever think about. I'm going to lose my father, and you're talking about murdering my brother!'

'All right, that's enough,' Jack said. 'Maybe I spoke out of turn, I'll accept that. But I'll tell you this, Susannah—if you think I could be in the same room as that so-and-so who ruined my daughter and speak politely to him, you're wrong. And that's my last word on the subject.'

But he could not silence his thoughts as easily as his tongue. He remembered Amy's bruised and battered face, and the memory was physical pain. Charlie's fists had inflicted the blows, but it was Jimmy who had got Amy into the state where marrying Charlie had seemed a sensible idea. And it was Jack who had agreed to it, his prickling conscience reminded him.

Susannah met his outburst with cold silence. She did not speak to him again until that evening when she was getting ready for bed. As she sat brushing her hair she spoke, addressing the mirror in front of her rather than turning to face Jack.

'I want to take the boys with me. I suppose you'll begrudge me that, too?'

Jack's first impulse was to say the boys were to stay at home, but he made himself give the question careful consideration before answering. Susannah took his silence as a refusal, and slid around on her stool to glare at him.

'He *is* their grandfather, you know. I know you hate my whole family, but you can't deny my father the right to see his own grandsons again before he dies.'

'I don't hate your family, Susannah,' Jack said wearily. 'Anyway, you're right, the boys should go and pay their respects. You can take them. I'll miss them,' he added quietly.

Susannah turned back to the mirror. 'I notice you don't say you'll miss me.'

Jack studied the rigidly upright back view that confronted him, and his mind treacherously cast up a memory of fondling Susannah's smooth flesh through the folds of her nightdress. All the time he had thought he was being gentle, and she had accused him of forcing her. Even if he had the opportunity he was no longer sure he could raise the energy, but on the cold winter evenings the thought of holding a warm body close was often tempting. But not tempting enough to risk having that accusation flung at him again. 'That's the way you want it, Susannah.' He rolled over to his usual perch on the extreme edge of the bed to put the view out of his sight before he could be driven to say something he might regret. He would keep to himself the knowledge that, rather than miss her, he would enjoy the peace and quiet.

Thomas and George greeted with dismay the announcement that they were to accompany their mother.

'We don't *want* to go to Auckland! We want to stay with you,' Thomas told Jack.

'You've got to go with your ma,' Jack said, his own reluctance to part with the boys making him irritable. 'I won't hear any arguments.'

'I won't go. I just won't,' George said. 'You can't make me.'

'That's enough of that talk, boy, if you don't want a hiding,' Jack warned, hoping to forestall an outburst from Susannah. 'Your grandpa's ailing and he wants to see you. You won't be away for long.'

'I'm not going to no special school up there, anyway,' George declared, confusing Jack for a moment until he recalled the arguments with Susannah over sending the boys away to school.

'Don't make us go, Pa,' Thomas pleaded. 'You're going to kill the pig soon, and you said we could help this year. *Please*, Pa. Ow!' He clutched at his reddening cheek.

Susannah stood over him, threatening to follow her slap with a second one. 'Do you think I *want* to take you, you hateful little devil? The pair of you are little brutes, you'll probably shame me before my whole family, but I've *got* to take you. I'm not going to have Constance parading her brood around and saying what a pity it is that I couldn't bring my children. You're Father's grandchildren just as much as hers are, and you'll do as I tell you. Little brute!' She raised her hand again.

Thomas backed away out of her reach. There were tears in his eyes that Jack knew were not just from the pain of Susannah's slap. Thomas always looked stricken after one of his mother's outpourings of abuse, while George managed to maintain a defiant attitude. It was the biggest difference between Jack's two young sons: George no longer cared what his mother thought of him, but Thomas still wanted her to love him.

'Stop it, Susannah,' Jack said. 'I've told the boys they're going with you, and that's the end of it. There's no need for any yelling and screaming. Tom, pull yourself together. And you watch your tongue, young George, or you won't be sitting down for a while.'

He glanced at Susannah; there was no chance of settling the boys down while she was glaring so fiercely at them. 'Time you boys chopped a bit more firewood,' he told them. 'Come on and I'll show you where I want it stacked up.'

When the door was safely closed on Susannah, Jack put an arm around Thomas's shoulders. 'Now listen, Tom. I can't go up there with your ma because... well, it just doesn't suit. You have to go so you can look after her for me. We don't want to send her off by herself, do we?'

'Yes,' George muttered in a voice obviously not intended to catch his father's ear.

'I didn't ask you, George. But I'll explain this to the pair of you, then I want to hear no more about it. Your ma's upset because her pa's crook. I'll tell you both straight—he's going to die. Now, that's upsetting your ma, because she's fond of him. That's why she's a bit scratchier than usual. She wants to go up and see him before he passes on, and she wants the pair of you to see him too. And you're going to do it. Now, for pity's sake try not to upset her. All right?'

Both boys nodded.

'That's my good fellows,' Jack said, giving them each an affectionate cuff. 'And make a good job of that firewood, too, or you'll be chopping another lot tonight instead of eating your dinner.'

He stood on the wharf and waved them off a few days later, watching the boat until it was out of sight. Strange how those boys of his could still seem like little fellows even though they were shooting up like weeds. There seemed to be some grit in his eyes; at least there was something making them prick uncomfortably as he tried to catch a last glimpse of the boys before the boat disappeared around a bend in the river mouth.

Silly to think that the house was going to seem empty until the boys were home again. It was certainly not going to be quiet; John and Sophie's three boys would see to that, and Jane would probably bring her brood up to visit more often while Susannah was away. He had to resort to using his fingers while he ran through the names of Harry and Jane's children; there were five of them now, with one-year-old Louisa the latest arrival. There would be no shortage of little ones around, with the noise and agreeable chaos they generated. But he would miss those young boys of his.

He gave a surreptitious wipe of his sleeve across his eyes, glancing around to see that there were no prying stares, and turned to walk over to the buggy. Tomorrow, he decided, he would go and visit Amy. There was nothing like seeing his girl to cheer him up.

Susannah's father died two weeks after she went up to Auckland, and she and the boys were away for five weeks altogether. Thomas and George came home rather subdued from their first close contact with death, as well as from the weeks of being confined to their grandmother's house or her small garden instead of the acres of bush they were used to treating as their playground, but they bounced back with the resilience of the young. They had the sense to suppress any signs of exuberance in front of their mother, but as soon as they had changed into their old clothes and were safely out of her sight they headed for the nearest patch of bush at a run, whooping with delight at freedom regained.

Susannah, too, was quiet as Jack drove them home, but her silence was taut and tight-lipped. The black cloth of deep mourning accentuated her sombre air as she sat beside him with her head held high, her body exuding the peculiar rigidity that Susannah seemed so much more capable of than any other woman he had ever known.

Jack felt awkward in the face of her austere silence, and he avoided Susannah for the rest of the day, knowing he was being cowardly as he did so. But he could not hide from her when they were alone in their bedroom. He sat in bed and watched her putting away her clothes, still moving with that uncanny stiffness even though she was now wearing a loose nightdress in place of her unyielding day clothes.

'You all right, Susannah?' he asked.

'Yes,' she answered, hardly opening her mouth long enough for the clipped monosyllable to escape.

'You seem a bit upset.'

'It hasn't exactly been a pleasure trip.'

'No, I know it hasn't.' He waited for her to say something else, but she continued unpacking in silence. 'You're a bit worn out from the boat, too. You want to take it easy for a couple of days.'

'There's not much chance of that in this house, is there?' She shoved the wardrobe door closed, then sat down to brush her hair, tugging at it with a savageness that made Jack wince.

'Your family all right?' he tried.

'Don't try and pretend it matters to you whether they are or not.'

Jack hid his irritation with an effort. 'I'm just trying to—' He saw a quick heave of her shoulders. 'You are upset, aren't you?'

'No. Leave me alone.'

'Susannah, it's only natural you should be upset about your pa. You don't have to try and make out you're not.'

Susannah turned to face him. 'Why should I be upset about Father? He never liked me. He never even wanted me. I was meant to be a boy. He told me that often enough—how he had to wait all those years for a son. I was just a nuisance. I wasn't even pretty, not like Constance. He never called me his little doll like he did her. He never wanted me to sit on his lap.'

Jack struggled to make sense of her outburst. She seemed to be distressed over things that must have happened nearly thirty years before. 'Now, don't talk like that, Susannah. It doesn't seem right, saying those things about your pa.'

'Don't speak ill of the dead? Why shouldn't I? He never had anything good to say about me.'

'Well, you want to forget all that now, especially if it upsets you. Anyway, you had a nice time with your ma, didn't you? It's good that you could spend a bit of time with her, help take her mind off things. And she'd have liked seeing the little fellows.'

'Mother didn't show much interest in the boys. And she had plenty of visitors calling, she didn't seem to have any great inclination to talk to me.'

'She must have been pleased to have the little fellows around,' Jack protested. 'They're her grandchildren.'

'That doesn't matter to Mother. It was different the other time I took them, when they were tiny. You couldn't tell if they were boys or girls at that age. But she's not interested in them now. Not with Constance's children to fuss over.' Susannah's lip curled slightly. 'Constance has daughters. She's got two boys as well, but it's the daughters that Mother worships. Three of them, and according to Mother they're the most accomplished creatures you can imagine. Pretty and talented, and the apples of Mother's eye. She wasn't a bit interested in a pair of great clumsy boys.'

Jack felt a rush of indignation at the notion that his sons could be considered inferior to any other children, but he had no intention of encouraging Susannah's mood. She seemed to have brought decades worth of resentment home with her. He struggled for useful words, but could find none.

'Mother never thought anything I did was as good as Constance,' Susannah said. 'She used to say what a pity I wasn't pretty like Constance, or had a nice singing voice like her. It was always my fault when anything went wrong. She'd always beat me, never Constance. She'd say Constance was too young to know any better, and it was up to me to keep an eye on her. Now she thinks Constance's children are better than mine. Because I haven't got daughters. Because I'm not pretty.' There was a rawness in her voice as she finished.

'I never thought your sister was as good looking as all that,' Jack said. 'No better looking than you are.' That, he realised, did not quite sound like a compliment. 'You're a fine looking woman, Susannah.' Not a beauty like Annie had been, but then there was no one like his Annie. And Annie had never had the proud carriage of Susannah; the ability to wear fine clothes as if she had been born to them. Not that she had ever had the chance to learn.

Susannah seemed hardly aware of his presence. 'And to have *her* speak to me like that,' she said in a voice so low that Jack barely caught it. 'All those nasty little remarks. She always smiled when she said them, too.'

'Who? You're not talking about your ma, are you?'

'No. Charlotte.'

Now, who on earth was Charlotte? Jack couldn't recall ever hearing her mentioned before. He had certainly never heard Susannah speak of anyone with such a weight of bitterness as she had used for this mysterious Charlotte. He was tempted to ignore Susannah's mood and hope she would snap out of it, but the sight of her lips trembling as she stared into the mirror troubled him.

'What did she do to upset you?' he asked, sure that no good would come of the question, but unable to resist the prompting of his conscience.

Susannah spoke without looking at him. 'What do you care? You're not interested in what happens to me.' There was a bleakness in her voice that spoke of unhappiness far more plainly than her usual wounded tones.

Jack leaned back against the pillows and sighed. 'I'm asking you, aren't I? I wouldn't ask if I wasn't interested. Hop into bed, Susannah, you're getting cold sitting there.'

To his surprise, for Susannah was not usually eager to obey him, she rose from the chair and sat on the edge of the bed, moving almost like a sleep walker. But she made no move to lift the covers and slip beneath them.

'She was so sly about it,' she went on in the same low voice. 'She'd smile that conceited smile of hers and say, "Oh, how *nice* it must be living in the country. What a relief never having to worry about keeping up with the fashions." Or, "I do envy you, Susannah, not having to think about whether a dress is stylish or not. Life must be so much simpler. Why, I sometimes spend an hour of a morning deciding what pair of gloves to wear." Then she'd pull off a glove and show off whatever diamond ring she happened to be wearing that day. And she'd look at me as if I were an old scullery maid or something.'

'She sounds a nasty piece of work. You don't want to take any notice of people like that.'

'How could I help taking notice of her? She was there every day, then they'd come around of an evening. She'd get Constance joining in with her, too—Constance said people seem to age faster in the country. She thinks I look old and dowdy. And I *do*,' Susannah said despondently.

'You?' Jack said in genuine amazement. 'You're the most stylish woman I've ever seen!'

'How would you know?' Susannah snapped. 'What would you know about style or fashion?' She looked away, and her eyes became unfocussed. 'What would I know about it myself? Buried in a place like this. I've turned into an old frump.'

'Don't talk like that, Susannah. You've let this Charlotte upset you. You want to forget about her.'

'I *can't*. I keep thinking about those things she said. I never thought anyone could be so nasty to me.'

'Who's this Charlotte woman, anyway? Why was she hanging around there all the time, getting you down?'

Susannah's expression became wary, then defiant. 'She's James's wife.'

The heat of his anger took Jack by surprise. He did not trust himself to speak for a moment, and when he did his voice came out as something close to a growl. 'So he's got married, has he? The next girl's father was a bit too fast for him, eh? Got caught before he could put a bastard in another girl and ruin her?'

'Don't be disgusting. Anyway, if you must know, they haven't any children.' Her face turned bitter again. 'Charlotte had the cheek to say how gauche my sons are—"natural", she called them, but she said it to be nasty—and she hasn't even got any children herself.'

'Why did he marry her, then, if he didn't have a gun at his head? What makes this Charlotte good enough for your precious brother when my daughter wasn't?'

'Because her father's rich.' Susannah spat the words. 'That's why. He certainly didn't marry her for her sweet nature.'

The old hurt and anger was like bile in Jack's throat. 'I didn't know I was meant to buy a husband for my girl.'

'He just sat there and let her say those things to me,' Susannah said, her face a mixture of pain and bitterness. 'He never once said anything to stop her.'

'I've heard about enough talk of him, Susannah.'

She went on as if to herself. 'He didn't seem to care. He didn't even want to talk to me.' There was no trace of anger now, just the confused pain of a child unable to comprehend why it was being punished. 'We used to be so close. He used to love me, I know he did. Now he doesn't care.'

'That's enough,' Jack said, but he might as well not have spoken.

'I used to give him my allowance when he'd spent all his. I used to buy him things he wanted when he couldn't talk Father into it. He'd dance with me at balls when no one else wanted to. There were always plenty of men wanting to dance with Constance, but hardly any of them ever asked me. But James always would. We'd dance and dance, and he'd make me feel so proud.' She managed a crooked little smile. 'He was so tall and handsome. I always felt proud to be dancing with him, even if he was my brother. He said he liked dancing with me better than with other girls. I was the best dancer he knew. He'd tell me I was pretty. He made me feel like I was. No one else wanted me, but he did.' Her face crumpled. 'Now he doesn't want me either. He doesn't care.'

'He should have married Amy,' Jack muttered.

'I wish he had!' Susannah's voice rose to a shriek. She turned away from him and stared at the wall. 'I wish he had,' she echoed in a whisper.

She seemed to be muddling up things that had happened twenty or thirty years ago with what had upset her over the previous few weeks, and getting herself in a dreadful state in the process. Her anguish spoke for itself, but Jack had no idea how to cope with it. Especially when he was fighting hard to keep his own anger silent. It was time she pulled herself together.

'Settle down, Susannah. You're a grown woman with two young ones of your own, there's no need for you to be going on with a lot of nonsense. You'll make yourself ill if you keep running things over in your mind. You've had a bit of a rough spin up there, I can see that, but you want to just forget all that and get yourself back to normal. Auckland's a wearying sort of place, especially when you've got family troubles.'

'I'm not going up there again. They don't want me.' She turned a defiant face to Jack. 'I'm never going there again.'

'Please yourself. Hop under the covers so I can put the lamp out.' He did not wait to see if she would obey before he plunged the room into darkness.

He felt the bed move as Susannah lay down and pulled the blankets over herself. 'You don't want me either,' she said quietly.

Was she going to keep him awake all night? 'Wouldn't do me much good if I did.' He had not meant to sound so bitter, but the words could not be called back.

'No one does.'

He heard the small sounds of Susannah weeping and trying to hide it. He could picture tears pooling in her eyes and running down into her pillow, and he felt the bed move from the tremor that ran through her body. For a moment the urge to roll over, put an arm around her and draw her close was almost overpowering, but he resisted it. The time when he and Susannah could have given each other comfort was long past.

5

November 1897

By the spring of 1897 the new co-operative had had two successful seasons, and all the effort Frank had put into persuading the farmers of the district to place their faith in the venture had been well and truly justified. The establishment of the co-operative had, as it turned out, coincided with the first signs of recovery from what would afterwards be called 'The Long Slump'; thus the suppliers found themselves getting a greater share of the price fetched by their butter at the same time as the price itself was steadily increasing.

Charlie had become a supplier to the factory for the simple reason that there was nowhere else to sell his milk. He refused to become a shareholder, repeating his refusal over and over again until Amy was heartily sick of the subject. She carefully refrained from reminding him that he had never actually been invited to become one. But although he was denied a share in the profits of the co-operative, Charlie benefited in a modest way from the higher prices paid for his milk.

Amy had to rely on the snippets of information she gleaned from Lizzie or from her brothers to find out that the factory was doing well; Charlie never discussed such matters with her. She had hoped that the lightening of any worries he might have had over money would cause him to mellow somewhat, particularly towards the children, but he seemed to be as demanding as ever, and as reluctant to praise.

Charlie had little respect for 'book learning', but he still expected his sons to do at least as well as the other children in the valley school. When Malcolm failed his Standard Three examination at the end of 1896 Charlie delivered a beating, but he had no words of praise for David when the younger boy did well in the same test.

The new minister (as Reverend Simons was still called after two years in the town) was considered something of a scholar by his parishioners, and Amy suspected this was part of Charlie's continued animosity towards him. Reverend Simons' sermons tended to contain words of more syllables than most of the congregation felt comfortable with, but it was his subject matter that most excited Charlie's outrage.

'Trying to stop a man having a drink after a hard day's work,' was his constant grumble. 'Interfering in a man's honest pleasures.' For a time Amy had thought he might cease going to church entirely, thereby curtailing her only regular outing. But among Charlie's crudely articulated theories on how to manage a wife was the idea that women needed regular church-going to keep them in a suitably cowed frame of mind. And as he did not allow Amy to go any further than Lizzie's house unaccompanied, that meant he had to take her.

Charlie was not the only man irritated by Reverend Simons' preoccupation with the evils of alcohol. Mr Bateson, the town's brewer and newspaper editor, had made good his declaration that he would not darken the door of the church again while Reverend Simons held sway there. But the antagonism between these two men did not stop with Mr Bateson's absence from church. That was just the beginning.

Mr Bateson's reports of the fortnightly meetings of the Ruatane Gospel Temperance and Mutual Improvement Society, founded and chaired by the minister, could not be described as complimentary. While the *Ruatane Herald* dutifully reported each meeting in language that at first glance seemed innocuous, hints of animosity were there for anyone who cared to search for them.

The journalistic feud started off harmlessly enough, with disparaging comments in the *Herald* about the level of education of a visiting speaker at one of the temperance meetings, who had been more distinguished by his enthusiasm than by the quality of his grammar. Charlie read the criticism aloud with relish, despite the fact that Amy was quite sure he had no idea what was wrong with the unfortunate speaker's choice of verb forms.

The following Sunday, Reverend Simons denounced from the pulpit those who claimed to be above their neighbours, taking as his text the Gospel account of the Pharisee and the Publican. He announced that anyone was welcome to attend meetings of the Society, explicitly including brewers, particularly those who considered they had a superior command of grammar, in his invitation. Reverend Simons also informed his congregation that one of the Tauranga newspapers was now running a regular column they might find 'Somewhat more edifying than the local journalistic fare'. When Amy managed to sneak a glance at the newspaper in question on her next visit to the store, she soon found the column under the pseudonym 'Pericles'. The style of the prose told her that the author was none other than Reverend Simons.

From then on, she read the column whenever she had the chance, which was only if the newspaper happened to be lying around when she visited Lizzie or one of her sisters-in-law. She enjoyed reading 'Pericles' ' opinions on social issues such as the low wages paid to women, the evils of secular education, and of course the ever-present matter of alcohol and the violence and misery it led to. The column was certainly a good deal more entertaining than the 'Ladies' Page' of the *Weekly News*, which was the only reading matter Charlie ever shoved in her direction.

While Mr Bateson did not take up Reverend Simons' invitation to attend any temperance meetings, he continued to take an avid editorial interest in the goings on of the Society and its members. When the opportunity came for him to expose a small scandal, he pounced on it.

The front page of the next issue of the *Ruatane Herald* carried an article about a crop of barley grown in Ruatane that season. The barley was of such good quality that it had fetched an excellent price from a large brewing company in Auckland, and according to the editor other local farmers might well be inspired to grow similar crops.

What made this news of particular interest to Mr Bateson was the fact that the farmer concerned was the Vice Chairman of Reverend Simons' beloved Temperance Society. Mr Bateson made much of the word 'Vice' in the guilty party's title. His article affected shock and outrage that a man who was obviously considered a pillar of the community should be producing a crop to supply an industry so vilified by that very Society in which he held office.

Reverend Simons was hard put to defend his deputy against a charge so demonstrably true. In his capacity as 'Pericles' he railed against the aspersions being cast on the man's character, but at the same time he admitted that selling a crop to the brewers could be seen as incompatible with holding office in a Temperance Society. And his next sermon told the local farmers in no uncertain terms that if any of them were tempted to grow barley for brewing, they should examine their consciences carefully.

'For do not forget,' Reverend Simons thundered from the pulpit, 'the day will come when we will all be judged. And on that day, how will you be able to face your Maker and confess that you grew a crop that drags women into the most hideous form of degradation, turns men into beasts who fight one another and desert their families, that is the root of so much that all men know is evil? Better that the crop be cast into the fire than the grower's soul be damned for eternity.' There was no barley grown in Ruatane the following season.

Reverend Simons did not save his admonitions for the grown men. He was particularly earnest towards those youths of the town who were dragged along to church by their parents, exhorting them to resist the blandishments of evil companions who would draw them from the paths of righteousness and into dishonour. There tended to be a good deal of noisy foot scuffing from his intended audience when the minister made such remarks, more from suppressed resentment than from any sense of remorse.

Malcolm's animosity towards the minister was based as much on the length of Reverence Simons' sermons as on their subject matter. He squirmed and scowled all through the harangues that often stretched close to forty minutes, lacking his father's ability (which most of the adult men in the congregation shared) to nod off inconspicuously after the first few minutes. And after church he always joined in eagerly with Charlie's complaints about the minister, enjoying the novelty of being allowed to criticise an adult in front of his father.

Amy hated to hear Malcolm scoffing about Reverend Simons, but it would have been useless for her to try and scold him when he was only parroting his father's opinions. So she held her tongue and hoped he would learn respect for the minister as he grew older, though her own good sense told her that was as unlikely as Charlie's joining the Temperance Society.

She knew something untoward had happened when Malcolm and David came into the kitchen one afternoon giggling over some shared secret, then abruptly fell silent when they saw her watching them.

'What are you two laughing about?' she asked.

'Nothing,' Malcolm muttered. 'Shut up, Dave,' he grumbled, digging David in the ribs as the younger boy let a giggle escape.

'But it's so funny,' David protested. 'Ma will think it's funny too.'

'Have you been getting up to mischief, Mal?' Amy asked.

'I haven't done nothing,' Malcolm said, fixing her with a resentful glare. 'You always think I've done something wrong. You're just like Pa.'

Amy could not help but wince at his thrust. 'Please yourself, then. Don't tell me if you don't want to.'

'They had a parade, Ma,' David said, full of excitement. 'Then they had a big fight, and there was a bonfire, and fireworks, and—'

'You're telling it all mixed up,' Malcolm said in disgust. 'Tell it properly.'

David screwed up his face in concentration. 'But I forget all the bits,' he admitted. 'You tell her, Mal.'

'All right, then,' Malcolm said grudgingly, but he grinned as he turned to Amy. 'You know it was Guy Fawkes last night?' Amy nodded. 'Well, it was in the paper that there was going to be a big fireworks display and things at the cricket ground.'

'Yes, I heard your father say something about that, but I didn't see it. I think I used that paper for lighting the fire.'

'Well, it didn't just say fireworks. It said there'd be a speech by... what's that funny name?' he asked David.

'Per... Perry-something,' David offered.

Awareness was slowly dawning on Amy. 'Not Pericles?'

'Yes, that was it,' said Malcolm. 'He writes things in the Tauranga paper, but everyone knows it's really old Simons. Anyway, Bateson put it in the newspaper that this Perri-what-you-said was going to make a speech, and there'd be a band and everything. They put signs on the hitching rails and things, too. So everyone went out to watch, and then there was a big parade with a cart from the brewery, and all the fellows like Des and his mates walking around it, and—'

'Mal, how do you know about all this?' Amy interrupted.

'I just heard,' Malcolm said with a scowl.

'Who did you hear it from?' she persisted. Malcolm said nothing, just glared at her. 'It was that Des Feenan who told you, wasn't it?'

'Maybe.'

'You haven't been to school today, have you? You've been off with those boys again.' But Malcolm clearly had no intention of answering. She sighed and returned to the vegetables she was chopping. 'All right, don't tell me. Finish the story, anyway.'

Malcolm went on eagerly. 'They had a sort of band, with whistles and kerosene tins and things. And Bateson was riding along with them. And right on top of the cart they had a sort of dummy sitting on an old chair.' He broke into uncontrollable giggles, and was unable to speak for a few moments. 'They had it done up like a minister!'

'I thought they might have,' Amy murmured.

'Bateson was calling out to everyone that the dummy—you know, Perri-thing—was going to make a speech. Then Sergeant Riley came out and told them to go home, but they didn't take any notice. Riley got scared, and he sloped off.'

'Tell Ma about the fight, Mal,' David prompted.

'I was just going to. Then a whole lot of men turned up—Des said they're in that dopey Temperance thing. Or their wives are, and they made them come out and fight. They had a really good fight. I wish I'd been there. Des reckons he broke someone's arm.'

'But Des got a tooth knocked out, you said,' David put in.

'He reckoned it was worth it, though. The other men wrecked the dummy and tipped the cart over, then they went off. Bateson and the others had to carry the dummy to the cricket ground, but they had a good bonfire and burned it. And they had heaps of fireworks, too—dear ones from Auckland, Des said.'

'I wish I'd seen the fireworks,' said David. 'Have you seen fireworks, Ma?'

'Course she hasn't! She hasn't seen anything,' Malcolm said before

Amy could admit that she had never had the chance to see fireworks. 'Someone's going to sort old Simons out, anyway, he needn't think he's so smart. He never came near them last night, he was too scared. Coward.'

'Reverend Simons must be nearly sixty, Mal,' Amy said. 'It doesn't make him a coward just because he didn't want to fight a mob of young... young *larrikins*. They should be ashamed of themselves.'

'Just 'cause they were having a bit of fun. You're an old misery like Simons.' Evidently remembering the success of his earlier jab, he repeated it. 'You're like Pa.'

'I don't mind people having fun, Mal,' said Amy. 'I want you to enjoy yourself. I just don't—' she stopped as she realised Malcolm had gone outside, David trailing in his wake. She sighed, and went back to her work. It as much use expecting Malcolm to take any notice of her as it was wishing that she could have seen the fireworks.

Amy lay in bed staring into the darkness, wondering what had woken her so abruptly. The night seemed as tranquil as it should, the distant sound of a morepork only serving to accentuate the silence around the cottage.

So why was she suddenly wide-awake and wary? She lay very still, probing the silence until she heard it again: a slight jingling of metal against metal. The sound of someone shifting things about in the shed that held the horses' tack.

Moving as quietly as she could, she pushed the covers back and crouched on her bed to look outside. She could not see the shed from her window, but now that her senses were attuned she could hear other noises. Again there was the metallic jingling, and a muffled curse as whoever was carrying the bridle tried to stop it making a noise as it swung. Then footsteps sounded, rustling through the long grass between the shed and the horse paddock.

Just as it occurred to her to wonder why Biff had made no challenge to the intruder, the dog gave a short bark that seemed more questioning than aggressive.

'Shut up, Biff,' she heard a low voice say. With a mixture of distress and resignation, Amy recognised that voice: it was Malcolm prowling around outside, doing his best to catch his pony and ride away without waking anyone in the cottage.

Her mind raced while she listened to him catch Brownie and lead the pony over to the fence to mount. If she rushed out to try and stop him she would be sure to wake Charlie, and he would be dangerously angry at such flagrant disobedience from Malcolm. But if she let him go off by himself he would be getting into Heaven alone knew what sort of mischief.

She sank down on the bed, helplessness washing over her. Malcolm might survive the escapade unscathed, or he might not; he would have to take his chances. He was a big boy for twelve; he could probably hold his own in the company he chose to keep. And if Charlie were to storm out there and find Malcolm sneaking off he would half kill the boy; she knew that with utter certainty. She tried to take comfort in the knowledge that at least Malcolm was too young for whoring.

Biff gave a whine of excitement as the sound of hooves told Amy that the pony was moving down the track. 'Make him shut up,' she heard Malcolm urge, and for a moment she wondered why the boy was talking to himself.

Only for a moment. 'Shh, Biff,' came a higher-pitched voice through the darkness. 'Lie down! Good dog.'

Amy scrambled back to her knees to peer out through the window, forgetting to move quietly. She strained her eyes to make out the figures in what little moonlight shone through the ragged clouds as the pony moved off down the track.

Not my little Davie! Not my little boy. Amy leaned out the window, trying to catch a last glimpse of the boys, until she realised she was in danger of falling right out. She collapsed limply onto the bed. *Not Davie. Not Davie.*

It was no use hoping she would get any sleep that night. She got up and crept through the house, running her hand along the walls to feel her way in the darkness, until she was in the boys' bedroom. The moonlight was brighter there; she gave a start when she saw two lumps in the bed. A step closer showed her that the lumps were the boys' pillows, slipped under the blankets in a clumsy attempt to disguise their owners' absence. The childishness of the gesture almost made her weep. Those boys were ridiculously young to be out on their own after dark. Especially David.

She paced up and down the tiny room until her legs ached with weariness, though her mind raced as frantically as ever. Then she sat on the boys' bed with her back against the wall and her arms wrapped around her legs, looking at the strange shadows moonlight made out of the familiar objects in the room.

It smelt of little boys: of the dirt she scrubbed out of their knees every Saturday night only to find it as ingrained as ever by Monday afternoon. The horsy smell that hours spent riding bareback left clinging to their clothes. The doggy smell of Biff from the times when David sneaked him onto the bed. And there was the smell that hers was the only nose in the house sensitive to pick up: a faint trace of urine from the last time David had wet the bed after she had thought he was too old to need a napkin at night. No matter how many times she aired that mattress the smell remained. Its association with infancy reminded her of the sickly-sweet milky smell that had hung around the boys when they were babies. Tiny little babies nuzzling at her breasts, relying on her for protection. They were still little boys, for all Malcolm tried to act so grown-up. And they were out there in the night with no one to look after them.

She shivered and hugged herself more closely, then stifled a cry as she felt something brush against her. 'Ginger,' she whispered. 'You gave me a fright. Do you want a cuddle? I do, anyway.'

She lowered her knees to make a lap. The big tabby climbed onto her, circled around until he was comfortable, then lay down with his head resting against her chest. Amy felt rather than heard his rumbling purr as she stroked him. Her stomach was warm where Ginger lay, and the warmth slowly spread through her as she leaned against the wall and settled down for the long, weary vigil.

David clung tightly to Malcolm as they cantered along the beach, moonlight silvery on the water now that the clouds had cleared. The wind slipped past Malcolm to bite at David's unprotected ears. He pressed his face against Malcolm's back, warm through his jacket, to try and hide from it.

'Don't wriggle,' Malcolm called without turning his head. 'You'll put Brownie off his stride. It's heavy for him, carrying both of us.'

David did his best to keep still, but he could not resist leaning a little to one side to peer down at the sand as it disappeared under Brownie's hooves. The pony stumbled slightly, and another yell from Malcolm had David sitting bolt upright and clinging tighter than ever.

His heart was pounding with excitement as he looked about him, eyes wide at the strangeness of his surroundings. He had travelled along this stretch of beach far more times than he could remember, but everything looked so different in the moonlight that he could hardly identify a single landmark.

He had never been out at night without his parents, and never beyond the valley even then. He had listened wide-eyed to Malcolm's tales of outings with his friends: of wild races on their horses, stolen kegs of beer, wrestling matches that turned into fights, and daring raids on the choicer orchards of the district. The other boys were all older than Malcolm, and David had known that there was no hope they would accept a ten-year-old like him as part of their group.

And then yesterday Malcolm had sworn him to secrecy with the most solemn oaths and told him of tonight's escapade, then (wonder of wonders) told him that if he wanted he could come too. If he wanted! All that day David had thought he would burst, he was so full of pride and anticipation.

He had been determined not to fall asleep while he and Malcolm lay in bed waiting until it was safe to creep from the house, but Malcolm had had to shake him awake when the time came. There was no trace of sleepiness in him now, though. Not now that he was having the first real adventure of his life.

Brownie's hooves rattled noisily over stones as they left the beach and met the road into Ruatane. As soon as they had crossed the bridge Malcolm slowed the pony to a walk, and David made out a shadowy group of figures. There were about a dozen youths, all much bigger than him. As they spoke in loud whispers he recognised a few voices, but could only put names to Des Feenan and the heavy-browed youth beside him who by his likeness to Des must be his brother Liam. Liam Feenan seemed to be the oldest there. Most of the others were town boys, David knew; the sort his mother called 'larrikins'. The ones who were old enough to go into the pubs tended to spend their evenings in one of Ruatane's two hotels, sometimes buying up beer to share with their younger cronies who hung about hopefully outside.

Tonight they were all united by the expectation of trouble. Though they spoke in low voices, David could sense their excitement. His own heart beat faster as he looked around at the other boys, most of them towering above him now that he had slid from Brownie's back.

'What's he doing here?' Des demanded of Malcolm. David did not need to see his face to know there was a sneer on it.

'You said we should bring as many fellows as we could,' Malcolm said, a trace of belligerence in his voice. 'So I brought my brother. What's wrong with that?'

'Aw, bloody hell,' Des said in disgust. 'We don't want little kids here! What say he starts bawling and wants his Mama?'

David felt his face burning as the other boys gathered round and stared at him. He wanted to protest that he was as tough as any of them, but when he opened his mouth no sound came out except a small squeak that was lost in the murmur of voices.

'He won't,' Malcolm insisted.

'How old is he?' one of the other boys asked.

'Twelve,' Malcolm lied.

67

'I thought you were twelve, Mal,' Des said dubiously. 'How can he be twelve too?'

'I'm thirteen.' Malcolm awarded himself the extra year with such assurance that no one disputed it.

'Aw, leave him alone, Des,' Liam Feenan decreed, secure in his own superiority of age and height. 'Mal's always ready for a bit of action, his brother can't be too much different. What's your name, boy?'

'Dave,' David said, trying to make his voice deeper than its usual soprano.

'Have a taste of this, then, Dave. This'll give you a bit of spunk.' He shoved a flask under David's nose. The younger boy took a step backwards in surprise. The acrid smell from the flask burned his nostrils, and reminded him uneasily of his father in his most terrifying moods.

Malcolm leaned close to whisper in his ear. 'Drink it,' he hissed. 'Show them you're not a Mama's boy.'

David snatched hold of the flask and took a gulp of whatever was in it. He nearly choked as a line of fire etched its way down his throat, burning a passage into his stomach, but he managed to smother the sound so that it came out as a strangled cough. He wiped his hand across his mouth and handed the flask back to Liam, affecting an air of nonchalance as though he were used to drinking liquid fire.

'He knows how to drink, anyway,' Liam said with an approving chuckle, tucking the flask back in his jacket pocket. 'Let's get on with the fun.'

There was something lying at Liam's feet that David at first took to be a bundle of old clothes, but when Liam gave it a kick David saw it was a crude effigy made out of clumps of straw tied to resemble arms and legs. The effigy wore a dark jacket, and a length of rope had been tied around its neck. 'I pinched the coat from Simons' porch when the old bugger was out the other day,' Liam said. 'Thought it might come in handy. Looks better on this thing than it did on the other bloke, eh?' He lifted his handiwork aloft to admire it the more easily. 'Time this fellow went home. Too late at night for him to be out by himself. He might get in a bit of bother.' David laughed with the others, though he had no idea what the older boy meant.

His chest swelling with pride at being accepted by such company, David listened intently as Liam outlined the plan. Malcolm had been vague on the details of the night's escapade, apart from telling David they were going to have some fun at Reverend Simons' expense. David was not greatly enlightened by Liam's explanation, but it seemed that they were to creep around to the minister's house, make their way into his paddock, and there do whatever damage they could manage without risking their own persons.

The explanation was interrupted by frequent swigs from the keg that stood at Liam's feet. From time to time other boys snatched up the keg and took long swallows. Malcolm darted in and made a grab for it, took a swig, then passed it to David.

The beer tasted sweet after the harsh whisky, and David gulped at it gratefully. As he handed the keg back to Malcolm, the burning in his throat extinguished by the cool beer, he remembered belatedly that his mother always said beer was the first step on the road to strong drink. Strong drink, he knew, meant whisky; well, having tried it once he would be in no hurry to taste it again. But he would not like his mother to know what he had done. He wouldn't want her to be upset with him.

He pushed the thought aside. His mother would never know, he and Malcolm had sneaked away so quietly. She would think they were both fast asleep. He gave an excited little giggle as he thought about just where he was and who he was with. Malcolm dug him in the ribs and told him to be quiet.

When the boys who had come any distance had tethered their horses under the bridge, the group made its way to the vicarage. The keg of beer made the rounds several times as they walked along the dusty road, and David took his turn with the rest of the boys. The road seemed to have an unreasonable number of large rocks in it, all of them eager to try and trip him up, and he had become mysteriously clumsy. By the time they reached the gate that led into the vicarage paddock, his feet had received several painful wrenches. But for some reason that he could not quite fathom, it all seemed very funny. Several times Malcolm had to shush him as he broke into foolish giggles.

Instead of lifting the wire loop that held the gate closed, the bigger boys began to kick and shove at it. The gate's hinges did not put up much resistance, and it was soon lying at a drunken angle while they clambered over it. Two of the biggest boys completed the job by taking hold of the gate and hauling at it until they had wrenched it right away from its post and flung it to the ground.

The vicarage was only a few yards away across the grass, with a fence separating its garden from the paddock that served as grazing for Reverend Simons' horse and his house cow. David could make out the shapes of the trees that shaded the house, darker shadows against the gloomy sky. There was a small byre in the corner of the paddock nearest the house; a sign that the minister clung to the English custom of keeping his cow under cover at night and in bad weather even in the mild Bay of Plenty climate. The byre's jutting roof was high enough to shelter a horse in bad weather while still leaving room for its usual occupant. On this calm evening the horse was on the opposite side of the paddock from the boys who had invaded its domain, but apart from a snort of protest it ignored them.

'What are we going to do now?' one of the boys asked Liam.

'How about we chase his horse out,' another boy suggested, earning David's disgust at his ignorance. The boy obviously knew nothing about horses; clearly he was a town boy from a family too poor to have a horse.

'Don't be stupid,' Malcolm said. 'If you chase it out it'll just hang around in the road then come back in the paddock. It's not going to run off anywhere.'

'Who are you calling stupid?' the other boy demanded. 'Cheeky little bugger! Want me to push your face in the cow shit?'

'Shut up, the pair of you,' Liam said. 'You can fight it out when we're finished here.' The keg of beer made the rounds again while Liam looked around the paddock. He caught sight of a neat haystack. 'Right, let's get stuck into that.' Liam led the way to the stack and dropped the effigy he had carried from the bridge. He snatched up a pitchfork that had been left lying beside the pile of hay, and with a jerk thrust it into the stack.

As if the thrust of the pitchfork had been some kind of signal, all the boys threw themselves at the stack, tearing at it with their bare hands. For a moment David stared in shock, remembering all the stacks he and Malcolm had helped build. But he pushed aside the uncomfortable picture of what their father would do to them if he caught them demolishing haystacks, instead launching himself into the task. He was soon caught up in the frenzy of destruction, laughing with delight as the stack was reduced to an untidy sprawl of hay and trodden into uselessness in the dirt of the paddock.

All efforts at silence were abandoned now that excitement and a good deal of beer were having their effects on the boys. When the stack had been destroyed they rushed to the fence separating the paddock from the house and surged over it, David falling flat on his face in the process. He picked himself up and ran on, heedless of his bruised knees.

Liam suspended his effigy from the verandah rail, the rope above its jacket holding it like a noose, and shoved it so that it began to swing. He took the pitchfork that he had carried from the ruin of the haystack and stabbed it into what would have been the dummy's chest, laughing as he did so.

There was something about Liam's laugh that sent a small shiver through David; or perhaps it was the way the older boy thrust the pitchfork with such relish. Crudely made as it was, the dummy looked too much like a man as it swung wildly on its rope, the weight of the protruding pitchfork making its motion erratic.

'Time Mr Simons came out to see his visitor,' Liam said. 'Let's wake him up.' He gathered a handful of gravel from the path that led up to the vicarage's front door and hurled it onto the roof, where it made a satisfyingly loud rattle against the corrugated iron.

The other boys joined in, and for several seconds the noise of gravel on the roof was like a hail storm. David forgot the uneasy feeling Liam had given him earlier. He hurled double handfuls of gravel until he realised the other boys had stopped.

A dim light flickered through the etched glass panel of the front door, then the brighter light of a hurricane lamp flared up as it was lit from the flickering candle. The door was flung open, and the tall figure of Reverend Simons emerged. His face looked unnaturally white in the lamp light, contrasted against his dark clothes and with his black hair unruly around it.

'What's going on?' he demanded, shouting even louder than he did in his most impassioned sermons.

Authority rang from Reverend Simons' voice, and David was used to obeying authority even in its most impenetrable forms. He shrank instinctively away from the anger in that voice until he had put several of the other boys between himself and the black-clothed figure on the verandah.

'Thought you might like a visitor. He doesn't say much, but he could tell you a few things about what happens to interfering old busybodies,' Liam called. He sauntered up to the verandah and shoved at the dummy.

Reverend Simons gave a start as the effigy began swinging, but he soon regained his outward composure. 'Get out of here,' he said. 'Go on, get on home, the lot of you.'

'Aren't you going to ask your visitor in for a drink?' Liam taunted.

'If you're not off this property in one minute I shall be forced to summon the sergeant,' Reverend Simons said.

'Huh! He'd be too scared to show his face. Even if we did let you out of here.'

'I'm warning you, lad.'

'You?' Liam took a step closer, placing his foot on the edge of the verandah. 'What are you going to do, old man? How are you going to stop me coming inside if I want to?'

'Hey, leave him alone, eh?' another boy said, tugging at Liam's sleeve.

'You said we'd just give him a bit of a fright.'

Liam shook off the hand. 'Shut up. You can go slinking home to your mam if you want. I reckon this old fellow's got a bit of money stashed away inside. I reckon he could share it around. What do you say to that, old man?'

Reverend Simons stood his ground and fixed Liam with a steely glare. 'I say you're to leave my property immediately.' His voice was as steady as if he were talking to a stray cat instead of a hulking youth.

Liam stepped up onto the verandah and stared back at the minister. They were much the same height, though Liam was broader across the shoulders. He reached towards his jacket pocket, and suddenly David knew without having to see it that there was a knife in there.

Liam shifted on his feet slightly, and the lantern light glinted on the long blade. David's mouth had gone dry. He stared mesmerised at the tableau, hardly daring to breathe for fear that he might break the spell.

'Hey, what's going on?' This time the voice came from behind the group of boys, from the street facing the vicarage's front gate. 'What was all that shouting about? There wasn't a house in the street we couldn't hear you from.'

David looked in the direction of the voice, and saw five men standing in the road. The one who had spoken was holding a large stick.

'Gilbert,' Reverend Simons called out, unmistakable relief in his voice. 'I've a few visitors I didn't invite.'

'You young rascals! What do you think you're up to?' The man Reverend Simons had called Gilbert opened the front gate and began advancing up the path, the other men close behind him. David saw that as well as a lantern each they were carrying an assortment of spades, sticks and shovels; each item looked quite capable of serving as a weapon.

He only had a moment to take in these details. As the men approached them, the boys abandoned any notions of bravery and took to their heels, clambering back over the fence into the paddock rather than confront the men who barred the way to the front gate.

David had little experience in escaping from such situations, so he was slower to react than the others. It was only when he heard Malcolm call his name that he turned and ran after them. But he was nimbler than the bigger boys, and it took him only moments to fling himself over the fence.

As he landed in the paddock, for a terrible moment he thought one of his pursuers had grabbed hold of him. He gave a desperate wrench, and there was a ripping noise as he tore himself free of the large nail that had snagged his trouser leg. It came loose with a suddenness that sent him sprawling. He scrambled upright and began to run, giving a yelp of pain when he found that he had twisted his ankle in the fall.

'See if we can catch any of them,' one of the men called. A wave of panic rose in David as he realised that with his twisted ankle he could not possibly outrun them. The other boys were already at the outer gate of the paddock; he would be the only one who would fall into the hands of those angry men. It would be like being beaten by five copies of his father.

He had to get away. Despite the pain in his ankle, David forced himself to run. Their eyes a little blinded by the hurricane lamps they carried, the men could not see in the dark as well as he could. He had a few seconds before they would catch sight of him; not long enough to get out of the paddock and back to the bridge, but time enough to find a hiding place.

The cow gave only the mildest of snorts as David wriggled between her and the manger full of hay, hardly disturbed from her standing doze by the arrival of one small boy. She allowed David to pat her flank, then he crouched against the manger and tried to make himself even smaller.

'It's no use, Gilbert, they're well clear by now.' David jumped when he heard Reverend Simons' voice just outside the byre.

'None of them hiding in this shed of yours?'

'No. Esmeralda would have made a fuss if they'd come near her, she's not used to anyone but me handling her.'

Esmeralda? David had never heard such an outlandish name for a woman, let alone a cow. He crouched in the darkness, feeling the warm breath of the cow dampening his hair, and his heart filled with gratitude that Esmeralda had not betrayed him.

'Did you recognise any of them?' one of the men asked.

'Not really,' Reverend Simons said. 'I think I've seen that hulking great fellow who seemed to be the ringleader—he pulled a knife, by the way—probably hanging around the hotels, but I couldn't put a name to him. And then there was… well, I didn't get a good look at any of the others, but I rather thought one of them had red hair.'

'Not a lot of redheads around here.'

'No.' The minister was silent for a moment. 'Mrs Stewart's older boy has red hair.'

'Mal?' The other man sounded dubious. 'Charlie Stewart wouldn't allow his boys out at night, he doesn't stand for any nonsense from wife or child from what I've heard. Probably a boy from town, just one you haven't seen before.'

'Perhaps.' Reverend Simons sounded unconvinced.

'I don't know, Gil, I've seen Mal hanging around with those Feenans a few times,' one of other men put in. 'They're usually pretty close to any mischief going on.'

'Maybe you're right, then. I know this for a fact, anyway—Charlie'd flay the boy alive if he found out he'd been here.'

'Well, I've no proof. I shouldn't go accusing anyone in particular. But I'll certainly keep my eyes open from now on, see if any undesirables are loitering around.'

'You do that. And if you ever have any trouble, just sing out.'

'I'm most grateful. Would you good men like to pop inside and sample the cup that cheers but does not inebriate?'

The other men declined Reverend Simons' invitation, pleading anxious wives as an excuse. The sound of their voices soon faded away into the distance, and David knew he was once again alone with the cow.

'Thanks, Esmeralda,' he whispered, reaching up to rub behind one furry ear. 'Thanks for keeping quiet.' The cow turned her head towards him, and in the moonlight that crept through cracks in the wall he saw that she had large, soft eyes with a surprisingly knowing expression.

David eased himself upright from his cramped position and sat on the edge of the manger while he thought about what to do next. He wriggled his ankle experimentally and found that while it was still tender the worst of the pain had gone.

He did not blame Malcolm for leaving him there; if Malcolm had stayed they would probably both have been caught. He was glad the other boys had got away; glad that by now Malcolm must be cantering along the beach, well clear of danger. But it was going to be a very long walk home.

David tried to picture the route in his mind. He would have to creep along the dark streets back to the bridge, and from there down to the beach. He hoped there would be enough moonlight to guide him along the sand; there were two or three small streams to cross, easily forded on horseback but probably none too easy by foot. And what if he missed the track up into the valley? Malcolm seemed to know the way, and Brownie could probably find his way home by himself if he had to. But David was not sure that he would be able to pick out the rough beginning of the track by himself and in the dark. How far down the coast might he get before he realised his mistake?

He had to do it; he had to try and find his way home. If he sat in the byre all night he would be found there in the morning, and the most hideous vengeance would descend on him; first of all from the minister,

74

and later from his father. The thought terrified him, and he stood up ready to make a start. But the picture of walking all those miles alone and in the dark crowded in on him, his fear made sharper by the jolt of pain in his foot when he put his weight on it. Alone and in the dark. Mysterious nighttime noises swarming around him. Shadows holding nameless terrors. Large tears welled up in his eyes and made warm trails down both cheeks.

A rustling outside the byre made him jump. He started to slide back down into his hiding place until a hoarse whisper stopped him.

'Dave? Where are you?'

'Mal!' In the surge of relief, he almost forgot to keep his voice low. 'I'm in here with Esmeralda.' He pushed past the cow and almost bumped into Malcolm as his brother rushed into the byre.

The cow gave an aggrieved snort at the sudden invasion. David took hold of Malcolm's arm and pulled him back outside. 'She doesn't like strangers,' he explained. 'I heard the minister say that. She didn't make any noise when I went in there, though. She's a nice cow.'

'It's just a cow,' Malcolm said with a shrug.

'No, she's prettier than Pa's ones. I think she's got a bit of Uncle Frank's sort of cow in her.'

'Never mind about the cow, let's get out of here. Why are you walking funny?'

'I hurt my foot. It doesn't hurt much, but I can't go fast.'

'Idiot! Put your arm around my shoulder, then, I'll give you a hand. And shut up till we're out of here, I don't want anyone hearing us.'

They crept back to the bridge where Brownie waited patiently, chewing on a mouthful of the scrubby grass that grew there. Malcolm gave David a leg up, and led Brownie by the reins until they were across the bridge. Malcolm climbed onto Brownie's back, using the bridge railing as a step, then guided the pony down to the beach and coaxed him into a gentle trot.

'Brownie'll be stiff after standing all that time in the cold,' he said. 'I won't canter him for a bit.'

David held on around Malcolm's waist, enjoying the warmth of his brother's closeness. 'Thanks for waiting for me, Mal.'

'Course I waited for you! I couldn't have gone home without you, could I? What would I have told the old man?' He turned his head slightly to give a quick glance at David. 'I got a heck of a fright when I got back to the bridge and I couldn't find you. I thought those men had caught you.'

'I was scared they would.' David gave a small shudder, and clung more tightly.

'Don't squeeze like that,' Malcolm said, squirming. 'Gee, it was funny, eh? Old Simons was that scared when Liam said he wanted to come in. He must have just about wet himself.'

David did not usually argue with his brother; Malcolm's two year advantage of strength and skill in fighting had always discouraged disagreement. But his nagging doubt would not allow him to keep silent. 'Mr Simons was quite brave, you know, Mal.'

'Eh? How do you mean?'

'Well, he just stood there and looked at us. He didn't look scared, or sing out, or anything like that. And he's really old, he must be nearly as old as Grandpa. He couldn't have done anything if Liam had gone for him, but he just stood there. Don't you reckon that was brave?'

Malcolm chewed this idea over for some time. 'I guess maybe it was,' he admitted. 'Anyway, it was good fun,' he added stoutly. He peered at the moon through the low cloud. 'I'd better start cantering him soon. We want to get home before it gets pitch dark.'

It was no use trying to talk while the pony cantered, and in any case David did not feel much like speaking. The memory of crouching alone in the byre waiting for the hand of justice to fall slowly faded, until all he was aware of was the muffled, rhythmic thud of hooves on sand. The sound was soothing in its repetitiveness, and David let his eyes close, knowing he could trust Malcolm to guide the pony safely over the rough parts of the beach.

He woke to find Malcolm tugging at his arm. 'Get off,' Malcolm whispered. 'We're home.' David slid from the pony's back and looked around dazedly, surprised that he had slept for so much of the ride.

He waited while Malcolm unharnessed Brownie and carried the pony's tack to the shed, then the two boys walked up to the house. David trailed along beside Malcolm, stumbling with weariness. Now that the excitement was long over and bed was an imminent prospect it was hard to drag one foot in front of the other. The pain in his twisted ankle was hardly more than an occasional twinge now. There was a growing discomfort in his belly; David was too naive to recognise the bloated feeling overlaid with nausea as the after-effects of a good deal of beer mixed with a large gulp of whisky.

'Fancy Pa lying in bed snoring, and all the time we were out having fun,' Malcolm whispered. 'Him and Ma never even knew we were gone!'

David giggled at the thought, and at the pleasure of sharing a conspiracy with his big brother. Malcolm shushed him, and they crept on tiptoe up the front door steps and into their silent bedroom.

A white shape moved suddenly in the darkness. David choked back a yelp of alarm and snatched hold of Malcolm's arm before he realised what the shape was.

'Ma,' he whispered in dismay.

'Where have you two been? What have you been doing?' She sounded frantic, though she kept her voice to a low whisper.

'What are you doing sneaking around after us? Poking around in our room? Just bugger off and leave us alone,' Malcolm flung at her.

She pushed past him to the door and quietly slid it to, Ginger making his escape just before the door closed. Then she lit the candle that stood on the chest of drawers and turned to face the boys.

David had never seen his mother looking like this. Her hair was loose and sleep-rumpled from the time she had lain in bed before the boys had unknowingly disturbed her, and her face looked pinched and cold after the long hours of waiting for their return. But it was her eyes that distressed him most. They were wide-open and wild-looking, full of pain and the marks of fear.

'You've been out getting in trouble, haven't you? All right, don't tell me. I can't make you. I know you've been drinking, Mal, I can smell it on you.' She turned to David, and her eyes went even wider. 'David, you smell of it too!'

He could find no words to explain. His adventure no longer seemed exciting and heroic; in the face of his mother's pain the whole affair was small and mean. The beer sloshed uncomfortably in his belly, and when he opened his mouth to say something, anything, that might excuse him a little, instead of words a loud belch emerged.

His mother turned on Malcolm. 'You've no right, Mal. You've no right to take Dave out with you like that—leading him into Lord knows what sort of company. He's only a little boy—he doesn't know any better. And you've made him drink!'

'He didn't make me, Ma,' David put in. 'I wanted to go with him. Honest I did.'

But his mother took no notice of him. 'If I told your father, Mal—'

'You won't. You're too scared of him,' Malcolm said scornfully.

She shook her head. 'I don't like seeing him hurt you, that's why I never tell on you. But maybe I should. If you're going to start dragging David into this sort of thing, I might just have to tell him.'

'I don't care if you do,' Malcolm said. David looked at him in alarm. His brother might not care, but David had no desire to taste their father's retribution. 'He'll just give me another hiding. I don't care if he does or not.'

'He might do more than that, Mal. If he finds out what you've been up to, he might just take Brownie off you. You won't be able to go out with those awful boys without a horse, will you? You'll—'

'You bitch!' Malcolm hissed, his face twisted in fear and anger. 'You want Pa to take Brownie off me! You never want me to have any fun. You're always nagging and whinging at me. You're just an old bitch. I hate you!'

She took a step back as if he had struck her. 'Don't, Mal,' she whispered. 'Don't say that to me. Please don't.'

'I do! I hate you! If you make Pa take Brownie off me I'll… I'll…' He flung himself down on the bed and pummelled at the mattress, unable to put his distress into words, then sat up, his face a mask of agony. 'I'll hate you if you do.'

'All right,' she cried out, her voice rising in pitch till it would have been a shriek if she had not forced it into a whisper. 'I won't tell him, you know I won't. Do whatever you want, then. Turn into a drunkard— and a lecher when you're old enough. I can't stop you doing any of it.' She seemed to collapse in on herself till she looked even smaller than usual. 'Just don't hate me, Mal.' Malcolm turned his face away, refusing to meet her pleading expression.

'Take your trousers off, David,' she said, her voice low again. 'You've got a huge rip down that leg, and you haven't got any more clean pairs. I'll get them mended before your father takes you milking. Even he couldn't help but notice a rip like that. Anyway, you'd catch a chill wandering around with your trousers all hanging open.'

She took the trousers when David had stepped out of them. 'He might notice the smell on your breath, too, if it's still strong in the morning. Wait a minute.' She left the room briefly, returning with two sprigs of mint which she placed on the chest of drawers. 'Chew this when you get up, that'll hide the smell a bit. Now you'd better try and get to sleep. You're not going to feel much like getting up in the morning.'

She paused in the doorway, looking back at the two of them with her face framed in the light of the candle she carried. Malcolm had turned his face to the wall, but David was held unwillingly by the hurt in her eyes.

'I didn't think you'd do anything like this, David,' she whispered. Then she was gone.

Despite the tiredness of his body, David could not sleep. He tossed and turned until Malcolm gave him a sharp dig in the ribs and told him to lie still, but forcing his body to stop moving did not ease the restlessness of his mind.

He was still wide awake when his mother slipped quietly into the darkened room and put David's newly-mended trousers on the end of the bed. He pretended sleep while she smoothed the covers over the boys and tucked them in deftly, and as she stood looking down at them he risked peeping through his closed lashes.

She was standing very still, one hand hovering over him as if she would have liked to touch him. There was enough moonlight coming through the window for David to see the silvery trail down each cheek that told him she was crying.

She turned away and left the room as quietly as she had come. David stared at the door she had closed behind her. His mother was crying, and it was his fault. He had made his mother cry.

He felt so sick and wretched with guilt that it took him several minutes to realise there was another reason than remorse for the grinding discomfort in his belly.

'What are you doing?' Malcolm asked drowsily as David tumbled out of bed and made a rush for the door.

'I feel crook. I think I'm going to throw up.' He raced outside, nearly falling down the front steps in his haste, then stood in the dew-damp grass and gave in to the lurching in his guts.

It took some time for him to empty his stomach into a watery mass that soaked into the ground at his feet, the solid remains of his dinner unrecognisable lumps floating in the sticky puddle. When he had finished he felt weak, his stomach aching from the effort of repeated retching, but his head was clearer.

His mother was crying. She was always kind to him, never angry, and she always tried to stop his father from hitting him. She cried when his father beat him or Malcolm, and then she would try to make it up to them with something specially nice to eat. Whatever David did, she praised and encouraged him. He had never thought he would see her look at him with such hurt and confusion in her eyes.

He stole around the outside of the house and in the back door, then through the kitchen until his hand rested on the handle of his mother's door. He tried to turn the handle silently, but he had barely taken a step into the room when she called out.

'Who's there? What do you want?' Her voice was soft, but he thought she sounded a little frightened.

'Ma?'

'David.' She made the word sound flat and tired. 'Go back to bed.'

'But I want to—'

'You've got to get up in a couple of hours. You're going to be very tired, and you'll probably have a headache. Don't make it worse by being silly now.'

'I want to say sorry, Ma. Please let me say it.'

She was silent. David crept over to her bed, the bare boards cold under his feet until his toes reached the rag rug. Hesitantly he lifted the covers, and when his mother made no protest he crawled in beside her.

She smelt of the dried lavender she kept in the drawer with her nightdresses. Her long, soft hair brushed against his neck as he pressed against her, tickling him pleasurably.

'I'm sorry, Ma.'

She gave a small sigh and slipped her arms around him, pulling him close till his back rested against the curve of her body. 'Davie, why did you do it?'

'Don't you like me any more?' He heard his voice tremble.

She held him tighter. 'It's all right. I wish you hadn't gone out drinking like that, but whatever you do I'll still love you.' She placed a soft kiss on the top of his head. 'Do you understand why I don't want you to do things like that?'

David thought back to the turmoil of his night. It no longer seemed like an adventure. Instead of the excitement, he remembered the disquieting look of hatred on Liam Feenan's face, eyes glittering with whisky-fed courage. Then the fear of crouching alone in the cow byre. And after that, the horrible retching from which his abdominal muscles still ached.

'I think so. Yes, I do,' he said with sudden certainty. He rolled onto his back and stared solemnly at the white shape of her face in the darkness. 'Ma, I'm never, ever going to drink again. Not even when I'm grown up.'

'Well, you might feel differently when you're a man. But at least leave it till then.'

'No, I'm *never* going to,' he insisted.

'Oh, Davie, what would I do without you?' She almost sounded as though she was crying again, but her voice was happy, and that was all that mattered. 'You'd better go back to bed, darling. Try and get a little bit of sleep.'

He did not want to leave the warm softness of his mother's bed, not just yet. 'Can't I stay with you? Just for a bit?'

She laughed, a muffled sound of pleasure. 'All right, then, just for a little while. I'll wake you up in time, anyway. I've been awake all night waiting for you, I don't think I'll get to sleep now.'

David laid his head on her soft chest and slipped into an untroubled sleep.

6

Some months before her latest baby was due, Lizzie had discovered that her usual nurse, Mrs Parsons, planned to be away from Ruatane in December when the baby was expected. Encouraged by Amy, she had sent Frank to ask Mrs Coulson if she would oblige.

'She didn't really want to,' Lizzie reported to Amy after Frank's mission. 'She said she doesn't do many deliveries at people's places any more, she just has women to stay with her. She says she's getting a bit old to do all the housekeeping and looking after the other children and all that. Frank talked her round, though.'

'It'll be lovely having Mrs Coulson here,' said Amy. 'I'll be able to come and see her lots.'

'Come and see *me*, you mean,' Lizzie said in pretended indignation. 'Me and the new baby. I should hope that's more important than some old nurse.'

'That's no fun, I see you nearly every week, and you having another baby's no novelty,' Amy teased.

'It still is to Frank,' Lizzie said. 'Every time I have one, you'd think it was the first baby ever born. He doesn't get in a real state like he used to, thinking I was going to break or something, but he's still like a little kid with a toy whenever we get a new baby.' She let her hands rest on the mound of her belly. 'Me, I'll just be glad that's over with for another couple of years.'

But the smile that played around Lizzie's lips gave the lie to her attempt at sounding blasé. 'It'll be nice to have a little one around again.'

Amy did not manage to be present at the birth of Lizzie and Frank's new daughter; Rose arrived too suddenly for that, on the evening of a sunny day in early December after a bare two hours of labour. But Amy paid her first visit the next morning, walking briskly down the road while the dew still lay in the shady places.

Mrs Coulson greeted her with a warm embrace, and Amy let her head rest on the older woman's chest as if she were a small child. 'It's been far too long since I saw you, my dear,' the nurse said.

She released Amy, and turned towards the bench. 'I'll just finish these few dishes, then you can come and see my latest little one. Not that I can take much credit for this one, mind you—she's the sort of baby who comes out looking like she's done it all before. And such a bonny little thing.'

'Is Lizzie all right?' Amy asked. She took the dish towel from Mrs Coulson and dried the last few plates.

'Right as rain. You'd hardly know she delivered just last night—I can see I'm going to have trouble keeping that one in bed for two weeks. Most women relish the chance to put their feet up, but not her.'

'Lizzie doesn't like missing anything,' Amy said. 'If you tell Frank she's to stay put, he'll make sure she does. He takes good care of Lizzie.'

'I do like him,' said Mrs Coulson. 'He's such a dear. He fusses around Mrs Kelly all the time, seeing that she's comfortable. I didn't want to take this job on, not with all the other children to cook for and clean up after, but Mr Kelly looked so worried when I tried putting him off. I just couldn't say no to him.'

'I told Frank he should ask you,' Amy confessed. 'I said you were the best nurse in town. I hoped I'd be able to come and see you if you did decide to look after Lizzie.'

'Yes, Mr Kelly said you'd praised me to the skies,' Mrs Coulson said, giving Amy a fond smile. 'Anyway, Mrs Kelly's mother took the two youngest boys off home with her last night, so there's only three of them to do for. And the girls are old enough to help. You've finished those dishes? Come and see the little one, then. Mr Kelly's up there with them, he can't bear to stay away for long.'

She led the way up the passage, and Amy followed her into the front bedroom. 'Here's a visitor for you, Mrs Kelly,' Mrs Coulson said.

The nurse was right, Amy thought; Lizzie showed little sign of her recent exertions. She was sitting up in bed waving one hand around to illustrate a point she was making to Frank, while he held her other hand in both of his. A small, blanket-wrapped bundle lay in the cradle close by Frank's chair.

'Come and look at my daughter, Amy,' Frank said, taking advantage of the fact that Lizzie had just paused to draw breath. 'Isn't she a beauty?'

Amy knelt beside the cradle and carefully lifted the blanket to admire the tiny baby. 'She's lovely.' She stroked her hand over the little girl's fuzz of dark hair and planted the softest of kisses on her cheek. 'She's not going to be fair like Maudie, is she?'

She rose to sit on the bed and embrace Lizzie as Frank moved his chair to make room. 'You look so well,' Amy told her.

'Of course I am,' said Lizzie. 'It was all over in no time at all. I could just about get up tomorrow.'

'No, you won't,' Frank said before the nurse had a chance to protest.

'You'll stay in bed till Mrs Coulson says you can get up. I don't want you wearing yourself out. Maybe you should try and have a sleep this morning.'

Lizzie pulled a face at him. 'I didn't say I was going to get up, just that I could if I wanted. Don't be such an old fuss-pot.'

'You see that she behaves herself, Mrs Coulson,' Frank said. He rose to his feet. 'Well, I'd better get this milk down to the factory or we'll have the bank turning us off the property.'

'I should think so,' said Lizzie. 'I'm sure Mrs Coulson doesn't want you under her feet all morning.'

'I don't know about that,' Frank told her with a grin. 'At least I'm keeping you quiet so you can't go bossing her around.'

He silenced Lizzie's indignant protests by leaning down to kiss her, then made his way out of the room.

Mrs Coulson left Lizzie and Amy to chat while she smoothed the covers over the sleeping baby, checked to see that Lizzie's bleeding was normal, and folded a pile of clean napkins.

'Look at these lovely flowers lying here with no water,' she said when she went to put the napkins in a drawer. 'I didn't see them earlier.'

'Frank brought them in when he came up from milking,' said Lizzie. 'See the pink roses? He said Rose and me should have some roses, 'cause that's her name, but he could only find a few.'

'I saw a nice vase in your parlour before, I'll put these in some water,' Mrs Coulson said. She gathered up the flowers from the dressing table where Frank had left them, then bustled out of the room.

'Rose,' Amy said, looking down at the baby. 'That's a pretty name.'

'Mmm. It's a good thing I had a girl this time, we couldn't think of any more boys' names. But I've had Rose's names picked out for ages. Rose Amy, we're going to call her.'

'Lizzie, I didn't know you were giving her my name,' Amy exclaimed in delight.

'I would've done it years ago, but I had the two boys in a row, then we managed to put off having Rosie for a bit. Three years we've got between Danny and her. I had more than two years without a baby on the way, that's the longest time in all the years we've been married.'

Amy kissed her on the cheek. 'Thank you for naming her after me.'

'Well, it's about time, isn't it? Three daughters—it's time I gave one of them your name.'

Amy studied Lizzie's face, wondering if her cousin remembered that Amy had given her own daughter Lizzie's name. *Ann Elizabeth. I wanted to give her the best names I could think of.* 'You know, Lizzie, you look better than ever,' Amy said, making her voice light. 'It suits you, having babies.'

'Oh, I should be used to it by now,' Lizzie said. 'I've had six of them, after all. Rosie was no trouble at all. It gets easier every time, really.'

Amy laughed. 'I'll take your word for it. You're the expert, anyway. I've only had four babies.'

They chatted away about the new baby, and Amy was so engrossed with Lizzie and Rose that she was vaguely surprised when she realised Mrs Coulson had come back into the room with Frank's flowers in a vase. The nurse was studying Amy with an expression that struck her as rather odd. Mrs Coulson put the flowers on the dressing table and left again without saying a word.

Despite her insistence that she was completely back to normal, Lizzie began showing signs of drowsiness after a few more minutes.

'It's just left over sleepiness from the chloroform,' she assured Amy after a large yawn had escaped her. 'I'm not really tired at all.' She yawned again, and gave Amy a rueful grin. 'Well, maybe I am a bit. I might have a little sleep before Rosie wakes up again.'

Amy smoothed the covers over Lizzie and tucked her in, then went out to the kitchen, where Mrs Coulson was peering uncertainly into the various drawers and cupboards.

'She's having a sleep,' she told the nurse. 'She's been trying to make out she's not tired, but she could hardly keep her eyes open. Silly thing,' she said affectionately. 'Shall I show you where things are?'

'Oh, that'd be a big help,' Mrs Coulson said. 'It's going to take me long enough getting the meals ready without having to find everything first. I'm afraid I'm not as fast as I used to be.'

Amy persuaded Mrs Coulson to sit down while she explained the arrangements of Lizzie's kitchen and larder, then she helped the nurse prepare the vegetables for lunch. When they finished, they shared a cup of tea on the verandah. 'Take your time doing the rest,' Amy said. 'You won't need to finish getting lunch on for ages.'

'Thank you, dear. I won't have anything to do this afternoon except looking after Mrs Kelly and the little girl. Mrs Kelly said not to start on dinner until her other girls are home from school. She wants them kept busy cleaning up the kitchen and peeling potatoes and suchlike, so they won't get up to any mischief while she has to keep to her bed.' The nurse laughed at the notion. 'I don't think there's much mischief goes on in *this* house. Mrs Kelly keeps them all in line.'

'Yes, she does,' Amy said, smiling. 'She's a good mother. And doesn't she look well? You must have done a good job with Rosie.'

'Oh, there was nothing to it. She hardly needs a nurse, she takes to it so naturally. There's no challenge at all delivering babies for someone like Mrs Kelly, it's as easy as shelling peas. Not like battling away with yours,' she said, giving Amy a pensive smile. 'Those great big boys of yours! What a struggle it was.'

'Mmm,' Amy agreed. 'I'm not made for childbearing, am I?'

'Not really, dear. Especially not with a great big husband like yours. It's a good thing you've stopped bearing.' She gave Amy a thoughtful look. 'You haven't had a child for a long time now.'

'No, I don't seem to get with child any more,' Amy said, avoiding Mrs Coulson's gaze.

The nurse reached out and patted Amy's hand. 'Well, that's your affair, my dear, but I'm sure it's for the best. You certainly look well these days, not like that pale little creature you used to be. And so frightened! I'll never forget that first day your husband left you at my house. I thought you were going to run away from me out into the rain and give birth in the garden, you were such a fearful little thing.'

'Oh, I was,' Amy said. 'I didn't think I'd be able to bear the pain and everything, not after... well, I thought it'd be awful. But then you were so kind to me, I wasn't scared any more. Not until I had to go home again,' she added in a low voice.

'I know, darling,' Mrs Coulson said softly. 'It wasn't easy for me to send you home after David was born, not when you'd told me how your husband behaved after you had Malcolm.'

'I shouldn't really have told you about that.' Amy smiled at Mrs Coulson and laid her head on the older woman's shoulder for a moment. 'You're so easy to talk to, that's the trouble. Anyway, it doesn't matter now. That's all over.'

'So it is, my dear. I'm glad he's seen a bit of sense, however you've managed it. Anyway, never mind all that business,' she went on briskly. 'How are those boys of yours getting on? I never see anything of you these days, and I do take an interest in the children I bring into the world, you know.'

Amy sighed. 'I don't know what to say about Mal, really. Oh, they're both strong and healthy, and they've grown so tall. They both take after Charlie for size. But Mal...'

She shook her head. 'I don't know what to do about him. He's getting into bad company, getting up to goodness knows what mischief. I just don't know what to do.'

'It's natural for you to worry about your children, dear—I've never known a mother who didn't. But are you sure you're not painting it a bit blacker than you need? How old is Malcolm now? Thirteen?'

86

'Twelve. Only twelve.'

'Well, what boy of twelve doesn't get up to a bit of mischief? It's all part of growing up.'

'Not like this. I don't expect him to be perfect, honestly I don't. But I'm so worried about him. Those boys he mixes with—they drink, you know, and Mal's much too young for that. And this latest thing—did you hear about what happened at Reverend Simons'?'

'Those boys who knocked down his haystack? Now, that was a bad business—I heard one of them threatened the poor minister with a knife.'

'I think Mal was with them—I'm almost sure he was. He sneaked out after dark, then he stayed out all night. And he came back all dirty and stinking of drink. As soon as I heard what'd happened in town I knew that's where Mal must have been. And he took David with him.' She clenched her fists at the remembered hurt and anger.

'David too! Oh, my poor girl, what a time you've been having with the pair of them.'

'No, Dave's all right,' Amy said. 'Mal talked him into going out with him that night, but Davie promised me he'll never do anything like that again. I think he was more scared than anything, poor love. I don't need to worry about him. Just Mal.'

She sighed. 'I haven't done much of a job with Mal. I've tried my best, but he just won't take any notice of me. I've never been a very good mother to him.'

'You're being too hard on yourself,' Mrs Coulson protested. 'Boys can be a trial—I should know, I had two of them to bring up on my own. They need a firm hand—at least you've got your husband around for that.'

Amy shook her head. 'Charlie couldn't be any harder on Mal without killing him. He's always expected so much of him.' She frowned, musing. 'Charlie waited a long time for a son, and I think he must have thought everything would be just right when he got one. He wants Mal to be perfect—he always has, right from when Mal was just a little fellow. So whenever Mal does anything wrong, Charlie jumps on him. He's given him some awful hidings.'

'I think any father would be angry with his son for sneaking off at night and getting up to that sort of thing. I can't say I blame Mr Stewart for that.'

'Charlie doesn't know about it,' Amy confessed.

'I'm not sure you should keep something like that to yourself, dear,' Mrs Coulson said carefully.

'I have to.' Amy closed her eyes for a moment, then went on in a steadier voice. 'I don't ever tell on Mal. No, don't tell me I should. I mightn't be much of a mother to him, but I'm doing my best. Mal gets plenty of hidings when he doesn't really deserve them, I'm not going to make him get any more.'

'A bit of firmness doesn't do a child any harm, dear. Look at Mrs Kelly's children—you couldn't find a livelier bunch, full of fun the lot of them, but I don't think Mrs Kelly puts up with any nonsense. You're an affectionate little thing, it's no wonder you get upset when your boys get a hiding, but—'

'What am I meant to do when I see Charlie bashing Mal's head against the wall?' Amy interrupted fiercely. 'And punching and punching him till his face was bleeding? Am I meant to stand and watch my son being killed?'

Mrs Coulson broke the silence that fell between them. 'I'm sorry, dear. I've no business telling you how you should raise your children. I've never lived with a man like your husband—I'm inclined to forget just how bad he is.'

'No, I'm sorry,' Amy said. 'I shouldn't have talked to you like that. You were just trying to help, I know. But I worry about Mal so much, I get a bit touchy when anyone says anything against him.'

'Forget I poked my nose in, then,' Mrs Coulson said.

'It doesn't make Mal behave better when Charlie beats him, you see, it just makes him angry. He hit Charlie once.' Amy heard Mrs Coulson give a sharp intake of breath. 'It was awful. That was when Charlie threw him against the wall, he was so wild with Mal for taking a swing at him. Mal was much smaller than Charlie then, and I was there to stop them, but if they ever have another fight like that…'

She let the thought stay unvoiced. 'I keep hoping if I can just stop Mal and Charlie from fighting it'll all come right one day. Mal's a good boy underneath it all, really he is. He's got in with bad company, but maybe he'll grow out of it. I just have to try and stop him getting in trouble with Charlie.'

Amy saw again in memory the look Malcolm had fixed Charlie with as the blood from his father's blows ran down his face. 'I have to try,' she repeated quietly. 'Mal's getting bigger all the time—stronger, too.'

'You've a lot on your plate, haven't you?' Mrs Coulson said, concern written in her face.

Amy forced herself to smile. 'I'm sorry, I shouldn't be laying my troubles on you like this. I've got lots to be thankful for, really. Dave's hardly given me a moment's worry all his life. He's a real comfort to me.

Maybe I could bring him to see you one Saturday while you're here, if Charlie'll let him off working for a bit.'

'That'd be lovely, dear.'

'And I'll come and see you again tomorrow if I can manage it.'

Amy glanced at the angle of the sun, and was surprised to see how much of the morning had slipped away. 'I'd better get back home or I'll be in trouble.' She kissed Mrs Coulson goodbye and went into the house for a last peek at the sleeping baby before setting off down the road, turning at Frank's gate to wave goodbye.

The nurse stood on the verandah and watched until Amy was out of sight.

'Your wife's coming along very nicely,' Mrs Coulson said to Frank as the two of them sat in the parlour. 'I've told her if she's a good girl she can get up for a bit tomorrow.'

'She'll like that,' said Frank. 'She always gets a bit restless when she's been stuck in bed for a few days—starts to think she's missing out on things.'

It was five days since Rose's birth, and Lizzie was directing the household as well as she could from her bed. As far as Frank could tell things were running as smoothly as they always did, but Lizzie was growing increasingly impatient of the passive role forced upon her. The only sign of weariness left over from the birth was that she tended to nod off soon after finishing her evening meal. When she did, Frank would slip from the bedroom with her empty plate and leave her to doze in peace while he joined Mrs Coulson in the parlour until it was closer to his own usual bedtime.

'It'll just be to sit quietly, mind, not go rushing about wearing herself out. And only if she has a nice sleep in the morning first.'

She leaned a little closer to Frank and spoke in a low voice, as if afraid Lizzie might overhear. 'Mind you, she hardly needs to stay in bed at all, she's getting over it so well. But it's not good for a mother to get up before the proper time, it can end up disordering her insides. Anyway, it doesn't do any harm for a woman to have a bit of a rest while she's got the chance—and she'll be busy enough when she does get up and about again.'

'I'm glad to see her having a rest.' Frank glanced at the door into the passage, beyond which Lizzie lay sleeping. 'She works so hard all the time.'

'It's a rare man who notices,' Mrs Coulson said. 'Your wife's a sturdy girl Mr Kelly, she'll be right as rain in no time.'

'She'll be tired again, though. She's at it from dawn to dusk, washing and ironing, cooking and scrubbing. And then she spends all evening sewing.'

'Six children is quite a number. She's got to keep you all decently clothed. She wouldn't do that by keeping her hands folded in her lap.'

It was hard to picture Lizzie's hands sitting idle. They always seemed to be tending a baby, preparing food, or using a needle and thread. And that was when they were not wringing out clothes or clutching a scrubbing brush. They had lost a little of their usual work-roughened look since Lizzie had been confined to bed, but Frank knew they would soon be as red and chapped as ever.

'I'd like to do a bit better for her,' he said, half to himself.

'She seems happy enough.'

'Oh, Lizzie never complains. She just says it's a load of nonsense when I talk about wanting to make things easier for her. That doesn't stop me wanting to do it, though.'

'Well, the work's got to be done, and it's no use railing against it. But you shouldn't fret yourself, Mr Kelly. Those two girls of yours are a big help to your wife already, and they'll be even more use when they're a bit older.'

'Monday's the worst,' Frank said. 'All those clothes for her to wash. And with the girls at school she has to do it by herself. I carry the basket of wet things for her, and I help her hang the clothes out sometimes, but she won't let me do anything else. She's just about dead on her feet sometimes by Monday night.'

'Washing is a trial,' Mrs Coulson agreed. 'Especially with a good-sized family like yours.'

'And then she has to get up on Tuesday and iron everything. All those frilly pinafores and things. I don't know how she manages it all.'

'She manages because she has to. I must say she's a good deal luckier than some women, Mr Kelly. It's not every woman whose husband worries about her.'

'Worrying's not much use. I want to *do* something for her. I've been thinking about it a lot lately, ever since we found out there was another baby on the way. I've been wondering...' He gave Mrs Coulson a sidelong glance, trying to decide whether to risk confiding in her. But the nurse did not seem the sort of person who would laugh at his fruitless thoughts.

'I wish I could get her a servant,' he said.

'A servant?' Mrs Coulson echoed. 'What, you mean like Mrs Leveston with her parlour maids and scullery maids all in their uniforms?'

'No, not all flash like that. I was thinking of someone just to sort of help Lizzie out with the heavier work.'

'Oh, you mean like I have one of Mrs Finch's girls in to help me from time to time? Now, that's a kind thought,' Mrs Coulson said, smiling fondly at him.

'I was thinking Lizzie mostly needs the help on washing and ironing days, and maybe for the scrubbing and things. Not every day.'

'So you really just want someone to come around say three days a week?'

'Yes. That'd be just right, I think.' He frowned as his enthusiasm gave way to reality. 'The trouble is, I can't see any way to get one for Lizzie. I mean, it'd have to be a family who didn't live too far away—it's no good asking a girl to come out all the way from town in time for washing day. But I don't think any of the mothers around here can spare any of their daughters. It'd be like asking Lizzie to do without one of ours three days a week.'

'Mmm, that's a difficulty. What you want is a girl from the sort of family who'd sooner have a few extra pennies a week than another pair of hands around the house.'

'But I want one who'd be good at the work,' Frank said. 'Not one whose family wouldn't miss her because she's no use.'

'Well, there are some fathers around who don't have the sense to appreciate their daughters—though precious few mothers, I'll grant you.' She frowned as she puzzled over the problem. A thoughtful look came into her face. 'I wonder,' she said. 'Yes, that mightn't be such a bad idea.'

'Have you thought of someone?' Frank asked.

'I think perhaps I have. Maisie might be the girl for you.'

'Maisie? I don't think I know her. What family's that?'

Mrs Coulson hesitated a moment before answering. 'Maisie Feenan. Now, don't go getting in a state, Mr Kelly,' she said, seeing Frank's look of horror. 'I know they're not much of a family, but I'd like you to think about it, not just say no straight off.'

'But… bringing one of the Feenans into the house?' Frank said. 'Lizzie'd raise the roof!'

'Well, just who did Mrs Kelly have in mind as a servant, then?'

'Heck, it's not Lizzie's idea! Once or twice when I've tried bringing it up she's just said it's a lot of nonsense. And that was without anyone talking about bringing Feenans here!'

'But you said yourself you haven't many girls to choose from. Do you want to get someone to help your wife or not?'

'Yes, I do. I really want to make things easier for Lizzie. But a Feenan?'

'Oh, Maisie's not such a bad girl. At least she didn't used to be—it's quite a while since I last saw the poor child.' Mrs Coulson sighed, and her face seemed to grow older. 'I remember her when she was just a little thing. I delivered her, come to that—though that father of hers waited till his wife was more dead than alive before he fetched me to her, poor creature. Lord knows how I pulled her through.'

'Did he begrudge the money to pay you?' Frank asked in horror.

'Well, he never *did* pay me, so he must have. Not that the Feenans ever have two pennies to rub together. She came through it somehow, though, and little Maisie too. Such a tiny thing she was, I didn't think they'd rear her. But she's tougher than she looks, that one, for all you'd think a breath of wind would knock her over. I used to see her at Mass from time to time—her mother managed to get there once in a blue moon, Lord knows how. Maisie used to be quite a happy little thing in her own way, when her mother was still alive. God rest her soul.'

'She's got no mother?' Despite himself, Frank felt an upwelling of sympathy for the unknown Maisie. 'That's hard on a girl, losing her ma.'

'Yes, it is. Maisie's father left it too late the next time the poor woman managed to carry a child to term. She was too far gone with childbed fever before I even heard about it.'

Mrs Coulson dabbed at her eyes with a handkerchief. 'Goodness knows how Maisie's getting on now. I haven't seen her in… oh, it must be a year or more. I'd hate her to end up like her sisters.'

'What happened to them?' Frank asked, a sense of fatalism growing upon him.

'I'm afraid they've both ended up living in the Royal Hotel.' She gave Frank a sidelong glance to check that the significance was not lost on him. 'It's hard to blame the poor girls, with the home they came from. But I hate to think of little Maisie ending up the same way.'

Frank stared at the rug under his feet and thought about his own daughters, secure in the warmth and shelter of a loving home. The idea of any young girl ending up as one of the Royal Hotel's whores did not bear thinking of. 'This Maisie's had a rough spin, hasn't she?'

'Go and see her, Mr Kelly,' Mrs Coulson urged. 'It can't do any harm just to meet the girl and see for yourself if you think she'd do for the job.'

'I suppose not.' The trouble was, Frank thought to himself, no matter how unsuitable she might be it was not going to be very easy to say no to this Maisie.

Frank climbed down from his spring cart to study the ground before him. At the sight of the deep ruts he admitted defeat. The track to the Feenans looked rough enough to provide a challenge to a pack horse, let alone any sort of wheeled vehicle.

He knotted the reins and left the horse to snatch what grazing it could from the rank weeds that grew beside the track; Grey was too steady a beast for Frank to worry that he might wander. After giving the big gelding a pat on the neck, Frank set off on foot towards what looked from this distance more like a heap of discarded timber than a dwelling.

There was certainly nothing worthy of the name of pasture in the rough paddocks around the track that might tempt Grey towards sweeter grazing. A few morose-looking sheep cropped the weeds in a dejected fashion, so scrawny that they looked as though it would take the whole flock to make a decent meal for a family. The Feenan farm was close to the sand-hills that marked the edge of the beach, and the sandy soil did not support anything recognisable as grass. At times the water table rose high enough for brackish water to seep into the lowest of the paddocks, killing off what green stuff had managed to take root.

As he drew close to the house, a frenzied barking interspersed with snarls started up. Frank's steps faltered, but he reasoned that the dog would already have him by the throat if it were roaming free, so it must be chained. Of course, if someone chose to let it off the chain… Well, he could not hope to outrun a large dog for long enough to reach his horse, so it was too late now to think of taking to his heels.

The remains of a fence lay in front of the house. Frank looked around for a gate of some sort, then gave up and clambered over the sprawl of rotten wood, the task made harder by the bramble that had worked its way into the ruin of the fence. He could now see the dog that was making so much noise, a beast of dubious ancestry that strained at the length of rope tied around its neck. Frank hoped the rope was stronger than it looked, but as he eyed the dog uncertainly a stream of abuse issued from the house. The dog lay down on the ground, contenting itself with growling under its breath.

There was a large field of potatoes near the house; the only obvious source of food within sight. A disturbed patch of ground inside the fence looked as if it might once have been a vegetable garden, but the only trace of its former role was a knotted vine with a few rotten pumpkins along its length. The smell that met Frank's nose as he approached told him the Feenan's privy was not only closer to the house than most people considered desirable, but had also not been dug deeply enough to deserve the usual name of 'long drop'. That smell was challenged by a noisome pile of refuse beside the house; Frank did not study it closely, but he could not avoid noticing the hordes of flies crawling over the waste heap.

Climbing onto the house's verandah presented something of a challenge; if there had ever been steps, they had long since collapsed. Frank reached out to grab at a post to haul himself up, pulling his hand back just in time when he noticed the post had snapped through the middle so that its upper and lower sections pointed in different directions. He wondered briefly how the roof of the verandah managed to stay upright, but a glance at the said roof told him 'upright' was too generous a term.

He clambered onto the verandah and walked up to the front door, which was hanging drunkenly from its one surviving hinge. Knocking on the door itself seemed likely to detach it altogether, so Frank banged on the wall near the doorway.

He waited for what seemed a long time, then banged again.

'All right, don't knock the flaming door down,' someone grumbled. The door was dragged open a crack, and a woman peered around its edge. 'What do you want?' she asked.

'Um, I wanted to see…' Frank realised that he had no idea what Maisie's father's name was. Asking for 'Mr Feenan' would undoubtedly be too general to be useful. 'Is Maisie's father home?'

'Ah, the useless bugger never stirs far—except to go to the pub when he's got a few shillings. Kieran!' she yelled, so loudly that Frank gave a start, but there was no answer from inside.

'The lazy sod's asleep by the fire,' the woman said. 'He had a skinful of some gut-rot last night, he's still sleeping it off.' She looked Frank up and down with an appraising stare that made him feel vaguely uncomfortable, as if he had left his trouser buttons unfastened. 'I'm Bridie,' she volunteered.

Bridie Feenan looked to be several years older than Lizzie, though it was hard to tell through the black veil of hair that hung over most of her face, defying the pins thrust haphazardly into the mass. The boniness of her shoulders showed through her dress, and there was a rip in the bodice that had been roughly pinned. She might once have been pretty, but there was no trace of it left except in the brightness of her eyes.

'Frank Kelly. Pleased to meet you.' He extended a hand, then let it drop awkwardly when Bridie made no move to take it. 'I need to see… Kieran, was it? Is he your brother?'

'So me mam always maintained. Is it money you're after from him? You might as well clear off right now if it is.'

'Oh, no, nothing like that. I just want to talk to him about Maisie.'

Bridie gave him the same appraising stare. 'She's a bit young for you, isn't she?' She laughed at his discomfiture. 'You'd better come in, then.'

She moved away from the door and turned to walk down the dim passage. Pausing only to check that his buttons were indeed safely fastened, Frank followed. After he caught an inadvertent glimpse of Bridie's legs through the long rent in the back of her skirt, he was careful not to look at her as she led the way.

A man who looked to be in his early forties lay slumped in a chair near the open fireplace that clearly served as cooking facility.

'Kieran,' Bridie shouted, leaning close to him. 'Here's a fellow come to see you. Says his name's Frank Kelly.'

Kieran stirred a little, then settled more comfortably. 'Tell him to bugger off,' he muttered.

'He won't bugger off till he's talked to you. Something about Maisie.'

Kieran opened his eyes a fraction, put one arm over his face as the light hit them, then cautiously lowered his arm and scowled at Frank. 'What's the little baggage been up to?'

'Nothing,' Frank said. 'I've never met her. I just wondered… it's for my wife, really, except she doesn't know about it yet… I wondered if Maisie would like a job.'

'You want to pay for the girl?' Kieran asked, his face lighting up with interest.

'Oh, yes, I'd pay her all right. I want someone to help my wife around the house, just three days a week. Washing and ironing, and scrubbing, all that sort of business.' Frank's eyes were drawn to the rough wooden floor, where mud and food stains alternated to form a lurid pattern. That floor showed no sign of ever having made the acquaintance of a scrubbing brush. 'I was thinking I'd give her three shillings a week to start off with—only if she's suitable, though,' he added hastily.

'Three shillings, eh? She'll be suitable, all right,' Kieran said. 'When do you want her to start?'

'Um, I'd like to see her first,' Frank hedged. 'I want to be sure she's the sort of girl my wife's after.'

'Where's the little trollop sneaked off to?' Kieran demanded of his sister. Bridie shrugged. 'Well, find her! Are you deaf, woman? This fellow wants to pay money for her!'

Bridie disappeared through the back door. She was gone long enough for Frank to look around the kitchen, though he soon wished he had

95

not. A huge saucepan full of potatoes stood near the fire, waiting to be put on to boil. Although the potatoes had been given a cursory peeling, judging from the clods of dirt that floated above them washing had not formed part of their preparation. Various unidentifiable portions of animal entrails lay on the table (which was only marginally cleaner than the floor); they looked like the sort of scraps Lizzie would throw to the cats, though the flies crawling over them seemed enthusiastic enough.

'Where have you been, you useless baggage?' Kieran shouted as Bridie returned, propelling ahead of her a small girl whom Frank assumed must be Maisie. With a sudden burst of energy, Kieran rose from his chair and crossed to the doorway in two strides. He took a handful of Maisie's hair and dragged her by it into the centre of the room. 'Here's a fellow wants you to go and work for him,' he told his daughter.

Frank studied Maisie with a sinking heart. She was tiny; not as tall as Maudie, and far slighter. Her hair fell matted around her face, so low on her forehead that it was difficult to see her eyes at first glance. Her whole face seemed to be spread with a layer of grime, with more clearly delineated patches of dirt on her chin and both cheeks. Her dress only had one sleeve, a ragged-edged armhole showing where the other sleeve had once been attached, and the longest of the skirt's tattered edges barely reached her grubby knees.

Maisie turned such a baleful glare on Frank that he almost quailed before it, until he studied her more closely. The girl had managed to school her face into an expression of defiance, but what looked out of those dark, brooding eyes was naked fear.

'Don't want to,' she muttered. Her head jerked to one side as her father's hand lashed against her cheek, leaving a red mark visible through the dirt, but she did not utter a sound.

'You ungrateful little bitch,' Kieran roared. 'Don't you be telling me what you do and don't want. You'll do as I say, girl.' He took hold of Maisie's arm and forced it up behind her back until she winced, though she still made no sound. 'Tell the man you want to go and work for him.' He yanked Maisie's arm higher. 'Tell him!'

'Hey, there's no need for that,' Frank said, resisting the urge to plant his fist in the man's face. 'If she doesn't want the job it doesn't matter. Let go of her arm, eh?'

'She'll want it, all right,' Kieran said, giving his daughter a menacing look, but he released Maisie's arm, where his thick fingers had left clear, red impressions on the pale skin. She rubbed at her skinny arm and stared at Frank.

'She's very young,' Frank said doubtfully. Maisie did not look the sort of sturdy girl he had pictured helping Lizzie carry loads of wet washing.

'She's fourteen, though I'll grant you she doesn't look it,' Bridie said.

'Always was a little runt, right from when she was born,' Kieran put in. 'She's tougher than she looks, though. She'll do the work you want her for.'

Frank studied the waif in front of him and sighed inwardly. Maisie seemed as unsuitable a girl as he could possibly have imagined, but he knew that if he rejected her she would pay the price in her father's wrath.

'Shall I tell you what I want you to do, Maisie?' he asked. He would gladly have taken her into his arms for the sort of cuddle his own daughters delighted in, but that would only frighten her more. 'My wife's very busy, you see. We've got six little ones, and she's so much washing and cleaning to do, I thought it'd be good if I could get someone to give her a hand. Do you think you could do that? Come around to our house three days a week to help Mrs Kelly?'

'Maisie knows all about washing and all that,' Kieran said expansively, though his own shirt bore no sign of ever having been laundered. 'She's the girl for you.'

Maisie stared hard at Frank. 'All right,' she said, and he felt he had passed some sort of test. 'When do I come?'

'Start tomorrow if you like, that's one of Lizzie's scrubbing days. Do you know the track up the Waituhi Valley?'

'No,' Maisie said, her glare making him feel irrationally guilty.

'It's easy to find—you just head down the coast till you come to a good-sized creek, then turn up the valley. Mine's the first farm you come to. It's not that long a ride.'

'Can't ride,' Maisie said shortly.

'Hmm, it's a bit far to walk.'

'Don't you worry about that,' Kieran cut in. 'She's a great walker, our Maisie. She'll be there tomorrow, all right.'

'I'll be looking out for you, Maisie,' Frank said. He smiled at her, and was rewarded with a slightly less baleful glare.

He drove his cart away from the Feenan's with a sense of escape, breathing deeply of the fresh air. This was not a place he would willingly return to, he thought as he glanced back over his shoulder. He was sure Maisie would be grateful for the chance to escape from it three days a week once she got used to the ways of more civilised people.

But his sense of relief was short-lived. True, he had got away from vicious dogs and drunken Irishmen unscathed, but that was no reason to feel so confident. Now he had to break the news to Lizzie.

7

January 1898

Frank carefully avoided any mention of his morning's visit, and Lizzie was too busy with her own concerns to notice any evasiveness on his part. It was not just reluctance to raise the subject before he had to; he did not want to give her the opportunity to send him straight back to the Feenans to tell Maisie that their arrangement was off.

He waited until the evening, when Lizzie was sitting in their bedroom with Rose at her breast. Suckling a baby usually calmed Lizzie, but tonight Rose was being difficult: refusing to feed, then crying fretfully when Lizzie made to put her in the cradle.

'I don't know what's wrong with her,' Lizzie grumbled as she guided a nipple into Rose's questing mouth for yet another attempt. 'She seems hungry, then she won't suck.'

'Maybe she's still getting the idea,' Frank said. 'She's only little.'

'She's a month old now, the others were all feeding properly by this age. I'm not used to this silliness. Oh, you're going to do it at last, are you, Miss?'

Frank sat on the bed beside Lizzie and slid an arm to enfold both her and the baby. 'You seem a bit weary today.'

'Of course I am, with this child of yours waking up half a dozen times last night,' Lizzie snapped, resisting Frank's attempts to pull her closer. She relented, and let her head rest on his shoulder. 'I've got out of the way of these broken nights, that's the trouble. And Rosie's not such a good sleeper as the others were. Never mind, the worst of it's over soon enough.'

'It's hard on you, though, while it lasts. It's not as if you can have a sleep in the daytime to catch up.'

'Hah!' was Lizzie's response to the ridiculous notion.

Frank stroked her hair. 'I've got a bit of a surprise for you.'

'Surprise? What are you on about?'

'Something to make things a bit easier for you. I went visiting this morning.' He took a deep breath, then went on quickly so as not to give Lizzie time to interrupt. 'I've sorted out a girl to come around three days a week and give you a hand with the work.'

'You'd no business doing that!' Lizzie said indignantly, pulling away from his grasp. 'I've told you I don't want anything to do with that nonsense. I'm not having some strange girl in the house.'

'But I've arranged it, Lizzie. I've told her she's to come.'

'Then you can just go back there tomorrow and tell her she's *not* to come.'

'I can't do that. She's coming tomorrow morning, first thing.'

'Oh, she is, is she? Without so much as asking my leave, you tell some girl to come here? Who is this girl, anyway?'

'Ah... her name's Maisie,' Frank hedged.

'Maisie? Maisie who? I don't know any Maisies.'

'No, you don't know this girl. You'll meet her tomorrow, though.'

Lizzie's eyes narrowed. 'What's her name, Frank?'

Frank gave her a sidelong glance, then looked at the wall. 'Maisie Feenan,' he confessed.

Lizzie was stunned into open-mouthed silence. She snapped her mouth shut and twisted around to glare at Frank, the movement dislodging Rose from her breast. 'Are you off your head, Frank Kelly? It's not enough that you go and get this mad idea I need some girl hanging around under my feet—you've gone and asked one of the Feenans?'

Rose began to complain noisily. 'Now you've got her going,' Lizzie said. She stood up and paced around the room in an attempt to comfort the baby, her full breasts threatening to escape from her nightdress as she walked back and forth. 'You've no right to ask that girl. I won't have it, Frank. I won't have her here.'

'Just try her out—give her a go and see what she's like. She didn't seem a bad sort of girl... well, not considering the home she's from. Let her have a go at helping you.'

'No, I won't,' Lizzie said. 'When she turns up tomorrow you can just send her packing. I'm not having one of those Feenans in my house, and that's that.'

Frank knew the folly of arguing with Lizzie. 'All right,' he said, feigning defeat. 'I'll do it if that's what you want.'

'It certainly is.'

'Yes, when she turns up I'll tell her I've changed my mind. Poor little thing, she'll be pretty disappointed.'

'I can't help that. You should have thought of that before you went to see her without asking me.'

'I'd better give her a day's money for her trouble, that'll help a bit.'

'What money? What do you need to pay the girl for, just for coming around here when she's not wanted?'

Frank was careful not to meet her eyes. 'It's not Maisie's fault you don't want her. I can't send her away with nothing.'

'I don't see why not. She won't be doing any work to earn it.'

'She'll have walked all the way here, then she'll have to turn around and go straight home again. It's not fair to waste her time for nothing.' Lizzie seemed a little off balance now; Frank pressed his advantage. 'Actually, I think I'd better give her a week's worth.'

'You'll do no such thing! The very idea, wanting to give a girl a week's wages just for turning up at the door!'

'Yes, I think I will. It's only three shillings.'

'Three shillings! You're not to give her that.'

Frank managed a heavy sigh. 'I don't want to upset you, Lizzie, but I'm going to give Maisie the money. I just wouldn't feel right with myself if I sent her away with nothing. I'm sorry, but I'm going to do it. And that's that,' he added in a deliberate echo of Lizzie's words.

'Ooh, you can be stubborn.' Lizzie glared at him, but Frank assumed what he hoped was a pensive air and stared at the wall rather than meet her gaze.

'Oh, all right, then,' Lizzie said. 'She can come and work tomorrow—just for the day, mind you—then you can give her a day's wages. That must be what, a shilling?'

'I think maybe I should give her a week's worth—'

'Don't you dare,' Lizzie said.

It was time to let her think she had won. Frank had already resigned himself to the chilly reserve any overtures for a cuddle would be met with that night; there was no sense getting himself into even more trouble.

'All right, then, a shilling it is. That should be enough to cheer her up a bit, make up for you not wanting her. Of course, you might change your mind and decide you do want her after all.'

'Not likely,' Lizzie said. 'The very idea, having some strange girl in my kitchen. 'A shilling, indeed! I'll see that she earns her day's wages,' she added grimly.

Next morning Frank was on his way back to the house after milking when he saw the small figure of Maisie Feenan coming up the track. He waited by the gate that led to the house, and as soon as Maisie drew close he went to greet her.

'Hello, Maisie, you're here bright and early.'

Maisie took a step backwards and scowled at him. 'You said the missus'd be here.' It sounded like an accusation.

'Yes, Mrs Kelly's home, she's inside. Come on and I'll introduce you.' He made to take Maisie's arm, but she darted out of his reach.

Putting her strange manner down to shyness, Frank led the way to the back door and into the kitchen.

'Here she is, Lizzie,' he said with a brightness that was somewhat forced. 'This is Maisie. Maisie, this is Mrs Kelly.'

Frank watched anxiously as they sized each other up. Maisie did not make an impressive figure. She wore the same ragged dress he had seen her in the previous day, and looked even grubbier than she had then. And she was painfully thin, he realised. Seen next to the robust Lizzie, Maisie's gauntness was far more noticeable than it had been in her own home. She scarcely looked capable of bearing her own weight, let alone wielding a scrubbing brush.

Lizzie gave Frank a withering look, which told him exactly what she thought of his idea of a suitable servant. She turned back to Maisie. 'So you're going to do some work for me today, are you?' she asked. Maisie nodded. 'I suppose you know all about scrubbing floors, do you?'

'I can do it,' Maisie said, her attempt at defiance sounding pathetic in Frank's ears. Her eyes darted around the kitchen, taking in the details of the unfamiliar room, until she saw the table and what lay on it.

'We'll see about that. You might as well get started, I'll show you where...' Lizzie broke off. 'Are you listening to me, my girl?' Maisie's head jerked around to face her for a moment, but then the girl's gaze slipped away again.

Lizzie followed Maisie's fascinated stare. She had not yet put away the bread and meat she had used to make school lunches for the older children, and it was that that had caught Maisie's attention. Frank saw Lizzie's puzzled expression as she noted how intently Maisie was staring at the food.

'Did you have a decent breakfast?' she asked.

Maisie looked away from the food, and rubbed her wrist over her mouth to wipe away a small trail of saliva. 'Didn't have no breakfast,' she muttered.

'Why not?' Lizzie asked, visibly shocked. 'What does your mother think she's doing, sending you off without anything in your stomach?'

'Haven't got a mother. She's dead.'

Lizzie was taken aback. 'Well... someone must look after you. Who gets the meals on in your house?'

'Aunt Bridie does, 'cept when she's too busy. She was milking the cow. She let me have a bit of milk out of the bucket.'

'A bit of milk doesn't fill a growing child!'

Maisie was not listening; she was staring once again at the food on the table.

Casting another reproachful look at Frank, Lizzie took hold of the loaf and cut two thick slices from it, which she spread generously with butter then filled with several pieces of cold mutton. 'You can't scrub floors on an empty stomach. Come on, girl, get this inside you.'

For a moment Maisie stared in disbelief at the sandwich in Lizzie's outstretched hand. Then she darted forward to snatch at it and ran over to the opposite corner of the room, where she stood by the wall and swallowed hunks of sandwich as rapidly as she was capable of forcing them down.

'What on earth are you doing?' Lizzie asked. 'Why do you want to run off with your food like that?'

Maisie gripped her sandwich more firmly than ever. 'Didn't want no one to take it off me,' she said, her words indistinct through a mouthful.

'We're not likely to take it off you, are we? Honestly, you look like one of the cats when I throw them some scraps. Come here and sit at the table like a civilised person, for goodness sake—you'll get indigestion eating like that.'

Maisie looked uncertainly from Lizzie to Frank, then crept over to the table, clutching what remained of her precious sandwich in two grubby hands.

'Here, you'd better have this to wash it down,' Lizzie said, pouring a large mug of milk. She watched Maisie finish eating and gulp down the milk. 'Do you want another sandwich?'

Maisie gave her an incredulous look. 'Yes,' she said in a voice that shook slightly.

'Well, what do you say, then?' Maisie stared blankly at her. Lizzie pursed her lips. 'Ask for it properly.'

'I want some more to eat like that stuff,' Maisie said.

'And what do you say?'

'I don't think she knows what you mean, Lizzie,' Frank put in. 'She thinks you're teasing her.'

'Of course she knows.' Lizzie looked thoughtfully at Maisie. 'Didn't your mother ever teach you how to ask for things nicely?'

Maisie shook her head, then screwed up her face in concentration. 'Please?'

'That's better.' Lizzie made another sandwich, and watched it disappear almost as rapidly as the first. 'You're just skin and bone, girl.' She turned to Frank and shook her head. 'She's not strong enough. I can't make a little scrap like her scrub the floors for me.'

'I *can*. I *can* scrub them. You've got to let me,' Maisie said, fear in her eyes.

'Oh, I do, do I?' Lizzie glanced at Maisie's hands, which were wrapped around the remnants of her sandwich. 'Look at the state of you! I should have made you wash your hands before I gave you that. And your face! I can hardly tell what colour you are under all that dirt. Here, hold still a minute.'

She snatched up a damp cloth from the table, pushed Maisie's hair back from her forehead and rubbed vigorously. Maisie tried to squirm out of her grip, but Lizzie was well experienced in handling wriggling children.

'I'll have to chuck this cloth in the wash,' Lizzie said. 'Look at this big smudge here.' She moved the cloth to a dark patch on Maisie's cheek. The girl let out a yell, and Lizzie took a step back in surprise.

'What's wrong with you?' She peered more closely at Maisie's cheek, which was now partly hidden by the girl's small hand. 'That's a bruise, isn't it? How did you get a whopper like that?'

'Me dad give it me,' Maisie said. 'I don't care. I didn't even bawl.'

'What'd he do that for?'

"Cause I said I didn't want to come and work here.'

'But you do want to work here now?'

'Yes.' Maisie stared boldly back at Lizzie, the effect marred by a tremble in her lower lip.

'I see.' Lizzie looked over Maisie's head at Frank and raised her eyebrows.

She sat down beside the girl and spoke in what for Lizzie was an unusually gentle voice. 'Well, Maisie, if you're as keen as all that, you can have a go at helping me today. Then Mr Kelly'll give you a bit of money to take home—that should cheer your father up. But I don't need anyone helping me regular—Mr Kelly got that wrong, you see. He'll pay you for today, but you can tell your father I don't need you to come again.'

'What'd I do wrong?'

'You didn't—oh, for goodness sake don't start crying, girl. Whatever's wrong with you?'

'I'm not crying.' Maisie sniffed noisily and wiped her nose on her sleeve. 'Me dad said if I didn't do the work proper, so you'd keep me on regular, he'd break my arm. He will, too—he broke my sister's arm once. She ran away then,' Maisie added enviously.

She sniffed again. 'I don't care if he does break my arm. I don't,' she insisted, though no one had spoken to contradict her. 'I won't go back to the house today, anyway. I'll just run off and hide in the bush for the night. Me dad'll probably get drunk tonight. He might forget about breaking my arm,' she added in a small voice.

'She means it, Lizzie,' Frank put in. 'He was halfway to breaking her arm yesterday because she answered him back.'

Lizzie glared at him. 'I'd just about believe you two've cooked this up between you.' But Frank could see the concern mixed with her irritation. 'Haven't you got any work to do, Frank Kelly? I've had enough of you hanging about getting under my feet.'

Frank hovered in the doorway. 'I suppose I should get on with—'

'Yes, you should,' said Lizzie. 'We've got a lot to do here. Off you go—and I don't want to see you back before lunch-time. You're not to come in tracking footprints all over my wet floor.'

'What about my morning tea?'

'Too bad about your morning tea,' Lizzie said. 'Well, I might put some scones and a pot of tea out on the verandah for you later. I can see I'm going to be too busy with Maisie to stop for a bite myself.'

Humility was the safest course. Frank let himself be ordered out of the house without protest.

He obediently stayed out of the house all morning, though he cast many anxious glances towards it whenever his work took him nearby. When Lizzie at last called from the back door to let him know lunch was ready he rushed up at once, arriving in the kitchen slightly breathless.

He stopped short in amazement. Maisie's hair had been combed and coaxed into an order he would not have thought possible, and she now had a half ponytail tied with a pink ribbon. She was wearing a much-mended dress he vaguely remembered having seen on Maudie the previous summer. It hung loosely on Maisie's gaunt frame, but compared to the rags she had arrived in it was like a ball gown. Her face shone with cleanness. She sat at the table with Danny on her lap, holding a mug of milk for the three-year-old.

'Lizzie, you're a marvel,' Frank said. 'Doesn't she look nice? You look really good, Maisie.'

'Don't scowl at Mr Kelly like that when he pays you a compliment.' Lizzie admired her handiwork before turning to Frank. 'Yes, she looks a lot better, all right. I should hope so, the trouble she gave me! I'd just as soon try bathing one of the cats as clean her up again.'

'I didn't like it when you pulled my hair,' Maisie grumbled.

'I only pulled it because of all the knots. I washed it for her—I had to catch and hold her head under the water before she'd let me. And then I had to threaten her with the belt so I could comb it. I gave her a good stand-up wash, and she smells a lot better now I've burnt that dress she came here in. That old one of Maudie's is too big, but it doesn't look so bad. Stand up, Maisie, and show Mr Kelly what your new dress looks like.'

'No,' Maisie muttered, glowering at Frank.

'Don't be silly. Come on, stand up.'

Lizzie reached out to lift Danny from Maisie's lap. At her sudden movement, the girl flinched and cringed away. 'Stop that,' Lizzie said sharply. 'She does that whenever I go near her, Frank. All I've done is wave the belt at her a couple of times.'

'She's not used to you yet.' Frank slid his arm around Lizzie's middle and gave her a kiss on the cheek. 'Will you show me your new dress, Maisie? I'd like to see it on you.'

Maisie stared, seemingly fascinated by the sight of his and Lizzie's easy closeness. 'All right.' She stood up, and turned around when Lizzie told her to, all the time keeping carefully out of reach.

'You look nice, Maisie,' Frank said. He studied Lizzie anxiously for any sign of weariness, but if anything she seemed exhilarated by her skirmishes of the morning.

Lizzie slipped from his hold to sit down at the table with Danny on her lap.

'Has Maisie been helping you all right?' Frank asked.

Lizzie cast a glance at the girl. 'Well, Maisie's learned a lot of things this morning. She's learned that floors get scrubbed—'

'It wasn't even dirty,' Maisie said.

'And I intend to see it stays that way. She's learned how to use a scrubbing brush. I *think* she knew what a bucket was before. Let's see, what else? She's learned how to use a range—'

'I never seen one of them before,' Maisie put in more brightly.

'She burned her arm on the top of it because she didn't know it was hot. She didn't make a fuss, though. And she's learned how you wash vegetables *properly*.'

Lizzie glanced back at Maisie, then quickly plumped Danny on Frank's lap. She reached out and grabbed hold of Maisie's wrist just as the girl was lifting a handful of meat towards her mouth. 'And now she's going to learn how to use a knife and fork,' Lizzie said, forcing Maisie's hand back down onto the plate. '*And* that we say grace before meals in this house.'

Frank said grace, then Lizzie ignored Maisie's scowls and muttered complaints and insisted that the girl pick up the utensils lying neglected on either side of her plate. Supervising Maisie's use of the unfamiliar tools meant lunch took much longer than usual, but, as all Lizzie's children except baby Rose had learned, she was quite prepared to keep the whole family waiting until one recalcitrant member had realised the error of his or her ways.

When lunch was over at last, Frank persuaded Lizzie to walk outside with him while Maisie cleared the table.

'Has she been any use at all to you?' he asked. 'I hope she hasn't just been a nuisance. I did it for you, you know, getting Maisie around here.'

'Oh, she's just what I needed,' Lizzie said, her voice dripping with sarcasm. 'Another little girl who needs looking after. Except this one's barely house-trained.'

'I'm sorry, love. I'd better take her home tonight and tell her pa you don't want her back. If I tell him it's nothing to do with Maisie, it's just that you don't want anyone to help you, he shouldn't give her a hard time.' Especially, he thought to himself, if he sweetened Kieran Feenan's mood with ten shillings instead of the three he had promised. 'She's had a good feed, and you've given her a decent dress, so she hasn't done too bad out of it.' But he could not help suspecting that, even with an unexpected windfall, Kieran would find an excuse to take out his anger on the defenceless Maisie.

'Don't be an idiot, Frank. Do you think I want to send that waif home to get her arm broken? You said yourself he'd do it. He might take a swing at you, come to that.'

'I don't want to have her here if she's just going to make more work for you.'

'Oh, one more child to look after isn't going to make much difference. Anyway,' she relented, seeing Frank's worried face, 'she wasn't too bad. She scrubbed as if her life depended on it once I showed her how. And she seemed quite fond of the little ones.'

'She doesn't seem to like me much,' Frank said.

'She's scared of you, anyway. I wouldn't be surprised if she thinks you might interfere with her.'

'Eh? What'd I do to make her think that?'

Lizzie pulled a face. 'I've an idea that child has seen a lot of things a girl her age has no business knowing about. Goodness knows what goes on in that house. Whatever it is, she doesn't have much time for men, I think.'

'But... I never went near her.'

'Oh, don't worry, she'll get used to you. I'm going to have to tell her to keep her mouth shut around the children, though—I won't have them hearing that sort of talk.'

'So you're definitely going to keep her on, then?'

'I've already said I will—don't make such a fuss about it, for goodness sake. She doesn't seem a bad girl, even if she is bog Irish.'

Frank drew her close to his side. 'You're a wonder, Lizzie. I hope she'll be a help to you, though. That's what I got her for, not for you to look after her. I've wanted to get you a servant for ages.'

'Servant, indeed,' Lizzie snorted. 'She'll be all right, I expect.' She glanced back at the house. 'I'll say this for her, anyway—that girl certainly can scrub.'

8

August 1898

By the time winter was showing the first signs of giving way to spring, Maisie's regular presence in the Kelly house was taken for granted by the whole family. She had lost much of her skittishness in Lizzie's company, and to Frank's relief she had learned not to back away in fear whenever he came within a few feet of her.

Lizzie had got into the habit of setting aside a generous portion of breakfast for Maisie on the three days a week the girl came. Maisie also had lunch with the family, as well as plenty of Lizzie's baking at morning and afternoon teas, and the sharp edges of her gauntness softened as the months wore on. She still had a deceptively frail appearance, and it was clear that she was unlikely ever to achieve the sturdiness of Lizzie's children, but she no longer looked half-starved.

As well as being slightly built, Maisie was tiny. Maudie towered above her by several inches, despite being two years her junior. It was the contrast between the two girls that led Lizzie to study her oldest daughter in an increasingly speculative way.

'Maudie's starting to develop,' she told Frank one evening.

'Develop what?'

'A bosom, of course. Haven't you noticed?'

'She's not!' Frank said in amazement. 'She can't be, not at her age!'

'It's only a couple of tiny little bumps, but it's starting, all right. Not all girls start developing that young—she takes after me for that,' Lizzie said, a touch of pride in her voice. 'I was early, too.'

'Trust you to be. I never knew girls started that young, though,' Frank said. 'A little thing like Maudie.'

'Not as little as all that. She's twelve now, you know. She'll be able to leave school this year if she passes the Standard Four exam.'

'That'll be good, too—she'll be able to give you more of a hand. Twelve, eh? Gee, the time slips away. I remember the day she was born like it was yesterday.' He reached out to take Lizzie's hand in his, smiling at the memory of becoming a father.

'I wouldn't be surprised if she starts getting her bleeding before too long,' Lizzie commented.

'She can't be due for that,' Frank protested. 'Not my little Maudie!'

'Well, it's hard to say. But I don't think it'll be more than a year or so before that young Miss starts. Mind you, there's Maisie gone fourteen and no sign of it—her chest's flat as two fried eggs, too. She hasn't even started getting any hair down below yet.'

'Lizzie!' Frank remonstrated. 'You shouldn't be telling me all that stuff about Maisie! She'd be really embarrassed if she knew you'd told me that.'

'But she doesn't know, does she?' Lizzie pointed out. 'And you're not likely to tell her.'

'I should think not! Heck, I won't know which way to look next time she comes.'

'Don't be so silly. She won't know I've told you, so she won't be worried. Anyway, I think it's a disgrace.'

'What is?' Frank asked.

'Maisie, of course. Fancy letting a girl get to fourteen without doing anything about seeing that she grows up decent. She was more than half wild when she started coming here. It took me weeks to teach her to so much as wash herself properly—I don't think the girl knew what soap was for till I got her in hand, let alone having any decent manners.'

'You've done wonders with her since. She's turning into a real young lady.'

'Well, I don't know about that,' Lizzie said doubtfully. 'But she's certainly more fit for polite company now. She doesn't eat with her fingers any more, and I've taught her not to scratch her private parts when there's other people around.'

'She never did that in front of me.'

'Think yourself lucky, then. I had to throw out a few batches of biscuits she'd helped me with when I caught her doing that—I didn't fancy letting anyone eat them. It took a few whacks across the knuckles with the wooden spoon to get her out of the habit. Mind you, she probably doesn't get as itchy these days, not now she's got clean drawers to put on.'

'Poor little mite, going all those years with no one to look after her properly. Our girls are pretty lucky, eh?'

'Yes, they are,' said Lizzie. 'I think it's a mother's duty to make the best of her daughters.'

'You don't need to worry about ours. They're all pretty neat already.'

'That doesn't mean they couldn't be better. I've been thinking about Maudie just lately—it's time I did a bit of work on that girl.'

'How do you mean? There's nothing wrong with Maudie.'

'She's growing up, Frank. I've got to do my best for her, you know. Otherwise before you know it she'll be fifteen or sixteen and it'll be too late.'

Lizzie's words would have sounded ominous to Frank if they had not been so ridiculous. 'Too late for what?' he asked. 'You make it sound like something awful might happen to her!'

'Too late to see that she gets the right sort of husband, of course. It's nothing to laugh about.'

'Lizzie, she's twelve years old! She's only a little girl.'

'She won't be twelve for ever, will she? It doesn't hurt to think about these things.'

'I'll tell you this,' Frank said, suddenly serious, 'if I so much as see a man looking at her with anything like that on his mind, he'll get a kick where it'll do him most good. I'm not going to have anyone hanging around my little girl.'

'You needn't think I'd allow any of that sort of mischief. Amy was only fifteen when her troubles started, and the old people all thought she was too young for them to have to worry about. I'm going to keep a good eye on all my girls, don't you worry about that.'

'Don't go talking about husbands, then, for goodness sake! Let her go on being a little girl for a few more years.'

'It's all very well saying that, but when it *is* time to be thinking about a husband for her, who's she going to get?'

'My girl could get any man she wanted,' Frank said. 'Finding one good enough for her would be the problem.'

'Well, I wouldn't be so sure about that. I mean, look at Maudie—what's she really got going for her? She's all right to look at—'

'She's a real beauty.'

'No, she's not, Frank. Maudie's got quite a nice face, there's nothing wrong with her looks, but she's certainly not a beauty. There's plenty of other girls around Ruatane the men'd go for before they took a second look at her. Jane and Harry's older girls, say—they're both better looking than Maudie.'

If it had been anyone but Lizzie daring to say it, Frank would have been decidedly angry. 'I don't know about that,' he said huffily. 'Not everyone likes red hair.'

'Say what you like, Frank, it's not you who'll be marrying Maudie. Oh, I dare say we'd find some fellow who'd take her cheerfully enough—someone with a rough bit of farm, and maybe half a dozen brothers to share it with. Maudie'd do for a fellow like that. But I want better for her.'

'I should think so! I'm not going to give my daughter away to the first fellow who asks for her.'

'That's if anyone *does* ask for her. Now, look at you—you're an important person around here these days.'

'I don't know about that, either,' Frank said with a laugh.

'Yes, you are! Chairman of the co-operative and all that, and breeding all these champion cows. You're a... what's the word? A prominent citizen,' she intoned solemnly.

'Shall I tell your pa that next time I see him?' Frank said through his mirth. 'He'd have a few words to say about that. "Big-headed" would be about the kindest of them.'

'Never mind Pa, what does he know about anything? Stop interrupting all the time. What with you being so prominent, I think we could do pretty well for Maudie. But we've got to make a young lady of her first.'

'I don't know what you're on about. What's meant to be so bad about Maudie?'

'Well... I don't exactly know,' Lizzie admitted. 'But there's nothing *special* about her. And don't say there is,' she added, forestalling Frank's protest. 'Of course she's special to us, she's our daughter. But there's nothing to set her apart from the other girls around here, and that's what she needs.'

'I can't say I agree with you, Lizzie. Don't go getting yourself in a state over it, eh? She's still a little girl.'

'I'm not getting in a state. I'm going to *do* something about it. I've decided I need to talk to someone who knows about this sort of thing.'

'Who's that?'

'Who do you think? Who do we know who's been to the sort of school they send young ladies to?'

Frank puzzled for a few moments. 'Um... Lily?' he offered.

'I would ask Lily—I'd rather, come to that. But she's the size of a house right now, with the baby due this month. I don't want to bother her. And she'll be tired after the baby comes, she doesn't take to bearing all that well, so it'll be no use asking her for months and months. No, I'm going to take Maudie to see Aunt Susannah.'

'Hey, hang on a bit, Lizzie,' Frank protested. 'I don't want Maudie turning out like Susannah, even if she does think she's such a fine lady.'

'Don't talk rot. As if I'd let Maudie get haughty like that! I'm just going to get Aunt Susannah to tell me how young ladies are meant to behave, that's all. Where's the harm in that?'

'Well, I suppose...' Frank said doubtfully. 'I'd just as soon you didn't.'

'I'll go on Friday,' Lizzie announced. 'Maisie's coming then, she'll be able to watch Danny for me. I can sit Rosie on my lap for riding, she's still little enough for that. I'll keep Maudie home from school, that'll put her in a good mood for a start. Right, that's settled, then.'

'I don't want to go and see Aunt Susannah,' Maudie grumbled as she rode beside Lizzie.

'So you've said half a dozen times. Say it once more and I'll give you a hiding when we get home,' Lizzie said briskly. 'You should be grateful to me for taking you visiting like you were grown up, not moaning all the time.'

'But Aunt Susannah's so *boring*. All she ever talks about is dresses and Auckland and all that stuff. And she'll just look down her nose at me the way she does, like I smell funny or something.'

'Well, you *don't* smell funny, not with your clean drawers on, so take no notice if she does. And it's time you started taking more interest in dresses, my girl—I think you'd run around in trousers like your brothers if I let you.'

'Wish I could,' Maudie said sulkily. 'Boys have all the fun. We don't have to stay long, do we?'

'We'll stay as long as I want, and you'll behave yourself like a young lady.' She saw Maudie's lips move, but did not catch the muttered complaint. 'I'll tell you this just the once, Maudie—you play up for me there, or disgrace yourself in front of Aunt Susannah, and you'll get a good hiding when we get home.'

This time she heard Maudie's muttering. 'Probably will anyway. Usually do.'

'You wouldn't if you behaved yourself better,' Lizzie told her in what she considered a perfectly reasonable fashion.

Susannah was alone in the kitchen when Lizzie walked through the back door holding the sleeping Rosie, Maudie trailing at her heels.

'Oh, it's you,' Susannah said. 'And which one's this? Maud, is it? You've so many I have trouble telling them all apart.'

'Hello, Aunt Susannah,' Lizzie said, turning her most winning smile on her startled aunt. 'We thought we'd come and see you, didn't we, Maudie? I've decided it's time Maudie started learning to mix properly so as she'll pick up some nice ways, and of course you were the first one I thought of.'

'Was I?' Lizzie was pleased to hear the note of surprise in Susannah's voice.

'Of course. I was talking to Frank about it just the other night, and I thought to myself, who around here's got really nice manners? Who's like a real lady? So here we are.' She beamed at Susannah.

'I see,' Susannah said, looking a little dazed.

Lizzie lowered her voice in a confiding manner. 'I need some advice about Maudie. I was hoping you might help me—as long as it's not too much trouble?'

'No, it… it's no trouble at all,' said Susannah. She graced Lizzie with a tight smile. 'You'd better come through to the parlour, then. Sophie will be back shortly, she's off getting meat out of the safe. I'll have her make us some tea.'

She led the way towards the parlour. Lizzie took hold of Maudie's arm as they followed Susannah up the passage. 'Now, look at the way Aunt Susannah holds herself. That's how a lady walks, see? Not stomping around as if she was a boy like you do.' Susannah turned to usher them into the room, a small smile of satisfaction on her face.

Lizzie watched Susannah take her seat, then turned to Maudie. 'Did you see the way Aunt Susannah sat down then? Wasn't that ladylike? You don't see *her* legs just dangling anywhere so people can see right up her dress, do you?'

Susannah looked horrified at the very notion, and Maudie squirmed in her chair. 'You don't walk like Aunt Susannah,' Maudie said.

'Yes, well, neither will you when you've had six children,' Lizzie said. Maudie pulled a face at the idea.

'Just what exactly is it you want from me?' Susannah asked, interrupting the tense moment.

Lizzie leaned forward as far as the plump baby on her lap would allow. 'Like I said, some advice. I want to make a lady out of Maudie,' she announced portentously.

Susannah studied Maudie for a moment, then turned to Lizzie. 'That's rather ambitious of you.'

'I know she's a bit rough around the edges. That's what I need the advice for, so you can tell me how to smarten her up. Frank's getting to be quite *prominent* around here,' she said, enjoying the sound of her favourite new word. 'I'm going to see that Maudie gets the chance to meet the right sort of person, you know?'

Susannah met her eyes. Lizzie saw that her meaning had not been lost, though it had gone right over Maudie's head. 'She's rather young for you to be thinking about that sort of thing, isn't she?'

'No sense leaving these things till the last minute. Anyway, there's not going to be much point seeing that she meets this right sort of person if she puts them off straight away, is there? I mean, people like that must be used to girls with a bit more going for them.'

'Hmm,' Susannah said thoughtfully. 'Well, she'll have to learn not to scowl so, for one thing. A face like that would frighten off anyone who got within ten feet of her.'

'Maudie!' Lizzie said sharply. 'Don't you go pulling faces.'

Maudie looked down at her lap and began tugging at a loose thread in her dress. 'Don't like you talking about me like I wasn't here,' she muttered. 'You make me sound like one of Pa's cows.'

'Her manners could certainly do with some polishing,' Susannah said.

Lizzie gave Maudie a warning glare, and turned her attention back to Susannah. 'What do you think I should do with her, then? How can I make a lady out of her?'

'Well, let me have a good look at her. Stand up, Maud, let me see you properly.'

'Hurry up, Maudie,' Lizzie said. 'Do what Aunt Susannah says.'

'That's right. Walk around the room a little—now stand still, and turn around slowly. All right, that'll do. Just stand there while I look at you.' Susannah stood up and walked around Maudie, studying her from every angle.

'What do you think of her?' Lizzie asked.

Susannah took a few steps back from Maudie and stood with one hand on her chin. 'She's not a bad looking girl,' she allowed. 'You could almost call her pretty. Her hair's her best feature, being blonde. A pity it's not wavy.'

'It just won't hold a curl,' Lizzie bemoaned. 'I've tried and tried with rags. Mine was just the same, though.'

'Still, curls aren't everything.' Susannah took another long stare at Maudie. 'I don't know how much you're going to be able to do, but you're quite right to want to make the best of her. I'd have liked a daughter,' she said. A wistful note, which Lizzie did not normally associate with her aunt, came into Susannah's voice.

'You should try having three of them,' Lizzie said. 'They're just as much of a trial as boys, only in different ways.'

'Yes, well, I never said I had any ambitions to be a brood mare,' Susannah said, the wistfulness disappearing as suddenly as it had come. 'I don't know where I would have found the time to teach a daughter the finer things of life, anyway—not that it would have been much use to her in *this* house. I suppose you've a good deal of time on your hands for this sort of business, now that you have a housemaid.'

'Housemaid, indeed,' Lizzie scoffed. 'Maisie's not a housemaid. It's more like having another child around the place—though Maisie's a hard worker, I'll grant her that.'

'Can I sit down now, Ma?' Maudie asked plaintively.

'Not until Aunt Susannah says you can. And stand still—don't keep shifting from one foot to the other like that.'

Rosie stirred in Lizzie's arms and let out a fretful cry. 'Don't worry about her, she'll settle down again when I've given her a feed,' Lizzie told Susannah, and began unbuttoning her bodice.

'Wouldn't you rather go into another room for that?' Susannah asked, looking away in distaste. 'You can use the bedroom if you like.'

'No, I'd just as soon feed her here,' Lizzie said. She waited until Rosie was suckling, then turned her attention back to Susannah. 'You went to one of those proper schools for young ladies, didn't you?'

'I certainly did. "Mrs Sanderson's Academy for Young Ladies",' Susannah said dreamily. 'Those were the happiest years of my life, I think.'

'Well, what sort of thing would they teach Maudie if she went to a place like that?'

'Ma!' Maudie protested. 'You said I could stop going to school this year! I don't want to go to some ladies' school.' She pulled a disgusted face.

'I don't know that they'd take you, dear,' Susannah murmured.

'I warned you, didn't I, Maudie?' Lizzie said, pointing a threatening finger at her daughter. 'We'll have a talk about you playing up when I get you home.' Maudie managed a defiant look with obvious difficulty. 'Anyway, I'm *not* going to send you away to school. You can stop home and help me for a few years. I was just *trying* to ask Aunt Susannah— before you butted in with your twopence worth—what they teach girls at those special schools.'

'All sorts of things,' Susannah said. 'Oh, it was wonderful there. Deportment, now—Mrs Sanderson was very strong on deportment.'

'What's that?' Lizzie asked doubtfully.

'How one carries oneself. Take Maud, here—see how she slouches when she's standing still?'

'Stand up straight, Maudie,' Lizzie ordered. Maudie made a half-hearted attempt at doing so.

'Now walk about the room, like you were doing before—see?' said Susannah. 'Her shoulders drop as soon as she starts moving. And she takes such long strides, too, not ladylike at all. She should float along, so that under a long dress you wouldn't see her limbs moving at all.'

'Show her how to do it,' Lizzie asked. Susannah obliged readily enough, gliding up and down the centre of the parlour. 'Now *that's* how a lady walks,' Lizzie told Maudie.

'Mrs Sanderson was always getting me to show the other girls,' Susannah said. 'She said I had the best deportment of any pupil she'd ever had. I was *much* better than Constance.'

'How can I make her do it, though?' Lizzie asked. 'I can't be looking at her all the time to see if she's walking properly.'

Susannah sighed. 'I'm afraid it's too late to do much about her. She'll never be really elegant in her movements, you have to start training a girl earlier than twelve for that. But you can certainly improve on her—oh, do sit down, Maud, I can't bear to see you pulling those faces any longer.' Maudie collapsed heavily into her chair with an exaggerated sigh of relief.

'A backboard would be ideal,' Susannah said, warming to her subject. 'I don't suppose you know what that is—it's a stiff board you fasten to the girl with a sort of harness, so that she can't help but stand up straight. Daily practice with a backboard would do wonders for her posture. You'd have no chance of finding one of those in Ruatane, I'm afraid.'

'I was thinking of putting her in stays early,' Lizzie said, ignoring the affronted look Maudie shot at her. 'Would that do the trick?'

'Not really. Stays wouldn't cure her of being round-shouldered. In fact, I'd advise against putting her in them till you've sorted out her posture. No, what you should do is make her walk with a book on her head.'

'Eh? How will that help?'

'You can't keep a book on your head without standing perfectly straight and gliding. Yes, you make her practise that every day until she can walk... oh, say up and down your passage twice each way without dropping the book.'

'Right, we'll do that,' Lizzie said, relieved to have found something well within her resources. 'Now, what else would she learn at this school?'

'The sort of things that help a girl mix in cultivated society.' Lizzie waited for Susannah to elaborate. 'Dancing, of course—'

'There isn't much dancing goes on around here,' Lizzie said thoughtfully. 'They don't even seem to have the hay dance any more most years. If they have one next year I might let her go to it as long as there's someone there to keep a good eye on her.'

'Singing, too. A young lady ought to be able to entertain when she's in company.'

'You do singing at school, don't you, Maudie?'

'Yes,' Maudie agreed cautiously.

'That's all right, then. She can sing. What else?'

'French. Cultivated people can always speak a little French. It's such an elegant language.'

This came as something of a shock to Lizzie, who had never found any shortcomings in English when she wanted to express herself. She quickly rejected the idea as useless.

'Well, no one around here speaks any French—except you, of course. And maybe Lily, though I can't say she's ever mentioned it. So there's no need for Maudie to talk it. Anyway, she's got enough to say for herself in one language without learning another one—especially when I wouldn't know what she was saying in it.'

'Yes, it would probably be wasted on her. If you really want her to mix in polite company she should learn an instrument, you realise.'

'A what?'

'A piano, of course. She should be able to play.'

'Oh,' Lizzie said, taken aback. 'Is that really important?'

'It certainly is,' Susannah said. 'No girl could be considered at all cultured without that.'

'We haven't got a piano, Ma,' Maudie said, the look of triumph in her face goading Lizzie into more enthusiasm than she might otherwise have felt towards the idea.

'Then maybe we'll just have to get one,' she snapped. 'Yes,' she said, enjoying the startled expressions Maudie and Susannah both wore, 'I remember your pa saying years and years ago that he'd like to buy a piano. Now might be just the right time.'

'Your husband must be doing well if he can contemplate that sort of purchase,' Susannah said. Lizzie could not decide if disbelief or grudging admiration was uppermost in her reaction.

'He is,' Lizzie said. 'He's doing very well. And he'll like the idea of getting a piano—I expect he'll see about ordering one right away. Does it take long to learn it?'

'To become proficient, yes. It takes years.'

'Well, she mightn't have to be really good at it. Just so as she can play a few nice songs, that should do the trick.' Lizzie was warming rapidly to the idea; playing the piano was such an unusual skill amongst the people of her acquaintance that she was quite certain it would set Maudie apart from the other girls of Ruatane. 'Do you think she'd be able to pick it up by herself?'

'Certainly not! She'd need a proper teacher.'

'Hmm. I don't suppose you could...' Lizzie said, doubting the merits of the idea even as she spoke.

'Oh, I couldn't possibly take on teaching piano,' Susannah said quickly. 'It's so long since I had the chance to play myself. Anyway, I simply haven't the time.'

'Never mind, I'll get Lily to teach her,' Lizzie said. 'I know she can play, she's mentioned it from time to time. And she used to be a teacher, so teaching piano'll be no trouble to her. She won't be able to start for a while, she's a bit poorly just now.'

'Yes, the poor woman,' Susannah said.

'By the time this piano arrives she should be feeling brighter. It'll be really nice, having songs around the piano,' Lizzie said, forgetting for a moment the main object of acquiring the instrument. 'You and Uncle Jack will have to come down and join in,' she added, expansive in her gratitude.

'Perhaps I will,' Susannah allowed. 'I can't speak for your uncle, he's never shown any leanings toward culture. How I did use to love musical soirées.'

'What are they?' Lizzie asked. 'I'll get Frank to buy a piano, but I don't know if he'll want to get those what you said.'

'You don't buy soirées,' Susannah said, pursing her lips. 'It means evening. It's French, you see, that's why it sounds so elegant. S-o-i-r-e-e, soirée. A soirée is a social gathering, when you have a few selected people around for the evening to share some cultured conversation and enjoy pleasant music together.'

'That's a good idea,' Lizzie said. 'Now that's a good excuse to ask people out—the sort of people I want Maudie to mix with. Soyrees, that's what we'll have.'

'Soirées,' Susannah corrected.

'Yes, soyrees. Afternoons might suit better than evenings, though, especially in winter. People don't always want to be out late at night.'

'Then they won't be soirées, will they?' Susannah pointed out.

'That won't matter. Like I said, no one around here except you and Lily can talk French, so no one's going to worry about that. I'll have to start thinking of some people to ask.'

Maudie managed to keep silent until she and Lizzie were out of sight of Jack's house on their way home, when she turned a resentful face on her mother.

'That was awful. You and Aunt Susannah talking about me like that. And her bossing me around—"Walk up and down, turn around, stand still". And saying I walk funny! I don't want to walk like her. She walks like she's got no legs.'

'That's how ladies walk. You're going to learn to be a lady,' Lizzie said.

'I don't want to! And I don't want to learn how to play a stupid piano, either. I'm going to tell Pa I don't want to. I bet he won't make me.'

'There's no use taking that tone with me, my girl. And don't think I've forgotten about you playing up for me—in front of Aunt Susannah, of all people! I warned you there'd be trouble if you didn't behave yourself, didn't I?'

Maudie glowered at her. 'I don't care.'

'I'll see that you care about it when we get home. I'll have to hunt some books out, too, for you to practise that special walking with.'

'I'm not going to do that,' Maudie said mutinously.

'Oh, yes you are. You're going to practise that every day till you've got it right.'

'I'm not,' Maudie insisted. 'I'm not going to walk around with books on my head. I'd feel really dopey.'

'You'll be in trouble if you don't do as you're told, Edith Maud.'

'I don't care. I'm already in trouble, so you keep saying.'

'That's no reason to make it worse, is it?'

'I've only got one backside,' Maudie muttered. 'I don't see how you can fit any more hidings onto it.'

'You'll find out if you're not careful. I don't know what's got into you today! Honestly, you're getting just like your grandpa, always wanting to have your own way. It's all for your good, you know—I'm only thinking of you.'

'You are not!' Maudie said indignantly. 'How's it meant to be for my good, doing all those awful things to me?

'Awful things, indeed! What's so awful, for goodness sake?'

Maudie gave her a look heavy with reproach. 'You want to make me walk stupid—and you'd like to send me away to a horrible school, 'cept you know Pa wouldn't make me—and you want to make me wear stays, and Aunt Susannah said to put me in a harness, and–and–and,' she ran out of breath, then took a deep gulp to finish her tirade on, 'and you want me to learn the *piano*.' She dug in her heels to give her frustration tangible expression. The startled horse pricked its ears forward and broke into a canter.

Lizzie made no attempt to catch up with her errant daughter. The baby snuggled against her made it impossible to ride faster than a walking pace, even if she had been inclined towards racing.

As Lizzie expected, Maudie's burst of energy did not last long. She slumped in the saddle, and the horse slowed to an amble so sluggish that the steady plod of Lizzie's mount soon caught it up. Maudie had let the reins go slack; it was only her horse's eagerness to get home that kept it moving at all.

'Wish I could go back to school next year,' Maudie said morosely as they neared the schoolhouse.

'Don't talk rot,' Lizzie said. 'You must have asked me a dozen times this year if you could leave school.'

'That's 'cause I'm sick of doing all those stupid sums and things. And having to do homework all the time, too. If you're going to make me do all those awful things I might as well stay at school.'

'I've had just about enough of your moaning for one day,' Lizzie said in mounting irritation. 'After nagging and nagging to leave school, now you reckon you want to stay there. Well, you can't and that's that. It won't hurt you to help me around the house a bit more, anyway.'

'That's all you want me for. Scrubbing floors and washing clothes and looking after babies. Ugh!'

'What's wrong with looking after babies? I'd like to know what more useful work a girl could do.'

'It's not fair,' Maudie complained. She gave the reins a half-hearted flick; the horse ignored her. 'Miss Metcalf makes me do homework, then you make me look after babies. I'm sick of being bossed around all the time. Why don't I ever get any fun?'

'It's for your own good, my girl. I'm going to a lot of trouble over this, you know—and your father's going to pay a lot of money for this piano, too—and it's all for your sake. Now, you should—'

'I don't *want* to learn the piano,' Maudie interrupted. 'I just want to… oh, I don't know,' she said, tears of frustration welling up in her eyes. 'I just wish you'd leave me alone.'

Lizzie was not one to be easily moved by tears, especially when she could see they were more a result of annoyance than unhappiness. But it was time to use a little subtlety, since further threats were likely to rouse her daughter to fresh heights of obstinacy.

'Well, Miss Sulks, what do you want, then? If it's so awful at home, what would you do about it if you had the chance?'

Maudie looked up suspiciously. 'How do you mean?'

'If you could do whatever you want—and I'm not saying you can, mind you—what would you do? Well?'

'I don't know… I… I'd just like to please myself for a change. Instead of having people boss me around all day,' she added, giving Lizzie a sidelong glance.

'And how would you do that?' Lizzie pressed. 'Since I'm not about to let you run my house for me, how do you think you'd be able to get your own way like you seem to want?'

'I suppose…' Maudie grasped at an elusive notion. 'I'd like my own place,' she said slowly. 'Yes, my own place,' she repeated. 'Then *I* could say how things were going to be, 'stead of just doing what you say all the time. That'd be good,' she said, her eyes bright.

'Now you're starting to use your head a bit, instead of just whinging all the time. And how do you think you're going to get this place of your own?'

'Well, I suppose… I suppose I'll get married,' Maudie said, looking mildly surprised at the realisation.

'I certainly hope you will. I don't intend to have you on my hands all your life. Right, then, when the time comes to try and find some man who'll put up with a sulky little miss like you—and don't get too carried away about it, either, you're only twelve, so you've got a few years to go yet—what sort of man would you like to marry? Well? A *prominent* man like your pa, or maybe someone like Maisie's father?'

'Ugh! I wouldn't marry one of the Feenans! I want a nice house and pretty clothes and things.'

'I thought you weren't very interested in clothes.'

'I would be if I could choose them for myself instead of just what you say I have to wear. I'm going to have all sorts of nice things when I get married.'

Lizzie pounced. 'And what makes you think you can afford to be fussy? Why should the sort of man who's got a flash house—or at least got the money to buy one—ask you to marry him?'

She pressed on without giving Maudie time to answer. 'If you're going to set your sights that high, you'd better have something to offer. There's not many men in Ruatane with much go in them, they get snapped up pretty smartly. Oh, you get the odd one coming here from the city who's got a bit of money, I suppose you'd fancy one of them?'

'I might,' Maudie said. 'If he was good looking.'

'And what sort of girl do you think men like that are used to mixing with? Farm girls with rough manners? I should say not! They're used to balls and drawing rooms and soyrees. And girls who can play the piano,' she finished triumphantly.'

She had the satisfaction of seeing her daughter lost for words for several seconds. 'But… but you can't play the piano, and Pa asked you,' Maudie said at last.

'Your father is a wonderful man,' Lizzie said. 'And everything he's got, he's managed through his own good sense. The farm hasn't always made the money it does now, with the Jersey cows and all. I don't think I had more than one new dress the first three years we were married—not that I minded, either. We had each other, and we had you lot, and that was all we cared about. If you think you can find another man like your father, then good luck to you, because I don't think there's another living. And you'd have to be prepared to put in a good few years struggling and making do before you could have those fancy things you're hankering after.'

Maudie's lack of enthusiasm for this picture was clear from her expression.

'But if you want it all on a plate,' Lizzie said, 'then you've got to make a good impression right from the start. And *that's* why I want to make a young lady of you. Of course, if you're happy to take whoever's left over after the other girls have had their pick, then that's your look out. Just let me know and I'll stop worrying about you.'

Lizzie let Maudie mull over these notions as they plodded on down the road, contenting herself with watching thoughts play over her daughter's face. They were not far from the turning to Frank's farm before Maudie turned to her mother and asked in what was clearly meant to be a nonchalant way,

'Do you think it takes long to learn the piano?'

9

Amy glanced up from the pile of washing waiting to be hung on the line, and saw Jack walking slowly towards the back door of Charlie's cottage.

Glad though she always was to see her father, Amy could not help wishing he had chosen a more thoughtful time to visit. The short days of late winter, especially when the sky was as leaden as the one currently lowering over her, gave few enough hours of sunlight to get her washing dry, without having to surrender time unexpectedly.

But she would far sooner cope with wet washing than risk letting her father think he might be unwelcome. Jack's visits had become less frequent over the last year or two, as the walk across the paddocks became more of an effort. Even from a distance Amy could see how much slower his steps were now, bearing little resemblance to the vigorous stride she remembered from her childhood.

She abandoned the tin bath of washing and hurried down the hill to meet Jack just as he reached the doorstep. 'I didn't know you were coming over today, Pa,' she said, careful to show no sign of agitation as she let him enfold her in a hug.

'Well, I haven't seen you for a bit. I missed you at church yesterday.'

'I thought you would. Charlie said he didn't feel like going—he was a bit grumpy about the sermon last Sunday. He'll have forgotten by next week, though.'

'I don't like it when I don't see you. I get thinking about things,' Jack said, his face taking on a grimmer expression.

Amy disentangled herself from his embrace and led him into the house, noticing how he leaned against her for support as they climbed the steps and with what relief he sank into a chair. 'Pa, you mustn't worry about me. Anyway, John was over just the other day—Friday, I think it was—so you knew I was all right.'

'I wanted to see for myself.' His frown gave way to a wry grin. 'Anyway, I wanted some better company. The air's pretty frosty at home.'

Amy set out the tea things. 'A bit grumpy, is she?'

'Worse than usual these last few days. And Monday's a bad day at the best of times—washing seems to get women in a black mood. Even Sophie's inclined to look a bit sour by the end of a Monday.'

'It's hard work, Pa. And there's lots to do, with all the little ones at your place, even with three women to share it.' She cast a rapid glance out the window, and was relieved to see that the sky had grown no more threatening.

Jack followed her glance and seemed to notice for the first time the traces of fluster in her face. 'I'm an old fool, aren't I? Coming over here bothering you on a washing day. I suppose you're flat out with it. I'll go home, leave you in peace.' He made to rise from his chair.

'Don't go, Pa,' Amy said. 'I was thinking I'd love to take the weight off my feet for a minute, just before you came.' It was true enough; no need to add that she had planned to wait until her latest load of washing was safely pegged out. 'Stay and keep me company.'

'I'm not getting in your way?' Amy shook her head emphatically, and he leaned back in the chair. 'Keeping you from your work, though.'

Amy brought the teapot to the table and sat down. 'It doesn't matter, I'll get it finished later. I've only got the four of us to do for, anyway, not like the mob at your place.' She smiled at him. 'Two boys and a man—just like when I had you and John and Harry to look after. And they get just as dirty as you lot always did, too. No wonder Susannah gets fed up with you.'

Jack made a grimace. 'You'd think she had the whole town to wash for, the fuss she's been making. Slaving like a servant, she says. She's been worse than ever since Lizzie came to see her the other day.'

'Did she, Pa? I didn't know Lizzie ever came to see Susannah.'

'She came one other time a couple of years ago. They had a bit of a set-to then, I seem to recall.'

'I wonder what that was all about,' Amy said, at a loss as to why Lizzie would ever have chosen to visit Susannah. 'Is that why Susannah's in a mood, then? Did Lizzie upset her?'

'They seemed to get on all right this time—Susannah didn't say anything about rowing with her, anyway. Lizzie brought her oldest girl to see her—Maudie, is it? Some nonsense about improving the girl's manners.' He gave a sigh. 'It seems Frank's gone and got a servant girl for Lizzie.'

'Yes, I know. It's just Maisie Feenan, she comes to help Lizzie three days a week. I don't like Feenans, but Maisie's quite a nice girl now Lizzie's cleaned her up.'

'Well, whoever she is, I've heard more about her the last few days than I needed to. "Even Frank Kelly has enough consideration for his wife to get her a housemaid. He doesn't expect her to work like a slave." I just about know it off by heart now.'

'Poor you.'

'As if *that* wasn't enough, she tells me Frank's going to buy a piano now.'

'Is he?' Amy said, astonished. 'I hadn't heard about that! Are you sure, Pa?'

'I should be—I've been told about it a dozen times a day since she heard, not to mention at night.' He shook his head. 'I never thought I'd be expected to come up with a piano.'

'You shouldn't take any notice. Susannah probably doesn't even want a piano, you know. It's just something to talk about.'

'I expect you're right. If it wasn't a piano it'd be something else. I'm the worst husband there's ever been, it seems.'

'You're not,' Amy said fiercely. 'You mustn't listen when she says awful things to you.'

'Oh, I'm pretty good at being deaf when it suits me,' Jack said, with an attempt at his old heartiness that it pained Amy to see. He gave a rueful grin. 'Maybe I should have offered her to Charlie when he came sniffing around for a wife, instead of you. She'd know all about husbands then, wouldn't she?'

'Pa, you say some terrible things,' Amy scolded, laughing with him. 'Susannah really *would* be wild if she heard you say that.'

'How do you think they'd have got on? Maybe they'd have suited each other. They're both pretty good at looking down in the mouth.'

'I think…' Amy hesitated, unwilling to spoil the joke. *I think he would have killed her.* 'Well, maybe she'd have worn him down, you never know. They might even have got on all right.' She could not help but laugh at the preposterousness of the idea. 'Or maybe he'd have thrown her out, sent her back to you. That's if she didn't leave first,' she added, giving her father a grin. 'Charlie's even worse than you for getting his clothes mucky, and that's saying something.'

'Where's he got to, anyway?' Jack asked, the merriment draining abruptly from his voice.

Amy shrugged. 'Off over the back of the farm, I think. He won't be back for a while.' She slipped her arm through her father's for a moment before pouring their tea. 'This is nice, Pa, just the two of us. It's like when I was at home.'

'Wish you still were,' Jack said gruffly.

'So do I, sometimes,' Amy admitted. 'But I wouldn't have my boys then, would I?'

'You'd be safe, though.' He took a gulp of the hot tea and put his cup down heavily on its saucer. 'I never should have let him have you. I should have—'

'Don't, Pa,' Amy interrupted. 'Don't go upsetting yourself over me. I'm all right, really I am. We get on all right now, Charlie and me.'

'When I think of what he did to you, I'd like to—'

'Stop it, Pa. He never lays a hand on me.'

'I know I'm getting old, girl, but my mind hasn't gone yet. Never lays a hand on you! I'll never forget the marks of his fists that day. If I'd been a younger man... if I'd told the boys what he'd done they'd have killed him, you know.'

'Yes, I know,' Amy said.

'By the time they found out about it you'd healed up all right, they never knew the state I saw you in. Maybe I should have told them,' he said grimly.

'And left me with two fatherless boys to bring up, and my brothers in jail, maybe getting hung for it? You did the right thing to keep quiet. He doesn't hurt me, honestly he doesn't—oh, yes, he did back then, we're neither of us likely to forget that. But that was a long time ago. He hasn't laid a hand on me since that day. It's true, Pa, cross my heart and hope to die.'

She turned away from his gaze and put several cakes on a plate for him. 'Let's talk about something happy, not all that awful old stuff. I haven't been over for a while, how's everyone getting on? Vicky must be getting big.'

'Now, which one's Vicky?' Jack asked, frowning in thought. 'Is that Harry's youngest girl?'

'That's right. It's easy to remember, she was named after the Queen because she was born around Jubilee time.'

'I get them a bit muddled up,' Jack admitted. 'I lost track of them a while back, especially those two smallest ones of Harry's.'

'There's too many children at your place,' Amy said, laughing. 'You just about need them all to wear signs around their necks with their names on.'

'They don't come up to the house much. You know what Harry's like with Susannah. I go down there a bit, to see the children. Jane always makes a fuss of me, says she likes the little ones to see their Grandpa.'

He smiled at the thought. 'Harry and John both did all right for themselves. Sophie never has much to say, but she's good-natured. They're nice girls both of them, Jane and Sophie.' He took hold of Amy's hand. 'I like my own girl best, though.'

Amy squeezed the hand holding hers. 'I wish I could come and see you more, Pa. I seem to be so busy all the time, even though I've only got the four of us to keep house for.' She did not add that she could

126

never be sure if Charlie would allow her to go out.

'You were always such an affectionate little thing,' Jack mused. 'You were a great one for sitting on my lap.' He gave her a look that was almost shy. 'I suppose you're too grown-up for that now.'

'Would you like me to?' Without waiting for his answering nod, Amy slipped from her chair and settled herself on his ample lap. 'Mmm, that's nice.' She wound her arms around his neck and pressed her face against his chest, feeling the tickle of his beard. 'I'm not too heavy for you, am I?'

'Of course you're not, a little scrap like you. You never did grow very big, did you? I suppose you've finished growing now.'

'I should hope so,' Amy said with a laugh. 'I'm a bit old for growing!'

'You must be over twenty now.'

'Twenty? Pa, I'm nearly thirty!'

'You're not,' Jack said in astonishment. 'You can't be!'

'I am, you know. I'll be thirty in October. Doesn't it sound old?'

'Thirty,' he echoed. 'I don't know where the years have gone. Seems just the other day you were crawling around on the floor like that youngest one of Jane's—Vicky, is it? No wonder I'm feeling old, with my little girl nearly thirty.'

'Well, at least I'm going to stay little. How do you think I feel, with those great big boys of mine? Every time I turn around they seem to grow another inch. They make *me* feel old. Tom and George are shooting up too, aren't they?'

'Like weeds,' Jack said. 'They throw off when I call them the little fellows, now they're taller than I am. They take after their ma for being tall.'

Amy reflected silently that it was the only thing her young brothers did seem to take after their mother in; that was something to be grateful for.

'They're only little fellows really, though,' Jack said pensively. 'They're a sight younger than John and Harry—there's twenty years between John and Tom, you know. That's something to think about.'

'How do you mean, Pa?'

'I've got to do right by them all. If a man goes taking a new wife and fathering sons when he's old enough to be their grandfather... well, it's up to me to treat them all fair.'

'Of course you do,' Amy said, made uneasy by the troubled note in his voice.

'Twenty years, you see,' Jack said, seemingly as much to himself as to Amy. 'It wouldn't be fair, now, would it? I can't give the little fellows the same as John and Harry, not when the older boys have worked twenty years longer. And it'd be no good splitting the farm four ways, anyway—they'd none of them get a decent living out of it then. But I've got to provide for the young ones, too. They're good little fellows, and they're my boys as much as John and Harry are.'

His meaning was clear to Amy now. 'Pa, don't talk like that. You don't have to think about that sort of thing for years and years yet.'

'I'm not getting any younger, girl,' Jack said, squeezing her hard for a moment. 'I've got to get all that business sorted out, not go leaving everyone to squabble over it when I'm gone.'

'They wouldn't!' Amy said, shocked at the notion.

'Well, maybe the boys wouldn't. There might be others who'd make a fuss. I want it all down in black and white, in proper lawyer talk so no one can argue about it.'

'Please don't talk about it—I don't want to think about that.' Amy wound her arms more tightly around his neck. 'What would I do for hugs if I didn't have you?'

Jack gave a tired laugh. 'All right, that's enough miserable talk, then. Don't know why I'm going on to you about it, anyway.'

He seemed to struggle to find a cheerful subject to raise, and Amy's heart was still too full of his references to his own mortality for her to contribute one. 'You still keen on those books of yours?' he said at last.

'They're like my friends,' Amy said, managing to smile. 'I just about know them all off by heart, I've read them so many times.'

'You should shout yourself some more, then,' Jack said, as if it were the simplest thing in the world.

'I haven't got any money, Pa,' Amy said gently, anxious not to let him think it worried her.

'You must have a little bit—doesn't he give you any for yourself?'

Amy shook her head. 'If I need a new dress he'll usually let me charge up some material. He wouldn't give me money to spend how I liked, though.'

'Miserable sod,' Jack muttered.

'He doesn't know any better, Pa. And what do I need money for, anyway? I've got enough to eat and a roof over my head.' She would not dream of troubling her father by admitting with what longing she sometimes studied advertisements for book shops in the *Weekly News*.

'I suppose so,' Jack said. He looked at her thoughtfully, until Amy distracted him with more of her cakes and questions about the goings-on at her old home.

They chatted away, sharing memories of the times that they both regarded with nostalgia. Much as Amy was enjoying her father's company, as the time wore on she cast surreptitious glances at the clock with increasing concern, aware of the pile of washing still to be pegged out. If it got much later it would be time to start preparing lunch, and she would have no chance to catch up on her work.

That would be difficult enough, but another thought began to trouble her. Jack had looked weary when he had arrived at Charlie's door, and she was sure he had been favouring one leg. She did not like the idea of letting him struggle home by himself, not with all the fences to negotiate. But going with him would mean first finding Charlie and asking his permission for the outing, then taking up a large chunk of what was left of the morning trudging at her father's slow pace across the paddocks. Even if she ran back afterwards, she would have difficulty getting Charlie's lunch on the table in time.

A noise at the back door made Amy give a start. She leapt up and looked guiltily towards the door, expecting to meet a disapproving glare from Charlie at being caught on her father's lap.

To her surprised relief, it was not Charlie who appeared in the doorway but her young brother. Thomas stood looking around awkwardly, and Amy rushed to give him a welcoming hug.

'I have to stand on tiptoe to hug you now,' she said. 'Tom, I'm so glad to see you—you never come over here usually.'

'So why have you turned up today, boy?' Jack asked, surprising Amy with the sternness of his voice. 'Not that I don't know.'

'I… I just thought I'd like to…' Thomas trailed off and stared at his own feet.

'That brother of yours sent you over here, didn't he?' Jack said. 'Told you to come looking for me?'

'No,' Thomas said. He raised his eyes, met his father's gaze and dropped them again. 'Yes,' he admitted.

'I thought as much. John seems to think I'm like a child that needs to be on leading-strings these days—well, I'm not as far into my dotage as that. I don't need to ask my own son's leave to come and go, do I?'

'Pa, don't growl at Tom,' Amy said, seeing how troubled Thomas looked. 'John just wondered where you were, there's nothing wrong with that, is there?'

'Don't like my own son checking up on me,' Jack muttered, so like a petulant child that Amy had to hide a smile.

She took hold of Thomas's hand and pulled him a little further into the room. 'Now, aren't you glad John thinks enough of you to care if you're all right?' she asked. 'And Tom's come over here specially to find you. I bet you wouldn't like it if none of us bothered where you were or what you were doing.'

'Suppose not,' Jack said.

'Of course you wouldn't. Anyway, I'm glad Tom's come over, it gives me a chance to see him. Sit down with us, Tom, so we can talk for a bit. You can have some cakes if Pa's left us any.'

'Maybe I should go straight home again,' Thomas said, eyeing the cakes in question with obvious longing. 'I've been gone a while—I went over to Uncle Arthur's first.'

'You can stay long enough to eat a couple of cakes,' Amy told him. 'John's not going to be as worried as all that. Then you and Pa can keep each other company on the way home. I really had better get on with this washing in a minute, Pa.'

'Come and sit down, then, Tom,' Jack relented. 'I suppose it's not your fault if that brother of yours is such an old woman. I'm going to give him a piece of my mind when we get home, sending you out after me as if I was a straying cow.'

Jack and Thomas left a few minutes later. Amy stood in the doorway and waved them out of sight. Jack had one arm flung around Thomas's shoulders in what looked like an easy gesture of affection, but Amy saw how heavily he was leaning on his son for support. She wondered if her father could have got home unassisted without risking a fall; John was right to be keeping a careful eye on him, even if it did ruffle Jack's pride.

Her father had grown old. It pained Amy, for all she knew she should accept it as natural. She did not want to lose him; could not imagine life without the man she had adored since her childhood. She remembered him swinging her high in the air; spinning her around while she squealed in delight. Now walking across a few paddocks left him so weary that he needed the support of a strong, young pair of shoulders to help him home.

And instead of the father she remembered from the early days, always hearty and joking, was a wistful old man who talked candidly of his own death. Amy searched her apron pocket in vain for a handkerchief, then gave up and wiped her eyes on her sleeve like a child.

Frank had greeted Lizzie's announcement that she wanted him to buy a piano with astonishment rapidly succeeded by delight. It was so unlike Lizzie to ask for anything remotely impractical that at first he doubted the evidence of his senses.

He wasted no time in finding out how to about ordering a piano, anxious not to give Lizzie's pragmatic nature the chance to reassert itself.

He pored over the advertisements in the *Weekly News*, becoming more and more mystified by the effusive descriptions each vendor gave of their own particular range. It was only when Lily had recovered somewhat from the birth of her latest baby that Frank was able to enlist her expertise to help him make a decision and send off his order.

After that it was a matter of waiting. Maudie soon became so impatient for the arrival of 'her' piano that Frank was convinced his daughter must be concealing hitherto unsuspected musical gifts.

At last a telegram arrived telling Frank he could expect his piano when the *Waiotahi* made its next trip to Ruatane.

'I suppose the spring cart will do for hauling it home,' he said to Lizzie the day before the boat was due in, eyeing his small cart doubtfully. 'I'm not too sure, though. Pity I haven't got a big dray like the one they use at the factory.'

'Borrow that one, then,' Lizzie suggested.

'Hmm, maybe I could ask the manager,' Frank said. 'See if he needs the dray tomorrow.'

'Never mind *asking* him, you tell the man. You're the Chairman, aren't you? He's got to do as you say.'

'He doesn't really,' Frank said, smiling at her confidence. 'He doesn't work for me—well, no more than he does any of the other farmers. Still, borrowing the dray's not a bad idea. I'll have a go.'

The factory manager raised no objections when Frank called on him the next morning, and even lent one of his assistants to help with loading the piano. Frank eyed the tall, well-muscled youth with some relief. He had brought an eager Joey along with him, ostensibly to help but mainly as an excuse for the boy to escape a day's school; but Frank knew that however keen Joey might be, his ten-year-old strength was going to be of only limited use.

One last passenger clambered onto the raised board at the front of the dray when Frank stopped in Ruatane's main street. During a conversation a few weeks earlier with Mr Callaghan, the bank manager had mentioned that if Frank wanted any help getting his new piano in tune he should speak to Mr Hatfield, who as well as being the town's jeweller, watchmaker and photographer was the nearest thing Ruatane had to an expert piano tuner. This was the first Frank had ever heard of a piano's need for tuning. He had at once decided to have Mr Hatfield on hand when the piano arrived rather than risk doing any damage to his valuable new possession.

Mr Hatfield had shut up his shop for the afternoon to accompany Frank. He sat on the dray clutching a black bag on his lap, his pale blue eyes alight with interest. When they arrived at the wharf, he startled Frank by the confidence with which he issued instructions to the *Waiotahi*'s captain, as well as to Frank and his team of helpers, as they manhandled the large crate off the boat and onto the dray.

'It's a monster,' Frank said, staring at the crate in awe when they had it safely loaded. 'I only wanted a medium-sized sort of piano, I hope they haven't sent me an extra big one. We'll never get it in the parlour.'

'It's just well-packed, Mr Kelly,' Mr Hatfield said. 'That just goes to show you're dealing with a reputable firm in Auckland, and they've gone to the trouble of packing the instrument correctly.'

That was all very well, Frank reflected, but there was still the matter of getting this monstrous crate home, and its contents into the house. He studied the large dray, grateful that he had not made a fool of himself by arriving at the wharf with his hopelessly inadequate cart.

By the time he had negotiated his awkward load the first few miles, Frank had a more profound awareness than ever before of just how many ruts there were along the track, and just how deep some of them were. Several times along the way they had to stop and lend their strength by pushing the dray from behind while Joey pulled on the bridle of the lead horse. If the track had not been unusually dry for September, Frank doubted if they would have managed the task at all. When Mr Hatfield mildly made the suggestion that a bullock wagon might have been more suitable, Frank had to bite back the retort that it would have been more useful to suggest it a few weeks earlier. Instead he kept silent, and told himself he was going to get this damned piano home if it took him all night.

It did not take all night, though it did take a good two hours longer than Frank had expected. They at last brought the dray to a halt outside the house, the annoyances of the trip home almost forgotten in the relief that it was over.

Lizzie rushed outside when she heard them coming up the last part of the track. She exclaimed in amazement at the size of the crate. There was clearly no chance of getting it inside, so when the men had carefully lowered it onto the grass Frank sent Joey running to the tool shed for a crowbar to wrench the crate open.

'It's in bits!' Frank said in dismay when they had lifted the lid off the crate, revealing several mysteriously-shaped objects of varying sizes, all well-wrapped. 'What am I meant to do with a piano in bits?'

'You can figure out how to fit it together,' Lizzie said with the utter confidence she always showed in Frank's abilities. 'Joey, run and get a hammer and nails for your father.'

'Oh, that won't be necessary, Mrs Kelly,' Mr Hatfield said. 'Goodness me, there's no need to take to the instrument with a hammer! Now, if you gentlemen will lift these pieces out—carefully, mind—and carry them through to the parlour, we'll have this set up in no time at all.'

Frank saw Lizzie fix Mr Hatfield with one of her most disapproving glares for the watchmaker's temerity in daring to order Frank around, but he was only too happy to be told what to do by someone prepared to be an expert. Mr Hatfield seemed unaware of her censure, and Lizzie was soon too busy making sure they had a clear path through the house and into the parlour to remember to be annoyed with him.

Under Mr Hatfield's brisk instructions, they unwrapped the pieces of the puzzle and fitted the various parts together until they assumed a shape that Frank recognised with relief as a genuine piano, and a medium-sized one at that.

'Gee, it looks good, doesn't it?' he said, standing back to admire his new possession. Lizzie was already attacking it with a polishing cloth, removing spots that were invisible to Frank as well as raising a shine on the swirling pattern of the wood. When she had finished, Frank was sure the piano must be the most beautiful ever seen.

'It needs a few nice ornaments on the top, it looks a bit bare like that,' Lizzie said, her eyes roving around the room in search of candidates. She had seized a small vase of flowers and a photograph of Frank and her with the three oldest children before Mr Hatfield managed to intercept her.

'Just before you do that, Mrs Kelly, I'd better see about getting this instrument in tune for you, don't you think?'

'How do you mean?' Lizzie asked. 'What's wrong with it?'

'Well, at the moment I think you'll find its sound doesn't match up to its fine appearance.' He raised the cover, revealing the keyboard, and played a succession of notes that even to Frank's untrained ear sounded flat and discordant.

'That's horrible,' Lizzie said. 'I can't have soyrees for people to listen to that! I hope this piano isn't a dud, Frank.'

'So do I,' Frank said, thinking of the extravagant amount he had paid for the piano.

'Oh, I'm sure it's perfectly sound, Mr Kelly,' Mr Hatfield said. He opened his bag and took out a device that looked to Frank like a mistreated table fork. After enjoining silence from his interested audience he struck the fork, creating a clear note. He chose one key near the centre of the keyboard and fiddled with the small peg behind it, making tiny adjustments until the sound of the key seemed indistinguishable from the sound made by the tuning fork.

He then spent what felt like hours to Frank, though it was probably closer to thirty minutes, alternately striking keys and adjusting pegs until he seemed satisfied with the sound produced by every key.

'That should be sufficient,' he said, carefully replacing the piano's cover. 'Would you like to try it out now? Which of you plays?'

'Oh, we can't play,' said Lizzie. 'We got it for Maudie, really—the other girls, too, when they're older.'

'Ah, the delightful Miss Kelly,' Mr Hatfield said, his watery eyes lighting up with a smile. 'I'm sure she plays like an angel.'

'Well, she doesn't yet—she's going to learn, though. I'll get Lily on to it as soon as she's feeling herself again. It shouldn't take Maudie long to pick it up.'

'How about you play us a tune, Mr Hatfield?' Frank suggested.

Mr Hatfield shook his head. 'I'm afraid I wouldn't give an audience any pleasure. No, it's many, many years since I touched a piano except to tune one—I don't even get a great deal of practice at that these days. I wouldn't attempt to play. Not now.' His eyes took on a faraway expression. Frank sensed the older man was recalling memories that gave mingled pleasure and regret.

Lizzie prevailed upon their helpers to stay for a generous afternoon tea, then Mr Hatfield took his seat on the dray beside the factory lad, managing to look as though he were seated in a fine carriage rather than a rough wagon, and Frank and Lizzie waved them off.

Frank patted Lizzie's hand where it rested on his arm. 'Well, we've done it, eh? I never thought I'd be able to get you a piano.'

'I never thought I'd want one. It's for the girls, really, but it'll be nice to have a few songs of an evening.'

Frank met her eyes and grinned. 'Let's go and look at it again.'

They went into the house and examined their piano in shared pride. 'It's a beauty, all right,' Frank said with deep satisfaction.

Lizzie put two lace doilies on top of the piano, and placed her chosen vase and photograph on them. 'It takes up a fair bit of room. But it does look nice. Now, the next thing's to get Maudie taught. I'll get Lily to come down tomorrow afternoon—she'd like to see the piano, and I can ask her when she can start teaching Maudie.'

'Do you think she'll feel up to coming?' Frank asked. 'Bill said she's still a bit frail when I saw him the other day.'

'She'll be all right. Bill's nearly as bad as you for fussing. An outing'll do her good, anyway. I'm going to write her a note right now, tell her to come down tomorrow. Joey can take it up there.'

Lily duly arrived the next afternoon. She came with a substantial escort; as well as Bill and their two younger children, Arthur interpreted the invitation as applying to himself and Edie as well.

'Trust Pa to turn up,' Lizzie grumbled when she saw who was driving the buggy. 'He's always got to go poking his nose into everything. Now, don't you go letting him bother you if he starts making remarks about you buying a piano. You know what he's like.'

Lizzie knew her father well. His first words when he had brought the buggy to a halt were, 'Thought I'd better come and see what you're throwing good money away on now, before the bank manager takes this place over for you. Some people have got more money than sense, it seems.'

'And *some* people know how to mind their own business,' Lizzie retorted.

Frank silenced her with a hand on her arm before Arthur had time to bristle in response. He grinned good-naturedly at Arthur's attempts at cutting remarks. 'I don't know about sense, but I've got a piano,' Frank told his visitors. 'Come and take a look at it.'

Bill jumped down from his seat and lifted Lily from hers, keeping an arm around her solicitously once he had her safely on the ground. 'You right, Lily?' he asked. 'I don't want her to go tiring herself out,' he announced to his audience. 'She hasn't really got over everything yet, you know.'

'I'm quite all right, Bill, you mustn't fuss over me,' Lily assured him. She smiled, but Frank thought she looked more drawn than even the sleepless nights the three-week-old baby in her arms was giving her could explain. He gave silent thanks for the robust good health that made Lizzie thrive on childbearing. But Lily's cheeks were pink with excitement, and she looked toward the house with obvious eagerness.

Bill showed signs of weariness himself, though he gazed at his new son and long-awaited namesake with unmixed pride.

'Little beggar doesn't want to sleep at night,' he told Frank as they walked towards the house. 'He's going to be a handful, this fellow.'

'We got spoiled with Arfie and Emma,' Lily added. 'They were such good sleepers almost from the beginning. Especially Emma, weren't you, darling?' she said to the three-year-old who was skipping along at Edie's side.

'I don't remember young Arthur being any trouble,' Arthur put in, ready as ever to rise to his grandson's defence. 'He's always been forward for his age, that boy.'

Bill rolled his eyes at Frank behind Arthur's back. They dropped behind Arthur and the women, so that they could talk without being overheard. 'You know, I sometimes wonder if Pa remembers whose son Arfie is,' Bill said in a voice too low for his father to catch. 'You'd just about think he was Arfie's Pa himself, the way he goes on about him.'

'Don't let Lizzie hear you say that,' Frank replied equally quietly. 'She gets a bit funny sometimes about your pa making such a fuss over your kids.'

Bill grunted. 'It's nothing to be jealous about. Pa can be a real pest over it—I can't even give Arfie a bit of a hiding if Pa's around. "Leave the boy alone, he didn't do any harm." When I think of the things I used to get hidings for!'

'That's what Lizzie says when Arthur sticks up for Maudie,' Frank said, grinning at Bill's affronted expression. 'You and her are a bit alike, you know.'

'Don't know about that,' Bill said. 'Lizzie was always better at keeping out of trouble than I was—she was pretty good at not getting caught, anyway.'

He stared at Lily, who was leaning on Lizzie's arm with Edie hovering close at hand. 'I wish Lily was more like Lizzie, though—not in her nature, that'd be like sleeping with Pa as well as working with him all day. I just wish she was a bit stronger. She doesn't take this childbearing business too well. Sometimes I wonder why she lets me touch her, with all that to put up with.'

'They're tougher than us. Even the frail ones like Lily—she doesn't look strong, but she must be, just to get through it. I know what you mean, though—I still worry about Lizzie every time, even after six of the little beggars.'

'Well, Lily's not going to have six,' Bill said. 'I want her around to rear the ones she's got.' He pulled a face. 'Leaving them alone's easier said than done, though, eh?'

'I'll say,' Frank agreed.

'Whatever are you two gossiping about? Hurry up, you can have a chat later,' Lizzie called from the doorway, for once forgetting to show wifely meekness in front of her father. Frank exchanged a rather shamefaced grin with Bill, and did not enlighten Lizzie on the subject of their conversation.

As soon as baby William had been settled down on Frank and Lizzie's bed, Lizzie ushered the family into the parlour.

'Here it is,' she announced, indicating the piano with a flourish.

'Oh, it's beautiful,' Lily exclaimed. She rushed forward and stroked the smooth wood of the piano with a touch that was almost reverent. 'A

Broadwood,' she murmured. 'I didn't think I'd ever see one again.'

'It's the sort you said to get, isn't it, Lily?' Frank asked.

Lily dragged her attention from the piano. 'It's exactly right, Frank. I must confess one reason I suggested a Broadwood was that it's the sort I used to have—though it's one of the best makes, too. But this is even lovelier than our old one.'

'Did you have a piano, dear?' Edie asked. 'Whatever became of it?'

'I sold it when Mother died,' Lily said. 'Mother couldn't bear to part with it, because it had been Father's. But there was no point in my having a piano, not when it didn't seem likely I'd ever have a settled home.' She cast a smile towards Bill that was full of gratitude. 'I've a home now, of course. And I think I've almost forgotten how to play, anyway.'

'You'd better not have,' Lizzie put in. 'You've got to teach Maudie.'

'I'll do my best,' Lily said. 'I should be able to start her off, at least.'

'Can we have a tune, then?' Frank asked. 'I'd like to hear what it sounds like.'

'I haven't let any of the children touch it,' said Lizzie. 'No grubby fingers on the piano. Frank had a go last night, though.'

'I did not,' Frank protested. 'Heck, I wouldn't have a clue where to start. I just pressed a couple of those key things. It sounded pretty awful.'

'I'll say,' Lizzie agreed, with more enthusiasm than Frank thought was strictly necessary. 'Play us something, Lily.'

'Oh, I don't know if I can,' Lily said, suddenly shy. 'It's been so long.'

'Go on,' Lizzie pressed. 'Play the sort of thing people dance to.'

'Something lively,' Frank suggested.

'A nice, romantic song, that's the sort I like,' Edie put in.

'Something from Scotland,' Arthur said. 'A good jig, that's what people like to hear.'

Lily's eyes swivelled between the speakers, and as the requests became more insistent she began to look alarmed. 'I'm not sure if I can...'

'Hey, leave her alone,' Bill said, glaring around the room. 'Lily, you don't have to play anything if you don't feel like it. Do you want to sit on the sofa for a bit?'

'No, I'm all right. I'd like to try playing something, though it probably won't sound very nice. I'm afraid I don't know any jigs, Father,' she said to Arthur.

'That's all right, my dear,' Arthur said magnanimously. 'You play whatever you like, then.'

'That's right,' said Bill. 'Play something you like, never mind anyone

137

else. And only if you feel up to it.'

Lily perched on the high stool Frank had placed in front of the piano. 'Oh, I don't know if I can remember anything,' she murmured. 'I wonder if I could manage that Chopin sonata...' She lifted the cover and stroked the keys gently, making no sound. 'How does it start?' she said to herself. 'Let's see.'

She played a few notes hesitantly, and shook her head. 'No, that's not right. It must be...' Her fingers hovered above the keyboard for a moment, then began moving over the keys, at first slowly then with gathering assurance.

After the first few seconds her audience sat in rapt attention, even little Emma staring open-mouthed at her mother. Frank had never heard any sound like it; never imagined that human hands could produce music of such beauty. It soared with passion, then plunged into delicious melancholy, but all the while remained graceful and delicate.

When the last notes died away there was utter silence in the room. Frank had just recovered himself enough to think of thanking Lily, and asking if she could play again, when he saw how oddly her head was drooping over the piano, as if she were suddenly very weary.

'I'd forgotten,' she said in a whisper. 'I'd forgotten what it's like. It's been so long since—'

'Mama?' Emma said, her childish voice high and bewildered. 'Why you crying, Mama?'

So she was, Frank realised in alarm. Lily blinked rapidly, but several large tears had already escaped to start coursing down her cheeks. Emma twisted out of Edie's grip and rushed to her mother, burying her head in Lily's lap while Lily's arms reached out blindly to pull her close.

'Mama's being very foolish,' Lily said, forcing back a sob with an effort so fierce her voice sounded almost harsh. 'Mama's very lucky, isn't she? She's got you, and Papa, too, she's no business crying like a silly girl.' She fumbled in her sleeve till she found a handkerchief, and mopped up the tears. 'See, Mama's not crying now. Don't be upset, darling.'

Lily looked around at the sea of concerned faces and gave a watery smile. 'I'm afraid I'm making a fool of myself. I'm sorry, I didn't mean to be a bother. It's just... it's the music, you see,' she said, as if willing them to understand. 'I'd forgotten about the music.'

Her face crumpled once more with threatened tears. 'I'm sorry,' she repeated helplessly. She stood up, hoisting Emma aloft though the effort of lifting the sturdy three-year-old made her wince. 'I think Will's stirring, I'd better go and see to him.'

Lily rushed from the room with Emma in her arms to tend to the supposedly wakeful baby, though no one else had heard any sound from him. Bill stood up and made to follow her, but Lizzie put a hand on his arm.

'I'll see to her, Bill. Don't worry, she'll be all right. I might get her to lie down for a bit. Do you want to take a look at her, Ma?'

'Yes, I think I'd better. She might have hurt herself with all this rushing around, she's not really over the other business yet,' Edie said. 'Although I thought she seemed bright enough today, I don't know why she's suddenly taken strange like that.'

When the men were alone in the room, Arthur strode towards the piano. 'Women get like that when they're bearing,' he explained with the air of one claiming the wisdom of superior years. 'Though I must say Lily's usually a sensible woman, it's not like her to get weepy.'

'No, it's not,' Bill said in a low voice. 'It's not like her at all.'

'This thing must have cost you a few bob, Frank,' Arthur said.

'A bit,' Frank allowed. He had no intention of admitting to Arthur the full extent of his extravagance.

'Humph! You must have money to burn these days.'

'A piano's not burning money,' Frank said, smiling amiably. 'Anyway, it'll last for years, it's not as if we'll ever need another one.'

Arthur bent down to peer at the keys, fingering them idly. 'I suppose it's a well-made sort of thing.' He lifted the ornaments Lizzie had placed on top of the piano, and Frank realised he was about to open the lid.

'Hey, be careful,' Frank said, earning a glare in return. 'Um, I mean, I think it's a bit delicate in there.'

'There's no need to take that tone with me,' Arthur said. 'I think I know as much about machinery as you do.' He raised the lid and peered inside.

Frank cringed as he watched. 'Do you want to come and have a look at my new calves?' he asked in an attempt at distraction.

'No, thank you,' Arthur said with great dignity. 'I've seen enough of your cows to last two lifetimes. And I seem to remember being dragged around those calves the last time I was here.'

'They've grown since,' Frank tried, but without any great hope of success. Arthur had bent down to look under the keyboard now, without having bothered to replace the top cover.

'I'd like to see them, Frank,' Bill said.

'Well... all right, then.' Frank cast a last, anxious glance over his shoulder as he and Bill left the room. If Arthur put finger-marks on the piano, Frank would at least be able to pretend ignorance when Lizzie complained afterwards. As she undoubtedly would.

He was easily distracted from the fate of his new piano by the pleasure of showing off his calves. 'Maybe you can give me a hand thinking up a few pedigree names for them—Lizzie and me've run out of ideas. I've got some beauties this year,' he said as they approached the paddock. 'Plenty of heifers, too. One of them's—'

'How much does a piano cost, Frank?' Bill cut in abruptly.

Frank stopped in mid-stride. Giving evasive answers to Arthur was fair enough, but he knew it was not nosiness that had prompted Bill's blunt question.

'Forty pounds it cost,' he admitted. 'And that's without the freight.'

Bill gave a low whistle. 'As much as that?' He shook his head dejectedly. 'Pa's very fond of Lily, but he'd never run to forty pounds. I never knew the music meant that much to her,' he said quietly.

'She's more than welcome to come and use the piano any time she wants,' Frank said. 'I don't mean teaching Maudie—just any time she feels like having a play on it.'

'It won't be like having her own, though. I sort of had an idea that if it wasn't too much I might be able to put a bit aside—Pa comes to light with the odd bit of money sometimes, says "Shout yourself a drink" or something—then talk him into coughing up a few pounds to make up the money.' Bill snorted. 'I'd never save forty pounds out of it if I never bought another drink in my life. Forty pounds!' he repeated, awed by the sum. 'We've got to cart a hell of a lot of cans of milk to the factory to get forty pounds.'

Or sell two or three heifers, at the price he expected to get this season, Frank thought to himself, but he said nothing aloud. Bill was lost in his own thoughts for a while, then collected himself.

'Hey, you must think I'm an ungrateful bugger,' he said, managing to laugh. 'Thanks, Frank, that's good of you. I'd like to see her play. I'll bring her down when I can get away—she's not going to be up to riding for a long while yet.'

'She's really good, eh? I mean, I knew she could play, but not like that.'

'Yes, she is,' Bill said. 'She doesn't talk about it much, but she told me one time her piano teacher said she could have been a... what did she call it? A concert pianist. You know, going round the place playing in front of important people.'

'Really?' Frank said, greatly impressed.

'Mmm. Her ma wouldn't let her, though. Said she didn't approve of girls going on the stage. Anyway, it would've cost money to start with, and they never had any.'

He gave Frank a wry grin. 'She should've married a rich bloke like you, eh?' Seeing Frank's embarrassment, Bill clapped him on the back. 'Well, maybe Pa'll go soft in the head one day and let me get some of these fancy cows of yours up at our place instead of just borrowing your bull to get a few half-breeds. Then we could start selling calves for heaps like you do. Let's have a look at them, anyway.'

'This is the best one, right here,' Frank said. He stroked the soft muzzle that had been thrust towards his hand as soon as they climbed into the paddock. 'I'm not going to sell this one. Isn't she a beauty? See the line of her back, and the build of her. She'll be a good milker, this one—a good bearer, too. She's got such a pretty face, I wanted to put Elizabeth in her name somewhere, but Lizzie says she doesn't fancy having a cow named after her.'

'Call her after Lily, then,' Bill suggested. 'Hey, that's a good one— Jersey Lily, like that Lillie Langtry woman—you know, the actress the Prince of Wales was meant to be so keen on.'

'It's just right,' Frank said. 'It's an easy name for people to remember, too, when I start showing her. Jersey Lily—I'll write that down when we get back.'

They lingered outside for some time, with Frank enjoying the chance to show off his calves as well as discuss some of his plans for further improving the herd. He vaguely noticed the older children's arrival, and was surprised to realise that it was late enough for school to be over, but neither of them was in any great hurry.

Bill was back to his usual cheerful self by the time they returned to the house. He became even brighter when they joined the others in the parlour and found Lily there.

The family had gathered around the piano, and Lily sat playing a pretty tune to which Edie seemed to know a few of the words. Emma was perched on her mother's lap, making playing awkward, but Lily insisted that the tune was so simple the little girl was not getting in the way.

'Are you feeling a bit better now, love?' Bill asked. Lily smiled at him.

'Much better, thank you. I'm sorry I made such a show of myself before.' She ran her fingers up and down the keys and laughed aloud at the sound they made. 'It's *lovely* to play again! I've forgotten so much, but it's coming back already.'

'Aunt Lily's going to teach me, too,' Maudie said. 'Will you teach me a bit today, Aunt Lily?'

'Oh, not today, dear,' Lily said. 'I've got to go soon, Arfie'll be on his way home. Perhaps next week—'

'No, not that soon,' Bill cut in. 'I don't want you wearing yourself out. You have a few goes just playing—it's good to see you enjoying yourself. But it's going to be like work if you've got to start teaching Maudie right off.'

'I think I could manage,' Lily said. 'Though I must confess I'd like to get some more practice in first.'

'*Please*, Uncle Bill,' Maudie pleaded. She slipped a hand through Bill's and leaned her head on his arm in a manner that Frank always found utterly irresistible. He turned away to hide a smile.

But Bill extricated his hand after giving Maudie's a brief squeeze. 'It's no good trying that on me, Maudie. I've known your ma all her life, I know all those tricks.' If he noticed the indignant glare Lizzie directed at him, he gave no sign of it. 'You can wait until you finish up at school in December, that's soon enough. Aunt Lily'll be feeling stronger by then.'

'But that's *months*,' Maudie said, her eyes wide with the injustice of it. 'Aunt Lily, that's so *long*.'

'I'm sorry, dear, but we'll have to do what Uncle Bill says,' Lily said, earning an approving smile from Arthur, but Frank caught the grateful look she cast at Bill. He could see that Bill was right: Lily was not up to coping with Maudie's exuberance just yet.

Maudie's view of the world did not include the notion that women did their husbands' bidding unquestioningly. 'What's the point having a piano if I can't learn to play it?' she complained. 'And I've been walking with a book on my head for *ages*,' she added, a remark that meant nothing to most of her audience. 'I want—'

'Now, Maudie, that's enough,' Frank said mildly. 'Aunt Lily'll start teaching you as soon as she feels up to it. I hope you'll come down and play whenever you feel like it, though, Lily,' he added. 'I'd like to just listen to you.'

'But Pa,' Maudie said, trying another target. 'Why can't—'

'Maudie!' Lizzie cut in sharply. 'Don't you go contradicting your father. I'll have a word with you about that later. I think it's time you started peeling a few potatoes—go on, you get out to the kitchen.'

Maudie gave her mother an aggrieved look, and made her way slowly out of the room, scuffing her feet against the carpet as she went.

She had recovered her usual composure by that evening, when Lizzie let the three oldest children sit in the parlour with her and Frank. In between prattling away about her day at school, Maudie sat and admired 'her' piano, gloating at the sight.

'We can start having people out as soon as I've learned to play it, can't we, Ma? *Interesting* people,' she said archly.

'We'll see,' Lizzie said. 'There'll be time enough for that once you've left school. There's no need to go breaking your neck over it, Maudie. I don't think anyone's going to find a girl of twelve *interesting*. Even if she can play the piano.'

Frank thought he saw the tip of Maudie's tongue briefly poked in her mother's direction, but she was not so foolish as to let Lizzie see it.

Beth went off to the girls' bedroom and returned with the two large porcelain dolls Frank had bought in Auckland the previous year. Maudie picked hers up and began dressing it in another set of clothes, forgetting about the piano for the moment.

Lizzie took the children off to bed a little later. 'They still like those dolls, eh?' Frank said when she returned from tucking them in.

'I should hope so, the money you must have paid for fancy things like that. They're lovely dolls, though.'

Frank smiled fondly at the memory of the two girls playing. 'They're still little girls, you know, Lizzie. Fancy you thinking Maudie's got ideas about a husband at her age! She's keener on dolls than anything.'

'That's just practice,' Lizzie said, full of assurance.

'Practice? What for?'

'Having babies, of course.'

Frank was rather shaken by this. 'But...' He trailed off, unable to think of an argument to refute it.

He gave a thoughtful look in the direction of the girls' room. 'How old were you when you started thinking about that sort of thing, then?'

'Oh, older than her,' Lizzie said. She gave Frank a quick glance, her lips curved into a smug smile. 'A little bit older,' she amended.

10

September 1899

Charlie screwed up his newspaper and pushed it away, at the same time reaching out to cut himself another slice of bread from the loaf.

'Bloody Government,' he grumbled. 'You know those mad buggers are getting into a war now?'

Amy pushed the butter closer to his hand. 'In South Africa? So they really think it's going to come to war?'

In the urge to air his disapproval, Charlie had forgotten his usual disregard of anything Amy had to say on subjects of consequence. 'If Seddon has his way. He's offered to send soldiers over there, so it says in the paper. To fight the bloody Queen of England's war! What business has that German woman got poking her nose around in Africa, anyway?'

Amy had long since given up cringing over Charlie's disrespectful remarks about the Queen. She sometimes worried that her boys might repeat one of them in front of a more loyal audience, but she knew better than to try rebuking Charlie. 'It's to do with land, isn't it? I read something about it a little while ago. They've got diamond mines there, and—'

'That's enough of your prattle,' Charlie cut in. 'What would you know about it? You keep to your pots and pans, woman, that's the place for you. That's the stupidest thing Seddon ever did, giving women the vote,' he said sententiously. 'Makes them think they're as good as men. Seddon's a bloody fool, and I've always said it. Still, what can you expect? He's an Englishman.' He spat out the word as if it was a term of abuse, which in Charlie's mouth it usually was.

'They haven't given women the vote in England yet,' Amy pointed out, indulging in a rare jibe.

'It's a bloody wonder,' was the best response Charlie could manage. 'You remember that, boy,' he said, turning his attention to Malcolm. 'Watch out for Englishmen. They're land grabbers and thieves, the lot of them.'

Malcolm grunted in response, toying idly with his fork and keeping his eyes fixed on his plate. He did not often speak at the table, even now that he had permission to.

Both boys avoided speaking to their father; the difference was that Malcolm occasionally found himself unable to resist uttering some complaint or argument. David had the advantage of being away at school much of the day; now that Malcolm had left school, he and his father were thrust into one another's company through most of the long hours of daylight.

'They took the land and murdered good Scots, and now they want to send good colonial boys off to fight their war in Africa,' Charlie said. 'Send New Zealand boys to get slaughtered instead of their own.'

Malcolm interrupted his father's pontification. 'Can I go in to town this afternoon?'

'No, you can't,' Charlie said, stabbing at the pat of butter and smearing a lump on his bread.

'Why not?'

'Because I bloody say so!'

Their eyes met across the table. Amy gave a shudder at the animosity in their mutual glare. So alike, her husband and her son, and so capable of arousing one another's fury. If she did not know them both so painfully well she would think they hated each other; Malcolm believed it, she knew. There were still sparks, rarer all the time and invisible to anyone but Amy; still tiny signs that Malcolm craved his father's approval. Another year or two and even those would be gone.

'Would you like some jam, Charlie?' Amy asked, anxious to break that hostile locking of eyes. She pushed the open jar until it nudged against his hand.

'No need to shove it at me like that,' Charlie grumbled, but it had the desired effect. He grabbed at the jar and spread a thick layer of jam on his bread, and by the time he turned his attention back to Malcolm his glare had lost much of its ferocity.

'You needn't think I'm letting you go out when you haven't done your work properly,' Charlie said.

'What'd I do wrong now?' Malcolm asked.

'That bottom paddock you were working in this morning. You did a shoddy job planting those potatoes—I'll be lucky if half of them sprout, chucked in the furrows any old way like that.'

'Did my best,' Malcolm muttered. He shot a resentful glance at Charlie, then dropped his gaze to the table.

'Your best,' Charlie scoffed. 'If that's your best you'll have to wake your ideas up, boy. You can do the rest this afternoon—and if you don't do it right you'll be taking them out tomorrow and putting them in properly. You hear me?' Malcolm muttered something unintelligible. 'What'd you say, boy?' Charlie demanded.

Malcolm raised his eyes to glare at his father again. 'You never let me go out. I never get any fun.'

'You've got to earn it first. You'll stop home till you do your work right.' He stared grimly at Malcolm, as if waiting for the boy to argue, but Malcolm had lapsed into sullen silence.

'If you start doing your jobs properly I'll take you out myself.' Charlie seemed to be waiting for Malcolm's response with more interest than his offhand manner suggested. 'You hear me, boy?' he said when there was no reply. 'I'll take you to the hotel sometime. Buy you a drink. Maybe shout you something else,' he added, glancing at Amy with a look that dared her to argue the point.

Don't you take my son whoring, Amy wanted to protest, but there was no need.

'No thanks,' Malcolm muttered.

'What the hell's wrong with you?' Charlie said. 'I offer to take you out and you don't want to go? You were grizzling about it five minutes ago. What do you bloody well want, then?'

'I want to go out with my mates. Not with you.'

Charlie narrowed his eyes to scowl at Malcolm, but Amy sensed the hurt underlying his anger. 'You're an ungrateful little bugger, aren't you? You watch your step, boy, or I'll teach you to—'

Just as Amy's mind raced in search of some way to distract Charlie again, she heard the sound of running steps approaching the house. She rose to see who was coming in such a hurry, but the door was flung open before she had the chance to touch the handle.

Thomas stood in the doorway, his eyes wide and staring. One leg of his trousers had a long rent over the knee, as if he had fallen heavily on that side. Amy saw a patch of blood seeping through the torn fabric.

Awareness jolted through her like a stab of pain at the sight of Thomas's face, twisted as it was with fear and grief. She did not need his words to tell her what had happened.

'Amy, you've got to come home right now,' he choked out through a threatened sob. 'John said for you to come. It's Pa. I think he's...' His face crumpled. He slumped forward into Amy's outstretched arms, his words muffled against her body.

Jack had risen early that morning, as he did every day outside the brief luxury of the winter months when only the house cows were milked. John and Harry had taken to suggesting that he have a lie in of a morning, that there was no need for him to come milking with them every time, but Jack was having none of it.

'I've got to keep an eye on you boys, see that you make a decent job of things,' he always told them, and his older two 'boys', who were nearer forty than thirty, usually shared a grin and said no more on the subject for a day or two.

Sometimes when the mornings were particularly chilly he would regret what he thought of as his determination and his sons privately called pig-headedness. But it was not that easy, Jack had found, to give up the management of the farm he had broken in largely with his own hands and where he had spent most of his adult life. To let John and Harry take over would be to concede defeat at the hands of old age; though in his more candid moments he admitted to himself that he was contributing little more than his presence when there was any heavy physical work to be done.

Susannah was still sleeping soundly. He studied her for a moment when he had finished dressing. She retained a surprising measure of rigidity even in sleep, her body perched as close to the edge of the bed as she could lie without falling out.

Even in sleep she managed to reject him; her stiffness and her awkward position showing with what reluctance she shared his bed at all. His own body had left a hollow close to the opposite edge, and he remembered with painful clarity the way that bed had looked in the old days. The days when he had had Annie. No separate hollows then; the bed had slumped in the middle so markedly they had often joked that one day it would collapse altogether. The nights had never been too cold in those years; not with Annie's warm body pressed close to his.

Susannah stirred in her sleep, relaxing a little as if she sensed he was no longer in the bed. Jack left the room quickly to avoid waking her. On the rare mornings he was careless enough to be still in the bedroom when she woke, he was always punished with a chilly glare, as Susannah showed him all over again how much she resented his temerity for having slept with her. It was not a pleasant way to start the day.

He was irritated with himself when he found that the boys were all down at the cow shed ahead of him; it had been a matter of pride with him for many years that he was always the first person in the house to wake. By the time he had hurried down from the house he was short of breath, and the tightness in his chest that seemed to follow any exertion lately was so painful that it took an effort of will to hide it.

'Must have slept in a bit,' he said gruffly as he took his seat on the milking stool vacated for him by George. 'Don't know why I did that.'

'No, I think the rest of us were a bit early this morning,' John said, brushing aside his father's discomfiture. 'I know I was, anyway.' He gave an exaggerated yawn. 'Can't seem to sleep properly just lately, Sophie's so restless at night. She says the baby's keeping her awake.' He snorted in amusement. 'The little beggar gave me a heck of a kick last night when

I was trying to give Soph a cuddle. He must be jealous of his old man.'

'Might be a girl this time,' Harry pointed out.

John shrugged. 'Suppose so. We've sort of got used to boys, after three of them in a row. Sophie'd probably like a girl, someone to give her a hand around the place.'

'Sophie's a good girl,' Jack said, only too aware of how much more uncomfortable his home would be if it were not for Sophie's patient acceptance of the lion's share of the work. A few more weeks and she would be too large and cumbersome to do the heavier work, forcing Susannah to do whatever could not be avoided altogether. Jack dreaded the thought of the sour moods he was going to have to put up with when that happened.

'Mmm, Sophie's pretty good,' John said. 'I just wish she'd start sleeping properly again.'

'Jane was moaning I've been keeping her awake lately,' Harry put in, looking so pleased with himself that if they had both been just a little younger Jack would have been strongly tempted to give him a kick.

'Yes, we all know about you and Jane,' John said in a long-suffering tone. 'She hasn't locked you outside for a while, eh?'

Harry glared at his brother, then turned his scowl on the others when the younger boys burst out laughing and Jack indulged in a grin. 'She hasn't done that for years,' he said huffily, then gave up his attempt at dignity and joined in the laughter, even though it was at his own expense. 'Boy, that was a good row,' he said with deep satisfaction.

'Why do you and Jane fight all the time?' George asked.

'We don't,' Harry said. 'Jane just gets worked up about things sometimes.'

'You think they're bad now?' John said. 'You fellows are too young to remember what they used to be like. Harry used to have to buy another load of plates and things just about every week, Jane was that keen on throwing them at him. And she used to black both his eyes, and—'

'Hey, hey, don't get too carried away,' Harry protested. 'She never did that! She wasn't much good at throwing things, either—she always used to miss me.'

'Did she really give him a black eye, John?' George asked, not quite willing to accept Harry's word on the subject.

'No,' John admitted. 'Makes a good story, though.'

'Bloody cheek,' Harry grumbled, but he grinned as he said it.

Jack enjoyed their banter, though he could not find the energy to take part in it. It was as much as he could do to sit quietly and milk, and he was aware that he was getting through fewer cows than the others. The boys were making it easy for him. There was no need to get up from his stool when he had finished with each cow; instead Thomas or George would let the cow out of its bail and lead the next one in, tie it securely, then dart on to the next bail.

He got up stiffly when the milking was finished, for a moment regretting the pride that had made him leave his walking stick in the porch. But Thomas was at his elbow before he had taken half a dozen steps, the boy's shoulders ready for his father's arm.

'That's my right-hand man,' Jack told him, gripping Thomas's shoulder.

Breakfast was a noisy affair. John's sons were lively children, and they greeted their father boisterously, while Sophie looked on placidly. The youngest, four-year-old Colin, demanded to be tossed on his father's knee and squealed in raucous delight when John obliged. It was good to see them all happy and healthy, but Jack found himself wishing for a little peace and quiet. He almost sympathised with Susannah when he saw her pained expression as she rubbed her temples.

'Oh, do be quiet, George,' she said when George began explaining to Jack in great detail what sort of engines the newest boat in the Northern Steamship Company's fleet had. 'I can hardly hear myself think as it is, without you prattling on with such nonsense.'

George pulled a face at her, but turned away before Susannah had the chance to see his scowl. He went on talking, his only concession to his mother's complaint being a slight lowering of his voice.

'And there's the *Terra Nova* too, that's the paddle steamer. Did you know it—'

'George!' Susannah snapped. 'I told you to be quiet. Really, I've no idea why you want to talk about that sort of thing. Boats, indeed! Anyone would think you were a common tradesman.'

'I was just talking, that's all,' George said. 'Dunno what's wrong with talking.'

Nothing fazed that boy, least of all criticism from his mother, Jack thought in quiet admiration mixed with a tinge of envy. George had the happy knack of ignoring Susannah altogether when she did not force herself into his awareness. Not like Thomas, who in his mother's presence tended to lapse into such utter silence that anyone who did not know him well might have thought him stupid.

'Mama, Mama, I want some milk,' Colin clamoured. He slid from John's knee and ran across the kitchen to Sophie, who was standing by the bench pouring milk into a jug. He almost tripped in his haste, and steadied himself against Susannah's knee as he rushed past, oblivious to the disapproving glare he earned.

Susannah placed her hands to her head again. 'That child has the most penetrating voice,' she said tightly. She reached out a hand to smooth her skirts where Colin's chubby fists had grabbed at them, and gave a small scream when she saw the sticky blotches on the fabric. 'Look at my dress! Just look at it!'

'You've got a bit of jam on it,' Jack said.

'I didn't put jam on it. Sophie, that child of yours has been putting his fingers in the jam jar again. He's smeared it all over my dress.'

'You shouldn't stick your hand in the jam, love,' Sophie said mildly. 'You get all mucky.' She wiped Colin's hands and face with her apron, removing a small portion of the jam that had adhered to the child.

'Goodness knows how I'm going to get this clean,' Susannah complained. 'He's rubbed it right in! I do wish you'd watch him, Sophie.'

'It's just a bit of jam, Susannah,' John said, fixing her with a hard stare. 'There's no need to go on about it.'

'I'll have to soak it, I think. This dress is years old, but I've so few nice ones. Really, I've never known such a grubby child.'

John's eyes narrowed at the slur. 'He's no different from any other kid. It's no good wearing fancy clothes with little ones around. You're just asking to get them dirty, dressing up like that. You should know that yourself.'

'I always went to the trouble of keeping my sons clean when they were small,' Susannah said.

'Yes, well, you had precious little else to do with yourself,' John shot back, and Susannah had the sense to subside into dignified silence.

But the wounded look she directed at Jack spoke volumes. He rehearsed silently the complaints he would hear when they were alone in the bedroom that evening. 'Of course you wouldn't trouble yourself to defend me when your son abuses me.' 'No one cares what I have to put up with.' 'You begrudge me any decent clothes, even when your grandchild ruins the few I've got.'

The thought of it wearied him. There was no way of avoiding those complaints, but at least he could escape from Susannah's accusing face for the moment. He rose from his chair, wishing he did not have to lean quite so heavily on the table to do so.

'I'm going out for a bit,' he announced.

He noticed Thomas catch John's eye, and saw the glance that passed between them. Thomas sent a questioning look at his older brother, and John gave a barely perceptible nod.

'Where are you going, Pa?' John asked.

'Just for a bit of a walk. Any objection?'

Thomas stood up. 'I'll come with you.'

'No, you won't,' Jack said, more sharply than he had intended. 'I just want a spot of fresh air. And some peace and quiet,' he added, with the briefest of glances in Susannah's direction.

'That's a good idea,' said John. 'Tom could probably do with an airing, too. Take him along.'

Jack glared at his eldest son. 'I'm going outside for a pee,' he said in a dignified tone, earning a tight-lipped look of disgust from Susannah. 'I don't need anyone's help for that, thank you. And when I've finished passing water I'm going for a walk *by myself*.'

He relented a little at the sight of Thomas's hurt expression. 'Maybe you and I'll go over and see Amy later, Tom. You can give me a hand over the fences. All right?'

'Don't forget to put your coat on, Jack,' Susannah called as he opened the back door, startling Jack with her show of concern. 'I don't want you keeping me awake at night coughing,' she added, spoiling the gesture.

Jack did put a coat on against the morning's chill, and after a brief hesitation he took up the walking stick that leant against the porch wall. There was no use denying it: making his way over the rough ground without the aid of a stick was just too difficult, whatever the urgings of pride told him.

After relieving himself behind the nearest tree, he looked about him to decide where to walk next. He considered the steep hill that rose near the house, then rejected the idea, knowing he would soon be painfully short of breath if he attempted the climb.

Besides, a large part of that walk was clearly visible from the house. One of the boys would be sure to stumble 'accidentally' across his path before he had gone far.

Instead he went as briskly as he could towards a patch of bush a few minutes' walk away. He glanced over his shoulder just before he reached the trees and was pleased to see that no one seemed to be watching him, then plunged into the shadows.

Many tracks had been worn through the bush over the thirty-odd years that Jack had had the farm. He wandered idly, letting his feet take him where they wished. It left his mind free to wander down its own paths, calling up old memories as well as mulling over the present.

'That son of yours has turned into a real old woman, Annie,' he grumbled, and was mildly startled to realise he had spoken aloud. He looked around, assuring himself that he was not being observed.

'That'd really get John thinking my mind's gone, eh? If he heard me talking to you like you were right here? Course I know you're not. Still, you're good company.'

He walked on. As he started more carefully observing the path his feet had chosen, details of his surroundings began to seem familiar.

'This was one of your favourite walks, wasn't it? You and I used to come along here a lot. Haven't been here for years. Now, let's see if I can find that spring you always thought was so pretty.'

Only a few large trees remained here, in a spot so easily reached from the house, but the ferns were thick and the undergrowth lush. There were many young saplings, too, as the bush recovered from the heavy felling of earlier years. Jack had to watch his step in the places where the track had become overgrown, but it was no hardship to go slowly. He was in no hurry.

'John'll send Tom out looking for me if I'm away long, you mark my words,' he said to the empty air. 'Amy says it's because they're fond of me. I suppose she's right. Suppose I should be grateful they bother about me at all.

'They're good little fellows, Tom and George. You'd have liked them, Annie. Funny, I have trouble remembering they're not yours sometimes. Wish they were.' He frowned as he tried to do a mental calculation. 'I don't know, maybe you would've been too old for bearing by the time they came along.'

He shook his head at his own words. 'No, I can't imagine you as an old woman. Not you. How old were you when I lost you? Twenty-seven, was it? Do you know, Amy tells me she's thirty now? Thirty-one this year, she says. I can't credit it, her being that age. She's that much like you, I just about call her Annie sometimes. She's a good girl, she's always got time for her old pa.'

He closed his eyes briefly as a wave of pain passed over him. 'I didn't make a very good job of looking after our girl. Giving her to Charlie like that! I must have been half stupid. I shouldn't have let that *Jimmy*,' he spat out the name, 'near her in the first place. Old fool! Couldn't see what was going on under my own nose. It wouldn't have happened if you'd been spared.

'Of course, Jimmy wouldn't have been anywhere near the place if you'd still been here, Annie. Neither would Susannah.' He recalled one of the last things Annie had said to him, while she had still had the energy to do more than gasp agonisingly for each breath.

I hope you find someone else, Jack, she had whispered faintly. *I won't mind. I don't want you to be lonely when I'm gone.*

'You shouldn't have said it, Annie. You should've told me not to be

152

such a fool. As if any woman could take your place!' His eyes grew too blurred to see, and he slumped against a tree trunk for support. 'You shouldn't have died, Annie!'

The sense of loss was so bitter he could taste it. He tried to swallow it down past the lump that had suddenly formed in his throat. 'I should have looked after you better, Annie,' he said, his voice hoarse with pain. 'I wouldn't have lost you if I'd taken better care of you.'

He stood caught up in his thoughts until the peace of his surroundings slowly penetrated. 'Telling me off for being an old misery, are you?' he said, feeling the weight of grief lift a little. 'You always were a great one for making the best of things. Our girl's like you in that, too. She says she's happy enough. And she's got the little boys, that keeps her cheerful.'

Clear in his mind was the picture of Annie holding Amy in her arms, her face alight with joy at having a healthy daughter at last. 'Pity she didn't have a girl, though. A woman likes to have a daughter, eh? Still, I'm glad he hasn't kept her bearing. Never did like the idea of him having her like that.'

He roused himself and walked on a short way, until the trees gave way to a small clearing. A trickle of clear water bubbled out of the ground and seeped into a moss-edged pool, which in turn fed a tiny streamlet. 'This is the place,' he said, pleased with himself at having discovered it. 'Here's your spring, Annie!'

He found a dry spot and eased himself to the ground, leaning heavily on his stick for balance. His heart was beating uncomfortably fast from the exertion; only after a few good, deep breaths did it begin to slow.

'It's taken it out of me, this walk. I'm not going to feel up to going back for a while. Never mind, they can do without me for a bit. Maybe Tom'll track me down, anyway. I wouldn't mind a hand getting back.'

He scooped up a mouthful of water from the pool, gasping at its coldness. 'Still tastes good, eh? Nicer than the stuff out of the barrel. We used to have picnics here sometimes, remember? Never needed to bring anything to drink, just had this good water. Used to bring the little ones along. Not every time, though.' He smiled at a sudden memory. 'Seem to remember getting up to a bit of mischief here once or twice. Must have left the boys with your ma.'

He gave a deep sigh. 'Shouldn't be this tired after a bit of a walk. I'm getting old, Annie. Old and worn out. Still, it's no good moaning about that, eh?' He looked around at the trees ringing the clearing, soft greens soothing his eyes as the silence eased his mind. A bellbird burst into a sudden outpouring of joy, and it could have been the same bird he and

Annie had listened to all those years before.

'There's no rush to get back. Nothing the boys can't do by themselves. I might stay here till lunch-time. What do you think, Annie?'

A deeper sense of peace hovered over him. Jack lay back against the grass and closed his eyes. 'You're still there? Come on, then. Keep me company a bit longer.' He patted the ground at his side, and without thinking why he did so he curled his arm slightly, as if to make room for someone.

A feeling of warmth gradually spread through him as he lay there. It might have been merely from the spring sunlight that poured into the clearing, though it was strange that he was so much warmer on one side than the other. The side where he had curled his arm. He sighed comfortably, and his mouth curved into a contented smile.

He was still smiling when Thomas found him, hours later. He looked so at ease that Thomas hesitated, unwilling to wake his father. It was only when he brushed Jack's arm and saw how limply it rolled away from his touch that he realised just how deep this sleep was. And how final.

11

September – October 1899

The days that followed her father's death passed in a blur of misery for Amy. She wept till her eyes were red and swollen, crying herself to sleep at night then waking to renewed awareness and fresh tears.

Somehow she stumbled through her regular tasks, the habits of years guiding her hands while her heart and mind were elsewhere. Meals were cooked and served, clothes washed, and the house kept clean and neat, but at the end of each day she had only the vaguest memories of having done any of those things.

From time to time one of Jane's daughters would appear in the doorway bearing a cake or pie, or a plateful of biscuits. The girl would dart into the kitchen and put her plate on the table, then slip out again as silently as she had come, shy in the face of Amy's grief.

And when she could spare time from her own tasks Lizzie would arrive for brief visits, giving Amy her only source of comfort in those dark days. Lizzie seemed to sense how to help without the need of many words. If Amy was working when she arrived, Lizzie would don a spare apron and work at her side. If she came into the kitchen to find Amy briefly abandoning herself to grief, head on her arms while she sat at the table and sobbed, Lizzie would push a chair close to hers and sit quietly with an arm around her while Amy nestled against her cousin's soft body and wept.

The only thing that saved Amy from breaking down during the funeral service was her anxious concern for Thomas, white-faced and with blood on his lip where he had gnawed through the skin in his desperate striving for self-control. His mouth trembled, and his knuckles were white where he gripped the handle of the casket as he bore his father's weight for the last time.

But he held back the tears as he walked slowly behind John and Harry, with George opposite him looking bewildered, as if he had yet to take in the fact that their father had gone. Behind Jack's four sons, grasping the last two handles of the casket, came Arthur, bowed slightly under the weight; and opposite him Malcolm, made solemn by his first close meeting with death and by the responsibility of helping carry his grandfather's body. For one of the very few times in his life, Amy was proud of her son.

When the funeral was over and Jack had been laid to rest beside his Annie, it seemed the depths of Amy's grief had been plumbed and she could start the slow climb back from the darkness. The weariness of misery began to slip away, and she became more conscious of those around her.

Charlie had barely spoken to her since Jack's death, confining himself to occasional muttered comments about 'bawling women'. Once she had recovered sufficiently to take any notice of him, Amy was grateful for his silence. Forbearing to berate her was the closest thing to kindness she was likely to see from Charlie. Malcolm, she knew, would be missing his grandfather, but she gave up after a few hesitant attempts to talk to the boy. Contempt for his mother had been too firmly fixed in his mind after years of hearing her reviled by Charlie for him to be willing to share his feelings with her.

David was silent, too, and this puzzled Amy. She slowly grasped that he had become shy of her; afraid of making her more unhappy by anything he might say. She had not realised just how much she had missed him until David, seeing that she was no longer likely to burst into tears without warning, began once again to share with her the small details of his day.

'You've got home quickly, Dave, you must have ridden really fast,' Amy said one afternoon two weeks after the funeral when David came into the kitchen out of breath.

'I did. I… I wanted to see you for a bit, Ma,' he said, looking down at his feet.

'I'll get you some milk and cakes while you put your working clothes on, then we can have a little afternoon tea, just you and me. Hurry up, though, Mal's already gone down to fetch the cows in, so we haven't got all that long.'

David was soon back, his shirt untucked and several buttons left undone in his haste.

'Look at you, Dave!' Amy said, smiling at the state he was in. 'There's not that much of a rush. Here, I'll sort you out.' She tidied his clothes, and finished by running a smoothing hand over his hair, which had gone awry during the process of getting changed. 'There, you look nice now.' She took the opportunity to plant a swift kiss on his cheek.

David sat down at the table and took a gulp of milk. 'You look sort of… happier today, Ma.'

'Well, I couldn't stay that miserable for ever, could I?' Amy tried to sound light, but her voice betrayed her with a slight catch.

'I don't like it when you're sad,' David said.

'I know, darling. I'm sorry if I've upset you. But I loved Grandpa a lot, you see, and I miss him. I can't help being sad when I think about him.'

'Grandpa was nice,' David said. 'He never used to get wild.'

'Well, I suppose he must have sometimes. I only remember nice things about him, though. It's like there aren't any bad things to remember.' Amy slipped an arm around David and pulled him close to lean on her shoulder. 'When I think about when I was a little girl,' she said, as much to herself as to him, 'it seems like no one was ever horrible to me, or frightened me. I had Mama and Granny—I only remember Mama a tiny bit, but I know she was nice. Mama and Granny died, but Pa was still there. He was always there to look after me, you see. And now he's not there any more, it's like… well, it's like I can't ever be a little girl any more. It's all gone away.'

'But you're grown up, Ma,' David said, sounding confused.

'I know, Davie.' She gave him a squeeze, and released him. 'That doesn't stop me being silly, does it? I wouldn't have you if I was still a little girl. Now, tell me why you were in such a hurry to get home today.'

David toyed with a biscuit. 'It's 'cause of tomorrow. I didn't want to leave it till then, though, because you said you had to go over to Grandpa's place.'

'That's right, I do. The lawyer's coming out from town to explain about Grandpa's will, and Uncle John said he wanted me to come over for it.'

'So by the time you get back Pa and Mal might be here, too. I thought if I got home early today, I might see you before Mal comes up… or Pa. Mal might throw off at me if he finds out.'

'What about, Dave? And what's so particular about tomorrow, that you specially wanted to see me then?'

David looked stricken. 'It's your birthday, isn't it? I thought it was tomorrow.'

'Is it? I suppose it is,' Amy said in mild surprise. 'I haven't been thinking about the date just lately. Anyway, I'm too old to worry about birthdays any more.'

'I wanted to buy you something, but I haven't got any money.'

'Oh, Dave, you don't have to buy me anything! You remembering's enough of a present.'

'But I did want to, Ma. Something nice, so you wouldn't be so sad any more.' He looked down at the floor for a moment before meeting her eyes again. 'You know how the girls have to do sewing at school?'

'Yes, I remember that. I used to get annoyed, the way we only had half as much time on arithmetic as the boys because of doing needlework. I was always trying to get through my sewing really fast so I wouldn't miss out on the work.'

'Beth does hers quite fast. She finished the last thing early, and Miss Metcalf said she had to make another one the same.'

'Poor Beth! It's boring sewing the same thing over and over.'

'She said she didn't mind. She said I could have it, so I'd have something to give you. But Beth said could it be from her as well, because she made it,' David added conscientiously. 'I've been catching her horse after school every day to pay her back, but it's an easy horse to catch.'

He reached into his pocket and pulled out a small package, painstakingly wrapped in a square of gingham fabric and tied with leftover lengths of ribbon. 'Beth wrapped it up, too. Happy birthday, Ma.' He held his package out shyly.

'Oh, Davie! I don't expect presents! Thank you, darling—and you must thank Beth for me, too.' She began carefully unwrapping the little package.

'I hope you'll like it, Ma.'

'I'm sure I will.' Amy untied the last knot and folded back the cloth to reveal a square of embroidered canvas, daintily stitched with a pattern of flowers, and with a few words cross-stitched in the centre.

' "Mother is the Heart of our Home," ' Amy read aloud. She swallowed hard against the lump that had formed in her throat.

'Do you like it?' David asked anxiously.

Amy reached out and drew him close again. 'Davie, I think it's the nicest present anyone's ever given me. Thank you, darling.' She kissed him on the mouth, and felt his lips pressed soft and warm against hers.

'Don't tell Mal,' David said when she released his mouth. 'He'll think it's soft. And Pa might go crook, too.'

'I won't tell anyone. It'll be our secret. I'll keep it in my bedroom— I'm going to put it on my chest of drawers, so I'll see it as soon as I wake up. I wish I could get a frame for it.'

'Uncle Frank put the other one Beth made in a frame for Aunt Lizzie,' David said. 'She's put that one in the bedroom, Beth said. She's got one just the same that Maudie made, that one's in the parlour.'

'And I suppose in a few years she'll have another one, when Rosie's old enough for sewing,' Amy said, smiling. 'All those daughters of hers! I've just got you, Davie. And Mal, of course.' *But Mal doesn't love me like Davie does. He doesn't even like me very much.*

David turned away to take another biscuit. Amy studied the smooth curve of his cheek. With his long, dark lashes and full lips, he could almost have been a girl if it were not for the hair cropped too short for his curls to show. *Such a pretty baby Davie was.* But was it David she was remembering? Or the little one she had had for those few weeks? *Ann. Do you give presents to your new mother to show her how you love her? Does she tell you how clever you are? Does she love you?*

A noise close to the back door made them both jump. Amy hastily thrust her present and its wrappings into her apron pocket. 'That'll be your pa—you'd better go out before he comes looking for you.' David stood up to leave, and Amy went into her bedroom to install the embroidered square in pride of place on her chest of drawers.

'Is it all right if I go next door now?' Amy asked Charlie the following afternoon. 'Mr Jamieson's coming out, remember? You said I could go.'

'That's right, the lawyer fellow. I suppose so. Don't know what they want you for.'

Amy shrugged. 'John said he wanted the whole family together for it. I don't suppose it'll take long.'

'There's maybe some trinkets of your ma's the old fellow's left you. Aye, that's probably it.'

'I don't think so. There was Granny's brooch, but I've already got that. Mama didn't have any jewellery of her own, except her wedding ring. I remember Pa saying that was the only jewellery he could ever buy her.' She twisted the ring that had formed a groove in her finger over the years she had worn it. 'I've got her wedding ring, too.'

'Aye, your pa wanted you to have that. Saved me wasting good money on a ring for you, anyway. Well, Lord knows why they want you there, but you'd better go or one of those brothers of yours will turn up looking for you. See you're back in time to get dinner on, mind.'

'I will.'

'It'll be interesting to see how your pa's left the farm,' Charlie said thoughtfully. 'What with four sons to split it over. See if you can follow what the lawyer says about that. I doubt if you'll fathom it, though.'

'I'll see if I can manage, if it's not too hard for me.' Amy turned her back on him and set out for her old home.

The lawyer was already there, seated in the chair opposite John's, when Amy came into the parlour. Mr Jamieson had seemed an old man to her when she had been a little girl, but the intervening years did not seem to have left any mark on him. His white hair was as thick as it had been then, and his shoulders no more stooped. He rose when she walked into the room and shook her hand, murmuring condolences that were an echo of those he had already given her at Jack's funeral.

The house was full of her father's presence; every corner of it brought some memory. Even the sight of John sitting in their father's old chair close to the fireplace seemed incongruous, and Amy half-expected Jack to come into the room and give his oldest son a sharp telling-off for his impertinence. But Susannah's black dress and her own mourning outfit, as well as the black arm bands worn by the men, were a sombre reminder of what they were all there for.

Harry beckoned her to the place beside him on the couch, well away from the chair Susannah had chosen, while Thomas and George made do with two footstools. There was no sign of Sophie; Amy guessed that she had gone to spend the afternoon with Jane, keeping her condition out of sight of their visitor.

Mr Jamieson took his seat again, then cleared his throat and placed a hand on the document that lay on a small table beside him.

'Now that Mrs Stewart has arrived, we'll make a start, if you don't mind?' He looked around the room, checking that he had everyone's attention. 'Mr Leith's will is quite straightforward—he was clear about what he wanted, my only contribution was putting his wishes into the correct form. You'll all have the chance to study this copy in detail when I've gone, but I'd just like to explain the main points, while you're all together. Mr Leith…' he fell silent for a moment, then gave them a rather sad smile. 'Jack,' he corrected himself, 'asked me to do that the last time he came into my office before he passed away. I'd known Jack a long time. Since before you were born, Mrs Stewart—not that that's so very long ago,' he amended hastily.

He picked up the will, glanced at it as if to check that his recollection was accurate, then replaced it on the table.

'Thomas and George won't come of age for some years yet.' The two boys exchanged a wary glance at being mentioned by name. 'Jack decided Mrs Leith should be their legal guardian until that time.' Amy saw George pull a face, but Thomas's expression was unfathomable.

'Of course I am,' Susannah murmured. Mr Jamieson studied her thoughtfully, as if weighing his words.

'Jack considered the options for some time,' he contented himself with saying. 'Well, to get on to the estate itself. It consists entirely of this farm, along with the livestock and equipment that goes with it. The farm has been left jointly and equally to Jack's sons. That is, half each to Mr John Leith and Mr Harry Leith.'

Susannah gave a sharp intake of breath. 'Do you mean to say,' she said in a tightly controlled voice, 'that my husband has left my sons out of his will?'

'Not at all, Mrs Leith,' Mr Jamieson answered. 'Your late husband was extremely anxious to do the right thing by all the members of his family. He took care to provide for your sons as well as he was able. We had some lengthy discussions on the value of the farm, and the fairest way to share that value out.' He gave Susannah a long stare, as if assessing her likely reaction to his next words.

'He's left the two boys the sum of two hundred and fifty pounds each, to be held in trust until they come of age. I'm one of the trustees for the bequests, and you are the other, Mrs Leith.'

'Two hundred and fifty pounds each,' Susannah said tautly. 'That's considered a fair share for my sons, is it?'

'Yes, it is,' Mr Jamieson said, meeting her gaze coolly. 'Based on the value of the farm, as well as I could calculate that with the bank manager's help, and taking into account just how much longer John and Harry have spent working on the property than their younger brothers have. There's also the fact that the farm would have to support four families in a few years if it were divided up that way. Jack felt that giving the younger boys their share in cash was the fairest way to go about it.'

'I see,' was all Susannah said, her lips compressed into a thin line when she had spoken. Amy could see that it was only her determination not to lose her dignity in front of the lawyer that kept her silent.

'As to yourself, Mrs Leith,' Mr Jamieson went on, 'Jack has made provision for you to have an annuity of twenty pounds a year for the rest of your life. Or until such time as you might marry again,' he added, his bland expression giving away nothing of what his opinion might be on the likelihood of that event. 'And, as their guardian, you'll receive the interest on your sons' bequests until they come of age.' Susannah acknowledged this with no more than a nod, her expression turned inwards as if she were doing calculations in her head.

'Mrs Stewart.' Amy gave a small start at being addressed, having been no more than an observer till now. Mr Jamieson gave her a smile of genuine warmth. 'I've left you till last, though your father talked about you first of all. You realise there isn't a great deal he could do for you?'

'Oh, I didn't expect anything,' Amy said. 'I mean, I'm settled and everything, and I knew the farm was for the boys.'

'Nevertheless, your father had no intention of leaving you out. He spoke at some length about wanting you to have something to call your own. It's not a large amount, but you're to have an annuity as well. Ten pounds a year.'

'What?' Amy stared at the lawyer in astonishment, till she realised that her mouth had dropped open. She composed herself as well as she could before speaking again. 'But... but I didn't expect... I didn't think...'

161

Mr Jamieson smiled. 'You'll have some time to get used to the notion. Your annuity will be paid into the bank four times a year, so you'll have to see Mr Callaghan about getting an account there in your own name. I'll go along with you for that, if you like. Your father was most particular that it was to be your own money, to do with just as you wish. He wanted me to tell you that.'

'Thank you,' Amy said faintly, unable to find words to say more.

Mr Jamieson left soon afterwards, and while Susannah was showing the lawyer out the front door Harry took the opportunity to slip out the other way.

'That's right, leave me to put up with Madam,' John grumbled half-heartedly.

'I'll end up doing something I shouldn't if I hang around here,' Harry said darkly. He gave Amy a hurried embrace and left just as Susannah could be heard closing the front door.

When Susannah came back into the parlour, instead of taking her chair again she stood by the fireplace and cast a cold stare around the room. Her gaze took in each of them, but when she finally spoke she was looking at the far wall rather than at any of her companions.

'I never thought he'd leave his own sons out of his will. Oh, I'm not surprised he's left me almost nothing, but his own sons!'

'He hasn't left them out,' John said. 'He's left them what he thought was fair.'

'Fair! Why is it fair for my sons to be given a few pounds while *you*,' her glare was clearly meant to take in John and the absent Harry, 'get the whole farm? That's why he did it, of course—because they're *my* sons. I never knew he hated me so much.' Amy could not decide just how sincere that catch in Susannah's voice was.

John gave a barely audible groan. 'Two hundred and fifty pounds each, Susannah. You might think that's not much, but I can tell you it's going to mean a hell of a mortgage on this place. Not that we grudge it,' he added hastily, casting a look at Thomas and George. 'They're Pa's sons, same as we are. It's only fair that the farm pays for them to get a start in life.'

'A start!' Susannah stalked back and forth in front of the fireplace, clasping and unclasping her hands. 'He should have thought about *that* years ago, while they were still young enough to benefit from a proper education. It's rather late now to be talking about a *start* in life, without the money to do it properly.'

'Well, you'll have to make the best of it,' John said, his patience clearly wearing thin. 'Pa told Harry and me what he'd decided, and he said it was the best he could manage. He worried himself sick over it, I don't mind telling you, and he didn't need extra worry. He's had enough to trouble him.'

Susannah drew herself up to her full, impressive height. 'Do you *dare* reproach me?'

'What if I do?' John asked, the challenge clear in his voice, quietly though he spoke.

Susannah stared back at him for a long moment, sizing up her opponent. But Susannah was no fool, and John was not his father. She knew she had no claim on him, nor any weapon to use against him now that he had assumed the role of head of the house. She turned away, taking refuge in self-pity.

'A woman alone in the world has no friends, I should have realised that,' she said, her voice trembling slightly. 'I shall simply have to carry the burden of bringing up my fatherless boys on my own, since the rest of you care nothing for them.' A dramatic wave of her arm indicated her sons, who were squirming with embarrassment on their stools. 'As, it seems, their father cared nothing.'

John did not bother answering, but Thomas did. He stood up and walked a few hesitant steps towards his mother. 'Don't talk about Pa like he was awful,' he said. 'Pa didn't mean it like that, I know he didn't. Honestly, Ma, he didn't mean to—'

Susannah rounded on him, eyes blazing as she found a safe victim. 'Don't *call* me that,' she hissed. 'You call me Mother, or keep silent. I won't have it, do you hear me? Talking like a rough, common farm boy!' She spat the words as if they were the deadliest of insults.

Thomas stared at her, clenching and unclenching his fists, and for a moment Amy thought he was going to cry. But the twisting of his face was from a rare anger, fanned by Susannah's abuse.

'That's what I am, isn't it?' he shot back at her, his voice tight with emotion. 'I'm a farm boy. That's all I've ever wanted to be—a farmer, just like my pa was. What's so bloody wrong with that?' He gave a yell as Susannah's hand lashed across his cheek, the slap so savage that within seconds the outline of each finger had made a crimson streak.

Amy was shaken out of the daze the news of her unexpected legacy had thrown her into. She rose from her seat to put a arm around Thomas. The boy turned to one side rather than look at his mother, who seemed poised to fling more bitter invective at him. John forestalled her next outburst by speaking first.

'Susannah!' he said sharply. 'Have some respect for the dead, for God's sake! Pa's barely cold in his grave and you're brawling in his parlour.'

'It was his fault,' Susannah said petulantly. 'I won't tolerate language like that from my own child.'

'You shouldn't have goaded him into it,' said John. 'You can't expect us to put up with you bad-mouthing Pa like that.'

His eyes locked with Susannah's, and it was Susannah who dropped her gaze first.

'You won't have to suffer me for much longer,' she said, facing the empty fireplace as she spoke. 'I shall be moving out of this house as soon as possible.'

Amy watched the signs of politeness fighting a brief, and losing, battle with honesty on John's face. 'I think that's for the best,' he said after a few moments. 'I think that's what Pa intended.'

'No doubt,' Susannah said. 'It may take me a few weeks to find something suitable, I hope you won't find my presence in your house too burdensome for that long?'

'Take as long as you like, Susannah,' John said, his teeth only slightly gritted. 'You're welcome to stay as long as you need to.'

'I suppose I should thank you for that. I shall take advice on finding a house as soon as I can.'

'Will you go back to your people in Auckland?' John asked, expressing a polite interest that Amy knew he did not feel.

'No,' Susannah answered quickly, startling Amy with her vehemence. 'I've no reason to go there. Anyway,' she added, 'I could hardly attempt to live decently on twenty pounds a year in Auckland. The rents are much lower in Ruatane. I shan't need a great deal of room just for the three of us, two bedrooms would be sufficient.'

Amy saw Thomas's face set in determined lines, as if he were schooling himself to an unpleasant task, but George erupted to his feet, knocking over his stool in his rush.

'I'm not going!' He turned to his older brother for support. 'John, we don't have to go with her, do we?'

John raised his eyes to the ceiling for a moment. 'Give me strength,' he muttered. 'Yes, you do,' he told George. 'If that's what your ma wants, you've got to do it. You heard what the lawyer said—she's your guardian now. That means you have to do what she says.'

He turned to Susannah. 'If you did want the young fellows to stay here, that'd be fine with me and Harry. I mean, this is the only home they've ever known—it's only natural they want to stay.'

'No,' Susannah said. 'Even you will allow that it's my right to decide where my sons should live.'

John sighed. 'Yes, it is.'

'*I* think it's only natural that they should want to be with their mother,' Susannah said, echoing John's phrase. 'They'll be coming with me, and that's an end to the matter.'

'But I don't *want* to,' George protested. 'I want to stay here—you do too, don't you, Tom?'

'No doubt,' Susannah said. She regarded each of her sons in turn. This time Amy was sure that the hurt in Susannah's expression was genuine, though her voice was quite steady. 'I was foolish enough to expect better of my own children.'

Amy was dabbing at the bleeding cut a roughness on one of Susannah's fingernails had made on Thomas's cheek. He waited until she had lowered her hand from his face before speaking. 'I...' Thomas began hesitantly. He turned to face his mother and spoke more firmly. 'I want to go with you, Ma–Mother.'

'You don't!' George said. 'I bet Pa never wanted us to go away with her. He probably meant Mother to go off and leave us here—yes, that must have been it. He left that money for Ma so she could live somewhere else. He can't have meant for us to go too, though, 'cause he knew John and Harry couldn't run the farm without us.'

'He did, George,' Thomas said. 'I know he meant us to go with her. He told me he did.'

'When?' George asked.

'It was...' Thomas frowned, struggling to recall the memory in detail. 'It was last year, I think, when Pa started getting real slow about walking and things. It was just him and me one day, I think we were going round the calves. He said a bit about how he had to leave the farm to John and Harry, but he'd sort it all out properly for me and you.'

'He seems to have discussed the matter with everyone in this house except his own wife,' Susannah remarked, but got no response.

'He never said it to me,' George protested. 'Why'd he only tell you, Tom?'

'Because he thought you might make a fuss about it. Like you are now,' Thomas added; George pulled a face at him. 'I didn't want him to talk about dying and all that.' His voice cracked, and he regained his self-control with a visible effort. 'So I sort of kept trying to talk about something else, but he made sure he told me that stuff anyway. And then he said...' He turned and looked at Susannah with a steady gaze. 'He said he wanted me to look after you. So I'm going to.'

She looked back at him in some surprise. 'I suppose you think I should be grateful.' Thomas shrugged and walked away to lean on the mantelpiece, turning his back on them all.

Susannah swept towards the door, the stiff, black crepe of her dress making a rustling sound as she moved. 'I'm going to lie down for a while, to try and recover my nerves,' she announced as she left the room. 'It has been a very trying afternoon.'

'There's no arguing with *that*,' John agreed quietly. 'She made damned sure it was… hey, how about you fellows get out of those fancy clothes of yours and see about getting the cows in?' he told Thomas and George. 'We've all done a bit much sitting around today. Tom,' he added, catching hold of his young brother's arm before the boy had taken more than two steps. 'You did the right thing, boy,' he said, patting Thomas's arm, and sounding so like their father that a lump came to Amy's throat.

The boys left the parlour at a half-run after farewelling Amy, readily taking the opportunity to get out of the house. 'I'm a fine one to talk about people bad-mouthing,' John said when he and Amy were alone in the parlour. 'I know I shouldn't go crook about her in front of them, but she makes it pretty hard not to sometimes.'

'John,' Amy said, 'this money Pa said I'm to have—is it all right? I mean, I don't want you and Harry giving me money you can't afford, and going short yourselves. You said you'd have to get a mortgage to pay for Tom and George's money.'

'It's only ten pounds a year, Amy,' John told her with a fond smile. 'The farm's not doing as bad as that! No, we can manage that no trouble at all. Why shouldn't you get a share, anyway? He was your father as much as ours. I wish it could be a bit more, that's all.

'Harry'll moan a bit about Madam's money,' he went on. 'Still, it's all talk—he knows as well as I do that Pa had to provide for her. Anyway,' he added in a low voice, 'I'd gladly spend twice that much to get her out of the house.'

'It'll be peaceful, won't it?' Amy said. 'I hope Tom and George'll be all right, though.'

'Yes, I feel a bit of an ogre saying they've got to go with her. You know, Pa thought about making me their guardian instead of her. He nearly did it, too—that's what the lawyer was sort of hinting about. But then he said how Tom and George are all Susannah's got, and it wouldn't be right to take them off her.'

'She would've been hurt if Pa had done that. Poor Tom, though, you know how he takes things to heart. I hope they'll all get on together.'

'Tom needs to stick up for himself with her a bit better. It was good to see him standing up to her before.'

'Yes, it was,' Amy said. 'And I think she got a surprise, Tom saying he wanted to go with her. Maybe she'll appreciate him a bit more.'

'Maybe.' John sighed wearily. 'I tell you what, it would all have been a lot simpler if Pa had lasted a few more years. Harry and me are going to miss the young fellows, specially with milking. Still, it can't be helped. I'll get Boy on to it—he's a bit young to be doing the morning milking, but he's big for his age, he should be right. And Harry says Dolly'll be finishing school this year, he'll get her on to the milking twice a day then, too. They won't be as fast as Tom and George, but we'll muddle along somehow.'

He walked to the back door with Amy, and caught hold of her hand when she stood on tiptoe to kiss his bearded cheek. 'Amy, just because Pa's gone, I wouldn't want you to think anything's changed here for you.'

'How do you mean?' Amy asked, puzzled by his sudden solemnity.

'I know Pa must have said this to you, and I'm saying it too—if you ever want to come back home, you've got a place here.'

'John, you're as much of a worrier as Pa was,' she scolded him affectionately. 'Anyway, my home's where my boys are. That's where I belong now.'

'Well, if it ever gets too much for you, you just remember you're welcome here. We'll have plenty of room now,' he added with a grin.

'Only until the next baby arrives,' Amy reminded him. 'Or maybe the one after that.'

John shrugged. 'I don't know, we don't have them as fast as all that. Not like Harry and Jane, anyway—you know he's talking about building on to his place again?'

'That'll be the third time!'

'I know. I'll get roped into helping him, too. He can wait till winter, though. Anyway, Amy,' he added, serious again, 'there's always room here for you, whatever happens.'

'Thank you.' She kissed him once again, laughing at the tickling of his beard. 'You're an awful lot like Pa, you know.'

The walk back to Charlie's house gave Amy time to get her thoughts in order, and to adjust a little to the astonishing fact that from now on she would have money of her own. Never again would she have to ask humbly to be allowed to spend a few shillings on fabric for a dress, then be faced with the alternatives of a curt refusal or grudging permission for which she would be expected to be pathetically grateful. Perhaps… perhaps she would even be able to afford to buy herself some new books. It would be up to her to decide just what to do with the money.

And that, she knew, was exactly what her father had intended.

David had not yet returned from school, and Malcolm seemed to be keeping out of his father's way, but Charlie came into the kitchen moments after Amy's own arrival, before she had had the chance to go into her room and change out of her good dress. She pulled on an apron over her mourning gown and buttered scones for their afternoon tea while she waited for the kettle to boil.

Charlie sat at the table watching her. 'How did it fall out? How's he left the land?'

'He's left the farm to John and Harry,' Amy said, not looking at him. 'And Tom and George are going to get some money when they come of age.'

'Mmm,' Charlie said thoughtfully. 'I suppose that was the best way to sort it out, with having the two families.'

'Pa thought it was the right thing to do.' She arranged the scones on a plate. 'Tom and George are going to move into town with Susannah. Pa's left her money so she'll be able to rent a house.'

Charlie grunted, clearly losing interest in the subject.

Amy put the plate on the table, and crossed to the range to fetch the teapot. She gripped the handle of the heavy pot so tightly that her knuckles whitened as she carried it to the table. Only for the briefest of moments did it occur to her that she might keep her own bequest a secret. Better to get it over with now than risk Charlie's finding it out from someone else.

'Pa's left me some money, too.' She set the pot down on the table, the thud serving to punctuate her announcement.

'What did he want to do that for?' Charlie asked, startled.

'Because he loved me.' She stood and faced him rather than taking her own seat. If she remained standing, he would not tower over her.

Charlie made a noise of disgust that showed what he thought of such sentiment. 'How much is it?'

'I'm to get ten pounds a year.'

'Every year?'

Amy nodded.

'That's not bad. It's not a hell of a lot, but it'll come in handy. There's a few things I can do with that.' A look of smug satisfaction settled over his face. 'Aye, a bit of cash will come in handy, all right. I might look into getting a new—'

Letting him speculate on all the ways he could use her money would only make him angrier when he found out the truth. 'It's my money, Charlie.'

His eyes narrowed. 'What's that supposed to mean?'

'Pa wanted me to have that money, so I'd have something of my own. It's not yours to spend, it's mine.'

'Stop talking your bloody rot! You're my wife—you've no business saying what you will and won't do with money. I'll have the law onto you if you try keeping it from me.'

'The law says a woman can have money of her own, whether she's married or not. It didn't used to be that way, but they changed it so that men couldn't take their wives' money off them. You can't have mine.'

'You...' He gathered breath for the assault. 'You thankless little bitch! All the years I've provided for you—fed and clothed you, kept a roof over your head, with precious little out of you in return. And now you've the chance to be a bit of use, you've the gall to say you won't do it! You've no right!' He thumped on the table, spilling milk from the jug with the force of his blow.

Amy stared coolly back at him, the firm conviction that she was in the right sustaining her calm. 'You're not going to spend my father's money on whores.'

'Thankless, good-for-nothing little bitch,' he flung at her, but there was more of self-pity than anger in his voice. 'If you'd do your duty by me there'd be no need to waste money on dirty whores. Don't you go throwing that in my face, or I'll show you—'

'No, you won't, Charlie,' she said, her voice calm. 'Not if you want me to stay, anyway. Though if I'm as useless as all that, perhaps you'd be better off with a housekeeper—you'd have to pay wages then, of course.'

He dropped his gaze from hers, and rended a scone savagely with his teeth.

'I'll clothe myself from now on,' she said, taking her chair at last. 'I doubt if you've ever spent more than a pound or two in a year on clothes for me, but I'm happy enough to pay for my own now. I don't really see how I can pay for my share of the food, when it mostly comes out of the garden or from the animals, but if you want I'll pay a share of the bill at the store.'

'No,' Charlie said sullenly. 'I'll not have the storekeeper poking his nose in my business, laughing behind his hand when he sees my wife waving her money around.'

'Just as you wish, then.' She took a cloth and wiped up the pool of milk around the jug.

Charlie shoved his chair back from the table, this time toppling the milk jug completely. 'Damn you and your haughty ways,' he snarled. 'I'm going out to the cows—they've more sense than you, at any rate.'

Amy began mopping up the fresh batch of spilled milk, and did not answer.

'I'll maybe be going into town tonight,' he said, clearly hoping for a reaction.

But Amy went on mopping up milk, acknowledging his announcement with a brief nod. 'Just as you wish, Charlie.'

12

November 1900

The debut of Lizzie's soirées was severely delayed by Jack's death, which plunged the whole family into mourning for many months. Lizzie then held a few musical gatherings for her own branch of the family, knowing better than to ask Amy to abandon deep mourning before a decent time had elapsed.

It was more than a year after her father's death before Amy was persuaded to attend a soirée, the first that was to have guests drawn from a wider sphere than the Leith and Kelly families.

'You want to go to a *what?*' Charlie said when Amy asked permission. 'Talk sense, for God's sake, woman!'

'A soyree, Lizzie calls it, but I don't know if that's the right word or not. She says that's what Susannah told her it's called. It's just a sort of evening tea—or afternoon, I think, I know Lizzie's had one or two in the daytime over winter. I think everyone just sits around and talks, and listens to the piano.'

'Sounds a load of nonsense. Night time, you say?' Charlie said suspiciously. 'I'll not have you going out after dark by yourself.'

'It stays light till quite late—I could be home before it was really dark if I hurried.' Amy saw his face set into stubborn lines, and knew that a refusal was looming. 'Lizzie invited you, too,' she said, trying another tack. 'She said you can come if you want.'

'What would I want to be listening to some silly girl playing the piano for?' His eyes narrowed. 'There'll be men there, will there?'

Amy's heart sank a little. 'Yes,' she admitted. 'Frank, of course. And maybe Uncle Arthur, and Bill—Lily'll be doing most of the playing, because she knows more songs than Maudie. I'm not sure who else.'

'All men with their wives there, then?'

'I think so.'

'Will they have a decent drop to drink?' he asked, a glint of enthusiasm showing. 'I was thinking I'd maybe go into town tonight—there'd be no need if Kelly's laying it on.'

'No, Lizzie said they only have tea at soyrees.'

'Serving men tea,' Charlie grumbled. 'Must be a womanish lot if they'll put up with that.'

'May I go, Charlie?' Amy asked, turning the discussion back to the main purpose.

'No, you're not going out by yourself at night. I don't want you wandering around in the dark.'

Amy had been uncertain whether she wanted to go at all; Charlie's refusal made the outing appear more desirable. 'What say I took Dave with me?' she asked. 'It'd be nice for him to come, he gets on well with Joey and Beth. And I wouldn't be going out by myself then.'

'Suppose you couldn't get up to much mischief if he goes with you,' Charlie said, clearly becoming bored with the subject. 'All right, go off and sit with a lot of giggling women. See you get your work done first, mind. And you're to be home by nine o'clock.'

He would not be home himself till long after that, Amy knew. But nine o'clock was late enough to keep David out, and it would be for the best if the boys were safely in bed and out of sight when Charlie came home from an evening's drinking. She thanked him with the best show of meek gratitude she could muster, and began to look forward to the unusual luxury of an evening out. Having David to herself on the trip to and from Lizzie's would make it even more of a treat.

She contrived to serve the evening meal half an hour earlier than usual, so that she and David were away by soon after six o'clock. She sat behind him on the patient Brownie's back (David had inherited the pony when Malcolm graduated to a bay of sixteen hands) with her arms around David's waist, enjoying the warm feel of his body against hers. This was to be her first outing since leaving off deep mourning. When she glanced down at her skirts it was strange to see herself clad in pale yellow cotton instead of the familiar black cloth she had worn for a year.

They arrived at Lizzie's house to find themselves well and truly the earliest of the guests, and in the midst of a flurry of activity, and Amy realised she had had no need to be in quite such a rush.

'Oh, good, you've brought Dave with you,' Lizzie said. Amy felt the bulge of Lizzie's latest pregnancy when they embraced, and a downward glance showed her that Lizzie's state was visible to a moderately sharp-eyed observer. 'I can do with another boy helping. Mal hasn't come, has he?'

Amy shook her head. 'No, he said he'd have an early night.' David gave her a swift glance, then turned away, but not before she had seen his expression. It told her what she had already guessed: Malcolm had no intention of staying home that evening. She tried to comfort herself with the reflection that Malcolm probably had enough sense to stay away from whatever hotel his father was likely to be drinking in.

'That's all right, Dave'll do. Dave, you and Joey carry those chairs through to the parlour, then you can help your Uncle Frank—he's moving the sofas for me. Beth, open the door a bit wider for them. That's the way.'

David was loaded down with two kitchen chairs and sent off to the parlour before he quite realised what was happening, while Amy hung her cloak on a hook behind the door.

'Lizzie, you've got so much food!' she exclaimed. 'How many people are coming?'

'Hmm? About seven, I think, not counting children. Maudie, fetch me another plate for these cakes. Let's see, there's you, of course, there'll be Bill and Lily, Tom's bringing Aunt Susannah, and I've asked two teachers out from town. Teachers can all play the piano, see, so they can spell Lily when Maudie's not playing.'

'No fellows,' Maudie grumbled. She carried a plate to the table and began arranging small cakes on it. 'What's the point of having a soyree with no fellows? That's what *I'd* like to know.'

'Stop your moaning, girl,' Lizzie said. 'I've told you and told you, this one's a sort of practice. We don't want to go inviting a whole load of strangers till we know we've got it all sorted out properly. It doesn't matter if we get the odd thing wrong with just family and a couple of teachers.'

'Suppose so,' Maudie allowed. 'Can I have a new dress when we have a soyree with fellows, Ma?'

'We'll see,' was Lizzie's noncommittal reply.

'And can I pick what sort of dress it is?'

'No, you can't. You're too young to know what's suitable.'

'But Ma—'

'That's enough buts for tonight. And mind you don't start going on about fellows in front of your pa. You know he doesn't like to hear you talking like that.'

'Pa thinks I'm a baby.'

'That's because you act like one sometimes.' Lizzie glanced at the clock. 'Look at the time! The visitors will be here soon, you'd better get changed, Maudie.'

Maudie gave her mother a meaningful look. 'I want to wear my white muslin,' she said, her tone so emphatic that Amy knew this was not the first time that evening the subject of Maudie's dress had arisen.

'Well, you can't,' Lizzie said. 'You're going to wear your pink dress. That's the prettiest one you've got, and you want to look your best for the soyree.'

'But I *told* you, Ma, I asked Aunt Lily the other day, and she said I should wear—'

'That doesn't matter. *I'm* telling you you're to wear the pink, and that's all there is to it.'

Not in Maudie's opinion, it seemed. 'But you said to ask Aunt Lily about style and things, because she comes from the city and she went to a fancy school. You *said* that. And I showed the pink dress to Aunt Lily, and she said—'

'I've heard just about enough of what Lily has to say for one night,' Lizzie cut in, her voice rising. 'Your Aunt Lily doesn't know everything there is to know about things, I might state. She was nearly thirty before she managed to find a husband, and she probably never would have if I hadn't shoved her under your Uncle Bill's nose.'

The moment the words were out, it was clear that Lizzie regretted her rare loss of self-control. Maudie stared wide-eyed at her mother.

'What a nasty thing to say! Ooh, Aunt Lily would be so upset if she knew you'd said that about her.'

'Well, she won't hear unless any big-mouthed girls go carrying tales, will she?' Lizzie said. 'There's no need for you to go butting into your elders' affairs.'

Lizzie looked around the room for a distraction, and found it in the younger children. 'Mickey, it's time you and Danny went to bed—you can put them to bed, Maudie. Give Danny's face a good wash first, he's got custard all round his mouth. And you can check if Rosie's settled.'

'There's too many babies around here,' Maudie remarked to the room at large before she took a reluctant Danny by the hand and dragged him down the passage, not before shooting a dark look at her mother.

'That girl can be very provoking,' Lizzie said. 'Going on about her dress like that, and making me say that about Lily! You girls watch your step tonight, I don't want anyone else annoying me,' she told the attentive Maisie and Beth, both of whom nodded vigorously.

Her composure recovered, Lizzie turned back to Amy. 'Fourteen, if you please, and going on like she'll be an old maid if she's not married before the year's out,' she said, aggravation and pride present in equal measures in her voice.

'You were just the same,' Amy said. 'Except there was only ever Frank for you. What can I help with, Lizzie?'

'Oh, I think it's about ready. Have you finished those sandwiches, Maisie?'

'I've made *hundreds*,' Maisie said. She indicated her mountain of sandwiches to Amy. 'See how fancy they look? I've cut all the crusts off,' she added, awed at such extravagance.

'The pigs'll soon clean the crusts up,' said Lizzie. 'Let's see—yes, those look all right, Maisie. I suppose they might be a bit thick.'

'I did them thin as I could,' Maisie said.

'I know you did. Aunt Susannah said make them dainty, but it's hard to cut bread thin when it's nice and fresh like that. Never mind, they look good with the crusts off.'

'I'm staying the night here,' Maisie told Amy self-importantly. 'I've never stayed the night before.'

'Yes, it'll be too late for her to walk home by the time we've finished,' Lizzie said. 'She can share with Rosie tonight, it's only a little bed but Maisie doesn't take up much room. Where'd you put your nightie, Maisie?'

'Haven't got one. I just sleep in me drawers, or I keep my dress on if it's cold.'

'Well, you're not sleeping in your drawers here! I'll sort out one of Maudie's for you—no, Beth's would probably fit you better. I'll do that later.' Lizzie scanned the laden table. 'Let's see, we've got ham, and pies, and some cold chicken, then there's all Maisie's sandwiches, and cakes for after. That should be enough. Right, everyone into the parlour, and we'll wait for the visitors. Beth, put those kittens back.'

'But I wanted to show them to Dave,' Beth said, a tiny, squirming kitten in each hand. 'See them, Aunt Amy? They're so little.' She held out one of the kittens, the image of Amy's Ginger at the same age. Amy took it carefully in her hands and stroked it.

'Well, you can show him another time. We don't want kittens in the parlour tonight, climbing on everything. Someone would only tread on them, anyway. Put them back in the box, love.'

Beth obediently gathered up both kittens and put them into an overturned crate that had been made into a bed for the kittens and their anxious mother.

Maudie came out a few minutes later, wearing a bright pink dress and a scowl. 'Aunt Amy, don't you think this dress is *awful?*'

It was certainly eye-catching, Amy thought; she suspected that was the main reason Lizzie so approved of the dress. No one would ignore Maudie while she was wearing a dress so well-endowed with frills and in such an intense shade. And the huge sleeves would ensure that she took up more of the room than anyone else present. 'Oh, no, it's not awful, Maudie,' Amy said. 'It's a very cheerful sort of dress. I would have loved one like that at your age.'

'Maybe it would have been the fashion back then,' Maudie countered. 'No one's wearing these silly big sleeves now. And this horrible colour! I look stupid in this thing.'

'I'll tell you what, you look ugly with that scowl on your face,' Lizzie said. 'No one would look twice at you with a face like that, even in that pretty dress. I went to a lot of trouble making that, my girl, and I don't want to hear another word about it tonight. Is that understood?'

Maudie mumbled something that might have been compliance, but any reply Lizzie was going to make was interrupted by the arrival of Bill and Lily.

Lizzie scolded them soundly for coming in the back door. 'That's for everyday. You should come in the front door when it's a soyree.'

'I did try and tell you, Bill,' Lily said to her unrepentant husband when Lizzie had hurried the family through to the parlour.

'Well, we'll come in the front door next time,' Bill said.

'If you're asked again,' Lizzie retorted. '*You* can come, Lily, but you can only bring him if he behaves himself.'

'Yes, I'll leave you at home to look after the children,' Lily added with a sidelong smile at Bill. 'I feel rather wicked leaving them tonight at all— it's the first time I've ever left Will.'

'They'll be all right with Ma,' said Bill. 'I bet you Pa'll keep Arfie up late, that's the only trouble.'

'And then he'll be in a mood tomorrow,' Lily said with a sigh. 'Well, that'll serve me right for leaving them, won't it? I do love the chance to play, though. I had a lovely session with it when I came down for Maudie's lesson yesterday. Oh, Frank, that new music's wonderful,' she added.

'I just sent away for the ones you said to,' Frank said. 'I should've got you to write the names out for me, though, it was a beggar trying to figure out how to spell them. I wrote them like you said, Showparn and all that, but the names on the music don't look much like what I wrote.'

'It doesn't matter, it's all wonderful—especially this one with the terribly long name.' Lily leafed through the pile of music on her lap and lifted a few sheets aloft. 'T-c-h-a-i-k-o-v-s-k-y,' she spelt out. 'Goodness knows how you're meant to pronounce it! But it's stunning music, and so hard to play! I had a delightful time struggling with it yesterday.'

'Is it the sort you can sing along with?' Lizzie asked.

Lily laughed. 'No, not at all, I'm afraid. Don't worry, I won't play any of that tonight. And I'm not going to try and make Maudie learn it, it's much too hard.'

'I'll say,' Maudie agreed. 'It's got no tune in it, either. Just all those notes bumping into one another.'

'Well, they sent some nice, easy music too, so there'll be plenty for Maudie and I to work on over the next few months. I don't know what possessed the music shop to send you such difficult music, Frank. I did say to ask for easy pieces. Actually, I don't recall even asking you to order any Chopin, come to that.'

'Well, I told them to pop in a bit for a really good player,' Frank admitted. 'I mean, you've been going to all the trouble of teaching Maudie for us, it's only fair if you get to play the things you want to as well. I remembered you saying that name Showparn, and I just hoped they'd send some other music you'd like as well.'

'They certainly did. Thank you, Frank, that was kind of you. I'd better get the music set up before the real visitors arrive. Will you help me with it, Maudie?'

Lily turned to Maudie and looked at her properly for the first time since her arrival. Her smile was replaced by a puzzled expression. 'Oh, you're wearing that dress. I thought we decided your white one would be better.'

Maudie shot an 'I told you so' look at her mother. 'Ma said I had to wear this thing,' she said in a long-suffering tone. '*I* wanted to wear the white one.'

'I see,' Lily said, the slight smile on her lips showing just how well she understood. 'Well, I'm sure your mother knows best. I'm terribly out of date with styles, it's so long since I took any notice of them. And I've no girl of my own old enough to worry about fashions. It's a pretty shade,' she added, but Amy saw the uncertain expression with which Lily studied the slash of colour the dress made. Maudie, too, saw her aunt's expression, and cast a resentful glance at her mother.

The two teachers arrived, and did not need any coaching to come to the front door. There was a time, Amy reflected as the unfamiliar women were shown in by Lizzie, when she would have had to fight down resentment at being forced to meet someone who had achieved what she had wanted; she was relieved to find that she could study the teachers with dispassionate interest. Their lives were so different from her own that jealousy seemed meaningless.

She even managed to feel more amused than irritated when Lizzie explained to the visitors that Amy and Lily had both been teachers. 'So you'll all have a lot to talk about,' Lizzie said.

'I wasn't a teacher,' Amy said. 'Lizzie's always telling people I was,' she added with a smile in Lizzie's direction. 'I was going to be a pupil teacher, but I never even got that far. I'm interested in hearing about it, though.'

But there were few opportunities to talk about teaching that evening. Lizzie installed the women, whom she introduced as Miss Denton and

Miss Harding, gave them each a cup of tea and proceeded to instruct them in the names, ages and characteristics of her six children, before moving on to give them a potted history of the creation of Frank's Jersey herd and explain Frank's role as founder and chairman of the co-operative.

By the time Lizzie had extracted brief life histories from her visitors in return, it was late enough for Susannah's non-appearance to be remarked on.

'Well, we can't wait all night for her,' Lizzie said. 'I don't want to keep Beth up much longer, and I want her to hear some of the music before she goes to bed. Lily's going to start teaching her as well as Maudie next year. Now, you pay attention, Beth, don't go talking to Dave in the middle of the songs.'

She turned to face the teachers again. 'Which one of you wants to play first?'

Miss Denton gave a giggle. 'Well, I wouldn't mind playing something, but I'd rather not be first.' Her blonde hair was pinned up in a mass of tight curls at the back of her head, and the curls shook as she laughed, threatening to tumble around her face. She looked no more than twenty. Amy felt the weight of her own thirty-two years more heavily than usual.

'You can have a go, then,' Lizzie told Miss Harding.

Miss Harding stifled a small yawn behind one hand. 'I'm afraid I don't play,' she said, earning a shocked look from Lizzie.

'Oh,' Lizzie said. 'I thought teachers all played piano. Do you play something else?'

'I'm afraid not,' Miss Harding said.

'I expect you like singing, then?' Lizzie prompted.

Miss Harding shook her head. 'No, I'm not at all musical. I prefer to leave that sort of thing to people with a gift for it.' She smiled at Lizzie, apparently quite complacent about her lack of talent. Amy had to hide a smile of her own at the indignant expression that flitted across Lizzie's face.

'Alice plays rather well,' Miss Harding said, drawing a giggle of protest from Miss Denton.

'I'm pleased to hear it,' Lizzie answered. Amy could see that as far as Lizzie was concerned Miss Harding had gained her invitation to the soirée under false pretences; there was little chance that a woman so shamelessly lacking in musical gifts would be invited again.

'You'd better get on with it, then, Lily,' Lizzie said. 'Then Miss Denton can have a go when you want a rest. Maudie's going to play for us later,' Lizzie announced to the room at large, making it clear that this was to be considered the highlight of the evening.

Lily took her place at the piano, beckoning Maudie to stand at her side to turn the pages of the music.

She began with a brisk little gavotte, but came to an abrupt halt when Maudie leaned across her to turn the first page. 'Oh, Maudie, those sleeves!' Lily said, startled by the sudden brushing of Maudie's leg-of-mutton sleeve against her face. 'I'm sorry, dear, but we're going to have to do something about them. Here, let me try and flatten this one down a little.'

Lily wrestled with the stiff fabric, creasing it visibly, while Maudie scowled at her mother. 'I didn't want to wear this dress,' the girl muttered, uncowed by the answering glare she aroused.

'I know, dear,' Lily said soothingly. She slipped two pins out of her bonnet and used them to hold the sleeve flat. It gave the dress an oddly asymmetrical look, but reduced the unwieldy effect of the excess fabric. 'It should be all right now. Let's go on, shall we?'

She began the piece again, though not before Amy had heard Miss Denton say to her friend, 'I used to like those sleeves when they were in fashion. I haven't seen such full ones for years.' Amy saw from Maudie's expression that she had heard it, too; it was fortunate that Maudie was soon too busy turning pages to be able to make any sharp remarks in return.

Lily played several pieces, then announced that she was ready for a rest. 'Would you like to play now, Miss Denton?' she asked.

Miss Denton gave a nervous laugh. 'I'm not sure that I want to now that I've heard you, Mrs Leith. I'm afraid you're all used to better than I can manage.'

'Oh, don't say that,' Lily protested. 'Really, I'm not as good as all that! Anyway, I'm sure you must know lots of the newer pieces that I've never heard—it must be twenty years since I went to any sort of concert. Do let me hear you.'

'Yes, you'd better play,' Bill put in. 'I don't want Lily getting too big-headed, with you praising her up like that—there'll be no living with her soon.'

'Honestly, Bill, fancy saying that to Miss Denton!' Lily scolded. 'Take no notice of him, Miss Denton, he's an awful tease sometimes.' She tried to grimace at Bill, but it turned into a smile instead.

Miss Denton let herself be persuaded to play, choosing some pieces from those she had brought with her. Amy knew she was no judge of music, but she could tell that there was a huge difference between Lily's playing and Miss Denton's. When Lily played, Amy was tempted to close her eyes and let the music take away her awareness of where she was and even who she was. Miss Denton's playing had nothing like such power, but she played capably and the tunes she chose were pleasant. They were indeed tunes that none of her audience except Miss Harding had heard before, most of them taken from the Gilbert and Sullivan operettas that Amy had read of in the newspapers from time to time.

'Some of those would be good to teach Maudie,' Lily said when Miss Denton paused between pieces. 'They're such cheerful tunes, and they don't sound too difficult.'

'Oh, they're terribly easy,' Miss Denton said. 'The ones I play, anyway! And they've lovely words, too. I love singing Gilbert and Sullivan. I'd rather sing than play, actually. Would you like to try it, Mrs Leith?' she asked, seeing the interest with which Lily was studying the music.

Now it was Lily's turn to protest. 'I don't think I could, just like that, not when I've never seen it before.'

'Oh, do try,' Miss Denton urged. 'It really is very easy, especially this one.'

'Come on, Lily, you're dying to have a go at it,' Bill said, while Miss Denton stood up and offered the piano stool with a flourish.

'Now you're all siding against me,' Lily complained, but she took the vacated stool readily.

After a few hesitant bars, Lily was confident enough to tell Miss Denton to begin singing. Lily's playing and Miss Denton's pleasant soprano made an enjoyable combination. The whole family applauded after the first song, insisting on several more.

Lizzie studied Lily and Miss Denton as they performed. During a pause in the music, she leaned across to speak to Amy in a low voice. 'I think Maudie should get into singing—you see the one singing much better than the one sitting down at the piano. Yes, I think I'll start her on that.'

Maudie caught her mother's remark and darted a glare at her. 'Not in this dress I won't. I'm not making a spectacle of myself.'

'You'll do what you're told, my girl. And I think it's a lovely—'

'Maudie, come and turn the pages for me,' Lily broke in, cutting short the discussion. Maudie and Lizzie had to make do with casting occasional hostile glances at each other while the music continued.

Just as Lizzie was threatening to serve supper without waiting any longer for her, Susannah arrived at last. She swept into the parlour on Thomas's arm in a rustle of lilac silk, pausing in the centre of the room long enough for everyone to take in the full effect before she took the chair Bill gave up to her, acknowledging his attention with a gracious nod of her head.

'We'd just about given up on you, Aunt Susannah,' Lizzie said. 'I thought you must've changed your mind about coming.'

'Really?' Susannah said. 'Oh, you must remember I've lost touch with a lot of your farm ways now I'm living in town. When I lived in Auckland I'd never dream of arriving at a soirée before eight o'clock.'

'Well, people in Auckland don't have to get up and milk cows in the morning,' Lizzie answered tartly. 'Never mind, you're here now. Let's get on and have supper, then, we're all starving. Maudie, you and Maisie can go and fetch it, and Beth—oh, look at the poor little mite.' Her voice softened at the sight of Beth sprawled on Frank's lap sound asleep. 'She's not used to staying up this late.'

Sensing their attention, Beth sat up and rubbed at her eyes. 'I wasn't really asleep,' she said unconvincingly, looking around in confusion. 'I liked the music.'

'Off to bed, love,' Lizzie told her. 'Maudie, put your sister to bed, she looks as though she'll fall over if she tries going by herself.'

Beth put her arms around Frank's neck and gave him a rather damp kiss, then let herself be led off by Maudie, pausing long enough to give her mother an even sleepier embrace.

'You haven't met these ladies, have you, Aunt Susannah? This one's Miss Denton, she can play the piano. And this is Miss Harding. She can't. Miss Denton, Miss Harding, this is Mrs Leith. And Tom's her son.'

The new acquaintances shook hands. 'It's so nice to meet someone new,' Susannah said. 'Ruatane's such a small town, it's a treat to see a new face.' She gave a little laugh. 'Of course, after so many years on the farm, Ruatane seemed quite a city to me at first! To be able to walk down the street to the shops, or to go visiting of an afternoon—oh, it was like coming to life again!'

She caught her breath and looked around warily, clearly wondering if her delight in her new state was a little too overt; she was, after all, in the same room as two of Jack's children. But no one spoke to rebuke her. Susannah turned her attention back to the visiting women and began interrogating them on the latest fashions in Auckland.

Amy managed to hide her rush of hurt; the way Susannah had spoken made it sound as though Jack's death were almost a cause for celebration.

The change in Susannah over the first year of her widowhood had been striking, Amy reflected. Their paths rarely crossed now, other than glimpsing one another at church; the one or two invitations to visit that

Susannah had issued expressed the demands of politeness rather than any desire for Amy's company, and they both knew it. Since leaving the farm, Susannah had acquired a sprightliness that Amy had never seen in her before. Now as she spoke to the teachers, clearly aware that she was the most elegant person in the room, she was positively glowing. For the first time, Amy thought she might be glimpsing a little of what must have attracted her father to Susannah in the first place.

'And this is your son?' Miss Denton said, smiling at Thomas. 'I think I must have seen you in town—Mabel, doesn't Mrs Leith's son look familiar?'

'Yes, he does,' said Miss Harding. 'I suppose we must have met on the street.'

Thomas shrugged. 'You might've seen me at work. Everyone seems to come in there, I don't remember who I see half the time, what with trying to get the sums right.'

'Thomas has taken a position at the bank,' Susannah said, endowing each word with great significance. 'He has very good prospects there, the manager is terribly pleased with him.'

'Mother,' Thomas said, squirming with embarrassment. 'You said you wouldn't go on about that.'

'And why shouldn't I take some pleasure in my son's achievements? You're doing very well, and I don't see why I shouldn't tell people. Heaven knows your brother gives me nothing to boast about.'

'Oh, you've another son as well, Mrs Leith?' Miss Denton asked politely.

Susannah sniffed. 'One would hardly know I did, for all the notice he takes of the fact.'

'Now, Mother.' The resignation in Thomas's tone made him seem older than his eighteen years. 'We agreed you wouldn't talk about that, remember? You'll just upset yourself.'

'I'm only answering Miss Denton's question,' Susannah said. 'I'm afraid my younger son has seen fit to abandon his mother.'

Thomas gave a sigh. 'My brother works on a boat,' he explained to the two women, who were both looking suitably shocked at Susannah's announcement. 'Mother doesn't approve.'

'I should think not,' Susannah said. 'Working with such rough, common men! And me never knowing where he is or what he's getting up to. We hear nothing of him for weeks on end.'

'He was home last week, and he'll be back next Tuesday,' Thomas amended. 'He's doing pretty well, too, saving his wages. He wants to buy his own boat one day.'

182

'He needn't think he's using his inheritance for that,' Susannah said. 'He won't see a penny of it till the day he turns twenty-one. I *hope* he'll have learned a little sense by then, though I sadly doubt it.'

'It's steady work,' Miss Harding offered. 'People will always need boats to travel on and get things delivered.'

'Oh, I don't deny it's steady,' Susannah said. 'And I dare say it's suitable enough work for a certain class of boy. I did, however, have hopes of better things for my sons.'

Miss Denton broke the brief, awkward silence. 'Well, you've Thomas, here, haven't you? No wonder you're proud of him.'

Susannah gave Thomas a look that, to Amy's mild surprise, seemed to have genuine affection in it. 'Thomas is a great comfort to me. I don't know how I'd manage without him.'

'Don't start on that again, Mother,' Thomas complained. But Amy could see that he enjoyed his mother's praise, despite the embarrassment.

Maudie chose that moment to offer a plate of sandwiches to Thomas. He took advantage of the distraction to move further away from Susannah and her captive audience. Amy got up and followed him, and they stood close together so that they would not be overheard.

'She still hasn't come round to the idea of George working on the boat, then?' Amy asked quietly.

Thomas shook his head. 'I don't think she ever will—not unless he ends up owning a fleet of them, anyway. I don't know, sometimes I think she enjoys having something to go crook about. You know what she's like.'

Amy did indeed, but she was careful not to criticise Susannah to Thomas. 'You and her are getting on well these days, anyway.'

'We have our ups and downs,' said Thomas. 'Once or twice she's tried going on about Pa—we had a couple of rows about that, she's stopped doing it now.' He cast a pensive glance at his mother. 'It's funny how things turn out. I never thought she liked me when we lived on the farm—she used to be a lot grumpier with me than with George. Now she's... well, she's not too bad. I think it was the farm, mostly. She hated it there, you know, really hated it. I don't know why.'

'I suppose it was just different from what she was used to. She might calm down about George when she gets a bit more used to that, too.'

'Maybe,' Thomas said doubtfully. 'If he doesn't come home for a week or two she says he's abandoned her, then when he does come she gives him such a hard time he's breaking his neck to go again. Last time he was here they'd been carting a lot of hides, and I don't think they'd cured them properly. Mother went on and on about George stinking the place out, and not being fit for polite company.' He pulled a face. 'He did stink, too. Don't know why she was complaining, she didn't have to sleep with him.'

Amy laughed at his expression. 'If she was Lizzie, she'd have held him down and scrubbed him. Poor old Tom, caught in the middle.'

'I'll say I am. George makes it worse, you know—he stirs her up on purpose sometimes. He likes a fight. There was one time a couple of months ago, the two of them were having a real set-to. She said he was no better than a common sailor, and he called her a… well, never mind. She'd put dinner on the table, and she said she didn't know why she went to the trouble of feeding him, and he reckoned the food wasn't worth eating, anyway. He ate plenty, though. She was nagging at him about having dirty fingernails, and Lord knows what else. Said she thought she'd left dirty men behind when she got us off the farm.'

'That wouldn't have gone down too well.'

'No. Anyway, it got worse and worse—they were really shouting at each other after a bit. George said if she was going to make his life a misery he wouldn't come home any more, and she said she didn't know why he bothered. She didn't mean it, but she said it anyway. Then George said why didn't I come away on the boat with him—he said there's plenty of work to do, he'd get me a job no trouble.'

'Your mother wouldn't have thought much of that! You're not really going to, are you, Tom?'

'I promised Pa I'd look after her,' Thomas said, a set expression on his face. 'Anyway, I don't know if I fancy working on a boat—I get too seasick. Right then, though, I told them I was fed up with the pair of them, and maybe I'd go and get a job in Dunedin or somewhere else a heck of a long way from both of them, anything for a bit of peace and quiet. George stormed out and slept on the boat that night, and I went off to bed early, so that was the end of that row.'

A smile stole on to Thomas's face, and he shot a glance at Susannah. 'She got me breakfast next morning. I usually just get myself a bit of bread and butter of a morning, you know how she likes having a lie in. But she got up early and made me a real breakfast, bacon and eggs like we used to have on the farm, and she brought it in on a tray. Breakfast in bed, eh! I'd never had that before. She didn't talk about what everyone had said the night before, but she sat on the bed and watched me eat breakfast, and she started talking that rot about being proud of me and all. And she said she'd be really lonely if I left her. She even gave me a kiss. She needn't have worried, though. I told Pa I'd look after her, and I will.'

Amy slipped her hand onto his arm and gave it a squeeze. 'Pa would have been proud of you, too, Tom.' To say more would embarrass him, so she changed the subject. 'How's your job going?'

Thomas shrugged. 'It's all right, I suppose. Mr Callaghan's pretty good to work for, but I get a bit sick of having to wear a collar and tie every day. Not like on the farm. I don't have to get up so early, that's one good thing. I'm sort of used to getting up early, though,' he said with a rueful smile.

'I wish you'd come and see me sometimes. I never see you now.'

'Why don't you come and see us, then?'

'It's a bit far to walk, Tom! And you know Uncle Charlie's not one for visiting, so I couldn't get him to take me.'

'I suppose not. I'd like to come out here more, but it's hard to get the time. She likes me to take her visiting on my day off, and she wouldn't want to come to the farm.' He looked towards the corner of the room where Frank and Bill were deep in discussion, with David and Joey close by trying to look knowledgeable. 'I wonder how Frank's cows are getting on.' Amy could see in his face how eager he was to be part of the conversation.

'Go and ask him,' she said, giving him a small push. She went back to her chair in time to hear Susannah press an invitation to visit on the two teachers. Susannah's animation had not lessened, and Amy felt herself to be a dull little mouse in comparison.

Maudie put a tray of food onto a small table and sat down beside Susannah. She reached out and brushed the folds of lilac silk, then pulled her hand back guiltily when Susannah gave a start at the touch.

'It's a lovely dress,' Maudie said. 'You always wear nice things, Aunt Susannah.'

'Thank you, dear,' Susannah said, gracing Maudie with a smile. 'This is the first time I've worn this one, actually. I had it made only last week. I must say it's rather a relief not to have to wear black any longer, though I did make the effort to have decent mourning clothes.'

Lamplight played on the slight sheen of the silk. The dress was beautiful, Amy thought. The style was quite plain, allowing the lovely fabric to show to best advantage. It fitted tightly over the bodice, emphasising Susannah's full bosom and narrow waist, then fell in soft folds. The sleeves were close-fitting, too, ornamented at the shoulders with tiny epaulettes and ending in ruffles of white lace at the cuffs.

Amy looked at her own dress with a critical gaze. It was clean and tidy, and the pale yellow was a pleasant enough colour, but cotton was not silk. The dress was beginning to fade in a few places, betraying its long life. She glanced again at Susannah's gown and allowed herself to speculate on the notion of making a silk dress. She had only had one in her life, and the blue dress still hung in her wardrobe, old-fashioned even by country standards but far too good to throw out.

She had yet to adjust to the phenomenon of having her own money. Material for her mourning clothes, along with a black bonnet, had been her first expenditure, soon followed by a frame for the present David had given her; then in the middle of winter her boots had developed a hole and had had to be replaced. After the third quarterly payment of her annuity, she had plucked up the courage to send away for a volume of poems advertised in the *Weekly News*, and had then been so horrified at the postage charge added to the cost of the parcel that she had not dared buy anything since. Now, seeing Susannah's dress, she felt the stirrings of a desire for pretty things of her own that she had suppressed for all the years of her marriage. Perhaps, she whispered to herself, she could even afford a sewing machine like the one that was now Lizzie's pride and joy. Perhaps she would not have to be a drab little mouse all her life.

'Such a pretty colour,' Maudie said, daring to touch the dress again. Amy saw Susannah give Maudie's hands a hard stare then visibly relax on seeing their well-scrubbed state. 'Do you think this colour would suit me, Aunt Susannah?'

'No, I don't think so,' Susannah said. 'It's too—' She stopped abruptly and gave Maudie a closer look. 'Goodness me, what a… striking dress.' She floundered briefly, then managed, 'It's very… bright.'

'It's horrible,' Maudie said, dismissing the dress with a flick of her hand. She cast a challenging look in her mother's direction, but Lizzie was too busy discussing small children with Lily to notice.

Maudie leaned forward and fixed Susannah with an earnest gaze. 'Aunt Susannah, what do you think would suit me best?'

Susannah gave Maudie an appraising glance. 'Not what you're wearing, anyway. At your age, simple styles are nicest. You've pretty hair and a reasonable figure, you don't need such elaborate frills and ruffles.'

'Ma,' Maudie said triumphantly, loud enough to catch her mother's ear, 'Aunt Susannah thinks this dress is horrible, too.'

'Well, I wouldn't put it quite that strongly,' Susannah demurred before Lizzie had a chance to respond.

'I think it's a lovely dress,' Lizzie said. 'I went to a lot of trouble over that dress, I'm sure I don't know why it's suddenly such a monstrosity.'

'Hardly a monstrosity,' Susannah said, with an obvious effort at tact. 'But I do think you could do better. That pink is far too bright, with your fair colouring. You'd be better with soft colours—pink by all means, just not so… well, lurid. Blues, too. Not lilac like this, it wouldn't look right with those pink cheeks of yours. Actually, green would suit you rather well.'

'I've got another dress,' Maudie said eagerly. 'The one I wanted to wear tonight—it's white muslin, quite plain, only it's got green ribbons on the bodice. Do you think that's the right sort of dress for me?'

'Yes, that sounds very suitable.'

'I suggested she wear the white muslin,' Lily said. 'I'm sorry, Lizzie, but I do think it suits her better.'

'But it's so plain,' Lizzie protested. 'No one would look at her in a dress like that.'

'A simple dress would set her off far better,' Susannah said. 'She's young, and she has some good features. This dress hides her best points instead of helping one notice them.'

'Oh.' Lizzie was briefly at a loss for words, but Maudie's superior expression was not something she chose to look at. 'Anyway, I still think it's a lovely dress,' she said as though that were an end to the discussion. 'Maudie, it's time you played us some of your songs. Hurry up, it's getting late. Quiet, everyone, Maudie's going to play now.'

Maudie played her first piece, Lily watching her with a proprietorial air. 'I do wish she wouldn't play extra loud when she's not sure of the notes,' Lily whispered to Amy, but she clapped as enthusiastically as everyone else when Maudie finished the piece.

'She's coming on well, isn't she?' Lizzie said. 'Aunt Susannah, doesn't she sit up nicely when she plays? She's got that deportment real good now. You should see her with a book on her head—she can get right up the passage and back without dropping it. Maudie, show everyone how you can walk with a book on your head.'

Before Maudie had a chance to voice the indignant refusal written on her face, Susannah spoke.

'Walking with a book is just an exercise in gaining good deportment, Lizzie,' she said, looking pained. 'It's not something to do as a party piece.'

'I just thought you'd like to see it,' Lizzie said; a little huffily, Amy thought.

Maudie started her second piece before her mother had the chance to make any more suggestions. She played more confidently this time, and when she had finished she turned to give the company a bright smile in response to their applause.

The smile disappeared when, in the brief silence that followed the burst of clapping, Susannah could be heard to murmur, 'Oh, that dress.' Maudie glared at her mother, a wasted effort as Lizzie was looking elsewhere, and for a moment Amy thought she might burst into tears.

Instead the girl slipped quietly from the room. Amy hoped Maudie would not expose herself to everyone's stares by having eyes too obviously red from crying when she returned.

She need not have worried on that count. In a surprisingly short time Maudie was back, no sign of tears on her face as she strode into the room with her head held high, wearing a white muslin dress with green ribbon bows on the bodice.

'Oh, *that's* better,' Lily and Susannah said in chorus. Amy suspected that their response would anger Lizzie as much as Maudie's defiant action. 'Yes, that's just the sort of thing I had in mind,' said Susannah.

Maudie shot a look of triumph at her mother, to be met with a hard stare in return.

'Maudie, pick up those empty plates and take them out to the kitchen,' Lizzie said in a deceptively mild tone. 'I'll be out in a minute to help you stack them up.'

Maudie did as she was told, with the slightest toss of her head as she went. Lizzie followed her a moment later.

Frank crossed the room to stand close to Amy. 'What's up with those two?' he asked quietly. 'They've been looking daggers at each other all night. It's something or other about Maudie wanting a new dress, isn't it?'

'Something like that,' Amy murmured back. 'Shall I go out there and try and calm them down?' she offered, though without any great hope of success.

'I wish you would,' Frank said. 'It's no good me interfering when they get like that.'

Amy could hear raised voices before she was halfway down the passage. When she entered the kitchen she found the two combatants had locked gazes across the table, each bristling with injured pride.

'You deliberately went against me in there,' Lizzie said. 'You tried to show me up in front of everyone.'

'Me show you up? What about you, making me wear that awful dress?'

'It's getting late, Lizzie. Why don't you and Maudie talk about it in the morning?' Amy said. They ignored her.

'You're getting too big for your boots lately, Miss,' Lizzie said. 'It's about time you started showing a bit of respect.'

'Why should I?'

'Because if you don't, I'll have to teach you a lesson.'

'I don't see why I should take any notice of you,' Maudie said, her eyes blazing. She was unfortunate enough to have inherited something of her grandfather's temper as well as her mother's overbearing ways; Lizzie would never have defied her own mother so openly. 'I'm not a little kid any more for you to boss around.'

'You can start calling the tune when you've got your own place, but you'll do as I say while you live in my house or there'll be trouble.'

Maudie stamped her foot. 'I never *will* get out of here if you have your way. Who'll look twice at me wearing awful dresses like you want? And then you go making a fool of me in front of everyone, talking about walking with a book on my head! I just about *died* of embarrassment.'

'I think I know more about what's suitable than a slip of a girl like you.'

'You?' Maudie said. 'What do you know about style or anything? I know the things that look nice better than you do—Aunt Susannah and Aunt Lily both said the dress I picked was much nicer than that awful one. You don't even care about how you look, let alone trying to tell me how to dress.'

Lizzie's eyes narrowed. 'I don't care for your tone. Don't you go setting yourself up above your betters, my girl.'

'I'm not,' Maudie flung back recklessly. 'I'm only setting myself up above *you.*'

Amy gave a gasp. 'I think you'd better say sorry to your ma, Maudie,' she said in the ominous silence that followed Maudie's outburst.

'No,' Maudie said. 'I'm *not* sorry.'

'You will be,' Lizzie said, her voice dangerously calm.

'Lizzie, don't be too hard on her,' Amy said. 'She didn't mean it, I'm sure. She's probably over-tired, with all the excitement tonight.'

'It's none of your business, Amy,' Lizzie said, her gaze never leaving her daughter's. 'Maudie, you can go back into the parlour now and play some more songs.'

'I only know those two well enough to play in front of people,' Maudie said, sullenness in her voice as her anger subsided.

'Then play the same two again,' Lizzie said sharply. 'Then you can say good night to everyone and go off to bed. You'd better not go to sleep, though, because I'll be having a word with you later. Off you go.'

It was time for Amy and David to leave before Maudie had finished her second recital. Before she went, she whispered to Frank that Lizzie and Maudie had had a serious falling out.

*

Even with Amy's warning, Frank was surprised when, after all the guests had finally gone, Lizzie said, 'Stay here in the parlour a minute, Frank. I want to have a word with Maudie before I go to bed.'

'Can't it wait till tomorrow?' Frank asked, thinking longingly of a warm bed and a good sleep.

'No, it can't. It won't take long. Maisie, just stack the rest of those dishes on the bench for me, we won't wash them tonight. Then you can go and tell Maudie I want to see her.'

Frank sat in the parlour and waited while Maisie carried the dishes out and Lizzie went off to their bedroom. A few minutes later he heard voices raised briefly, soon followed by the unmistakable sound of leather against bare flesh.

'I've finished, Frank,' Lizzie called. He left the parlour just as Maudie rushed from her parent's room. She careered into Frank and flung herself against his chest, sobbing.

Frank put his arms around her and stroked her hair, uncomfortably aware of the budding breasts pressed so firmly against him. Maudie was growing up more quickly than he would have wished; she could not be much younger than Lizzie had been when he had first started courting her. 'Never mind, love,' he said awkwardly. 'Never mind.'

'Maudie,' Lizzie called from the bedroom. 'Go to bed. You've got a big pile of dishes to do in the morning. And don't try playing up to your father, either.'

Frank gave Maudie a final squeeze, then disentangled himself from her embrace and watched her go into the room she shared with her sisters.

'What'd you get?' he heard someone ask in a hoarse whisper; he recognised the voice as Maisie's.

'Mind your own business,' Maudie answered, the last word lost in a sob.

Frank went into his own bedroom and closed the door. 'Poor little thing.'

'Rubbish,' Lizzie said, pulling pins out of her hair as she spoke. She had already taken off her shoes and stockings and undone the buttons of her bodice. 'She's been asking for that all evening.'

'What'd she do wrong?'

'Oh, all that fuss she made about the dress. Playing up in front of Aunt Susannah, not to mention those teachers. And then to come out in the other one like that! And she gave me some fearful cheek in the kitchen.' She shook her hair loose and began sliding off her skirts.

Frank waited for a moment to hear the rest. 'Is that all?' he asked when he realised there were no more crimes to be revealed.

Lizzie stopped undressing for a moment. 'What do you mean, "all"? That's bad enough, isn't it?'

'Well, I didn't really follow all that stuff about the dress, and I know she shouldn't give you cheek, but... I don't know, it just doesn't seem a lot to get a hiding for.'

'I think I'm the best judge of that,' Lizzie said. 'If you had your way, that girl would never have had a hiding in her life. Goodness knows what she'd be like if I hadn't been firm with her. The cheek of the girl! Do you know what she came out with just now?'

She went on without giving him the chance to speculate, her words punctuated by the shedding of undergarments. 'I told her we wouldn't have another soyree for months because she'd played up like that, and do you know what she said? She stood there and looked me in the eye, and she said, "That's not why we're not going to. It's because you're having a baby." Did you ever hear such audacity? I didn't know what to say for a bit.'

'But Lizzie,' Frank said, struggling not to laugh, 'it's true! You told me yourself this'll have to be your last soyree till the baby comes.'

'That doesn't mean I want a slip of a girl saying it to me! Honestly, I don't know where she gets such ideas from.' She tugged her nightdress viciously over her head.

'I suppose she used her own two eyes. She's seen you with child enough times to have figured out what it means when you start swelling up like this.'

He fell abruptly serious when he saw that Lizzie seemed to be getting in something of a state. 'Now don't go upsetting yourself,' he soothed. 'It's not good for you, with the baby and everything.' He stood behind her, slid his arms around where her waist should have been, and held her till he felt the stiffness start to relax out of her body.

'That's better, isn't it?' he whispered, kissing her hair near her ear. He slid his hands down till they rested on the hard bulge of her belly, wondering if he would be able to feel the first small flutterings of life there. Lizzie leaned back against him, her body warm against his. She seemed to grow warmer and softer whenever she was with child. 'You're nice with a baby in you,' he murmured.

'You won't say that when I'm the size of a house. Hurry up and get undressed, Frank, I want to go to bed. And don't you go getting any ideas, either. I'm too tired.'

191

'I'm pretty weary myself.' Frank gave a yawn. He got undressed and into his nightshirt as quickly as his tiredness would allow, then climbed into bed and put the lamp out. 'I didn't think they'd all stay so late.'

Lizzie pressed against him, a stray tendril of her hair tickling his face. She had managed to get into the centre of the bed, taking up more than half, but Frank had long ago given up trying to claim a fair share. 'Neither did I. Amy and Dave went too early, really, I think Charlie must have told her she had to. But those teachers stayed pretty late. And as for Aunt Susannah! I thought she was never going to go. Tom must've said half a dozen times that they should be off.'

'Then in the end he stood up and said, "Come on, Mother, we're leaving now,"' Frank said. 'She gave him a bit of a sour look, but she went all right. I think I would've fallen asleep on the sofa if she'd stayed much longer.'

'Me too.'

'She seemed to have a pretty good time. Being a widow seems to suit your Aunt Susannah.'

'Mmm,' Lizzie agreed drowsily. 'Being a wife never did, anyway.'

She was quiet for some time. Frank was on the verge of sleep when she spoke again. 'You know, that dress doesn't fit Maudie very well.'

'Doesn't it?' Frank roused himself to say, though it was difficult to take an interest in the subject of Maudie's clothes at such an hour.

'Not really. It was all right when I made it, but she's getting bigger in the bosom.'

'Can't you let it out or something?'

'Oh, I don't think I'll bother. I might give it to Maisie—she can make it a bit smaller and take the hem up. She won't care whether it's in the fashion or not.'

Frank struggled to clear his head enough to take in what Lizzie was saying. 'But wasn't that what all the fuss was about? Because you like that dress and Maudie doesn't?'

'Don't worry, Frank, I don't expect you to understand about style and all that. Maudie can wear that dress for another couple of months, then I'll give it to Maisie.'

'Please yourself.'

'Mmm.' Lizzie pressed more closely against him. Frank gave up another few inches of bed to her before he realised what she was doing.

'Frank?' she whispered a few minutes later, this time rousing him from actual sleep.

'What?'

'It was a really good soyree tonight, wasn't it? It all went off so well.

It'll be good when we can have another one.'

Frank sighed at the thought of how few hours remained till he would have to get out of his warm bed. Just now, an early night seemed a precious thing. 'If that's what you want, Lizzie.'

13

It took all Frank's powers of persuasion to convince Mrs Coulson to attend Lizzie at the birth of her seventh child. The nurse protested that she had retired from such work; she was too old to commit herself to riding out to the farm in the middle of the night (which was, as she added with the wisdom of long experience, when most babies in isolated spots chose to be born); and she was certainly too old to run a household of nine while Lizzie was bed-ridden.

But Lizzie wanted Mrs Coulson again, and that was enough to make Frank persistent. He made repeated visits to her house, countering every argument with one of his own. He would bring her out to the farm a week or two before Lizzie was due, so there would be no need for a nighttime dash. The girls would do all the work; there would be no need for her to do anything but look after Lizzie.

His visits continued, until finally one day the nurse flung her hands up in front of her face in a gesture of defeat and said, 'All right, Mr Kelly, you win. You've worn me down.'

Frank beamed at her. 'I knew you'd come around in the end.'

She smiled back. 'It was what you said about Mrs Kelly that did the trick, you know—how you'll be nervous enough anyway, but you'd be worried sick about her if she couldn't have the nurse she wanted.'

She patted him on the arm as she led him to the door. 'Any man who still worries about his wife after seven babies deserves to have whatever he wants, in my opinion.'

Mrs Coulson found Frank as good as his word when the time came. She spent a pleasant few days helping Lizzie with the last of the preparations for the new baby, then little Kate obligingly arrived a week earlier than expected, and with a minimum of fuss.

In fact she found the Kelly home even more pleasant to stay in than on her previous visit, when she had delivered the now three-year-old Rose. This time Maudie was only too eager to take over her mother's role, and Maisie stayed with the family throughout Mrs Coulson's sojourn. Beth, too, made herself useful when she was not at school. Mrs Coulson found the household functioned smoothly, with no more than a light supervisory touch from herself.

She enjoyed the company of the children all day when she was not attending Lizzie and the new baby, and in the evenings when the little ones were all safely in bed it was delightful to sit in the parlour and chat with Frank until it was time for them to retire.

Maudie took advantage of her mother's confinement to sit up later than Lizzie normally allowed, insisting that her self-appointed role as lady of the house gave her the right. Not to be outdone, Maisie announced that, because she was older than Maudie, she should be allowed to sit up at least as late. Mrs Coulson and Frank both took the cowardly way out and let the girls have their way, only sending them to bed half an hour before their own bedtime.

It was that last half hour of the day that Mrs Coulson enjoyed most. Frank was anxious not to disturb Lizzie's rest, so he was careful to wait until she was deeply asleep (with the help of a sleeping draught supplied by the nurse) before he crept in to join her. That gave Mrs Coulson the pleasure of Frank's company in the pleasant lull at the end of the day, and she could not recall when she had last enjoyed herself so much.

It was more years than she cared to remember since she had shared a fireside with a man; though Frank reminded her far more of her sons than of her long-dead husband. She found it easy to become fond of Frank; so easy that she reproached herself for becoming soft in her old age. She had let herself get fond of Charlie Stewart's little wife, and all that meant was that she fretted about the poor girl whenever she thought of her.

That was another advantage of staying with the Kellys, of course: it gave her the chance to see her little favourite most days. Amy seemed calmer than she had in the past; certainly the trembling fear of her husband that she had so barely concealed in the old days had gone. She seemed worried about that older boy of hers, though she said little enough about it, but such worries were no rarity in a woman with a boy of fifteen. When Mrs Coulson looked at Frank, so anxious for his wife's comfort and so unfailingly patient with his children, she could not help but wish gentle little Amy Leith had found such a husband instead of somehow having Charlie Stewart forced on her.

She tried to keep herself too busy all day to have time to dwell on such thoughts, though it was hard to find enough to occupy her in this well-ordered household. In fact her work seemed so easy, with the most difficult job being to keep Lizzie from getting up too soon after the birth, that Mrs Coulson began to feel a little guilty about taking Frank's money for what was almost a holiday. There must be something she could do more useful than a vague 'keeping an eye on the girls'.

As the nurse moved quietly around Lizzie and Frank's bedroom one day, the only sound that of the sleepy breathing of Lizzie and her new daughter, she thought of a small task she might perform. That chest of drawers was unlikely to have had the newspaper lining each drawer changed for several months; she could not imagine Lizzie had been able to bend down to the lower drawers recently.

She fetched some paper from the kitchen, then emptied out each drawer in turn, replacing the old newspaper with fresh sheets and putting the clothes back as neatly as she had found them, until she had worked her way down to the lowest drawer.

As she lifted out the last piece of newspaper, a smaller sheet of paper fluttered towards the floor, unfolding as it fell. Mrs Coulson snatched at it, then turned the sheet over and glanced idly at the writing that covered its other side.

The first glimpse told her that what she held was a letter. Mrs Coulson was not in the habit of reading other peoples' private correspondence, and she was about to fold the letter up and put it back where she had found it, when two phrases caught her eye.

The first was 'Miss Leith'. The nurse immediately recognised this as referring to Amy; it did not occur to her that it might equally as well have meant Lizzie. When another phrase leapt out at her, all thoughts of replacing the letter unread were abandoned. 'Parting with the baby.'

After a brief, guilty glance at Lizzie to check that she was still asleep, Mrs Coulson slipped from the room and into the parlour, where she was unlikely to be disturbed at this time of day. She sat down in the chair furthest from the door and devoured the letter from beginning to end.

The reference to Amy as Lizzie's 'sister' puzzled her for barely a moment; she knew Lizzie had no sisters, and she knew that the cousins were closer than many genuine sisters. She read on rapidly, every sentence helping mould the vague suspicions of Amy's fate that she had held for years into full-formed comprehension. So there had indeed been a child born before Amy's marriage; a child she had had to part with, a little girl. Mrs Coulson had no difficulty in putting a name to this child, though none was given in the letter: Ann. The name Amy had cried aloud in each of the labours Mrs Coulson had attended her in. The name of her dead mother.

'She had been very wronged,' the writer of the letter had said. Yes, Mrs Coulson was quite sure of that. But the wronging had not stopped with the conceiving of a child. It had led to the misery of a forced marriage with that brute of a man.

But why make the girl marry Charlie Stewart? The letter did not help Mrs Coulson answer that question. Scandalous as it was for an unmarried girl to have a child, that was no reason to marry her off to such a man. Her family had managed the birth and farming out of the child so discreetly that Mrs Coulson had never heard so much as a whisper of it in the gossip-prone little town; if whoever had wronged Amy had managed to get out of reach before her family could catch him and make him do right by her, why not keep the girl quietly at home with them once she was over the ordeal?

That dreadful marriage was all Susannah Leith's doing; of that the nurse was certain. She had drummed into Amy such a sense of shame that the girl had let herself be pushed into Charlie's bed. Anger at Susannah welled up until Mrs Coulson stopped her thoughts in their tracks. Whatever else she might be guilty of, Susannah had not got Amy with child.

So who had fathered a child on that girl then refused to marry her? On a farm that far from town, few enough men would have had the chance. A girl as young as Amy would never have gone beyond the end of the valley unaccompanied; when would she have been able to spend time alone with a man not part of her family?

Her family. A thought too horrible to be entertained slowly began to seep into Mrs Coulson's mind. No, it wasn't possible. It couldn't be.

She hurried back to the bedroom and replaced the letter in its drawer, put a fresh sheet of newspaper on top of it, then piled the clothes back where they belonged. Lizzie stirred a little, and the nurse left the room.

But replacing the letter did not settle her troubled thoughts. Who had got Amy with child? Why had the fact that her stepdaughter had borne a child out of wedlock made Susannah Leith so desperate to get her out of the house? Why not let it all be forgotten once they had placed the baby with a good family? Why go to such lengths to get rid of Amy?

Mrs Coulson had lived in many places and seen many things, some of them things she would rather forget. She knew that dreadful things happened in families; over the years she had sometimes heard dark rumours of girls being misused by their fathers. Had that happened to Amy?

The very idea made her feel physically ill. Amy had loved her father; Mrs Coulson had seen that clearly enough when Jack had come to visit his daughter and her new babies. And he had certainly been fond of her. But so he would be, she reflected, if he had been taking his pleasure with her.

It was a dreadful thing to think evil of the dead, and this thought was indeed evil. He couldn't have. And yet...

And yet it explained it all so neatly. All Amy's talk of having done such dreadful things. The pains taken to place the baby in Auckland, instead of pretending it was Jack and Susannah's own, as most families would have done. Susannah's claim that Amy had 'brought it on herself', and her haste to get Amy married off no matter how unsuitable the husband.

The few encounters Mrs Coulson had had with Susannah had told her that Susannah Leith was a woman with little warmth, and with none of even such affection as she was capable of being directed at her husband. Nothing could excuse such behaviour by a father, but it was not beyond Mrs Coulson's imagination to comprehend, however dimly, how a man saddled with such a cold wife might seek comfort elsewhere. And perhaps he had sought it with his pretty little daughter, as warm and affectionate a girl as Mrs Coulson had ever known, and who was said to be the image of her dead mother.

Mrs Coulson went outside, hoping that the fresh air would lift her thoughts above the foul rut they had fallen into. She worked in the garden for a time, pulling weeds and picking fresh flowers for the house, and when that was done she rushed on to other activities. Anything to take her mind off the idea that Amy had had such things done to her by her father.

But her frantic attempts at busyness were no use. She tired her body, but her mind raced on. She was a little sharp with the children, and unusually silent with Lizzie as she tended her.

She was still on edge when Frank came home for his afternoon tea, somewhat late and disappointed at finding Lizzie asleep.

'Well, I can't sit with my girls just now, so how about you come and have a cup out on the verandah with me,' he said. Mrs Coulson agreed, welcoming the distraction.

'Lizzie's doing well, isn't she?' said Frank. 'She seems a bit tired—she's sleeping more than she did after the others were born—but she's looking good.'

'She's doing very well,' Mrs Coulson said. 'And it's good for her to take the chance of a decent rest while she can. She'll get little enough opportunity once she's up and about again—though she's lucky to have the girls to help her. They'll probably be even more useful next time.'

'I don't think there'll be a next time,' Frank said. 'I mean, it's good Lizzie takes it so well and all that, but there's no denying it wears her out. And seven children's enough for any man.'

'It's certainly a blessing to have seven healthy children.' She gave Frank a sidelong glance; she had seen how affectionate those two were towards each other. 'They do have a way of coming along, no matter what people decide.'

'Well, we'll have to see about that,' said Frank.

'It takes a certain amount of… restraint from time to time,' Mrs Coulson said carefully. 'Particularly on the part of a husband.' That was as far as she could go, even with so amiable a man as Frank Kelly, and it was far enough to have embarrassed them both.

'It's been good this time, while she was carrying Kate,' Frank said. 'It's the first time I've ever managed to get Lizzie to take it easy. Now Maudie's home all the time—and we've had Maisie staying quite a bit, she's been a big help to Lizzie—Lizzie didn't have to rush around as much as she did with the others. She even took to having a lie-down in the afternoons once she got big, she'd never done that before.'

Maisie came out onto the verandah, carrying a tray with tea cups and a plate of biscuits. 'Talking about me?' she asked. 'I heard you say my name—you don't want to take no notice of him,' she told Mrs Coulson, casting a cheeky grin in Frank's direction.

'It was all nice things, dear,' Mrs Coulson said, smiling at Maisie. 'Mr Kelly was saying what a help you are to Mrs Kelly.'

'Maisie?' they heard Maudie calling imperiously from the kitchen. 'Hurry up, I want you to start on these spuds. I've just about finished doing the meat.'

Maisie rolled her eyes. 'She's worse than the missus, that one. I'm coming, wait your patience!' she shouted back. 'I'll be glad when the missus starts running the place again.' She made a show of setting out the tea things slowly and deliberately, then headed back towards the kitchen in no great hurry.

'That daughter of yours is rather fond of telling everyone what to do,' Mrs Coulson said. 'She's in her element, now that she thinks she's running the house. I'm afraid I just let her have her head—it doesn't seem worth arguing over. Anyway, it's good practice for when she does have her own household to run.'

'I suppose so,' Frank said, clearly with no great enthusiasm for the idea of Maudie's leaving his house.

'For goodness sake don't tell Mrs Kelly I'm letting Maudie think she's in charge of things,' Mrs Coulson added. 'Your wife thinks I'm being quite firm with them all.'

'No, there's no sense letting Lizzie get herself in a state over it. Her and Maudie are inclined to row a bit at the best of times.'

Mrs Coulson picked up her cup of tea. 'I just can't get over what you've done for Maisie Feenan,' she said, remembering the girl who had placed the cup in front of her a few moments before, her black hair so shiny that it caught the light as she moved, and her eyes sparkling with mischief. 'She's a different girl since she starting spending time here. So clean and neat, and she's looking so healthy.'

'She's still pretty scrawny compared to Maudie, but I suppose she has filled out a fair bit. She was just a little scrap of a thing in rags the first time I saw her, and as scared as a wild kitten. It's nothing to do with me, though, it's all Lizzie's doing. She's fed her up and taught her manners and all that.'

'Well, she's done a wonderful job of it,' said Mrs Coulson. 'Even giving her decent clothes. Oh, Maisie's terribly proud of that bright pink dress Mrs Kelly gave her, she showed it to me the day I arrived.'

'That was Maudie's dress, her and Lizzie had a row about it because Maudie didn't like it. I'm glad Maisie's so fond of it. She keeps it here, doesn't she?'

Mrs Coulson nodded. 'Yes, in your daughters' wardrobe. I doubt if she's got anywhere at home to keep it that isn't filthy.'

'Mmm,' Frank said. 'I've noticed when she goes home for a couple of days she comes back all dirty and worn-out looking. I don't think they've got proper beds to sleep in at her place. Lizzie says Maisie always spends the first half hour or so after she gets here giving herself a good scrub and getting changed.'

'That's another good habit Mrs Kelly's taught her, cleanliness.'

'I'd sort of like to have her here all the time,' said Frank. 'We're a bit short of room, though, with all the girls. Anyway, her pa'd probably make a fuss about it, 'cause he wouldn't get her money any more. I think I'll have to buy Maisie off him if I want to have her come and live here—I wouldn't call it that, but it's what I'd be doing.'

'Well, a few more years and Maisie will be able to please herself where she lives. In the meantime, I think she's happy enough spending half her time here.'

She shaded her eyes to look down the valley towards the sea, a band of blue with the sun striking sparks of light off it. 'It's been a beautiful day. It's hard to believe we had that dreadful storm the other night.'

'Yes, it's blown itself out well and truly,' Frank said. 'I had a few branches knocked off some of the trees, but nothing too bad. I heard Charlie down at the factory the other day saying he'd lost some shingles off his roof in the middle of the night.'

Mention of Amy's husband brought the dark thoughts Mrs Coulson had been steadfastly suppressing bubbling back to the surface.

'Mrs Stewart said something about that when she came down yesterday,' she said, finding herself almost reluctant to say Amy's name aloud. 'I gather that husband of hers was in rather a sour mood over it.'

'Hard to tell the difference with Charlie.'

'Yes.' A silence fell between them, as if the mention of Charlie had cast a cloud over both their moods. 'I'm very fond of little Mrs Stewart,' Mrs Coulson said at last.

'She's nice,' said Frank. 'Lizzie and her are like sisters, too. When Lizzie was sick that time, Amy was down here helping look after her, and she had Joey staying with her so she could feed him. I didn't know whether I was coming or going, I was no use to anyone. She was really good about it all. And she had enough on her plate without all that.'

'I'm sure she did.' She sensed there were things Frank was leaving unsaid, but she did not feel like probing what was behind his words. 'Where were you this afternoon, Mr Kelly?' she asked, making a determined attempt at cheerfulness.

'Oh, I've been down at the school,' Frank said, brightening visibly. 'A bunch of us were having a good look over it—me and Bill, and Lizzie's cousins, and a couple of other men with kids there. I've been thinking for a while it's time that place got done up, it's just been a matter of getting a few others stirred up enough to do something about it.'

'That's a very worthy idea.'

'It's close to falling down, the state it's in. The floor's gone all uneven the last couple of years, and the roof leaks, and it's that draughty in winter. Stinking hot in summer, too. We're going to redo the floor and the roof, and pull all the rotten boards off the walls and put decent ones on. Probably have to replace a couple of the windows, too.'

'It'll be a different building when you men have finished with it. I think that's very good of you, making time to do that.'

'Well, just about half the kids in the place are mine,' Frank said, with a touch of exaggeration but with understandable pride. 'Don't want my kids trying to learn their lessons in an old shack like that.'

He grinned, then glanced almost shyly at Mrs Coulson. 'I've had some good times at that school,' he said, looking like a boy caught in some harmless mischief.

'Really? Did you enjoy your schooldays a lot?'

'No, I wasn't much good at school. I only went for a couple of years, anyway. No, I was thinking about other times... one time specially.'

His grin was infectious, and Mrs Coulson felt herself smiling in response. 'And what time was that, Mr Kelly?' she prompted.

'They used to have dances there, when there were a whole lot of us around the dancing sort of age. I took Lizzie to one—no, I didn't really, Bill brought her—anyway, Lizzie and me...' another shy grin, 'that was when we started courting properly.'

'I see. No wonder you're so fond of the place, then. Was there rather a lot of that going on at this dance?'

'I suppose there was. I didn't take much notice of anyone but Lizzie. Let's see, who was there? I don't think Sophie was, her and John got together later. And of course Lily didn't turn up till years after that—her and Bill were all Lizzie's doing, anyway. I've an idea Jane was, though—yes, that's when her and Harry met, I think.' He screwed up his face in thought. 'Oh, I can't remember—seems like everyone was there. Even Charlie turned up, goodness knows why. I remember he shoved past me and Lizzie when he got there, he must have been in a hurry for the beer. He sure wasn't there for the dancing.'

Frank grinned sheepishly. 'Not that I can talk. I was a dead loss at it, Lizzie's feet must've been covered with bruises by the time I'd finished with her. There was hardly room to dance, anyway, but some of the others managed all right. I remember seeing Harry dancing with Jane, and of course Amy and Jimmy were…'

He stopped abruptly, and suddenly seemed intensely interested in the biscuit on his saucer. Mrs Coulson let the silence rest between them for several long moments before she asked in a voice of studied casualness, 'Who's Jimmy?'

Frank examined the fascinating biscuit more closely. 'Oh, he was just a bloke who came and stayed at Jack's place that summer.' If that was an attempt at sounding indifferent, Mrs Coulson thought, then Frank Kelly was an extremely bad actor.

He offered a scrap more. 'He was Susannah Leith's brother, that's why he went to stay with them. He was younger than her, though—about the same age as me, I think.'

If she had not been so eager to disprove her dark conjectures, Mrs Coulson might have told herself that it was none of her business; that she must not pry. Instead she went on probing, gently but relentlessly. 'And they had something of a romance, did they? This brother of Mrs Leith's, and young Amy Leith?'

She heard Frank's feet scuffing against the boards of the verandah. 'Something like that. It didn't come to anything.' He shot a guilty glance at the nurse, and Mrs Coulson decided that Frank was as bad a liar as he was an actor. 'Well, he went away at the end of the summer. It didn't come to anything good, anyway.'

'I see,' Mrs Coulson said, and indeed she did. 'I imagine Miss Leith was rather upset about it all.'

'Yes, I… I think she was. I didn't see much of her around then.'

Mrs Coulson could see an inward struggle reflected in Frank's face;

debating whether or not to say more, she guessed.

'We… we don't really talk about that stuff much,' he said at last. 'About Jimmy and all that. I mean… well, it was a long time ago, and…'

He looked at Mrs Coulson with a troubled expression; she sensed he was trying to decide how much she knew or had guessed. 'It's Charlie, really. Amy's had a lot to put up with over the years, and he's grumpy enough without people bringing up all that old stuff. It's better not to talk about it.'

'I'll say nothing outside this house,' Mrs Coulson assured him. She slumped back in her chair as a wave of relief washed over her.

So that young rogue had lured Amy into wrongdoing, then somehow managed to get away before his guilt had been discovered. It was a shameful deed, but not as uncommon as people liked to pretend. Mrs Coulson had delivered too many supposedly seven-months babies to believe that all brides went to the altar as virgins, and not all fathers managed to make sons-in-law out of their daughters' deflowerers. She had been young and in love herself once, though it seemed more than a lifetime ago; she knew what it was to feel temptation. It might be sinful, but it was natural. She no longer had to imagine what was so hideously unnatural: the idea of a father making his daughter do service as a wife.

She considered the whole story as dispassionately as she could, picturing each of the main characters in her mind. 'Mrs Leith's brother, eh? And it all came to nothing. I wonder why. Wasn't young Amy good enough for him?'

Frank's face set into an expression sterner than she would have thought him capable of. 'Maybe he thought she wasn't. He was pretty fond of himself, I think. I tell you what, though—he was wrong about that. She was too good for him. Much too good.'

14

May – August 1901

Amy had taken a mild pleasure in the beauty of the day, drinking in the sense of calm that came from the smoothness of the distant sea and the stillness of the air. After the wild weather of a few days before, the contrast could not help but lift her spirits.

Even Charlie seemed not entirely unaffected by the improved weather; certainly he seemed a little less impatient with the boys than usual. Amy allowed herself to hope that perhaps the worst was over between Charlie and Malcolm.

It was only when a storm of another kind broke that Amy discovered just how ill-founded her optimism had been.

The family were sitting down to morning tea. Amy knew it was too much to hope that Charlie and Malcolm might have a civil conversation, but she was heartened that at least they were not actively annoying each other. The noise of hoofbeats coming up the track took them all by surprise. Charlie scowled at the sound.

'One of your bloody relations coming poking their nose in here again,' he grumbled, but Amy shook her head.

'I shouldn't think so. John and Harry don't ride over here, it's just as fast to walk, and it won't be Lizzie, she's not up and about yet. It might be someone to see you.'

Amy went to the back door to see who their visitor might be, but Charlie pushed past to get outside first. He shaded his eyes as he looked down the track to where a man on a large, black horse was riding towards them. 'What's that bloody policeman want?' Charlie muttered under his breath, but as soon as Amy caught sight of the tall figure she was sure she knew just why Sergeant Riley had ridden all the way out from town. Or at least who he had come to see.

It's Mal. What on earth has that boy got up to now?

Sergeant Riley dismounted and tied the reins to the nearest fence. 'Morning, Stewart,' he said curtly. 'How'd'ye do, Mrs Stewart,' he added, tilting his hat in Amy's direction.

'What can I do for you?' Charlie asked, not bothering to hide his irritation at the unwelcome visit.

'It's not you I'm wanting to talk to, Stewart. It's that son of yours. And there's the boy now.'

Amy turned to see Malcolm and David peering out the back door.

'Malcolm Stewart, you come out here,' the policeman boomed. 'I want

204

a word with you, boy.'

For a moment Malcolm looked as though he were considering escape, but he seemed to think better of the idea. He walked towards the waiting adults, the hint of a swagger in his gait given the lie by the nervous glances he shot in his father's direction. David crept along in his wake, but no one had eyes for the younger boy.

'What's my boy got to do with you?' Charlie demanded.

Sergeant Riley ignored him, fixing his steely glare on the edgy Malcolm.

'What do you know about this business with the minister, boy?' he asked.

Malcolm frowned in a confusion that Amy was sure was unfeigned. 'Dunno what you're talking about.'

'What's happened to Reverend Simons?' Amy asked.

'Haven't you heard?'

Amy shook her head. 'I haven't been out of the house for days, except going to Mrs Kelly's.'

Charlie cleared his throat. 'I heard someone rattling on about that down at the factory the other day. Had his house broken into, didn't he? Got roughed up a bit, too, I heard.'

'Nasty business,' Sergeant Riley said. 'You know the poor fellow's been as good as bedridden with the rheumatism these last few months?'

Amy nodded. Reverend Simons' age had begun resting heavily on him over the last year, and it was now all he could do to struggle to church once a month to take a communion service. She had missed his fiery sermons, though she knew that Charlie regarded the minister's affliction as something akin to divine retribution for having preached such foolish doctrine.

'Well, it seems a bunch of young ruffians decided to turn his place over for him. They got in there the other night and found his strongbox—there was little enough in it, from what I can make out, but they helped themselves to it. They must have thought the old fellow wouldn't put up much of a fight even if he did wake up. They were wrong about that,' he said with satisfaction. 'Simons wasn't too bad at all with the rheumatics that night, and he heard the hooligans. He knocked one of them down with a poker and gave another one a good clout with it before they got it off him. Must have been four or five of them, by all accounts.'

'Is he all right?' Amy asked anxiously.

'It was touch and go for a couple of days there. He couldn't speak till last night, that's the first chance I've had to get the full story out of him.

Doctor says he'll be all right now, though you wouldn't have thought so the other day. Those young thugs kicked him till he was black and blue, and he had a lump on his head the size of a duck's egg when Mrs Finch went in to do his bit of cleaning the next morning. He'd spent the night lying on the passage floor, and a powerful cold night it was, too. Mrs Finch thought it was a corpse she'd found. He's a tough old fellow, that one.'

'Poor Reverend Simons,' Amy said.

'That's all very well,' Charlie cut in, 'but what's it to do with us?'

'That's what I intend to find out,' Sergeant Riley said grimly. He turned back to Malcolm. 'Well, boy? What have you got to say for yourself?'

'I didn't—I wasn't—you don't—' For a few moments Malcolm could not manage a coherent sentence. 'I don't know nothing about it. I wasn't there. I didn't know anyone did that. And anyway, I wouldn't beat up some sick old man,' he finished on a defiant note.

That, at least, Amy was prepared to believe. Whatever other mischief Malcolm might be capable of, she had never seen any hint of bully in him. Malcolm was much more likely to take on an opponent far too strong for him, most notably his father, than to pick on a weak one.

'No?' Sergeant Riley said sceptically. 'It'd be the first piece of trouble you weren't mixed up in for a good while, lad.'

'You want to watch what you're saying, Riley,' Charlie said. 'My boy's never been near the minister's place. He'd never have had the chance, even if he was inclined to. I don't allow my boys out at night,' he finished on a self-satisfied note that made Amy cringe, given what she suspected would come next. 'I sometimes let the boy go out of a Saturday afternoon if he's done his work properly, but I keep my sons home of an evening.'

Sergeant Riley stared at Charlie in blank disbelief for a moment, then looked from Malcolm to his father in growing amusement.

'You young rascal,' he said, forgetting to look stern for the moment. 'Been pulling the wool over your father's eyes, eh?' He faced Charlie with a challenging air. 'Keep them home of an evening, do you? I tell you what, Stewart, if this son of yours has been staying home at night he must have a twin out there somewhere. I've boxed that boy's ears more times than you've had hot dinners when I've caught him playing up in town—given him a few good kicks in the backside, too. Begging your pardon, Ma'am,' he added, touching his hat in Amy's direction.

'What the hell are you talking about?' Charlie said, still bewildered rather than angry.

'I'm talking about this larrikin son of yours, you great fool. When there's a window broken, or stones thrown on someone's roof, or a fight in the street, Malcolm Stewart's never far away. And it can't have been more than a fortnight since I told him the next time I catch him doing furious riding in the town I'll put him in the lockup overnight.'

'He couldn't—I don't—' Charlie spluttered briefly, then subsided into silent confusion. He stared at Malcolm with his mouth hanging open in utter perplexity.

'Well, lad?' Sergeant Riley said, all amusement gone from his voice. 'You want to tell your father what you've been up to? What about that fight you were in last month outside the Royal, when someone said those ruffians from Tauranga had knocked around one of the wh... ah, one of the women from the hotel? Though it's not a fit story for a lady's ears, so you'd maybe better not tell it in front of your mother. And what about when I caught you jumping that horse of yours over my fence? Horse must be as mad as you are—that fence is damned near six feet high. He cleared it, too,' he added with grudging admiration. 'Only fell off trying to get back over it again. I took my belt off to him when I caught him—I bet you were pretty sore riding home after that.'

He snatched hold of Malcolm's ear, twisting it till the boy grimaced in pain. 'Now, tell your father and me what you've been up to. This isn't some bit of mischief I can sort out with a good kick, boy. This is jailing business—it'd be a hanging matter if the old fellow hadn't pulled through, you know. I want to know who else was with you.'

'I didn't,' Malcolm said, his face screwed up in anger as well as pain. 'I never went near there. I didn't!'

Amy felt her own anger rising. 'Mal wouldn't do something like that,' she protested. 'Why are you so sure it was him, anyway? Why don't you go and see those Feenan boys? I bet it was one of them.'

Sergeant Riley gave her a patronising look, loosing his hold on Malcolm's ear slightly as he did so. 'Of course a mother always takes her child's part, to be sure. But I can assure you, Mrs Stewart, your son's the sort of lad that trouble seems to follow wherever he goes.'

'That doesn't mean he attacked Reverend Simons,' Amy shot back. 'I don't believe Mal did that at all. I don't think he knows anything about it. It was those Feenans, I'm sure it was.'

'And I'll be going to their place next if I get no satisfaction here,' Sergeant Riley said. Amy detected a trace of reluctance at the idea of entering the Feenan's den. 'I wanted to see to the most likely culprit first.'

The most likely! Amy was lost for words at the notion that Malcolm was considered a more likely perpetrator of such deeds than any of the Feenans. She looked from Sergeant Riley, still holding Malcolm by the ear, to Charlie, where she saw fury slowly mounting as he digested the policeman's revelation of how Malcolm had been spending so many of his nights.

Vengeance was going to descend on Malcolm from at least one direction, but she was determined to make sure that it would not be an unjust vengeance. Malcolm was not guilty of the attack on Reverend Simons; of that she was certain. Now, how was she to convince Sergeant Riley?

Her mind racing, all her protective instincts roused to the task, she grasped at an idea.

'When did this happen?' she asked. 'When did they break into Reverend Simon's house?'

Sergeant Riley frowned. 'Mrs Stewart, I know it's all a terrible hard shock to you as a mother, but you're going to have to accept that your boy's a bad lot. Now, I'll tell you something that's going to come out at the trial—the minister told me last night about something that happened years back, that time he had a pack of larrikins throw stones on his roof and suchlike. He should have told me back then, and I've an idea he didn't mean to let it slip last night, only with him being poorly he forgot himself.' He gave Amy an appraising look. 'I think the old fellow's got a soft spot for you, Ma'am.'

He paused a moment, as if for dramatic effect. 'He told me he caught sight of one boy in particular that other time. A boy with red hair.' He snatched a handful of Malcolm's hair and gave it a shake, jerking Malcolm's head. 'Not a lot of boys with red hair in this town, are there, Mrs Stewart?'

If he had hoped to shake Amy's assurance, he was doomed to disappointment. She had suspected Malcolm's involvement in the earlier incident for years; it did not make her any the more willing to believe he had attacked a helpless old man.

'When did it happen, Sergeant Riley?'

He scowled at her persistence. 'Tuesday night, it was, if you're going to make such a fuss over knowing.'

'Tuesday!' Amy said triumphantly. 'Then it wasn't Mal, it wasn't! Charlie, it wasn't Mal. Charlie!' She had to raise her voice to rouse him from his stupefaction. 'Tuesday was the night we had that bad storm, remember?'

'A bit of bad weather doesn't keep the larrikins off the street, Mrs Stewart,' Sergeant Riley put in, but she ignored him.

'We lost all those shingles, remember?' she hurried on. 'And you woke up with the rain coming in on your face. You and the boys had to get on the roof to fix it, and I was holding one of the lanterns so you could see your way up the ladder. You and the boys, Charlie! You had them both out there—you were up and down the roof all night, on and off. Mal was here the whole time, you know he was. Tell Sergeant Riley—please, Charlie, tell him.'

Charlie shook himself slightly. 'Aye, she's right. The boy was here. He wasn't out of my sight for more than an hour at a stretch that night.'

'And you'd be willing to swear to that, would you?' Sergeant Riley asked.

'Aye, I'd swear it,' Charlie said heavily, his voice sounding distant. 'I'd swear it,' he said again, glowering at the policeman.

'I thought you would.' Sergeant Riley released his hold on Malcolm's hair with every sign of reluctance. Malcolm took a few steps backwards, rubbing his scalp and looking from his father to the policeman.

Sergeant Riley cleared his throat and drew himself up to his full height, which brought his head almost to the same level as Charlie's. 'Now, it seems your boy wasn't in on this, Stewart, but I'll give you a word of advice.'

'I don't want your bloody advice,' Charlie muttered.

'I'm giving it to you anyway. It's men like you that make my job harder, you know. Here's this boy of yours into every bit of mischief he can sniff out, and you not knowing where he is of an evening. It's a disgrace, Stewart, and I don't mind telling you so. Letting your boys run wild like that—no good will come of it.'

Charlie's mouth worked, but he could find no words, not when he was so patently in the wrong. Amy watched his fists clenching and unclenching in impotent fury. She knew that the longer this went on, the worse it would be for Malcolm when the policeman finally left the family alone.

Sergeant Riley watched Charlie's reaction, a satisfied smile slowly spreading over his face. 'Now, I know you're feeling a fool over being caught out like this, Stewart, but it's better to find out where you've been going wrong now than later. Another year or two letting your son run wild, and he'll—'

'Sergeant Riley,' Amy cut in. 'I think you've said enough.'

'Begging your pardon, Ma'am, but it's your husband I was talking to, not you. Now, as I was saying—'

'My husband doesn't want to hear any more.' Charlie would not like her speaking out, she knew, but that was less of a risk than allowing

Sergeant Riley to work him up into an even worse temper. 'Hadn't you better be getting off to the Feenans'?' she asked. 'You wouldn't want whoever really did hurt Reverend Simons to go running off before you get the chance to arrest him, would you?'

Sergeant Riley gave her a disapproving glare, but Amy stood her ground and looked up into his scowling face. It was Sergeant Riley who dropped his gaze first.

'I can see you've got your hands full with this lot, Stewart,' the policeman said, letting his gaze rest on Malcolm then on Amy before giving Charlie a pitying look. 'I wish you luck with them.'

He glared once more at Malcolm. 'I'll be keeping an eye out for you, boy. It'll be more than a clip over the ear next time I see you up to no good.'

'No need for that,' Charlie said. 'You won't be seeing him.'

Sergeant Riley gave a grunt. He nodded distantly in Amy's direction, then stalked over to where he had tethered his horse. He was mounted and away before two minutes had passed, leaving the family staring after him in silence.

The deceptive peace did not last long. Charlie gave a shake of his head as though to clear his thoughts, then took a step towards Malcolm.

'Make a fool of me, will you, boy?' he said in a low growl. 'Running wild at night with me thinking you're in your bed. You little bugger!' He snatched hold of a handful of cloth at Malcolm's throat and shook him by it.

'He didn't hurt Reverend Simons,' Amy said. 'He didn't do that! Charlie, don't—'

Charlie turned on her. 'I don't care a damn about the bloody minister! I don't care if somebody slits the fool's throat. This little bugger,' he gave another shake, wrenching the handful of cloth upwards so that Malcolm had to stand on tiptoe, 'he's made a fool of me! You'll pay for that, boy.'

He released his hold, and Malcolm staggered backwards. The boy said nothing in his own defence; there was nothing he could say. He stared back at his father, waiting for what was to come with something approaching resignation.

Charlie's fist lashed out against the side of Malcolm's head, knocking him to the ground. Malcolm clambered to his knees, but made no attempt to rise. Charlie loomed over him, then caught sight of David, who stood transfixed with fear.

'And what about you, eh?' Charlie demanded, catching hold of David's arm and pulling the younger boy close. 'Have you been sneaking off behind my back, too? Well?'

'N-no,' David said in a frightened squeak that was barely audible.

'No, he hasn't,' Malcolm said, his first words for many minutes. 'Dave never comes out with me. Says he doesn't want to. Leave him alone.'

Charlie released David, and swung his arm in a heavy, back-handed slap across Malcolm's mouth, jerking the boy's head to one side. Malcolm raised his hand to his mouth. When he lowered it, Amy saw blood on his lip.

'Keep your mouth shut, boy,' Charlie snarled. 'You've shamed me, you know that? I've had to stand on my own land and listen to that bloody Irishman tell me how to bring up my own son! You've brought shame on the name of this family.'

And that was Malcolm's crime in his father's eyes, Amy knew; not the misdeeds the policeman had spoken of, but exposing his father to Sergeant Riley's thinly veiled contempt. 'Charlie, please—' she tried.

'Shut your mouth, bitch, or I'll shut it for you. This is your doing. It's your bad blood coming out in the boy.'

Amy's stunned reaction seemed to give Charlie some satisfaction. 'Aye, it's your ma's bad blood coming out in you,' he said, turning on Malcolm again. 'Teaching you to bring shame on an honourable name. I'll beat it out of you, boy. I'll beat it out of you if I have to kill you to do it.'

He took hold of Malcolm's arm and half-dragged the stumbling boy after him. Amy turned away from the sight, but she could not drown out the screams that soon assailed her ears; the sound of Charlie avenging his own bruised pride on his son's flesh.

Malcolm got a beating that left him incapable of walking for a day, then unable to sit down without grimacing in pain for almost a week. It had been inevitable that Charlie would eventually find out about the boy's delinquency; perhaps, Amy hoped, it could all be forgotten now.

But she had reckoned without the strength of Charlie's outrage. The wound to his pride had gone deep, and left a smouldering resentment that refused to cool. Charlie's face was habitually stern, but now it seemed constantly set in ominous lines. Sometimes of an evening he might appear to forget his grievance, particularly after the boys had gone to bed and he could bury himself in a newspaper, but a visit to town, or to the dairy factory, was almost guaranteed to bring him home flushed with renewed anger and eager to take it out on someone.

The other men must be teasing him, she soon realised. It seemed that Sergeant Riley had lost no time letting it be known around Ruatane how laughably ignorant of his son's doings Charlie had been, and the men were taking full advantage of what must have been the best joke they had heard in years. Over the weeks that followed, Amy often wished she could have a few moments alone with some of those men and tell them just how much trouble their little jokes were causing.

'I'll show you who rules in this house,' Charlie had thundered at his silent audience the morning after Sergeant Riley's revelations, and his first attempt to prove his authority was to ban Amy and the boys from leaving the farm for any reason. Churchgoing ceased; Charlie went to the store by himself; and, worst of all in Amy's eyes, she was forbidden to visit her family.

But it was not as simple as Charlie had thought to keep Amy in seclusion. When they noticed her absence, her brothers simply came to see her more often. They both probed her as to whether Charlie was ill-treating her, and John openly checked her face for any telltale bruises despite Amy's assurances that Charlie had not touched her.

'He's grumpy about Mal, that's all,' she told them. 'I'll come and visit again soon, but it's no use me asking him just now.'

Irritating as Charlie might find John's and Harry's increasingly frequent visits, he could usually manage to make himself scarce as soon as one or both of them appeared. But after a week of Amy's enforced isolation, another visitor began paying calls that Charlie found much harder to ignore.

Lizzie had no intention of losing all contact with Amy just because she was tied to the house by a tiny baby. As soon as she realised that Amy did not seem to be coming to see her any more, she despatched Frank to check up on her. After that first visit, while Charlie's interdiction lasted Frank duly appeared twice a week to see that all was well.

He and Amy would sit in the kitchen perched stiffly on their chairs, Amy careful to keep the table between them, making awkward attempts at conversation while Charlie hovered in a corner like a disapproving maiden aunt pressed into duty as chaperone. It would have been difficult to say which of the three of them found Frank's visits the most unpleasant, but it was Charlie who gave in first.

'Time you went visiting Kelly's wife,' he said after he had kept Amy confined to the house for close to a month. 'I'm fed up with that silly bugger hanging around here.'

Soon after that, Charlie began taking his family to church again, as well as occasionally letting them come with him to the store, though the boys were still banned from leaving the farm except under their father's supervision; even going next door to visit their cousins was outlawed.

Amy had thought that the easing of Charlie's restrictions on her own movements might mean his mood was softening at last, but she soon found she was wrong. Charlie clung tenaciously to his sense of grievance. He had never been easy to live with; now he had become almost unbearable.

To Amy it meant being snarled at and abused more often and with more venom than she had become used to, but that was no great trial to bear. She wished he would not use such language in front of the boys, but he did not use any words they had not heard dozens of times before from him.

David felt his father's heavy hand more than usual. In Charlie's current mood, any perceived slowness to do as he was told, or the slightest imperfection, real or imagined, in the way the boy did his work, was liable to earn him a slap across the head.

But it was Malcolm who was the real target of his father's ire. Charlie would not leave the boy in peace; much of the time he seemed almost deliberately to be goading Malcolm into earning himself another beating. Whether they were working together or merely sitting in the same room, Charlie would constantly berate the boy. If Malcolm answered back in his own defence, as often as not he got a blow that knocked him to the ground.

Malcolm would have had even more of such treatment had he not displayed a level of self-control that at first astonished Amy. But as she anxiously watched his dealings with his father, she became aware of the brooding resentment growing in him. The boy might be saying little, but his feelings were running a deep and increasingly bitter course.

She watched and fretted, painfully aware of her powerlessness to do anything to influence either of them. It was only a matter of time before Malcolm and Charlie had a nastier falling-out; and all Amy could do was watch and wait.

When it came, the day she had been dreading seemed at first no different from any other. Over breakfast Charlie took exception to Malcolm's surly expression and gave the boy a clout across the head, but that was no great novelty.

The trouble began soon after Charlie returned from a visit to town that had taken up much of the middle of the day. He had decided to go shopping by himself; when she smelt the beer on him Amy knew he had spent more time at the hotel than in the store. He had forgotten most of the things she had asked him to buy.

'You boys fed out the hay yet?' Charlie asked as he sat having a much-delayed afternoon tea. Amy saw the boys exchange glances, as if daring each other to be the one to answer. Malcolm gave a quick shake of his head.

'You told them to wait till you came home, Charlie,' Amy put in quietly.

'Useless pair of brats,' he grumbled through a mouthful of scone. 'Can't trust you to do anything.' He pointed an accusing finger at Malcolm. 'I can't trust *you* out of my sight, boy. You've brought shame on this family, you know that?'

'Would you like another scone?' Amy asked, putting one on his plate without waiting for an answer.

'It's a fine thing when a man can't have a quiet drink without some clever bastard asking me if I know where my son is. That's a bloody fine thing, isn't it?' Charlie glared at the three of them in turn before shifting his attention to the new scone.

Amy passed one to Malcolm, giving his hand a surreptitious pat of encouragement as she did so. Malcolm jerked away from her, the movement knocking the scone onto the table. He snatched it up, but not before it had left a small trace of jam on the cloth.

'Watch out, you useless bugger,' Charlie growled. 'Don't go chucking your food all over the table.'

'It doesn't matter,' Amy said. 'It's only a little bit of jam, it'll wipe off.'

'I can't trust you to do anything, can I?' Charlie said, warming to his theme. 'You can't even eat your food without making a mess of it. What's wrong with you, boy?'

Malcolm stared down at his lap and said nothing.

'Didn't you hear me?' Charlie said, his voice close to a shout. 'I asked you a question, boy. What's wrong with you?'

The boy raised his eyes for a moment to glare back at his father, then dropped his gaze again. 'Nothing,' he muttered.

'Nothing! Nothing! You're a disgrace to me, you know that? You're a bloody disgrace!' Charlie thumped on the table to emphasise his point. His hand came down so hard that his tea cup shook, splashing tea into the saucer and from there onto the table cloth.

The brown stain on the cloth only served to make Charlie angrier. 'Now look what you made me do, you little bugger!'

'I'll pour you a fresh cup,' Amy said, reaching for the half-empty one. 'That one must've been getting cold, anyway.' She was about to grasp the cup when Charlie half rose in his chair, leaned across the table and gave Malcolm a blow on the side of his head.

Malcolm snatched at the cloth in a frantic attempt to catch his balance, the force of the blow almost knocking him from his chair. The plate holding the remaining scones flipped its contents jam side down onto the table. At the same time four tea cups tipped over, one of them rolling off the edge of the table and crashing to the floor.

Charlie looked at the ruin of Amy's neatly-set tea table in silence for a few moments. When he opened his mouth she expected a fresh tirade, but all he said was, 'What a bloody mess.'

Amy began picking up broken china and mopping away the worst of the devastation. Charlie might have meant the table and the floor around it, swimming in tea and soggy scones, or his family; either would fit just as well. 'It doesn't matter,' she said. 'I'll clean it up.'

Charlie stood, and walked a few steps across the room. 'Get outside and get that sled loaded up with hay,' he told the boys, his back to them as he spoke. 'Make yourselves useful for once.'

Malcolm had his hand clutched to his head where Charlie's blow had fallen, his face screwed up in pain. He lowered his hand and stared at his father with a venom that sent a cold stab of fear through Amy. For a long moment she thought he was about to spit abuse at Charlie. But David tugged at his sleeve and Malcolm seemed to think better of it. The two boys went outside without a word.

Charlie lifted a bottle of whisky from a high shelf, took a long swallow from it and wiped his mouth on his sleeve. 'Bloody kid,' Amy heard him mutter.

'You could let the boys feed out by themselves, Charlie,' she said quietly. She did not want his company around the house, but even less did she want her boys forced to spend the rest of the afternoon with him in his current mood.

He took another swig before putting the bottle away again. 'I don't want to let that boy out of my sight any more than I have to. Don't want him bringing more shame on me.'

Amy bit back the urge to ask what shame Malcolm could bring while feeding hay to cows. When Charlie had gone outside she stood in the doorway and watched until he was out of sight, the sense of impending disaster growing as she remembered the look she had seen on Malcolm's face.

The short days of winter meant the sun was already close to the top of the hills when Charlie returned to the house. He came rather later than Amy had expected, and he came alone.

'Where are the boys, Charlie?' Amy asked, setting out their dinner plates. There was no immediate answer. When she looked up at his face she saw a small trail of blood running from the corner of his mouth down into his beard. Her stomach twisted with a sick fear.

Charlie sat down heavily at the table. 'He's got to learn. He's got to learn not to cross me.'

Amy closed her eyes for a moment as she struggled for calm. 'Where are the boys?' she repeated. 'What's happened?'

Charlie thumped his fist on the table. 'The boy took a swing at me, that's what happened! He did that one other time—I warned him then he'd better not try it again.' He fingered his cut lip gingerly. 'The little bugger took a swing at me,' he muttered.

'And what did you do to him?' Amy asked, her voice tight with fear and barely-concealed anger. A saint would have had difficulty putting up with the treatment Charlie had been giving his son lately; and Malcolm was no saint.

'Taught him a lesson he'll not be forgetting in a hurry. He'll not be trying that trick again. And don't you go giving me your hoity-toity looks, either, woman. I gave the boy a good hiding, that's all. You get a move on with my dinner or you'll maybe be getting one yourself.'

Amy's instincts told her to ignore his bluster, to rush out of the house and go looking for the boys, but she fought the urge for long enough to dish Charlie's dinner up and place it in front of him.

She heard rapidly approaching footsteps, and was halfway to the back door when David came in, his face taut with fear and a large, red mark cutting a slash across his cheek.

'Ma, I think there's something wrong with Mal,' he blurted out, panting a little from his run. 'He won't get up, and he's making funny noises.'

'Bawling, is he?' Charlie said. 'That'll teach him. Let that be a lesson to you, too, boy—you'll get the same if you cross me.'

But David did not mean his brother was sobbing; Amy could see that clearly enough. 'Show me where he is, Dave,' she said. She sat on the doorstep to pull on her boots, then hurried off with David, doing her best to keep up with his long-legged trot as he led her down the hill from the house and across two paddocks.

Malcolm was slumped forward on the ground, his head on one arm and his other arm flung out to the side. Amy crouched beside him. Her stomach heaved when she saw the sticky mass of blood that covered his face, oozing out of the swollen, pulpy mess that she knew to be his nose only from its position. A bubbling sound interspersed with odd little choking coughs came from his mouth. She would have vomited on the spot if she had had time for such luxuries.

'He's choking on the blood.' She lifted Malcolm's head as gently as she could and slid her fingers into his mouth, reaching around inside to be sure she was clearing it properly. She pulled out a handful of mucus and half-congealed blood, and Malcolm took a great gulp of air, followed by a brief fit of coughing that set a fresh burst flowing from his nose.

Amy laid his head in her lap and stroked his hair with her clean hand, smoothing down the red tufts Charlie's rough attempts at barbering produced, while Malcolm's breathing gradually steadied. He gave little sobs of pain with each breath, but the hideous bubbling sound had faded into something closer to human. 'Oh, Mal,' she murmured as she cradled his head. 'My poor Mal.'

'He's going to be all right, isn't he, Ma?' David asked, his eyes wide and staring.

Amy gave a deep sigh. 'I think so, Davie. Not for a while, though. And he's not going to look the same as he used to, either. Your pa must've hit him really hard this time. What happened?'

'He was wild—I've never seen Pa that bad. He was going on at Mal, all that stuff about shame on the family and everything. Well, he just went on and on, and Mal got fed up with it—I would've, too. He told Pa to shut up, and Pa gave him a clout—he knocked Mal down, then he went over and got his stick. Then Mal got up and started yelling and screaming, and he sort of threw himself at Pa, and he gave Pa a couple of really good punches.'

'Not as good as the ones he got back, though.'

'No. Pa just stood still for a bit, like he didn't know what'd happened, then he started hitting Mal.' David's face clouded. 'I thought he'd sort of gone mad, Ma. He hit Mal and knocked him down, then he picked him up and hit him again, and he just went on and on. He didn't say anything, just hit him. I tried stopping him, honest I did—I yanked on his arm and yelled at him to leave Mal alone, but I couldn't make him stop.'

'Is that how you got that?' Amy asked, pointing to the red weal across David's cheek.

David fingered the mark as if registering its presence for the first time. 'It must've been. Yes, that's right, he gave me a crack with the stick when I grabbed his arm. Then he carried on hitting Mal.'

Malcolm gave a groan and moved his head a little, trying to raise it, then lay still again. Amy stroked his forehead. 'Listen, Mal. I'm going to take you up to the house and put you to bed now—you'll have to help me, Dave, we'll just about have to carry him. We'll try not to hurt you, but… well, I don't think we'll be able to help hurting you a bit. We'll be as quick as we can.'

She and David each slipped an arm under Malcolm's shoulders and hoisted him upright. He gave a short scream, the sound bubbling out through his blood, but he made no attempt to resist. He stumbled along between them, Amy and David taking as much of his weight as they could. David had to stoop as he walked to try and match his level more closely to Amy's, as well as shortening his stride, as they carried their awkward burden back to the house, up the front steps and into the boys' bedroom.

Amy put both pillows lengthwise on the mattress and they eased Malcolm onto the bed, his body leaning against the pillows.

'I'll get him something for the pain,' she said as soon as they had settled him. 'I don't want to try cleaning up his face before I've put him to sleep. Hold him still, Dave, I don't want him to hurt himself.'

She hurried through the parlour and into the kitchen. Charlie looked up from his plate as she came in.

'You've taken your time. I'll have my pudding now.'

'It's on the range. You'll have to get it yourself,' Amy said. She dragged a chair over to the high shelf she kept medicines on and lifted down the laudanum bottle, realising as she did so that she was the only person in the house not tall enough to reach the shelf merely by standing on tiptoe; she had always been careful to keep medicines out of the boys' reach when they were small, and the habit had stuck.

'What the hell's got into you? You watch your tongue, woman—have to get it myself, will I?'

'Yes, you will.' Amy did not look at him as she spoke; she was too busy getting together a bowl of water and some clean rags, as well as a spoon for the laudanum. When she had the things assembled, she paused for a moment and glared back at Charlie. 'Do you know what you've done to Mal?'

'Gave him a hiding, that's all. There's no need for you to be carrying on with a load of nonsense. He's got to learn that—'

She cut in before he could get into full flow. 'Charlie, you've broken his nose. You might think that's teaching him a lesson. I think it's… well, never mind what I think. I doubt if you're very interested in that.'

'I've not done any such thing! I've maybe given the boy a bleeding nose, and that's no more than he was asking for, but I—'

'You've broken his nose,' Amy repeated doggedly. 'I know what it looks like, I remember a boy at school got his nose broken once. It wasn't his father that did it to him, though,' she added bitterly. 'I'm going to patch him up as well as I can, and you're going to have to dish up your own pudding for once.' She left the room without waiting for a reply.

It was difficult to get Malcolm to swallow the laudanum, but she managed to get as large a dose as she dared into him, though she spilt half as much again before she had finished. While she was waiting for the drug to take effect she noticed for the first time traces of blood on the back of his shirt.

'What's this from, Dave?' she asked, her fingers brushing against the marks. Even her soft touch was enough to make Malcolm groan afresh.

'That was after Pa knocked him down. He started belting him with the stick. I tried to stop him then, too, Ma—he said he'd give me the same when he finished with Mal, 'cause he was wild at me for butting in. But he...' David looked at the red marks and swallowed audibly. 'He broke the stick on Mal. Suppose he'll cut a fresh one for me tomorrow.'

Amy bit back the words that sprang to her lips. She did her best to avoid criticising Charlie to his sons; it had never been more difficult. *Couldn't you have done one thing or the other, Charlie? Punch him or belt him, but not both.* 'He might forget about you before tomorrow,' she said when she could trust her voice again. 'Look, Mal's gone to sleep now. You hold his head still for me while I wash his face.'

They were soon too busy tending Malcolm to exchange more than an occasional word. Slowly and carefully Amy washed away the blood and mucus until she could see the battered mess that remained of his nose. She shuddered as she handled the mangled flesh, painfully aware of her lack of skill in what she was attempting.

She knelt beside the bed and moved her fingers delicately over Malcolm's face, moulding the nose into something as close to its original shape as she could manage, trying to tell herself that the work was not so very different from a complicated piece of embroidery. She felt small pieces of bone under her fingers and gently pressed them into what she thought must be their proper positions, stopping to mop up blood whenever it began oozing again.

When she had done as much as she could, she wadded clean strips of bandage around her handiwork to hold it in place, then sank back on her heels and took a deep, shuddering breath. Her fingers felt cramped after the long minutes of painstaking work; she flexed them tentatively.

'Well, that's the best I can do,' she said, her voice shaking with weariness. 'Dave, do you think you can get his boots off without moving the rest of him? I don't think I can manage just now.'

David did the job as carefully as she would have herself. By the time he had finished she felt strong enough to go back to the kitchen and fetch them both something to eat; she did not feel particularly hungry after the gruesome work, but she would need her strength for the night ahead.

Charlie was in the parlour, pretending to be engrossed in his newspaper; he looked up as she passed through, but did not speak.

She and David ate sitting on the floor with their backs against the wall, Amy keeping a close eye on Malcolm for any sign that the laudanum might be wearing off. She had lit the lamp on the boys' chest of drawers, and the light fell across Malcolm's head, accentuating the brightness of his hair and the white bandages that stood out starkly against his bruised flesh.

'You'd better sleep in my bed tonight, Dave,' she told him when they had finished eating. 'I'll be sitting up with Mal.'

'I'll sit with you, Ma,' David offered. 'I'll keep you company.'

She squeezed his arm. 'No, you'd better not. You're going to need your sleep. You'll have to help your pa by yourself until Mal's better, you know—you don't want to be slow and start annoying him.'

David gave her a look full of trepidation at the thought. She sent him off with his nightshirt tucked under his arm, and began her next task. She unbuttoned Malcolm's trousers and untucked his shirt and vest, wincing when she had to pull the cloth away from the stripes of dried blood marking the track of Charlie's stick, but Malcolm was too deeply unconscious to show any sign of feeling.

Amy was still engrossed in washing Malcolm's back and buttocks when she heard a step too heavy to be David's. The bedroom door opened.

'Close the door, Charlie, the wind's cold tonight,' she said, not raising her eyes from her task. 'I don't want Mal getting a chill on top of everything else.'

She heard the door pushed to, and looked over her shoulder to see that Charlie had taken a step towards the bed. He stood there awkwardly, as if unsure whether to come closer or retreat.

'How is it with him?' he asked, his voice gruff.

Amy said nothing until she had finished her washing. She stood up and pressed her hands against her back, aching from the time spent crouching over Malcolm.

'I don't know. I've done the best I can to patch him up, but I'm no nurse. I'd like the doctor to see him.'

Charlie stared at her as if she had gone mad. 'And have that bloody quack telling me how I should be bringing up my son? It's bad enough every other fool in this town passing remarks. I don't go running for the doctor every time I give the boy a good hiding!'

'You don't usually break his nose,' Amy snapped, her nerves stretched too taut for caution. 'Well, if you won't go I can't make you. You might as well go to bed, then. I'd be obliged if you try not to make too much noise when you get up tomorrow, the laudanum might be wearing off a bit by then.'

Charlie took a step closer. 'I didn't think I'd hit him as hard as all that,' he said, staring down at the unconscious figure with its hideously swollen face.

'You're a strong man, Charlie. I should know that, of all people. At least you didn't knock any of his teeth out. That's something, I suppose.'

'He shouldn't have driven me to it!' There was an edge to Charlie's voice that gave the lie to his bluster. 'It wouldn't have happened if he'd behaved himself. He's got to learn.'

Amy looked at him without speaking, and he turned aside from her steady gaze. 'What am I meant to do?' he demanded as if she had voiced a criticism. 'Let my son take a swing at me and do nothing about it?'

'He won't be taking swings at anyone for a while. Does that make you happy?'

'He's got to learn!' Charlie repeated, a hunted look on his face. 'He's got to do as he's told. When I was his age my father would have—'

'When you were his age, your father was dead,' Amy cut in.

He frowned in mingled suspicion and puzzlement. 'What's that supposed to mean?'

Amy turned her back on him and leaned down to check Malcolm's breathing. 'It means I don't think you really remember how you felt about things when you were Mal's age. It doesn't matter, though, does it? I'm too stupid to have anything sensible to say about it.'

She tucked the blankets more snugly around Malcolm's still form and frowned down at him, wondering if he would be warm enough. 'I'd better get in with him,' she murmured.

'You're going to stay with him all night?' Charlie asked.

'Of course I am. I could hardly leave him by himself in this state, could I?'

She smoothed the blankets, fussing unnecessarily over the task but reluctant to start undressing while Charlie stood there. He opened the door, and lingered in the doorway for an awkward few moments before blurting out,

'If he's taken poorly in the night... if you think it's needful... come and wake me. I'll fetch the doctor.'

'All right,' Amy said shortly. 'I won't trouble you unless he gets worse.'

She waited until the door was shut, then put out the lamp, slipped off her outer clothes and climbed under the covers to hold Malcolm close all through the long, sleepless night.

Amy hovered over Malcolm, unwilling to let him out of her sight for more than a few minutes at a time until she was sure he was recovering. It was many nights before she dared leave him alone and return to the comfort of her own bed.

But Malcolm had the strength of a healthy fifteen-year-old to draw on, and his body healed more rapidly than she had dared hope. The swelling on his face turned to bruising in a hideous range of colours, then gradually faded until all that was left to show what had happened was his misshapen nose, flattened below the bridge and with a pronounced tilt to one side that Amy knew would be permanent.

She kept him drowsy with laudanum, to shield him from pain but also to put off the time when he and his father would have to face each other again. Even when she allowed him to regain full consciousness, for days afterwards Malcolm lay on the bed in a silence that seemed unnatural. If she spoke to him he did not reply, but she saw the traces of brooding thoughts in his eyes.

There was no mirror in the boys' room, so it was only when Malcolm was at last well enough to take his first tentative steps, leaning heavily on Amy's arm, that he had the chance to catch sight of his face in the mirror that hung over the fireplace. He stood stock still and stared at himself for a long moment.

'I'm sorry, Mal,' Amy murmured. Malcolm's mouth twisted, and he turned his back on the image.

Amy knew that Charlie had been shaken by the extent of the injuries he had inflicted. Once or twice while Malcolm was still regaining his strength, she thought she saw Charlie's hand tense to slap the boy, and felt her stomach tighten with apprehension. Each time he seemed to think better of it, but Amy did not trust his forbearance to last.

And when she watched Malcolm stare at his father, a chill came over her. He barely spoke to Charlie, rarely bothering even to answer direct questions, but the look in his eyes was something darker than Amy had ever seen there. Deep pools of resentment welled up in those eyes; a brooding sense of injury that showed no sign of healing. No forgiveness was asked for by Charlie; certainly none would be given. Malcolm did not speak his feelings aloud, but Amy could read them in his face.

The first hint of spring was in the air and Charlie had gone into town to settle his account at the store the day Amy found Malcolm putting the bridle on his horse.

'Mal, don't,' she begged. 'Please don't go out. You know your father said—'

'He won't know,' Malcolm cut in. 'You're not going to tell him. Anyway, I don't care what the old bugger says. I'm going out to see my mates.'

'Please, Mal. I don't want him to hurt you again.'

Malcolm carried on adjusting the buckles on the bridle as if he had not heard, but she saw his mouth tighten. When he mounted she put a hesitant hand on the horse's neck in a last, silent appeal, but Malcolm knocked her hand aside and kicked the horse into a trot.

For all his brave words, Malcolm was careful to be home well before his father. He walked with a swagger as he came into the house, attracted by the scent of the freshly-baked biscuits Amy had ready for him.

Malcolm pulled a chair out from the table and flopped into it. His jacket fell open as he slouched against the chair back, revealing the worn leather belt fastened around his trousers.

And revealing something else. Amy leaned across to put a plate of biscuits in front of him, and the plate slipped from her hand to thud heavily onto the table.

'What's that on your belt?' she asked, staring in horror at the grubby handle protruding from a leather sheath.

'This?' Malcolm took hold of the handle and pulled out a long, wicked-looking knife. 'It's my new knife. It's a beauty, isn't it?'

'Where did you get it?'

'Des gave it to me. He said it used to be Liam's. Liam left his knives behind when they took him off to jail. Des reckons the one he's got's even better than this one, but I like mine best.'

He ran his fingers lightly up and down the blade with its nicks and scratches, his touch almost a caress.

'Mal, I... I don't want you having that,' Amy said, her voice trembling. 'You don't need a knife. It's a dangerous thing—an evil thing.'

'Mind your own business,' Malcolm said. 'Silly bitch,' he added in a voice so reminiscent of his father's that Amy briefly closed her eyes against the pain it gave her.

He held the knife up in the air, turning it this way and that to catch the light. 'It's good having a knife,' he said. For a moment Amy thought she saw a glitter from the blade reflected in Malcolm's eyes. 'People don't give you any trouble if you've got a decent knife. Or if they try it, you just sort them out.' He patted the blade against his hand in a slow, rhythmic thud.

15

September 1901 – May 1902

Amy passed each day in a kind of waking nightmare, rushing blindly from one task to the next, never allowing herself to relax her vigilance. Seeing Charlie and Malcolm together made her feel sick with fear, but if they were together and out of her sight it was even worse. At least if she could see them she could judge their moods; see for herself if either of them was showing signs of an anger that might be lethal.

She had witnessed many skirmishes between Charlie and Malcolm over the years, but now she was sure there would only ever be one more fight between them. It would have to be the last, because at the end of it one of them would be dead, with that horrible knife of Malcolm's plunged into his body.

That knife. It dominated her thoughts all day and much of the night, now that she could no longer sleep soundly for the fears plaguing her. Malcolm wore it constantly, only leaving it at home when the family went to church. When Charlie was around Malcolm left it undisturbed on his belt, but often when his father was absent Malcolm would take the knife out while he sat at the table and finger it lovingly, polishing it against the cloth of his trousers.

Charlie was still stronger than Malcolm, though they were becoming more evenly matched as the years began to tell more heavily on Charlie and Malcolm grew towards his full strength. Perhaps Charlie would be able to wrench the knife off Malcolm and turn it against his son in lethal self-defence. Or perhaps Malcolm would thrust it between his father's ribs and revenge all the beatings he had ever had, then find himself on trial as a murderer.

Both prospects were horrifying, and Amy threw herself into the task of preventing that last, fateful fight. It was no use trying to talk to either husband or son; an utter lack of respect for her was one of the many characteristics they shared. All she could do was try to keep them both as even-tempered as she was capable of. She devoted all her energies to that duty, knowing all the while that she was only putting off the evil day, not preventing it.

She tried to avoid even the smallest failings that might rouse Charlie's temper. Meals had always been driven by his fussy appetite; now she was careful to prepare only the foods she knew to be his favourites. She returned to the habit she had picked up in the fear-filled first weeks of her marriage of having Charlie's plate loaded and ready to place in front of him the moment he walked in the door at mealtimes. She made his bed and folded his clothes with more than her usual fastidiousness, and tried to anticipate any small tasks he wanted done before he had the chance to ask for them, whether it was fetching his newspaper, buttering a piece of bread, or pouring him a mug of beer.

Amy took to carrying morning and afternoon teas down to wherever Charlie and the boys might be working. She did it because she could not bear to have them out of her sight for long, but even more because she wanted to make sure Charlie did not drive himself too hard with the heavier chores and work himself into a temper. At least she could see that he stopped every two hours or so and ate a generous helping of the cakes and biscuits that he liked best.

So desperate was she to try and sweeten Charlie's temper that Amy gave long, hard consideration to the idea of offering to return to his bed. It was agonisingly difficult to overcome the revulsion that welled up as she pictured such a return; all but impossible to think coolly about what she would be sacrificing.

To return to that bed, with all its memories of pain and degradation. He would climb on her and hurt her, then beat her when she did not please him. That would not stop him from getting her with child; her fruitfulness would betray her within weeks. She would soon find herself constantly ill and wretched again, just as she had been during those years when miscarriages had come every few months, draining away her health and strength with each outflow of thick, clotted blood.

And for what? Would she be helping Malcolm by giving up the sanctuary of her own little bedroom? When Amy got beyond the sick horror of the picture and forced herself to think dispassionately, she knew it would be worse than useless. She had never made Charlie happy when she did share his bed; he had always seemed to get more frustration than pleasure out of her. Cool logic agreed with her instinctive reaction: she would be better off leaving Charlie to take whatever pleasure he got out of his occasional visits to the whores, while she did her best to please him by running his house as well as she possibly could.

It wasn't enough. Even as she rushed around doing the extra work she so desperately hoped might avoid the impending disaster, she knew that all she was doing was delaying it. Sooner or later Charlie would become irritated with Malcolm again and would try to give him a beating. And that would be the end.

There was no question of Amy's leaving the farm when Charlie and

226

Malcolm were both home, not when it would have meant leaving the two of them alone together. But when she realised one day in early November that she had not seen Lizzie for weeks, she knew she would have to get permission to pay her cousin a visit the next time Charlie went out.

Much as she loved Lizzie, it was not the desire for her company that saw Amy set off down the road soon after Charlie had left on a trip to town. If she let too much time go by without seeing Lizzie, Frank would be despatched to check up on her, and a visit from Frank was guaranteed to put Charlie into a sour temper.

The familiar walk seemed much more of a chore than usual. By the time Amy turned off the main track to walk up to Frank's house she was puffing with exertion. When she hit her foot against an unexpectedly large stone and stumbled, nearly dropping the plate of biscuits she carried, she realised that she was almost running. It took an effort of will to make herself slow to a steady walk. She seemed to be doing everything at a frenetic pace lately, driven by fear and by the urgent necessity to meet everyone's wants.

She saw Frank a paddock away, walking behind the plough while Joey and the two younger boys followed after him, dropping seed potatoes into the furrow as it was opened up. Frank waved, then passed the reins over to Joey and started across the paddock towards her at an easy lope.

Amy stood and waited for Frank to join her, feeling even more edgy at the forced inactivity. She wanted to get this visit over with; to put on as bright a face as she could to reassure Lizzie, then get back to the house well before Charlie was likely to return.

Frank climbed over the fence between them. 'It's good to see you, Amy. Lizzie'll be pleased you've come, she was saying just the other day you hadn't been down for a while.'

'I haven't been able to get away lately—I can't stay long today, either.'

'No? Never mind, you can stay for a cup of tea, can't you?'

'Just a quick one, yes.'

'That's good. I'll come up with you, it's a good excuse for me to knock off for a bit. Here, I'll carry that for you.'

He took the plate from Amy, and they walked towards the house together. 'Better not leave the kids at it by themselves too long, it's pretty hard work on the plough,' Frank said, glancing back towards the boys. 'It's good for Joey to have a go at it by himself, though. He doesn't need his old man breathing down his neck all the time.'

Frank smiled as he looked over his shoulder at the children. 'He's a real help to me, that boy. I was telling him just the other day he's my right-hand man.'

Amy studied the look of contentment on Frank's face and tried not to feel envious. 'It's nice the way you and Joey are friends,' she said.

'Mmm? Yes, I suppose we are. He's my best mate, really, Joey is. Except Lizzie, of course.' Frank's smile broadened. 'That's a bit different, though.'

They came to a paddock where a huddle of golden brown calves trotted up to the fence to watch them pass. 'Have you seen my new calves?' Frank asked. 'We've got a really good lot this year—one or two champions there, I hope. See the one over the back with the white mark on her nose?'

He talked on animatedly, but the words did not reach Amy. Through the sound of Frank's voice, quiet though full of enthusiasm, her own thoughts jarred discordantly.

I used to wish Mal and Charlie could be friends. I used to think maybe they would, like Frank is with Joey. Now I just wish they won't kill each other.

'Don't you think so?' Frank fell silent, and Amy realised he had asked her a question.

'What? I'm sorry, Frank, I didn't hear you. What did you say?'

Frank gave her a rueful grin. 'Never mind, it doesn't matter. I'm just going on about my cows again, take no notice. Lizzie says I—'

A shrill voice interrupted him. 'Papa, Papa!' Amy looked over at the house, now only a few yards away, to see the small figure of Rosie running towards them as fast as her plump little legs would carry her. She cannoned into Frank and began tugging at his trouser leg. 'Up, Papa,' she demanded. 'Pick me up.'

'You come back here, Rosie!' Maudie stood in the doorway with her hands on her hips, looking sternly at her little sister. 'Don't you go running off like that—and you with one of your chests, too. You know Ma said you should stay inside.'

'She's all right, love,' Frank called back. 'We'll bring her in. Hey, stop it, Rosie.' He made a feeble attempt to fend off the sturdy four-year-old, who was trying to climb his leg as if it were a tree. 'I'll drop Aunt Amy's cakes.'

Amy retrieved her plate from Frank's precarious grasp. 'I've got them. Pick her up, Frank, she's desperate for you to.'

'Come on, then, monster.' Frank bent down for Rosie to fling herself into his arms. She clung around his neck and pressed her face against his chest as he stood upright, his hands making a seat for her. 'Gee, you're getting heavy, love.' Rosie beamed, and clung on all the more tightly.

'She's got a bit silly like this since Kate came along,' Frank said, giving

228

the little girl a squeeze. 'Wants cuddling all the time, and Lizzie's been busy with the baby. This one gets a bit jealous. You'll find Kate's grown since you saw her last, Lizzie says she'll be crawling in a few weeks. She never seems to stop feeding, Kate doesn't.'

The baby was behaving true to form. When Amy walked ahead of Frank into the kitchen, to be relieved of her plate and greeted with kisses by Maudie and Beth, she found Lizzie sitting at the table nursing Kate. Lizzie told Amy where to sit down, exclaimed over the length of time since her last visit, admonished her not to leave it so long before the next one, promised to let her hold Kate when the baby finished feeding, and told Maudie to put the kettle on. She paused for breath, and to change the baby to her other breast.

'Don't make a pot specially for me, Lizzie,' Amy said, anxious at the thought of how long it might take the full kettle to come to the boil. 'I can't stay long.'

'Oh, you've got time for a cuppa. Anyway, you'll want a cuddle of Kate before you go. Beth, help Aunt Amy off with her bonnet. You've left an eye in that potato, Maudie, peel it properly.' Amy saw Maudie poke her tongue out very slightly in Lizzie's direction when she was sure her mother's gaze was turned elsewhere.

'Have you finished already, Frank?' Lizzie asked.

'Just about finished making the furrow. I've left Joey working the plough, there's not far to go. When they've got the spuds in I'll hitch Blackie up instead, give Blaze a rest. I can cover the spuds by myself, I thought I might send the boys down the creek for a swim before lunch. They've worked pretty hard this morning.'

'Can Beth and me go for a swim too, Ma?' Maudie asked. 'It's *so* hot in here, I'm just about melting.'

'We'll see,' Lizzie said. 'If you get those vegies done in time. Done properly, too—no eyes left in the spuds. And no poking tongues, either,' she added, earning an affronted glare from Maudie.

'Your ma's got eyes in the back of her head,' Frank told Maudie. Amy noticed Rosie craning her neck to look behind Lizzie's head. Seeing no sign of this second set of eyes, the little girl nestled back into Frank's lap.

Amy sat between Lizzie and Frank, willing the kettle to come to the boil so that she could gulp down a cup of tea and leave. She perched on the edge of her chair, voices buzzing all around her while she sat locked in her own uncomfortable thoughts.

Maudie and Beth talked quietly to each other as they worked, and Lizzie and Frank cuddled a little girl each while they chatted away about the events of the morning. Lizzie did up her bodice when Kate had

229

finished suckling, so used to the task after rearing seven babies that she could fasten the buttons without looking. The sweet smell of milk came from her; a smell that usually made Amy feel calm and a little drowsy. Today it only made her feel even more out of place.

Was that kettle never going to boil? Amy shot a glance at the clock. 'I'd better go, Lizzie. Never mind the tea, I'll have some with you another time.'

'Don't be silly, of course you've got time for a cup,' Lizzie said. 'Beth, that water must be just about boiling, check it for me. Anyway, you've brought those nice biscuits.'

'You eat them. I'll fetch the plate next time I'm down. I've got to go, I've been away too long already.'

'Rubbish, you've hardly been here five minutes. And if you're that worried about the time one of the girls can double you home. You just sit there and have a nice cup of tea.'

'I want to go now, Lizzie.' Amy had meant to sound determined, but her voice came out as little more than a whimper. 'I want to go home.' She stood up, using the edge of the table to steady herself, and blinked rapidly in a vain attempt to clear the tears that had begun blurring her vision.

'Amy, whatever's wrong with you today? Don't you feel well?' She was aware of Lizzie's face looming nearer, studying her closely. 'You look a bit awful—see those rings under her eyes, Frank? Haven't you been sleeping properly, poor love?'

Amy stared around at the sea of faces that surrounded her. Lizzie hovered solicitously, Frank was looking at her with concern, and Maudie and Beth had left their work to see what was wrong; even Rosie and the baby looked worried. She tried to smile, to brush aside their anxiousness with a light remark, but suddenly it all seemed too hard. The brittle persistence that had held her steady through the sleepless nights, the days full of nagging fear, crumbled under the combined weight of affection pressed on her. To her dismay, she felt warm tears begin to spill down her cheeks.

'I'm sorry,' she choked out. 'I can't help it. I can't make him get rid of it. I just can't!' She sank down into the chair with her arms on the table, laid her head on her arms and abandoned herself to racking sobs.

It took Lizzie only the briefest of moments to take charge of the situation. 'Right, you girls, you get outside,' she told Maudie and Beth. 'I'll finish those vegies myself. You can go down to the creek—you might as well have a swim if the boys are going to. Take Rosie with you—keep a good eye on her, though, and make sure she doesn't get cold. See you stay well away from the boys, mind.'

The chance of escaping even part of the work of preparing vegetables for a family of nine was too good to miss. The girls gave their mother no opportunity to change her mind before they darted from the room with their little sister in tow. Lizzie sat close to Amy with one arm held firmly around her, watching till the girls had closed the back door behind them.

'Now, what's going on?' she asked. 'You look dreadful, now I come to take a proper look at you. Has he been hitting you?' Cold anger sounded in her voice.

Amy shook her head, and swallowed painfully past the lump in her throat. 'It's nothing like that. Charlie hasn't touched me. He never touches me.' She spoke with her face still pressed against her arms. 'It's Mal. It's that awful knife. One of them's going to get killed, and then the other one'll get hung, and I can't stop them. I don't know what to do!'

Lizzie sat holding her till the storm had passed. Then she helped Amy to sit upright and gently drew out of her the whole story of the knife and the threat it held.

When she had unburdened all the details of her looming fear, Amy rested in the circle of Lizzie's arm and watched Frank and Lizzie exchange wordless glances full of meaning. She saw Frank ask a question with his eyes, and Lizzie raised her own heavenwards for a moment, then gave a quick nod as if resigning herself to an unpleasant task.

'Amy, do you think...' Frank began hesitantly, 'how about if Mal came and stayed with us for a bit? Just until him and Charlie calm down about all this stuff. It might help if you could just get him out of the house for a while.'

Amy's heart gave a great leap, as for a moment the prospect of relief from the nightmare hovered before her. She came back down to earth with a thud. 'It wouldn't be any good. Charlie wouldn't let Mal come and live here, he'd just fetch him home again. We couldn't keep him away from Mal, not when it's so close.'

She looked at the two faces studying her with such kind concern. 'Anyway, I don't think I could bear to send Mal to you. He's not—' *Not a bad boy*, she had been on the verge of saying. She caught back the words, unwilling to lie even to defend Malcolm's character. 'He can't help it. He's never really had the chance to be any different from how he is. But he can't come here, even if Charlie would let him. Mal's not like Joey, Frank. He'd only make your life a misery.' Or even worse. Hideous enough to imagine Malcolm attacking his father; how much more dreadful if he should plunge that knife into Frank.

'Well, I suppose you know best,' Frank said. Amy detected a hint of relief. 'I wish we could give you a hand some way or another, though. Do you think it would do any good if I had a talk with Mal? You know, just sort of tried to make him see it's not a great idea for him to be waving a knife around?'

He meant it so kindly. Amy could not tell him that, after herself, Frank was probably the last person in the world Malcolm would take any notice of. Not when ever since babyhood he had heard Charlie call Frank 'idiot', 'fool', and worse terms of abuse. 'Maybe,' she said. 'Yes, if you're talking to Mal sometime, maybe you could try that, Frank. Thank you for thinking of it.'

'I don't know, Frank, he probably wouldn't take much notice,' Lizzie said, more willing than Amy to be blunt. 'It's a pity we don't know anyone else he could go to. You know, somewhere miles and miles away like, say, Auckland. Well, I suppose you do know a few people around the place to do with selling the cows,' she added doubtfully.

'I don't think I know anyone well enough for that,' Frank said, clearly uncomfortable.

'No,' Amy said, shaking her head. 'I couldn't even let you two try and put up with Mal, and you're family. I wouldn't expect you to ask anyone else, Frank.'

She sighed. 'I wish I could send him away somewhere. Somewhere he'd be safe, but he couldn't spoil things for anyone else. I don't see how I can do it, though. I think we're all stuck together.'

'We might sort something out yet, Amy,' Lizzie said. 'Frank's good at thinking of things.'

Amy thanked them warmly, but she went home as troubled as ever. Lizzie and Frank wanted to help her, but there was nothing they could do except be kind. The problem was hers to solve, and she had no real hope of finding a solution in time.

If only she could find somewhere safe for Malcolm. Somewhere a long way from his father. As she walked back up the road the words echoed futilely inside her head: *if only*.

Amy was not actively listening to the boys' conversation as Malcolm and David sat at the table over their afternoon tea some weeks later. She stood at the bench preparing vegetables for their evening meal while the boys chatted. It occurred to her to be grateful that Malcolm and David never seemed to fight with each other; probably because they had always had such an obvious common enemy in their father.

Malcolm seemed quite animated by whatever they were talking about. Amy slowed down the pace of her slicing and chopping to listen more closely.

'So they really beat the daylights out of those other fellows, eh?' Malcolm said, his eyes bright. 'How do you say what they're called?'

'Bo-ers, it must be. Yes, the paper said the Boer fellows just ran off in the end, and our fellows chased after them and shot half of them. They caught the rest and locked them up. They reckon the New Zealand soldiers are the best riders over there.'

'Lucky buggers,' Malcolm said. 'And what else did it say? Where'd they go riding next?'

David shrugged. 'I don't know. I didn't read any more after that.'

'Why not?' Malcolm demanded.

'Well, that's where the paper was ripped. Someone else must've used the rest of it.'

'Have you still got that piece? You might've forgotten some of it.'

David cast a discomforted glance in Amy's direction. 'No, I used it. There wasn't much paper in the dunny, so I couldn't save that bit.'

'Idiot. Well, if you find any more good stuff about the war, you'd better hang on to it. Specially stuff to do with—'

But the sound of Charlie's tread on the back door step put a stop to further conversation about the war for the moment. Any mention of the subject was inclined to draw a tirade on the evils of the English government, and the scandal of colonial governments sending their own boys over to fight what Charlie always referred to as 'the bloody King of England's war'.

Amy had taken little enough interest in the war during the two years it had been going on. It seemed a remote thing, too far away from her own small world to have any relevance. In any case, over the last few months she had had a far more important war to contend with: the simmering battle between Charlie and Malcolm. But the memory of Malcolm's face, bright with interest as he pressed David for details of the fighting, aroused an answering spark in Amy. What was forming in her head was too tenuous to be called an idea, but it was the germ of one.

She watched Malcolm closely, and a few days later saw something so unexpected that it briefly robbed her of speech. Charlie had left his newspaper crumpled on the floor beside his chair when he went out to take the milk to the factory, leaving the boys to finish their breakfast. Amy carried their plates to the bench while David went outside to the privy. When she turned back to the table she saw Malcolm peering intently at Charlie's newspaper, retrieved from the floor. He had pressed out the worst of the creases, and now sat with his face close to the page, tracing his finger along the words as he silently mouthed them.

'Mal, you're reading,' Amy said when she had recovered her wits. 'You never read.'

'Shut up,' Malcolm muttered, lifting his eyes from the page to glare at her. 'Aw, damn it, now I've lost my place.' He ran his finger along several lines until he found the sentence he had been wrestling with.

Amy had not seen Malcolm so much as glance at a printed page since she had coached him through his stumbling attempts at the Standard Three examination. He was clearly struggling to cope with whatever he was reading. She crept up behind him, avid to see what had so caught his attention.

As she had suspected, the newspaper article was a report of recent progress in the war. It was full of the florid language that always seemed to accompany such reports; words of far too many syllables for Malcolm to cope with. She heard him muttering vague approximations of the words under his breath, his face screwed up with effort.

'Do you want me to help you with that, Mal?' she asked.

'No,' Malcolm said. A moment later he asked in what seemed meant to be an offhand way, 'What's c-cal… calvry mean, anyway?'

'Calvary? That's to do with the Bible. Does it really say that?' She looked over his shoulder at the spot where his finger pointed. 'Oh, that says cavalry. That means soldiers riding horses.'

'I know what it means,' Malcolm said indignantly. 'They just write it a dopey way.' He struggled on with the report, once or twice seeming about to ask Amy's help with other words, but though she hovered ready to assist he did not speak to her.

At last he crumpled the paper in disgust. 'That's just stupid, the way they write that stuff. It doesn't make any sense. How can people read about it if it doesn't make sense?'

'I'll read it out to you if you like. Why are you so interested in all that?'

Malcolm turned on her. 'Why don't you mind your own business?' He flung the newspaper to the floor and stalked outside, slamming the door behind him.

Amy stared thoughtfully after him. Abandoning the bench of dirty dishes, she went outside, pulled on her boots and chased Malcolm's retreating form.

When David appeared around the corner of the house, Amy stopped her pursuit of Malcolm just long enough to ask David to take the slops bucket to the pigs for her.

'And can you take a little while over it?' she asked. 'I want to have a talk with Mal.'

Malcolm's stride was much longer than hers, but he was drifting aimlessly, apparently lost in thought as he ambled along with his hands thrust into the pockets of his jacket. 'Wait for me, Mal,' Amy called after him when she was well in earshot.

'Bugger off,' Malcolm shouted back over his shoulder.

Amy quickened her pace. When Malcolm saw that she was gaining on him he walked away more purposefully, but Amy followed doggedly.

'Leave me alone, why don't you?' Malcolm called. He broke into a run, leapt across a drain in his path, and disappeared over a slight rise.

Amy had no prospect of succeeding in such a leap. Instead she climbed down into the drain and crossed it slowly, lifting her skirts to keep them out of the mud in the bottom. She went over the rise and found Malcolm sprawled on the ground in a sheltered hollow that looked towards the sea, propped up on his elbows and scowling at her approach.

'Why don't you bloody leave me alone?'

Amy sat down beside him, careful to choose the side that meant she did not have to look at his knife. 'Tell me about the war, Mal. Tell me why you're so interested in it.'

Malcolm turned on her. 'What would you know about it? Silly bitch. Just bugger off.'

Amy closed her eyes for a moment, and took a deep breath. 'Let's play a game, Mal. How about you pretend just for a minute that I'm not your mother? Pretend I'm an ordinary person instead. Then you won't have to go to the trouble of talking nasty to me all the time. Now, come on. Tell me about the war.'

'Will you clear off if I do?' Malcolm asked, glaring at her.

'Well, I won't go away if you don't.'

Malcolm spat on the ground. 'Nagging old bitch,' he said, but without any real venom. He looked away from her and began speaking in a low voice, so that Amy had to lean towards him to catch his words.

'It's good over there. No one telling you what to do all the time. There's lots of fighting and stuff—there's wild animals, too, lions and tigers and things. And you can ride and ride, just on and on as far as you like.' He turned to Amy. 'What's "veld" mean? It was in the paper.'

Amy was suddenly reminded of the inspector's examinations she had gone through while at school. Producing the right answer was more important now than it had been all those years before.

The word seemed vaguely familiar, as if she had come across it years and years before. She closed her eyes and pictured the old schoolroom.

Miss Evans stood at the front, holding open a large book with an engraving of a grassy plain, a lion stalking across the centre of the page.

She opened her eyes. 'I know what it means! It's what they have in Africa instead of the bush—I think they've got jungle, too, but in the dry bits they have veld. It's like hundreds and hundreds of paddocks all joined together, but no fences or anything. Just open country as far as you can see.'

The intensity of longing she saw in Malcolm's face startled her. 'Just on and on for ever,' he murmured. 'Just get on your horse and ride for ever.' He was gazing out towards the sea, but Amy knew it was not the ocean that he saw in his mind's eye. 'And no old bugger thumping you all the time. No bloody cows to milk day in, day out. You just get to please yourself.'

'I think you'd have to do what the men in charge told you,' Amy said gently.

'Bet they don't break your face if you don't.'

'No, I suppose they don't.' It was time to bring matters to a head. 'Mal, do you think you'd like to go over there?'

'What's the use of talking like that?' Malcolm hurled at her. 'Course I bloody would! I can't, though, can I? I'm stuck in this dump with the old bugger. Him and his bloody cows.'

'You want to go to South Africa?' Amy pressed. 'You really, really want to go?'

She saw what looked suspiciously like tears glinting in the corners of Malcolm's eyes. 'You think I want to stay in this dump all my life? Never see anything or do anything?' He scowled at her. 'What would you know about it, anyway? You've never been anywhere.'

'I went to Auckland once.' *Stupid*, she told herself the moment the words were out, regretting the childish impulse that had made her rise to his bait.

'I don't remember that,' Malcolm said, eyeing her dubiously.

'It was before you were born. Before I got married. It was a long time ago, don't take any notice.' Amy reached out and put a hand on his arm. 'Mal, maybe you could go over there. If you want it that much, I think we should try and—'

Malcolm shook her arm off. 'I *can't*,' he interrupted, hoarse with emotion. 'I'm stuck here. You've got to pay money. Dave read a bit about it in the paper. There's too many blokes wanting to go, so they only take you if you've got money. You have to pay for your gear. You're meant to bring your own horse, too.'

'I know,' Amy said. 'I've been reading about it since I saw how interested you were in the war.' She watched his face closely, eager to see what his reaction would be to her next words. 'I could give you the money, Mal.'

His eyes opened wide, then narrowed in suspicion. 'You? Where would you get money from? The old bugger wouldn't give it to you any more than he would me.'

'I've got my own money.' She held up a hand to stem the questions she saw poised on Malcolm's lips. 'Never you mind how I got it or where it's from—it's my money, and it's my business how I spend it. Your father knows I've got it, but he doesn't like me talking about it to people.'

She frowned in thought. 'Twenty-five pounds for your gear, I read that somewhere. And money towards a horse, too, that'd be even better. I'm sure I haven't got that much in the bank. Never mind, I'll manage. I'll get the money from somewhere.' It would be no use trying to borrow money from the bank, she knew; the manager would want to get Charlie's permission, since Charlie would be liable for any debts she incurred. *Frank'll lend me the money*, she realised with relief. *He'll keep it secret from Charlie, too.*

She smiled at the look on Malcolm's face, suspicion slowly being replaced by a dawning hope. 'I'll get the money for you, Mal. You can have your adventure.'

'But...' Malcolm opened and closed his mouth several times. Amy sensed that he did not want to risk changing her mind by anything he might say. She watched as curiosity overcame his caution. 'Why?' he asked. 'Why do you want to give me the money?'

'Mostly because I want to get you away from your father,' Amy said. 'I'm scared, Mal. Scared of what you two might do to each other. And I'm tired of being scared and not being able to do anything about it.'

'He's not going to try that with me again,' Malcolm said, fingering his knife as he spoke.

'Maybe not. He won't if you're not here.'

She put her hand back on his arm; this time he let it stay there. 'There's another reason, too. I didn't know how much it meant to you till just now. It's really important to you, isn't it? You really want to go away and have adventures.' Malcolm looked away almost shyly, and gave a quick nod.

'I used to have a head full of dreams, too, when I was your age. No, that's not right,' she corrected herself. 'When I was your age I married your father. I'd finished dreaming by then. Well, when I was a year younger than you, say. I had all sorts of fine ideas about where I'd go and what I'd do.' Amy made herself smile in an attempt to ward off tears. 'I never did any of them.' She fell silent, lost in old memories.

'But you're going to, Mal,' she went on more firmly. 'You're going to do what matters to you. And that's why I'm going to give you my money.'

She basked briefly in the warmth of Malcolm's delighted expression, then held up a warning finger. 'Except you must promise me two things first.'

A guarded look came over his face. 'What do you want?'

'We'll have to keep it all secret from your father, of course, or he'd stop you going. And you must promise me you'll never tell him where you got the money from—even when you get back from the war you mustn't. There'd be an awful fuss if he found out.'

'I won't tell him,' Malcolm agreed readily. 'I don't talk to him 'cept when I've got to. Anyway, he doesn't even think we should be in the war,' he added in tones of disgust. 'All that crap about Scotland and stuff.'

'He's got his reasons. You should ask him about it one day, if you and him ever get to be friends. About what happened to his family when he was little.'

'That was *years* ago. Who wants to hear about all that?'

'Well, maybe you'd understand him a tiny bit better if you did. Never mind that for now, just remember you mustn't tell him about the money. All right, that's the easy one. Now, I want you to promise me that when you get back you'll try to make your father happy. I know it's not easy,' she said, forestalling his protest. 'No one knows that better than me. But do your best. That's all I'm asking.'

'Mightn't come back,' Malcolm muttered. 'Not if I can get a job somewhere else. I don't want to work for the old man all my life. Him and his bloody farm.' He spat on the ground to punctuate his words.

For years Amy had watched Charlie drive himself almost to exhaustion, breaking in more bush land, building up his herd, and trying to improve the small patch of land that was so precious to him. Always his driving force had been 'It's for the boy'. A piece of land that belonged to him, that no one could take from him, and that he could leave to his son. David was little more than a bonus; an extra demonstration of his father's manhood. Malcolm was the first-born, the son Charlie had yearned for. She was grateful that Charlie was not there to hear what his son thought of his inheritance.

'Maybe you'll both feel different about it all when you've been away for a year,' she said. 'That's how long you have to sign up for, you know.

You and your father might miss each other.'

'Him?' Malcolm said. 'He hates my guts as much as I hate his.'

Amy shook her head. 'You're wrong, Mal. Your father loves you more than anything or anyone else in the world.'

'He's got a bloody funny way of showing it,' Malcolm said, years worth of bitterness in his tone.

'I know. That doesn't stop it being true.'

Malcolm scowled. 'He's given me some awful hidings.'

'I know, Mal.' *Me too*, she added silently.

'Why's he so rotten to me, then?'

Amy sighed. 'Don't ask me to explain your father to you. I've never understood him properly myself. I think he's just not good at showing what he feels.'

'He's always been pretty good at showing me.'

'Well, not good at showing nice feelings, then.' She smiled wistfully. 'I wish you could remember how he used to be with you. When you were born he was so proud you'd've thought he'd burst with it.' She closed her eyes and saw again the wonder in Charlie's face as he gazed down at the little red-headed bundle in its cradle. 'Having you was the one thing I ever did that was completely right in your father's eyes. He was pleased when Dave was born, but not like he was with you. You were the first. You were perfect. You even looked like him.'

'Can't help that,' Malcolm muttered.

'He used to love telling people about you when you were little. He was so proud of you.'

'He wasn't,' Malcolm argued. Amy heard old pain in his voice. 'Do you remember that time I won the race?' he asked, not looking at her as he spoke.

'Oh, yes! Racing against all those big boys, and you with just a little pony like Brownie. And you beat them all! Your father was so proud. He must have told everyone in town a dozen times over what a good rider you were.'

'He never told me.' Malcolm's face twisted. 'He's never said anything good to me all my life.'

'It's just the way he is, Mal. It doesn't mean he doesn't *think* good things about you. It's just the way he's made.'

'He's made rotten, then.'

Amy let silence rest between them for some time. 'I think you and him might feel different when you get back,' she said at last. 'You'll be older, and... well, he'll get a bit of a shock with you going away. You'll both have a chance to think about things.'

'I'll still hate him.'

'I hope not. I don't think you hate him now, anyway. You've just got used to thinking you do. But I still want you to promise, Mal. Promise me you'll try and get on with him. Even...' She faltered, struggling to accept the idea that Malcolm might find a life for himself that had nothing to do with the farm. 'Even if you decide you don't want to live with us any more. At least come back and talk to your father, try and explain things to him. You owe him that.'

'I don't owe him nothing!'

'Maybe you owe it to me, then. Promise, Mal.'

'Oh, all right. I promise.'

'That's my good boy. And one more thing—'

'Hey, you said two things,' Malcolm protested.

Amy laughed softly. 'So I did. Well, you don't have to do this one. I'd just like you to. Can I have a kiss? Please?'

'Of course you can,' Malcolm said, taking her aback with his enthusiasm. He gave her a child's kiss, wet-lipped and full on the mouth. Amy clung to him for a moment, then let him go.

Malcolm flopped down on the grass and regarded her with bemusement. 'Fancy you having money and me never knowing. I used to think your name was "silly bitch", you know.' He gave Amy a grin that was a little too close to a sneer for her to feel quite comfortable with it. 'Till I was about five or six, that's what I thought it was, 'cause that's what the old man always called you. Maybe you're not so silly after all.'

'No, maybe I'm not,' Amy said.

Matters moved quickly once the thing had been decided. Frank readily agreed to lend Amy the extra money she needed for Malcolm; he was reluctant to call it a loan and not a gift, but Amy insisted that it would be a proper loan, and that she would begin paying it back as soon as the next instalment of her annuity was in the bank. She busied herself with sewing two fresh sets of underclothes for Malcolm, as well as seeing that all his clothes were neatly mended.

'They'll only have to do you till you get your uniform,' she said. 'Except the drawers and vests and things—I don't think they'd have those in a uniform.' She pulled out a photograph she had carefully torn from a newspaper, showing a soldier. 'Won't you look handsome dressed like that?'

She saw a tiny look of pleasure on his face. No one else would call Malcolm handsome; he resembled his father too much for that, and the ruined nose Charlie had given him had not improved his looks. Amy could never have come out with such a thing if love had not coloured her vision of him.

All their planning; all the secret conversations when Charlie was out of the house and she had Malcolm and David to herself. Sometimes she hardly dared hope that Charlie would not guess what they were up to; would not intercept some telltale glance that passed between her and Malcolm. But Charlie stayed blind, and the time for Malcolm to go drew nearer.

Amy had all the details mapped out weeks before the day came. She chose a day when the *Waiotahi* would be sailing from Ruatane on a morning tide, and would meet the boat in Tauranga with only a short time to wait. Then Malcolm would go on to Auckland, stay the night there in a boarding house whose address Frank had given Amy, and the following morning would make his way to the army camp. Amy wrote out the times and dates for Malcolm, and carefully went over the timetable with him until she was sure he understood it.

She finished packing his things the afternoon before he was to leave. She had made a bag out of canvas, large enough to hold his clothes but not so big as to be awkward to carry slung over his shoulder. The money that he would need to produce for his equipment she sewed into a special pocket inside his jacket, while she calculated what his travelling expenses were likely to be and made him a wallet to hold the necessary money.

The boys went off to bed as usual, to be roused in the early hours by Amy. The three of them crept out of the house and over to the horse paddock. Amy stood shivering slightly in the chilly night air while David helped his brother catch the horse and get its bridle on.

Malcolm and David shook hands a little self-consciously, then Amy hugged him before he mounted and reached down for the bag David held out. 'Now, remember,' Amy whispered, 'you're to leave your horse in Mr Moody's paddock, and tell him your pa'll come in and collect it later in the week.'

'Yes, I know,' Malcolm said with a trace of impatience. 'Don't go on about all that.' She and Malcolm had argued off and on for several days about the horse, with Malcolm protesting that the horse was his and he had the right to take it with him. Amy had argued equally strongly that Charlie most certainly considered the horse to belong to him, and would be even angrier than he was going to be over Malcolm's defection if the horse went too. Anyway, she pointed out, she had given Malcolm extra money to make up for his lack of a horse. After a few days of this, Malcolm had surprised her by abruptly ceasing to argue and agreeing to leave the horse behind.

'Well, I'll see you fellows later, then,' Malcolm said, his excitement audible even through his whisper. 'Hope the old man doesn't give you too much trouble.'

'Bye, Mal,' David said, raising his hand in a half wave. 'Have a good time over there, eh?'

'Take care, Mal,' said Amy. She reached out her hand towards his leg. But she had left it too late, and Malcolm was already beyond her reach.

She put an arm around David's waist and drew him close. They stood together, listening to the hoof beats fading, until they could no longer hear anything but their own breathing.

'It's going to be funny without Mal,' David said. Amy heard a wistful note in his voice.

She put her other arm around him and squeezed, enjoying the warm feel of his body against hers.

'Yes, it'll seem strange not having him. The time'll go quickly, though, I'm sure it will. A year's not as long as all that.' Amy took a deep breath of the cool night air and felt a sense of peace settling over her. 'I'll tell you one thing, Dave—it'll be quiet without him, anyway.'

When daylight came and Malcolm did not appear at milking time, David managed through vague, evasive answers to give his father the impression that his brother had simply slipped out in the night and David did not know exactly where he was. Charlie drew his own conclusion: that Sergeant Riley had made good his threat to lock Malcolm up the next time he caused trouble in the town. He grumbled loudly that he would 'teach that boy a lesson' when Malcolm appeared again.

Amy said nothing until she was sure Malcolm must be safely away on the boat, then she produced the farewell note she had had to badger him into writing.

'This was in the boys' room—it's in Mal's writing,' she said, trying to convey an ignorance of the contents as she handed the folded sheet to Charlie. She had eventually had to write the note herself, with Malcolm copying her writing word for word in his own clumsy scrawl. The note was terse, saying only that Malcolm had enlisted and was off to fight. 'I hope you will be proud of me one day,' it ended. Amy had struggled to get Malcolm to write those words.

'It'll make it a bit easier for Dave if you write a proper note to your father,' had been the argument that finally persuaded him. 'Your father's going to be angry over all this, and it'll be Dave who gets the worst of it.'

If you can make your father just a tiny bit less wild, he mightn't be as hard on Dave.'

Charlie raged loudly against Malcolm's desertion, roaring threats against the boy that would have frightened Amy if Charlie had not been impotent to carry any of them out. He ranted more loudly than ever when he found that Malcolm had, after all, taken the horse with him. There were dark threats for a day or two of 'getting the law onto the young bugger for horse thieving,' but Amy knew it would come to nothing. Even if Malcolm had not already left the country, Charlie was not going to expose himself to Sergeant Riley's open scorn by admitting that the boy had once again made a fool of his father.

'His name will not be mentioned in this house,' Charlie announced. 'He defied me, and he'll pay for it. He's no son of mine while he carries on like that.'

In a melodramatic illustration, he took the photograph of himself, Amy and the boys from the mantelpiece and flung it into the empty fireplace. Amy rescued it when Charlie had gone outside, and put it on the chest of drawers in her bedroom where it would be safe from any further grand gestures by Charlie.

The rule that Malcolm's name not be mentioned did not seem to apply to Charlie; he raised the subject of the boy's disgrace several times a day. But Amy and David both knew better than to disobey him; they were careful not to refer to Malcolm within Charlie's hearing, nor to show any reaction to even the more outrageous of his threats.

Charlie's outbursts gradually subsided into intermittent grumbling. He scowled and swore, and threatened David with dire retribution if he so much as thought about following his brother to the war; but as the fury of the first few unpleasant weeks diminished, Amy began to suspect that Charlie was almost enjoying his sense of outrage. He was the wronged father, burdened with a thankless son, and one day his son would see the error of his ways.

'That boy didn't know when he was well off,' became a familiar refrain. 'He'll learn. Now he's gone off with those bloody English generals, he'll see what a damned fool he's been.' Amy and David knew to keep quiet during such litanies; it was not their opinions that were wanted, merely their presence as an audience.

'He needn't think I'm taking him back, either,' Charlie often continued. 'Not till he gets down on his knees and begs me to forgive him. Aye, I'll not take him back till he does that.'

A look of satisfaction tended to creep over his face at this point, rather spoiling the intended effect of a bitterly wronged parent. Charlie was convincing himself more and more, Amy knew, that Malcolm would come back as the penitent prodigal son, pathetically grateful for Charlie's goodness and ready and eager to be everything his father wanted of him. She hoped that when the year was up she would be able to persuade Malcolm into a sufficiently meek demeanour.

But that was a whole year away, and in the meantime Malcolm was safe. It was an odd way to think of war, she knew; but then hers was an odd family. Until they settled their feud, Malcolm was in more danger from his own father than from some nebulous enemy.

In any case, the war seemed to be going well. In the two and a half years since it had begun Amy had never taken much interest, but now she avidly followed the details of every skirmish. She gathered up the newspaper as soon as Charlie discarded it, and when he was safely out of sight she and David would study the columns of war reports, discussing each item and speculating aloud on whether or not Malcolm might have been at any of the engagements reported. If Charlie gave them no opportunity to read the news in peace during the day, sometimes she would creep into David's room after dark. They would read the newspaper by candlelight, then whisper to one another of the adventures they imagined Malcolm might be having.

'See this bit about the New Zealand fellows galloping around guarding that train?' David said one night. 'I bet Mal's doing stuff like that. Racing around all over the place, keeping the Boer fellows away. No one rides better than Mal.'

Amy was more interested in the fact that the soldiers seemed to have seen no sign of the enemy, reinforcing her conviction that Malcolm was safer in Africa than he had been at home. He had perhaps had more opportunity for fighting in Ruatane's main street than he was getting over there. But the riding, she was sure, must be all Malcolm could have wished for.

'He must be just loving it,' she murmured. 'Galloping for miles and miles like that. It's just what he wanted to do.'

'He's lucky,' David said, and Amy was surprised to hear something like longing in his voice. 'It must be fun doing all that.' His voice, already a whisper, became almost inaudible. Amy was unsure whether she had heard the next words properly: 'I wish I could.'

She put the candle down carefully and gave David a searching look. 'You wouldn't really go away and leave me, would you, Davie?'

'No. Not till Mal comes back, anyway. Maybe I could go over there for a bit then.' The eagerness in his voice gave Amy a pang. 'Then Mal can look after you. I wouldn't want you to be here by yourself with Pa.'

Amy laughed softly, and laid her head on his shoulder. 'It's not me who needs looking after, it's you boys. There's no need to worry about me. Anyway, you're much too young to go off to war—even Mal wasn't really old enough, you know.' She was comfortably certain the war would be over well before David was old enough to follow in his brother's footsteps.

'I know it's hard for you with Mal away,' she whispered. 'Your pa hasn't been easy to get along with, has he? Thank you for being so good about it, darling.'

She felt David shrug. 'He's all right, I suppose. Just grumpier than he used to be. If I don't say much, he doesn't take much notice of me.'

That was the best David had ever hoped for from his father, Amy knew: to be ignored. Even that small expectation had been harder to achieve since Malcolm's departure, with David thrust into his father's attention far more than usual. It was fortunate that David was blessed with a placid nature; he had had more need of it lately.

But Malcolm was safe. Amy was so convinced of this that she felt not the slightest hint of concern on the May afternoon when Charlie had an unexpected visitor.

She was working in her vegetable garden at the time, pulling weeds from between the rows of carrots, and Charlie was repairing a piece of harness in the shed nearest the house.

'What does that bugger want?' she heard Charlie grumble. He had discarded the harness and was walking towards her. Amy looked up from her weeding to see Sergeant Riley coming up the track on his black horse. 'If that boy's been getting in trouble I'll bloody well—Dave!' he shouted. 'Get over here!'

David was a paddock away, feeding chaff to the two draught horses. 'Can I just finish doing this?' he called back. 'I won't be long.'

'It won't be anything to do with Dave, Charlie,' Amy said. 'It's probably nothing to do with us at all.'

She could hardly have been more mistaken. As Sergeant Riley pulled his horse to a halt in front of them, Amy was puzzled to see how discomforted the policeman appeared. He dismounted and stood looking from Amy to Charlie, chewing at his under lip.

'Afternoon, Stewart,' he said at last. 'Mrs Stewart.' He raised his hat to Amy, but instead of putting the hat back in place he held it to his chest. 'I've...' he trailed off awkwardly, then began again in an oddly formal tone. 'I've some unpleasant news for you. Unpleasant,' he echoed, looking down at the ground for a moment before fixing his gaze on Charlie.

'It's about your son.' Amy saw Charlie dart a glare across the paddock to where David was still feeding the horses. But the strangeness of Sergeant Riley's manner had already told her that this was no high-spirited indiscretion of David's the policeman had come to report. Coldness crept through her.

'It's Mal,' she said in a whisper.

Sergeant Riley's eyes flicked to hers. He looked away as if unwilling to confront what he saw there. 'I'm afraid so,' he said, his eyes apparently focussed on a point several feet behind Charlie. 'I've had a telegram just this morning.'

He reached into the pocket of his jacket and pulled out a piece of paper. 'It was the enteric fever that took him—it's taken a lot of the boys. He… passed away a week ago, but the news is a while getting back to us.' He lifted his gaze from the telegram, and for a brief moment his eyes looked straight into Amy's.

'I'm sorry,' he said. 'That boy drove me half distracted, but I'd never have wished anything like this on him.'

He turned to Charlie, who had neither moved nor made a sound since Sergeant Riley's announcement. 'He was a brave lad. You should be proud of your son.'

Amy saw Charlie give a slight shudder, as if dragging himself back to awareness of his surroundings. He stared at the telegram Sergeant Riley held out to him, but made no move to take it.

'I've no son of that name,' he said, his voice no more than a hoarse whisper. 'He defied me. He's no son of mine. I've no son.'

He walked towards the house with an unsteady tread, the telegram fluttering to the ground as Charlie turned his back on it.

Amy was vaguely aware that Sergeant Riley was speaking to her, but she could make no sense of the sounds; not through the thick fog filling her head. She stumbled after Charlie, half running to try and catch up to him, scarcely noticing that Sergeant Riley was mounting, eager to escape; nor that David had finished with the horses and was walking over to where the telegram lay abandoned.

'Charlie,' she called, but he ignored her. 'Charlie, wait.'

She went into the kitchen in time to see Charlie going through to the parlour, clutching a whisky bottle in one hand. He jarred against the doorpost, then went staggering on into his bedroom.

'Don't, Charlie,' she begged. 'Don't shut me out. I want to talk to you about Mal. We have to talk. Charlie!' Her voice came out as a ragged scream. 'He's my son too!'

The door slammed. Amy slumped against it, the wood rough against her face. She could hear the pounding of her heart, making a counterpoint to her thoughts. *It's my fault Mal's dead. He wouldn't have gone away if I hadn't given him the money. I've killed my son.*

'Ma?' The sound was thin and stretched, quite unlike David's usual voice. She looked up to see him standing there, the telegram clutched in one hand. 'It says Mal's dead. He can't be dead, can he? It's a mistake or something, isn't it? Isn't it, Ma?'

She felt his anguish like a cruel hand squeezing her own heart, and gasped with the pain of it. All through David's life Malcolm had been there, the big brother to trail after and try to keep up with. The world without Malcolm in it, without even the knowledge that Malcolm was riding across the plains two oceans away, was beyond his imagining.

'I'm sorry, Davie,' she whispered, and with the words she felt hot tears spill from her eyes. 'I'm sorry.'

She stumbled towards him with her arms outstretched, and they fell into a close embrace. For a long time they stood locked together, bodies convulsing with shared sobs, as the early darkness of winter began to creep into the house. Through the closed door, softly at first, then gradually building into throbbing, wailing roars of pain and loss, she heard the sound of Charlie weeping for his son.

16

May – July 1902

Charlie did not emerge from his room until late in the following afternoon. He seemed to have aged years overnight, Amy thought as he walked into the kitchen with an oddly shambling gait. His shoulders were more stooped, his face grey, and his eyes were red-rimmed within their swollen lids.

She and David had muddled through the farm work that could not be left for even one day, like tending to the horses, stopping only to help each other prepare rough attempts at meals when hunger drove them to. David's face showed the telltale swelling hours of weeping had left, and she knew her own must bear similar signs. David had finally fallen into an exhausted sleep somewhere in the cold, dark hours of the night, his head resting in Amy's lap while she sat in an armchair, but sleep had been beyond Amy's reach while grief and guilt warred for mastery.

Of the three of them, Charlie was the only one who had achieved unconsciousness for more than a few hours, but the whisky-induced stupor had clearly done nothing to ease his spirit. They stood and stared at one another for a few moments, while Amy struggled to find something useful to say. But it was Charlie who broke the silence first.

'His name will not be mentioned in this…' His voice cracked. He shuffled over to a chair and slumped onto it. 'In this house. He went against me. He's no son of mine.'

He raised his gaze to study Amy and David. His eyes narrowed as he took in her black dress and David's arm band.

'There'll not be any mourning worn for him,' he said. 'He's no part of this family. Get that thing off, boy.'

Amy put a hand on David's arm, knowing he would object. She felt his muscles stiffen beneath her fingers.

'Get that bloody thing *off*,' Charlie said when David was slow to respond, thumping the table to emphasise his words. The thump was a feeble parody of the sort of gesture Charlie usually made, barely rattling the dishes on the table.

'Let me, Dave,' Amy murmured, tugging at the black cloth. She squeezed his arm encouragingly and slipped the offending band into a pocket of her apron.

'And you can fetch me a drink before you get out of your crow's weeds,' Charlie said, turning his attention to Amy. She was fairly sure he had meant something other than the cup of tea she set before him, but although he frowned at the cup he picked it up without complaint. He took large gulps of the hot tea, gnawing absently at the day-old bread spread with butter and jam that was the best food Amy could offer him at short notice.

Weariness made it difficult to be sensible. Amy felt an irrational urge to fling herself at Charlie's feet and beg forgiveness for having robbed him of his son; to do something to try and comfort him. But she recognised the futility of the impulse even as the strength of it brought tears to her eyes. She could offer Charlie no comfort; still less could she hope to draw comfort from him.

That did not mean he was going to rob her of the right to mourn Malcolm. She served Charlie in silence, and waited until David had left the room before she spoke.

'I'm going to wear mourning,' she said quietly.

He gave her a look that was clearly meant to be forbidding, but there was no power in it. 'I say you're not.' He waited for her answer; when she gave none he spoke again. 'You can get out of your weeds right now. Go on, get on with it.'

Amy shook her head, calm in the knowledge that in this, at least, she was doing the right thing.

'Defying me, are you?' He scowled at her, the weary droop of his mouth spoiling the effect.

'I don't want to go against you, no. But I will if you make me.' She sat down opposite him and held his gaze, though the pain of loss that she saw in his face made her wince. 'Charlie, our son—'

'He's no son of mine,' Charlie interrupted, his voice cracking as he repeated the harsh litany.

She closed her eyes for a moment. 'All right, then, *my* son. My son's dead, and I'm going to mourn him properly. You don't have the right to stop me.'

The bitterness in his stare made it hard to keep her eyes fixed on his face. 'Since when did you care a damn about my rights?'

He turned away. 'Please yourself, then. Wear black for the rest of your life if you want, like some old crone. It's no affair of mine.'

No more was said about her mourning clothes, though Amy knew the town must be talking about Charlie's lack of any outward sign of being in mourning himself, and even more about his rebuff of anyone's attempt to mention Malcolm's name in his presence. But other people's gossip was the least of her concerns.

All the trouble and worry Malcolm had given her over the years seemed insignificant. He was the child she had carried inside her for nine long months, and who had ripped her open in his eagerness to enter the world. He was the little boy she had taught to walk and to talk, and had nursed through all his childish ailments. He was the son Charlie had longed for; the one she had put so much effort into protecting from his father's anger, and whose wounds she had patched up when her protection failed. He was her son, and he was dead.

She had not been there to nurse him through that last, fatal illness. He had gone off to a foreign country to find adventure; instead he had found himself a grave. And it was her fault. She had sent him there. The pain grew even sharper when, a mere two weeks after they heard of Malcolm's death, the papers were full of the news that the war had been won.

But she could not let herself wallow in grief, not when she had Charlie and David to worry about. David had been left distraught by the loss of his brother, and being forbidden to mention Malcolm's name in Charlie's hearing made it even harder for David to cope.

Amy gave him all the opportunities she could to talk about his brother. They passed many hours sharing whispered memories in the darkness of David's room. Often David's dog and Amy's cat crept into the room to keep them company in a silent sympathy broken only by an occasional scratching of fleas.

Only a few nights passed before David asked the question that Amy realised must have been preying on his mind.

'Ma, did it… do you think it hurt Mal?'

Amy sat in the darkness and considered the question, anxious to give an honest answer without upsetting David. 'I don't know,' she admitted. 'I don't really know what that enteric fever's like. I hope it didn't…' Her voice betrayed her, and she had to wait a few moments before she could go on.

'It's a fever, though,' she said, clutching at a sudden memory. 'I remember your Uncle John had a fever once, years and years ago—it was when he cut his foot open. I looked after him. The fever didn't hurt him, it made him get muddled in his head. Maybe Mal didn't really know what was going on, not when…' *when he was dying.* 'Not right at the end.' She hugged him tightly. 'Let's hope not.'

'That sounds right,' David said, his voice full of optimism. 'I bet he had a good time, anyway.'

'What?' Amy was startled out of brooding on Malcolm, alone and feverish, by David's abrupt change of mood. 'How do you mean, Dave?'

'Before he got sick. I bet Mal had a good time. You know, riding around and all that. Like you and me used to talk about.'

He made it sound like something they had talked of years ago, though it had been their main topic of conversation just the previous week. 'So we did,' Amy said, snatching gratefully at the memory. 'Yes, I think he did have a good time. I think he had the best time of his life.'

'He got away from the old man, anyway,' David said, resentment giving his voice an edge. 'Pa was rotten to him. And he doesn't even care about Mal being dead—he won't even let us talk about him.'

'Oh, he cares all right,' Amy said softly. 'Your father misses Mal as much as we do. Maybe even more.'

'Why won't he talk about him, then?'

'Because… oh, I don't know how to explain it. Because he doesn't like showing his feelings. It's just the way he's made.' She knew David would not understand her fumbling attempts to explain his father any more than Malcolm had. 'He loved Mal a lot. I know sometimes he didn't act like it, but that doesn't mean he didn't feel it. And now he feels this. He feels it really, really hard. But he doesn't know how to talk about it.'

'Mal used to reckon he hated Pa,' David said. 'Specially when Pa gave him really bad hidings. Mal'd say he didn't care what Pa did, or what he said or anything. And after he got the knife he'd reckon he was going to do Pa in one of these days.'

'Shh, Dave, don't talk about that. It's best to forget those things.'

'But it was funny, Ma,' David went on earnestly. 'Mal'd say that, about not caring what Pa did and all that. But then sometimes I'd hear him crying. Only when it was really late at night and he thought I was asleep. I never let on I heard him, he would have been wild if I'd said anything about him bawling. But I think…' He was silent for a moment. 'I think he did care. He just didn't want anyone to know.'

Amy sighed. 'I think you're right. That was the main trouble with Mal and your father, you know. They were too much like each other.'

Consoling David was not difficult; not when he instinctively turned to her for comfort, eager to share his thoughts and feelings. David mourned for his brother, but he would get over the loss in time, Amy knew, especially with his youth and easy-going nature to help him.

But Charlie troubled her deeply. When the trembling hands and grey face of his whisky binge disappeared, Amy began to see the real scars Malcolm's death had etched in him. The mouth that had habitually been set in a stern, unyielding line now took on a twist so bitter that she found it almost painful to look at. When he thought no one was watching him, Amy would often see a brooding resentment in his eyes. She sensed the course his thoughts were taking. All the wrongs, real and imagined, that he had ever suffered were epitomised in this one gross betrayal. The one thing in his life that had mattered to him above all else had been stolen from him. He might be unsure whether his enemy was the English race; the New Zealand government; some mindless, all-powerful fate; or even himself; but that made his resentment none the less bitter. Whomever he blamed for it, he would never be able to forgive the betrayal.

He stubbornly refused to talk about Malcolm. In the early days after the dreadful news, any attempt by Amy to raise the subject was met with a snarl that, if she persisted, turned into roars of abuse. Later, when he was apparently calmer, he was no less obstinate.

'Don't know who you're talking about,' was his usual answer. 'I've no son of that name.'

Charlie spoke less than he had in the past. Sometimes a whole day passed with no more than a dozen words exchanged between himself and Amy. He seemed reluctant to mix with other people any more than he had to, often sending David to take the milk to the factory instead of going himself, and constraining Amy to beg a ride into town with John or Harry when she needed to visit the store. Occasionally Charlie went out to one of the hotels for an evening, but most of his drinking was done alone in his room.

He would no longer attend church, but he usually grunted an indifferent assent when Amy asked if she could go. On one of her trips to church with her family, Amy heard the news that had caught the imagination of Ruatane's townsfolk.

'John says they're going to put up a monument,' she told Charlie over lunch. She studied his face as she added, 'A monument to Mal—to my son,' she amended when she saw his scowl deepen.

Charlie said nothing at first, but she could see that the idea had caught his interest. 'What do you mean, a monument?' he asked after a pause. 'Are they going to put up a statue?'

Amy shook her head. 'Not a statue. A big stone, sort of like a tombstone. We can't get him back to bury him here, but there's going to be a proper stone to him in the cemetery.' The idea had already given her comfort; it had troubled her that Malcolm was buried in a graveyard halfway around the world whose name she could not even pronounce, and where she would never be able to place flowers on his grave. Now, at least, there would be a solid memorial. 'People are putting in money for it, and as soon as they've got enough they're going to send away for a special stone.'

'I'll have no part of it,' Charlie said. 'They needn't think I'm paying out good money for it, either.'

'I don't think anyone's going to ask you, Charlie.'

There seemed no difficulty in raising the money. Malcolm had been the only soldier from Ruatane to have gone to South Africa, and the locals readily forgot the boy's misdemeanours in the excitement of commemorating him. By July the monument was ready, and its dedication had been planned. And Amy was preparing herself for a battle.

She waited until the evening before the dedication to make her approach to Charlie, making sure that David had gone to bed before she raised the subject.

'The memorial's ready,' she began. Charlie made no comment, merely rustled his newspaper noisily as a sign that he did not want to listen.

'They're having a special service tomorrow afternoon—a dedication, they're calling it. They're going to have speeches and things.' A grunt was the only reply, though she knew he was following every word.

She took a deep breath. 'I want to go to the service.'

'Well, you're not,' he said from behind his newspaper.

'I should go—I think it's the right thing to do.'

He lowered his newspaper and glared at her. 'Are you deaf as well as stupid? You heard me. You're not going, and that's that. The boy's...' his voice cracked a little. 'He's nothing to do with us. He's no son of mine.'

'I think I'm the best judge of that,' Amy said, irritation briefly getting the better of her. 'Well, you stay home if you want, Charlie, but when the whole town's gone to the trouble of putting up a monument to my son, I think I should be there to see it dedicated.'

'I've had about enough of you, you nagging little bitch!' he shouted. 'I don't care a damn what you think! You're stopping home tomorrow.'

Amy bent over her sewing and made a show of concentrating on a difficult seam.

'You hear me?' he demanded. 'Got it in that dopey head of yours yet?'

'Yes, I understand.' She waited a moment before adding, 'John's coming over tomorrow.'

'What's he want here?'

'He's coming to fetch me. I thought you mightn't want to come, so John said he'd pick me up. Harry'll probably come, too—the whole family's going in tomorrow.'

She looked up from her sewing to meet his gaze. 'You can tell them why I can't go. They might make a fuss about it.'

His fingers gripped the edges of the paper so tightly that Amy saw his knuckles whiten. She watched the flow of thoughts across his face, knowing he was trying to decide whether to enforce his ban anyway.

Discretion won over pride. 'Suppose you might as well go,' he said. 'Get you out of my sight for a bit.'

Amy wished she could leave it at that and be grateful, but she had not quite finished the argument. 'And I'll take Dave with me.'

'No, you won't. I've work for him tomorrow.'

'Charlie, it's a service for Dave's brother. Don't you think he should be there for it?'

'No.' He looked at her, clearly waiting for her to say something else, but Amy stared back in silence, wondering if he would realise the obvious for himself.

Comprehension dawned. 'Did you tell that brother of yours Dave'd be coming too?'

'Yes, John's expecting Dave. He'll come looking for him if he's not around.'

He scowled at her, but Amy saw defeat in his face. 'You and your bloody family! To hell with the lot of you! All right, take the bugger with you. I don't care what you do, just shut up your whining.'

'Thank you,' Amy murmured as she resumed her sewing.

It was victory of a sort, but she wished it could have been achieved with less animosity. A vague feeling of unease troubled her for the rest of the evening and all the following morning.

Charlie had made himself scarce some time before John rode up to the house. 'So he's not coming, eh?' John asked Amy while they waited for David to catch a horse and lead it over to them.

Amy shook her head. 'Don't mention it in front of Dave. He's upset about it all—you know, how Charlie won't let anyone say Mal's name and all that. And now with Charlie not coming to the service, when Dave knows everyone's going to be there. I've been frightened him and Charlie are going to have a row about it.'

'Well, I won't say anything. Can't speak for anyone else, though.' John hoisted Amy behind his saddle for the short ride down to the main track, 'You forget about the old fellow for this afternoon, eh? You look as though you could do with a rest from it all.'

It was David who really deserved the rest, Amy thought as she sat squashed companionably between Sophie and Jane on the way into town, each of her sisters-in-law holding a child on her lap. The two farms' worth of Leiths made quite a procession down the valley, with buggies full to overflowing while most of the riding horses carried a small child or two as well as a larger rider. David was quiet for the first few minutes, but Amy saw his face gradually lighten as he began talking with his cousins.

It was good to see David have a rare opportunity to let down his guard. He was still a month short of fifteen, but he had been forced into a wariness that seemed unnatural in a boy so young. Not that David looked much like a fifteen-year-old. He was only four months older than Dolly, the nearest in age of his cousins, but he appeared several years older than any of them.

David seemed to have filled out his long, lanky body in a rush over the last few months, Amy thought as she studied his lean, well-muscled frame. The extra work since Malcolm's departure had forced him into rapid growth. All his shirts were becoming too tight for him, with the muscle he had acquired. His face was still boyish, but his body was unmistakably a man's.

He had borne more of the burden of Charlie's moods than she had lately, Amy knew. She only had to cope with Charlie at mealtimes and during the usually silent evenings; David had to work with him all day long.

Charlie had never been an easy man to please, but now it seemed that David could do nothing right. If the boy took pains over his work he was slow and stupid; if he hurried, he was making a shoddy job of things. And there was one failing David had in his father's eyes that no amount of hard work could ever atone for: he was not Malcolm.

Amy knew there had been a great deal of interest in Malcolm's monument, but she had not been prepared for the size of the gathering at the town's cemetery. Every house in town must be empty, she thought as she gazed around at the sea of faces. Gratitude brought a brief rush of tears, but she fought them back, anxious to show a calm demeanour.

She took David's arm and let John steer her through the crowd with his hand on her other shoulder, people falling back to make room for them. She heard murmurs all around her as they walked, snatches of audible words among them:

'Hasn't come.' 'His own son's service, too.' 'Such a shame, poor woman.' 'Miserable old bugger.'

The last voice, clearly a man's, was hurriedly 'Shushed' as they passed, but not before Amy had seen David's face stiffen. She gripped his arm more tightly, and felt John give her shoulder an encouraging squeeze as they came to the centre of the crowd around Malcolm's memorial.

It was a comfortable feeling, standing surrounded by so many people who wished her well. All her family were there, Lizzie and Frank nearly constituting a crowd in their own right with their seven children. Almost everyone else she knew at least by name, and all around her she saw kind faces. She noticed to her surprise that a girl she barely knew by sight was crying quietly, her cheeks wet with tears. Amy was touched by the girl's show of grief, though she was sure it must be no more than a reaction to the emotion around her.

Charlie should be here. He should be here to see how everyone wants to be kind to us. Instead, she knew, he was sitting at home brooding on the wrongs the world had done him. She could think of no way to draw him out of his dark solitude.

Fretting about Charlie would not help her behave with proper dignity. Amy studied the tall, black marble stone while she waited for the service to begin, impressed at the size of the memorial. It had Malcolm's name and the years of his birth and death, as well as the fact that he had died while serving in the war, with a verse near the base just above an inscription stating that the stone had been erected by the people of Ruatane. There was nothing to say who Malcolm's parents were.

Reverend Simons used a stick to guide his steps now, but he was still as capable as ever of noisily denouncing sin from the pulpit of his church. Today he was in a softer mood. He said a prayer for the repose of Malcolm's soul, the words a set form from the prayer book, but kind sincerity in his voice. When he followed this prayer with a short thanksgiving for Malcolm's life, Amy was pleasantly surprised at the apparent fervency of the assembly's 'Amen'.

The minister ended with a prayer dedicating the stone to Malcolm's memory, then spoke briefly to the assembled crowd, emphasising the gratitude for Malcolm's sacrifice that the stone represented. It was a mark of the community's goodwill, he told them, that so many people had contributed so generously. He sounded quite detached until, right at the end of his talk, he looked straight at Amy and said,

'I'm sorry that Mr Stewart wasn't able to be here today, Mrs Stewart.'

Amy met his gaze and gave a small shrug. She heard the renewed murmurs aroused by the minister's words, and was glad when they were silenced by the next speaker's striding forward.

Sergeant Riley looked rather self-conscious at having been thrust into the role of representing officialdom at the service, but the solemnity of the occasion did not make him any less forthright than usual.

'Most of you'd know that Mal Stewart was no friend of mine,' he began, raising a low murmur of shock. Amy felt a tiny smile tugging at her lips. She would have thought less of Sergeant Riley if he had pretended otherwise.

'That doesn't mean I can't admire courage when I see it,' he said, raising his voice a little to cut through the murmurs. 'I called that boy a lot of names in my time, but I never called him coward.' His mouth twisted in a wry grin. 'Mad, maybe, especially when he was on the back of a horse, but never a coward. He was one of the bravest kids I ever knew.'

He looked around at the faces staring back at him. 'I'm sure he made a fine soldier. He did us all proud, and it's only right that we've put this up,' he patted the memorial, 'to say thank you to him. And to his family.' His eyes met Amy's, and he nodded thoughtfully at her. 'He was a fine boy in his own way, Mrs Stewart. You can be proud of him.'

I'd sooner have him alive. But she gave as good a smile as she could manage.

Sergeant Riley stepped back into the crowd, and Amy saw people looking expectantly in her direction. It was time for someone from Malcolm's family to speak, she realised. Time for Charlie to speak.

'Looks like I've got to say something,' John murmured in her ear. 'Haven't made a speech since I got married—can't remember what I said then, either.' He took a step forward and cleared his throat noisily.

John was a man of few words, and Amy was grateful for the readiness with which he took over the responsibility Charlie had abdicated. He told the crowd that Malcolm's family were grateful for the memorial, and for the numbers that had turned out to remember Malcolm. After three sentences he had exhausted his fund of oratory. He thanked everyone once again, and stepped back to Amy's side with obvious relief.

'Thanks, John,' she said quietly, taking his hand in hers and squeezing it.

'Just don't ask me to do it again in a hurry, eh?' John grinned at her and put an arm around her shoulders. 'You all right?' Amy nodded, leaning against his broad chest and reflecting on how much it was like snuggling against their father had been. 'Good girl.'

He looked around at the crowd, which was already beginning to disperse. 'We'd better hang around here for a bit, let them get a head start on us. It'll take them a couple of minutes to get the hall set up properly.'

'What for, John? Aren't we going home now?'

'Didn't I tell you? They're putting on afternoon tea in the church hall for us, tea and cakes and all.'

'Oh. I didn't think we'd be out for that long.'

'I suppose we don't have to turn up,' John said doubtfully, but Amy shook her head.

'Yes, we do. Don't worry, it'll be all right. He won't mind if dinner's a bit late just this once.' And if he did mind, she would just have to manage him. She could not insult these good people by refusing to be guest of honour at their tea.

Lizzie took charge of Amy at the afternoon tea, shooing David away to talk to his cousins. Amy saw him deep in conversation with Beth soon afterwards, and when she next caught sight of him he was in a corner talking earnestly with George. She was glad to see David animated again; the constant reminders of Malcolm's death all through the service had left him looking tense and drawn with the effort of holding back tears.

She spent the next hour or so giving polite answers to well-meaning questions, smiling and nodding at people, and being plied with tea and a variety of cakes and sandwiches. It was a relief when she found John at her side again.

'Time we were going, I think,' he said. 'No one else'll leave till we do. I'd better grab Dave off George before that mad brother of ours has him on the boat and halfway to Auckland.'

Amy smiled at the notion; whatever things she might have to worry about, David's getting an attack of wanderlust was not among them.

The sun was not far above the western hills when Amy and David made their way up the track to the house, David leading the horse by its reins so that he and Amy could walk together. They spoke in low voices, both tired and subdued from the events of the afternoon, till they rounded the last bend in the track and saw Charlie standing there.

'You took your time,' he said, with a baleful stare at each of them.

'I'm sorry, Charlie, I didn't think it'd go on so long. I'll start getting dinner on right now, it shouldn't be too late.'

Charlie made no answer, instead turning his glare on David. 'I didn't tell you you could take one of my horses.'

'Didn't think you'd grudge it,' David said, not looking at his father as he spoke.

'You should have bloody asked me. You hear me, boy?'

'Yes, I hear you.' He turned away and led the horse towards its paddock, leaving Charlie scowling at his retreating back. David stopped on his way to let an excited Biff off the chain. The dog capered along beside him like a pup, making an odd counterpoint to David's uncharacteristically stolid tread.

Amy went into the house, and Charlie soon followed her. Rather than waste time changing out of her formal mourning clothes, she made do with slipping an apron over the heavy black cloth.

Charlie sat down at the table, taking a biscuit from one of the tins he had left open there. 'Anyone turn up?' he asked between bites.

Amy untied the long, black ribbons of her bonnet and placed it on a chair, then began peeling potatoes. 'The whole town, I think. I've never seen so many people in Ruatane. And they all said such nice things about… him.'

'Never had a good word to say for him when he was alive,' Charlie muttered.

Amy stopped peeling for a moment, her knife poised over the potato. 'No, I suppose they didn't. But that's what happens when someone dies. People forgive everything once you're dead.' She shot a glance at him over her shoulder. 'Most people do, anyway.'

Charlie gave a grunt and rose to his feet. 'Better get that boy doing some work. Needn't think he can waste the whole day, just because he got away with sneaking out like that.'

'Give him a chance to get out of his good clothes first, Charlie. And it was my idea to take him into town with me, remember.'

He stared at her through narrowed eyes. 'Aye, I remember, all right. I'll not be forgetting it in a hurry.' He stalked out of the room, pausing in the doorway to add, 'Won't stop him getting a kick in the backside if he doesn't get on with his work.'

Well, it wouldn't be the first kick, and probably not the last. Amy tried to get on with her work without brooding over Charlie and David, but her hands carried out the familiar tasks without involving her mind. Why did she feel so uneasy? Charlie was in a sour mood, but that was no novelty. She should be used to the pall of smouldering anger that hovered about him. Hovered as though it was waiting for a target; something to focus itself on. She shuddered at the memory of the dark look he had given her as he had left, though she had nothing to fear for herself. He would not dare raise a hand to her.

But there was David to think of. Dear, patient David, whose patience was showing signs of wearing. Whose nerves must be taut after all the events of the afternoon. She knew she was being like an old mother hen with one chick, but how could she be otherwise when David was the only child she had left?

David had changed into his working clothes, and he and Charlie were mending the fence just behind the house. From time to time Amy heard their voices through the open kitchen window. She gradually became aware that it was only Charlie's voice she was hearing, and that it was growing increasingly loud.

This was not the time to let Charlie try and pick a fight with David. Perhaps she could distract him until tomorrow, when he would have begun to forget that David had gone out against his will.

Abandoning her pots of vegetables, she hastily buttered some scones that Charlie had not found when he raided the tins earlier. She spread a generous layer of strawberry jam on each one, then took the plateful outside and over to the fence, where she waited for a good moment to interrupt. Biff came over to her and rubbed against her legs, looking at her plate with open longing. She broke off a corner of one scone and gave it to the delighted dog.

David was holding a fence post upright while Charlie held his heavy hammer above it, ready to drive the post into the ground. Charlie looked drawn with fatigue, and the tightness of his mouth showed that his mood was as grim as Amy had feared. She saw his chest heaving with effort, and she tried to think of a way of suggesting that he should tell David to do the heavy work.

David was as tall as his father, now that Charlie had become increasingly stooped, Amy realised with a start. Young though he was, he had almost come into his full adult strength, while Charlie must be close to sixty and looked even older.

But Charlie would not thank her for telling him he was getting old; the best she could do was give him an excuse to stop working for a few minutes. 'Would you like a scone, Charlie?' she asked.

'Suppose so.' He made a grab at one, smearing jam on his hand in the process. He devoured the scone in two bites, and reached for another.

'You don't need any,' he said, knocking David's hand away when the boy reached out towards the plate. 'You'll have been stuffing yourself all afternoon, I'll be bound. You've been no bloody use to me today, anyway.' He wiped his hands on his trousers and took a fresh grip on the hammer. 'Time we got back to it.'

Charlie took a stand close to the post and raised his hammer. 'Hold that thing steady,' he told David. 'Don't let it move till I've got it well in.' He took a massive swing at the fence post. Amy saw the muscles of his upper arms bulging through his shirt sleeves. The stroke fell with a crack of metal against wood. But it was unsteady, for all the force behind it, and the post went into the ground at an angle.

'I told you to hold the bloody thing,' Charlie shouted. 'Can't you do anything right?' David looked down at the ground, biting his lower lip.

'Well? Haven't you got a tongue in your head? Don't stand there like a bloody ninny.'

'I did hold it steady,' David muttered towards his feet.

Charlie's hand lashed out, leaving a red welt on David's cheek. Amy was sure his anger was as much at his own weakness as at any imagined failing on David's part. 'Don't talk back to me, boy. I say you let the thing slip. You're a useless bugger, aren't you?' His voice rose. 'You're bloody useless. You'll never amount to a damned bit of good. You're not half the boy your brother was.'

After Charlie's roar, the silence seemed all the more unnatural. He let the hammer fall from his hand and took a step backwards, his face half turned away. Amy saw his mouth working with emotion.

David was staring at his father with his eyes wide and his teeth bared slightly. He looked uncertain whether to scream in rage or burst into tears at the brutal injustice of it. Charlie had broken his own rule that Malcolm was not to be spoken of by flinging the cruellest of insults in David's face.

Amy put the plate on the ground, went up to him and rested a hand on his arm. 'He doesn't mean it,' she said softly. 'Don't take any notice. Please, Davie.'

She felt the stiffness gradually ease out of him. Amy slid an arm around his waist and leaned against his chest, grateful once again for his patient nature. 'Thank you, darling,' she whispered, standing on tiptoe to plant a kiss on his cheek.

That was the first mistake, she realised afterwards. She was usually so wary of showing David affection in front of Charlie, but shock had made her careless. She had believed Charlie was too lost in his own thoughts to take any notice, but when she glanced in his direction she saw him studying them with his lip curled in disgust.

'Look at you two. You make a pretty sight, don't you? The mammy's boy and his bitch of a mother.'

Amy felt David stir against her. She tried to pull away from him, to break the guilty tableau, but he put a possessive arm around her.

'Don't talk to Ma like that,' he said in a low voice. From the ground at his feet, Biff gave a barely audible growl. Amy saw the hair along the dog's back rise.

'I'll talk to her how I please. And I'll have none of your lip, boy. You get out of here,' Charlie said, turning his eyes on Amy. 'Go on, bugger off, you meddling little bitch.'

'I said don't talk to her like that.' David's voice was louder this time. He let his arm drop from around Amy and took a step towards his father. 'She shouldn't have to listen to that.'

'Oh, aye, you and your precious little ma,' Charlie said, his voice dripping with scorn. 'I could tell you some things about her if I had a mind to. You'd maybe think a bit different about her then.' He cast a venomous glance at Amy.

And that was her second mistake, she told herself over and over again when it was too late to do anything about it. She let Charlie see that his words frightened her, and her fear gave him a weapon, turning an unthinking remark into a threat.

'Aye, maybe I will,' he said thoughtfully. 'It's maybe about time the boy found out a few things about you. Well, boy? Want to know what your ma used to get up to before I got hold of her? Want to know how she was no better than a whore?'

Don't, Charlie. Please don't. She tried to speak, but no sound came.

'You shut your mouth!' David shouted. 'You say one more word like that about Ma and I'll shut it for you.'

'It's no more than the truth. Can't keep the truth quiet for ever, eh, bitch? Whoring's bound to come out in the end.'

'I told you to shut up!' David screamed. He crossed the ground between them in two long strides. Before Amy had gathered voice enough to cry out to him she saw his long arm snake towards his father. David's fist connected with Charlie's jaw in a sickening crunch.

Charlie staggered back, stunned as much by the fact of the blow as by the strength behind it. He stared at David in blank disbelief, then with a roar of rage launched himself at the boy.

At the same moment, Biff gave a snarling bark and ran at Charlie. Before the dog had time to reach them, David deflected his father's blow with a thrust of his left arm then delivered another punch with his right fist that knocked Charlie to the ground. When he tried to rise, he found Biff snatching at a mouthful of his sleeve while David stood over him, his fist still clenched.

'Stop it!' Amy screamed. She picked up her skirts and ran towards them. She took hold of Biff's rope collar and hauled on it until the dog released Charlie's sleeve; then, holding the collar with one hand, she tugged at David's arm till he let his fist drop. 'Come away, Dave! Charlie, he didn't mean to hurt you,' she said to the figure still sprawled on the ground. 'He just got in a state, with Mal's service today and everything.'

She pulled both David and Biff away a few steps, and held her breath as she watched Charlie slowly get to his feet. His eyes locked on David's, but he made no move towards the boy.

'Get out,' he said in a voice so low that it was more of a growl. 'Get out of here.'

'Go over to your Uncle John's, Dave,' Amy said urgently. 'You can stay the night with them.' And in the morning, perhaps it would all be forgotten. Even as she formed the thought, she knew it was hopeless.

'You've got ten minutes, boy,' Charlie said. 'Pack your clothes and get off my farm. You'll get out of town if you know what's good for you. If

I ever see you on my land again I'll blow your bloody brains out.'

Amy felt herself go cold as the meaning of his words sank in. 'No,' she whispered. 'Don't send David away. Not Dave. Please, Charlie, please! He didn't mean it! He's sorry now, aren't you, Dave? Tell your father you're sorry. Please, Davie!'

'I'm not sorry!' David blurted out. 'I'll do it again if he talks to you like that.'

'Ten minutes, boy,' Charlie repeated. 'And take that bloody mongrel, too, or I'll cut its throat.'

'All right, I will!' David shouted. 'I'll clear out, just like Mal did! That's why he went off and got killed—just 'cause he wanted to get away from you.' He flung the words over his shoulder as he went away at a half run, Biff loping at his heels.

'You go on your own two feet, too,' Charlie called. 'You touch any of my horses and I'll have you hung for a horse thief.'

'Davie, no!' Amy cried after him. She ran as fast as she could, but by the time she reached the house David was already in his room, pulling clothes out of the drawers and making an untidy pile on the bed. He seemed unaware of the grazes Amy could see on his knuckles, legacies of his fist's encounter with his father's jaw.

'Don't go, Davie,' Amy sobbed, flinging herself on him. 'Don't go away.'

David stopped his work to take her in his arms, pressing her cheek against his chest. 'I've got to,' he said, his voice taut with emotion. 'I've had enough of him. I'm not putting up with it any more.'

He gripped her so tightly that it almost hurt, then abruptly held her at arms' length. 'Come with me, Ma! I'll get you away from him. I can look after you—I'm going to get a good job somewhere. I'll show him who's useless! There's places you can make heaps of money—George said today there's mines you can work in, they pay heaps—he said the boat goes near there, he'd get me a ride any time. The boat's going tomorrow, and I'm going to be on it. You come too—George'll take you too.'

Amy waited for the flood of words to subside, shaking her head as he spoke. 'I can't, Davie. I can't just up and leave like that. You'll have enough to do looking after yourself without me to worry about.' She put her hands over his, willing herself into calm as she tried to think about what was best for David.

It was like the years of sickening fear for Malcolm all over again. Charlie would never forgive David; and David would be as stubborn in his turn. It was no use to consider sending him to live with John; it would only be a matter of time before he and his father fought again, and more seriously, if they were separated by no more than a few fences. It wouldn't be fair to try and keep David close to her.

'I think you're right, Dave. I think you've got to go.' Her voice cracked on the last word. 'It's Waihi you're thinking of,' she said, barely managing to school herself into a semblance of calm. She began folding David's clothes, glad of something to occupy her hands. 'That's where the mines are. You'll have to get off the boat at Tauranga and then… oh, I don't know, perhaps there's a coach or something.'

'You come too,' David insisted.

Amy shook her head. 'Where would I stay? The people who run the mine might only have places for men for sleep. They wouldn't want someone turning up with their mother. You'll have to think about learning the work and everything, and getting to know strange people.' Her little boy, among strangers. She bit back tears, knowing that David would not keep his own control if she let hers slip.

'Well… maybe I can't take you just now. But I'll send for you, Ma. I'll make lots of money for us, and I'll get a proper house for you to live in, then I'll send for you. Will you be all right with him till I can get you away?'

Amy gave him a watery smile. 'Dave, I'd been looking after myself around your father for a lot of years before you got big enough to thump him on my account. Don't you worry about me.'

She went to fetch something for David to carry his clothes in. There would be no chance to make him a neat bag like the one she had sewn for Malcolm. She tipped a pile of mending out of its drawstring carrier and onto her bed, then brought the bag to David's room and packed his clothes into it. It was the one in which she had carried her own belongings to Charlie's house on the day of her marriage, she realised as she drew it closed.

'This is all the money I've got just now,' she said, reaching into her apron pocket and pulling out a few coins. 'Only one and threepence. I haven't got any in the bank. I gave it all to Mal. Maybe this'll buy you your dinner tomorrow.' She pressed the coins into his hand and closed his fingers over them. 'George can get you on the boat for free, can't he? You'll have to ride with the cargo, though. Maybe he'll lend you a bit of money, too—I can pay him back soon. I'll be getting my next quarter's worth of Grandpa's money this month, I'll be able to send you some then.'

'I won't need your money, Ma. I'm going to get a good job.'

'You'll have to eat till you get one. And you'll have to pay for the coach. Dave, you mustn't go into town tonight—I'm sure it's going to rain, and you'll catch your death walking all that way on a cold night like this. Stay the night with your Uncle John.'

'No, I'll stay with Uncle Frank,' David said. 'I'll be closer on my way to town for tomorrow morning. Anyway, Beth's got a kitten with a broken leg, and we thought we'd have a go at setting it. I told her I'd try and get down to give her a hand this week.'

Amy watched him throw the bag over his shoulder. 'You'll write to me, won't you? I'll want to know how you're getting on.'

'Every week,' he promised. 'Maybe more than that.'

'I don't think your father would let me get letters from you, though. You'd better send them to Uncle John, or maybe Uncle Frank. Ask Uncle Frank to lend you some money, too—that'd be better than asking George. But be sure and tell him I'll pay it back as soon as I can.'

She hurried along at his side, trying to match her steps to his long ones, as they walked from the house to the beginning of the track. Amy tried to think of the sensible advice David might need now that he was to make his own way in the world, all the while knowing she was ill-equipped to give such advice. But the words filled up the silence that would otherwise fall between them; words would stop her from breaking down in front of David.

Charlie had gone back to working on the fence. They had to pass him to get to the track. 'You still here?' he growled.

'I'm going, don't you worry.'

Charlie spat on the ground. 'Good. I don't want to see you round here again.'

David stopped in his tracks and stared long and hard at his father. 'I'm going, all right. But I'll tell you this—if I hear you've laid a hand on Ma, I'll come back. And I'll kill you.' He said it in a low, calm voice; not as a threat, merely as a statement of fact. Amy could see that the words had shaken Charlie, despite his attempts to seem unconcerned.

'Get out of here,' he said, and turned his back on them.

Amy flung her arms around David's neck and gave him a long, lingering embrace. When she released him, she had to bite her lip to hold back the sob that begged to be allowed out. 'Take care, Davie,' she said, her voice made small by the tightness in her throat.

He bent to press his mouth against hers one more time, then straightened up and walked off down the track, the dog bounding along beside him in oblivious delight at the outing. Amy stood and watched, the back of her hand pressed to her mouth and her shoulders shaking with sobs.

'Good riddance,' she heard Charlie mutter, and suddenly she could not bear to be within sight of him. She ran to the house, stumbling over the rough ground with eyes half blinded by tears, rushed into her bedroom and slammed the door behind her.

She braced her back against the door, then looked about wildly for some way of blocking it. Tomorrow she would have to face the aching emptiness of the house without David, but tonight she was not going to be in the same room as Charlie.

She dragged her heavy chest of drawers over to the door, wedging it against the hinges and into the corner of the room, so that any attempt to force the door open would only press the chest harder against the wall. She had scarcely finished shoving it in place and was leaning against the chest, catching her breath, when she heard Charlie come in the back door shouting for her.

'Hey! Where the hell are you, woman?' he called. 'You got that dinner on yet?'

She made no answer. Instead she stood silently, listening to the sound of his footsteps on the kitchen floor. He hammered on her bedroom door, his fist making it shake.

'You're in there, aren't you?' His voice came muffled through the wood. 'Having a sulk, eh? Well, you can bloody well get out here and get my dinner on. I'll not put up with your nonsense tonight.'

Again she said nothing, but pressed her body more firmly against the chest.

'I'm warning you,' he called. The door handle turned, and the door opened a fraction. Charlie shoved on it, but the chest did its work. The harder he shoved, the more solidly it was wedged against the wall.

'You little bitch!' he roared. 'You get out here or you'll be sorry.' The handle rattled again. Amy heard a stream of abuse directed at her, then there was a brief silence.

'Well, bugger you, then,' he yelled at last. 'Think I need you? I managed for myself before I ever had you to plague me, you useless, good-for-nothing little slut!'

She heard pots and plates being rattled, as Charlie snatched things off the shelves.

'You can stay in there and starve, and good bloody riddance to you! I can get my own meal on,' he called. She could tell from the fainter sound that he had his back turned to her. The rattling and banging went on, interrupted by a crash and a curse as what sounded like a mug fell to the floor.

He couldn't get his own meal; of that she was quite certain. It was more than seventeen years since he had last had the need to, and his kitchen was a very different place from what it had been then. She doubted if he so much as knew how to work the range. He could boil the kettle for himself, and get a slice of bread, but anything beyond that would have taken him all evening to manage.

It did not take Charlie long to realise the same thing. 'Shit,' she heard him cry out. She guessed that he had burnt his hand. He slammed his fist against her door; she felt the force of it right through the chest of drawers. 'Bugger you!' he roared. 'Bugger you! Think you're the only woman in the world, do you?'

The back door slammed, making the whole house shake. Soon afterwards she heard the sound of Charlie riding away down the track, and knew that he was taking himself into town to eat at a hotel. And perhaps to gratify himself with a whore afterwards, if he did not get too drunk first. He would not be back before the early hours of the morning.

Amy sank to the floor and clutched her arms around herself, her back resting against the chest. The room was in darkness now. She gave a violent shudder as the night chill took hold of her. The house was so quiet that she could hear the sound of her own breathing.

I've lost all my children now. The thought seemed punctuated by the rhythmic throbbing in her head. *First it was Ann.* The memory of the tiny baby in her arms, and the empty cradle and her emptier heart after the baby had been snatched away, drew a ragged sob from her throat. *Then Alexander. They never even let me see him. Then all those babies. I hardly had the chance to know I was carrying them, then they were dead. And Mal. I sent him off for his big adventure, and it killed him. And now David. They're all gone now. All gone.*

Another sob, then another, and the flood of grief was upon her. She flung herself on the floor, her face soon smeared with tears while her body shook with the violence of her sobs. Grief racked her till she thought she had no more strength to weep, and then strength came from somewhere and she wept again.

'David!' she screamed aloud, the name ripping a path through her constricted throat, and the pain of screaming left her exhausted. She lay with her face against the floorboards, her hands clenching and unclenching on the empty air. At that moment, it was hard to think of any reason to go on living.

17

July – November 1902

But even if it no longer had any meaning, life was not something she could slip out of like a worn, old dress. Amy came to herself in the early morning cold and stiff, her throat raw with weeping, and her body aching after a night spent on the bare floor. She was alive, and the world had to be faced.

She undressed in the dark, and clambered into bed in her underwear, too weary for the bother of lighting a candle or putting on her nightdress. She did not know how long she had spent in the bed when she heard Charlie come home; nor how long it was after that before the habit learned over years woke her. It was time to get up, pull on some clothes, and make breakfast.

Amy ate her share as soon as she had cooked it, swallowing the food mechanically, hardly knowing what it was. She had cooked far too much, she realised as she dished it up, now that she had no growing boys to fill. The thought sent a fresh pang of loss through her, so acute that she felt it as a pain in her belly. It was not going to be easy to keep up the composed façade she intended to show Charlie. But she was determined not to give him the satisfaction of seeing her grief in its raw nakedness. Night and the privacy of her own room were the time and place for such self-indulgence.

She dished up an extravagant helping for Charlie and left it on the side of the range to keep warm, quite sure that he would sleep in a little after his outing of the night before. Her empty plate was on the bench with her knife and fork placed neatly on it by the time Charlie came out to the kitchen.

Amy felt his eyes fixed on her as she placed the plate in front of him. She busied herself with tidying the kitchen, filling the silence with the rattling of pots and plates. It took her some time to clear the mess Charlie had left after his abortive attempt to make his own dinner the night before, but she was glad of the distraction as she picked up the last shards of broken china from the corner where they lay half-hidden, wiped the spilt sugar from the bench, and swept up the heap of barley that had fallen to the floor when Charlie knocked over the bag. He seemed oblivious to the state he had left the kitchen in. *If I wasn't here, he'd have the kitchen worse than that. There'd be mud everywhere, too, if I wasn't cleaning it up all the time. After a couple of weeks, you'd think there'd never been a woman in this house.*

Charlie ate his food in silence, but he caught her eye when she reached across to take his empty plate. 'Don't think you can get away with that nonsense of yours again. Locking yourself in, and no dinner on the table and all. I'll let it pass this time—you were pining for your bairn,' he said with a sneer. 'Well, I've got rid of that young bugger, you'll not be seeing him again. And *you*,' he stabbed a finger towards her, 'can just behave yourself. Or I'll make you sorry for it.'

As if there was anything else he could do to hurt her, now that David was gone. She said nothing as she walked back to the bench, her mouth tight with the effort of holding back a retort.

'And that's enough of your sulking, too. I'll have no more of it.' He scraped his chair away from the table and walked towards the door. Amy stood with her back to him, waiting for the relief his absence would bring. 'What's the matter with you now? Eh? Cat got your tongue?'

'I've nothing to say.' Amy spoke the words to the wall behind the bench.

'Nothing that's any sense, I'll be bound. I'll have none of your whining and grizzling, woman.'

Amy turned to face him. 'You've sent my son away, Charlie. Don't expect me to thank you for it.' She regretted having spoken as soon as she saw the self-satisfied expression her words brought.

'I don't care a damn what you think of it.' He looked her up and down contemptuously. 'You look a right hag this morning.' Clearly pleased at having had the last word, he shoved the door closed behind him and went outside.

Amy finished clearing all traces of untidiness from the kitchen, then went back to her bedroom. A glance in her mirror showed there had been truth in Charlie's taunt. A few pins had survived the night to leave her hair roughly held up on one side, while the rest tumbled down in a tangled mass. Her eyelids were swollen and her face still bore traces of red blotches.

'Hag,' she whispered to the unsightly reflection. She turned away when the eyes in the mirror filled with tears. *Don't be such a baby. Dave'd feel terrible if he saw me in this state over him.*

She splashed cold water on her face and scrubbed it dry with a rough towel, then attacked her hair with comb and fingers until she had bullied it into submission. Her scalp was tender by the time she had finished, but she ignored its complaints as she stabbed pins into the heavy pile of curls.

This morning, tidying Charlie's room was a more disagreeable chore than usual; not because he had left it any more disheveled than he normally did, but because of her intense reluctance to have anything to do with him. She was careful never to go in there when Charlie was in the house, but just being in his bedroom brought her into a contact that was unpleasantly intimate. The room reeked of him, bringing back memories she would far rather forget.

The stink of stale urine told her that Charlie had used his chamber pot in the night. She hauled it out from under the bed to take outside and empty. A thick gob of spittle lurched drunkenly around the inside of the chamber pot as she carried it, greenish-brown amid the yellow of the urine. As she emptied the pot and rinsed it out, Amy wondered for a moment if Charlie had deliberately used it so as to make work for her, rather than walking the few steps outside. There was probably no active malice in it, she decided. After all, why should he take the trouble to go outside, exposing himself to the cold night air, when he had a wife to clean up after him?

She put away the clothes he had left lying on the floor, then made his bed, smoothing the sheets until no trace of a crease remained. The sheets still smelt faintly of soap from the wash of a few days before, the clean smell pleasant after the stink of urine. As she folded his nightshirt and placed it under the pillow, Amy remembered the musty smell of unwashed sheets that had filled her nostrils on the first night she had lain shivering with fear in this same bed. The sheets had been musty again when she had come home from Mrs Coulson's with her babies. *I don't think he even knows you're meant to wash sheets. If I wasn't here, he'd have this room smelling like an old goat in no time.*

There was no real need for her to go into the boys' room; certainly no work for her to do there. She went through anyway. Even if the room might never be used again, she could not bear to have it shut it up and ignored as if the boys had never existed.

There was so little left of them, a mere day after David's departure. The room still smelt of boys, but that would fade within days. She had already made the bed and tidied the room hours before David's fateful confrontation with his father, and the few clothes David possessed she had helped him pack, just as she had done for Malcolm when he had left.

The only visible reminder of the boys was the trophy Malcolm had won in the riding race at the A and P show so many years before, and which Amy still dusted every day then restored to its pride of place on top of the chest of drawers. She lifted it, and turned it to and fro so that the silver caught the light from the window, while she summoned up the memory of Malcolm's day of triumph and the way Charlie had soured it for him. But the trophy was showing signs of its age, despite Amy's careful polishing. It looked like a relic of someone long dead, and did little to lighten the bedroom's comfortless air. The room looked neat and tidy, and quite unoccupied.

Out of the old habit of neatness, she smoothed the faint creases in the coverlet that David's makeshift pack had left, and immediately regretted having added, however slightly, to the impersonal look of the room. She noticed something dark just visible where the coverlet met the floor. Amy knelt to retrieve it, and found it was a solitary sock, obviously dropped by David in his rush to pack and unnoticed by either of them until now.

Amy sank onto the bed and sat there with the sock in her lap, Malcolm's trophy resting against the neatly-darned black wool. A small silver cup and an unmatched sock; that was all that remained of the years the boys had spent in this room. They would not be hard to carry with her if she left.

So little to show that the boys had lived here, and little enough tangible sign of her own presence in the house. Her diligence kept the house from being overcome by dirt and general shabbiness, but that was a mere absence of squalor that any competent housekeeper could manage. There had never been any question of her being allowed to make the house reflect anything of herself; the only part of it that had ever felt as if it belonged to her was her own tiny bedroom, where Charlie never came and where she could have her few little treasures around her. If she bundled all her belongings up, they would not make too heavy a parcel. She could carry it easily enough if she left...

If she left. The realisation of what she was contemplating brought Amy's meandering thoughts to an abrupt halt. She had spent more than half her life in this house.

But what was there to hold her now? Even when Charlie's violence had driven her from his bed she had been reluctant to deprive the boys of their father, and to deprive Charlie of his sons, by leaving him. Now she had no children, and no father of her own to be upset by the scandal of an abandoned marriage. All she had to do was pack up her belongings, wait until Charlie went out, and walk away. He might rant and rave; might even be foolish enough to risk her brothers' vengeance by coming after her; but he would get used to her absence soon enough. Her bedroom, and the boys', would stand empty, and the house would soon become shabby and unkempt. It would be as if she and the boys had never lived there.

As if the boys had never existed at all. As if seventeen years of

271

childbearing and rearing, of being beaten and humiliated for six of those years, of struggling to protect her sons and give them all that she could of happiness and affection, had never happened. A small surge of revolt welled up in her at the thought of accepting such a defeat. It battled against the lure of never again having to spend a night under the same roof as Charlie.

It was a strong lure. She could go home again; back to the house where she had been happy. She could have her old room, sleep under her bedspread in her old bed, and make the room look as if she had never left it. It would be like going back to being a child again.

But she was not a child, and it was no use pretending otherwise. How could home be the same place it had been half a lifetime ago, with the memories of her lost children to haunt her? How could it be the same without her father there? It was John's house now, and much as she loved him, and however welcome he would make her, she knew she would be a burden to him if she came home. He did not need another woman around the house to help Sophie; what he did need was all the bedrooms in the house for his own children. It was all very well dreaming of having her old room back; she would be evicting two small boys from it if she did so.

And watching John's houseful of children grow up around her while she was as childless as if she had been barren would be even harder to bear than knowing herself to be a burden. Bad enough if he had nothing but sons, but there was Mary to make it even worse.

To her own mild surprise, after three boys in a row Sophie had produced a little girl. At three years old Mary was plump and sturdy like her mother, and almost as uncommunicative, but she had thick black hair, blue eyes, and a shy, pretty smile. Whenever Amy saw her, she was vividly reminded of David at the same age, before his beautiful curls had been shorn. And Mary stirred another memory that was equally poignant. Her hair might not be as long and wavy as Amy imagined her own daughter's to be, nor her eyes as huge or as startlingly blue, but if Amy had to live in the same house as her, Mary would be a constant, painful reminder of Amy's own loss.

The thought of living on in this house with Charlie, with no David to add any spark of happiness to her life, was not appealing; but surely it must be better than going home and having the old wounds torn open daily, and making a nuisance of herself into the bargain. She had no fear of Charlie; there was nothing he could do to hurt her now. If life held no great hope of pleasure ahead, at least she could minimise the pain.

'Frank! I want you to go into town, and you'd better hurry up or it'll be too late for today.' Lizzie's voice carried easily from the corner of the paddock where she stood to where Frank and Joey were repairing a stretch of fence, near the opposite corner.

Frank looked up from the work to watch Lizzie scurrying towards them, lifting her skirts to move more freely. The tone of her voice, not to mention her unusual haste, told him she was in a great state of agitation. When she was close enough for him to see her expression, he found it was not distress that had put that spark in Lizzie's eyes; it was excitement.

'I don't think I can go today, love,' Frank said, knowing as he spoke that she was unlikely to be put off quite so easily. When Lizzie got that look in her eye, she could be as hard to stop as the creek in flood. 'I want to get this lot finished this afternoon. I'll go tomorrow if you like.'

'No, that's no use, it might be too late by then. You can finish your fence tomorrow.'

'I don't know that I can—looks like it might rain tomorrow. What's the rush, anyway? What are you after in town?'

'Ma told me just now when I was up there.' Lizzie paused for effect, then made her announcement. 'The new doctor's arrived.'

'Yes, I heard that when I was in town the other day,' Frank said.

Lizzie's mouth briefly dropped open in shock. 'You knew he'd come and you didn't tell me?'

Frank shrugged. 'Didn't think you'd be interested. Mind you, I'm not sorry old Doctor Wallace's gone. He was a dead loss—he never did you a bit of good that time you were ill. It was your ma and Amy that pulled you through. He didn't even—'

'Yes, yes, never mind all that old business,' Lizzie said, cutting Frank's flow short. 'It's the new doctor I'm interested in. He's quite young, Ma said—not too young, though. And he's well off—he must be, anyway, being a doctor. And,' she beamed at Frank, clearly feeling that she had saved the best news till last, 'he's not married!'

Frank studied her in amusement tinged with irritation. He knew where all this was leading, and he did not particularly approve. 'Well, I don't see what that's got to do with you, Lizzie,' he said, trying unsuccessfully to make his voice stern. 'He mightn't be married, but you are. And I'm not about to start sharing you. Mind you, I might be able to get on with this fence a bit better if I did.'

'Oh, don't be so... so *awkward*,' Lizzie said, frowning at him. Frank knew he would have earned a more abusive name than 'awkward' if Joey had not been there to hear. 'You know what I mean. Now, I want you to go and see the doctor—Doctor Townsend, his name is, isn't that a nice name? He's from England. Anyway, go and see him, and tell him he's to come out tomorrow afternoon, about three o'clock. That'll give us time to get the lunch dishes done and everything, and the girls and me can do a load of baking.'

Frank was determined not to make it too easy for her. 'What do you want the doctor for? You're not sick, are you? You're looking a bit thin in the face,' he added with a total disregard for the truth.

'Of course I'm not sick! I want you to tell him—'

'Is one of the kids sick?' Frank asked, beginning to enjoy himself. 'I'll get him to come today if they are—no sense waiting till tomorrow if one of them needs a doctor.'

'No, today's too soon. Tomorrow'll be just right. I think I'll get Amy down, she could do with a rest from himself, and she can help me think it all out. I've got to sort out what Maudie'll wear, and I want her to make some nice biscuits—'

'Is Maudie sick? She shouldn't be doing baking, then, should she? What's wrong with her?'

'Maudie's *not* sick! I just want the doctor to come out so we can get to know him. That'd be neighbourly, wouldn't it?'

'He's not a neighbour,' Frank pointed out.

'No, but he's new. We should be making him welcome.'

'I don't know that I want to make him welcome. I don't know what sort of chap he is. I mean, he might be the sort of fellow who turns up and goes marrying people's daughters just because he likes the sort of biscuits they make.'

Joey let out a snort, and Lizzie glared at him. 'What's so funny, Joseph Kelly?'

'They'd have to be pretty good biscuits to make anyone want to marry Maudie,' Joey said, grinning at the notion.

'Who asked your opinion?' Lizzie said indignantly. 'Don't you go saying that when Doctor Townsend comes tomorrow, either. There's no need for anyone to be talking about getting married just yet, not the first time he comes out. Frank, you'd better hurry up, or it'll be dinner time before you're back.'

Frank leaned on a fence post and regarded Lizzie thoughtfully. 'Look, I tell you what,' he said in the voice of one being carefully reasonable. 'I'll go into town and see this doctor fellow,' Lizzie's face lightened as he spoke, 'if you'll finish off this fence for me. How does that sound?'

'Honestly, Frank, you can be so stubborn sometimes! As if a bit of fence matters more than your own daughter's future.'

He bowed to the inevitable. 'All right, Joey, you'd better run a message for your ma. I can finish this off by myself, it'll just take a bit longer. Your ma wants you to go and see this new doctor, and tell him he's to come out and marry Maudie.'

'How much will I say you'll pay him to take her, Pa?' Joey asked, his eyes glinting with mischief.

'Don't you go encouraging him, Frank! You're not to say any such thing, Joey. No, I've thought it out—tell him I want him to come and take a look at Rosie. She's got one of her chests.'

'Rosie's always getting one of her chests,' Joey pointed out.

'Then it's high time I had a doctor take a look at her. Anyway, don't pass remarks. Now, you go inside and put some clean clothes on—wear your Sunday jacket, too, I don't want him thinking we don't know how to behave. He's living in that house around the corner from the Masonic—you know, it used to be Walker's place. Tell him your mother wants him to have a look at your little sister, and he's to come at three o'clock tomorrow. Half past three would be all right. Can you remember that? Good. Off you go.'

She gave Joey a small shove to hurry him on his way, and watched him with a smug expression. 'That should work out nicely.'

'I don't know what your rush is,' Frank said. 'I shouldn't think the fellow'll be getting married to anyone else before the week's out.'

Lizzie turned on him. 'Frank, do you think this town's full of suitable men just lining up to marry Maudie? A nice young chap like this doctor, half the women in Ruatane will be after him for their daughters. And most of them live closer to him than we do. I'm not going to just wait around till someone else gets hold of him.'

'She's only fifteen. There's plenty of time for all that.'

'Sixteen,' Lizzie corrected him. 'She's sixteen. That's how old I was when you and me started keeping company. And how often will she get a chance like this?'

'Whenever there's a fellow with sense enough to know a fine girl when they see one. Anyway, I don't know if this doctor chap's good enough for my Maudie.'

'Then you'll get a chance to find out tomorrow. That's the idea of getting him out nice and soon, so we can have a good look at him. If he doesn't seem a decent sort of fellow, we won't have him again.'

'He'll have to be more than just decent if he thinks he's going to have Maudie... hey, I'm getting as mad as you,' Frank said, pulled up short by the realisation of how far he had let his thoughts wander. 'Who's to say this fellow even wants to get married?'

'Of course he does. He's the right age for marrying, he's got a good job, and he's got plenty of money. He must want to get married. How could he not?'

Frank studied her face, bright with conviction, and he broke into a smile. He drew Lizzie within the circle of his arm. 'Well, maybe because he doesn't know what he's missing out on. Poor beggar.'

As soon as she arrived at Lizzie's the next afternoon, Amy found herself being bustled into the girls' room, where Lizzie and Maudie were poring over the contents of the wardrobe. Lizzie carried Kate on one hip, while Rose wandered around at her feet occasionally tugging at Lizzie's dress in a vain attempt to get her mother's attention.

'Now, what do you think, Amy?' Lizzie asked. 'The blue one's nice, but I'm worried it might be a bit fancy for just an ordinary working day. We don't want the doctor thinking Maudie's got dressed up specially. Rosie, don't keep pulling my dress like that,' she said, brushing the little hand away. 'I'll get you a biscuit in a minute.'

'But Mama, I don't want—'

'Shh, girl, Mama's busy. Go outside and play if you like.'

'What about this one, Aunt Amy?' Maudie asked, pulling out a pale grey dress in fine wool, simple in style but with a prettily draped skirt.

'It's very plain,' Lizzie said. 'You want something a bit eye-catching.'

'Like that awful old pink dress you gave Maisie?' Maudie asked, a challenge clear in her voice. Amy spoke quickly before Lizzie could take it up.

'Why not wear the grey one with something to pretty it up?' she suggested. 'Have you got any nice sashes, Maudie?'

Maudie opened a drawer, and Amy rummaged through it till she found a sash in dusky pink. 'This one would look nice with it, don't you think?' She held the sash against the dress.

'Oh, yes, that's just right,' Lizzie said. 'It's pretty, but it doesn't look overdone.'

'And I've got a hair ribbon the same colour,' Maudie volunteered. 'But don't you think it might make me look like a little girl, Aunt Amy? Sashes and hair ribbons and stuff?'

Amy gave her a wistful smile. 'Don't be in too much of a hurry to grow up, Maudie.' But she did not want to spoil Maudie's obvious delight in the coming visitor. 'Shall I have a go at fluffing your hair out, so it looks all soft and full?'

'She's not having it up,' Lizzie said. 'I've told her we'll put her hair up come summer, when we let her dresses down. I'll put her in stays then, too.'

Maudie looked affronted. 'I don't want it up, anyway. It'd look stupid, putting my hair up while I'm still in short dresses.'

'I didn't mean putting it up,' Amy said. 'I just thought I could fluff it out. Here, I'll show you what I mean.'

She took Maudie's comb and began primping and fussing over the girl's thick, blond hair. A few minutes and a handful of hairpins later, she tied the pretty pink ribbon in place and stepped back to admire her handiwork.

'That looks lovely,' Maudie said in delight. 'Thank you, Aunt Amy!' She planted a kiss on Amy's cheek.

'You're good with hair, Amy,' said Lizzie.

'Oh, not really. I've had to figure out how to keep mine tidy, that's all. Mine's so thick, it'd be a real mess if I didn't manage it. I'm not really much good with clothes, you know,' Amy added. 'I'm not used to fancy things. You should have asked Lily, she's used to city fashions. Or even Susannah, come to that.'

'Humph!' Lizzie said. 'There's *some* girls who get a bit hoity-toity if people encourage them to think they know more than their betters. I don't let Lily give Maudie advice on how to dress any more. Anyway, you're quite right about that grey dress, and her hair looks lovely. Yes, she looks just right,' Lizzie said, studying Maudie. 'That's just how I wanted her to look. That should do nicely.'

Maudie bristled at her mother's proprietorial air. 'I don't know if I'm even going to like this doctor, you know,' she said loftily. 'He might be ugly, or have bad breath or something. Or he might just be boring. You needn't think I'm going to have anything to do with him if I don't like him.'

Instead of biting back as Amy expected her to, Lizzie regarded her daughter calmly. 'Oh, I wouldn't worry about that,' she said. 'If it comes to that, I don't suppose there's much chance he'll like you.'

Maudie opened her mouth, then closed it again. Amy saw the rush of thoughts across the girl's face as she mulled over this new notion.

'Time you got changed, then you can go and help Beth set those biscuits out on the plates, Maudie,' Lizzie said. 'We want it all to look just right. Put one of my aprons on over that dress. Mind you don't mess your hair up, either, now Aunt Amy's done it so nice for you. Rosie, do stop that,' she said, tugging her skirt out of Rosie's hand.

'Mama, why do I—'

'In a minute, Rosie. You just stay here with your sister—she'll give you some jobs to do in the kitchen in a bit. I want to have a little talk with Aunt Amy now.'

She led Amy out of the girls' room and into the front bedroom, then closed the door and put Kate down on the floor. 'Are you all right?' she asked, giving Amy a searching gaze. 'Not having any bother with him?'

'No, there hasn't been any trouble,' Amy said. 'Charlie hardly even talks to me, let alone saying anything nasty. I think he's too tired.' Charlie's loud gloating over having banished David had worn off as soon as the realisation sank in that he now had to do by himself the work the two of them had done together. By the end of most days he barely seemed to have the energy to eat his dinner, without wasting it on abusing Amy.

'That's all right, then.' Lizzie put her arm around Amy. 'I know it's not much fun for you, stuck there by yourself with him. And you miss Dave, of course.'

'Miss' was not a strong enough term. Amy did not have the words for the aching loss she still felt. The shock was over, now that David had been gone nearly four months, but the pain was still there. Even the sudden death of Ginger, thirteen years old and worn out by too many winters, a month after David's departure seemed part of the melancholy pattern. 'Oh, yes, I miss him all right,' she said softly. 'But he's safe. That's all that matters, really. I wanted Mal to be safe, and I made an awful mess of that, but Dave's all right. Even though I can't have him any more.'

'He'll come back one day.'

Amy shook her head. 'Not while Charlie's around. They'll never make it up, not those two. Charlie'll never forgive Dave, and Dave wouldn't come back without being asked. Not after the way Charlie talked to him.'

'Men are that stubborn,' Lizzie said, looking so stern that Amy could not help but smile.

'Don't worry about me, Lizzie. Dave's safe, and he's getting on all right. He's trying to save up his money, but they seem to take just about all he earns off him for board, poor thing. He says he's got plenty to get by on, though. And he writes faithfully every week, just like he said he would. He's a good boy.' The letters David sent her via Frank were a poor compensation for having lost him, but she drew every morsel of happiness she could from them. Her greatest pleasure was to sit in the boys' room when Charlie was away from the house, spreading out the letters on her lap and reading them over and over. 'Brooding', Lizzie had called it when she caught Amy at it, and perhaps it was, but Amy had no intention of giving it up.

'Well, as long as you're all right,' Lizzie said.

Amy gnawed at her lower lip while she tried to decide whether to speak about what was troubling her, then words came in a rush.

'Lizzie, you'll think I'm awful saying this. And I know Maudie's a good girl, I'm not trying to say she isn't. But… be careful with her. No matter what this Doctor Townsend seems like, be careful with Maudie. I'd hate anything to happen to her.'

'Of course you're not awful,' Lizzie said fiercely. 'And it's nothing to do with being a good girl, either—I know what men can be like. Oh, yes I do, don't you go looking at me like that. I wouldn't care if this fellow was the Prime Minister's son, I'm not letting him out of my sight with Maudie. Not until I know what his intentions are, anyway.'

'Give him a chance to know them himself, Lizzie,' Amy said, smiling. 'Give him a chance to meet her, anyway!'

'Well, there's no harm in thinking ahead, is there? It's no good just sitting back and waiting for things to happen.' Lizzie retrieved Kate from the floor and stood up. 'Come on, let's see if Maudie's doing things properly out there.'

Amy followed Lizzie out to the kitchen, to find that the boys had gravitated into the room, attracted by the smell of baking.

'Now listen, you boys,' Lizzie said, 'you can have some biscuits—just the plain ones, leave the fancy ones for when the doctor comes. Have plenty now, because you lot can stay outside when we have our afternoon tea. It'll just be the grown-ups then, and Maudie, because she's the oldest.' She looked thoughtfully at Beth. 'No, you can stay too, Beth. It'll be good for you to learn about mixing with different people.'

'Pity the doctor's not bringing a mate,' Joey said. 'Then you could see if the other fellow wanted to marry Beth.'

'One more word like that out of you, and you'll find you're not too big to get a hiding,' Lizzie said, narrowing her eyes at her oldest son. 'You can say good day to Doctor Townsend when he comes, but don't you go making any smart remarks in front of him. Oh, Rosie, don't start that pulling on my dress again! Do you want a biscuit or what?'

'No,' Rosie said in a whimper.

'Well, what *do* you want, then?'

'I want—I don't—I—' Rosie's words dissolved into a wail. Lizzie passed Kate over to Beth, sat on a chair and drew Rosie onto her lap. 'Come on, tell Mama what's wrong,' she said, suddenly gentle.

'I don't want the doctor to look at me,' Rosie sobbed. 'I don't want him to stick things in me.'

'He won't stick things in you! He'll just have a look at you, and try and see why you cough all the time. Then we'll have a nice afternoon tea, then he'll go home.'

'But—but he'll have great big needles and things,' Rosie insisted. 'And big, big knives. Doctors stick knives in you so they can see inside. I don't want him to!'

'Who told you that?' Lizzie asked.

'Mickey did! Mickey said the doctor would stick needles in me!'

'Michael Kelly, you stop right there,' Lizzie said, before a guilty-looking Mickey had got even halfway to the door. 'Have you been telling your sister stories about the doctor?'

'It was just a joke,' Mickey offered feebly. 'I didn't say anything about knives, either.'

Lizzie glared at him, and Mickey looked at his feet. 'I'll tell you a story if you're not careful. A story about a strap and a backside. Frightening your little sister like that! You tell Rosie you're sorry, and that it's not true.'

'Sorry, Rosie,' Mickey mumbled. 'It's not true what I said about the doctor.'

'Your father will have something to say to you, my boy, if I tell him what you've been up to. You just watch yourself.' Lizzie held Mickey's eyes for a few seconds before releasing his gaze. 'Right, off you get outside—no more biscuits for you today. There'll be no pudding tonight, either,' she called as Mickey made good his escape.

'Mama, I'm scared of the doctor,' Rosie said, sniffing noisily. 'He'll have needles.'

Lizzie wiped the little girl's nose and gave her a hug. 'Now, there's nothing to be frightened of,' she soothed. 'Mama will be there all the time the doctor's looking at you. Mama wouldn't let the doctor hurt you, now, would she?'

'No,' Rosie said in a small voice.

'That's all right then, isn't it? And if you're a good girl, you can have afternoon tea with the grown-ups afterwards. You'll like that, won't you?' Rosie gave a hesitant nod.

'I wouldn't worry if I was you, Rosie,' Joey put in. 'The doctor's not really coming to see you, you know. It's Maudie he's after.'

'Joey!' Lizzie and Maudie said in unison, each glaring at Joey. The boy grinned at his sister as he slipped out the door.

By the time the doctor's gig was seen coming up the track, Maudie was still wavering between eager curiosity and the desire to appear unmoved by her mother's suggestion that the visitor might not be impressed by her. When the knock on the front door came, she took refuge in aloofness.

'I'll stay out here and butter a few more scones,' she said when Lizzie called down the passage to her from the front bedroom. 'I'm in no rush to meet him.'

Lizzie gave Amy a knowing smile, then went to open the door to her guest.

Rosie was sitting up in her parents' bed, wearing her prettiest nightdress and looking overawed by the solemnity of the occasion. She stared wide-eyed at the doctor as Lizzie led him into the room. Amy patted the little girl's hand encouragingly, at the same time studying the doctor for herself.

Doctor Townsend looked to be in his late twenties. Curly brown hair framed a clean-shaven face, and his mouth seemed well accustomed to smiling. He had an air of authority about him that Amy found surprising in so young a man, but she sensed that it came from competence and brisk efficiency rather than from a domineering nature.

A handsome man, she thought, though not out of the ordinary. Until she saw his eyes. They were large and brown, and to Amy they spoke of an innate kindness that ran deeply through this man.

'This is Doctor Townsend, Amy,' Lizzie said, her eyes bright as she communicated a silent message of approval. 'Doctor Townsend, this is Mrs Stewart. And this is Rosie—she's got one of her chests. Whenever she gets a cold it goes straight to her chest. She gets more colds than the others, too, I don't know why.'

'How do you do, Mrs Stewart.' Doctor Townsend gave Amy a pleasant smile, then turned his attention on Rosie.

'Well, I can see there's nothing much wrong with you, young lady,' he said. Amy's heart warmed to him when she heard the gentle way he spoke to the little girl. 'Those beautiful rosy cheeks! Is that why they call you Rosie?'

Rosie gazed at him, too awed by the novelty of having a stranger in the house and by the bogey-man image her brother had painted of this man for her to be able to speak. She gave a little whimper.

'Don't be frightened, dear,' the doctor said. 'I won't hurt you.'

Lizzie crossed the room to sit on the bed beside Rosie and slip her arm around her. 'Don't be silly, love,' she chided. 'Mama's here.'

'I'd like to listen to her chest, if I could,' Doctor Townsend said. 'Mrs Kelly, could you unbutton Rosie's nightdress for me? Yes, that's just right.' Amy moved her chair to make room for the doctor to sit on the bed close to Rosie.

He put his bag on the floor and reached down towards it. 'Now, Rosie, I'm going to listen to your chest. It won't hurt, I'll just—' As he spoke, he pulled a contraption of rubber and metal out of his bag.

The moment Rosie saw it, her eyes grew even wider. She opened her mouth as if to scream, but instead she vomited loudly and copiously down the front of Doctor Townsend's jacket.

'Rosie!' Lizzie exclaimed. 'Look what you've done—on the doctor's nice jacket, too! Why didn't you tell Mama if you felt sick?'

'I don't want him to cut me up with that thing,' Rosie wailed. 'He wants to stick it in me!'

It took several minutes before Lizzie managed to calm Rosie down, and in the meantime Amy relieved the doctor of his jacket and took it out to the kitchen for the girls to clean. Doctor Townsend endeared himself further to her by his total lack of concern for his jacket; Rosie was his only care.

Once Rosie appeared reasonably calm again, Doctor Townsend took the contraption and held it up, too far from Rosie for it to be threatening. 'It's a funny looking thing, isn't it, dear? It's got a funny name, too. It's called a stethoscope. It's not for sticking in little girls, it's for listening to what goes on inside your chest. See, it hasn't got any sharp bits.'

He turned the stethoscope over in his hand, still holding it at a safe distance. As Rosie studied the thing dubiously, he showed her how it fitted into his ears. 'Do you think I could listen to your chest with it?' he asked. Rosie shook her head vigorously, and clung more tightly to her mother.

'Rosie, that's enough,' Lizzie scolded. 'Stop being so naughty.'

'It's all right, Mrs Kelly,' Doctor Townsend said. 'Rosie, would you like to have a go with it first?'

Curiosity overcame Rosie's fear. She released her tight hold on Lizzie and let the doctor slip the narrow tubes into her ears. He held the flat metal part against his own chest.

'I can hear a bumpa-bump!' Rosie said, her eyes alight.

Doctor Townsend lifted the plate off his chest before speaking. 'That's my heart beating. Can I listen to your bumpa-bump now?'

Rosie considered the idea. 'All right,' she said.

The doctor listened to her chest from the front and the back, tapped gently at it, and asked Rosie to cough for him. He turned her face to the light and looked in her mouth and up her nose, checked out her ears, and got her to move her eyes up and down while he studied them. By the end of the examination it was obvious that Rosie was thoroughly enjoying the fuss being made of her. She looked a little disappointed when the doctor packed away his stethoscope and closed up his bag.

'What do you think?' Lizzie asked.

'Oh, I don't think you've anything to worry about with her, Mrs Kelly. Her lungs are certainly a little congested, and from what you say that's probably become chronic. But I shouldn't think it'll slow her down much. Keep her wrapped up warmly in the cold weather, and perhaps keep her inside on the coldest days, and she'll always have those rosy cheeks. Don't send her to school in the worst of the winter weather, either.'

'I don't go to school yet,' Rosie piped up. 'I'm only four.'

'Are you?' The doctor managed to look astonished. 'A big girl like you! I thought you must be five or six.'

Rosie giggled in a self-satisfied way. 'Are you going to look at Maudie now?' she asked.

'Shh, Rosie,' Lizzie said quickly. 'No, he's not.'

'Did you want me to look at one of the other children?' Doctor Townsend asked. He glanced towards the door, where Lizzie's remaining six children had assembled, drawn by their varying degrees of curiosity. Doctor Townsend's smile faltered a little. 'Not all of them, I hope.'

'No, there's nothing wrong with any of them,' Lizzie said. 'Don't take any notice of her.'

'But Joey *said*,' Rosie insisted. 'He *said* the doctor was coming out to see Maudie. Are you going to do Maudie's chest, too? Maudie, the doctor's got a thing to listen to your insides with.'

Amy saw Maudie slink further into the passage and out of sight, her cheeks reddening.

'That's enough, Rosie,' Lizzie said. 'Don't take any notice of Joey's nonsense. You'll stay for afternoon tea, won't you, Doctor Townsend?'

'Well, perhaps I should be getting back to town.'

'No, you have to stay,' Rosie protested. 'You have to stay and have a grown-up tea with me.'

Doctor Townsend laughed. 'How can I refuse such a pretty invitation? Thank you, Mrs Kelly, I'd be honoured.'

'Right, bring the stuff into the parlour,' Lizzie told Beth. 'Is the kettle on? Good. Where's your father?'

'Pa said he wasn't coming,' said Joey. 'He said he's too busy.'

Lizzie's eyes narrowed. 'Tell him I said I want him to come up,' she said sweetly. 'I'd like him to come right now. Tell him the doctor wants to meet him, too.'

'Oh, I don't want to inconvenience Mr Kelly if he's busy,' Doctor Townsend said.

'Don't you worry about that,' Lizzie said, turning her most brilliant smile on the doctor. 'I know my husband's been looking forward to meeting you.'

Doctor Townsend looked somewhat puzzled by the contradiction of a man who was supposedly eager to meet him, but at the same time claimed to be too busy to do so. But he allowed himself to be ushered into the parlour and seated in the best chair. He was not to know that it was Frank's.

Frank greeted the doctor politely but with an unaccustomed reserve when he came in. The boys were banished outside, while Rosie pulled her little stool over to Doctor Townsend's chair. She sat at his feet and watched him adoringly.

Beth came into the parlour carrying a plate in one hand while she balanced Kate on her other hip. 'Shall I put her to bed, Ma?' she asked.

'Hmm? Yes, put her down, that's a good girl. Put a clean nap on her first if she's wet.'

Doctor Townsend smiled at the toddler, who was staring at him with big eyes. 'Is this one Maudie?' he asked.

'No, I'm Maudie.' Maudie walked in with a tray of teacups. It was her first opportunity for a close observation of Doctor Townsend, and she took full advantage of it once she had put the tray on a small table, looking him up and down with a glance that, while brief, was thorough. The doctor seemed momentarily taken aback, clearly having expected a much younger child. A flash of amusement showed in his face, to be quickly replaced by a bland smile.

'How do you do, Miss Kelly?' He stood up to shake Maudie's hand.

Amy could never recall having seen Maudie look timid before, but the smile she gave the doctor was decidedly shy. It lent a sweetness to her face that more than compensated for its lack of any startling prettiness.

Maudie took the seat closest to Doctor Townsend's, which Lizzie had carefully left free for her. 'Move out of the way, Rosie,' she told her little sister as she leaned across to pass a cup to the doctor.

'No,' Rosie said. 'He's my doctor, not yours. He didn't come to see you. He's not going to do your chest.'

'Rosie,' Lizzie said sharply. 'You can sit there quiet or you can go to your room. Not one more word,' she added when Rosie opened her mouth to protest. 'Have some of Maudie's nice cakes, Doctor Townsend. She made nearly all this lot by herself. She's a good cook.' Maudie blushed becomingly.

'Do you like them?' Lizzie asked, watching the doctor as he took a bite.

'Very nice, thank you. Oh, I don't think I need any more just yet,' he said as Maudie began loading up his plate.

'You've got to try one of those ginger ones,' Lizzie said. 'They're about the best ones of all.'

'And I take it you made these as well, Miss Kelly?' Doctor Townsend asked, obediently taking a ginger cake. Maudie nodded shyly.

'She's just about as good a cook as I am,' Lizzie said. 'I think it's important for a girl to be a good cook, don't you? She knows all about looking after a house, too, I make sure all my girls learn those things. And she's used to looking after the little ones.'

'Ma!' Maudie protested, squirming with embarrassment. 'Don't go on.'

'I'm not going on, I'm just discussing things with the doctor. I'm sure Doctor Townsend thinks it's important for girls to learn those things, don't you, Doctor?'

'Oh, yes, most important.' Doctor Townsend gave Lizzie a wry smile. 'You may find this hard to credit, Mrs Kelly, but there are some women who would take offence at any suggestion that their daughters should know how to cook.' His smile grew broader. 'Though I suppose all mothers have similar aims for their daughters, just different ways of going about it.'

The source of his amusement dawned on Amy. 'You mean like Mrs Bennet?' she asked, smiling as she realised it. 'When Mr Collins came to court Lizzie—not you, Lizzie,' she said before Lizzie had time to protest. 'It's in one of Miss Austen's books.'

The doctor's smile faltered for a moment, then came back more strongly. 'You're quite right, Mrs Stewart,' he said with a self-deprecating grin. 'How foolish of me to think none of you would have read Miss Austen.'

'Oh, books,' Lizzie said. 'I'm much too busy for that sort of thing. Amy knows a lot about books, though. She used to be a teacher.'

Amy did not bother correcting her this time; she knew she was not intended to be the chief object of the doctor's attention. *I haven't read that book for years*, she realised. *I must get it out again.*

'I think you might enjoy Miss Austen's work, Mrs Kelly,' Doctor Townsend said. 'You'd rather sympathise with Mrs Bennet, I suspect. Five daughters to see properly settled.'

'Four's enough, thank you. Have another cake. Frank, do you want some more?'

'Yes, I wouldn't mind. Nice cakes, love,' he told Maudie. Amy saw a slightly wistful look on his face as Maudie gave him only the briefest of glances in return.

'We're having one of our soyrees soon, Doctor Townsend,' Lizzie said. 'The week after next, I was thinking of. It'd be nice if you could come.'

'I'm sorry?' the doctor said. 'I didn't quite catch... what did you say you're having?'

'A *soyree*.' Lizzie looked puzzled. 'Don't you have soyrees in England? You know, a sort of musical evening—we sometimes have ours in the afternoon, though, because it's better for milking.'

'Oh, a *soirée*,' the doctor said. 'We used to pronounce it a rather odd way at home,' he explained smoothly.

'Soyree, that's right. Maudie plays the piano very nicely. She sings, too. And we have a nice supper, or an afternoon tea. You'll come, won't you?'

'Ah, I'm not sure if...' the doctor said. 'I'm very honoured to be asked, of course, but I... well, I might be away that week.'

'Well, you'll just have to come to the next one, then,' Lizzie said, nothing daunted.

Amy excused herself soon afterwards, knowing that she would have to rush to get Charlie's afternoon tea ready before he became impatient.

Frank could see that the doctor was wondering how soon he could politely leave himself, and he began to feel a little guilty about leaving their guest to Lizzie's none-too-subtle attentions.

'Lizzie, the doctor's a busy man,' he chided gently. 'There's times I can't get away, you know, like calving and things. I don't suppose you're interested in cows?' he asked the doctor, offering the only area of conversation in which he felt adept.

'I'm woefully ignorant on the subject,' Doctor Townsend said. 'I'd like to learn something about farming, though—it seems foolish not to take the opportunity while I'm living in a farming district. And from what I've heard, you're just the person to ask.'

'Frank's very prominent,' Lizzie put in. 'You know he's the chairman, I suppose?'

'Lizzie!' Frank said, embarrassed and pleased at the same time.

'Well, someone's got to tell the man!'

'Yes, I had heard that. I've also heard you're a very successful breeder, Mr Kelly—of cows, I mean.'

'I'm not too bad on kids, either,' Frank said with a grin, regretting the impulse when he saw Maudie and Beth giggle while Lizzie cast an admonishing look at him. 'I haven't done too bad with the cows, the herd's come on pretty well over the years. I don't suppose... would you like to see them?' he asked. Out of the corner of his eye, he saw that he was earning a glare from both Lizzie and Maudie.

'I don't think the doctor wants to see your cows just now, Frank,' Lizzie said sweetly. 'He'd like to just sit here and have another cup of tea.'

'Actually, I should be going,' the doctor said. 'But I would like to see your cows, Mr Kelly.' He pulled out his watch and studied it. 'I think… yes, I'd be delighted to see them.' He turned an enthusiastic smile on Frank, and Frank felt his heart warming to the young man in place of the mild resentment he had felt earlier.

'You realise I can't really tell one cow from another?' the doctor said as they walked out of the house together. 'You'll think I'm quite an ignoramus.'

'No, I don't know anything about doctoring, either. But cows are all different, once you get to know them. You get to the stage after a bit where you can tell whether a heifer's going to be a good producer right from when she's a calf. The bloodlines are important, too. But it's funny, you can get a cow who's a really good milker, but she doesn't always throw good calves. The bull's got a lot to do with it. And you've got to pick cows that have the good points the bull mightn't have. It's really…' Frank trailed off. 'Tell me to shut up if I'm being a bore.'

'It's not boring at all—it's fascinating! You must have to keep quite full records, I suppose, of what cows you mate and when?'

'Oh, yes, I do that. And production figures and things. And which ones calve easier.'

'You know them all by name, do you?'

'Yes, they've all got names. Remind me to show you Jersey Lily, she's named after Lizzie's brother's wife. It's a funny thing about her—she's got a little patch of white on her neck, and she always seems to throw a calf with the same bit of white. It's queer the way they pass on some things and not others.'

'I've always been interested in that sort of thing,' Doctor Townsend said. 'Actually I was reading something about it not long ago. There was work done by a monk, of all people. It was somewhere on the Continent, I don't remember just where. He wrote it years and years ago, but it's just come to light recently. It was mainly about peas, I seem to recall, but I wouldn't be surprised if the same sort of rules applied to cows.' He gave Frank a look of surprised pleasure. 'Do you know, you're the first person I've ever met whom I could talk to about this sort of thing without noticing them yawning after the first sentence.'

'I was just thinking much the same thing myself,' Frank told him with a grin.

'But you can stay for one more cup of tea, can't you?' Lizzie asked. 'You must be worn out, too, after Frank dragging you all over the farm. Sit down for a bit, why don't you?'

'I've enjoyed every minute of it,' Doctor Townsend assured her. 'And I'm afraid I really can't stay any longer—I just came back to thank you for your kind hospitality. And thank you for cleaning my jacket so nicely,' he told Maudie as he slipped it on, still warm from being dried by the range.

He made his farewells, and before Lizzie could make any further protest Frank was showing him out. 'Front door, Frank,' she hissed, but it was too late; Frank had already led the doctor to the back door.

'Bye, Richard,' Frank called as the doctor's gig pulled away.

'So I'll expect you later in the week,' the doctor called back. 'I'll hunt out that book we were talking about.'

'Yes, next time I'm in town I'll pop in. That'll be good.'

Frank went back to the house to find Lizzie and Maudie in the kitchen, both regarding him sternly.

'Well, a fat lot of use *that* was,' Lizzie said. 'You rushing him off like that, before Maudie even had a chance to talk to him.'

'You'll have a chance another time, love,' Frank told his scowling daughter.

'I hope so,' Maudie muttered. 'I'm going to get changed,' she said, stalking off towards the passage. 'Don't know why I bothered to get dressed up.'

'And he didn't seem to want to come to the soyree,' Lizzie said, frowning in irritation. 'I'm not sure what to do about him.'

'Oh, he's coming to the soyree,' Frank said, taking great satisfaction from the startled expression that came over Lizzie's face.

'But he said he couldn't come. He said he'd be away.'

'Well, he seemed to change his mind,' Frank said. 'I asked him while we were out with the cows, and he said he'd be glad to.'

Lizzie opened and closed her mouth twice, while she gathered her wits. 'But... but I thought you didn't even like him. You were that funny about us having him out here.'

'That was before I got to know him. I'm allowed to change my mind, aren't I?' Frank pulled her close and slipped an arm around her, letting one hand rest on her bottom. 'You think he's worth chasing after, don't you? You know something?' He patted the soft roundness under his hand. 'I don't think he's such a bad catch myself.'

18

Although Maudie was clearly put out that it was her father who was the attraction as far as Richard Townsend was concerned, it meant the doctor could be persuaded to visit the house, and for the moment she appeared to be content with that.

Richard was soon a regular guest at Lizzie's soirées, and after an initial reserve he seemed to enjoy the company of all Maudie's relations. He was an appreciative audience of Lily's playing. Frank would often see an expression of deep pleasure on Richard's face as he listened to Lily executing a particularly complex piece.

Fond father though he was, Frank did not try to deceive himself that Maudie's playing was anywhere near the level of Lily's, but Richard always managed to appear impressed by Maudie's attempts, too.

'He's got such lovely manners,' was one of Maudie's early comments on the man she already appeared to think of as her future husband. 'He's just so polite all the time.'

And so he was, Frank agreed. There never seemed to be anything unnatural or forced about Richard's behaviour, but somehow the man never said anything out of place or remotely likely to give offence. Frank supposed this must be the mysterious 'good breeding' he had sometimes heard spoken of. Even without Richard's pleasant looks and supposed money, the novelty of a man who never allowed himself to be seated in a woman's presence while she was standing, who opened doors for her and always expected her to precede him through any doorway, could not help but attract Maudie's interest. But, to her increasingly visible frustration, Richard showed her exactly the same polite attention as he did her mother; no less, and certainly no more.

By the time Richard came to his third soirée, early in the New Year, he was taking part more easily in the group's conversations.

'You're enjoying the music, aren't you, Doctor?' Bill remarked one evening, having noticed with approval how impressed Richard was by Lily's playing.

'It's very fine,' said Richard. 'I've never heard finer playing, Mrs Leith.' Lily gave a little laugh and tried to brush aside the compliment, but Frank could see that the doctor's praise pleased her. After all, he reflected, Richard had probably been to more concerts than the rest of them put together.

'Are our soyrees much different from the ones you used to go to in

England?' Lizzie asked.

A cautious expression crossed Richard's face. He accepted a cake from the plate offered him by Maisie before turning to Lizzie.

'I'd say yours were friendlier, Mrs Kelly. And smaller, generally. It makes it far easier to talk to everyone, I must say.'

'But they have the piano, and singing and everything, like we do?' Lizzie pressed.

'Oh, yes, music is always an important part of soi... of such occasions. Always a piano, of course, and sometimes a flute or a violin—or even both—to go with it.'

'A violin! I adore violin music. Oh, I'd love to play in a little group like that,' Lily said.

'Would you, love?' Bill looked surprised.

'Oh, yes! It's such a challenge, playing with a group. Not that I don't love playing on my own, of course,' she added with a reassuring smile at her husband. 'And if I had to choose one or the other, I'd much prefer to keep to playing alone. But a group's such a different challenge. I know,' she said, the laughter in her voice making it clear that she was bantering, 'why don't you find someone to teach one of the children the violin, Lizzie? Then we could start our own little group.'

Lizzie's expression showed that she was giving the idea more serious consideration than Lily had intended. 'I'll have a think about that. I've already started Beth on the piano, it's not worth changing her over. But maybe when Rosie gets a bit older we'll look into it.'

'Oh, I'd really rather you didn't, Mrs Kelly,' Richard said. He gave an embarrassed laugh when he saw the startled look Lizzie turned on him. 'I'm sorry, I didn't mean to sound as though I were laying down the law like that! It's just that I was witness to a rather unpleasant incident with a violin once.'

'What happened?' Lizzie asked.

'It was at a soirée I went to in Hertfordshire, at the home of a friend from Cambridge. They had a little musical group—a piano, I think it may have been two flutes, and the violin was being played by a young lady. She was rather new to the instrument, it turned out later, and that was half the problem. It seems she'd tightened the strings far too much, not knowing any better. Then when she was halfway through a piece, she tried tightening one a little more, and it snapped.'

'So she couldn't play it any more?' Frank said.

'Well, it was worse than that. The string whipped against her face, and dug right into her cheek. The poor girl got a dreadful fright, and it hurt her terribly. I had to give her a dose of morphine to settle her before I

290

could see to the cut.'

'Did she come right?' Lizzie asked.

'Oh, it healed up cleanly enough, but it left its mark.' He smiled in the direction of the girls' bedroom. 'I wouldn't like to think of little Rosie left with a scar like poor Lady Harriet.'

They all tut-tutted over the unfortunate story, but Maudie was the first to remark on one aspect of it. 'Doctor Townsend,' she said hesitantly, 'did you say *Lady* Harriet?'

'Mmm? Oh yes, I did.' Richard looked as if he had not meant to let that particular piece of information slip. 'Yes, her father's an earl. I must say "Lady" seemed rather incongruous for a girl of thirteen,' he added with a smile.

Maudie's voice came out as something close to a squeak. 'Do you…' She swallowed with difficulty and started again. 'Do you know lots of titled folk?'

'Not really,' Richard said, looking decidedly awkward. 'A few.'

'You're not…' Maudie was bright-eyed with the new idea that had just struck her. 'You're not titled folk yourself, are you?' Frank saw written clearly in her face the notion of herself as Lady Maudie.

Richard laughed. 'The only title I have, Miss Kelly, is the one I earned through my own efforts: Doctor. And I've never desired any other.'

'Oh.' Maudie looked only slightly downcast. 'But fancy mixing with all those people! I bet they've got such lovely clothes and things. And titled folk!'

'Believe me, Miss Kelly,' Richard said, 'people are much the same wherever one goes. And no matter what their titles. Mrs Leith, are we to have the pleasure of hearing you play again?'

After Lily obliged, the talk drifted on to other subjects. But Maudie's attention had not shifted, Frank noticed. His daughter was gazing at Richard with her mouth slightly open, and a look of adoration in her eyes.

Richard seemed to find the soirées pleasant enough, but he and Frank enjoyed each other's company far more when there were not quite so many people around. Remembering her own early successes with Frank, Lizzie began inviting Richard out for Sunday lunches. She always made it clear what a large part Maudie had played in the preparation of these meals, though with no greater reward from Richard than a polite show of appreciation.

Good though the food was at Lizzie's table, Frank soon saw that it was not the main reason Richard enjoyed his visits to the farm. Freed from even the slight veneer of formality that Lizzie managed to impose on her soirées, Richard was at first a somewhat bemused observer of family life in Frank's house, then an increasingly relaxed participant. The children soon came to take his presence for granted, which meant an end to Joey's knowing grins and supposedly witty remarks intended solely to bait Maudie. Rosie openly adored Richard, and after a few Sundays' worth of visits she was as likely to demand that she be allowed to sit on his lap as on her parents' or big sisters'.

Richard sometimes spoke of the countries he had visited in Europe, with their castles and palaces, museums and cathedrals, on what he referred to with a touch of embarrassment as his 'Grand Tour'. Maudie did not pine for faraway castles, but they gave Richard even more glamour in her eyes. She was besotted with him, and made little effort to disguise it, hanging on his every word. No matter how commonplace the subject, her expression showed that what he said was fascinating to her.

Richard went from looking rather uncomfortable at the attention to mild amusement, then after a month or two he seemed to have learned to ignore it. He was as polite as ever to Maudie, though he tended to avoid meeting her eyes any more than politeness demanded. But he had lost all sign of reserve with the family, now that he had been accepted as almost part of it. Frank would often see Richard watching the children with a soft smile playing around his lips.

'You like the kids, don't you?' Frank asked as the two of them were taking a stroll around the cows after one Sunday lunch.

'Mmm? Yes, I do. You've a fine family. You must be very proud of them.'

'Yes, I'm that all right. I tell you what, Richard—marrying Lizzie was the best thing I ever did.' Frank could not resist adding with a sly grin, 'Maudie's a lot like her ma, you know.'

Richard rolled his eyes. 'Frank, don't you start. You're not playing your part properly, you know. Mr Bennet never tried to help his wife marry off their daughters.'

'I must read that book one of these days, then I'd know what you're on about.'

'You know perfectly well what I'm on about,' Richard said. 'Though I must say you and Mrs Kelly are the best advertisement for marriage I've ever seen. And your children are the best advertisement for fatherhood.'

'And Maudie's just like her ma,' Frank pointed out, raising an answering smile from Richard. 'You must get lonely, living all by yourself.'

Richard looked pensive as he spoke. 'I didn't know I was until you started sharing your family with me.' He gave Frank a grateful smile. 'And now I don't really have the chance to be.'

'That's good. It's not much, though, just the odd lunch and soyrees and stuff. You're still by yourself most nights. I expect you miss your family, what with being so far from England.'

'Not really,' Richard said, much to Frank's surprise.

'But you must,' he protested. 'Gee, I'd hate to think of any of my kids being halfway around the world so I could never see them.'

'Frank,' Richard said, 'I suspect you have something of a false picture of my family. You're imagining it to be much the same as your own, aren't you?'

'Well, I suppose kids are kids, aren't they? I know your place must have been an awful lot flasher than this, though.'

Richard shook his head. 'That's not the sort of difference I was thinking of. Have you ever heard of Eton?'

Frank shook his head.

'It's a school in England. It's considered a very good school, and I suppose it is in its way. I certainly learned many things there, not all of them lessons from books. I was destined for Eton from an early age. To get me ready for it, I was sent to what we call a preparatory school, and I went there as a boarder. That meant spending ten months a year living at the school. I was seven years old.'

'Seven?' Frank echoed in amazement. 'Heck, that's not much older than Danny is! Lizzie'd never part with one of ours at that age. Neither would I.'

'No, I'm sure you wouldn't. But that's the way things are done in families like mine. And you know what, Frank? I didn't fret for my mother. I certainly didn't pine for my father—at that age I often didn't see him from one week's end to the next, but I remember being terrified of him even so. I suppose I saw Mother most evenings—she usually wafted into the nursery after we children had been fed and bathed, so that we could see her dressed for dinner. I think we were allowed to kiss her good night sometimes.'

Frank stared at him incredulously. 'I suppose it was good that you didn't fret for home, anyway,' he said, feeling that he should find something positive to say.

'Oh, I fretted all right.' Richard had a distant expression on his face. 'I remember crying my heart out every night for weeks when I was first sent away. Not for Mother, though. It was for my nurse. She was the nearest I had to what you'd think of as a mother. But I was the youngest, so when I went off to school she wasn't needed any more. When I went

293

home for the holidays she'd gone. I'm sure Father gave her a suitable payment when she left, and I believe she married some time later.'

His eyes met Frank's, and he smiled again. 'So perhaps you can see why I don't spend a lot of time pining for my family now.'

'Gee, I never knew there were families like that. I can't credit a mother... sorry,' Frank said awkwardly.

'You can't credit a mother who'd abandon her seven-year-old to the tender mercies of a boarding school,' Richard finished for him. 'No, I'm sure you can't. I certainly can't imagine Mrs Kelly doing any such thing. But I don't hold it against Mother. She didn't know any better.'

'I suppose not.'

'No, she didn't. And I don't think I did, either—not till I met your family, and saw how things could be done differently. Your way's better, Frank. If I was ever to have children, I rather think I'd like to bring them up as you do yours.'

Frank let the subject lapse, a little uncomfortable at having drawn such deeply personal recollections from Richard. But he suspected the younger man was thinking much the same as he was: if Richard wanted to give his children an upbringing so different from his own, he would be well-advised to choose a wife from the sort of family he so admired.

'How's that calf doing?' Richard asked, clearly eager to turn the conversation to other matters. 'The one you were worried about?'

'Oh, she's right as rain now. You wouldn't think she'd been frail when she was born. I nearly put her down—she was such a runty little thing I thought she'd never last—but Beth begged me to let her have a go at rearing it. She fed it up and dosed it with Lord knows what. It's all credit to her that the calf's so healthy now, she's got a real way with animals. She was with me when I delivered that one, that's why she got attached to it. I've told her that heifer's hers—Jewel, she's called it.'

'That's another thing that seems very different to me about your family,' Richard said. 'I can't imagine either of my sisters' ever being allowed anywhere near a calving cow. Most people seem to think girls should be kept in ignorance of such things.'

'Well, I don't know that it makes much difference—Lizzie had seen enough calves being born before we got married, and Lord knows how many I'd delivered, but we were still scared silly when it looked as though I was going to have to deliver Maudie by myself. Babies are a bit different from calves.'

Richard laughed. 'I'll have to take your word for that. Perhaps I could find out for myself next time it's calving season—would I be in your way if I came out and hovered around while you were helping the cows?'

'No, not a bit of it. Joey and me would be glad of the company—Beth, too, if she's hanging around. Then you can tell me if it's much different from babies. Do you deliver a lot of babies?'

'Not for quite a while. I used to in London, and I've helped at a few deliveries in Auckland, too. Only the difficult ones, of course—women prefer to be tended by other women if possible. I can't blame them for that.'

'No, I can't imagine Lizzie putting up with that unless she was really crook. Don't know that I'd like the idea myself, some other man poking around in her,' Frank admitted.

'That's how most husbands feel. I have an extra disadvantage, too. It troubles women—and their husbands, come to that—even more if... now, Frank, you mustn't take advantage of my saying this,' Richard said, suddenly looking rather defensive.

'Eh? No, of course I won't,' Frank said in mild confusion.

'Well, it's an extra disadvantage that I'm an unmarried man. Women seem to accept being tended by a doctor a little more easily if the man's married. I used to be called in to help at a hospital for poor women in London, and then from time to time I went to particularly difficult cases at the Magdalene homes in Auckland. Homes for fallen women,' he explained, seeing the blank look on Frank's face. 'Penniless women, and disgraced ones, can't afford to stand on their dignity quite so much, poor creatures. And if it's a matter of forceps or worse, there isn't a great deal the midwives can do for them.'

'All right, I won't say it.' Frank tried hard to assume an expression of innocence. 'I won't say you need a wife. Anyway,' he added, relenting when he saw Richard's slightly hunted look, 'I've no girls nearly old enough to be thinking about getting married. I'm in no rush to be rid of any of them.'

'I'm pleased to hear it,' Richard said.

Teasing anyone but Lizzie did not come naturally to Frank, and he said no more to Richard on the subject of marriage. And Lizzie was quite aware that she had spoken of Maudie's charms often enough for anyone but a simpleton to have grasped what a treasure her oldest daughter was.

Lizzie had weapons more subtle than words, however. She made sure that Maudie was always sitting close to Richard, whether at family dinners or soirées. She was careful about Maudie's clothes, though Frank cringed at the arguments this tended to ignite between Lizzie and Maudie, with Lizzie constantly veering towards the flamboyant while

Maudie fought for the understated. They usually managed to compromise on something that satisfied them both, though often not before Maudie had earned herself a session with the belt for what Lizzie considered particularly outrageous cheek.

Lizzie had studied Richard's reaction to the various delicacies offered at the soirées, and when she had noted the things he enjoyed most she made sure that they were served whenever he came. She no longer felt the need to remind him verbally what a good cook Maudie was, but she would not let him forget how good Maudie's food tasted.

After ensuring that Richard had heard Maudie's playing often enough to know what an accomplished young lady she was, Lizzie let Lily do most of the playing. Even to Lizzie's ears, Lily's playing gave more pleasure than Maudie could ever hope to offer.

'Do you think he's getting the idea yet?' Lizzie asked Frank the night before a soirée in March, six long months after Richard had first come to the house.

'He's got the idea, all right,' Frank said. 'He's just not too keen on getting married yet, that's all. Don't rush the lad.'

'He's taking so long, though. Maudie'll be seventeen this year, you know.'

'She's got a while before she's an old maid, Lizzie. Leave them to it, Richard'll see what a good catch she is before too long. Let him take his time.'

'He's doing that, all right,' Lizzie grumbled.

At first it seemed it would be a soirée like all the others that Richard had attended. There was to be the usual generous supper, the usual mixture of family and guests, and the usual musical entertainment. The difference was in Maudie.

Maudie's eyes were bright with the excitement of her first soirée since Lizzie had let her go into adult clothing. She had a new dress for the occasion, and Lizzie had let Amy talk her into choosing a fabric subtle enough not to offend Maudie's sense of style. It was made of silk in a pink so pale as to be almost cream, full in the pintucked bodice and the skirt, with a white lace collar and cuffs. The dress rustled as Maudie twirled in front of her father to show it off to him. Frank was startled to see how much more womanly Maudie's figure had suddenly become, until he realised that much of the effect was due to her new corset accentuating her curves.

'Do you like it, Pa?' Maudie asked. Her face looked almost unfamiliar under the soft folds of fair hair that Amy had pinned up for her. There was no denying it; his little girl was growing up.

'You look gorgeous, love,' Frank told her. 'Nearly as pretty as your ma.'

Frank saw Maudie watching Richard closely that evening, eager to see his reaction to her new finery.

'May I say how particularly fetching you look this evening, Miss Kelly?' Richard said as he held out a chair for Maudie. Maudie blushed prettily and murmured a thank you.

But although Richard paid her his usual polite attentions, they were no more than he gave to the other women present. Frank saw Maudie begin to look a little downcast as the evening wore on. She played most of her repertoire of items, and Richard clapped each one as heartily as he did Lily's. But no more heartily.

'What about giving us a song, Maudie?' Lizzie said shortly before supper. 'We haven't heard you singing tonight.'

'All right,' Maudie said, casting a hopeful look at Richard as she moved to stand close to the piano. 'What shall I sing, Aunt Lily?'

'This one about the little bird is rather sweet,' Lily suggested. 'You sing this one beautifully, dear.'

Maudie launched into an enthusiastic rendering of 'Titwillow'. 'Very nice,' was murmured around the room, as everyone applauded politely.

'Oh, what about this one?' Lily said, pulling out a sheet of music. 'You and I were practising it the other day, remember?' She played a few bars of music.

'Yes, I like that one—but you said it should really be a duet.'

'Well, yes, it would sound better as a duet. Never mind, dear, just sing the woman's part.'

'I don't know if I want to,' Maudie said, suddenly shy. 'It might sound a bit funny, just singing half the words.'

'Joey, your sister wants you to help her with the singing,' Lizzie said. Frank saw horror in his son's face, rapidly succeeded by rebellion.

Before Joey had the chance to voice his outrage, Richard came in smoothly. 'I think I know that one, Mrs Leith. I seem to remember singing it at school. I'll gladly take one of the parts—if everyone can put up with my voice, that is?' There were noises of encouragement from around the room, the loudest of all coming from Joey.

'I can play this one by ear, Doctor Townsend,' Lily said. 'You and Maudie use this for the words.' She passed the sheet to Richard.

Richard held the sheet at a convenient height for Maudie, though Frank wondered if his daughter needed to stand quite as close as she did to the doctor. Richard gave a slightly embarrassed laugh. 'I should confess that the last time I sang this piece was before my voice broke. I've only ever sung the part of the lady. You'll have to forgive me, Miss Kelly, if I stumble over some of the words.'

'Yes,' Maudie said in a small voice, gazing at Richard with her usual adoring expression. She looked, Frank thought, as though she would forgive Richard things far more serious than muddling the words of a song.

But Richard did not stumble, and Maudie's voice was not small when she sang. Their voices blended pleasantly, and Frank had been listening to them for some time before he realised they were singing a love song.

Neither of them was confident enough of the lyrics to lift their eyes from the sheet for more than a moment at a time, but when they did let their gaze leave it, Frank saw Richard's eyes slip to Maudie's as often as they did to his audience.

The two parts came together as the song ended, with both voices singing in harmony. 'Sweetheart,' they sang. 'Sweetheart.' Richard lowered the hand that held the music, and offered his arm to help Maudie back to her chair. As Frank watched, he saw their eyes meet. Richard's expression was at first thoughtful, then as he studied Maudie's face he broke into a smile. There was no trace of embarrassment or amusement in the smile; there was nothing but a deep warmth.

Maudie only had to wait until the following Sunday for Richard to give a more substantial sign of his newly-aroused feelings towards her. After waiting long enough for the generous lunch to settle, he spoke to Lizzie with an air of diffidence that Frank found surprising. It was shyness, Frank decided, rather than any doubt as to what Lizzie's answer might be.

'Would it be in order for me to ask Miss Kelly to accompany me on a walk, Mrs Kelly?'

Lizzie appeared to give the idea serious consideration for a few moments. 'Yes, I think that would be very nice, Doctor Townsend,' she said, while Maudie turned a beaming face on Richard. 'Maudie can show you some nice views. Beth can go with you, too.'

Maudie and Beth both turned faces full of unspoken protest on their mother, but Lizzie met their eyes with a set expression that told them how useless arguing would be.

'Of course,' Richard said, turning a smile on Beth that gave away nothing of how he might feel about the arrangement. 'I'd be delighted to have Miss Beth's company as well.'

'And me,' Rosie announced. 'I'll come too.'

'No, you won't,' Lizzie said. The somewhat hunted expression that had appeared on Richard's face as more and more of the family seemed about to be added to the party was replaced by one of relief. 'You can go another time, if you're good.'

'But he's *my* doctor,' Rosie said indignantly. 'Why can't—'

'That's enough, Rosie,' Lizzie interrupted. 'Not another word, my girl. And don't you pull faces at me, Rosie Kelly, or there'll be trouble.'

It was not, Frank reflected, the time to point out that he and Richard usually went for a walk themselves after Sunday lunch. It rather looked as though he was going to have to accept playing second fiddle to his daughter from now on.

Richard helped Maudie on with her cloak, though Frank had never before known her to have any difficulty putting it on by herself. He was holding Beth's cloak out to her when Lizzie spoke suddenly, as if an idea had just struck her.

'Wait a minute, Beth, I've got something I want you to do. Oh, you and Maudie go on ahead, Doctor Townsend,' she added. 'Beth can catch you up later.'

Maudie was not one to miss an opportunity. She slipped her arm through the one Richard held out to her, and led the way from the house at a brisk pace.

As soon as they were safely out of earshot, Lizzie turned to Beth. 'Now, there's no need for you to be treading on their heels. Give them a bit of a chance to talk. You stay within sight of them, mind, and make sure they can see you—him especially. But you don't need to go listening to what they say, or he'll be too shy to say anything.'

'Do I have to go with them, Ma?' Beth asked plaintively.

'Yes, you do, and I'll have no arguments. I'm not letting them go off by themselves Lord knows where.'

'But what say he wants to kiss her or something?' Beth persisted. 'I'll feel stupid watching them.'

Lizzie's eyes narrowed. 'If he tries something like that, you're to tell me. Your father will have something to say to Doctor Townsend if anything like that happens, I might say.'

'I can't tell on Maudie,' Beth protested. 'She'll go really crook at me if I do.'

'Don't you worry about Maudie, I'll see to her. Now, you get a move on before they get too far ahead. Just remember, close enough but not too close.'

Frank made do with the company of Joey and the younger boys when he made his round of the cows that afternoon, but he was curious enough about the outcome of Richard and Maudie's first outing to make sure that he was close to the house when they returned, Richard with a girl on each arm. Beth looked uncomfortably self-conscious at such an attention, though Maudie was leaning so heavily against Richard that he must have had little enough awareness to spare for her younger sister.

As soon as Richard had made his farewells and they had waved him out of sight, Beth spoke in a rush. 'He only took my arm like that just when we were coming back, Ma. I didn't get close to them the rest of the time, honest I didn't. I couldn't hear anything they said.'

'No, Beth was all right,' Maudie said, the rather foolish smile on her face making her look unusually silly. 'I just about forgot she was there. Richard made her come and walk with us just now, though—I think he felt sorry for Beth, having to tag along with us. He's so thoughtful,' she said, her smile more foolish than ever.

'That's a good girl, Beth,' Lizzie said. 'I knew you'd have the sense to make a good job of it. Now, come on.' She ushered the two girls into the house while Frank followed in her wake. He sat down at the table, wondering idly if Lizzie might offer to make him a fresh pot of tea, but all her attention was on Maudie. 'Tell me all about it,' she said. 'What happened?'

'It was lovely,' Maudie said dreamily. 'We went for such a lovely walk up the hill and… oh, I don't remember where we went. It was just lovely.'

'That's all very well,' Lizzie said. 'What did you talk about? What did he do? Did he hold your hand?'

'I'm not going to tell you all that! It's private!'

Lizzie's expression changed from eager curiosity to a grimness that startled Frank. 'Now, you listen to me, Maudie,' she said, leaning close to the girl. 'I don't want to hear any talk about things being "private" or "secret". I'm your mother, you've no business having secrets from me.'

'I don't see why I can't have my own private business,' Maudie protested. 'Why do you have to go poking your nose into everything?'

'Maudie, don't speak to your ma like that,' Frank put in, but he might as well not have spoken for all the notice Maudie and Lizzie took of him. Lizzie held Maudie's eyes, her expression so serious that Maudie's self-righteous air changed to one of uncertainty.

'I knew a girl once who said things were private,' Lizzie said solemnly. 'She had a young man she used to go for walks with, too. She wouldn't talk to anyone about it—it was all private and secret, you see. A terrible, terrible thing happened to that girl.'

'What happened to her?' Maudie whispered.

'Never you mind,' Lizzie said. 'I'll just tell you this—some people would say it would have been better if that poor girl had died. I'm not going to have anything like that happen to you. So let's hear no more about secrets, thank you very much. And now,' she dropped her solemnity as quickly as she had assumed it, 'how did you get on with him? What did you talk about?'

Maudie had clearly been too shaken by her mother's doom-filled tone to maintain her haughty air. 'He seemed to want to ask me a lot of things,' she volunteered. 'He asked me what sort of books I like reading.'

'That was a funny sort of thing to ask,' Lizzie said.

'I didn't really know what to say. I told him I always read the ladies' page in the *Weekly News*, but I think he meant proper books.'

'Hmm,' Lizzie said. 'You'd better go and see Aunt Amy and borrow her books. You've got to be able to talk about the things he wants to. What else did you talk about?'

'Um… he asked me what I like doing in my free time. Not that I ever get much free time, what with looking after babies and things,' Maudie added sourly, but without getting a reaction from her mother. 'I told him I quite like playing the piano, but he knew that already. We talked about music for a bit, but I think he likes the things Aunt Lily plays better than my stuff. I didn't really know what he was talking about when he started saying the sort of music he likes best—you know, all those foreign names. I just sort of nodded and smiled.'

'I hope you didn't just stand there like a dummy,' Lizzie said, her brow furrowed. 'I don't know why you have to decide to be shy just now, you've certainly never shown any sign of it before. He must be used to girls with something to say for themselves—I don't want him thinking you're a bit simple.'

'He wouldn't think that!' Maudie said. 'He's much too nice for that.' Her face softened into a smile. 'He really wanted to talk to me. We got talking about what I do in an ordinary day—boring things like cooking and washing and looking after the little ones. He seemed like he was interested, but he can't have been, really. And then he asked me things about the farm and stuff—he said I must think he's a bit strange, not knowing about milking and everything. Of course I said he's not strange. I think he's lovely. I didn't say that to him, though,' she added hastily.

'I should think not,' Lizzie said.

'Beth would've been better at telling him stuff about the farm. I didn't like to say that, though, not when I was trying to seem like I knew things.'

'I wish I could have,' Beth said. 'It was awful, just walking along by

301

myself. I felt really stupid.'

'Your turn will come,' Lizzie said.

Beth said nothing. Frank saw her studying Maudie's radiant face, her lower lip trembling slightly, and his heart went out to her.

'Hey, you're not in a hurry to get married, are you?' he asked. 'I can't go losing all my girls at once, you know.' He reached out an arm, and Beth snuggled into it and let herself be drawn close. 'Who'd help me look after the calves if they're a bit sickly? I don't know how I'd get on without you telling me what to do with them.' He planted a kiss on Beth's nose.

He was rewarded with a smile. Beth slid her arms around his neck and buried her face against his chest. 'I don't ever want to go away and leave you, Pa,' she told him in a muffled voice.

'Oh, don't talk silly, Beth,' Lizzie said. 'Goodness me, you won't even be fourteen till November! Don't you worry, I'll see you don't miss out when the time comes. So,' she said, turning her attention back to Maudie, 'it sounds like you got along quite nicely, even if you didn't have enough to say for yourself. You'll get over that, it's just a bit of silliness. Anyway, did he hold your hand or not?'

'No,' Maudie said, looking disappointed. 'Except he shook my hand when he said goodbye just now—he sort of gave it a bit of a squeeze, too.'

'Well, that's enough for him to be doing, when you've just started courting,' Lizzie said. 'Plenty of time for holding hands later.'

'Courting,' Maudie repeated dreamily. 'I like courting.' She gave a delighted little giggle.

'Do, you, indeed?' Lizzie said. Frank saw the self-satisfied smile that spoiled her attempt to sound stern. 'Let's see if you can pull your head out of the clouds long enough to make your poor father a cup of tea, my girl. And hurry up about it.'

Maudie gave a toss of her head as she walked over to the bench to do her mother's bidding. She impulsively rushed to Lizzie, flung her arms around her neck and kissed her. 'I do like Richard, Ma,' she said breathlessly. Then she was suddenly a young lady again, head held high as she made her way gracefully back across the kitchen.

'I feel a bit sorry for Richard,' Frank remarked to Lizzie as they got ready for bed one evening. Richard had paid one of his regular calls that afternoon, and Frank had watched the threesome making their way up the hill, Beth following dutifully at what her mother judged an appropriate distance.

'Why? Hurry up and get those laces undone, Frank, I'm dying in these stays.'

'Serves you right,' Frank said, though his fingers moved quickly to untie the knots. 'You were the one who said I was to pull them good and tight this morning.'

'I just wanted to look my best.'

'Oh, yes? Don't think I haven't noticed, Lizzie Kelly,' he teased.

'Noticed what?'

'You're always a lot keener on looking your best when Richard's coming out here. Oh, yes you are,' he said, cutting off her indignant response.

'Honestly, Frank, what a lot of nonsense you talk,' Lizzie said, her protest just a little too vigorous for Frank to be taken in by it. He was fully aware of the pleasure Lizzie took in any compliments paid her by the amiable young man who had become such a frequent visitor, though the knowledge gave him not the slightest pang. He was far too certain of his Lizzie to be anything but amused. 'Anyway,' Lizzie said, 'what do you mean, you feel sorry for him?'

'Well, you weren't too free and easy with the cuddles when we were courting, but you let me do more than shake your hand!'

'That was later. It was different once we'd got engaged.'

'You let me kiss you before then,' Frank argued. 'Remember that dance? I thought you might slap me for doing it, but you as good as asked me to do it again.' He grinned at the memory. 'Now I come to think of it, you did ask me to do it again.'

'Shh,' Lizzie hissed, looking meaningfully at the wall beyond which the girls slept. 'There's always ears flapping, and these walls are none too thick. Anyway, we'd been more or less keeping company for months by then.'

Frank let the subject rest until they were in bed, close enough to whisper with no fear of being overheard. 'I don't know how you think Richard's ever going to get around to doing anything except shake Maudie's hand if you never give them any time on their own.'

'There'll be plenty of time for that later,' Lizzie said. 'He can make his intentions known first. In the meantime I'm not taking any chances.'

'I don't know, Lizzie, I don't think you need to worry too much about Richard. He's a decent sort of fellow.'

'Humph! Don't think I've forgotten what *you* were like before we got married.'

'What's that supposed to mean?' Frank asked, too startled to be affronted. 'What'd I do?'

'It's not so much what you *did* as what you would've done if I'd let you get away with it. I know what young men are like.'

'I never did more than give you a kiss and a bit of a cuddle!'

'Yes, and that's only because I wouldn't let you get away with anything else. Oh, don't go getting in a huff about it,' Lizzie relented. 'It's not so much you I'm thinking of. It's that other fellow. I'll never forget what happened to Amy.'

'Richard's not like that ratbag.'

'Of course he's not. I wouldn't let him near the place if I thought he was. But he's young and he's a man, isn't he? There's no need to go putting opportunities in front of him.'

'He'd probably have more idea what to do with her than I had with you, too,' Frank said. 'What with him knowing about women's insides and all that.'

'Well, he's not going to know anything about Maudie's insides till they're decently married.'

There seemed little enough risk of Richard's finding out anything more than was proper. Unwelcome though it was to her, Beth took her role of chaperone seriously. Frank cast his mind back to the casual approach Bill had had to the same job so many years before, cheerfully letting the courting couple have all the privacy they wanted. He felt a warm sense of gratitude to his brother-in-law, and at the same time felt more sorry for Richard than ever.

But Richard persevered with his visits, and as time wore on Frank saw Maudie and Richard become more at ease with each other. When winter's approach sometimes made walks impossible, Lizzie would send the courting couple out onto the verandah to talk. This had the advantage of freeing Beth from her obligations, though it was harder to keep Rosie away. Kate, now two years old, had begun to follow Rosie's lead in wanting to hover around Richard whenever he came, but Lizzie always insisted that both little girls have a nap for at least part of his visits.

Maudie was so determined to make a good impression that Frank became used to the hitherto unknown sight of his daughter sitting in the parlour of an evening with a book on her lap, frowning with concentration as she struggled over the more difficult passages.

'I'm going to ask Aunt Amy for an easy book next time,' she grumbled one evening, flinging the book down in disgust. 'That one's as dry as anything—just some man going on about politics and stuff. As if anyone's interested in what he thinks.'

'Why'd she lend you that one, love?' Frank asked.

'Well, I suppose I did ask her for one of her hard ones,' Maudie admitted. 'I thought it'd sound good if I told Richard I was reading it. She said I might enjoy a novel better, she's got lots of them, too.'

'A novel's more suitable for girls,' said Lizzie. 'A nice, romantic one, that's what you want to read. I'll tell your Aunt Amy what to lend you next time.'

Maudie scowled in her mother's direction. 'As if you know anything about books.'

'That's enough of your cheek, my girl,' Lizzie said.

Frank was relieved to see Maudie subside into silence. Richard's attentions seemed to have given her more self-confidence than ever, and this added assurance was inclined to lead to trouble between her and Lizzie. Maudie often seemed to be going to bed in tears lately, after having overstepped the bounds of her mother's forbearance. Frank could never see any difference in Maudie's behaviour after these sessions, but Lizzie showed no sign of tiring of what seemed to him to be a losing battle.

It always troubled him to see Maudie unhappy. He could not deny the truth of Lizzie's assertion that he was soft on the children; on Maudie most of all, he knew. Maudie's tears had never lost the ability to wring her father's heart.

'Don't you think Maudie's getting a bit big for hidings?' he asked one night, after seeing Maudie rush sobbing from her parents' room.

'No, I don't,' said Lizzie.

'But she's growing up. She's got a real figure now and everything. It doesn't seem right, her still getting hidings like she was a little kid.'

'It's what's on the inside that counts. I'll think she's too old for hidings when she starts behaving like a sensible young lady.'

'I bet you didn't get them when you were her age.'

'Of course I didn't,' Lizzie said. 'Ma had no need to be giving me hidings. I always behaved myself.'

'You were too good at getting your own way without your ma catching on what you were up to, you mean. I don't know, I… I sort of think Maudie gets confused,' Frank said, struggling to put his thoughts into words.

'I'll straighten her ideas out, don't you worry about that.'

'No, it's you who makes her confused. I mean, one minute you're telling her to be all grown up and act like a young lady so Richard will like her, and next thing you've got her bending down so you can get stuck into her with the belt. It seems to me Maudie doesn't know if she's grown up or a little girl.'

'It seems to *me*,' Lizzie said, as imperturbable as ever, 'that Maudie's much too good at playing up to you. Don't you worry about her, Frank. I know what I'm doing.'

Arguing with Lizzie was rarely worth the effort. 'I suppose so. You're probably right,' Frank said doubtfully.

'You'll be able to come to tea next Wednesday, won't you, Doctor Townsend?' Lizzie asked Richard after one Sunday lunch in June. 'It's Maudie's birthday, and we're having a little birthday tea for her.'

'You will come, won't you?' Maudie added, looking up at Richard with a look that Frank knew he himself would have had no chance of resisting had it been directed at him.

'I'd be delighted,' Richard said, smiling back at her. 'I didn't know your birthday was coming up.'

'She'll be seventeen,' Lizzie said. 'Do you know,' she added as if it had just that moment struck her, 'that's the age I was when I got engaged. Remember, Frank?'

'Yes,' Frank said, grinning at the memory as much as at Lizzie's attempts at subtlety. 'Seventeen, and your pa said I could have you when you were eighteen. It was the longest year of my life, I think.'

'It wasn't a year, only nine months. Anyway, it's good to have a decent engagement, it gives lots of time to get everything organised. Seventeen, eh? Fancy Maudie being as old as I was when I got engaged.' Frank saw her dart a sly glance at Richard to see if her meaning had gone home, but Richard's expression gave away no sign of what he might be thinking.

Richard was the only guest at Maudie's birthday tea, but, as Lizzie lost no time in telling him, 'You're almost one of the family now, aren't you?' The short winter days meant that it was already dark before they had finished eating, so there was no chance for Maudie and Richard to have any time alone on the verandah that evening. The whole family was his audience when Richard took a small, carefully wrapped package from his pocket and held it out to Maudie.

'I've a small gift for you, Miss Kelly. I hope that's all right,' he added, looking to Lizzie for approval.

'It's very thoughtful of you,' Lizzie said. 'We don't usually bother with a lot of presents, what with having so many of them to buy for.'

Maudie opened the package, eagerness warring with her desire to appear refined. 'Oh, it's lovely,' she said, lifting something bright from a small box. 'Look, Ma, look at this lovely brooch. See the pretty colours? Look, Pa.'

Frank leaned over to see what lay in Maudie's palm. It was a brooch of finely wrought gold in the shape of tiny leaves and flowers, with patches of bright enamel for the petals. He vaguely remembered having seen it in Mr Hatfield's window the last time he had checked to see that 'his' pearls were still there. 'It's nice, love,' he told her. 'It's really pretty.'

'Thank you, Doctor Townsend,' Maudie said, her eyes shining. 'Thank you very much.' The tension in her body as well as her expression told Frank that she desperately wanted to show her gratitude. He had to hide a smile when she thrust out her hand to shake Richard's.

Richard made it into a graceful gesture by taking her hand in both of his and squeezing it for a moment. 'I'm glad you like it,' he said with a smile. 'After all,' he added, looking straight at Lizzie, 'I could hardly let so portentous a birthday as a seventeenth go by without doing something to mark the occasion, could I?' His smile grew broader.

For days after Maudie's birthday, it seemed to Frank that whenever he came into the house she and Lizzie were involved in deep discussions over the significance of Richard's having given her so fine a gift. He was mildly surprised to find Maudie missing when he came in for his afternoon tea a week after her birthday, but assumed that Lizzie had set the girl some task elsewhere in the house.

He had just settled comfortably in his chair and lifted his cup when they heard a wheeled vehicle approaching. Beth went to peer out the window, and looked back at her mother with her face full of alarm.

'It's Richard!' she said, as if this were a dreadful piece of news.

'Oh, no!' Lizzie said, startling Frank even more. 'What on earth does he have to come out today for? Frank, you'll have to talk to him.'

'I wouldn't mind,' Frank said. 'I don't usually get the chance these days. What's up, Lizzie?'

But Lizzie ignored him in her rush to smooth her apron, make an unnecessary attempt to tidy the table, and assume a rather forced smile as she went to open the door for Richard.

'Doctor Townsend, what a lovely surprise,' she lied. 'Do come in, we're just having a cup of tea.'

Richard came into the kitchen, looking almost as flustered as Lizzie. 'I shouldn't really... I was in the area...' His voice trailed away awkwardly. 'I had to go out to the Carr's today, to see how Mr Carr's leg was mending. You know he broke it in that bad fall he had? As I was so near... well, not as near as all that,' he added, looking somewhat abashed, 'I thought I'd take the opportunity to call in on you.'

'That was very nice of you,' Lizzie said, still looking uncharacteristically distracted.

'Sit down, Richard,' Frank invited. 'Have a cup of tea—it's still fresh.'

'I can't really,' said Richard. 'I've another patient to see on my way back to town. I shouldn't really have come at all, but I wasn't able to last Sunday, and it seemed a long time till next week, and I...' He smiled, and gave a helpless shrug. 'Well, suddenly I found myself coming up the road. I almost felt I couldn't help myself. I'm sorry, that sounds ridiculous, I know.'

'It's always nice to see you, Doctor Townsend,' Lizzie said. 'It's a pity you can't stay for a cup of tea.'

'No, I really shouldn't, but... is Miss Kelly in?'

'Maudie's in her room,' Lizzie said. She seemed to be avoiding Richard's eyes. Frank watched as she composed herself and looked back at the doctor with every appearance of confidence. 'She's not feeling the best, I'm afraid. I sent her off for a lie-down.'

Richard's face was abruptly full of concern. 'Is she unwell? I'll gladly examine her if you like, just to see if there's anything at all serious. In your presence, of course, Mrs Kelly.'

'No, no, it's nothing like that,' Lizzie said. 'Nothing I can't sort out myself, thank you.'

'Maybe Richard should take a look at her, Lizzie,' Frank said, startled at the news that Maudie was not well.

'There's no need for that,' Lizzie said. 'It's just the sort of problem girls get from time to time. I know how to deal with it.'

'I'm sure you do, Mrs Kelly,' Richard said. 'I... I'd better be going, then.' He cast a disappointed look in the direction of the passage door.

'Come out on Sunday, won't you,' Lizzie called to him from the porch as he walked towards his gig. 'Maudie'll be right as rain by then.'

'I'll look forward to it,' Richard called back.

As soon as he was out of sight, Lizzie let her smile drop. 'Ohh,' she said, clenching her fists in frustration as she and Frank went back into the kitchen. 'Why did he have to come today? Oh, that girl!'

'What's wrong with Maudie, then?' Frank asked, though by now he had guessed.

'And did you see the funny mood he was in? All excited like that. He was going to propose today, I'm sure he was. He might go and change his mind now—it might be ages till he gets his courage up again.'

'Why couldn't he see Maudie?' Frank pressed.

Lizzie gave him a sidelong glance. 'She was cheeking me. I can't put up with her answering me back all the time. I know you think she's too old for hidings, but I can't help that.'

'I didn't say a word, Lizzie.'

'You didn't have to. You've got that look on your face.'

The passage door opened and Maudie peered around it, her face swollen and tear-streaked. She had put on her nightdress, and was holding her dressing-gown closed with one hand. 'Ma? Was that Richard?'

'Yes, it was,' Lizzie said, still frowning in frustration.

'Oh, *Ma!* And I missed him! Oh, it's not fair! It's your fault, too.'

'That's enough of your cheek, Miss. It wouldn't have happened if you'd kept a civil tongue in your head.' She gave Frank a glare, as if daring him to argue. 'You get back in that room, my girl. I want a word with you.'

Maudie disappeared up the passage, followed by Lizzie, and Frank heard the sound of the girls' door being pulled to.

Frank did not make a practice of eavesdropping, but the temptation was too strong. His stockinged feet made no sound as he walked softly up the passage and stationed himself near the bedroom door.

'Now, listen, Maudie,' he heard Lizzie say. 'I had to give you that hiding today, you know I did, so let's have no complaints about it. But you're getting a bit big for hidings, you know.'

'Doesn't stop you giving them. Oh, fancy missing Richard!'

'I don't enjoy it, you know. No, I don't, so there's no need for you to look at me like that. In fact, I'm a bit tired of giving a great big girl like you hidings. You should be grown up enough not to need it.'

'Why do you do it, then?' Maudie challenged. 'Seems every time I do anything or say anything you jump on me. Seems I can't do anything right.'

'And why do you have to contradict everything I say? Be quiet for two minutes and listen.'

There was silence for several seconds, as though Lizzie was gathering her thoughts. 'I know I'm firm with you,' she said. 'It's for your own good, you'll know that when you've got children of your own. But I think perhaps it's time I started expecting you to be a bit more grown up.'

'What do you mean?' Maudie asked suspiciously.

There was another silence before Lizzie spoke again. 'I'll make a bargain with you, Maudie. If you'll try not to be so provoking—and I mean really try, mind you, you needn't think you can get away with murder—then I'll try not to give you so many hidings. If I can see you're really making an effort, I don't see why I can't stop them altogether. Now, I can't say fairer than that, can I?'

'I suppose not.' Maudie sounded doubtful. 'You mean it, Ma?'

'I certainly do. We're agreed, then? Good. Now, wash your face and get dressed. You can come out for dinner.'

'But you said I had to—'

'I can change my mind, can't I? Hurry up and you can give Beth and me a hand.'

Frank began to move away, knowing Lizzie would emerge shortly. Just before he slipped back out to the kitchen, he heard her say, 'Make sure you wear one of your nice dresses on Sunday, for when Richard comes out. I've an idea he might be going to get around to it soon.'

Frank heard Maudie's steps practically skipping up the passage, so eager was she to come back into the kitchen from the verandah, with Richard following more sedately. One look at his daughter's glowing face told Frank all he needed to know.

'Do you think the weather's dependable enough for a short walk, Frank?' Richard asked. 'I'd appreciate a few moments of your time.'

'A walk with me?' Frank said with a grin. 'That'll make a change.'

Frank chatted away easily about the farm and his plans, but Richard made nothing more than occasional polite responses until they had walked for several minutes. Frank saw him frowning in concentration, as if running through a speech in his head.

'Mr Kelly,' he began at last, then gave a smile when he saw Frank's startled expression. 'Frank,' he corrected himself. 'You should know that for some time now I've held your daughter in the highest possible esteem. And I have hopes that she is not completely indifferent to me. I feel I'm in a position to provide for Miss Kelly in the manner she deserves—I have the earnings from my practice, as well as an income from my father's estate, and I'd be more than willing to set out a copy of my accounts for you to study, if you so wish. It would make me very happy if I had your permission to make my feelings known to her. May I ask the honour of seeking your daughter's hand in marriage?'

It was some moments before Frank realised that his mouth was hanging open in astonishment. He shut it, at the same time giving his head a small shake to clear his thoughts. 'Gee, you made a good job of that, Richard. A heck of a lot better than I did of asking for her ma. Of course,' he added, the memory too full of amusement for any trace of bitterness, 'I didn't give you a hard time like Arthur did me. Not that you gave me much chance to. Gee, that sounded really good.'

'Can I take it that your answer is favourable?' Richard prompted.

'Eh? You mean can you have her? Yes, yes, of course you can. I'd never hear the end of it from her or Lizzie if I said no. You knew I'd say

310

yes, didn't you?'

'Well, perhaps I did. There's a due form to be observed in such things, though. And I was a little concerned that you might think Maudie was too young for proposals.'

'She's gone and grown up while I wasn't looking,' Frank said with a rueful smile. 'Fathers can't stop their daughters doing that, I suppose. I'll tell you this, though, Richard,' he added more seriously. 'I wouldn't give Maudie to just anyone, you know. It takes someone special to be good enough for my girl.'

'I'll do my best to be worthy of your trust in me.'

'I'm sure you will.' He clapped Richard on the back. 'We'd better get on, or Maudie and her ma will be coming out looking for us.'

They walked back towards the house, enjoying each other's company. 'Can I ask you something, Richard?' Frank said as a thought struck him. 'Are you meant to ask the girl first or her father first? I mean, you've already asked Maudie, haven't you? I could tell from the way she looked just now. I only ask out of interest, mind you. You seem to know how this sort of thing's done.'

'Well, I've never proposed to anyone before,' Richard pointed out. 'But as far as I know I've acted correctly. Maudie and I did reach a certain understanding before I spoke to you, but I don't think we could properly consider ourselves engaged until I had your permission.'

'So it's all right to ask the girl first?' Frank pressed.

'I believe so, yes.'

'It doesn't really make sense otherwise, does it? I mean, why go to all the trouble of asking a man for his daughter if the girl might turn around and say she doesn't want you anyway?'

'Quite,' Richard agreed.

'Arthur gave me a hard time about that, too. He caught on that I'd asked Lizzie before I asked him, and he went crook at me for it. He was just enjoying see me squirm, I think. Rotten old so-and-so,' Frank added fondly.

'Well, I'm glad you didn't feel the need to put me through the same treatment.'

'Richard, can I ask you something else? Maudie's my daughter, and as far as I'm concerned there's no finer girl in the world. But you must have met a lot of fancy girls in England, at dances and all. What was it attracted you to Maudie specially?'

'Oh, there're a lot of things to admire about Maudie,' Richard said, smiling. 'But I suppose... I think it's because Maudie is so different from the young ladies you're thinking of. They're elegant, of course, and sophisticated and witty and all the things that young ladies are supposed to be. But Maudie's just herself. She sits and walks like a real girl—a healthy girl, too, not some fragile flower who spends all her time at balls and never sees the light of day—and she says what she thinks in her own lovely, artless way. She's natural.'

He became aware of Frank's mirth. 'What's so amusing, Frank? Have I said something foolish?'

'No, you haven't,' Frank said, controlling the laughter that insisted on bubbling up. 'No, it's just... don't say anything like that to Lizzie, eh? About Maudie being natural and all that. Lizzie's gone to a lot of trouble to try and make Maudie like those other girls, she might get a bit funny if you let on that she's been going down the wrong track.'

'Thank you for the advice. I've no desire to offend Mrs Kelly.'

'Let's get a move on, then. If we get on with it, you'll have time to take Maudie for a walk before it starts getting dark.' Frank grinned at a fresh thought. 'I'm not promising anything, mind, but I wouldn't be surprised if Lizzie says you don't have to take Beth with you any more. Want to find out?'

19

June 1903 – October 1904

Maudie's wedding was to be the grandest that Ruatane had ever seen. The months of her engagement seemed scarcely long enough for all the planning and organising that had to be done to make sure the wedding was all that could be wished.

It was to take place in April. Lizzie had at first decreed that Maudie would have to wait until she was eighteen, just as Lizzie had, but the united forces of Frank, Maudie, and even Richard in a deferential but nonetheless persuasive appeal, soon convinced her that there was no need to make the young couple wait a whole year.

'An Easter wedding will be nice,' she announced as if it had been her own idea all along. 'That's about the same time of year as we got married. Anyway, June's too cold to have the reception outside.'

There were lists of guests to be drawn up and pored over, invitations to write, and a quantity of food to be organised large enough to feed a small army. But the thing that caused more excitement, and initially more trouble, than anything else was the matter of dresses.

He should have known better, Frank told himself afterwards. He had known Maudie all her life, after all. But somehow, when she sought him out one day to call him in for morning tea, wound an arm around his waist and planted a kiss on his cheek, he had not the least suspicion that she was motivated by anything more than affection.

'Pa,' she said, fixing him with her most winning smile, 'I can have a really, really nice dress for my wedding, can't I?'

'Of course you can, love,' Frank said. 'The flashest dress you can get. You can send away to Auckland for one if you like.'

'So I can have whatever I like?' Maudie pressed.

'I don't see why not. It'd better be something your ma likes, though,' he added, a hint of suspicion beginning to cloud his pleasure in Maudie's company.

Maudie's smile faltered. 'But I can have a new dress, can't I?'

'Yes, of course! I don't expect you to wear one of your old ones to get married in!'

'Thank you, Pa.' She put both arms around his neck and kissed him soundly, then took his hand and they walked up to the house together.

Frank had barely closed the back door when Maudie spoke in a rush. 'Pa says I can have a new dress, Ma,' she said triumphantly. 'He says I don't have to wear some old thing for my wedding dress.'

Lizzie fixed her daughter with a steely glare, then turned her eyes on Frank. 'Did you tell her that, Frank?' she asked, her eyes narrowing in a way he did not quite feel comfortable with.

'Well, yes, I did,' he admitted, wondering what he had let himself in for. 'It's her big day, Lizzie. I don't mind shelling out for a new dress.'

'See?' Maudie looked smug.

'All right,' Lizzie said, assuming a haughty air. 'If my wedding dress isn't good enough for you, then that's your affair. I've always looked forward to the day I could see you wearing that dress, but it seems it's not to be.' Her gaze took in first Maudie, then Frank; her expression spoke of one still forgiving despite having been wronged. 'We'll say no more about it.'

'Oh, good,' Maudie said with exaggerated relief. 'I've heard enough.'

'I didn't know you wanted her to wear yours, Lizzie,' Frank said guiltily. When Lizzie still pretended aloofness, he sat in the chair next to hers and took her hand in his own. 'It's only natural she wants a new dress for her big day, and I'm not going to have the chance to spoil her for much longer. Let her have what she wants.'

'I hope you're grateful, Miss,' Lizzie said in Maudie's direction, still sounding rather distant. 'You're very lucky to have such a generous father.'

'I know.' Maudie put her arms around his neck and kissed him; this time Frank was certain it was pure affection. At the same time Lizzie squeezed his hand. The household was at peace once again.

Never one to dwell on past defeats, Lizzie set aside any vexation at Maudie's refusal to wear her wedding dress and put her energies into seeing that Maudie's gown would be the talk of the district. Every illustration Lizzie and Maudie could lay their hands on, whether engravings from the pages of the *Weekly News* or pictures of Paris gowns from the journals that Susannah regularly ordered from Auckland, were spread out on the kitchen table to be pored over and discussed at great length. Amy was called in to add her opinion, and the three of them painstakingly reached decisions on fabric, style and trimmings.

Susannah's advice was sought as to who were the finest dressmakers in Auckland, and catalogues duly arrived from the chosen firms to take the place of the newspaper illustrations in dominating the kitchen table. Even when the dress had been selected, weeks of correspondence between Lizzie and the firm of dressmakers were still needed, giving Maudie's measurements and settling every detail of the dress's construction, before Lizzie could finally announce that things were arranged.

'They want you to send a deposit before they'll start, though, Frank,' she told him when the last letter arrived from the dressmakers. 'Then you can settle up the rest of it when it's finished.'

'Might be just as easy to pay it all now,' Frank said. 'How much is it, anyway?'

What he had thought of as a simple enough question was met at first by silence. He saw Maudie and Lizzie exchange what struck him as rather shifty glances.

'You tell him,' Maudie said to her mother. The potato she was peeling suddenly seemed to be utterly fascinating.

'All right, all right,' Lizzie said. 'It's…' She began boldly enough, then her voice subsided into a shadow of its usual self. 'Twenty-five,' she admitted.

Frank frowned in confusion. Surely a wedding dress that had involved so much fuss must be going to cost more than twenty-five shillings? Comprehension dawned. 'You mean… twenty-five pounds?'

'Guineas,' Lizzie said faintly.

'Heck!' The exclamation was out before he could call it back.

Maudie let her potato drop to the bench and crossed to her father. 'We could make it a bit cheaper, Pa. I could have a different sort of lace. The sort with silver in it's the dearest. I don't have to have that sort, it's only that it's the prettiest,' she finished, a plea in her face.

'You can have a gold-plated dress if you want, love,' Frank told her, smiling fondly at her anxious expression. 'I don't mind paying whatever it costs. I just got a bit of a start, that's all. I just… well, I didn't know a dress *could* cost twenty-five pounds. Guineas,' he corrected himself before Lizzie had the chance to.

Having accepted the startling fact that a wedding dress could cost more than a good horse, Frank was mildly surprised to learn that the rest of the dresses were to be made at home. And what a lot of dresses there were, he found. A new one for Lizzie, of course; her role as mother of the bride required something special. And all three of Maudie's sisters were to be bridesmaids, with matching dresses apparently essential.

'You'd better be a bridesmaid too, Maisie,' Maudie said. 'I'm having all the others, so I'll have you as well. Four makes a nice, even number, too.'

'What do I have to do?' Maisie asked suspiciously.

'Nothing much. Just walk along behind me and help with the veil and things. You can have a new dress.'

'Can I?' Maisie looked more enthusiastic. 'Whose?'

'What do you mean, whose?'

315

'Whose dress can I have? Yours or Beth's? Only, when I get one of yours I have to cut lots off the bottom, 'cause you're much taller than me. Beth's ones fit better.'

'One of your own, of course,' Lizzie said. 'All these dresses we're going to be making, it'll take no time to run up one for you as well.'

Maisie said nothing, and at first Frank thought she was indifferent to the idea. Then he saw that she was sitting quite still, tears trickling down her cheeks.

'Whatever's wrong with you, girl?' Lizzie asked. 'Don't you want to be a bridesmaid? You don't have to if you don't want to.'

'A-a n-new dress,' Maisie sobbed. 'A dress made s-special for me.' She sniffed noisily and wiped her nose on her hand, earning a reproving look from Lizzie. 'I never had nothing new before,' she said to the ring of faces staring at her. 'Not even drawers or anything.' She rose from her chair, crossed to Lizzie and put her arms around her neck. 'Thanks,' she said, her voice muffled against the cloth of Lizzie's bodice.

Lizzie fished a handkerchief out from her sleeve and held it over Maisie's face. 'Blow,' she ordered, wiping Maisie's nose when the girl had obeyed. 'No, I don't want the hanky back, tuck it up your sleeve. We'd better make you half a dozen hankies as well, since you don't seem able to find one when you need it. Silly girl,' she said, squeezing Maisie's thin shoulders.

Those dresses seemed to take over the house. For months on end, it was full of lengths of fabric, rolls of lace and yards of ribbon.

'Don't stand on the material!' a voice would yell at Frank whenever he entered the parlour. Pointing out that there was nowhere else to stand earned him a reproachful stare. If he found himself sitting or standing on a pin (of which there seemed to be thousands scattered around the house), he would be told that he should be more careful where he put his feet or backside.

'I'll be glad when this wedding's over,' he grumbled one day as he gingerly removed a pin that had entwined itself in his sock. The sewing effort had been transferred to the kitchen to take advantage of the morning light, and Amy had managed to get Charlie's permission to join Frank's womenfolk for a few hours, making the room even more crowded.

'I don't know why you've got to get underfoot all the time,' Lizzie said, her voice indistinct through a mouthful of pins as she struggled to get a straight edge on Rosie's hem. 'Oh, keep still for goodness sake, Rosie! I'll stick one of these in you if you keep wriggling.'

'I want to go to the dunny!' Rosie complained.

'Well, you'll just have to hang on. I'll have this pinned in two minutes if you'll only keep still—Frank, get off that lace!'

'I only wanted a cup of tea,' Frank said. 'Can't I have a cup of tea in my own kitchen?'

'No, you can't. Take it out on the verandah. Hurry up, Frank, you're in the way.'

'But the kettle hasn't even boiled yet! I can't make it till the kettle's boiled.'

'Why's Richard marrying Maudie, anyway?' said Rosie, her squirming showing that she had not forgotten her more immediate problem.

'Because he loves me,' Maudie said, looking up with a sunny smile from her task of pinning lace to Maisie's bodice.

'But why doesn't he marry *me*? He's my doctor, not yours. He never listens to your chest. *I* need my chest done because I get coughs.' Rosie frowned in concentration and summoned up a small cough. 'See?' she said triumphantly.

'Keep *still*, Rosie,' Lizzie scolded. 'Frank, what are you doing with those tins?'

'Just trying to get a biscuit. This tin's got nothing in it.'

'There's some afghan biscuits in that tin on the top shelf. Don't you go dropping crumbs on the material. Maudie's the oldest, Rosie. You'll have a nice young man of your own when you're her age.'

'It's not fair,' Rosie whined. 'She always gets things first, just 'cause she's the biggest. He's *my* doctor.' She stamped her foot just as Lizzie tried to place a pin, her movement wrenching the pin from Lizzie's hand and pulling a thread in the fabric. She wailed as her mother gave her a hard slap on the bottom.

Lizzie spat the mouthful of pins into her hand and put them to one side. 'Right, I've had enough of you,' she said above Rosie's wails. 'Lift your arms up.' She tugged the pink satin dress over Rosie's head and took the opportunity to plant another slap before quickly pulling on Rosie's everyday dress. 'Go to the dunny, then you can stand in the corner. And you can stop that bawling or I'll go and get the belt.'

'I want to get married *now*,' Rosie grumbled when she was safely out of her mother's reach on her way to the door.

'A good hiding, that's what you want. Frank, you're dropping the icing off that! Take it outside.'

'I want—' Rosie began again.

'None of you other girls are going to get married before you're thirty,' Frank exploded. 'It's going to take me twenty years to get over this bloody wedding!'

'What a *horrible* thing to say, Pa,' Maudie wailed. 'I thought you *liked* Richard.'

'*Take those biscuits outside, Frank!*' Lizzie shouted.

'But I want a cup of tea! Can't I have a cup of tea?'

'No! Go away!'

Amy rose from where she was kneeling to pin Beth's dress, took Frank's arm and steered him towards the door. 'I think you'd be better off out on the verandah,' she told him. 'I'll make you some tea when the kettle's boiled, and I'll bring it out with some of those nice biscuits of Lizzie's. I won't be long.'

By the time Amy came out with a tray a few minutes later, she could see that Frank was already regretting his outburst. 'Thanks,' he said as Amy set out his cup and saucer. 'Sorry about that fuss.'

Amy sat down beside him and patted his hand. 'That's all right, Frank. It must be getting on your nerves, all this business with dresses everywhere. Don't worry, in a couple of months you'll have forgotten everything except what a lovely wedding you gave Maudie.'

'It's a bit rough, getting you down here to help then you have to put up with us all yelling at each other.'

Amy thought of her own kitchen; of the mealtimes when she and Charlie might not speak to one another at all, now that he often had no energy to snarl at her. She did not make the pretence of seeking his company in the evenings, choosing instead to sit in her room reading, mending while the light held, or writing long letters to David, while Charlie sat in the parlour with his newspaper and a bottle.

'I don't mind,' she said. 'I like sharing your family. Even when you yell at each other.' She poured his tea and passed the cup to him. 'Not that you make a habit of it,' she added with a smile.

Frank ran a hand over his hair, took a gulp of tea and slumped back in his chair. 'I never used to. I tell you what, I really will be glad when this wedding of Maudie's is over. And I've got three more daughters to worry about!' He pulled a face, then laughed. 'No, I bet you're right. It'll be worth all the fuss to give Maudie her special day.'

'I'm sure it will.'

'Lizzie's loving every minute of it, too,' Frank said. 'Getting it all organised and bossing everyone around. I think it's pretty special for a woman when her daughter gets married.'

The silence between them had grown uncomfortably obvious before Amy could bring herself to answer. 'I suppose it is, Frank,' she said quietly.

'Sorry,' Frank said. 'I didn't mean to... sorry.'

Amy managed a smile with difficulty. 'Don't worry. Lizzie shares her daughters with me, so I'm lucky really, aren't I? It doesn't matter that...' *That I haven't got any daughters.* She could not bring herself to say the lie, certain though she was that Lizzie had kept Ann's existence secret from Frank.

'I suppose...' Frank trailed away. Amy was puzzled at how embarrassed he seemed to be. 'Sorry,' he finished feebly.

Maudie broke the awkward moment by appearing in the doorway.

'We've finished for now, so Ma says you can come inside if you want,' she announced to Frank, her sunny expression banishing all memory of the reproachful look she had given him earlier. 'Come and have morning tea, Aunt Amy.'

'I'd better not, Maudie. I told Uncle Charlie I'd be back by eleven. I'll just come in and say goodbye to your mother, then I'd better hurry. Oh, thank you, dear,' she said as Maudie passed a book to her.

'I liked that one,' said Maudie. 'It had a good story to it. Especially that bit about the mad wife in the attic—ooh, that was scary!'

'It didn't keep you awake at night, did it?'

'Oh, no, nothing keeps me awake. Though it might have if I'd been on my own,' she added thoughtfully. 'You can't be scared with four of you in a room, eh?'

'I've got another one by Miss Brontë, I'll bring it next time I come, shall I?'

Amy made her farewells and left. Frank and Lizzie waved her out of sight, leaving the girls to get morning tea ready.

'Fancy having to hurry back to that sour old so-and-so,' Frank said. 'Don't know how she stays as bright as she does, living with him.'

'And no Dave to cheer her up.' Lizzie frowned as she watched the small figure fade into the distance. 'I'm worried about her, Frank. It's not healthy, being stuck in the house with a man like Charlie.'

Frank remembered his own thoughtless remark guiltily. 'She seems all right.'

'Amy always *seems* all right—she doesn't like to worry other people. I'll just have to try and keep an eye on her. I don't want her going funny in the head.'

'Couldn't really blame her if she did.'

There were times when Frank thought that April would never come. But come it did, and the Easter wedding was everything Maudie and her mother had hoped for.

It was a perfect day, from the golden autumn weather to the beauty of the simple service and the bounty of the food and drink that followed it, the amount left over making a mockery of Lizzie's earlier anxiety as to whether there would be enough. A day that would bring a smile to Frank's face whenever he recalled it. And at the centre of everything, shining like a brilliant star, was his beautiful daughter.

The dress was part of it. When Frank first saw Maudie in the folds of white lace shot through with silver, so full and soft that she seemed to be floating rather than walking, he began to comprehend that a dress could just possibly be worth twenty-five guineas. But the face under the veil, bright with joy, could not have been bought at any price.

'I don't know if I can bring myself to give you away, love,' Frank told her as they prepared to make their grand entrance through the assembled guests. 'You're so gorgeous I might want to keep you for myself.' Maudie laughed aloud in sheer delight, gave him the last kiss he would ever receive from her as an unmarried girl, and tugged at his arm to hurry him up, showing him that she was more than ready to be given away.

After the service Maudie and Richard moved among their guests, Maudie bestowing radiant smiles on everyone she came near. Maisie and the younger girls, looking like bunches of blossom in their pink satin dresses, hovered about her from time to time as they helped carry plates and glasses, their prettiness accentuating Maudie's silver and white glory.

Maudie was stunning. She smiled and laughed, twirled to show off her dress, kissed people, and proudly displayed the gold band that had taken its place beside her engagement ring. It was the greatest day Maudie had ever had in her life, and she loved every moment of it.

It was no wonder, Frank thought, that Richard could not take his eyes off his new wife. All afternoon Richard watched Maudie with a bemused smile, as if he could hardly believe his good fortune. When their eyes met, as they often did, they would smile more brightly than ever, already sharing unspoken secrets.

By the time the sun had edged close to the hills few of the guests were showing any sign of wanting to leave, but Frank saw Richard and Maudie exchange a glance that had an obvious message in it. He was not surprised when the newlyweds sought him and Lizzie out soon afterwards, to say their goodbyes quietly before farewelling the crush of guests.

Maudie gave them both a rapturous embrace, tilting her veil a little askew in the process. It gave her a slightly rumpled appearance that

Frank observed with a smile. It was good to see a trace of his little girl again in this dazzling young woman. Richard gave Lizzie the warmest kiss she had ever received from him, and Frank observed with amusement the way it made her cheeks pink with pleasure.

'Take good care of my girl for me, eh, Richard?' Frank said as the two of them shook hands.

'I will,' Richard said, gripping his hand more tightly. His gaze sought out Maudie's as if he could not bear to let her out of his sight for more than a moment, and their eyes met again in that special smile. 'I will.'

Then it was time to follow them to Richard's gig and wave them off, calling good wishes after them as the horse trotted down the track, leading Maudie away from home for the first night she had ever spent beyond the valley.

The departure of the bridal couple did not mean the end of the celebrations. Even when the tardiest of the guests had gone home, Lizzie and the older girls had to put the house back in some semblance of order and see that the little ones were properly settled before going to bed themselves. It was close to midnight before Frank could slide his arms around Lizzie and feel her warm body nestling against him in the darkness, both of them too weary for immediate sleep.

'Funny to think she won't be coming back here, eh?' he murmured in Lizzie's ear. 'We won't even see her for two weeks.'

'Ridiculous idea,' Lizzie said, managing to sound disapproving even through her drowsy tone. 'Fancy going away like that when they've just got married! No one'll be able to visit them or anything.'

Richard had startled Maudie's relations at the beginning of their engagement by buying her an extravagantly beautiful diamond ring; they had been even more startled to learn that he intended to take her on a honeymoon. After spending their first night at Richard's house, they were to catch the boat for Tauranga the next morning on the first stage of their trip.

'I don't know, I think it's a pretty good idea,' Frank said. 'Going off by yourselves, sort of getting to know one another properly without everyone staring at you and wondering how you're getting on.' He gave Lizzie a squeeze. 'How about I take you on a honeymoon sometime, eh?'

Lizzie gave a snort. 'It's a bit late for that, isn't it? You must know me pretty well by now.'

'You could do with a holiday, though. And wouldn't you like to see somewhere different? Maybe Rotorua, like Maudie.'

'Don't talk rot, Frank. What's wrong with here that I'd want to go wandering off somewhere else? As if I could leave the little ones, anyway.'

'I suppose not.' Frank put the idea in the back of his mind along with a few other distant plans that Lizzie had little inkling of, to be saved for the day when the youngest children were no longer quite so young. 'Maudie looked really happy, didn't she? Not even nervous or anything. You had a talk with her about it all, didn't you?'

'Yes, I managed to shoo the other girls away for a minute this morning so I could tell her what she needed to know. Nervous? I think she was looking forward to it! The little minx,' she added complacently.

Frank yawned luxuriantly and pulled Lizzie closer. 'I always said Maudie was just like her ma,' he said, knowing that Lizzie was too sleepy to take the bait. 'I hope Richard wasn't as tired as I am,' he murmured as he reluctantly let sleep take him.

Frank was surprised at how flat the household seemed without Maudie. It took months for him to get over a mild sense of disappointment every time he came into the house expecting to see her and finding her missing.

Soon after Maudie's marriage, Frank decided the time had come to abandon the pretence that Maisie still lived with her family and only 'worked' for Lizzie. Lizzie had lost the help of her oldest daughter around the house, and Maudie's departure had left enough room in the girls' bedroom for Maisie to take her place. Lizzie readily agreed, and Maisie was delighted at the idea, fear of her father's reaction to losing his sole reliable source of income being her only worry.

Frank set off one day with Maisie bouncing behind him on the horse's rump and a wad of bank notes in his jacket pocket. When they arrived home an hour later, Maisie's face was wreathed in smiles but Frank was grim and silent.

'How much?' Lizzie asked when they were alone.

'Ten pounds. I think he expected me to try and beat him down or something, but I wasn't going to go haggling over Maisie as if she was a cow. I just gave him what he asked for. And I hope he drinks himself to death on it,' Frank said bitterly. 'I managed to slip her aunt five pounds, too, when that bugger was out of sight. She seems to be the only one who's ever taken any notice of Maisie around there.'

'You expected to pay about that, didn't you? What's got you in such a mood?'

'It's not the money. It's what that so-and-so said about it.' Frank banged his fist on the table in remembered anger. 'Do you know he as good as said I use Maisie as if she was a sort of live-in whore? He reckoned it wasn't a bad price to have a girl around whenever I want one, and he said I must be… no, I wouldn't repeat that stuff in front of you.'

'What a dreadful thing to say!' Lizzie said, outraged. 'Fancy saying such a thing about you! Ooh, I'd have given him a piece of my mind if I'd been there.'

Frank made a noise of disgust. 'I don't care what he says about me. You know what made me really wild? He thought it was funny. The man thinks I've been using his daughter like that for years, then he watches me take her away without batting an eyelid. He bloody well laughed! I just about knocked his teeth out for him.'

'Did Maisie hear him say any of that?' Lizzie asked, suddenly solemn.

'I don't know. I hope not. I'd sent her off to get her stuff before he started. She didn't seem to have much.'

'A spare pair of drawers—damp, I might add, I don't think they know how to give clothes a decent airing in that house. And a raggy old doll. She bawled when I wanted to take it off her and wash it, she said something about her ma making it for her. She's had it hidden under the house for years, it's just about falling apart. I might help her make a new dress for it when she's settled down a bit, that'll hold the insides in.'

Frank smiled gratefully at her, feeling his anger slip away. 'You're an old softie, Lizzie. Well, I'm glad I'll never have to go near that place again. Neither will Maisie. Gee, those girls are going to have tons of room in there, aren't they? All that stuff of Maudie's she took with her! Boxes and boxes of it.'

'She'll be taking Rosie, too, if she's not careful. Rosie's always asking Richard when she can come and live with him. Especially when she's in trouble with me. Kate's nearly as bad.'

'Rosie's still telling him off about not taking her on their honeymoon, too,' Frank said with a grin. 'You're going to have to watch her when she gets a bit older.'

'Daughters!' Lizzie said, spreading her hands wide in an extravagant gesture of defeat. 'Who'd have them?'

A new arrival in the district was always a welcome novelty, and when Lily announced that the latest teacher to arrive in town was distantly related to her, Lily's family were eager to make the young woman's acquaintance. They found her rather different from what they had expected.

'You know the new teacher's coming?' Lizzie said to Amy shortly before her next soirée. 'I had to ask her, what with her being Lily's cousin, but you don't need to take any notice of her.'

'Whatever do you mean, Lizzie?' Amy asked. 'What's wrong with her?'

'Oh, she's a funny sort of person,' Lizzie said, frowning in disapproval. 'Frank can't stand her.'

'Hey, hey, that's a bit strong,' Frank protested. 'I didn't say that. She's just… well, like you said, she's a bit funny. She's got this way of looking at you, Amy, like she's caught you out doing something you shouldn't have. I suppose it's to do with her being a teacher—she probably gives the kids at school a look like that when she's going to thump them. But I sort of felt guilty, the way she was staring at me.'

'And *nosy*,' Lizzie put in. 'She kept wanting to know what everyone's names were and how we were all related—she's sort of fussy, you know? Wanted to be sure she was getting it all right. You could see Lily was embarrassed, with her being a relation.'

'In the end Bill asked her if she was writing a book,' Frank said with a grin. 'That settled her down, she felt a bit stupid about that, I think.'

'Serves her right,' Lizzie said.

'I don't like people asking me a lot of questions,' Amy said uneasily. 'Still, I don't suppose she'll take much notice of me, I'm not very interesting. Is Maudie coming?'

'Humph!' Lizzie said. 'I suppose Mrs Townsend might just decide to drop in on us. I did tell her to come, but of course she takes no notice of what I say. I'm only her mother, after all.'

Frank caught Amy's eye and raised his eyebrows. 'Now, Lizzie, Maudie's all right,' he said. 'She's just finding her own ways of doing things around the house, that's all. It's only natural she wants to do that now she's got her own place.'

'And I know nothing about running a house, I suppose? That's why she argues with everything I tell her.'

'She's not as bad as all that. Give her time, she'll start asking you things.'

Lizzie's lips set in a thin, disapproving line. 'And another thing—that girl's got far too much time on her hands. Do you know,' she said, her voice tight with indignation, 'she gets a woman in to do her work for her?'

'Just the heavy work, Lizzie,' Frank said. 'Richard used to have Mrs Clark in to look after the place before him and Maudie got married, so he's kept her on to do the scrubbing and washing and things,' he explained to Amy.

'Heavy work, indeed,' Lizzie scoffed. 'How much heavy work is there to do with just the two of them, I'd like to know? I *think*,' she said, her voice dripping with sarcasm, 'I *think* she does the cooking herself. Though nothing would surprise me about that girl.'

'You know she does the cooking,' Frank said. 'Didn't she make us that nice lunch the other day? And Richard told me how he had to tell her not to cook him so much, because he's not out digging drains and suchlike all day. I think it's nice he's got someone to help her.'

'*I* was married twelve years before I got anyone to help me,' Lizzie said self-righteously. 'And I had six children to look after as well as a husband. Richard spoils that girl, and it's doing her no good at all. It's not good for a young bride to have too much time on her hands.'

'Why not?' Frank asked.

'It just isn't, that's all. Don't you think so, Amy?'

'I think it's lovely that Richard wants to look after Maudie,' Amy said, earning a look of exasperation from Lizzie and a grin from Frank.

'That's just what I think,' he said. 'I would've liked to have got someone to help you when we first got married, too, Lizzie. Richard's got the money, so why shouldn't he spend it on Maudie? There's nothing wrong with a bit of spoiling.'

'Well!' Lizzie said, glaring at them both, 'if you two are going to side against me, there's no point me saying anything, is there?'

'No point at all,' Frank said.

After Lizzie's comments Amy was expecting something of a dragon, but when Sarah Millish arrived at the soirée Amy saw an attractive young woman with an expression that, though disconcertingly direct, was certainly not sour.

'Oh, Sarah, come and sit next to me,' Lily said when Beth led Miss Millish into the room. 'No, I must introduce you to everyone before we sit down,' she added, taking her arm. 'Miss Millish and I are cousins, after a fashion,' she explained to the room at large. 'Miss Millish's father was distantly related to my mother, and he was very kind to Mother and me. Now, you've met Mr and Mrs Kelly, and this is their daughter Mrs Townsend, and her husband Doctor Townsend.'

Lily dutifully introduced Miss Millish to everyone in the room, giving Amy plenty of time to study the visitor before Lily reached Amy's insignificant corner.

Miss Millish was very tall, with dark hair piled above a pale face. Her eyes were large, and a striking dark blue. It was a very definite sort of face, Amy thought, with its prominent cheekbones, straight nose and rather broad jaw. There was a firm set to that jaw that gave the impression of someone who should not be crossed lightly.

'And this is Mrs Stewart,' Lily said when they came to Amy. 'She's

Bill's cousin, Sarah,' she explained. 'Mr and Mrs Stewart live on the farm next to Mr John Leith's—remember you were asking me the other day who lives there?'

'How do you do, Mrs Stewart?' Miss Millish took Amy's hand and turned a penetrating gaze on her from under well-defined eyebrows. Amy felt an irrational desire to say something clever to try and impress her, but all she could manage was to murmur a polite 'How do you do' and wait for her hand to be released. Amy was glad that she was at least wearing a smart dress tonight. It was of yellow silk, and she had made it on the sewing machine she had bought out of her annuity. It was not nearly as beautiful as her blue silk dress; Amy's confidence with the sewing machine did not extend so far, nor did her pocket run to the amount of silk she would have had to buy to imitate such an elaborate style; but it was a good deal less old-fashioned.

Lily made Miss Millish sit beside her, fussing over the guest and seeing that she soon had a cup of tea and something to eat. Amy began to suspect that Lizzie's assertion that Lily was embarrassed by her young cousin was something of an exaggeration, though she could see how the quick glances Miss Millish constantly darted around the room might be off-putting. She saw Frank squirm in his chair when he noticed Miss Millish studying him, though the teacher had the grace to look away when she saw how discomforted Frank looked.

The youngest girls were visibly struggling to stay awake. At a nod from Lizzie, Beth and Maisie ushered them off to bed. Beth came back into the room clutching an envelope; she sat at Amy's feet and held it out to her. 'Here's a letter from Dave, Aunt Amy, it came today.'

Amy smiled at Beth and took the letter from her. She glanced beyond the girl, and was mildly startled to see Miss Millish staring intently.

'Amy?' Miss Millish said. 'You're Amy?'

'Are you writing that book again, Sarah?' Bill asked, grinning at the sudden flush his words brought to Miss Millish's face.

'I-I'm sorry, Mrs Stewart,' she said. 'Lily may have told you that I'm very interested in names and their meanings. I suppose it comes of struggling away at my Latin for all those years. And... and I've a friend called Amy, and it's not a name one hears often. It's the French for "loved", did you know that? Amy,' she said, as if playing with the sound in her head. 'It's such a pretty name, isn't it?'

'I was named for my grandmother,' Amy said.

A smile spread across Miss Millish's face, banishing its severity and lending an extra prettiness. 'So was I,' she murmured. She took up her tea cup and appeared to give it her complete attention for some time.

Lily was called upon to entertain. She played several pieces before offering her place at the piano to Miss Millish.

'You play beautifully, dear,' Lily said when Miss Millish stopped for a rest. 'The last time I saw Sarah she was so small she had to be lifted onto the piano stool,' she told the audience.

'I play adequately,' Miss Millish said. '*You* play beautifully, Lily. You've a true gift.'

'It's thanks to your father that I play at all,' Lily said. 'He paid for my piano lessons, you know.'

'I remember his saying it was the most worthwhile money he ever spent,' Miss Millish said. 'Father loved music, though he didn't play himself. He often used to speak of your playing after you moved away.'

'He was a lovely man,' said Lily.

'Yes, he was.' Miss Millish's face was suddenly serious again. She gave herself a small shake. 'I'm sure you don't want to hear me play all evening. Mrs Stewart, do you play?'

'Oh, no,' Amy said quickly. 'No, I don't.'

'Perhaps you'd like to sing, then?' Miss Millish coaxed. 'Is there something I could accompany you in?'

'No, I don't sing either. I can't do anything, really,' Amy said, smiling ruefully.

'What rot!' Lizzie said. 'You can do lots of things! What about the lovely embroidery you've taught my girls to do? And bottling and things—Amy's won prizes for her jam, you know,' she told Miss Millish.

'I didn't mean things like jam,' Amy said. 'Everyone can do that sort of thing. I meant clever things like music.'

'Well, you could have played if you'd only had the chance to learn,' Lizzie said, undeterred. 'It was just that there was no one to give you lessons. Even the magistrate's wife said you were musical, remember? She looked at your hands and said you'd be good at playing the piano. And *she'd* know about that sort of thing.'

'Honestly, Lizzie, you make me sound like... oh, who was the girl?' Amy said half to herself, flustered by Lizzie's prattle. 'The one whose mother was always going on about how good she would've been at this and that except she'd never learned.'

'Anne de Bourgh,' Miss Millish said. 'Lady Catherine's daughter. That's who you mean, isn't it?'

'Who's she?' Lizzie asked the room at large.

'You've read Miss Austen?' Amy asked Miss Millish.

'Oh, a book,' Lizzie remarked. 'I might have known.'

'I've got that one, haven't I, Richard?' Maudie put in, clutching at her husband's sleeve to attract his attention away from his conversation with Frank.

'Hmm? Oh, *Pride and Prejudice*. Yes, darling, so you have. It's one of the books we bought for you in Tauranga, isn't it? It seemed a very suitable book for you to read. Will you play for us, Maudie? Your father hasn't had the chance to hear you for a little while.'

Maudie took Miss Millish's place at the piano and began playing, while Miss Millish moved a chair close to Amy's and sat down beside her. When Maudie had played her pieces, conversation in the room resumed.

'I've all Miss Austen's works,' Miss Millish said. 'She's quite delightful. Though I do find her heroines irritating at times, with their obsession over finding husbands. Miss Brontë is more satisfying—her women tend to find a career for themselves, even if they do become shackled with a husband later.'

'Are you shackled, Lily?' Bill asked, trying to look serious despite his grin. Lily shushed him frantically.

'Oh, I… perhaps I went a little far in saying that,' Miss Millish said. 'I'm sure marriage isn't always bondage. But you must admit that women are often denied their just place in society? That we're held down just because we're women?'

'Men and women each have their own place,' Lizzie said piously.

'But why should a woman's place be at the bottom?' Miss Millish demanded. 'Why should the course of a woman's life always be decided for her by the men around her? Mightn't the world be a better place if women were treated as the equals of men?' Her attention swung to Amy. 'Mrs Stewart, what do you think?'

'Me? Oh, I… I don't really…' Amy was disconcerted by the knowledge that all eyes in the room were upon her, then was abruptly angry at herself for appearing witless in front of this startling woman. 'I read somewhere,' she began hesitantly, and went on more boldly. 'It said that when things get better in countries, it's always when they start treating women more as equals. The man said you could tell how good a country was from the way they treated women.'

' "Through all the progressive period of human history, the condition of women has been approaching nearer to equality with men",' Miss Millish quoted. 'And didn't he put it well?'

Amy stared at her in delight. 'You've read John Stuart Mill?'

'I know that passage off by heart.'

'I've never met *anyone* else who reads John Stuart Mill,' Amy said, hardly able to believe it. 'No one I can talk to about him, anyway.'

'Somebody Stewart, is he?' Lizzie asked, unwilling to be left out. 'Is he a relation of Charlie's?' she said doubtfully.

Amy laughed. 'I shouldn't think so, Lizzie. I don't think they'd get on very well, either. No, he's a man who writes about that sort of thing—liberty, people's rights, all those things. He's *wonderful*. He really makes you think. I had to buy a dictionary before I could make anything of it, though,' she confessed.

'I've his complete works,' Miss Millish said. 'Perhaps I could lend you something? And Carlyle, too—he's rather dry after Mill, but it's interesting to compare the two.'

'I've heard of him, but I've never read anything by him.'

'I must lend you some of my books, then. Perhaps I could call on you?'

'Oh, I-I'm not sure,' Amy stammered, shy at the thought of exposing Miss Millish to Charlie's coarseness and to the plainness of their cottage. 'My husband doesn't… we don't get a lot of visitors. I'd rather just see you here, if that's all right?'

'Just as you wish.' Miss Millish spoke smoothly, though Amy was aware of the curiosity she was struggling to hide. 'And I *will* see you here,' she announced. 'I hope we'll see each other often.'

'So do I,' Amy said, smiling shyly at her new-found friend.

Amy had to leave before the other guests, constrained by the curfew Charlie had imposed. She was even more reluctant to leave than usual, since it meant curtailing such delightful conversation, but she said her goodbyes and went out to the front door, Lizzie going with her as far as the verandah.

'I've decided what's wrong with that girl,' Lizzie said in a low voice. 'Why she's so funny with everyone.'

'She's not funny, Lizzie,' Amy protested.

'Yes, she is. It's because of all that stuff she was talking, you know, about women being as good as men. She's one of those suffragist women. Except there aren't any proper suffragists left, what with us having the vote. But there're still women like her with funny ideas. That's why she hasn't got married, see? She's quite pretty, and Lily says she's got pots of money, being an only child and her father was rich. But she's full of those funny ideas, so she can't get on with men.'

'What a lot of rot you talk sometimes,' Amy said, unsure whether to laugh or scold. 'I don't notice you going around thinking you're inferior to men—you don't think you're inferior to anyone, and quite right, too. You don't let Frank boss you around.'

'I do what Frank says. Yes, I do,' Lizzie insisted, seeing Amy's expression. 'Well, except when he's wrong about something, then I just explain how he's wrong until he sees it for himself. Anyway, it's different once you're married, but there's no sense frightening off every man in creation. *I* think she doesn't like men at all. Look at the way she gives Frank those funny looks—no wonder he doesn't like her,' Lizzie said with the air of one who had demolished all arguments.

'Well, *I* like her,' Amy said. 'I like her very much.'

Lizzie regarded her thoughtfully. 'It was good to see you enjoying yourself tonight. Lord knows you can do with something to cheer you up. I wasn't going to ask that girl again, but if you and her are going to get on so well I might as well get her out to all the soyrees. She's pretty good on the piano, too.'

Amy put her arms around her cousin's neck and kissed her. 'Thank you, Lizzie. Thank you for everything.'

She hugged Lizzie tightly, and set off down the track with a lighter heart than she had had in years. The sun had set, but enough daylight lingered for her to re-read the letter from David, which she had only managed to skim while at the soirée. It was his usual sort of letter, telling her the everyday details of his life, what work he was doing and what he had had for dinner that week, and asking after the people he cared about. He never mentioned his father in his letters.

David's letters had been the brightest spot in her existence in the two years since she had lost him. For the brief period of reading his words, she held him to her once again. She would rub the paper between her fingers as if it held some essence of him; hold the pages to her nose and drink in the smell of the ink, trying to breathe in a trace of her son. She read his letters slowly, savouring each word, putting off the moment when the letter had to be folded and put away, and she had to face the fact all over again that she had lost David. The gentle pleasure of reading one of his letters was always followed by the sharpest of pains, when the soft underbelly of her senses lay open to the harshness of her reality.

But today that pain was muffled; the dull ache of an old wound instead of the stab of one newly reopened. Today there was the remembered pleasure of Sarah Millish's company.

'I've got a friend, Davie,' she whispered into the evening. 'A real friend I can talk to about books and ideas—all those things people like Lizzie think is just me being silly. I haven't had anyone like that since Miss Evans. She's nice, Davie. You'd like her.'

She hugged the letter to her chest as she hugged the memory of her evening. She would have to try and coax Lizzie into having soirées more often; or perhaps just into inviting Miss Millish out for an afternoon. If she did not ask for outings too often, it was usually possible to get

Charlie's permission to visit Lizzie. She mused on how long it might be before she could see her new friend again; surely not more than a week or two. For the first time in many months she had something to look forward to.

She saw Charlie in the middle of the newly planted potato paddock as she walked up the last part of the track, and was surprised that he was outside so late when little light remained. But it was a warm evening, and she knew he had difficulty finding the time to get all the potatoes planted now that he had to do it alone.

'I'm home, Charlie,' she called, cupping her hands to make the sound travel further. 'I'll get some supper on for you.'

He made no answer, not even turning towards her, though Amy was sure he must have heard.

He's probably in a mood. He's tired himself out and got in a mood. I hope he doesn't say I can't go to Lizzie's next time.

But it was no use brooding on such things. If he refused her next outing, she would simply have to keep asking until he tired of the game. Even if it took weeks, he would give in eventually.

She put the kettle on and buttered scones for his supper, spreading them thickly with jam. She was astonished to find herself humming as she worked.

The tea was in the pot, brewed and in danger of becoming too strong, and still Charlie had not appeared. Whatever was he doing out there? It was surely too dim to work now.

Amy went outside and retraced her steps to the potato paddock. Charlie was in the same spot she had seem him earlier. Exactly the same spot, she realised. She frowned, straining her eyes to see through the gloom. The same spot and the same position, crouched down as if he were studying the dirt of the paddock.

She scrambled over the fence and started across the furrows, picking up her skirts to move more freely. She walked faster, then broke into a run, almost stumbling in her haste to leap over the ridges of earth.

Charlie was slumped across a planted mound, his body an untidy heap and the fingers of one hand clawed into the soil. Amy dropped to her knees beside him, her heart pounding.

'Charlie?' she whispered. 'Charlie, what's happened to you?' Hesitantly she reached out a hand towards his face, sickly grey in the last of the daylight.

20

October – December 1904

Charlie twitched at her touch. He made a gurgling noise in his throat and his eyes stared at Amy without any sign of recognition. She crouched with her face close to his, frozen by those empty eyes.

As she watched, awareness slowly came into his gaze. The blank, lifeless stare was replaced by a look of confusion, as if he were trying to take in where he was and how he had come to be there.

'Charlie, you're all right!' Amy said, taking a great, sighing breath of relief. 'I thought something awful had happened to you. What's wrong? Did you have a fall?'

Charlie's confused, almost frightened, expression did not change. He opened his mouth to speak, but what came out was an unintelligible mumble. At the sound, he looked more fearful than ever.

'Don't try and talk,' Amy said. 'You must have fallen and hit your head. You've hurt your mouth, too, I think, that's why you can't talk properly just yet.'

She felt gingerly around as much of his scalp as she could reach, watching him closely to see if she was hurting him. She peered at her hands to see if there was any trace of blood on them; she could see none, but there was so little light left that she could not be sure.

'I've got to get you up to the house. Can you sit up? Here, I'll help you.'

She took hold of his arm and hauled him into a sitting position, feeling his weight drag at her. His other arm hung limp at his side.

'Can't... can't move my arm,' he mumbled, speaking with an obvious effort. 'Doesn't work.'

'You must have put all your weight on that side when you fell. Does it hurt?'

He frowned in confusion. 'Can't feel it. Can't move it.'

Amy ran her hand up the limp arm. As far as she could tell, the bones were still sound. 'Perhaps it's just numb from you lying on it. Your leg might be numb, too. Can you move it?'

She saw the strain on his face. 'No,' he said faintly.

Amy felt the leg as well as she could with Charlie's weight resting on it, and was relieved that it obviously gave him no pain. 'I'll have to help you, then. Put your arm around my shoulders and I'll get you up.'

He gripped her shoulder so tightly that Amy felt his fingers digging into her flesh. She sensed his fear. His strength had never deserted him before; Charlie had no experience of being helpless.

Amy felt pain clawing through her body as she heaved at Charlie's weight. His attempts to help himself, clutching convulsively at her neck, only made it more difficult. When she had him upright at last, the two of them swaying like a pair of drunks supporting each other, she had to stand still for several seconds, taking great gasps of air and waiting for her heart to slow.

One leg dragged uselessly as she led him across the paddock, through the gate and up to the cottage. She took him through to his bedroom, pulled back the covers with one hand while balancing him with her other arm, then eased him onto the bed as gently as she could. He sank back against the pillows and lay there watching her with those frightened eyes.

'Perhaps I should get the doctor to you,' Amy said, frowning. 'You must have had quite a fall. If I hurry I might catch him still at Lizzie's.'

'No!' That word came out clearly enough, though she was puzzled at how he seemed to screw up his face as he spoke. 'Don't want some bloody quack. You stay home.'

He might become distressed if she pressed the issue, and there could surely not be anything seriously wrong with him. A good night's sleep should see him over the strange numbness in his leg and arm, and though he might wake up with a headache if he had indeed hit his head, it would probably be no worse than the aftermath of a night's drinking.

She undid his boots and pulled them off, and briefly considered offering to help him undress. Best not to, she decided. It would embarrass both of them, and the worst he would do was crease his clothes by sleeping in them.

'Are you comfortable?' she asked. He gave a quick nod. She pulled the covers up over him and tucked them in. 'Try to get to sleep, then. You'll feel better in the morning.'

'Aye, I will,' he said, his voice oddly thick. She went out of his room, closing the door behind her.

Amy was jolted into wakefulness early the next morning by a crash, the sound muffled through the wall. She hurried through to Charlie's room and found him crouched beside the bed, leaning heavily on it, his kerosene tin of water on the floor beside the toppled washstand.

'My leg,' he said, staring wide-eyed at her. 'It's not working.'

'Still?' Amy helped him up so that he could sit on the bed. 'What about your arm?' She saw the effort on his face, but the arm did not move. 'You must have fallen really hard on that side. Are you sure you don't want the doctor?'

'No doctors. They're no bloody use.' He saw the protest on her lips, and gave her a look that would have been fierce had it not been so frightened. His words were slurred, as if he were drunk, but she could understand him easily enough. 'Knew a man once that broke his leg. They got the doctor to him. The quack sliced his leg off.'

'Charlie, he wouldn't do that.' But it was no use pressing the issue. 'All right, then, we'll leave it. Maybe it's going to take a day or two for you to come right. I think you should lie down, and I'll bring your breakfast in to you later.'

'What about my cows?' Charlie demanded. 'I've got to get the milking done.'

'I'll do it. I know how to milk, you know I do.'

'You'll go frightening my cows with those skirts of yours flapping. And you'll take all bloody day over it.'

'Not as long as you'd take with an arm and a leg not working.' He winced at that, but she had to be firm, even if it meant hurting his feelings. 'And I've lived here nearly twenty years, Charlie—since before any of those cows were born. I'm not going to frighten them.'

She set his washstand to rights and mopped up the spilt water, then turned to go back to her room to dress. Charlie sat on the bed, muttering away to himself.

'That cow with the black patch behind her ear has got a sore tit,' he said just as she reached his door. 'Be careful with her.'

'I will,' Amy said over her shoulder.

'The one with the black patch. See that you remember.'

'Yes, Charlie.'

'Don't you go hurting that cow.'

Amy paused in the doorway. 'I think I know as much about sore tits as you do. I certainly should do.' She left him puzzling over that, and hurried off to her room.

It did take her a long time to milk; much longer than it usually took Charlie. Her stomach was grumbling over its emptiness by the time she turned the last of the cows out of the shed and regarded the row of full milk cans with a sense of accomplishment.

The smug feeling did not last long. 'And what am I going to do with you?' she murmured to the row of cans. She sighed, and took up the smallest of them. It bumped awkwardly against her legs as she carried it up to the house. She left the can in the kitchen and went through to Charlie's room.

'I've finished,' she said. 'I know I took ages, but I've done it. I remembered your cow with the sore tit, too. But I don't know how we're going to get the milk to the factory.'

Charlie was sitting back against the pillows with the covers pulled over him. He looked up at her entrance with an oddly embarrassed expression, which changed to a scowl at her words.

'Bugger,' he muttered.

'I don't think I could lift the cans onto the cart, and—'

'You're not going down to that factory on your own,' Charlie interrupted. 'I'll not have men saying my wife's doing my work for me.'

'I didn't think you'd want me to. And it's too late to ask John to take it, he'll be well on his way by now.'

'Waste of good milk,' Charlie grumbled.

'Well, it can't be helped. We'll just have to feed it to the pigs. I'll save some for butter, though, so it won't all be wasted. I was thinking—would it be all right if I go over and see John later? I thought I could ask him to take the milk to the factory for us tomorrow, and maybe after that, too. Just till you're better.'

'Don't you go telling him you did my milking for me,' Charlie said, fear on his face.

'No, I don't need to tell him that. I'll just say you've hurt your arm so you can't lift the cans onto the cart. That's true enough, isn't it? I won't say anything about the milking.'

Charlie's mouth worked as he considered the idea. 'All right, you can ask him—just mind you hold your tongue about the milking. I don't want that family of yours wagging their tongues about me.'

'I'll be careful what I say.'

'And you tell him he'd better not be getting my milk muddled up with his, either,' Charlie added in something more like his usual manner.

'Charlie! John wouldn't go pinching your milk!'

'He'd better not, that's all.'

'I don't think you've any need to worry about that,' Amy said. 'Anyway, I'd better get breakfast on now, I bet you're hungry. I'll just get changed first, I'd forgotten how filthy you can get milking. Can you wait till breakfast's ready, or shall I get you a bit of bread and butter to be going on with?'

'I'll wait.' He met her eyes for a moment and seemed about to say something more, then looked over at the far wall.

'What's wrong, Charlie? Do you want me to do something for you?'

'No.' But she sensed that he was not telling the truth. He reminded her painfully of Malcolm as a little boy, trying to keep some guilty secret and making a poor job of it.

'Are you comfortable?' she pressed. 'Do you want me to straighten the sheet? It looks as though you've got it twisted under you.'

'Leave me be,' he growled, and made a feeble grab at the covers with his one good hand. He tried to scowl at Amy, but he seemed so astonishingly close to tears that his expression looked more like a plea for help.

'Let me.' Amy disengaged the covers from his feeble grip and pulled them down to reveal a large wet patch centred around Charlie's trouser buttons. The fabric of his trousers looked sodden, and the sheet immediately beneath the wet patch showed signs of dampness.

'I'm sorry, Charlie,' she said softly. 'I should have thought to ask if you needed a hand.'

'A man should be able to sort himself out,' Charlie said, his voice gruff with distress. 'Shouldn't need looking after like a baby.'

'Well, never mind all that,' Amy said, suddenly brisk. Overt sympathy would only distress him further; best to get on with making him comfortable. 'Let's get your nightshirt on, it'll be easier for you to manage in that. Come on, sit up first then I'll help you stand up.'

She crouched beside the bed and put her arms around him, helping him into a sitting position, then took hold of his legs and guided his feet on to the floor. 'That's it, swing your legs around. Now, put your arm around my neck and we'll stand you up. Oof! You're heavy.' She was filling the silence with meaningless words, but it suited her purpose of distracting Charlie from the indignity his helplessness forced on him.

She took off his jacket, then unbuttoned his shirt and pulled it off. 'Put your arms up,' she said as she held his nightshirt up, regretting her words a moment later as she remembered that one of his arms could not obey. 'No, don't,' she corrected herself quickly. 'I'd never reach up high enough if you did, not without standing on a chair.' She slipped the nightshirt on him, the numb arm heavy and awkward in her grip, then under the cover the long nightshirt afforded Charlie's dignity she undid his trouser buttons, slippery with urine, and pulled down the damp, smelly trousers with the drawers sticking to them. Taking up the towel from his washstand, she wiped him dry as well as she could without looking, then helped him into the chair beside the bed, slipping a pillow behind him to help him sit upright.

'There, that's better, isn't it?' He gave a quick nod, but was clearly reluctant to meet her eyes. 'Now I really had better get breakfast on—it's just about going to be time for me to start lunch as soon as we've had our breakfast at this rate. I'll change your sheet later—I might put your mattress out for an airing, too, it's ages since I aired it.'

Amy left him slumped in his chair, feeling his eyes on her as she went out of the room. She was tired from the unfamiliar work of milking, and

336

was tempted to sit down in the kitchen for a few minutes before starting on the meal, but it would be difficult enough to catch up on her day's work without indulging in a rest. She would have to start the afternoon milking much earlier than Charlie usually did, since she was so much slower at it.

I'll get faster when I get back into the way of it. Except Charlie'll be better before long, so I won't have to worry. It'll only be for a few days.

It was a nuisance; there was no denying it. So was having to see to the horses every day, and any of the other farm work that could not be ignored. But she was careful to hide any sign of irritation from Charlie; he was upset enough at his forced inactivity without her adding to his distress.

The day after Charlie's fall, Amy scrabbled in the wood pile and found a length of wood suitable to be used as a walking stick. She spent time every day propping him up as he stumbled around the bedroom trying to get the knack of using the stick, until four days after the fall he could manage to get about without her help.

They both took his new-found facility with the stick as an encouraging sign; it must mean he was on the road to recovery. His excursions extended no further than the parlour or the kitchen, but even that small range seemed a great advance after having been confined to the bedroom for days.

'I'll be taking over that milking again soon,' Charlie said. 'See what sort of a job you've been making of it.'

'Of course you will. Just another day or two. Just till that leg gets strong again.'

Amy looked forward to his recovery as eagerly as he did. She knew she was letting things slip in the house; tasks like dusting had become luxuries, and scrubbing could only be done in a cursory fashion.

Not that the floor had the chance to get as dirty as usual. Unlike Charlie, Amy always took her dirty boots off before coming inside. And Charlie did not bring any mud in, now that he spent all day inside dressed in nightshirt and socks. It was easier on both of them to keep him dressed like that; he could manage to use the chamber pot unassisted if he had no buttons to worry about.

The effort of fitting in all her extra work meant Amy struggled on without a real awareness of how time was passing. She was startled when she realised that over a month had gone by since Charlie's fall. His learning to use a stick had given a brief boost to their confidence, but there had been no visible progress since. He was still clearly incapable of any sort of work, and Amy began to wonder just how long it was going to be before he showed real signs of recovery.

She watched Charlie closely to try and gauge his thoughts. He still spoke of taking up his usual work again soon, but there seemed an increasing element of bluster in his assertions. Sometimes she would see his face twisted in frustration as he tried to perform some task that had been child's play to him before, but he kept his thoughts to himself and she did not press him.

They were speaking to each other more than they had in years, Amy realised. After the near silence that had existed between them since Charlie had ordered David out, the two of them would have appeared almost companionable to anyone who did not know them. She had to check that he was comfortable, whether he needed any help to get about, whether he could manage to eat his food using only a fork or spoon. Charlie was constantly asking her what she was doing with the animals, and telling her how she should be doing it. He might grumble over what he saw as shortcomings in how she did the work, but he no longer shouted or snarled.

Despite his forced inactivity, there seemed a constant weariness hanging over Charlie since his strange fall. A weariness and, Amy decided, a fear. There were times when she sensed he was close to tears. She could not bring herself to upset him further by suggesting that she tell her family just how helpless he was and ask for their assistance around the farm. It wouldn't be for much longer, she told herself. She could manage.

Most days Amy was too busy to be lonely, even with only Charlie for company. She saw John or Harry, or occasionally one of their sons, every day when they collected the milk, and when she made her rushed trips into town each week she sometimes bumped into Frank and Lizzie at the store. There was never time to exchange more than a few words with Lizzie, but Amy was careful to appear calm in front of her cousin.

'Yes, Charlie's all right. His leg's still giving him trouble, but he's not too bad in himself,' was the sort of innocuous answer she always gave to questions about Charlie's health. The troublesome leg was a convincing enough explanation for Charlie's continued absence from the factory and the town, and Amy was sure no one suspected how much of the farm work she was doing herself.

'You missed the last soyree,' Lizzie scolded during one brief meeting. 'You haven't been around for ages.'

'I know, I seem to have had a lot on lately,' Amy said. 'I'll try and get down sometime.'

'That cousin of Lily's was quite put out that you weren't there. You'd better come to the next one or I might have a bit of trouble with her. It's Saturday week, so don't forget.'

'Oh, Miss Millish! I was looking forward to seeing her again. I just couldn't, though, Lizzie, I'm sorry.'

'Come around tomorrow, why don't you? Even the kids have been asking where you are.'

'Tomorrow? I don't think I can tomorrow,' Amy said. 'Maybe another day.' She glanced at the clock above the counter, wondering how to get away from Lizzie without appearing rude.

'I'll have to come and see you, then.'

'No, don't do that!' Amy said hurriedly. If Lizzie found Charlie at home in his nightshirt in the middle of the day, their whole pretence that he was still doing his normal work would be uncovered in a moment. 'No, it's, um...' She scrabbled for an excuse that would not be a lie.

'It's not fair if you put yourself out coming to visit me,' she managed at last. 'I mean, there's only me and Charlie to do for, and you've got such a crowd at your place. And you've got Maudie to visit, too, now she's not going out much.'

Lizzie was not to be diverted. 'That's another thing,' she pounced. 'Maudie says why don't you come and see her? She might even take a bit of notice of you, Lord knows she takes precious little account of what I tell her.'

'I'd love to see Maudie. I just can't, though. She's keeping well, is she?'

'Seems to be,' Lizzie said, assuming an offhand manner. 'Of course, my opinion isn't—'

'Maudie's really well, Amy,' Frank cut in, giving Amy a conspiratorial wink. 'Blooming, you women call it, don't you? We're going around there after we finish this lot, why don't you come, too?'

'I... I've got to get home,' Amy said. 'But I will come and see you soon, Lizzie, honestly I will.'

She fretted for days over the idea of Lizzie's catching her out with a surprise visit, until at last she decided that she would have to find time to visit Lizzie herself.

'Lizzie's having a soyree tomorrow,' she told Charlie as she held a match to his pipe. They had become quite dexterous at getting the pipe going as a joint effort, since Charlie found it impossible to manage the task with one hand. 'May I go?'

Charlie puffed several times until he was satisfied the pipe was going properly. 'All right. See you're back in time to get dinner on, mind.'

Getting back in time for milking was the main issue, but Amy did not point that out.

The next afternoon she installed Charlie in the parlour with a rug over his knees and a tray with tea things beside him.

'Don't leave that tea too long or it'll get cold,' she said. 'Here's your paper, if you feel like reading. I've put extra milk in the jug, and here's a glass, in case you want a drink of milk later. Are you comfortable? Do you want anything else?'

'I'm all right,' Charlie muttered. 'Stop your fussing.'

'I'll be as quick as I can down there, but it'll take me a bit longer than going into town does. I mean, I've got to stay long enough to be polite. Are you sure you'll be all right by yourself?'

'Of course I will. I don't need a bloody nursemaid! You go off with your gabbling women.'

Amy's doubts over whether or not it was a good idea to go were banished by the delighted greeting she got from Sarah Millish when she entered the parlour.

'Oh, Mrs Stewart, you've come!' Miss Millish exclaimed. 'I was so hoping you would!' She rose from her chair and clasped Amy's hand. 'You must sit beside me—see, I've saved you a chair—I was trying to will you to come, you see. And it worked!'

Amy returned her smile, and willingly let herself be led to the chair next to Miss Millish's.

'I've brought some books I thought you might like,' Miss Millish said, reaching into a capacious bag by her chair. 'Here's Carlyle's *Past and Present*. It's dreadfully heavy going, but there's the odd gem buried among the obscurity. And this John Stuart Mill, you said you hadn't read this one, I think? Then I thought you might like a change from all that philosophy, so I brought some poetry, too. I'm sure you love poetry, don't you?'

'Oh, yes!' Amy said, taking the books eagerly.

'I *knew* you would. Mother never quite approved of Byron, so I used to keep this one hidden away, but there's no real harm in him. Such wonderful images! You must tell me what you think of it.'

'Honestly, Amy, I used to think you were bad enough about books, but the two of you together!' Lizzie said, smiling indulgently. 'Of course, it's no wonder you two get on—you've got something in common, what with Amy being a teacher too.'

'Lizzie!' Amy protested.

'Did you teach, Mrs Stewart?' Miss Millish asked in surprise.

'For goodness sake, Lizzie, every time a new teacher comes you tell her that,' Amy said. 'No, Miss Millish, I wasn't ever a proper teacher. I wanted to be one, and I helped at the school for a while, but it didn't work out. They needed me at home.'

'I see,' Miss Millish said, studying Amy thoughtfully. 'That must have been very disappointing.'

'Oh, I don't know,' Amy said, trying to make her voice light. 'It was a long time ago.' She met Miss Millish's eyes and saw the real sympathy there, and felt a sudden urge to be truly honest. 'Yes, it was. It was really disappointing.'

Amy shrugged. 'But it couldn't be helped. Thank you for bringing out these lovely books,' she said, eager to change the subject. 'I'm so looking forward to reading them. It's very kind of you, Miss Millish.'

'It's my pleasure,' Miss Millish said, squeezing her hand briefly. 'And you must call me Sarah! We won't sound like friends if you keep being so formal with me.'

'I'd like that. Thank you, Sarah.' Amy saw the younger woman's eyes on her in a searching gaze, and was tempted to ask Sarah to call her by her first name, too. But it did not seem quite correct to suggest it to a single woman so much younger than her.

'Aunt Susannah's coming today,' Lizzie announced while Beth and Maisie served tea and cakes. 'She'll be late, of course. She's always late.'

'I mightn't even see her, then,' Amy said without any trace of disappointment. 'I can't stay all that long.'

'And who is Aunt Susannah?' Sarah Millish asked, looking questioningly at Lily.

'She's Uncle Jack's wife, Sarah,' Lily said. 'His second marriage, do you remember? I explained it to you when you first came out to see us.'

'Didn't you take notes, Sarah?' Bill asked. 'I thought you were writing it all down for your book.'

'You'd best be careful, or you'll find yourself cast as the villain,' Sarah said, the faint suggestion of a twinkle in her eyes belying her stern expression. Lily smiled at her husband, and Amy thought she detected 'Serves you right' being shaped on Lily's lips.

'You've brothers through this younger Mrs Leith, haven't you?' Sarah asked Amy.

'That's right. Tom and George. Tommy might come out with Susannah, he usually takes her about.'

'And how old are they?' Sarah sent a challenging glance in Bill's direction before turning her attention back to Amy; he assumed an expression of wounded innocence.

'Let's see, Tom's twenty-two now and George is twenty-one. They had their birthdays in August,' Amy said.

'And for goodness sake, don't mention that in front of Aunt Susannah,' Lizzie put in. 'I don't want her starting on all that business about the money again. Frank thought it was quite a good idea, George putting the money in a boat.'

'Pa left Tom and George some money,' Amy explained, seeing Sarah's questioning expression. 'George got his share this year, when he turned twenty-one, and he bought part share of a boat. Susannah's never been very keen on him working on boats.'

'Transport seems a sensible investment to me,' Sarah remarked. 'It's certainly a necessity of people's lives. Father preferred property, but he had some investments in shipping, too.'

'I think Susannah's coming round over it,' Amy said. 'Tom keeps telling her how George'll end up as a real businessman now he's got into buying a boat instead of just working for someone else. She doesn't like to back down, though.'

'I almost feel I know Mrs Leith already,' Sarah said with a slight smile.

Susannah did arrive rather late, giving Amy ample opportunity to talk with Sarah. Amy enjoyed her outing so much that she was only vaguely aware of time passing. She glanced at the mantel clock and was just about to announce that she had better be leaving, when Susannah and Thomas arrived.

Trust her to come just now. I'll have to stay a couple more minutes, or it'll look rude.

It was not as if she had the chance to talk to Sarah again once Susannah had arrived. A guest who was reasonably fresh from Auckland was too much for Susannah to resist.

'Fashions, you must tell me about fashions,' Susannah said soon after their introduction. 'I follow the journals, of course, but one can never be quite sure they're completely up to date. Are bodices still full? What about sleeves?'

'Full and narrow, respectively,' Sarah told her. 'Colours? Oh, blue is very fashionable, I believe. I can't say I've taken much notice lately. A dark skirt and a white blouse suits me well enough in the classroom.'

'But you surely attend fashionable events in the city?' Susannah pressed. 'I understood you were from quite a… well, prominent family in Auckland.'

Sarah gave her a long gaze, clearly quite aware that the word Susannah had been tempted to use was 'wealthy'. 'Yes, I do my social duty when I'm at home. I can't say it's all duty, either,' she added, her stern expression relaxing. 'You said you're from Auckland yourself, did you not, Mrs Leith?'

'I lived there all my life until my marriage. Of course I did consider moving back after my husband died, but it wouldn't have been fair to Thomas. He has such a promising career in the bank.'

'Mother,' Thomas said in a long-suffering tone. 'I've told you and told you, you don't need to stay in Ruatane on my account.'

'As if I could leave you on your own! Thomas has been a great comfort to me, Miss Millish.'

'I'm sure he has.' Sarah turned an openly searching gaze on Thomas, then glanced from him to Amy and back again. 'You two aren't terribly alike, are you? Family likenesses are a strange thing.'

'Tommy takes after Pa,' Amy said, slipping an arm through Thomas's. 'People always say I'm like Mama.'

'Thomas gets his height from my family, of course,' Susannah put in. 'You may have heard of my father, Miss Millish. My maiden name was Taylor, my father was Thomas Taylor of Parnell. My Thomas is named after him.'

'Taylor? Oh, yes, I do know of your family, Mrs Leith,' Sarah said thoughtfully. 'Father did a little business with your father, I believe. And I think I've met your brother.'

Amy saw Susannah stiffen, and her stepmother stared around the room with something of a hunted air. But Susannah recovered her composure within seconds. 'You may have met my sister as well. She's Mrs Henry Kendall, her husband is a partner in one of the law firms in the city.'

With the conversation running on less perilous lines, Amy felt able to look about her again. Sarah's innocent indiscretion seemed soon forgotten by everyone except Amy. Susannah was clearly delighted at the chance to converse with a fellow Aucklander; Amy was surprised at how willingly Sarah seemed to give her attention in return. Sarah said little, but she listened to Susannah and watched her with every sign of interest.

It was foolish to feel hurt at being apparently passed over in favour of Susannah, but Amy could not quite suppress a pang. *I suppose I'm not very interesting. I can't talk about fashions and rich people, or balls and parties and things.*

As soon as she felt politely able to leave, Amy rose and made her excuses.

'Oh, you're not going already, Mrs Stewart?' Sarah looked genuinely disappointed, and Amy's sense of hurt evaporated in a moment. 'I thought we'd be able to talk some more.'

'I've got to, I'm sorry. It was lovely to see you. And thank you for the books—I'll bring them back as soon as I can.'

'There's no hurry at all,' Sarah said. 'Take as long as you want.'

She followed Amy out to the front door and saw her to the verandah steps. 'I hope I can see you again soon. I'm going home to Auckland in two weeks, and I won't be back till well into the New Year, so do come to Mrs Kelly's before I go.'

'It's hard for me to get away, but I'll see if I can.'

'And you'd rather I didn't…' Sarah began; Amy knew she was about to offer to come to Charlie's house. 'No, never mind, I'll just look forward to meeting you here,' Sarah said. 'You will come again soon, won't you?'

'I'll try,' Amy said her. 'I really will.' She was tempted to hug Sarah, but resisted the urge. It was hardly appropriate with a woman she had known for such a short time.

Amy was almost running by the time she got close to the cottage, knowing that she had stayed away longer than she should have. She would be milking well into the evening. It was fortunate that sunset came so late now that it was December. She hurried into the kitchen, slightly out of breath, and felt her calm mood evaporate in a moment.

The teapot lay on the floor with its lid beside it, close to the overturned sugar bowl. Wet sugar and tea leaves were mingled indiscriminately around the bowl, along with several broken biscuits. The kettle was perched precariously near the edge of the range, the damp patch on the floor below it showing where hot water had dripped.

Charlie sat slumped against the wall, his arm clutched close to his side. 'You took your bloody time,' he growled, his face twisted with pain as he spoke.

Amy put Sarah's books on the table and dropped to her knees beside him. 'What happened? Have you hurt your arm?' She took it in her hands as gently as she could, and raised the sleeve of his nightshirt to reveal an angry red scald.

'Kettle. Tipped the kettle over,' Charlie said, struggling to get the words out. 'Water went down my arm.'

Amy helped him onto a chair before fetching a strip of old sheet for a bandage. She spread a little butter on the cloth and wrapped it around Charlie's arm, tying it securely in place.

'It doesn't look too bad, but I bet it's sore. Why were you out here, though? Why didn't you stay in the parlour?'

'Wanted a cup of tea.'

'But I made you one before I left. You had a nice fresh pot there.'

'I wanted another one.' He gave her a defiant glare that was spoiled by the trembling of his mouth. 'And I wanted some different biscuits. You were gone a hell of a time.'

'I'm sorry, Charlie. You're right, I shouldn't have stayed so long. Was the kettle too heavy for you?'

Charlie looked confused. 'I don't know. I was filling the pot, and... I don't know. My leg gave way, or some such. I don't remember. It went black in my head for a spell.'

'I see.' Amy regarded him thoughtfully. 'I think you must have had another one of those falls. Perhaps you'd better go to bed, your head might start hurting.'

'Hurts now,' Charlie said, raising his hand tentatively towards his forehead. He winced as the pain of the burn struck him.

'Best if you lie down, then. This might help you get to sleep.'

She poured him a small measure of his precious store of whisky. They both knew without discussing it that there would be no more when this was gone; Amy could not possibly go into a hotel and buy liquor. She saved it for the times when Charlie seemed particularly miserable, then doled it out carefully. She held the glass to his lips as he sipped. When he had finished the drink she helped him to his bedroom and into bed.

'Try and go to sleep,' she said. 'If your arm hurts too much I'll give you some laudanum later.'

'Don't need laudanum.' He lay in the bed and stared at her. Amy was struck by how he seemed to have shrunk in on himself over the past few weeks. 'Don't you go staying out like that again.'

Amy sighed. 'I won't, Charlie. I won't go to any soyrees again. Not till you're better, anyway,' she added, but she knew it was no more than an empty formula. He was not going to get better.

Frank had hoped that Maudie's pregnancy would bring her and her mother closer together, but it seemed to have the opposite effect. If there had been a tension between them before, now they positively struck sparks off each other.

'Just let her sort herself out, Lizzie,' he said after a particularly tense visit. 'She's excited about the whole business, she'll settle down when she gets used to it.'

Lizzie sniffed. 'Well, I don't see why she can't take a bit of advice. It's not as if I'm trying to interfere, or anything. I'm only thinking of her. I've had seven children!'

'Yes, I know you have.'

'So I should know something about it, shouldn't I? But do you think she'll listen to me? Ha!'

It was no use trying to intercede between those two; he might find himself caught in the crossfire if he did. Frank could only hope they all survived the next few months relatively unscathed, and then pray that the pleasure of having a new baby in the family would allow all differences to be forgotten.

In the meantime, he found the tension rather wearing. Lizzie and Maudie seemed to watch each other like hawks, ready to pounce on any perceived failing.

'What's this?' Lizzie said over lunch at Maudie's one day, poking suspiciously at a piece of meat on her plate. 'It's got a funny colour about it. And you've put raisins in with the meat!'

'That's a curry,' Maudie said proudly. 'I found a recipe in the *Weekly News*.'

Lizzie took a small mouthful. 'Tastes a bit funny. I think that meat might be off. You want to tell that butcher his meat's off.'

'It is not off!' Maudie said. 'It's just spicy, that's all. They have food like that in India, don't they, Richard?'

'That's right, darling.'

'They probably don't know any better over there. Why'd you want to make it?' Lizzie asked.

'Richard likes that sort of food. Richard asked me to make one, didn't you, Richard?'

'Well, I did say it might be a nice change, if you felt like trying it,' Richard admitted, wincing at Lizzie's reproving expression. 'We once had a cook who'd been in India, she used to make the occasional curry. I didn't really think you'd try it out on your parents, though, dear.'

'Oh, your father can't eat this sort of thing,' Lizzie pronounced. 'A man couldn't do proper work on funny food like this. Don't eat it if you don't like it, Frank. I'll get you something nice when we get home.'

'You do like it, don't you, Pa?' Maudie turned a wistful face on him. 'I thought you'd like it.'

Maudie looked prettier than ever now that she was carrying a baby, Frank thought. She had a higher colour than usual, but that just made her eyes look brighter. The pregnancy was no more than a small bulge, barely visible through her loose dress, but he noticed Maudie's hand frequently rested on it in a proprietorial gesture. 'Um… it's a change, all right,' Frank said carefully. 'It's quite nice, really.'

'There, see?' Maudie cast a triumphant look at her mother. 'Pa does like it. You should make one sometime, instead of cooking the same old things all the time.'

Lizzie drew herself up to her full height. 'I *think*,' she said haughtily, 'that I know how to cook decent meals. I *think* I've fed a husband and seven children properly for twenty years. You'd better tell me if I'm not cooking you decent meals, Frank.'

'Lizzie, you're a wonderful cook,' Frank said, unsure whether the sinking feeling in his stomach was from the unfamiliar food or the sense of impending conflict. 'You know I love your cooking. That's how you hooked me in the first place, you know.' That brought a smug smile to Lizzie's face, though Maudie's lips tightened a little.

Frank took the coward's way out when the meal was over, readily taking up Richard's suggestion that the two of them have a stroll in the garden while the women cleared away the lunch things. Maudie had established a pretty border of flowers in front of the verandah, though the heavier work of the garden was left to a boy who came around once a week.

'I suppose we'll have to interfere if blood flows,' Richard remarked, casting a wary look towards the house. 'It's probably best to leave them to it otherwise.'

'I think that's for the best,' said Frank. 'We had a couple of cats like that once, snarling at each other all the time. Beth used to be in tears over them. They sorted it out by themselves in the end—they had a really good set to, then they curled up together and went to sleep.'

'I just hope it doesn't come to blood first.'

'I shouldn't think so,' Frank said. 'Maudie looks well, doesn't she?'

'Oh, she's in the peak of health. Of course, she was such a healthy girl anyway, she's taking pregnancy in her stride. She certainly doesn't need a doctor hovering over her and checking on her progress all the time—she puts up with it very graciously, though,' Richard added with a fond smile. 'A doctor does have some extra privileges when he's also the father.'

'The first one's really special,' Frank said, calling up pleasant memories of the time when they had first suspected that Lizzie might be with child. 'All kids are special, of course, but the first time… well, you'll see for yourself.'

'I'm looking forward to it.' Richard glanced in the direction of the parlour, where they could now hear Lizzie and Maudie setting out tea things. 'I suppose we should go inside,' he said reluctantly.

'Wait until they call us. No sense joining in till we have to.'

'Good idea. Shall we sit out here, then? I've had enough walking for now.'

They sat on the verandah, talking in low voices while vaguely aware of the two women moving about in the parlour. Maudie opened the parlour window, and the sound of the women's voices became clearer.

'You're having a rest of an afternoon like I told you to, I hope,' they heard Lizzie say.

'Richard says it's a good idea for me to rest, so I have a lie-down every afternoon,' Maudie answered.

'Does he just? Well, I hope you're getting plenty of exercise. Rest is important, but you've got to get enough exercise, too.'

'I know that,' Maudie said. 'Anyway, Richard takes me for a walk nearly every evening. We go for a walk along the riverbank where there's not too many people around.'

'Of course I never had to worry about whether I was getting enough exercise,' said Lizzie. 'I had that much work to do when I was your age, looking after your father and the house and all, I used to be worn out at the end of the day. I even used to help your father with the milking before I was carrying you. Not that I would have wanted it any other way. I thought it was my duty to look after my husband.'

'I look after Richard,' Maudie said sharply. 'Are you saying I don't?'

'It seems to me that you do what suits you. You don't scrub, do you?'

'Neither do you,' Maudie countered. 'Maisie and Beth do all the scrubbing. Anyway, I scrubbed enough floors for you to do me one lifetime. I think it's nice that Richard doesn't want me wearing myself out.'

'My name is coming up a little more than I'd choose,' Richard murmured to Frank. 'I do wish Maudie would leave me out of these discussions.'

'Humph!' Lizzie snorted. 'Richard spoils you. Anyway, you just see that you get enough exercise. It makes the whole business a lot easier when the time comes. And another thing, every day you should—'

'Oh, don't go on, Ma,' Maudie interrupted. 'I don't want to hear all that stuff. Richard's told me all about what I should and shouldn't be doing, I don't need you nagging at me.'

'I like that! I try to help you a bit, just like any mother would, and I'm accused of nagging! I'm only thinking of you, you know. I only want to be sure you have as easy a time of it as you can. I've been through it all myself, so I know what you need to be told.'

'I don't need to be told anything! Richard's explained it all to me.'

'Oh dear,' Richard said quietly.

'Richard? What does Richard know about having a baby? Correct me if I'm wrong, but I don't *think* Richard's a woman. I don't *think* he's ever had a baby.'

'There's no need to talk silly. Richard's delivered dozens and dozens of babies, he knows all about it.'

'Your father's delivered *hundreds* of calves. It doesn't make him a cow, does it?'

'It makes him an expert, though,' Maudie answered smartly. 'Cows don't deliver one another's calves, do they?'

'My wife has a quick mind, hasn't she?' Richard murmured to Frank.

'Afraid so. She's got a quick tongue, too,' Frank agreed.

'It's not the same,' Lizzie said. 'I'm sure Richard knows his work well enough, but it's not the same as bearing a child. There's things only a woman can tell you.'

'Richard says women forget what it was like afterwards. And it's so long since you finished having babies, you must have just about forgotten everything.'

'It's not as long as all that,' Lizzie said indignantly.

'Yes, it is! It's years and years. Kate'll be starting school in a year. I bet you hardly remember anything about it.'

'Seven children, I've had! I think I know something about the subject.'

'But you've finished having them. You've forgotten.'

'Forgotten, indeed! At least I knew something to forget in the first place! The cheek of it, a green girl like you speaking as if you know the least thing about bearing a child.'

'But I do,' Maudie insisted. 'Don't you ever listen to anyone? Richard's told me all about it. He even showed me in a book.'

'A book!' Lizzie said, disbelief in her voice. 'What's a book got to do with it?'

'Oh, it's a lovely book—it's got pictures of babies inside their mothers and how they get out and all sort of things. Richard explains things really well. He told me I probably know more about it than you do now.'

Richard looked pained. 'I didn't say it quite like that,' he murmured. 'And I certainly didn't expect to have it repeated against me.'

'Oh, he did, did he? You can tell Richard he can keep his opinions to himself, thank you very much.'

'Don't worry,' Frank whispered, seeing the younger man wince at Lizzie's fierce tone. 'Lizzie's got a soft spot for you, she won't hold it against you for long.'

'I sincerely hope not,' Richard whispered back.

Maudie obviously knew she had the advantage. She pressed it home ruthlessly. 'It's such a good book, Ma.' The challenge in her voice was clear from where the men sat. 'Richard would probably lend it to you if you wanted to find out about babies. Shall I ask him if you can read it?'

The silence that fell in the parlour was like the pause between lightning and thunder. Richard closed his eyes for a moment as though

349

in pain, then turned to Frank. 'Maudie has gone too far,' he pronounced, and Frank could only agree.

They waited for the explosion, but Lizzie said nothing to Maudie. Instead she appeared on the verandah a few moments later, wearing her coat and with Frank's jacket over her arm.

'Put your jacket on, Frank,' she said, thrusting it at him. 'We're going home.'

'Aren't you staying for a cup of tea?' Maudie's voice came through the window. 'I've made a chocolate cake.'

Lizzie did not answer her daughter. She turned to Richard and gave him a long, cold stare. 'There are some things, Richard, that can't be learned from books.'

'Oh, I'm very aware of that, Lizzie,' Richard said. 'Maudie,' he called towards the window. 'Come out here, please.'

There was a moment's silence. 'No,' Maudie said, her voice clear though quiet.

'Maudie,' Richard called again in a sterner tone, but got no answer. 'I'm sorry, she's a little overwrought today,' he said. 'I think perhaps she should lie down for a while.'

'I know what that girl needs,' Lizzie said grimly. 'And it's *not* a lie-down.'

Lizzie was still bristling with indignation as Frank drove her home, thinking somewhat regretfully about the chocolate cake as the buggy bounced along.

'The cheek of it,' Lizzie grumbled. 'A slip of a girl like her, talking to me like that. Show me books, will she?'

'Take no notice, Lizzie,' Frank urged. 'She'll come round. Richard'll have a talk to her.'

'And talking to me as if I was an old woman! Forgotten what it's like to have a baby, indeed! Too old to have one, she meant. I'm not even forty yet!'

'Just a young thing, eh?' Frank put the reins in one hand and slipped his free arm around her. 'Still my little bride.'

Lizzie held herself rigid for a moment, then softened against him and leaned on his shoulder. 'I'm not old,' she said, the plea clear in her voice.

'Of course you're not. You've hardly changed since the day we got married.' Lizzie's need for reassurance seemed far more important than a strict regard for the truth. 'Maudie's just showing off, that's all. She's full of herself because she's having this baby. She'll grow out of it.'

'The little madam,' Lizzie muttered. 'Too old, am I? Thinks she knows it all, that one.'

Lizzie said no more about Maudie during the rest of the day, but Frank saw a pensive expression on her face from time to time. She was still rather quiet when they went to bed.

Frank wondered what chance there was that Richard could talk Maudie into apologising to her mother. Precious little, he admitted to himself.

He put out the lamp and reached through the darkness to draw Lizzie close, eager to cuddle away any lingering distress. Lizzie moved towards him, pressing her body against his.

Lizzie was usually obliging when the calendar was on their side, but she was not normally an initiator. Frank was startled to find his nightshirt being tugged upwards and Lizzie's naked legs (her nightdress seemed to have migrated up towards her waist) busily entwining themselves around his. Her mouth sought his and pressed down hard.

It was even more pleasant than it was startling. Frank forgot that a few moments before he had felt sleepy; his blood was up and he responded with a vigour that gratified him as much as it surprised him. His only regret was that it was over so quickly.

He rolled onto his back and pulled Lizzie over to lay her head on his chest. He smiled in the darkness, enjoying the warm languor that was creeping through his limbs.

A vague sense of unease seeped into his awareness, bringing an unwelcome return to cold reality. 'Lizzie?' he said quietly.

'Mmm?'

'Was tonight a good sort of time? Did you look at your calendar?'

'It was a good time, all right.' He did not have to see her face to know there was a smug expression on it.

'I thought you said the other night that it wouldn't be safe till next week. Didn't you—'

'Never mind about that, Frank.'

'But didn't you say we shouldn't?'

'Oh, I don't know,' Lizzie murmured. 'I don't remember,' she added unconvincingly. 'You don't want to worry about all those dates. I don't think I'm as regular as I was, anyway—not like I used to be when I was younger. And what would it matter if I did get with child? I'm not too old.'

Frank mulled over her remarks. 'Let me get that straight, Lizzie. You don't remember if it's the right time or not—funny, really, you've always been good about the dates—you're not regular any more because you're getting on a bit, and you're not too old to have a baby. Is that about the size of it?'

'That's right,' Lizzie said, seemingly quite unaware of any contradiction.

'All right, then. Just as long as I've got it straight.' He felt his way towards her cheek, brushing away a stray lock of hair before planting a kiss on the smooth flesh. 'I suppose one more baby wouldn't hurt,' he whispered in her ear.

'Of course it wouldn't.'

'Just the one, though. Maudie'll have more babies after this one, you know. You can't expect to keep up with her.'

'It's nothing to do with Maudie,' Lizzie said. 'I was thinking I might like another baby, anyway.'

'First I've heard of it.'

He felt Lizzie's hand slipping down his body to where his nightshirt was still indecently high. 'Waste of time, Lizzie.' He retrieved the errant hand, held it to his lips and kissed it before disentangling himself from her to roll onto his side. 'Looks like you haven't changed since you were my little bride, but I'm not as young as I used to be.' He reached out and patted her bottom idly before settling himself for sleep. 'Wait till tomorrow, love,' he murmured.

21

December 1904 – February 1905

If she could have given up sleeping altogether, Amy thought there might just have been enough hours in the day to make a proper job of all her responsibilities.

Her world had become a small, enclosed space, compassed within the boundaries of the farm. She could not leave Charlie by himself for any other reason than the essential weekly trip into town for their stores. The anxious, hurried journey was an extra burden rather than bringing any sort of respite.

She had to impose a strict schedule on herself to have any chance at all of getting through the work each day. Even with the long hours of daylight that summer had brought, she was up before dawn every morning and did not sink exhausted into bed until well after dark.

The twice-daily milking was the most onerous task of all, punctuating her day with the hours it took to get the cows in, milk them, put them back out into the paddock and carry the cans up to the house. It was no wonder Charlie had looked so weary since he had sent David away, with twenty cows to milk by himself.

It had been hard enough for Charlie; with the extra milk production brought on by December's lush grass, Amy decided that for her it was simply impossible. She could not milk in the pitch dark, and she had to have the morning milking finished in time for John to collect the cans on his way to the factory. There were too many days when she had to carry them up to the house leaving a few cows unmilked, then go back down to the cow shed after John had taken the cans and finish the milking. The milk from those last few cows had to be used up somehow, and milking for the benefit of the pigs was not a useful way for her to spend the scanty time she had.

She did not tell Charlie she had dried off some of the cows. He would have taken the news badly, but it was hard to know whether he would have reacted by shouting himself into a rage or by sinking more deeply into the dull, silent misery that sometimes enveloped him.

He had wild swings of mood now, sometimes ranting against his weakness and any imagined failings in the way Amy was doing the work, and other days sitting hunched in his chair, or in bed if he refused to get up, saying nothing at all as he stared dully at the wall with his red-rimmed eyes. On such days it was difficult even to coax him into eating.

Amy knew the farm's income must be lower than it should since she had been forced to dry off some of the cows, so when John brought her the factory cheque early in the new year she was careful not to let Charlie see it. She took the cheque into town without even mentioning it to him, and handed it over at the store to settle their account.

The storekeeper opened his account book, studied the cheque again, then looked over the counter at Amy with an awkward expression.

'Ah, Mrs Stewart, it doesn't quite cover the account. It's not much short,' he added quickly. 'Two pounds, three shillings and fourpence, that's all. No need to worry about it, leave it till you get your potato money in.'

So her milking was not even bringing in enough money to pay for what they had to buy at the store. And as for harvesting the potato crop... Amy suddenly felt so weary that she leaned against the counter for support. But only for a moment.

'I'll sort it out, Mr Craig,' she told the storekeeper. 'I'll be back in a minute.'

Amy had the briefest of chats with Thomas at the bank, and was soon back at the store with a few notes clutched in her hand. She passed the money across the counter and watched Mr Craig write up the transaction.

'That's all settled, then,' he told her with a smile. Amy gave him a brief nod and hurried out the door to the gig. It was a good thing she had let the money from her father's legacy build up a little in her bank account. She wondered how long it would last now that it was going to have to bolster up the slender income of the farm.

The haymaking was a wearying time for Amy that January. She knew it would bring the greatest risk yet of her family's guessing just how frail Charlie was; haymaking was always a combined effort, but it was quite impossible for Charlie to be part of it at all.

The story she gave out, that Charlie's arm was giving too much trouble for him to be able to toss hay, sounded flimsy in her own ears. She waited anxiously for someone to make the connection that Charlie could surely not be doing much of the farm work if his arm was too painful for him to make hay. But the men were too busy getting on with the work (and, Amy suspected, too relieved at not having to put up with Charlie's unwelcome presence) for them to question her more deeply.

She did what she could to make up for the fact that Charlie was not contributing to the work, cooking great batches of cakes and pies and taking them over to the workers when they were on her brothers' farm as well as during the days they spent on Charlie's. It did a little to ease her own feelings of guilt that other people were having to work harder to make up for Charlie's lack, but it did nothing to help Charlie.

He was sunk in misery for the whole period of the haymaking. 'Useless. Bloody useless,' he muttered to himself, and if Amy tried to remonstrate with him he did not answer. She often heard him talking under his breath when he did not think she was in the room; she suspected that when she was out of the house he talked to himself even more.

She had to be sure he was comfortable and had everything he needed before she left him alone to take food down to the workers. Since his second attack, he had been too frightened to move from wherever Amy left him while she was out of the house. He would still hobble about on his stick if he knew she was there to pick him up if he fell, but when he was alone he stayed where he had been put.

Charlie would rouse himself to show a wavering interest in the work when Amy came back from the hay paddocks. He would ask her how the haymaking was going, then turn and gaze towards the window, and she knew he was not listening to her answer. He wanted to be outside with the other men; outside and strong again. She felt trapped enough herself; how much worse must it be for Charlie, who had been confined to three rooms of the house for months?

It was mainly a desire to rouse him from his melancholy that put the idea into her head, though she could not deny that she was becoming desperate for a proper outing and the chance to talk to someone other than Charlie. Being trapped on the farm had become even harder since she had heard that Sarah Millish was back from Auckland and had been asking after her.

Amy mulled over the idea for a few days, then decided it was worth a try.

'Lizzie's having a soyree tomorrow,' she told Charlie as she watched him slurping at a cup of lukewarm tea. Sometimes she held a saucer under his cup for him while he drank; today he was in an irritable mood and had refused the attention, instead dripping tea on his nightshirt.

His hand shook as he dropped the cup onto its saucer. 'You told me you wouldn't go to those things any more,' he said, his eyes full of fear. 'You're not going!' He raised his voice, but his attempt at anger was a shadow of its old self. 'You're stopping home!'

'I don't want to go by myself—I thought you might like to come with me.'

'Go to some fool tea party?' Charlie said in astonishment. 'Sit around with a lot of cackling women? Why would I want to do that?'

'It's not only women there, you know. Frank'll be there, and Bill. Richard, too—no, he won't, because of Maudie. Tommy might be, though. And Joey's just about grown up now, he's sort of like another man.'

'Don't want to go to Kelly's place,' Charlie muttered. 'Him and his cows and his sons. Don't want to listen to him bragging.'

'But wouldn't you like a change?' Amy coaxed. 'Wouldn't you like to talk to some men for a bit? You must be sick of being stuck here with me all the time.'

'Aye, I'm that, all right. Listening to your nonsense. It's enough to send a man touched in the head.'

He gazed towards the window with the familiar longing expression. 'We'll maybe go,' he allowed. 'We'll see tomorrow.'

Amy knew it had been a mistake to come within minutes of their arrival. She had become so used to Charlie's changed appearance that she had not considered how struck other people might be by it.

The strains of piano music from the direction of the parlour window told her that Lily was taking the opportunity of playing, even if the hot weather had driven most of her audience outside. Amy brought the gig to a halt and helped Charlie down, just as Mickey and Danny rushed over to take the horse out of its harness. She passed Charlie's stick to him and took his arm to lead him over to the others.

They rounded a corner of the house and came within easy sight of the verandah. Amy saw everyone staring at Charlie as he walked slowly beside her, leaning heavily on her arm for support.

Amy had done her best to make Charlie presentable for the visit. She had washed him as well as she could manage, using a damp towel and reaching around awkwardly under his nightshirt, then helped him dress in a set of clean clothes. She had washed his face, combed his hair and even his beard until he had slapped her hand away and told her to stop fiddling with him. He looked tidy enough, but she could do nothing about the dragging leg or the arm that hung limp and useless by his side, nor about the grey tinge to his skin and the extra lines deeply etched in his face.

But there was no chance of turning back now; she would have to make the best of it. Amy smiled as brightly as she could at everyone she saw, and found a chair for Charlie in the corner of the verandah where the men were gathered.

She tried to cover her awkwardness with bustle, fetching Charlie a cup of tea and a plate of cakes and making sure they were well within his reach.

'Now, I'll get out of your way and leave you men to talk,' she said. She moved away to the other end of the verandah, though not without an anxious glance back towards Charlie.

Frank cleared his throat noisily. 'It's good to see you out and about again, Charlie,' he said. 'I'm glad you've come.' Amy was grateful to Frank for the effort he was making. He was not glad to see Charlie at all, she knew; no one ever was.

Lizzie had commandeered almost all the chairs for the shadier end of the verandah, where the women were gathered close enough to the parlour window to get the benefit of Lily's playing. Most of the men were leaning against the verandah rail, or squatting facing the rail with the wall of the house for support. Frank sat on the top step of the verandah with Kate on his lap. Amy looked over at the men and saw the conversation flowing back and forth between them, Charlie's silence barely noticeable amidst the tide of words.

She felt her sleeve being tugged, and Lizzie drew her aside into a quiet corner.

'What's wrong with Charlie?' Lizzie demanded. 'He looks awful.'

'He's not the best today,' Amy hedged, hoping that Lizzie would not probe too deeply. 'He's feeling a bit down.'

'But he can't even walk by himself! And that arm looks pretty useless. How's he managing to get his work done?'

'He's having a bad day.' Charlie's grim expression told Amy that he, too, was aware of the speculation his appearance had aroused. 'Some days he's much better than this.'

'Are you managing, then?' Lizzie asked. 'You look pretty tired—you haven't been looking too good at all lately.'

'Yes, everything's all right.' Amy tried to project confidence into her voice. 'I get worried about Charlie when he's down like this, and I start feeling down, too. Don't worry, Lizzie, I can manage.'

'Well, you're to tell me if you need any help.'

'I don't need any help.' Amy slipped an arm through Lizzie's and kissed her. 'Thank you, but you mustn't worry.'

She wished Lizzie looked more convinced. Amy went on quickly, anxious to divert her cousin's interest. 'I thought you looked pretty pleased with yourself when we arrived, Lizzie. What have you been up to?'

Lizzie's eyes sparkled. She looked around to check that they were not being overheard, then brought her mouth close to Amy's ear.

'I'm not sure yet, I haven't told anyone else—except Frank, of course—but I think I might have a baby on the way.'

Amy's first reaction was a rush of sympathy, picturing for a moment just how horrified she would be to find herself pregnant, impossible though it was. But one look at Lizzie's face told Amy how delighted her cousin was.

'That's lovely news, Lizzie. I thought you might have had enough of having babies, but if it's what you want, then I'm really pleased for you.'

'Don't tell anyone, though. I don't want people hearing till I'm sure.'

'I won't,' Amy assured her. *I never see anyone I could tell, anyway.*

She looked around the lawn, shading her eyes against the light. 'Isn't Sarah here?' she asked, unable to keep the disappointment out of her voice.

'Humph,' Lizzie snorted. 'I might have known it's her you came to see. Oh, don't go looking all guilty about it, you know I like to see you enjoying yourself with her. She's inside with Lily, I bet she doesn't even know you're here. Beth, run and tell Miss Millish Aunt Amy's here.'

A moment later Sarah Millish appeared in the doorway and rushed to Amy.

'I'm so glad you've come,' she said, taking Amy's hand in both her own. 'I've been looking forward to seeing you ever since I got back from Auckland.'

'You'll tell me everything you did up there, won't you?' Amy asked. 'All the plays and things you went to, and outings and everything?'

'Everything,' Sarah promised, laughing. 'Even all the meetings I had with the people who look after my affairs for me, if you like—I warn you, you'll find them very boring.'

'Well, you two have got a bit to catch up on,' Lizzie said. 'I'll leave you to it.'

Sarah drew Amy over to two chairs close together, and they were soon talking animatedly. But Amy could not give Sarah her full attention; not when she had to keep glancing over at Charlie to see how he was coping.

Not too badly, she was relieved to see. He still had some food on his plate, someone had topped up his cup, and he was managing the tea without spilling more than a few drips on himself. He was even making an occasional monosyllabic remark in response to something said by one of the other men, and with Charlie known to be such a poor mixer no one would expect more of him than that.

Amy let herself relax a little in the pleasure of Sarah's company, until she realised the men were standing up and about to move away.

'Frank? What are you doing?' Lizzie asked in the sweet voice she usually tried to use when they had visitors. 'You're not going off somewhere, are you, dear? We're going to have some hot savouries in a minute, then we'll all go in and listen to Beth play a song.'

'I just thought I'd take these fellows up the back,' Frank said, casting a guilty look in Lizzie's direction. 'Tom hasn't seen this year's calves. We won't be long.'

'All right, dear,' Lizzie said, resignation tinged with a hint of warning. 'Just as long as you bring them all back before those savouries get cold. Kate, you can stay here with me, I don't want you getting that dress all muddy.'

'Yes, we'll only be a minute,' Frank said, giving Kate a small push in her mother's direction and looking eager to make his escape before Lizzie changed her mind. He noticed Charlie slumped in the chair.

'Ah, do you want to come too, Charlie?' Frank asked. 'I'll, um… I'll give you a hand if you like.' He held his arm out, embarrassment clear on his face.

'No, I don't,' Charlie said, scowling at Frank. 'I've cows of my own. I've no need to go traipsing around admiring yours.'

'Well, if you're sure…'

Charlie's face showed the answer clearly enough. Frank and the other men wandered off together.

Amy saw Charlie watch the men walk away, the harshness of his expression marred by the tremble in his lower lip.

'I'd better go and see to him,' she murmured. Seeing Sarah's look of surprise, Amy realised that Sarah had no idea who Charlie was. She looked Sarah squarely in the eyes. 'Come and meet my husband.'

'Your… that's your *husband*?' Sarah stared at her in obvious disbelief, then collected herself. 'I'm sorry, I didn't mean to sound like that. I just… well, I didn't realise.'

Amy gave her a rueful smile. 'I know,' she said simply. 'Let me introduce you to him.'

Sarah hung back, clearly reluctant, but Amy took her hand and led her over to Charlie.

'Sarah, this is Mr Stewart,' Amy said. 'Charlie, this is my friend, Miss Millish. She's Lily's cousin, she's come down from Auckland.'

Charlie gave a glance at Sarah, then stared harder, frowning. Sarah in her turn narrowed her eyes and stared back.

'Shake hands, Charlie,' Amy murmured.

He made no move to offer his hand to Sarah, instead turning his scowl on Amy.

'Bloody stupid idea of yours, coming here,' he grumbled. 'Sitting around listening to this lot talking about Kelly's cows.'

'I know, I'm sorry,' Amy said, trying to sound soothing. 'I didn't think they'd go off like that, either.'

'Wandering off looking at a lot of damned cows! Thinks he knows it all, that bugger does.'

'Shh, Charlie,' Amy said, uncomfortably aware of Sarah at her side. 'Shall I get you another cup of tea? Or would you like something else to eat?'

'I want a decent drop to drink,' Charlie said petulantly. 'I want a beer.'

'There isn't any. Wouldn't you like something nice to eat?'

'Why can't I have a beer? Kelly's meant to be made of money, why doesn't the miserable bugger put a bit of beer on the table?'

'Charlie, please don't talk like that. Lizzie doesn't like to have beer at soyrees. I'll get you some tea.'

Amy snatched up his empty cup, then took Sarah by the arm and tugged her away. 'I'm sorry, Sarah, I didn't think of him saying those words in front of you. He's got a bit upset today, you mustn't take any notice of the way he talks. He's not used to people, that's all.'

Sarah was staring at Charlie, her mouth slightly open. When Amy touched her arm she gave a shudder, and dragged her gaze back to Amy. 'I... I had no idea.'

Amy gave a small shrug. 'It's just the way he's made. I shouldn't have introduced you, but I thought it might take his mind off things. I'll get him some fresh tea and sit with him for a while, maybe you and I can talk some more later.'

She took the tea over to Charlie. 'Here's a nice, fresh cup,' she said, putting it down beside him. 'You'll feel much better when you've had this.'

'I don't *want* a cup of tea!' Charlie shouted. 'I want something decent to drink! Can't you understand plain English, you dopey bitch?' He thumped the arm of his chair, and to Amy's dismay he sent the cup toppling into his lap.

He yelled as the scalding tea struck him. Amy snatched the cup off his lap, then mopped up the hot liquid with her own handkerchief and one she took from Charlie's pocket. She was sure he had not spilt enough to do any real damage, but he had got himself into even more of a state now.

'Whatever's going on?' Amy looked up from tending Charlie to see Lizzie standing beside her. 'What's all the fuss about?'

'We just had a little accident with the tea. Charlie's all right now, don't worry. I'll get you another cup, Charlie.'

'I don't want tea. I won't drink it,' Charlie said, scowling at them both.

Amy looked at him helplessly, then turned to Lizzie. 'Do you think he could have a little bit of beer? I know you don't like having it at soyrees, but it might settle him down.'

Lizzie gave Charlie a hard stare. 'Such a fuss over a cup of tea. Oh, all right then, he can have one. Just one, mind you, so you'd better make it last,' she told Charlie.

'Thank you, Lizzie,' Amy said. 'I'll run and get it—the beer's in the kitchen, isn't it?'

'There's no need for you to go running about after him,' Lizzie said. 'You do enough of that the rest of the time.' She looked around to find the nearest child, and spotted Beth.

'Beth, go and get a mug of beer for your Uncle Charlie,' she said. 'Then you can sit and keep him company for a couple of minutes.'

'There's no need,' Amy said, but Lizzie took her arm and steered her firmly over to where Sarah sat.

'Now, you're to sit here and talk to Miss Millish,' Lizzie told Amy. 'You're to enjoy yourself. I don't want to see you getting out of this chair until those men come back. Miss Millish, you see that she doesn't.'

'I will, Mrs Kelly,' Sarah assured her, the hint of a smile hovering around her mouth. She turned her attention to Amy, and the hint became a full smile. 'Now I've got you all to myself again.'

Amy was torn between the pleasure of talking to Sarah and her concern for Charlie. She looked over at him every few moments, but Beth seemed to be coping well with the task her mother had assigned her.

Beth had brought the mug of beer, and now she was sitting on the verandah floor beside Charlie's chair with her legs tucked under her. She was talking quietly to Charlie, and though he was showing far more interest in the beer than in the girl at his feet, after a few minutes he began to pay her a little attention.

'He's talking to Beth,' Amy said in surprise.

'And why shouldn't he?' Sarah asked. 'She seems rather sweet.'

'Oh, Beth's a lovely girl, I've always been fond of her. But Mr Stewart's not used to little girls.'

'Isn't he?' Sarah gave Amy a quizzical stare. 'How old were you when you married him, Mrs Stewart?'

It took Amy a moment to grasp the significance of Sarah's words. 'I see what you're getting at,' she said with a rueful smile. 'I was older than Beth, anyway—nearly a year older than she is. I suppose I grew up in a bit of a rush.'

It was not a subject that gave her any pleasure to dwell on. Amy turned away from Sarah's searching gaze to look back at Charlie and Beth. Beth had disappeared into the house briefly and reappeared with a small lidded box, which she opened carefully and showed to Charlie. He peered inside it, then looked up at Beth. Amy saw him speak to the girl, and she nodded and seemed to be explaining something about whatever was in the box. Charlie listened in apparent interest.

'Trust Beth,' Amy said, smiling as she watched them. 'I think she's decided Mr Stewart's like one of those calves and kittens and things she's always patching up when they get hurt. She's always been like that, right from when she was a little thing. She used to get Dave...'

Her voice trailed away, and she swallowed hard to get past the lump in her throat.

'Dave's your son, isn't he?' Sarah asked. 'Lily told me about him.'

Amy nodded. 'He's not... I can't...' She lapsed into silence for a few moments, then began again. 'I'm sorry, Sarah, sometimes I get a bit upset when I talk about Dave. I'd just as soon not just now.'

'I've no desire to hurt you, Amy,' Sarah said. 'I'm sorry, I'm forgetting my manners,' she added quickly, her smile oddly stiff. 'Mrs Stewart, I meant to say.'

Beth scurried off to put her box away when the men returned from their stroll, and Lizzie soon enlisted her to help with passing the savouries around. Amy saw Charlie lift his empty mug towards Beth when she put some small pies on his plate, the request clear in his gesture. When Beth looked over at her mother for approval, Lizzie's lips tightened. She frowned at Charlie and shook her head firmly. Beth gave a helpless shrug and moved away from the men.

'Oh, dear,' Amy murmured. 'I hope he doesn't get in a mood again.'

She watched as Charlie stared morosely at his empty mug. He lifted his gaze to the men who had come back onto the verandah, and for a moment Amy thought he was going to try and join in the conversation.

But even if he had wanted to, it would have been difficult for Charlie to have any real part in the talk. Knowing that they would be going inside before long, none of the men bothered to sit down. Instead they chatted away standing up, and all Charlie could do was shift his eyes from one speaker to another until he grew tired of straining his neck with tilting his head so far back. He looked across the verandah at Amy, caught her eyes on him and scowled.

'I think I'll have to take him home,' Amy said.

'Must you go?' Sarah asked.

Amy nodded. 'I'm afraid I'd better. He'll only get in a state if we stay much longer. I shouldn't think he'd be very interested in the piano playing, either.'

She made to stand up, then reached out to take Sarah's hand. 'I don't think I'll be coming to any soyrees again,' Amy said, speaking quickly because she was not sure how long she could trust her voice. 'So I don't know when I'll be able to see you again. I… I'll miss you, Sarah.'

Amy felt her hand squeezed in return before she released Sarah's and stood up. She went over to Charlie and knelt beside his chair.

'We don't have to stay if you don't want to, Charlie,' she said, speaking quietly so as not to interrupt the conversation. 'Would you like to go home now?'

Charlie glared at her. 'Aye, I bloody well would like to. Stupid idea of yours, coming here.'

'Yes, I know it was,' Amy said. 'Never mind, we'll go home. Take my arm, I'll help you up.'

'Silly bitch,' Charlie grumbled, struggling to his feet with Amy's assistance. 'What have you got to be such a silly bitch for?'

'Shh, Charlie, shh,' Amy urged. 'Don't talk like that in front of people.'

'They all know you're a silly bitch. They all know you're no better than—'

'All right, Charlie, that's enough of that,' Frank broke in. 'Watch your language in front of the ladies, eh?'

Charlie scowled at Frank, and seemed about to find some fresh abuse to fling, then he turned away as if too weary to bother. 'Bugger the lot of them,' he muttered under his breath.

He caught Sarah's eyes on him, hostility clear in her gaze. 'What's she looking at me like that for?' he demanded, glaring back at her.

'I don't think she's used to hearing people talk like that,' Amy said. 'Come on, Charlie, we'll go now. There's no need to get in a state.'

'Do you want a hand, Amy?' Frank asked, taking a step towards her, but Amy shook her head.

'No, I can manage. Thank you for offering.'

'Can't I do anything?' he persisted.

Amy saw Lizzie bearing down on them, and knew she would have to move quickly to get Charlie away before he caused more of an upset. 'Yes, you can,' she told Frank, keeping her voice low. 'You can help me a lot. Act as if nothing funny's going on, so people won't stare at Charlie and me too much. And thank Lizzie for me, and tell her I'm sorry for leaving in such a hurry.'

She led Charlie away, catching Sarah's eye again for the briefest of

363

moments before they were around the corner of the house and out of sight.

Charlie sat in the gig grumbling away under his breath. 'Bloody Frank Kelly,' he muttered. 'Thinks he's smart, that bugger. Him and his cows.'

He appeared to notice for the first time that Amy was not answering. 'I never wanted to go there. It was your stupid idea.'

'I know it was,' Amy said. 'You're right, it was silly of me. I wanted to see the others, that's all. And I thought you might enjoy talking to the men. I'm sorry, I won't suggest it again.'

'I didn't want to go and see his cows,' Charlie said. 'Offering me his arm like I was an old woman! Bloody cheek.'

'He was only trying to help. He meant well.'

'Smart bugger. One miserable mug of beer, that's all I got! Miserable sod.'

Amy almost felt she would have managed to get angry with Charlie if she had not been quite so tired and disappointed. 'Well, it's more than any of the other men got, Charlie. No one else got any beer at all.'

That seemed to make him think. Charlie was quiet for some time, as if mulling over the idea.

'Who was the little lass?' he asked a few minutes later. 'The one that brought me the beer?'

'That's Beth. She's Lizzie's third, she's the next one down from Joey.'

'She's not a bad lass,' Charlie said, and from him, Amy knew, that was high praise indeed. 'She's got a wee bird in a box. She showed it me. Says she found it under a hedge and she couldn't find its nest. She's rearing it so she can let it go again. Funny little lass.'

'Beth's like that. She likes looking after animals that aren't well. She's always been good at looking after Lizzie's little ones, too.'

Charlie grunted, his attention wandering. 'Who's that sour-faced bitch?'

'I don't know who you mean,' Amy said, aware of the tightness in her voice. She could guess easily enough who had attracted Charlie's censure.

'That one you were talking to. Wouldn't be a bad looking woman if she didn't go around with that scowl on her face.'

'She doesn't usually look like that. I think she's quite pretty.'

'One of your relations, is she?'

Amy shook her head. 'No, she's Lily's cousin. Her name's Sarah, and she's my friend.' *And I don't know when I'll ever see her again.*

'Sour-faced bitch,' Charlie repeated. Amy made no reply.

They drove on in silence until they reached the track up to Charlie's cottage. The sight of the paddock full of potato plants brought the problem Amy had been brooding on for weeks full into her awareness.

'The potatoes are coming on well,' she remarked, careful to sound calm.

'Aye, they are. Should be a good crop.'

'There'll be a lot to harvest this year. An awful lot.' She glanced over at Charlie, but he was looking straight ahead at the track, refusing to meet her eyes.

'I don't know how I'm going to manage it,' Amy said quietly. Still he said nothing, just stared straight ahead, but she saw the corner of his mouth begin to twitch convulsively. 'The potatoes, Charlie,' she pressed on, knowing the subject had to be faced sooner or later. 'I don't think I can—'

Charlie turned on the seat and glared at her, his eyes wide and staring. 'I'll get my own bloody potatoes in,' he said, his voice rasping as if he were forcing the words out with difficulty. 'I'll not be in this state much longer. I'll get them in!'

Amy closed her eyes for a moment. 'All right, we won't talk about it. We don't need to worry about them for another month or so, anyway.'

'Think I'm useless, do you?' His voice was taut, the words barely audible for all the force Amy sensed behind them. 'Think I'm bloody useless?'

'No, I don't think that at all. Let's not talk about it.'

Charlie opened his mouth, but no words came out. His jaw hung slack, and his eyes stared blankly, then his head and one arm began twitching. Amy reined the horse in and took hold of his shoulders.

'Charlie? What's wrong?' She shook him a little. 'I'm sorry I started on about the potatoes, I won't talk about them again. Charlie!'

He twitched again, then gave a shudder. Amy watched awareness creep back into his eyes, followed by that familiar mixture of fear and confusion.

Amy held him tightly by the shoulders, fearing that he would slump to the floor of the gig if she let him go. 'Did it go black in your head again?' she asked softly.

Charlie frowned. 'Aye, it did.' The words came out slurred, as if his tongue had grown too thick for his mouth. 'Black.'

'Don't talk, then. You're all right now, but let's sit quiet for a minute, then I'll get you up to the house and put you to bed.' She kept an arm around his shoulders until he had regained some sort of control over the muscles that had gone lax so abruptly.

'There, that's better, isn't it?' Amy said, carefully letting him go when she felt him take his own weight again. He looked at her for a moment, then his eyes dropped to his lap.

Amy followed his gaze and saw the wet patch that was spreading across his trousers. 'Never mind. I'll get your nightshirt on you as soon as we're inside, you'll be all right then.'

She gave a brief glance back at the potato paddock, then looked in the other direction to where the cows were already lined up close to the gate, eager for the relief that milking would bring them.

'I hope you filled up on cakes and things down at Lizzie's,' she said wearily. 'Dinner's going to be very late tonight.'

'Did he start playing up?' Lizzie asked in a low voice as Amy and Charlie were moving away.

'Yes, he did,' Frank said, matching her quiet tone so that not even Rosie, who was swinging on the veranda rail close to them, could hear what they said. 'Amy said to tell you she was sorry she left in a rush like that.'

'Ooh, that man,' Lizzie muttered. 'Trust him to cause trouble. Honestly, he begrudges her a bit of pleasure with all the running around she does after him.'

Frank glanced across at Sarah Millish, and was startled to see the force of hostility in the look she was directing towards Charlie. Her knuckles showed white with the ferocity of her grip on the verandah rail.

He gave Lizzie a nudge. 'Look at that,' he murmured, indicating Sarah with a small gesture. 'She looks as if she'd like to throttle Charlie.'

Amy and Charlie disappeared around the corner of the house, and Sarah relaxed visibly. She turned towards Lizzie and Frank as if she had sensed their eyes on her.

'What a perfectly dreadful man,' she said, her voice clear though it shook a little.

'Yes, he's horrible,' Rosie chimed in. 'No one likes Uncle Charlie.'

'That's enough, Rosie,' Lizzie said. 'You get on and start picking up those plates before someone treads on them. Hurry up, girl.'

She turned towards Sarah with a stern expression. 'I try to bring my children up to be polite to adults, Miss Millish. It makes it difficult when they hear other people being rude in front of them.'

Sarah met Lizzie's gaze steadily. 'I'm very sorry if I caused you offence, Mrs Kelly. I certainly had no intention of doing so. But I'm afraid that some men make it difficult to keep within the bounds of correct behaviour. I shall have to try harder.'

She nodded to Lizzie, turned on her heel with a swish of skirts and went into the house.

'You were a bit hard on her, weren't you?' Frank said as he watched Sarah disappear. 'I've heard you say worse things than that about Charlie.'

'Not in front of the little ones,' Lizzie said. 'Anyway, that's different. She's no business passing remarks when she's only known us a few months. It's just because she doesn't like men, you know.' She saw Frank's quizzical expression, and pulled a face. 'Oh, I suppose you're right, I did bite her head off a bit. Charlie got on my nerves, playing up like that. That's the trouble when he's around, he always gets everyone upset.'

'I wouldn't like to have to live with him, that's for sure.'

Lizzie frowned. 'I didn't like the look of him. I don't know how Amy's managing.'

'That leg of his didn't look too good,' Frank agreed. 'I suppose he must be making do somehow, though.'

'I don't know about that. Amy said he wasn't too bad, but I'm not so sure. I think I'd better go up there sometime and see how she's getting on.'

'She mightn't want you butting in.'

'It's not butting in at all,' Lizzie said sharply. 'It's just keeping an eye on her. Don't you talk to me about minding my own business—I did that for years with Amy, and look what happened. He could have beaten her to death while I was minding my own business.'

'Shh,' Frank murmured, glancing around to see if anyone had heard, but the noise of conversation was loud enough to cover Lizzie's words. 'I know,' he said quietly. 'It's pretty hard for me to give Charlie the time of day when I think about what he did to her. But that was a long time ago, eh? She seems to manage him pretty well now—and he's in no shape to hurt her.'

'She's too soft hearted, that's the trouble. Oh, I don't know, I suppose I might worry a bit much about her. Still, I'll have to have a talk with her sometime.'

Frank made a noncommittal noise vaguely expressive of approval. He was fond of Amy, but he did not want Lizzie getting herself upset over her. Especially now, when she was probably carrying a baby. He did not relish the idea of having to dissuade her from ill-advised outings to Charlie's farm. Dissuading Lizzie from anything was never easy.

22

February – March 1905

Amy looked up from her plate and saw that Charlie was struggling to manage his fork. She had dished up what she could only loosely call a stew; the advantage of the meal was that she could leave it simmering on the range while she was out on the farm rather than in its flavour.

'Meat's a bit tough,' Charlie grumbled. His speech had become more slurred lately, though Amy was not sure how aware of it he was himself.

'Is it? Maybe I didn't cook it long enough.' She did not suggest that it was because Charlie had less control of his jaw these days, though she had seen signs of it since his last attack. 'Shall I cut it up smaller for you?'

Charlie shook his head. 'I can manage,' he said, casting a resentful glare at her.

'Whatever you want,' Amy murmured. It would have been far easier to look after Charlie if he had not had erratic bursts of trying to be independent. Caring for him was much like having a small child in the house again; except that she had never had to worry about offending her babies' dignity.

Charlie stabbed at a chunk of meat. His hand twisted awkwardly, the heel of his palm pitched onto the edge of the plate, and plate and food toppled to the floor.

He stared in disbelief at what had been his dinner a few moments before, helpless frustration in his face. 'Look what it's done,' he said across the table to Amy. 'That's my bloody dinner there!'

Amy stood up and carried her own plate around to him. 'Have mine.' She scraped what she could of Charlie's dinner off the floor onto his plate and emptied it into the slops bucket. The stew had left a sticky pool, adding to the undeniably grubby state the floor had got into lately. But she had enough to think about without fretting over a grubby kitchen.

'What'll you have?' Charlie asked, looking doubtfully at the food that had appeared before him.

'There's more potatoes in the pot, I can fill up on them.'

'You need meat,' Charlie said. 'You can't work without meat in your belly.'

'I've had quite a bit of it already. Anyway, those gristly bits are too hard for me to chew—leave those bits if you don't want them, just eat the vegies.'

'Why can't you chew the meat? What's wrong with you?'

'It's my teeth. I'm missing a couple at the back, I notice it when the meat's tough.'

Charlie stared at her, his mouth working as if he were puzzling through a problem. 'Teeth,' he echoed. 'The ones I knocked out.'

'That was a long time ago, Charlie,' Amy said quietly. 'Best to forget all that. Come on, eat up your dinner and I'll open a bottle of stewed fruit for afters.'

Charlie was clearly troubled. He reached for the clean fork Amy had given him, but his hand trembled too much for him to take a firm grip. 'I don't want it,' he said, shoving the plate away.

'Yes, you do,' said Amy. She pulled a chair close, cut the meat and vegetables into small pieces, and lifted a forkful to Charlie's mouth. 'Eat up.'

He scowled defiantly at her for a moment or two, then slumped back further in his chair, opened his mouth, and let himself be fed like a baby.

It took a long time to feed him, giving him time to chew each mouthful before offering the next. When the plate was empty at last, Amy noticed Charlie's jaw was still working convulsively, his face twisted with the effort.

She had noticed this apparent discomfort after eating since his most recent attack, but this was the first chance she had had to observe it at close range. Now she saw that one side of his jaw no longer worked properly, leaving a pocket of food wadded uncomfortably in a corner of his mouth.

'Let me,' she said. She reached a finger into his mouth and cleared out the food, dropping the wad onto his empty plate. 'You should have told me you were having trouble with that.'

Charlie's jaw eased visibly. 'A man doesn't want to be looked after as if he's a baby,' he muttered.

'I know, Charlie. But you must let me help you with things like that. I don't mind doing them for you. Just until you feel a bit better.'

She dished up the leftover potatoes onto her plate and bolted them down, then opened the promised bottle of fruit and served them both a generous helping. Charlie insisted on eating the dessert unaided.

By the time they had had a cup of tea and a few biscuits, Amy felt comfortably full. She resisted the urge to sit back in her chair and relax; she still had too much work to do before she would be able to crawl into bed that night.

'Do you want to go to bed now, or sit up for a bit?' she asked. Sometimes Charlie wanted her help to walk through to his bedroom;

after the fright he had had that evening with tipping his dinner onto the floor, Amy thought he would probably need her arm.

He frowned in thought, as if even so simple a problem taxed him. 'I'll go to bed now.'

Amy helped him up and steadied him by one elbow until he was in his room and sitting on the bed.

'I'll get you a clean nightshirt, that one's got stew on it,' she said. 'Can you manage getting changed?'

Charlie nodded. She was not sure just how he did manage to change into a clean nightshirt once a week, but somehow he did, with no help from her other than with his buttons. She worried that he might hurt himself straining with the clothes, but it seemed his shyness was stronger than his desire for help.

'Are you going to bed now?' he asked.

'Not yet. I've got a few things to do before that.'

'You look half dead. You should go to bed.'

Amy shook her head. 'I've the bread to make first. I've got to wash the dishes, too, and tidy up in the kitchen a bit.' And after that there was mending to be done, and a letter to David to be finished off if she could keep her eyes open long enough.

'Women's work.' He let her unbutton the front of his nightshirt, then watched her fetch a clean one from his chest of drawers. 'Man's work all day and women's work all night.'

'Not all night, Charlie. Just the things I don't get around to in the daytime. Anyway, I've got quite used to it now, I don't seem to need as much sleep as I did.'

She saw him staring at her, frowning in thought as he did so. 'You never...' he said uncertainly. 'You never complain.'

Amy made no answer. She placed the clean nightshirt on the chair beside his bed and made to leave the room.

'Why not?' Charlie asked, startling her.

'What do you mean?'

'Why don't you ever complain? God knows you've reason enough.'

From Charlie the question seemed so ridiculous that Amy felt a smile twitching at the corners of her mouth.

'You were never one to encourage complaining, Charlie. I learned that soon enough after I came to live here.' She gave a shrug. 'I suppose I just got out of the habit. That's no bad thing, is it? Complaining about things just gets a person down. Much better to get on with it. Good night.'

She felt his eyes following her as she slipped out of the room and closed the door behind her.

It was morning sickness that made Lizzie certain enough of her pregnancy to want to tell the world; or, more precisely, to tell her oldest daughter.

'I think we should drop in on Maudie this morning,' Lizzie remarked to Frank with a studied casualness as the two of them got back in the buggy after finishing their shopping. 'We haven't been around there for a while.'

Not since Christmas, in fact. After Lizzie had stormed out of Richard's house in high dudgeon, she had insisted that she would not go back there until she got an apology from Maudie. She had relented for Christmas, and the whole family had crammed into Richard's parlour on Christmas Day for a brief visit on their way home from church, but since then she had not crossed the threshold. Sometimes she chose not to come into town with Frank, and he always dropped in on his daughter on those days, but he had not been able to persuade Lizzie to relax her attitude of injured pride.

Until today. Frank did not press for an explanation as to why she had changed her mind about waiting for an apology they both knew would never come; he knew her reasons well enough.

Lizzie sat in Richard's parlour balancing a saucer on her lap and looking around the room with a brazenly self-satisfied air. Maudie watched her mother, until at last she could bear the mystery no longer. Lizzie had barely downed the tea when Maudie hurried her off to the bedroom, ostensibly to see some baby clothes Maudie had been making.

'And just what is Lizzie so pleased with herself over?' Richard asked Frank as soon as the two of them were alone. 'She looks like the cat that's swallowed the cream.'

'She does a bit, doesn't she?' Frank said. 'Well, we've got a bit of news, Lizzie and I have. Lizzie's got a baby on the way.'

'Ah,' Richard said slowly and thoughtfully. 'I see it all now.' He gave Frank a look that seemed intended to be reproachful, though Frank was aware of the smile that threatened to break through it. 'Someone's nose is going to be badly out of joint over this, you realise?'

'Maudie'll be all right about it,' Frank said. 'It'll be nice, the two babies being so close together and all.'

'It's easy for you to say she'll be all right,' Richard said drily. 'It's me who'll have to smooth the ruffled feathers, you know. I'm afraid I must say that I blame you, Frank.'

'Well, I had something to do with it,' Frank admitted with a grin. 'It was all Lizzie's idea, though.'

'I'm quite sure it was. Still, you must confess that you went along with it.'

'That's usually the best way when Lizzie gets her mind set on something.'

'So I've gathered. And is Lizzie keeping well?'

'She's not too bad,' Frank said, a trace of doubt in his voice. 'She's been having a bit of trouble with the morning sickness just lately.'

'Has she? I don't think Maudie realises quite how lucky she was over that—she had no nausea at all. Is it a real problem for Lizzie?'

Frank hesitated, torn between the vague worry he had over Lizzie's sickness and the promise she had extracted from him to say nothing to Richard or Maudie about just how unpleasant it was. After all, he told himself, it was only morning sickness, even if it seemed to be worse than Lizzie had had in her earlier pregnancies.

'She says she's all right,' he hedged. 'It won't last long, anyway.'

'Lizzie looks quite well,' Richard said. 'And she obviously enjoys the best of health normally. I'm sure she'll come through it all without too much trouble. Of course I'd be more than happy to help in any way I can—perhaps you'd like me to check her over?'

'I don't think that'd be a very good idea,' Frank said cautiously. 'I don't think either of us would be too popular with Lizzie if I suggested that.'

'No, I suppose not,' Richard agreed. 'But if you do think it's necessary at any time… well, just keep it in mind.'

Their conversation was abruptly halted when Lizzie and Maudie emerged from the other room. Lizzie's smile was more self-satisfied than ever, while Maudie was tight-lipped, as if holding back what she wanted to say only with the greatest of efforts. She kissed her mother goodbye without any real show of enthusiasm; Frank was relieved when she kissed him with her usual affection. Maudie had clearly decided for herself where the blame for her mother's pregnancy lay.

'We might pop in and see you next week,' Lizzie said as she and Frank set off down the path to the buggy.

'That'll be nice,' Maudie said through clenched teeth. When Frank glanced back from the garden gate, which he was holding open for Lizzie, he saw that Maudie was no longer looking at them. Instead she had turned towards Richard and begun speaking. At this distance Frank could not hear her voice; he could only see the movement of her mouth and a little of her expression. But that was enough for him to make a fair guess at just what she was saying to Richard.

Amy had been putting off the task of clearing one of the drains for weeks, but when a heavy fall of rain made the drain overflow into the paddock it ran through she knew it was time to do something about it.

She waited a few days until the ground had dried out somewhat, then took a shovel from one of the sheds and walked down to the paddock.

As soon as she started, she was reminded of just why she had put it off for so long. It was a filthy job, as well as exhausting. The thick sludge, half mud and half manure from the cow shed, clung to her boots with invisible hands, dragging at her as if trying to draw her down into itself. Taking a step meant heaving each foot up with an effort, the mud reluctantly releasing its hold with a loud sucking noise and a stench that made Amy retch until her nose grew too used to it for violent reaction. If she left her feet where they were for longer than a minute or two, she felt them slip down into the sludge until mud oozed over the tops of her boots.

Small, biting flies clustered around her face. The back of her hand was slimy against her skin when she gave in to the urge to rub it across her cheek. Each shovel full could only be gouged out of the drain with a shoulder-wrenching effort and a smell even worse than that stirred up by the movement of her boots. The reek of her own sweat, acrid as hot metal, cut through it from time to time.

It was a long, slow job, but Amy could see that she was more than halfway through when she was interrupted by a call from the direction of the house.

'Amy?'

From the paddock where she was working she could not quite see the house, but she recognised the voice as Charlie's. She thought she detected uneasiness in his tone, though it was certainly short of panic.

'Where the hell are you?'

There was more irritation than uneasiness in that yell. Amy sighed.

'I'm coming,' she called. She heaved her feet out of the cloying mud and began trudging back up to the house, her feet unnaturally heavy with the weight of mud clinging to her boots.

She stopped short when she rounded a corner and the house came into view. She could make out Charlie standing in the doorway, and a few steps away from him was a woman in a dark dress; a woman so tall that she was within a few inches of Charlie's height. Amy only knew two women that tall, and she was quite sure it was not Susannah who stood on the verandah waiting for her.

'Hurry up, for God's sake,' Charlie called. 'Don't keep the woman standing here all day.' He disappeared back into the house, pulling the door to after himself, clearly eager to escape the uncomfortable situation he had found himself in.

There was no help for it. Amy loosened the skirts she had tucked up into her drawers, shouldered her shovel and walked up to the house, aware of the eyes studying her as she came. When she got to the foot of the steps, she let the shovel fall to the ground and looked up to the verandah.

'Hello, Sarah,' she said quietly.

'Oh, God.' Sarah reached out almost blindly for the chair that stood near her and sank into it, her eyes never leaving Amy.

Amy came up the steps towards her, but thought better of taking the other chair. She would have to scrub it clean if she dropped any of her load of dirt onto it. Instead she sat on the top step of the verandah and studied the pattern of splattered mud on her skirts before raising her eyes to Sarah's.

'I would've smartened myself up a bit if I'd known you were coming.' Amy tried to smile.

'I didn't realise he'd be here—I just stepped in the door and he was sitting there, not even properly dressed,' Sarah said, clearly distressed. 'I thought he'd be out on the farm somewhere and you'd be here by yourself. I thought we'd be on our own, so we'd be able to talk. I wanted to… I thought I could… what on earth have you been doing?' she asked, staring at Amy with a kind of horrified fascination.

'Clearing out a drain. I'm not usually in a state like this, it's just that it's such a dirty job.' Amy was acutely aware of the unpleasant smell emanating from her.

'Why were you doing a job like that?'

'It was blocked,' Amy said simply. 'It needed digging out.'

'Yes, but why were *you* doing it? Why wasn't he?' Sarah indicated the house, and the absent Charlie, with a disapproving toss of her head.

'Mr Stewart's not feeling very well just at the moment. He's not up to the heavy work today.'

'Then why not leave it till he *is* feeling up to it? Why on earth do such a filthy job yourself? Goodness me, I know nothing about farming, but I can't believe clearing out a drain couldn't wait a day or two.'

Amy could think of no convincing answer. She gave a shrug and tried to change the subject.

'Would you like a cup of tea? Don't worry, I'll wash myself and put some clean clothes on before I touch anything in the kitchen.'

Sarah was studying her closely. Her eyes suddenly grew wide with comprehension. 'He never feels well, does he?' she said, then went on more rapidly. 'All this talk about bad days and good days—he doesn't have any good days. You're having to do all these filthy jobs for him, and you've been keeping it a secret from everyone.'

'He gets so upset,' Amy said helplessly. 'He doesn't want anyone to know. And he *is* better some days than others, really he is.'

'However have you been managing? Not very well, from the look of things. You look exhausted.'

'It's the drain, that's all. It's an awful job. I haven't finished it yet, either.' Amy had not meant to admit that, but the words slipped out before she could stop them.

'Let me help you, then,' Sarah said eagerly. 'I'm sure I could dig as well as you can—it can't take any great proficiency to dig drains. And it'd be easier for me than a little thing like you.'

'Oh, no, Sarah!' Amy said, horrified at the notion. 'I couldn't let you do anything like that! It's an awful job—I'm used to it, it's all right for me, but not for you.'

'I *want* to,' Sarah protested. 'I want to help you. Won't you let me?'

'No, I can't. I couldn't bear to see you do that. And what about your nice dress?'

'Clothes can be washed.'

'I wouldn't like the job of washing a pretty dress like that if you wore it in the drain. It's silk, isn't it? This is just an old cotton thing, it's just about rags already. Please, Sarah, don't even ask me to let you do something like that.'

'Well, there must be some way I can help. Something in the kitchen, perhaps?' Sarah latched eagerly onto the idea. 'Could I do some baking for you?'

'I don't think so,' Amy said. 'Charlie—Mr Stewart would get upset if there was a stranger in the house.'

'Oh, *him*. Doesn't he ever leave the house?'

Confronted with a straight question, Amy could not evade it. 'Not really,' she admitted. 'Only to sit on the verandah sometimes when it's fine.'

'Then there's nothing I can do to help you?'

'I don't need any help. Thank you for thinking of it, but I can manage, really I can. You mustn't worry about me. Why did you come today, anyway?'

'I've been up to visit Lily. I thought it would be a good excuse to come and see you. I never thought of his being here, sitting around in his nightshirt in the middle of the day. I know you said you didn't want me to visit you, but I thought I'd never have the chance otherwise, now you don't go to Mrs Kelly's any more.'

'I don't like to leave him by himself, you see.'

'I've brought you a book.' Sarah reached into the bag at her side and pulled out a leather-bound volume. 'Byron. Passionate verse is not particularly appropriate, I'm afraid,' she said, looking towards the cottage with resentment smouldering in her eyes. 'But there's no harm in dreaming, is there?'

There's no good in it, either. 'Thank you, that's very kind of you. I'm sure I'll enjoy it, but I won't touch it just now, not with my hands in this state. Could you put it up on the rail for me?'

Amy looked at the gold lettering on the book's spine, anticipating the pleasure of reading the verse inside. 'I don't know when I'll get it back to you, though—I don't get out much these days.'

'No need to return it. It's a gift. I sent away to Auckland for it.'

'Oh, Sarah! That's one of the loveliest things anyone's ever given me! Oh, I'd like to kiss you, but I don't want to get you dirty.'

'Faces can be washed more easily than clothes,' Sarah said, and before Amy could stop her she had knelt down on the top step and pressed her lips to Amy's cheek. 'There.'

She stood up. 'And now I think the best thing I can do is get out of your way. I'm sorry I barged in uninvited, I shan't make such a nuisance of myself again.'

'You're not a nuisance.'

'Oh, yes I am.' She studied Amy. 'I shall have to think of some way of helping you. I don't like the idea of your living in squalor.'

'There's no need for that. No need at all.'

'We'll see about that,' Sarah said.

Amy rose to walk with Sarah over to where she had tethered her horse.

'Sarah,' she said when the younger woman had mounted, 'I'd be grateful if… well, if you didn't tell anyone about all this. About Mr Stewart and everything.'

'Yes, I suppose you would,' Sarah said thoughtfully. 'I suppose you would.'

She rode away down the track, glancing back frequently over her shoulder and returning Amy's waves.

There would be no point in cleaning herself up enough to go inside and then getting filthy again. Amy went back to her drain and finished the job, then trudged back up to the house.

She was sitting on the porch steps pulling off her boots when the door opened a fraction and Charlie peered out.

'Has she gone?' he asked, looking around nervously.

'Yes, she has. I don't think she'll be back, either.'

'She'd better not be,' Charlie said, attempting belligerence. 'Poking her nose in my house! Coming in when a man's not even dressed.'

'She didn't know you were here. Didn't she knock?'

'Aye, she damned near thumped the door down, knocking and knocking. I thought she'd take herself off if I took no notice. Then the bold-faced tart barged right in! Said something about wanting to leave a note for you. Bloody cheek of it.'

'I think she got as much of a fright as you did. And if she didn't know you were in the house you can't really blame her for coming in. Never mind, she's gone now.'

'Bloody good riddance. Don't want your relations hanging around here.'

Amy tugged at a stubborn boot. 'She's not my relation, Charlie. She's Lily's cousin. I've told you that.'

'She's some relation of yours,' Charlie said, looking suspiciously at her. 'I can see she is. Don't you go telling me she's not.'

'Please yourself, then.'

Charlie screwed up his face as he watched her. 'You stink to high heaven.'

'I know I do. My nose is full of it. Sarah must have thought I'd been rolling around in the muck.' She looked at herself in disgust. 'I don't know what she thought of me.'

Even after she had scrubbed at her hands and face and changed into clean clothes, Amy felt dirty. It was as though the filth had seeped into her skin and become ingrained. She fancied that the fetid smell of the drain still hung about her.

Squalor, she thought to herself as she looked around her grubby kitchen. *That's a good word for it, Sarah.* She felt a sick sense of relief that Sarah had refused her unthinking offer of a cup of tea; and an even sicker sense of disgust at herself for having been caught in such a state. Tonight, she decided, she was going to have a respite from squalor.

'What are you doing with that thing?' Charlie asked when she dragged the tin bath into the kitchen.

'I'm going to have a bath. I haven't had one in weeks—no, months,' Amy corrected herself.

Charlie looked at her doubtfully. 'I can't fetch the water for you.'

'I know. I can manage, it'll just take me a while.'

It did take a long time to haul enough water, and boiling it used a fearful portion of the store of firewood that had taken such an effort to chop, but Amy was determined. By the time she had the last kerosene tin full of water heating, she had settled Charlie in the parlour with a cup of tea. She heaved the tin of steaming water off the range and tipped enough of it in to get the bath as full as she wanted, hoisted the tin back onto the range to keep it hot for the dishwashing, then stripped off and stepped into the bath.

The feel of hot water against her skin was blissful. Amy scrubbed at herself until she was pink all over, then leaned as far back as the little bath allowed and savoured the delicious sensation of being clean.

It was only when the water began to cool and her fingers were water-soft and wrinkled that Amy could bear to leave it. The roughness of the towel was pleasure rather than discomfort, making her skin tingle delightfully. Even her nightdress, warm from being draped over a chair close to the range, seemed to caress her as she pulled it on over her head.

The urge to share the unaccustomed pleasure of being so thoroughly clean was strong, especially when Amy saw how much hot water she had to spare; far more than she needed for the dishes.

She opened the door into the parlour. Charlie was sitting up in his armchair, ostensibly reading the *Weekly News* but in reality dozing fitfully. He looked up when Amy entered the room, and rustled his newspaper noisily. 'What do you want?'

'Would you like a bath? I've left the water in it, and I've got a load of hot to top it up with.'

She watched him consider the idea. 'I won't bother,' he said after a pause. But she saw the look of longing he cast in the direction of the kitchen; saw, too, the involuntary move to scratch himself under one arm.

'Are you sure?' she pressed. 'It seems a waste of water just for one. I'll help you,' she added quietly, knowing that that was the real issue.

'Don't want to be helped,' Charlie said gruffly; then more softly, as if he had not meant to speak aloud, he added, 'I wouldn't mind a bath.' Amy saw him glance towards the kitchen again.

'Come on, then,' she urged. She took his arm, and he let himself be helped up and led into the kitchen.

Charlie leaned against the edge of the table and watched her empty out a few bucketfuls of grey water from the bath and replace them with clean hot water.

'Hell of a job for you, hauling all that,' he said. 'Should be my job, that sort of thing.'

Amy lifted the kerosene tin back onto the range, enjoying the sense of relief when she relinquished the weight. 'Well, you've hauled plenty of bath loads for me over the years. I don't mind taking a turn.'

She stood in front of Charlie and reached up to undo the buttons of his nightshirt. He grabbed feebly at the nightshirt when she started to lift it, his face twisted in distress, but Amy easily won the unequal battle.

'Now, hurry up and get in that lovely hot water before it starts getting cold,' she said briskly.

He clutched at Amy, leaning against her as he stepped into the bath then carefully lowered himself into the water.

Amy knelt on the floor behind him, hoping he would be less uncomfortable if he could not see her. Charlie held himself stiffly upright, rigid with embarrassment, while Amy began soaping his back.

He said nothing for some time, and Amy left the silence undisturbed while she washed him. Then she heard him muttering under his breath, and she paused for a moment to catch his words.

'Man can't do for himself,' she heard. 'A man's in a bloody bad way when he can't wash himself.'

'There's no harm in getting someone else to help you with the awkward bits,' Amy said. 'Lizzie does Frank's back, you know.'

'She doesn't!' he said in astonished disbelief.

'She does, Charlie, honestly. Her and Frank have always done each other's backs, right from when they were first married. Lizzie told me that years and years ago.'

He digested her startling claim in silence, leaving Amy free to go on washing him. When she had finished his back she could no longer stay behind him, instead walking around on her knees until she was crouched close to his side. She worked her way around to the front of his body, doing his arms then his chest.

The hair on it was thick and grizzled, with no more than a hint of the reddish colour it must have had when he was a young man. It was hard for Amy to imagine Charlie as a young man; he had seemed old even when she was a child. Old, but powerful and frightening; now he was old and pitiable. Her only fear as she tended him was that she might inadvertently hurt him.

Her hands worked lower, to where the hair drew inwards to a narrower line down his belly. Below that, the hair spread out again into a patch of a darker colour. Amy's hands hovered uncertainly as she neared it.

While she hesitated, Charlie reached out with his good hand and snatched the soap from her. 'I'll do it myself,' he said.

She sat back on her heels and waited for him to finish washing his private parts.

Amy had never before seen a grown man at such close quarters. It seemed such a small, insignificant thing dangling there rather comically, brushing the surface of the water as if in imminent danger of drowning. It was hard to believe how terrified she had been of it, and how much it had hurt her. Hard to understand why letting a man put that silly little thing inside her had made her ruined in the eyes of the world.

He let her take back the soap to do his legs and feet, then she rinsed him off and helped him out of the bath. She felt him trembling as she rubbed him with the towel; even so small an exertion as having been bathed had left him exhausted. By the time she had a clean nightshirt on him he could hardly stand. He leaned heavily on Amy as she helped him into the bedroom and tucked him into bed.

'You should sleep well now, after all that,' she said. 'I've put an extra blanket on, I don't want you getting a chill from having a bath. Are you warm enough?'

He nodded, but seemed too tired to speak.

'I think I'll start having baths again,' Amy said. 'I'd forgotten how good it feels. We don't need to bother every week, not when it takes so long to fetch the water, but once a fortnight or so would be nice. Once a month, at least.'

'Makes a lot of trouble for you,' Charlie said indistinctly.

'It's worth it, especially if you'll share the water. I don't think I could be bothered doing it just for myself very often. It's nice to feel clean, isn't it?'

Charlie nodded. 'Feels good,' he murmured. 'Lot of bother. Glad you did it.'

He closed his eyes. Amy put out the lamp and crept from the room. She had already closed the door behind her before she realised with a start that Charlie had just come surprisingly close to thanking her for something.

Frank inched back the bedcovers and slid slowly towards the edge of the mattress, doing his best to get out without making the bed move. Despite his efforts, Lizzie stirred and opened her eyes.

'Don't get up, Lizzie,' he said quickly. 'There's no need. I can get myself a cup of tea easy enough.'

'I've always made you a cup of tea before you go out milking, and I don't intend to stop,' Lizzie said, her voice still a little blurred from sleep. 'Don't go making a fuss.'

'I wish you wouldn't—' Frank saw Lizzie move to sit upright. He darted around to her side of the bed, bashing his ankle against one of the bed legs in his rush, grabbed at the basin that rested on the bedside table, and managed to thrust it under Lizzie's mouth just as she began to retch.

It had become something of a routine, this morning drama of Lizzie claiming that she was quite well, Frank begging her to stay in bed, and the whole scene climaxed by a violent bout of vomiting. Frank crouched beside the bed holding the basin for Lizzie, his other arm around her shoulders, steadying her while her body lurched.

'Poor old thing. My poor Lizzie.'

A particularly violent spasm left Lizzie lying limp against his arm. He carefully wiped away the trace of vomit trickling down her chin and gripped her more tightly. 'No more babies after this, eh? I don't want to see you go through this again.'

Lizzie gave him a venomous look. 'If you think I'm ever going to let you touch me again, Frank Kelly—' She was interrupted by another bout of retching.

'I won't touch you,' Frank said wildly. 'I'll go and sleep with the boys or something. Heck, I'd just about cut the bloody thing off before I'd want to get you with child again. I won't—'

'Oh, shut up, Frank.' Lizzie held herself very still for a few moments, till it was obvious that the nausea had passed. 'Are you going to milk those cows, or are you just going to sit there all day like a great fool?'

'I'm going.' Frank reluctantly released her and stood up. 'Don't get up, eh,' he said, knowing it was useless, and Lizzie showed him how right he was by getting out of bed and putting on her dressing-gown.

'You boys hurry up and get dressed,' Frank heard Lizzie call into the boys' room as she went down the passage ahead of him. 'Don't keep your father waiting.'

She had the kettle on the range by the time Frank had finished dressing and had joined her in the kitchen. 'Do you want a piece of bread and butter to keep you going?' she asked.

'I don't feel hungry just now,' Frank said, the basin of vomit still too fresh a memory. 'Tea'll be nice. How about you sit down and let me pour it?'

'I'll pour it myself,' Lizzie said. 'I'd better do some bread and butter for those boys to have on their way down.' She sawed slices from the previous day's loaf.

Frank studied her, observing the signs of weariness left by her violent nausea.

'Lizzie,' he said carefully, 'you used to let me get my own cup of tea of a morning, you know.'

'Rubbish. I always get you one.'

'Not when you're expecting. It's true, Lizzie, don't scowl at me like that. It's fair enough for a woman to take things a bit easier when she's carrying, isn't it?'

'Oh, I suppose I might have slowed down a bit when I got really big,' Lizzie allowed. 'Maybe I did sleep in more when I was further along with the others. There's no need for that just yet, though. Not when I'm so well. And I always do well, I shouldn't think I'll have to take things easy at all this time.'

Frank knew that anything he said just then would only make matters worse, so he kept silent. He knew plainly enough just why Lizzie was so insistent that she was perfectly well: Maudie's glowing good health, and the ease with which she was sailing through pregnancy. Lizzie seemed to be taking Maudie's easy voyage almost as an insult; certainly as a challenge. Lizzie had never been one to ignore a challenge.

She plumped cups and saucers down on the table next to the teapot, then sat down heavily. 'Don't forget to do that message for me in town.'

'No, I won't forget,' Frank said absently, his mind more concerned with the unpleasant grey tinge of Lizzie's face, and with the unaccustomed angularity it seemed to have gained of late.

'Are you listening to me?' Lizzie said sharply. 'I want that done today. I'm going to get things sorted out for Amy.'

'Oh, for God's sake, never mind about Amy!' Frank exploded. 'It's you I'm worried about!'

'Frank, are you going to do it for me or not?' Lizzie demanded. Her eyes were suddenly wide, and she seemed to be panting slightly. 'I'll have to go in myself if you won't.'

'Hey, hey, calm down, love.' Frank got up from his chair and stood behind her with his arms around her shoulders. 'I didn't mean to bite your head off like that. I'll do your message, don't worry.'

'You'd darned well better.'

'I just don't want you upsetting yourself, not when you're not feeling the best. I just about told that Millish girl off, coming around here bothering you like that.'

'The girl's got a good head on her shoulders, for all she's got some funny ways,' Lizzie said. 'I'm glad she had the sense to come and see me.'

'I suppose so,' Frank said. 'I might look in on Richard and Maudie while I'm in town, see how she's getting on.'

'Don't you say anything to them about me sicking up a bit,' Lizzie warned. 'I don't want Madam poking her nose in, making nasty little remarks about me being too old to have a baby. She'll have Richard out here nosing around if you're not careful.'

'I won't say a word.'

'Good. It's not as if I'm ill or anything,' Lizzie said with more confidence than Frank could muster. 'It's only ordinary old morning sickness.'

Amy dressed quickly by candlelight, then prepared a bowl of bread and milk to take through to Charlie. She had realised he found it a long wait for breakfast by the time she finished milking, so had taken to bringing something to him before she went out.

It also meant she could help him on to the chamber pot of a morning; he had grown more unsteady on his feet lately, and on a few mornings he had been too frightened to get out of bed by himself. That meant a wet bed and a distressed Charlie, both of which made extra work.

Charlie was already awake when she went in, and anxious to relieve himself. Afterwards Amy helped him back into bed, then sat beside him and fed him the bread and milk with a spoon.

She slipped a finger into his mouth to clear out the wad of food that had become trapped on one side of his jaw, then watched as he lay back against the pillows and closed his eyes, trying to decide whether or not she could risk upsetting him.

He seemed a little calmer than usual. And the subject could not be put off for ever.

'Charlie?' she said quietly.

'Mmm?' He answered without opening his eyes.

'I thought I might have a word with John when he comes over today.'

'What about?'

'The potatoes.'

His eyes opened, and he glared at her. 'None of his business. You keep your mouth shut about my potatoes.'

Amy pressed on. 'Charlie, I've got to. No, really I have, don't look at me like that. I went down and had a look at them yesterday, they're ready for harvesting. I don't think I can do it by myself, not all that great paddock full. I thought if I asked John—'

'No!' Charlie broke in. 'Don't tell him!'

'Him and Harry'll be doing their own any time. They could come over and do ours too, they wouldn't mind.'

'Don't tell him. Don't tell him I can't do my own.'

383

'I think I've got to,' Amy said as gently as she could.

'Don't,' Charlie said, his mouth trembling. 'Don't tell him.'

'Why not? All they'll do is—'

'They'll fetch you away,' Charlie said in mounting distress. 'They'll fetch you away home with them if they find out I can't provide for you any more.'

'Charlie, they wouldn't!' Amy protested.

'They will! They'll fetch you away from me.' He was shaking with the force of his distress, his good arm twitching violently.

'Don't get upset, please don't.' Amy put her hands on his shoulders until she felt the shuddering die down. 'My family's not like that. They'd be glad to help. I know Harry talks a lot of nonsense, but he's good-hearted underneath it all. Anyway, I wouldn't go.'

'I couldn't stop them if they wanted to fetch you away.'

'Maybe not, but I could.'

Charlie frowned at her in a puzzled way. 'Don't know why you don't clear out. Everyone else has buggered off.'

Amy knew he was thinking of their sons. She said nothing.

'I wouldn't have him back, you know,' Charlie said more vehemently. 'Not if he went down on his bended knees.'

'I know. And he wouldn't come back unless you begged him to. Not after what you two said to each other. There's no use dwelling on it.'

'He defied me,' Charlie said. 'He went off to fight the King of England's war. I'll not have him back under my roof. Not until he begs me.'

It was some time before he noticed Amy staring at him in surprise. His face screwed up in confusion. 'Went off and…' he muttered under his breath, then shook his head. It seemed the task of unraveling the memories of his living son and his dead one was too difficult. 'Don't know why you don't clear off too.'

Amy studied him as he slumped back against the pillows. 'How could I, Charlie?' she murmured. She smoothed the covers over him and stood up to go.

'What about the potatoes, then?' Charlie asked, startling her with his sudden burst of lucidity.

'I'll manage them somehow.' She did not dare upset him again by pressing the point.

'How?' Charlie insisted. 'How will you manage them?'

'I suppose I could do a few every night after I do the milking. I should be able to manage half a row. I think the lantern would be bright enough to do it by.'

'Take you a hell of a long time.'

'Yes, I suppose it will. But I'll just have to do my best, won't I? See if you can get back to sleep, it's very early yet.'

The grubby kitchen silently screamed its accusation of neglect as Amy went through it on her way outside. *Granny'd really have a go at me if she saw the state of this house.* 'Well, Granny, you didn't have fifteen cows to milk night and morning,' she murmured to herself.

She wished the potato paddock were not so clearly in sight as she walked down to get the cows in. The plants seemed to be taunting her with their rampant growth; jeering at her foolish suggestion of harvesting them by the light of a lantern. They would be rotting in the ground before she had done a quarter of them, she knew; and with them she would lose her only chance of a cash crop for the year. Her annuity would not keep the farm going for ever. But she could not bear the thought of bringing on another of Charlie's terrifying attacks by pushing him too far.

She was so used to milking now that she could do it without engaging her mind more than peripherally. Open the gate. Herd in the cows. Lead them into bails and tie them two at a time. Squeeze out the milk. Empty the buckets into cans. Release the two cows. Lead in the next two. Her body moved of its own accord, the cows joining in the rhythm, as expert in the dance as she was.

The shed was warm, and damp with the breath of the cows, and the milk made a swishing sound in the bottom of the buckets. Often Amy was so tired when she did the morning milking that it was like moving in a dream, and she would finish the job with no memory of having done it at all. But this morning her mind was painfully active, chewing futilely at the problem of the potatoes. What was she going to do about those potatoes?

The cows lowed softly, the sound varied by an occasional snort. For a moment Amy thought she heard a dog in the distance, but decided it must have been a cough from one of the cows. She rested her head against the flank of the beast she was milking. *Swish, swish,* went the milk in the bucket. *What am I going to do about those potatoes?* went her chafing thoughts.

She became aware of a restlessness about the cows; they milled about more, and their lowing took on a note of urgency. 'Steady, girl,' she murmured to the cow beside her. 'I know I'm slow, but you'll just have to be patient.'

The cow lifted her head and mooed loudly, and Amy gave a start at the noise. The cow was twisting her head around towards the open side of the milking shed. Amy sat up on her stool to follow the animal's gaze.

She was looking right into the sun, and her eyes were dazzled. A man was silhouetted against the light; a man so tall and powerfully built that for a moment she thought it was Charlie, until she remembered abruptly that Charlie could no longer even stand unaided, let alone walk all the way down to the cow shed to tower over the animals.

'You shouldn't be doing this by yourself,' the man said, the voice a little deeper than she remembered, but still instantly recognisable. 'Better let me do it for you.'

Amy leapt from her stool and ran to him, oblivious to the cows that snorted in fright at her sudden movement. She flung herself at him, and found herself lifted aloft and swung round and round then clasped so tightly that she could hardly breathe.

'Davie,' she gasped, uncertain whether she was laughing or crying. 'Davie!'

David lowered her carefully and looked down at her with both hands resting on her shoulders, a broad smile spreading across his face.

'I'm home, Ma.'

23

March 1905

Amy stared up into David's face with tears of joy streaming down her cheeks, vaguely aware of Biff nuzzling at her. 'I can't believe it,' she whispered. 'I can't believe you're back.'

'Well, I am.' He leaned down to kiss her on the mouth. 'Believe it now?'

'Oh, Davie.' For a moment her heart was too full for words, then they began pouring out. 'When did you get back? How did you know to come home? Have you been looking after yourself? Did you have breakfast?'

'Hey, slow down, Ma,' he said, lifting his hand to halt the flow. 'How about I tell you while I finish off this lot for you?'

Amy looked about her at the cows pressing towards them. 'Do you know, I'd forgotten all about them?' She gave a little laugh. 'Fancy forgetting about milking!'

'Come and sit down, then.' David slipped his arm around her and steered her towards the cows.

'I think you've got taller,' Amy said. 'I thought you'd stopped growing before you went away.'

'No, you've got smaller. I'd forgotten what a little thing you are.' He dropped his bundle of belongings in a corner of the shed. 'Sit there,' he told Amy, pulling an old crate towards them and wiping the top of it with his arm. 'Gee, this stool's low,' he said as he sat down beside her, his long legs folding an alarming amount.

'Let me help you with the milking—I can't just sit here and do nothing.'

'Yes, you can. You look all in, Ma. You look like you're ready to drop.'

'I am a bit tired,' Amy admitted. 'But I just about feel like I could dance a jig now you're here! Oh, Davie, I've missed you.'

'I've missed you too.' He looked around him, at the cows and beyond them to the paddocks. 'I've missed everything, really. The farm, and the animals. Aunt Lizzie telling everyone what to do. Beth and those kittens and things she's always patching up.' His eyes came back to Amy. 'But specially you.'

Amy slipped her arm through his and leaned against him, feeling the muscles of his arm swell as he reached out towards the cow's udder. 'Your curls are back,' she said, reaching out to touch the thick, black hair. 'Your hair's got so long.'

'It's all right,' David said, a touch defensively.

'It's lovely. I've missed your curls. I might give it a bit of a trim for you later, though, just to tidy it up.'

'I don't need a haircut,' David said quickly. 'I had it cut a while back. Hope I can still remember how to milk—it's been a long time.'

'You'll remember,' Amy said. 'Once you've learned it you never forget how to milk. It's just about like walking.'

The milk resumed its swish, swish into the bucket, and David smiled. 'You're right, Ma. I haven't forgotten.

'I got back last night,' he told her. 'Uncle Frank met me at the boat. He said I'd better stay the night with them, so they could tell me about you and everything.'

'Just think of you being right here in the valley last night and me not knowing!'

'Well, Aunt Lizzie said I'd need a good night's sleep before I came up here, in case there was any trouble with the old man. She wrote to me, you know. That's why I came home.'

'Sarah must have told her,' Amy mused. 'Fancy her thinking to tell Lizzie.'

'Is that Aunt Lily's cousin? Aunt Lizzie said last night that's who told her. Anyway, I got this letter from Aunt Lizzie a couple of weeks ago. She writes just how she talks, you know—like if you don't do what she says right now you'll get a sore backside. I just about walked out of the bunkhouse and went looking for a lift to Tauranga then and there.'

'Whatever did she tell you?'

'She said Pa was dying and you were killing yourself trying to do his work.'

'She shouldn't have said that! It wasn't that bad! Your father's not dying, he's just not very well. I would've told you myself if he'd been as ill as that.'

'Mmm, when I calmed down a bit I thought she might have made it sound worse than it was so I'd get off my backside and come home. There was an old fellow there I was a bit friendly with, he got me talking about it, and I got it all straight in my head. He said I'd be no use to you if I went out wandering after a lift in the middle of the night. It was pouring with rain, too,' David added, smiling ruefully at the memory.

'You might have caught your death! I'm going to tell your Aunt Lizzie off next time I see her, upsetting you like that.'

'I don't know, she said she's going to give you a telling off for not asking them to help you. I think I'd put my money on Aunt Lizzie if it came to telling off.' He tightened his grip on the teats, making the cow snort in alarm. 'I feel like telling you off myself, Ma, getting yourself in this state,' he said, giving Amy something of a stern look. 'Why didn't you tell me how things were? Why'd you go on writing that everything was all right?'

Amy leaned her head on his shoulder and wound one of his curls around her finger. 'I didn't want to worry you. And I thought I could manage, really I did. I kept thinking your father would get better.'

'You should have told me,' David insisted. 'Look at the state of you— you've got those awful dark rings under your eyes, and you look like you haven't had a decent feed in years. I was a lot more worried getting a letter like that from Aunt Lizzie than I would've been hearing from you.'

'He didn't want people to know he wasn't managing. He got in an awful state if I ever mentioned it. I didn't want to upset him—he gets quite ill if he's upset.'

'*Him,*' David said bitterly. 'I don't care what happens to him. It's you I'm bothered about.'

'I didn't know if you'd come back even if I did tell you, Davie. Not with what you and your father said to each other. And I knew I'd never get him to ask you.'

'You should know me better than that, Ma.' He abandoned his milking briefly to put an arm around her and hold her close. 'I'd have walked all the way home if I couldn't have got here any other way, once I knew you needed me.'

The shed that Amy had spent so many weary hours in over the last six months had been transformed into a place full of warm pleasure. She and David had long bursts of rapid conversation, trying to cram almost three years of separation into an hour or two, interspersed with periods of companionable silence.

'Finished,' David announced, standing up and straightening his back. 'It's better than digging for gold, anyway.'

He let the last of the cows out into the paddock and took up two large milk cans to carry to the house. 'Where's the old man?'

'Your father's still in bed. He hasn't really been getting up lately.'

'Lazy old bugger. What's wrong with him?'

Amy took his arm. 'You'll find your father very changed, Davie,' she said, anxious to prepare him as best she could.

'What, has he turned into a nice old fellow? That'd be a miracle.'

'Don't talk like that,' Amy said. 'You'll only feel bad when you see him.'

'I'd never feel bad about him,' David claimed, but Amy eyed him doubtfully. Harshness, she knew, had no part in David's nature.

She led him into the house, the milk cans abandoned outside for the moment. They halted by the bedroom door. 'Let me talk to him first,' she told David. 'I don't want him to get too much of a shock.'

Amy slipped into Charlie's room, leaving the door open but with David out of sight to one side of it. Charlie was propped up against the pillows, his eyes closed but his breathing too uneven for sleep.

'Charlie?' she said quietly.

'Mmm?' His eyes opened. 'What do you want?'

'I've got a surprise. Something lovely's happened.' She sat on the bed and took his hand. 'Dave's here, Charlie. David's come home.'

Charlie clutched at Amy's hand, his face clouded in confusion. Amy called to David, and followed Charlie's gaze as he stared at the tall figure who appeared in the doorway.

His expression changed to a scowl. 'Thought I told you to clear out of here. Told you to bugger off and not come back.'

She saw David stiffen. 'I didn't come back for your sake, that's for sure. I came back to sort things out for Ma. I heard you were leaving her to do all the work these days.'

'Shh, David!' Amy stood up and hurried across the room to him. 'Your father's not well,' she murmured. 'Please don't upset him.'

She took David's hand and tugged until he let himself be led across the room. 'You'll let Dave stay, won't you, Charlie?' She was aware of David's irritation at the pleading note in her voice, but she had to tread delicately to avoid a conflict that would be as pointless as it would be unpleasant. David was staying; of that she was certain. Charlie was no longer in a position to order his son from the house. But she had to let him pretend he had some choice in the matter.

Charlie looked down at the bedcovers. 'Aye, well, your ma could do with a hand around the place.' He raised his eyes to stare straight at David again. 'You can stay if you do a decent job helping her.'

Amy squeezed David's hand hard to forestall the retort she sensed rising in him. 'Of course he'll help me. Won't you, Dave?' Prompted by another squeeze of his hand, David gave a curt nod.

She let David make his escape from the room, knowing he and Charlie would gain little pleasure from each other's company. They were going to have to learn to get along, one way or another, but there was no sense in rushing things.

Amy could hardly bear to let David out of her sight, grudging even the time he spent fetching the rest of the milk cans up from the cow shed. She filled the void with busyness, and soon set to work making the sort of breakfast for which she had had neither the time nor the energy for many weeks, cooking up great helpings of bacon and eggs.

'Haven't had a bite of bacon for a while,' Charlie remarked, eyeing his plate in surprise. She had cut his bacon into small pieces, but even so it took her a long time to feed it to him, waiting for him to chew each morsel as well as he could manage before offering the next one. He was tired out by the effort of eating before he had made much impact on the plateful.

'Never mind, I'm sure Dave'll finish up yours as well as his own,' Amy told him as she cleaned out the wad of half-chewed bacon from a corner of his mouth. 'You know what boys are like for eating.'

'Got plenty for yourself?' Charlie asked, sinking back against the pillows.

'Tons of it. I've probably made far too much, but I don't want Dave to get hungry.'

'You'll be having yours with him, will you?'

'Well, yes, I will,' Amy said, surprised at the question.

Charlie turned his head away. 'Aye, I thought you would.'

He closed his eyes, and Amy left the room as quietly as she could, assuming that he had fallen asleep in the disconcertingly sudden way he sometimes had.

'I had a bit of a talk with Uncle John,' David said when he came in for his breakfast. 'He said to go over there sometime soon, tell him all about what I've been up to. It'll be good to see them all again. He didn't say much, but I could tell he got a bit of a start when I told him about Pa not getting out of bed any more, and you having to do all the work. He said he'll have a word with you about that later.'

'He'll tell me off, you mean,' Amy corrected, but she laughed as she said it. 'I'm lucky your Uncle John isn't one for making long speeches, aren't I? I thought you might have gone down to the factory with him.'

David gave her a look that was almost shy. 'He asked me if I wanted to, but I said I'd just as soon not. I told him I'd start taking our milk myself tomorrow, but for today... well, I'd rather stay home with you today, Ma.'

It was pure delight to have a meal with David, the two of them eager to share old memories as well as go on with catching up on the years spent apart. They lingered over their breakfast, both reluctant to end their time together, until Charlie ended it for them by calling out from the bedroom.

'I'm coming, Charlie,' Amy called back. 'He wants me to help him with something,' she told David, careful not to mention that it was probably help with getting onto the chamber pot.

'Time I made myself useful, anyway, instead of sitting around here all day. What do you reckon I should do first, Ma?'

'Perhaps you should talk to your father about what he thinks you should do,' Amy said cautiously.

'Don't see why I should ask him,' David said. 'He just lies around in bed all day.'

'He doesn't want to be like that, Davie. He'd love to be able to get out on the farm again.'

'I'm not talking to him any more than I have to.'

'He'd like you to ask him, you know.' But Amy knew it was useless even as she spoke. 'Well, never mind that just now. Let's see, there's the cows to move, I was going to put them in the paddock next to where the sheep are today. Then I think the best thing you could do is take a look at those potatoes.'

David pulled a face. 'Potatoes. Gee, I used to hate digging the potatoes.'

'I've been worrying for weeks how I was going to do them on my own.'

'You would've killed yourself trying,' David said. 'I'm only glad I got back in time to do them for you.'

'So am I, Davie,' Amy said fervently.

She hurried into Charlie's room, aware that she had kept him waiting longer than she should have. 'I'm sorry I was a bit slow, I got talking to Dave. Now, do you want me to help you out of bed?'

'Aye, I do. You can find me a pair of trousers, too.'

He met her startled gaze with a look of defiance. 'I'll be getting dressed today. I've had enough of lying in bed.'

'If you feel well enough to get up, that's good, Charlie,' Amy said carefully. 'But are you sure you want to get dressed? It'd be a lot of bother for you if you had to get your trousers undone in a hurry.'

'I don't want to sit about in my nightshirt all day,' Charlie said, his mouth quivering. 'I want to get dressed.'

Amy sighed. 'All right, then, if that's what you want. Do you want the pot first?'

He nodded. Amy helped him onto the chamber pot, then back onto the edge of the bed when he had finished. She searched through his drawers for a set of clothes and laid them out on the bed.

Charlie was already trembling with the effort of being dressed by the time Amy had his shirt on him. She had to stop and let him rest before she could attempt to haul on his trousers. When he seemed strong enough she put her arms under his armpits and heaved him upright, letting him lean on her for support as she drew the trousers up and fastened the buttons.

She helped him out to the kitchen, and to a seat at the table. Charlie seemed more alert than Amy had seen him for weeks, aroused by David's startling arrival, but she watched him anxiously, sure that he had over-exerted himself.

His eyelids were drooping by the time Amy had lunch ready, but he roused himself when David came in, sitting up more erect and fixing his son with a hard stare.

'What've you been up to this morning, boy?' he asked.

'Made a start on the spuds,' David mumbled, turning away from his father's gaze.

'Good. You see you make a decent job of it, now. I don't want those spuds ruined. The first thing to do is—'

'Soup smells good, Ma,' David said, interrupting Charlie's discourse. 'You want a hand?' He carried the bowls from the bench to the table and took the seat furthest from Charlie's.

Amy had become so used to feeding Charlie that she did it without thinking, and he opened his mouth for the offered spoonful with an equal lack of thought. He had taken several mouthfuls before he shut his mouth abruptly, his eyes narrowing as he glared down the table at David.

'What are you staring at?' he said.

'Nothing. I'm not staring at anything.'

'You watch yourself, boy,' Charlie growled. 'You needn't think I'll be stuck in the house for ever. I'll be back about my work before too long, then I'll see what sort of a job you're making of things.'

David dropped his gaze to his soup, apparently interested in nothing beyond demolishing the bowlful, but Amy saw him cast occasional furtive glances at his father.

Charlie snatched his spoon from Amy's hand and insisted on trying to feed himself. It was a messy business, with soup stains soon appearing on the front of his shirt. He glared at David over his soup bowl, clearly looking for something to find fault with; some way of reasserting the authority that his body's treacherous weakness had robbed him of.

'You could do with a haircut,' he announced.

David bridled at once. 'No, I couldn't,' he said, and for a moment Amy saw the frightened child of three looking through the eyes of the young man of nearly eighteen. 'I don't need a haircut.'

'It's a little bit long,' Amy said, anxious to intervene before either of them became too excited over so trivial a matter. 'I've already told Dave I'll give it a cut, Charlie, there's no need for you to worry about it.'

By the time they had finished their pudding and a cup of tea, Amy sensed Charlie's discomfort, noting how he was squirming on his chair. Without bothering to ask if he wanted help, she offered her arm and got him up, then took him into the bedroom.

'Hurry up,' he said urgently as Amy undid his trouser buttons. He made the task more awkward by trying to use his good hand to help with the buttons, succeeding only in getting in Amy's way.

She almost managed to get him onto the chamber pot in time. 'You can't stay in those wet trousers,' she said as she helped him stand up again. 'Do you want me to get you another pair? Or would you rather have a lie-down after that big lunch?' she prompted. Much to her relief, Charlie let her undress him and put him to bed.

David was still in the kitchen, looking a little dazed by what he had seen over lunch.

'What's wrong with him, Ma?' he demanded as soon as Amy came in. 'I didn't know he was that bad when I saw him lying in bed. Why can't he walk by himself or use that arm? He can't even feed himself properly.'

Amy sat down beside him at the table. 'I don't know, Davie. I just don't know. It's like he's got really, really old suddenly, but it's not that.'

She poured them another cup of tea. 'At first we thought he'd had a fall and hurt himself, and he was just taking a long time getting better. But he never did get better. He's getting worse and worse. There's things he could do a few months ago that he can't do now.'

'Hasn't made him any better tempered, anyway. Grumpy old so-and-so.'

'I think it has, you know,' Amy corrected him. 'He takes a lot of looking after these days, but... you'll laugh at me saying this, but he's a lot easier to get on with than he used to be.'

'So he jolly well should be, having you waiting on him hand and foot, and doing all his work for him as well! What were you doing, trying to manage everything by yourself? Why didn't you get Uncle John and Uncle Harry to help you?'

'I thought it'd only be for a few days, then I thought maybe a week or two. Your father was so worried about anyone finding out that he couldn't do his work, it seemed the right thing to do to keep it quiet. And by the time I started understanding that he wasn't ever going to get better... well, I'd got used to doing things. He got in such a state if I ever said I should tell your Uncle John, and I couldn't bear to upset him. Not when he's got all that to put up with.'

'That old bugger would've worked you to death just so's he wouldn't be shown up. You're too soft, Ma.'

'Maybe I am,' Amy allowed. 'But it's just the way I'm made. And don't call your father names like that. It's not right.'

'Neither is how he's always treated you,' David said darkly.

After the embarrassment of having David watch him being spoon-fed, Charlie did not ask to get up for the evening meal. Amy fed him in bed before having her own meal with David. But when she went to tuck him in for the night he showed no inclination to settle, instead insisting that she help him out of bed and through to the kitchen. He did not want to be left out of things, and she could not blame him, though she would rather have had the time alone with David.

'Might have a drink tonight,' Charlie said. 'You can get me a drop of whisky.'

'It's a good excuse to celebrate, isn't it?' Amy said, moving to fetch the bottle and a glass. 'Having Dave come home like this.'

'As long as he makes himself useful around the place.' Charlie regarded the small amount of whisky in the bottom of his glass, frowning as though thinking out a puzzle. 'Give the boy a drink, too,' he announced.

Amy knew how generous an offer it was on Charlie's part. She watched David, unsure just how she wanted him to respond.

'No, thanks,' he said carelessly.

Charlie regarded him in stunned disbelief. 'What do you mean? I offer you a good drop of whisky and you don't want it?'

'No. I don't drink.'

'What sort of womanish notion is that? What's wrong with you?'

'Nothing's wrong with me,' David said, his voice hardening. 'I've never seen any good come out of guzzling booze, so I don't do it.'

Charlie seemed to shrink back in his chair under David's grim stare. 'Bloody fool notion,' he muttered under his breath.

Amy felt a warm rush of pride in David; she could only guess at how hard it must have been for him to have kept his childhood promise never to drink alcohol once he was living in a town full of hard-drinking men. But her pride was mingled with regret that Charlie should have had his offer rejected. Benevolent gestures did not come easily to Charlie.

Charlie retreated into silence, but his presence had a dampening effect on the conversation. His eyes swivelled from Amy to David as they spoke about such innocuous topics as Maudie's wedding, Harry and Jane's youngest child, and other family events David had missed. Once or twice Amy thought Charlie might have been about to say something, but he did not speak quickly enough and the moment passed.

Even when Amy had finished her work in the kitchen and they went through to the parlour, Charlie showed no desire to go to bed. He had not sat up so late for months. Amy put a three-day-old newspaper on his lap, and he pretended to read it, although no pages were turned. Several times she saw his head droop forward so far that his chin almost rested on his chest before it was abruptly jerked upright again.

At last he nodded off long enough for a short burst of snoring to escape him, waking himself up in the process.

'Would you like to go to bed, Charlie?' Amy asked. 'It's quite late, really.'

She watched him thinking it over. 'Aye, I'll go off now,' he said. Amy helped him up, and he had taken a hesitant step before he caught David's eyes on him.

'Time you went to bed, boy,' Charlie said. 'You'll be up early tomorrow.'

David shrugged. 'I'll go in a while. I might sit up a bit longer yet.'

Amy felt Charlie stiffen against her. 'Didn't you hear me?' he said in a low growl. 'I told you to go to bed.'

'I'll go when I'm ready.' David kept his voice low, but there was a challenge in it that Amy knew Charlie must have heard as clearly as she had. 'I don't need to be told.' His eyes locked with Charlie's.

Amy broke the moment. 'Well, *I'm* ready for bed,' she said, her voice sounding foolishly light in her own ears. 'Such a day it's been, with you coming home! I wish you would go to bed, Dave, we're low on kerosene and I'd rather not run that lamp out of it tonight.'

David turned his gaze away from Charlie. 'All right,' he mumbled. 'S'pose I am a bit tired, come to that. I didn't get much sleep last night. See you in the morning, then.' He got up from his chair, stretched, and moved towards the front door. When he glanced back at Amy, she met his eyes and sent him a silent message of thanks.

She caught herself trying to hurry through settling Charlie for the night, and felt a rush of guilt as she looked down at the frail creature in the bed. He had no one to look after him except her; she shouldn't begrudge the time she spent on him.

He stared up at her. 'You want to go out there and see your boy again, don't you?' It was half accusation, half pleading.

'Dave's gone to bed, just like you told him to.' She brushed a wisp of grey hair away from his forehead. 'You've overdone it a bit tonight, haven't you? You look tired.'

'I've no reason to be tired. Just lying in bed all day. No use to anyone.'

'Don't talk like that, Charlie, you'll only upset yourself. Dave's home now, so you can have a rest without feeling bad.'

She pulled the chair closer to the bed and sat down. 'Shall I stay here for a while? Just until you start feeling sleepy.'

'Suit yourself,' he said brusquely, but the plea in his eyes was clear enough. Amy leaned across to smooth the covers, then sat beside him in silence until she was sure he was asleep.

The parlour was in darkness when she crept out of Charlie's room, but Amy knew her way by memory. The front door creaked a little as she slid it open and pulled it closed behind her.

A sliver of light showed under David's door. 'Davie?' she said quietly. 'Can I come in?'

She heard his rapid footsteps. The door opened to reveal the small room lit by candlelight, with David almost filling the doorway. He stepped back, taking Amy's arm and drawing her in after him. Biff was lying on the floor beside the bed, thumping his tail at the sight of Amy. 'I hoped you'd come, Ma,' David whispered. 'I'd just about given up.'

'I had to settle your father down first—it was a bit much for him, all the excitement. I knew I wouldn't get to sleep if I didn't come and see you before I go to bed, though.'

'Pity he had to hang around all night.'

'He felt a bit left out, I think, with you and me talking around him. He doesn't usually want to stay up that late.'

'He just likes spoiling things.' David flopped onto his bed, his back against the wall and his long legs folded in front of him. Amy sat beside him and nestled into the crook of his arm.

'I'd better not keep you up too long,' she murmured. 'You do have to be up early tomorrow, you know.'

'I know. Stay a bit longer, though, Ma. I don't feel sleepy yet.'

'Neither do I.' Amy studied the effect of the flickering candlelight on his dark hair, and the play of light and shadows it made across his face, and she felt that she could sit there watching him for the rest of her life.

She was reluctant to spoil the moment, but she could not hide from her worries for long. 'Davie, I hope you're going to try and get on with your father.'

'I don't care a damn about him.'

'I'm not asking you to like him, just to try and get on with him. Try and think how it is for him—hardly able to get out of bed, or do anything for himself.'

'He's still a grumpy old so-and-so like he's always been.'

'He's not really, you know. He was a bit funny with you because it was such a shock seeing you again, especially with you and him having that awful fight before you went. And now you've come back bigger and stronger than ever, and he's got old and frail. He's... I think he's a little bit scared of you. Don't make him more scared. Try and be a bit nice to him.'

'I'm not going to pretend I like him.' David saw the look she sent him, and grimaced. 'I don't want him to be scared of me, though. There's no sense in that. Oh, all right, I'll try and get on with the old so-and-so.'

Amy pressed more closely against him. 'That's my good boy. I knew you'd do the right thing.'

'Funny, really, what he said this morning,' David mused. 'He said he wanted me to help you. It was just about the first thing he said. He never used to care about what you had to do.'

'He's changed a lot, Davie, he really has.'

'Maybe he has.' David yawned, remembering to put his hand over his mouth half way through.

'You're tired, aren't you, darling? I'd better let you go to bed.'

'I suppose so.' David held her more tightly. 'It's going to be funny, sleeping by myself. I've got used to a room full of fellows.'

'Remember how you used to sneak into my room sometimes when you were little?'

'Mmm.' David grinned at her. 'If I woke up feeling crook or miserable. I used to be scared the old man would find out, but I'd do it anyway. You always made it better.'

'You've got a bit too big for that.' The idea of curling up with David all night was deliciously tempting, but it would be wrong now that he had grown into a man.

'Big enough to look after you properly. You go and get some sleep, Ma. You can have a lie in tomorrow.'

'I'll make sure I'm up before you, so you can have a bite to eat before you go milking.'

'You don't need to, I could get something for myself.'

'I *want* to.' She wound her arms around his neck. 'I don't want to be away from you any longer than I have to. I thought I'd lost you, Davie. I thought I'd never see you again.'

'I'm not that easy to get rid of.' He yawned again.

Amy kissed him on the mouth. 'Good night. Sleep well.'

She disentangled herself from his arms and stood beside the bed for a moment, taking a last look at him. 'Thank you for coming home, Davie,' she whispered before she slipped from the room.

Over the next few days Amy had to put up with more scoldings than she had in years. John and Harry both came over to chide her soundly for not having told them what had been going on, and Lizzie managed to talk Frank into driving her up to visit Amy so that she could add a reproof of her own.

Despite her best efforts to appear suitably contrite, Amy found herself laughing at all her scolders. Nothing could upset her for long, not now that she had David back. It was only Lizzie who spoiled her composure, and that was from the unexpected mildness of her cousin's harangue.

'Are you all right, Lizzie?' Amy asked. 'You don't quite seem yourself today.'

'Oh, don't you start,' Lizzie snapped. 'I've got enough to put up with, what with Frank hanging around me like an old mother hen. I'm perfectly all right, I just had a restless night, that's all. It was so hot last night, I kept waking up in a sweat.'

'It wasn't as hot as all that,' Amy said in surprise. 'I had two blankets on.'

'Well, *I* was hot,' Lizzie said. 'I can't speak for the rest of the world.'

'Are you keeping well? You look tired.'

Lizzie glared at her. 'Of course I'm keeping well. I've always done so well having the babies, you know that. Don't talk rubbish.'

Amy abandoned the futile attempt at giving Lizzie advice. 'You take good care of her, Frank,' she said when she went out to see Lizzie off. 'She's not looking herself.'

'Don't you encourage him,' Lizzie grumbled. 'He's bad enough without you making him worse. You two are as bad as each other.'

Amy caught Frank's eye and they shared a smile, though Amy thought she saw a hint of concern in Frank's. Still, she reflected, it was true enough what Lizzie said: she had never found pregnancy much of a problem.

David threw himself into the work of the farm. As soon as the potatoes were safely harvested he began catching up on all the tasks Amy had had to leave undone, ranging from one end of the property to the other mending fences, digging new drains, and pulling weeds from the cleared areas. He seemed able to work all day and barely look tired by sundown, his youth and strength more than equal to the task.

Released from the farm work, Amy steadily worked through every room of the house, making good all the unavoidable neglect of the months since Charlie had become ill. She washed and scrubbed and dusted. Every dish in the kitchen was lifted from its place and given a thorough scouring, the floor was scrubbed till the wood was pale, and all the bedding was carefully aired. For the first time in months, she could look around her without being stung by shame.

And for the first time in months she could tend to her own appearance. Baths were no longer too laborious to be attempted more than once a month; with David to haul the water, they could indulge in the luxury of a weekly bath. Instead of having the state of her clothing vary only between mildly grubby after a cursory wash day and outright filthy from the farm work, she now had clean, sweet-smelling and neatly ironed clothes to wear. Her hair, instead of being an unwashed tangle hurriedly pinned up each morning, half of the pins giving up the unequal struggle before the day was over, was as soft, shiny and neat as she could have wished.

The rousing effect wrought on Charlie by the shock of David's return did not last long; he soon retreated to his room again, not emerging unless Amy coaxed him out to sit with her and David for a half hour or so. She did not like to leave Charlie in his room by himself all day, discarded and forgotten.

'It's good for him to have a bit of company,' Amy said when David complained half-heartedly about his father's brooding presence. 'He doesn't do any harm.'

'He doesn't do any good, either, sitting there scowling at everyone.'

'Well, he can't think of things to say, that's all. He gets a bit muddled in the head sometimes, remember. It'll only be for a little while, you know he can't sit up very long.'

But Amy could not deny that she gained far more pleasure from the times when she and David were alone together, with no Charlie to make Amy anxious and David unnaturally stiff. Those were the times she delighted in, whether spent chatting and laughing over their meals or whispering together in the parlour or in David's room after she had settled Charlie for the night.

They were lingering over their afternoon tea one day soon after David's return, so engrossed in their conversation that they did not hear the approaching rider until the sound of a horse's snort close to the house caught their attention.

Amy went to the door and down the steps, just in time to see Sarah Millish appear at the gate.

'Sarah!' she said in delight, running to take the young woman by the hand. 'I'm so glad you've come!'

'I rather thought you might want to berate me for interfering in your affairs,' Sarah said. 'Though if you'd wanted an apology you'd have been sadly disappointed—I've no regrets over letting Mrs Kelly in on your secret. But I had to assure myself that things are in a satisfactory state now.'

She studied Amy, taking in her pretty dress of flowered cotton, clean on that morning, and the heavy mass of hair carefully pinned above her face. 'Obviously they are. It seems I've done some good.'

'You did the best thing in the world. You got Davie back for me. Oh, you must meet him, Sarah!'

Amy tugged Sarah's hand, pulling her up the steps to the back door, but Sarah stopped in the doorway and would not be moved. Perhaps she was shy, Amy thought, though it was not a quality she had associated with Sarah before.

'Dave, come and meet my friend,' she said. David stood up and came across the room to join them. His arm rested easily across Amy's shoulders. She slipped her own arm around his waist and leaned against him.

'This is David, Sarah,' she said, her voice resonant with love and pride. 'This is my son.'

Amy was startled by Sarah's reaction. Her expression hardened and she fixed David with a stern gaze, until Amy felt him stiffen against her, clearly discomforted.

'So you decided to come home at last, Mr Stewart,' Sarah said. 'I hope you're taking some care of your mother after leaving her to manage on her own all this time.'

'I… yes, I think I am,' David said uncertainly.

'Of course you are!' Amy said. 'I don't know how I ever managed without you. Oh, Sarah, do come in and have a cup of tea with us. I'd love you to get to know Dave properly.' She was firmly convinced that no one with an ounce of sense could know David for any length of time without loving him.

'No, I won't,' Sarah said. 'You don't need my company, I can see that.'

Amy was interrupted before she had a chance to protest. 'Amy?' It was Charlie's voice coming from the bedroom; Amy always left the intervening doors open in case he needed her suddenly. 'Who's out there? I heard a horse.' There was a quaver of distress in his voice.

'Don't worry, Charlie, it's only a friend come to visit,' she called back.

'It's not that policeman, is it? He's not come about the boy?'

'No, nothing like that. It's just Lily's cousin, Miss Millish. I'll come and tell you about it in a minute.'

She waited a moment, but Charlie did not call out again, apparently pacified by her answer. 'He gets a bit muddled sometimes,' she explained, as much for David's benefit as for Sarah's. 'He slips back a few years and forgets what's happened in between. He's thinking about

Mal—that was our other son. Do come in, Sarah, you can keep Dave company while I settle Mr Stewart down. You'd like that, wouldn't you, Dave?'

'Ah… yes,' David said doubtfully.

'I've no desire to come into your house with *him* here,' Sarah said, casting a resentful glance in the direction Charlie's voice had come from. 'No, I shan't waste any more of your time. I wanted to see if things were well with you, and I've done that. You obviously don't need anything else from me. Good day to you, Mr Stewart,' she said coolly to David, giving him a cursory nod.

Amy extricated herself from David's encircling arm, ran down the steps and caught hold of Sarah's sleeve as the younger woman moved away. 'Please don't go, Sarah. I thought you and Dave could be friends.'

Sarah looked up at David, who was standing at the top of the steps appearing uncertain whether he should add his voice to his mother's or slink away from Sarah's disconcertingly direct stare. 'He's very like you, isn't he?' Sarah said, her voice suddenly pensive. 'It's quite a startling likeness.'

She turned her gaze back on Amy. 'Come out with me,' she said, taking Amy aback with the unexpectedness of the request. 'Come and visit Lily.'

'I can't, Sarah.'

'Why not? You've no need even to saddle up—my mount would hardly notice the extra weight of a little thing like you. We could talk on the way.'

'I'm sorry, I just can't. I can't really leave Mr Stewart, you see.'

'Couldn't *he* look after his father for an hour or so?' Sarah asked, casting a disapproving look in David's direction.

'I… I don't like to leave him,' Amy said lamely. She could not tell Sarah that Charlie would be frightened to be left alone with his son; nor that she was unwilling to ask David to give his father the sort of delicate assistance Charlie now needed.

'Really?' Sarah looked over Amy's head to meet David's eyes and hold them with her own. 'I do hope you do something other than sit around the house all day, Mr Stewart,' she said, raising her voice slightly to be sure David would hear. 'I would have thought one man under her feet was more than enough for your mother.'

'You will come and see me again, won't you, Sarah?' Amy asked.

The stiff formality Sarah seemed to be striving for was marred by an odd fragility; as if she might even give way to tears if she let her rigid self-control slacken. 'I really don't see how I can. And I fail to see what you might need from me now.'

'I want to be able to talk about books and things. I want someone to make me really think.' Amy put a hesitant hand on Sarah's arm. 'I want you to be my friend.'

Sarah allowed her stiff manner to relax slightly, and even managed a small smile. 'I want those things, too. Those things and more. We shall have to find some way of achieving that, Amy. Mrs Stewart,' she corrected herself.

David came up behind Amy when Sarah had moved away, resting his arms lightly on her shoulders.

'What'd I say wrong, Ma?' he asked. 'Boy, she seemed to have it in for me.'

Amy turned to face him, slipping her arms around his waist. 'You didn't say anything wrong. Sarah's... well, I've never seen her quite like that, but some people find her a bit hard to get on with.'

'I'll bet they do,' David said with feeling. 'When she tells you off you really feel told off. And she's got that way of looking at you—she's sort of like Aunt Susannah, you know.'

'She is not!' Amy protested. 'She's not a bit like Susannah.'

'Well, there's something about her. It might be just the way she makes you feel a bit small.'

'Your Uncle Frank thinks it's because she's a teacher. Maybe it makes her a little bit bossy.'

'A teacher!' David pulled a face. 'Yes, I suppose that's why she's so scary. Must have made me think of old Miss Metcalf.'

He stared thoughtfully in the direction Sarah had gone. 'She's a lot better looking than Miss Metcalf, though. Better looking than Aunt Susannah, too.'

'I should think so!' Amy studied David's expression. 'Do you think she's pretty?'

'I suppose she is a bit.' He grinned down at Amy. 'Not as pretty as you are.'

'You mustn't tease me, Davie,' Amy said, laughing. 'I'm too old to be pretty. Would you like to get to know Sarah better?'

David grimaced. 'Don't know about that. I think she might put me off my meals, telling me off all the time.'

'Your Aunt Lizzie's got an idea that Sarah doesn't like men. She's certainly got no time for your father.'

'Neither has anyone else,' David said sourly. 'That doesn't mean there's anything wrong with her. Did I hear her ask you to go out with her, Ma?'

'Yes, she did,' Amy admitted. 'She wanted me to go up and see Aunt Lily with her.'

'Why didn't you go?'

'I can't leave your father, Dave, you know that.'

'You can if you want to. I wouldn't mind looking after the old bugger to give you a break.'

Amy sighed. 'You can't even talk about him without calling him names. You can't expect me to leave him with you when you won't show him a little bit of respect.'

'He doesn't deserve any respect.'

'Maybe he doesn't. But he needs it just the same. If I left him with you he'd go getting upset, and he might even make himself ill. Never mind, don't let's talk about it. I'll see Sarah another time.'

'Is she going to come and visit you again, then? I'll make sure I'm out of the way if she does.'

'I wouldn't worry, Davie,' Amy said, smiling ruefully. 'I don't think she'll come again in a hurry.'

She slipped reluctantly out of David's embrace. 'I'd better go and see how your father is.'

24

May – July 1905

From the paddock where he and the boys were working, Frank could see Danny near the house talking to a small boy on a large horse.

The conversation did not last long; the boy wheeled his horse around and set off at a trot, while Danny ambled back up to his father and brothers.

'What'd that boy want, Danny?' Frank asked.

'He had a message from Richard. Do you know what? Richard gave him a shilling just for riding out here!' Danny said, his eyes large with the magnitude of the sum. 'A whole shilling!'

'Well, what was the message?'

'Eh? Oh, he said Maudie's had a baby,' Danny said, his off-hand tone showing how little interest the news held for him.

'She's had it? Well, how is she, then? Is she all right? Is it a boy or a girl?'

Danny shrugged. 'Dunno. Fancy getting a shilling just for riding out here.'

'The boy must've said more than just that she's had the baby, Danny! Richard would've told him more than that.'

Danny shrugged again and looked blank. 'I didn't know she was having a baby.'

'Well, you can go and tell your ma the message,' Frank said. 'She'll go crook at you for not getting it all straight, mind you. Tell her I'll be down shortly for my morning tea. I'll let her finish having a go at you first.'

'Do I have to, Pa?' Danny asked, a dim awareness of how he might have been remiss showing in his eyes.

'Yes, you do. Get it over with, Danny, that's usually the best way.'

When Frank arrived in the kitchen a few minutes later with the two older boys, he found Danny backed into a corner of the room with Lizzie, Maisie and Beth all confronting him, varying degrees of aggression in their faces.

'He must have told you something more than that,' Lizzie said. 'Richard wouldn't have sent a silly message like that, not saying anything about the baby.'

'Fancy not asking the boy, Danny,' Beth said, pursing her lips in disapproval. 'And not asking him if Maudie's well or anything.'

'Didn't that boy say *anything* about the baby?' Maisie pressed.

'Of course he did,' Lizzie said. 'Danny was just too stupid to remember it properly. I've a good mind to give you a belt, Daniel Kelly.'

'He might… he might have said it was a girl.'

'Yes, and he might have said it was a calf or a lamb for all the notice you took,' Lizzie snapped. 'Don't you go trying to slide out of it now, making things up.'

'I'm not making it up,' Danny protested. 'I remember he said Richard gave him a shilling, anyway. A whole shilling just for—'

'And you'll get a clip over the ear if you say that once more,' Lizzie interrupted. 'You might get one anyway.'

'Hang on, I've remembered,' Danny said, his voice rising to a squeak. 'He said—hang on, I'll get it straight in a minute. He said, "Doctor Townsend said to tell you Mrs Townsend has a fine little daughter and they're both in the best of health". That's what he said, that's just the right words. He said it like he'd learned it for a lesson.'

'Then he's obviously got more brains than you have,' Lizzie said. 'Not that that's saying much.'

She turned away from Danny and sat down heavily at the table, not responding when Frank took the seat next to her and placed his hand over hers.

'That's good news about Maudie, isn't it?' Frank said, a certain forced brightness in his voice. He longed to see an answering brightness in Lizzie's face.

'Mmm.' Lizzie barely glanced at Danny as he made his escape from the room with every sign of relief, giving the lie to the menace she had directed at him a few moments before.

That seemed to be the pattern of Lizzie's moods lately: a fit of bad temper followed by apathy. Lizzie's justice, though unfailingly strict, was for the most part reluctantly acknowledged as fair by her children, but outbursts of bad temper were something new and unwelcome. Frank was sure he had sometimes caught a shadow of pain flitting across Lizzie's face before these moods, but she always denied it fiercely if he risked asking.

'Would you like to go in and see her this morning?' Frank prompted. 'We can leave it till this afternoon if you like, if you're feeling a bit tired just now.'

Lizzie's reaction startled him. 'I can't go in. You know that perfectly well.'

'But… but you want to go and see them, don't you?' Aware of the close interest the girls were paying to their conversation, he tilted his head closer to Lizzie's ear so that he could speak more quietly. 'I mean, I know you're not going into town any more these days, but this is a bit special, eh? You could wrap up warm and no one would see what shape you are.'

'I'm not going to go parading myself around the town.'

'There's no need to do that. Just straight in to Richard's and out again, that's all. It might cheer you up a bit.'

'I don't need cheering up,' Lizzie said, scowling at him. 'There's nothing wrong with me.'

'No, no, I know there's not,' Frank said quickly. 'But Maudie'll expect you to come in, love.'

'Oh, too bad about her. Stop nagging me, for goodness sake, Frank. You go in yourself, get out from under my feet. Then you can tell me how they all are,' she added, letting her unconvincing mask of hardness slip for a moment.

'I'll leave it till this afternoon,' Frank said. 'You might've changed your mind by then.'

She did not, of course. One thing that had not altered about Lizzie was her reluctance to change her mind. Frank had to admit defeat and set off without her that afternoon, though he did not go alone. Beth begged to be allowed to go with him, and once he had checked that Lizzie could spare her, Frank welcomed the company.

Beth was never noisy, but she seemed unusually quiet as they rode along. Frank noticed a suspicious redness in her eyes; noticed, too, the red mark on one cheek.

'What's wrong, love?' he asked. 'You don't seem too bright.'

Beth shrugged. 'I had a row with Ma. I didn't mean to,' she said, a plea for understanding plain in her eyes. 'I don't know what I said wrong.'

'It's all right, you probably didn't say anything wrong. Your ma's just a bit tired, that's all.'

'She slapped me,' Beth said in a small voice.

'I don't suppose she meant to. Try and keep out of her way when she gets in a mood like that.'

'Don't see how I can,' Beth murmured.

Richard greeted them at the door, signs of weariness around his eyes but a look of quiet wonder in his face.

'Come and see my beautiful girls,' he said, hurrying Frank and Beth through the house. 'You've timed it perfectly—they're both awake, though Maudie's looking rather sleepy. You two will liven her up, I'm sure.'

Maudie was sitting propped up against the pillows, her arms curved protectively around the tiny baby she held. She looked up at their approach, her eyes alight with the excitement of her new state.

'Look at her,' she said. 'Isn't she beautiful?'

Frank and Beth hovered over Maudie and the baby, making suitably appreciative noises. To Frank the baby looked much like any other, special only because it was Maudie's, but that was reason enough to make a fuss over it.

'We're going to call her Lucy,' Maudie said. 'We've had that name picked out for ages. She's so lovely, I had to be sure I had a pretty name for her. She looks like Richard, don't you think?'

'Oh, I hope not,' Richard protested laughingly. 'I'd much rather she looked like her beautiful mother. What do you think, Frank? You're the only one of us who knew Maudie at the same age.'

Frank's thoughts went back to the sight of Lizzie holding the newborn Maudie in her arms, the same delight shining out of her eyes. He wished fervently that Lizzie's pregnancy was safely over, the child something for her to enjoy instead of a creature that seemed to be causing her nothing but discomfort.

'She's sure to take after Maudie,' he said, realising that some answer was required of him. 'She'll probably have a bit of you in her too, though, Richard.'

'I hope she has Richard's curls,' Maudie said. She took her eyes from her baby for a moment to look beyond Frank. 'Where's Ma?' she asked, a slight frown marring her smooth forehead.

'She didn't come, love.' Frank winced at the sight of Maudie's face hardening at his admission. 'She was a bit tired today. She might come another day,' he said, knowing how feeble that was as a sop. 'She sent her love, though.' No, she hadn't, he realised as he said it. Lizzie had been in one of her frighteningly quiet moods when he had left, and she had sent no message at all.

'I thought she'd come,' Maudie said, hurt and bewilderment clear in her voice. 'I thought she'd want to see her own grandchild.'

'You can come out and see us soon,' Frank said. 'Once you're up and about again.'

'Maybe,' Maudie said in a clipped tone. 'Richard, I think I might give Lucy your mother's name for her second name,' she said, as if the matter were of only slight interest to her. 'Lucy Caroline sounds quite nice, doesn't it?'

Richard shot a brief glance at Frank before answering. 'If that's what you want, darling,' he said carefully.

Frank and Richard left the sisters to carry on fussing over the new baby, while they went out into the parlour for a celebratory drink.

'Maudie looks well, Richard—she seems to be getting over it quickly. Did everything go all right?'

Richard stared over the top of his glass into the unseen distance, a soft smile playing about his lips. 'Maudie was… magnificent. There's no other word for her. To think I've had the cheek to accuse her of being childish at times—only when we've had the very occasional disagreement,' he added hastily, and Frank nodded sagely.

'I'll never dare call her such a thing again,' Richard went on. 'I very much doubt if I've her courage. Pity your poor daughter, Frank,' he said, smiling ruefully at him. 'It's no easy thing, having a doctor for a husband.

'She went into labour yesterday morning. She was so excited about it, every time she had a twinge her face lit up and she practically danced around the room. She's a funny little thing at times. Well, I put the sign up on the gate saying I was unavailable, talked Maudie into taking things a little more quietly, and we set ourselves to waiting.'

'Takes a while, doesn't it, with the first one.'

'Yes, it does. As I said, Frank, pity your daughter. Chloroform is a wonderful substance, but I've seen far too many babies born barely conscious and struggling for breath from the midwife's being too generous with it. I explained that to Maudie as well as I could, and told her that if she thought she could bear it I'd like to avoid giving her any till well on in the labour. I did stress that I didn't want her to suffer unnecessarily, but I'd just like to minimise the use of the drug.

'Maudie sat there looking at me, her eyes huge with the excitement of it all, nodding wisely at everything I said. And she certainly took me at my word. The trouble with theories, Frank, is that often when one comes to put them into practice they don't seem quite so fine. Especially when they relate to someone you happen to love dearly. As soon as Maudie's pains were strong enough to make her cry out, I rushed for the bottle of chloroform and offered it to her.'

'I would've, too,' Frank said.

'Maudie was having none of it, though. She sat there clutching at her stomach and shaking her head at me. You know what she said? "It's not as bad as getting a hiding from Ma, and I've put up with plenty of those. I want to do what's best for the baby." She must have had some fierce sessions with her mother if it was true,' Richard added, frowning slightly.

'They've had some bad set-tos over the years,' Frank admitted. 'Especially when Maudie really started getting a mind of her own.'

'I suspect that my wife was born with a mind of her own,' Richard said with a wry smile. 'I put her to bed a little after sunset, when I could see that things were progressing more rapidly. Do you know, she kept on refusing the chloroform almost until the end? It was only when the baby's head was quite visible that Maudie said, "It's worse than a hiding now, Richard."

'She let me take the pain away then, thank goodness—I was beginning to think I'd have to force it on her.' He sat back in his chair and smiled dreamily. 'Then it was just the baby and I, working together. It's quite an experience, Frank, bringing my own child into the world. I had no idea it would feel like that.'

'You're lucky to be able to,' Frank said, remembering being unceremoniously banished from the bedroom when Lizzie was in labour.

'I know I am. I think I'm the most fortunate man that ever lived, and I'm savouring every moment of it. I'll arrange for a nurse to come in from tomorrow, so that Maudie can be suitably fussed over, but I told her that I wanted to be her nurse and do everything for her just for the first day.'

He laughed softly. 'Do you know, I don't think I slept at all last night? What with checking on Maudie to see that she was resting comfortably, and looking at that baby of ours every few minutes, the night had slipped away before I'd quite realised.'

'I wish they'd let me stay with Lizzie.'

'Ah. Lizzie.' Richard's voice lost all trace of its dreamy tone. 'It's a pity Lizzie was unable to come today,' he said carefully. 'I'm afraid Maudie's rather hurt over it.'

'I know she is,' Frank said distractedly. 'Lizzie was a bit tired today…'

He trailed off, sick of the lie. Lizzie was more than merely tired.

'I'm worried about Lizzie. She's not well.'

Richard looked startled. He studied Frank's face closely. 'Frank, I'm terribly sorry. I've been too full of my own thoughts even to notice how anxious you are. Whatever's wrong?'

Frank sighed. 'I don't know. I wish I did. It just doesn't seem to be going right for her this time.'

'She's not still getting morning sickness, is she?'

Frank shook his head. 'No, she stopped that in the end, thank God. She had it much worse than she's ever had it before—you'd have thought she was going to heave her whole guts out some mornings.'

'What seems to be the problem, then?'

'I can't get her to tell me, that's the trouble,' Frank burst out. 'I know things aren't right with her, but she won't admit it. Whenever I ask her, she says everything's just fine, and she keeps saying how well she's always done before.' He grimaced. 'It makes it worse when she says that.'

'How do you mean, Frank?'

'Well, whenever she says it, I think that's right, she's had seven babies, and everything's gone well for her. It makes me feel like we're... I don't know, like we're tempting fate having another one. Like maybe this'll be the time things don't go well.'

'There's no reason to think like that,' Richard said. 'The fact that Lizzie's always taken childbearing so well must be seen as a good sign.'

'I know it sounds dopey. It's just what I keep thinking all the time. Things hurt her, I can tell they do, but she won't admit it. She goes all quiet sometimes, and that's not like Lizzie. I've seen her holding her head when she thinks I'm not watching, I know she's getting a lot of headaches. Really bad ones, I think. It makes her pretty sour with the kids, but I know she can't help it.'

'Headaches?' Richard frowned. 'I don't quite like the sound of that. You haven't noticed any unusual swelling around her face or her hands, have you?'

'She always gets a bit of that when she's expecting. I thought it seemed a lot worse than usual this time, though. Her wedding ring's looking tight as anything on her finger, but I'd never dare tell her to take it off. There's another thing, too.'

'You'd better tell me the worst, then.'

'I don't know this for sure, but I think she's had some bleeding. I saw her with a bit of rag in her hand one morning, and she was looking at it with her face white as a sheet. I thought I saw red on it, but she shoved it away somewhere before I could get a decent look.'

Richard nodded slowly. 'I think you're right to be concerned.' Frank could see how carefully he was choosing each word. 'Now, you mustn't be unduly alarmed, I'm sure there's every reason to hope all will go well with Lizzie. But it would do no harm for her to take extra care of herself. And I'd like to have a look at her.'

'There's no chance of that,' Frank said, shaking his head. 'She'd go up the wall if I even suggested it. That's the trouble, I can't talk to her about it. She just says there's nothing wrong with her, and if I start going on about it she gets in a state. If she even knew I'd told you she'd make a heck of a fuss. Hey, you mustn't tell Maudie, eh? I'd never hear the end of it from Lizzie.'

'No, there doesn't seem much sense in distressing Maudie over it, especially just at the moment. And anything I'm told about medical matters is always treated in the strictest confidence. You're quite sure

411

Lizzie wouldn't let me examine her?'

'She'd slap you if you suggested it.'

'And I gather from what you're saying that there's not much chance of your persuading Lizzie to take better care of herself.'

'Not when she won't admit there's anything wrong with her,' Frank said miserably. 'She's that set on having everyone think she's well. She shouldn't be having this baby at all. I shouldn't have let her talk me round.'

'Lizzie's a little hard to say no to, isn't she,' Richard said, smiling slightly. 'Well, it seems to me that since she won't do it for herself it's up to you to take care of Lizzie.'

'I'd do anything to make her right again. What does she need?'

'From what you say, she's having problems with the circulation of her blood. It's not uncommon during pregnancy, especially when women have had a large number of children previously. The only thing you can really do for her is make sure she rests.'

'That's easier said than done.'

'Yes, I suppose it is. Ideally, I'd like to see her more or less take to her bed until the child's born, but I suppose that's out of the question. Get her to rest as much as you possibly can, though.'

'I'll try. I don't know how much good it'll do.'

'Now, you mustn't be too distressed over it all. Lizzie's a healthy woman, she's every chance of getting over this pregnancy as well as she has all the others, just as long as she takes things a little easier than usual.'

He hesitated a moment before going on. 'I should warn you, though, Frank, that it's possible she might lose the child. I don't like the sound of the bleeding you described. It's certainly not a foregone conclusion, it's perfectly possible that you'll have another healthy child in four months' time. But you must be prepared for the alternative.'

Frank sighed. 'Do you know, I don't really care? It sounds a rotten thing to say about one of my own kids, I know, but I can't think past Lizzie. As long as she's all right, I can't get worried about whether the baby pulls through or not. Except Lizzie won't be all right unless the baby is.'

'She'd be upset, of course.'

'She'd be more than upset. I suppose losing a baby must mean a lot more to a woman than it does a man, after carrying it all that time. But if anything happens to this baby, I think… I just about think Lizzie might go funny in the head.'

'It's surely not that bad,' Richard protested.

'I don't know. It means an awful lot to her, having this baby. It's like… well, I suppose that's the big thing in Lizzie's life, having the children. She's that proud of having seven of them, and rearing them all. And ever since she got this idea in her head of wanting another one, it's as though nothing else matters. She wouldn't be so bad if she wasn't crook with it, of course. She's worried about the baby, but she won't talk about it. And she shouldn't be having another bloody baby at all! All because she…'

'All because she wanted to show Maudie that she wasn't too old to have another child,' Richard finished for him when Frank trailed off awkwardly. 'Yes, I do realise Maudie's role in all this. It seems an odd reason to go through childbearing, but, as you say, women view these things differently. It must have been dreadfully galling for Lizzie to have her daughter crowing over her the way Maudie did. And Lizzie's hardly the type to admit defeat over something so important to her.'

'I just wish it was all over and Lizzie was all right again.'

'We'll do our best for her. Try to make her rest, and keep me informed on how she is. If things begin to look more serious, then I might have to speak to her myself.'

'I don't think that'd do any good, Richard.'

'Well, perhaps not. Try not to worry too much—though I know that won't be easy. Lizzie was clearly in the peak of health before she began having these problems, and that's the best possible reason to believe she'll come through it all beautifully.'

'I don't…' Frank began, but he stopped himself. There was nothing Richard could do except offer advice, and Frank was guiltily aware that he was casting a shadow on Richard's happiness by dwelling on his own troubles. He had always been a worrier where Lizzie's health was concerned, he knew; perhaps he was being foolish about it.

Perhaps. 'You're probably right,' Frank said with a false heartiness. 'Let's go and look at my granddaughter again, shall we?'

Amy stirred away at a bowl of pudding mixture, her main attention directed at the book propped up on the table in front of her.

' "I stood in Venice, on the Bridge of Sighs;
A palace and a prison on each hand:
I saw from out the waves her structures rise
As from the stroke of the enchanter's wand" '

she murmured aloud, savouring the feel of the words in her mouth. Since Sarah had presented her with the unexpected gift, Amy had read the book through from beginning to end more than once, and knew several passages off by heart. *That's lovely. I wonder what Venice looks like,* she mused.

She was so absorbed in her visions of a magical city, palaces on every side, that it took her a moment or two to become aware of Charlie's voice when he called out from the bedroom.

His distress was unmistakable, though she could make out no coherent words. Amy hurriedly put down the bowl and ran to his room. Charlie seemed to be straining to lift himself up from the pillows, his eyes wide open and staring.

She knelt beside the bed and put her hand on his arm. 'What's wrong, Charlie? Does something hurt you?'

His mouth opened and closed, but for the moment he seemed unable to form words. Instead he stared avidly at her, as if drinking in the sight.

'I... I thought...' he said, his voice hoarse. He closed his eyes and fell back limply against the pillows. 'I don't know,' he said faintly.

'Did it go black in your head again? Did you get a bit muddled?'

'Black.' He was silent for a time, his forehead creased in thought. 'Aye,' he said eventually. 'Went black.'

'Never mind, you're all right now, aren't you?' Amy soothed. 'How's your head?'

'Hurts a bit.'

Amy rose to leave the room. 'I'll wring out a cloth in water for your forehead, that'll help.'

'No!' His eyes opened suddenly, and he stared at her with something close to panic in them. 'Stay here.'

She knelt by the bed again. 'I'll stay as long as you like—I just thought you'd like me to take the hurt away. You mustn't get upset, you'll make your head worse. What's wrong?'

'It went black.' His hand shook where it lay on his chest, and Amy took it in her own. 'I couldn't hear you.'

'I was just in the kitchen. I came as soon as you called out.'

'I couldn't hear you,' he repeated. 'I thought you'd gone.'

'Where would I have gone, Charlie? I don't go out and leave you alone, you know that. I'm always here.'

'I thought you'd run home to your pa's. Thought you'd run off.'

Amy knelt beside him, squeezing his hand and wondering how many years his mind had wandered back. 'I wouldn't do that,' she said after a few moments. 'I wouldn't go away.'

She watched as the panic slowly slipped out of his face, to be replaced by a puzzled frown.

'Your... your pa's dead.'

'That's right. It'll be six years this September.'

He lapsed into silence for some time. 'No,' he said at last. 'You won't run off. Not now your boy's home.'

'I wouldn't have done it before, either. This is my home, too, you know. I won't leave you, Charlie.'

When David came into the house an hour later, he found Amy's bowl of pudding mixture still lying abandoned on the table. He followed the sound of her voice through the house and into Charlie's room.

He stopped just outside the door, brought up short by the astonishing sight of his mother sitting beside his father's bed, holding his hand in one of hers as he lay back with his eyes closed, and reading quietly from the book that lay in her lap.

> ' "Since my young days of passion—joy, or pain,
> Perchance my heart and harp have lost a string,
> And both may jar: it may be, that in vain
> I would essay as I have sung to sing." '

'Ma? What are you doing?' David asked when he got his voice back.

Amy looked up, startled, and put a finger to her lips. She bent low over Charlie's face, checking that he was indeed asleep, then gently laid his hand on his chest. She tiptoed from the room, closing the door behind her.

'You were... you were reading poetry to the old man,' David said, hardly able to credit what he had seen.

'He was upset, and I wanted to settle him down. I knew I might have to sit with him for quite a while, and it's hard sometimes to think of things to say to him, especially when he gets muddled.'

'But... *poetry*? To *him*?'

Amy smiled at the look on David's face. 'I think he quite liked it. I don't know if he was taking much notice of the words, but just the sound of them's nice. I'd just got him off to sleep when you came in.'

She walked out to the kitchen, and David followed her, still in a kind of daze. He sat down at the table when Amy took up her neglected bowl, and he studied her as she worked.

He enjoyed watching her. All through the three years he had been away from home, his mother's face had never faded in his mind. It was his earliest memory, the vision of that face bent over him, eyes full of love, as he lay drifting off into sleep. She had often looked sad over the years, and sometimes frightened, but he had never seen cruelty or hardness there.

David picked up the book of poetry that now lay on the table, and turned it over idly in his hand, studying the brown leather cover with its gold lettering. He had a very early memory, made misty by distance, of his mother reading to him when he had been too young to understand the words properly. Clearer than the memory of the stories was the memory of what had always ended the reading so abruptly: his father's voice calling out from the kitchen or the parlour, its harshness making her cringe, ordering her to come out and wait on him.

In all his childhood memories, David could only recollect two moods in his father: anger, or indifference. David had always aimed at being ignored, and had usually managed it. It was easy enough now that he had no reason to fear his father for David to ignore him in his turn, but the sight of his mother having to spend all day tending to the old man's every need brought back half-forgotten, brooding resentments.

She seemed so tranquil, her face smooth and her eyes deep pools of calm as she worked away, pouring the pudding mixture into a basin. She looked up to find David's eyes on her, and her mouth curved into a smile.

She leaned over and gave him one of her quick, impulsive kisses, then passed him the almost-empty bowl and its wooden spoon.

'You can lick the bowl out if you like. I missed having you to give the bowls to when you were away.'

David took it readily; hard work and an eighteen-year-old body that had only recently finished growing gave him a healthy appetite. He scraped away enthusiastically, but kept his main attention on his mother, watching her move about the room.

She was looking much better than she had when he first came home, he thought, taking pleasure in the knowledge that he had helped make her well again. She had looked close to exhaustion then; now she was the mother he remembered from years ago. And she was far too good to be spending her days waiting on his father.

'Why don't you go out for a while, Ma?' he asked.

She gave a little laugh. 'Dave, I'm in the middle of getting dinner on! I'm not going to go rushing off somewhere. Anyway, I don't go out, you know that.'

'Well, you should,' David insisted. 'Not right now, but maybe tomorrow. I don't like to see you stuck here with the old man all the time.'

'I don't mind staying home, not now you're back. And I don't mind looking after your father, either. He's not much trouble.'

'But... it's not right,' David said, struggling for the right words. 'You'll go funny in the head or something, never getting away from him.'

He saw the protest on her lips, and pressed on quickly. 'Why don't you go down and see Aunt Lizzie? You know, Beth was saying when I was there the other day how she wished you'd come down.'

She was slicing vegetables now, making neat little movements with the knife that left a growing pile of slices. 'Did she? That was nice of her. Tell Beth to come up and see us here sometime.'

'No, she wants you to go down there. She said Aunt Lizzie's been really grumpy lately, Beth thought you might cheer her up.'

'I don't see that I'd be any better at that than your Uncle Frank.' She frowned suddenly. 'Aunt Lizzie's all right, isn't she? How did she seem to you?'

David shrugged. 'She's getting pretty fat, but I think she's about the same apart from that. I don't know, I suppose she might be a bit quieter than usual.'

'She's probably tired. Still, she's got the girls to help her, she should be all right. It's a pity I can't get down there, though. I miss seeing her.'

'You should, Ma,' David pressed. 'I know Beth wants you to.'

'Well, I just can't. I can't leave your father on his own.'

'Can't you just forget about him for once?' David said, frustration making him sound harsher than he had meant to. 'Aw, heck, I could look after him for you, come to that. One of the kids could double you home from Aunt Lizzie's, so you wouldn't be gone all that long.'

She shook her head and gave him a rather sad smile. 'It's nice of you to offer, Davie. But I couldn't leave him with you.'

'Why not? What's he need doing that I couldn't do for him? I can fetch cups of tea and things.'

'He'd get upset. He wouldn't like to be left with you.'

'Too bloody bad about him, then. Tell him he can just put up with it. You need a rest from him.'

'It wouldn't be fair on him.' She put her knife down and looked at him for a long moment before she spoke. 'Remember what I told you the first day you came home? He's scared of you. Don't you know that?'

'What's he got to be scared of? I hate the old bugger, but I wouldn't knock him around or anything.'

She came back to the table and sat down beside him. 'Think about it, Davie. If you decided to be rough with him—if you decided to get back at him for some of the hidings you used to get—what could he do about it? He couldn't do anything, and he knows it. *I* know you wouldn't hurt him, but he doesn't.'

'Trust him to be a nuisance,' David grumbled. 'Stupid old bugger.'

'Stop it, David,' Amy said, startling him with the unfamiliar sharpness of her tone. 'You shouldn't talk about him like that, you really shouldn't. He's your father.'

'That's not my fault.'

'No,' she agreed, suddenly sounding weary. 'I suppose it's mine.'

He had upset her; though he was not quite sure how he had done it, he felt guilty nevertheless. 'I'm sorry, Ma.'

'There's no need for you to be. You're right, it's not your fault.'

She stood up, moved back to the bench and began attacking the vegetables again. David watched her, chewing at his lip as he thought about what she had said.

It was becoming difficult for him to associate the terrifying father of his childhood with the sick, old man who spent most of the time shut away in his bedroom. Hard, too, to sustain the resentment he had held within himself for so long.

'I suppose...' he began, softer words hovering on his lips.

Then his mother turned her head slightly, part of her face falling into shadow. It was only a trick of the light, that darkness down one side of her face that looked so disconcertingly like a large bruise, but at the sight the old bitterness seethed.

'Why do you bother about him, Ma?' he demanded. 'Why don't you just leave the old bugger to look after himself?'

She turned those huge, blue eyes of hers on him, and David saw in them a plea for understanding. 'Because he's old and sick, and he needs me,' she said simply.

'But the way he's treated you!'

She looked at him almost blankly, as if she could see no connection between the two things.

David got up and walked across the room to her. 'Listen, Ma. There's things you don't take any notice of when you're little—things you just forget. But what with me being away all that time, it made me think about things. Made me remember them again. I remember something that happened when I was really little.'

He saw her puzzled expression change to one of concern.

'What thing?' she asked. 'What do you remember?'

He ran a finger gently down her cheek, noting the fine, fine lines at the corners of her eyes and the few grey hairs just discernible above her forehead. 'There was one time your face was all black and blue. It was swollen up so bad I could hardly tell it was you, and it seemed to be like that for ages. You told Mal and me you'd fallen over, didn't you? Why'd you tell us that?'

'I did,' she said quietly. 'I did fall down.' She gave what seemed meant to be a laugh, though there was no humour in it. 'It was a bit hard to stand up after what happened.'

'He beat you up, didn't he? Not just like those times he slapped you or gave you a bit of a shove. He really got stuck into you—really knocked your face around. You know what? When I figured out what he'd done, I wanted to kill him.'

He saw the pain in her face at the old memories he had dredged up; saw, too, the way her hands slid down her body to rest on her belly, and for the first time he realised it might have been more than just her face that his father had attacked.

'What did he do to you?' he demanded. 'Where did he hurt you, Ma?'

She gave a small shudder, as if hauled abruptly back to the present by the sound of his voice. 'It was a long time ago. There's no good in talking about those things now.'

'And then you wonder why I don't want anything to do with him. You want me to be *nice* to him.' He spat the word out as if it were an obscenity.

She put her hands on his arms and looked up into his face. 'He did those things to me, Davie, not to you. I've forgiven him. Why can't you?'

He could think of nothing useful to say. Mumbling an excuse, he went outside and found himself enough work to keep busy for what remained of the afternoon.

She was too soft, David told himself. To think of her tiring herself out looking after the old man, and refusing to leave the house for fear it might upset him. After what he'd done to her! The memory of her ravaged face kept his smouldering anger warm.

But the trouble was that it was difficult to keep that memory fresh. Try as he might, it insisted on being overcome by the picture of her face as it was now: tranquil, and always full of kindness. She didn't have it in her to be hard.

After what his father had done to her... she had forgiven him. That was another picture he was having trouble remembering: his father's face contorted with rage. His father was that frail old man in the bed now. The father he remembered would never have sat and listened to poetry.

He caught her frowning anxiously when she came back from feeding the old man, and she was quieter than usual over dinner.

'What's wrong, Ma?' David asked.

'Oh, you'll tell me I'm silly, but... well, I'm a bit worried about your father. I like him to come and sit in the parlour with us of an evening, but he doesn't want to tonight. He's feeling low after he had that nasty turn this morning.'

'Yes, you're silly,' David said with a grin, hoping to raise an answering smile, but she seemed too preoccupied to notice.

She took their empty plates to the bench when they had finished their pudding; she stacked the dishes but made no move to start washing them. 'I'd better sit with him tonight. I don't want him in there by himself all the time. I can do the dishes and sort out the bread later.'

'You'll have to stay up pretty late,' David said, but she was already walking towards the door.

'It doesn't matter,' she said over her shoulder. 'I don't have to get up as early as I do in summer. There's biscuits in the tins if you're still hungry.'

Then she was gone, the room unpleasantly empty without her. David helped himself to a selection of biscuits and settled down to eat them, but there was not much pleasure in eating alone.

He heard his mother's voice, a gentle murmur too soft for him to make out any words. What did she find to say to the old man? Was she reading him poetry again?

She spent so much time looking after his father; it seemed unfair that she should have to carry the whole burden. David knew he would never be able to talk her into leaving the house and having a rest from her work if it meant leaving his father on his own.

Amy abruptly stopped speaking when David came into the bedroom, looking up in surprise from the chair she had pulled close to Charlie's bedside. They both stared at David as he stood in the doorway.

'I... um... I thought you might like some biscuits, Pa,' he said awkwardly. The biscuits were crumbling a little from being clenched in his hands, but he didn't think his father would notice.

'That's nice of you, Dave,' Amy said. 'Isn't that nice of him, Charlie? Would you like some?'

Charlie studied David suspiciously, clearly unwilling to believe that his son would be offering him anything out of pure affection. 'What sort are they?'

'The ones with jam in. There's one of those coconut ones, too. Here.' He held out the biscuits, then realised he would have to take them right up to the bed, since his father could not get up by himself.

'Bring them here,' his mother said. She took a biscuit from him and began breaking it into small pieces, which she fed to his father one at a time, waiting for him to chew each piece slowly. 'Sit down,' she urged. 'Come and talk to us for a bit.'

David saw the hope in her eyes, and he could not reject it. He sat on the edge of the bed, looked at his father, and tried to think of something to say.

'I went around the cows this afternoon,' he said, snatching with relief at a subject they shared a concern in. 'They look pretty good.'

Charlie grunted, and eyed David warily, but he was unable to feign a lack of interest. 'Got enough feed for them?'

David nodded. 'Yep, there's still plenty of hay. The grass isn't bad for the time of year, either.'

'How's that one with the bit knocked off the top of one horn? She was lame in a hind leg last time I saw her.'

'Which one's that?' David asked, puzzled. The herd was not large, and he was sure there was no cow with a damaged horn.

He felt Amy squeeze his arm, and saw her lips form the word 'pretend'. He nodded in sudden understanding: his father had slipped back a few years. Charlie might have been remembering a cow of ten, twenty or even thirty years before. 'She must be all right,' he said with studied casualness. 'None of them look lame.'

'Good.' Charlie frowned in thought. 'How long till they calve?'

'Another month or so.' David hesitated, then, encouraged by the gratitude he saw in his mother's face, plunged on. 'I'll have to get you to tell me what to do when the calving starts. I've never done it by myself.'

Out of the corner of his eye he saw his mother looking from his face to his father's and back again, her eyes shining. It seemed a fair enough return for the labour of trying to have a civil conversation with his father.

She stood up and took a step back from the bed. 'Shall I leave you two to talk about the farm?' she asked. David knew the plea in her voice was directed at him. 'I've got things to do in the kitchen.'

It was his last chance to escape, and he let it pass. 'Yes, you go and get your other stuff done, Ma. I want to ask Pa about the cows.'

Once he had started, it was not as difficult as David had expected. He soon realised that his father's attention frequently drifted, so it did not matter if he repeated himself or even whether or not he made a great deal of sense. It was the company Charlie wanted; and the attention, and the sound of an amiable voice.

His father dozed off briefly from time to time, only to wake with a start. David was beginning to wonder how long he was going to have to sit there, when he saw that Charlie had at last fallen into a slumber that looked as though it would go on longer than a few moments. David stood up, careful not to make the bed move, and crept out of the room with elaborate caution.

He glanced at the clock as he went through the parlour, and was astonished to see that he had only spent half an hour with his father; he had thought the evening must be almost over.

His mother looked up from kneading the bread dough as David came into the kitchen. 'I think he's asleep,' he said, sinking heavily into a chair. 'Boy, that was hard work.'

'Thank you, Davie, that was lovely of you.' She leaned across the table to kiss him, then returned to pounding her dough. 'I've wished and wished you'd start getting on with your father.'

'Well, you needn't go thinking I like him. I don't know, I suppose the old so-and-so doesn't do much harm these days.'

He watched her working away at the dough, and he thought about the hours and hours she spent looking after the old man. 'How about you go and see Aunt Lizzie tomorrow, Ma?'

'Don't start that again, please don't. I can't leave your father.'

'But I'll look after him for you. I was all right with him tonight, wasn't I?'

'Well, yes, you were,' she admitted. 'You were very good with him.'

'So you could go out, couldn't you?'

She slapped her dough down on the table with a thump. 'Davie,' she said gently, 'I appreciate you spending that time with your father tonight, I really do. But it was only half an hour, you know. I don't think I could leave him with you much longer than that. And anyway, he knew I was here in the house, so he wouldn't have got frightened.'

'But I only did it so's you'd be able to go out. Heck, you don't think I wanted to sit and talk to him, do you?'

'Don't be annoyed with me, darling. I've got to try and do the right thing, that's all.'

David clenched his fists in frustration. 'Ma, I wish you'd go out. I hate the way you're stuck here with him all the time. I hate it.'

'Well… maybe I will go and see her sometime,' Amy said, but David caught the evasiveness in her voice.

'Tomorrow,' he pounced. 'Go down there tomorrow.'

'Oh, I don't think I could go that soon. I'll go another day.'

'When?' David pressed. 'The next day?'

'No, I…' She hesitated, caught his eyes on her, then the dough abruptly seemed to claim her full attention. 'I'll go another day. Some day when your father's feeling better.'

'You might be waiting a long time for that, Ma.'

'Then I'll just have to wait.'

25

July – September 1905

'Here you are, Pa, you can hold Lucy,' Maudie announced, clearly quite certain that she was bestowing the highest possible honour. She put the warm little bundle on Frank's lap and curved his arm around the baby. 'She'll go to sleep in a minute, she always does after she's had a feed, but I'll let you hold her first. Mind you keep your hand behind her head like that. That's right, you're getting the hang of it.'

'You know, I've held a fair few babies over the years, love,' Frank told her, smiling.

'Not *my* baby you haven't,' Maudie countered smartly.

It was the first time she had entrusted Lucy to him, and Frank tried to appear suitably grateful for the distinction. Lucy was, in fact, his main excuse for calling as often as he did these days; though there was no need for him to feign an interest in his grandchild.

At six weeks old, Lucy was becoming more responsive, and therefore more captivating, by the day, and Frank fondly imagined that she already recognised him. Her hair was showing promise of inheriting the curls that Maudie coveted for her, but her smile was her mother's, and as capable of winning over Frank as Maudie's had always been.

Maudie sat and beamed at the two of them. 'Lucy looks a bit like you, you know, Pa. Don't you think Lucy's got Pa's nose, Richard?'

'Oh, I think you're a much better judge of such things than I am, darling,' Richard said. 'Women always seem far more able to see likenesses than men.'

Much as he enjoyed Maudie's company, Frank was relieved when she gathered up the now drooping-eyed Lucy and took her off to the bedroom. Lucy was a delight, and he was already in love with her, but she was not his real reason for the visit.

'How's Lizzie?' Richard asked as soon as Maudie was safely out of earshot.

Frank sighed. 'Much the same. I think she's a bit worse, but it's hard to tell. She's that swollen up, you'd swear she's ready to drop that baby any day. I don't know how she's going to put up with two more months of it.'

'I've my doubts about your putting up with it, come to that,' Richard remarked. 'You're looking rather weary yourself.'

'She doesn't sleep properly, that's half the trouble. And I just can't get her to rest in the daytime—she says she's got to keep the girls in order.

She's not doing the really heavy work any more, Lizzie's not stupid, but she wears herself out just organising everyone. And half the time she's clutching at her head because it's aching—not that she'll ever admit it is, mind you.'

'I could give her something for that. I know you're quite sure she wouldn't let me near her to check her over, but do you think she'd take medicine if I mixed something up?'

Frank shook his head. 'There's no way in the world she'd take it. I can just hear her saying it now—"I never had medicines or doctors or any of that nonsense with the other babies, and I'm not going to start it now."'

Richard smiled at Frank's attempt to imitate Lizzie's affronted tone. 'She certainly hasn't lost her spirit, has she? You should take comfort from that. And the further through her pregnancy she gets, the more reason to believe you'll have another healthy child come September.'

Frank made a noncommittal sound. The trouble with that line of reasoning was that the further through her pregnancy Lizzie got, the larger, more uncomfortable and more tired she got, too. But he knew that Richard was doing the best he could, given that he was unable to see Lizzie or even prescribe anything for her.

'If you could get her to rest more, that would be the best possible treatment,' Richard said. 'Far better than any medicine. Even half an hour's doze of an afternoon would be better than nothing.'

'I'll have a go,' Frank said, certain that it would be as futile as all his other attempts.

'I like to see that Maudie has an afternoon nap even now,' Richard said. 'She may be having a lie-down at the moment, while Lucy's sleeping. Lucy's a good baby—or so I'm told by her mother, who knows far more about such things than I do—but she does have the unfortunate habit of waking up in the middle of the night demanding food. And of course she draws all her nourishment from Maudie, so Maudie needs to conserve her strength.'

'She looks well, anyway, and the baby's growing.'

'Oh, yes, Maudie's taken to motherhood as enthusiastically as she does all sorts of things. Though I'm not a great deal of help to her now that Lucy's arrived, and I'm afraid I've rather disappointed Maudie with my ignorance from time to time.'

'How do you mean?' Frank asked.

'Well, I was quite the expert when she was expecting, and of course bringing Lucy into the world was very much a joint effort. But my knowledge of child rearing runs out at the moment of birth—leaving aside illness, of course, and there's no question of that. Fortunately for us all, Maudie is more than competent at such mysteries as changing napkins and generally keeping Lucy clean and contented, but I let her down badly when she wants advice about… well, aspects of her body, shall we say? Things that give her discomfort. And feeding the baby—I can see as well as you can that Lucy's thriving, but I really can't be of any use when Maudie asks me if she's putting Lucy to the breast properly, or why it sometimes hurts her when the baby suckles. I can give her a salve when her nipples crack, but I've no idea why they got into that state.'

'She needs her ma,' Frank said, calling up vague memories of Lizzie complaining of such things after Maudie's birth.

'Exactly,' Richard said with a sigh. 'Such a waste that Maudie should be deprived of all Lizzie's knowledge and experience. I do wish those two weren't so determined to be estranged from each other, but it's no use you and I trying to force the issue.'

'I'd have a go, but with Lizzie being poorly I don't like—'

Frank stopped abruptly at the warning glance Richard sent him. He looked over his shoulder to see that Maudie had appeared in the doorway.

'Lucy's sound asleep,' she announced. 'I'll leave having my rest till later, though. I didn't want to miss seeing you, Pa.'

She looked from Frank to Richard and back again, amusement on her face. 'Why are you two so quiet all of a sudden? Were you talking about me or something?'

'Well, you know you're a subject of great interest to us both, darling,' Richard said, trying with only limited success to make a joke of it. 'We weren't really—not exclusively, anyway.'

'What's that supposed to mean?' Maudie said, still amused. 'You look awfully guilty, Richard—and you're even worse, Pa. Whatever have you two been up to? You were talking nineteen to the dozen when I was in the passage.'

'I'm afraid I can't really tell you,' Richard said uncomfortably. 'I can only…' He trailed off, caught Frank's eye and gave a shrug expressive of helplessness.

Maudie's expression changed from amusement to puzzlement, and then to mild irritation, all in a moment. 'What on earth are you on about? Pa, why's Richard looking at you like that?'

'Because I told him not to tell you, love,' Frank said, tired of the deception. 'It started back before Lucy arrived, and Richard and me didn't want to upset you. It's your ma. She's not well.'

'We're not at all sure it's serious, you mustn't get upset,' Richard put in quickly, seeing the look of shock creeping over Maudie's face.

'What's wrong with her?' Maudie asked, her eyes fixed firmly on Frank. 'What's wrong with Ma?'

'It's all to do with the baby,' Frank said, struggling for the right words. Embarrassment made him drop his gaze to the floor. 'It's a strain on her, carrying it and all that. Richard says there's something wrong with her blood.'

Maudie turned on her husband. 'You've known for ages and ages there was something wrong with Ma, and you never even told me! Richard, how could you?'

'Maudie, please don't get in a state,' Richard said. 'You must understand—'

Maudie stamped her foot. 'You've no right not to tell me! You've no *right!*'

Her last word was nearly a scream, and Richard flinched visibly; Maudie was capable of surprising volume when the urge took her. 'Maudie, dear, you mustn't—' he began, then he took the wiser course of abandoning words for the moment. He crossed the room to Maudie and took her in his arms, and when she tried to twist out of his grip he held her all the more firmly. 'Shh, shh, it's all right,' he soothed. 'I don't believe your mother's dangerously ill. I'm sorry, sweetheart, we should have broken it to you more gently. Come on, sit down and we'll tell you properly.'

He drew Maudie over to the sofa and sat with one arm tightly around her. 'You know I can't tell you things that I'm told in confidence. I've explained that to you, haven't I?'

'Even when it's my own mother?' Maudie asked, her voice unsteady.

'Even then. I could say nothing until your father chose to speak.'

'It's my fault, love, you shouldn't go crook at Richard,' Frank said. 'I told him not to let on to you.'

'I'll say it's your fault,' Maudie said, her anger returning now that the shock had lessened. Frank realised with a sinking feeling that it was all turned on him. 'Honestly, Pa, you should have known better. Fancy letting Ma have a baby at her age! No wonder she's not well. I don't know what you were thinking of.'

'Well, it was sort of… I couldn't really…' Frank flailed around for words, feeling more awkward by the moment. It was not a subject he was comfortable discussing with his daughter.

'Babies do have a way of coming to a married couple whether they're intended or not, my dear,' Richard put in, but Maudie was having none of it.

'Humph! Ma never does *anything* she doesn't want to. She always gets her own way. Fancy her even wanting another baby at her age! Seven would be plenty for most people. It's stupid of her, wanting another one. Just because she wants to be better than other people. Just because she...'

Maudie trailed off. As Frank watched, her face went pale. 'Because she wanted to show me she could still do it. Because I went on and on at her about being too old. It's my fault.'

'No, darling, you mustn't say that,' Richard said, hastening to reassure her.

'It's not your fault, love, your ma might've had another baby anyway,' Frank put in, but Maudie brushed them both aside, her sensible nature reasserting itself.

'Yes, it is. It's my fault—and hers for taking notice of me. Oh, don't go looking all worried, Richard, I'm not going to get in a state over it. That's no use to Ma, is it? You can make her better, can't you?'

Richard shook his head. 'There's not really a great deal I can do. Apart from the fact that your father's quite sure she wouldn't let me near her, what she needs more than anything is plenty of bed rest.'

'Pa, you're not letting her tire herself out, are you?' Maudie asked. 'Why don't you make her rest?'

'Well, she says she's got to get the girls organised, see that everything gets done properly and all that,' Frank said. 'And anyway, love, it's not that easy to make your ma do something she doesn't want to. I've tried telling her, but... you know.'

'Honestly, you men are as bad as each other,' Maudie said, her tone expressing utter disdain for the entire sex. 'I'll just have to do it myself.'

She extricated herself from Richard's arm and stood up. 'Did you ride in or bring the buggy, Pa?'

'I've got the spring cart—I had that much to get at the store, I knew the buggy would be no good.'

'Well, that's all right, then, there'll be room for me and Lucy. Now, Richard, you can come and pick us up later. An hour should be long enough—it doesn't matter if you're a bit longer than that, but make sure it's at least an hour.'

'But... but Maudie, dear, are you thinking of going out to the farm with your father?' Richard asked, looking mildly dazed by the sudden turn of events.

'Of course I am. It's no good you taking me out, Ma'll catch on that something's up if we come together. Anyway, she doesn't want to see you. I'll tell her you had to go and see someone out near the farm, so I got a ride out with Pa and you're to fetch me later. It's all right, Richard,

I've got it all worked out. Now, I'd better get my stuff organised.'

'Wait a minute, please, darling,' Richard said, halting Maudie in her swift progress towards the door. 'I'm not sure that I want you to go out there today.'

Maudie turned and stared at him in evident disbelief. 'What are you talking about?'

'Weren't we speaking just the other day—no, it was only yesterday—about outings? Don't you remember? I said then that I'd rather you didn't go on carriage rides for another week or so—and that was *carriage* rides, for goodness sake, not a cart! Maudie, I don't want you bumping along all that way. I'm worried you'll hurt yourself. I think you'd better stay home.'

'Oh, don't talk rot, Richard.'

'Maudie!' Richard said, visibly shocked.

'Well, you are. I'm perfectly well—you said yourself that I'm a picture of health. I bet thousands of women ride around in carts when they've just had babies.'

'That may well be true, but those thousands of women don't happen to be my wife. And what about Lucy? You're always saying you don't like to wake her up once she's settled, and now you're going to take the poor little mite out on a bumpy old cart when she's fast asleep.'

Richard was doing his best, but Frank could see that he had lost the battle almost before it had begun. The note of desperation he had allowed to creep into his voice was a sure sign of that, and Maudie was far too good at this sort of thing to miss such a sign. As an involuntary observer of these marital negotiations, Frank tried to make himself as inconspicuous as possible, but he took a healthy interest nevertheless.

Maudie folded her arms and gave Richard a look that expressed exasperation, amused disbelief, and settled determination all at once. 'Pa's cart isn't bumpy, Richard. It's a very nice cart. And Lucy will *like* riding in it. Babies always like riding in wagons and things, everyone knows that. She'll be off to sleep again in no time.'

'But Maudie, darling, listen—'

'No, *you* listen. Ma's sick. Of course I've got to go out there. How could I not go?

'Now,' she went on briskly, clearly believing that she had stated an inarguable truth, 'I've got to get Lucy organised, and get a few things ready. Pa, you get the horse hitched up and you should be ready to go by the time I am. Don't forget, Richard, I'll need about an hour, and you can come out any time after that.'

She swept out of the room in a rustle of skirts, leaving Richard looking more dazed than ever.

'I think I've just gained a new understanding of what's meant by an irresistible force,' he said. 'I suppose pointing out that it's not particularly convenient for me to go out to the farm today would be completely useless.'

'I expect so,' Frank agreed, careful to hide his amusement.

'Well, I've always said part of Maudie's charm is that she's so natural—that she's never reluctant to show her feelings. I suppose I can't really complain when I experience the raw edge of it. Though I can't say I've ever been accused of talking rot before,' he added reflectively. 'Maudie has certainly become more strong-minded since she gained the status of a mother.'

He turned his attention on Frank. 'And what do you think of the idea of your daughter's descending on the farm like a whirlwind this afternoon?'

'As long as they don't have a row—and I don't think Maudie'll try and start one, not when she's worried about her ma—it should be pretty good. It'll perk Lizzie up no end, seeing Lucy at last.'

'Oh, yes, I'm quite prepared to believe that my daughter is capable of effecting a miraculous improvement,' Richard said with a smile. 'And I'd be as pleased as you would to see a reconciliation between Maudie and her mother. I've just found myself slightly left behind the rapid course of events. I'm still trying to adjust to the fact that a woman who not three hours ago was being described to me as "a terrible woman—you don't know what she's really like", and Maudie couldn't possibly try and make it up with her—this same woman is now the prime moving force in Maudie's life.'

'She's changed her mind, Richard. They do that, you know. The best idea's not to make a big thing of it. They only get upset if you start saying "But you said such-and-such" and all that sort of talk.'

'No doubt,' Richard murmured.

Frank had the cart ready to go, and he and Richard were standing by it, when Maudie emerged from the house with Lucy in one arm and a large basket looped over the other. Richard relieved her of her burdens while Frank gave her a hand up onto the front of the cart.

'Lucy hasn't even woken up,' Richard said in surprise.

'No, I didn't think she would,' said Maudie. 'Lucy's a very good baby, you know.'

Richard gave a snort. 'I think Lucy is already a member of that conspiracy known as womankind.'

'Probably,' Maudie said idly, her mind clearly on other things. 'Put that basket down next to the flour, Richard, it won't tip over there. Yes, that's right. All right, I'm ready for Lucy now.'

She held out her arms, and Richard passed the baby up to her. 'Now, do be careful, Maudie. Don't go tiring yourself out, or getting upset.'

'Oh, don't be silly. Honestly, you can be a real old fuss-pot sometimes.' But Frank saw the smile she gave Richard, and the way she tilted her face to receive his kiss.

'And you, Mrs Townsend, can be a real little minx,' Richard said as he disengaged from the kiss. 'Frank, you be sure and take proper care of my girls. You will drive carefully, won't you?'

'As if they were the Crown Jewels,' Frank assured him.

Lucy woke as the cart moved off, gave a surprised hiccup followed by a huge yawn, then closed her eyes again and went back to sleep. It could have been Lizzie sitting beside him, the infant Maudie on her lap, Frank reflected as his mind drifted back nineteen years.

Except that he could not remember when he had last seen Lizzie wearing the calm smile that adorned Maudie's face. The thought jolted him roughly back to the present.

'You won't upset your ma, will you, love?' he asked. 'She's easily upset lately, since she hasn't been feeling the best.'

'Of course I won't upset her. Don't you worry, Pa, I know what I'm about.'

Frank had no intention of missing the encounter between Maudie and her mother. As soon as they had pulled up near the house, he called the boys over to see to the horse and cart and to bring in the stores, while he took Maudie's basket and walked up to the back door with her. Lucy had woken when Maudie climbed down from the cart. She looked up at the sky with an expression of mild surprise as Maudie carried her along at a brisk walk.

Lizzie was standing beside the table, leaning on its edge for support. The grimness of her expression, and the apprehensive looks on the faces of Beth and Maisie, told Frank that he and Maudie had interrupted a tense scene.

Beth's and Maisie's expressions lightened the moment they saw Maudie and Lucy. They fell on their visitors with exclamations of delight, fussing and cooing over the baby.

Maudie let them have a few seconds of admiring Lucy, then brushed them aside and walked up to her mother.

'So you're here, are you?' Lizzie said, eyeing Maudie suspiciously, as if trying to fathom her motives. 'I didn't expect to see you out here.'

'Richard's got to come out this way today, so I got Pa to give me a ride. Richard will pick me up later.' Maudie gave her mother a glowing smile, and held out the child in her arms like a benediction. 'I've brought Lucy to show you.'

Frank held his breath, hoping that Lizzie would not spoil the moment with a sharp remark. But the temptation of the baby was too much.

'Give her here,' she ordered, holding out her arms. Maudie handed the baby over, and gazed contentedly on the sight of Lizzie holding Lucy.

'Isn't she beautiful?' said Maudie.

'Mmm, she looks pretty healthy,' Lizzie allowed. 'Feeding well, is she?'

'Oh, yes, she's a real little pig. Sit down, why don't you? She's pretty heavy.'

Lizzie stiffened. 'I'm all right. I don't need to sit down.'

'Well, I do. I'm tired out after that ride, I haven't been that far from the house for months.' Maudie collapsed dramatically into a chair, and pulled out the one beside her for Lizzie. 'Come and sit down, Ma, I'll get a crick in my neck looking up at you.'

Lizzie hesitated for a moment, then took the offered chair. Frank sat down opposite her, a silent observer of the proceedings.

'I'm that dry—make us a cup of tea, you girls,' Maudie said. She watched for a moment to see that they were doing as she told them, then turned her attention back to Lizzie.

'She's big for her age, don't you think?' she asked, tucking the blanket more snugly around Lucy.

'Not bad. Not for a first baby,' Lizzie said guardedly.

Frank could only watch in quiet admiration as Maudie got Lizzie talking about Lucy and about babies in general. Maudie had always been good at persuading those who loved her (other than her mother) to see things her way, but in the year since her marriage she seemed to have developed a far lighter touch in dealing with people.

Maudie more than carried her share of the conversation, but at the same time Frank saw her observing Lizzie closely. He knew she was noting the lines that pain and fatigue had etched around Lizzie's mouth, and the puffiness of her face. Lizzie's left hand was visible on top of Lucy's blanket; the skin around her wedding ring looked red and swollen.

Maudie fussed around with her basket while Beth was setting out their tea things, then she brushed her sister aside and poured when she judged the tea had drawn. She kept Lizzie talking, and kept watching her carefully.

A huge yawn seemed to take Lizzie by surprise when she had barely finished her first cup of tea. By the time they had had a second cup, she was visibly struggling to hide the yawns.

'Doesn't it make you sleepy, holding a baby?' Maudie remarked. 'I always start yawning when I've had her on my lap for a while.' She leaned close to Lizzie and spoke in a conspiratorial tone. 'Can we go up to your room for a bit, Ma? I wanted to ask you a couple of things. You know, about feeding and all that.' She looked around the room, taking in Frank and the girls with an air of disdain. 'We can't talk about those things out here.'

Lizzie let Maudie relieve her of Lucy, but Maudie did not affront her mother by offering to help her stand up. It was hard for Frank to watch Lizzie struggle to heave herself upright, but he would only annoy her if he offered his arm.

They disappeared up the passage, and Frank heard the bedroom door closed firmly behind them.

There was work he could usefully be doing, but he was reluctant to leave the house while those two were in it. The boys could manage well enough without him for a little longer.

Maudie emerged some time later, creeping down the passage with exaggerated care and closing the passage door after her.

'Ma's asleep,' she said with a self-satisfied air. She put Lucy on Frank's lap and looked around the room.

'Right, now I'm going to get you lot organised,' she declared. 'You big girls first, then I'll round up Rosie and Kate. Now, you two—'

'How'd you do it, love?' Frank interrupted when he had recovered from the shock of her announcement. 'How'd you talk your ma into having a sleep? She goes crook as anything if I ever say she should have a lie-down.'

Maudie reached down into her basket and pulled out a small bottle. 'I put some of this in her tea. It's wonderful stuff, it knocks you out in no time.' She passed the bottle across to Frank. 'Here you are, you'd better look after it, Pa. Put it somewhere safe, mind—you don't want Ma finding it. You don't need to give it to her every day, so it should last a while. Every other day should do.'

'But… it's some sort of medicine, is it? You went and slipped your ma some medicine on the sly? Did you ask Richard if you could?' Frank corrected himself before Maudie had a chance to answer. 'No, I know you didn't, he was with me the whole time. Maudie, you shouldn't go dosing your ma like that—specially not now, the state she's in.'

'Oh, don't go making a fuss,' Maudie said. 'It's some stuff Richard used to give me when I was expecting—I think it's just laudanum or something. Some nights I couldn't get off to sleep, and I was getting really tired. So it must be all right for Ma.'

'I don't know about that,' Frank said. 'You just see that you ask Richard if it's all right.'

'But he'll only go on about it,' Maudie said, reluctance clear in her voice. 'There's no need to go worrying him.'

'Well, if you don't tell him I will. And I'm not going to give your ma any of this stuff till Richard says it's all right. I don't care if he does tell you off.'

'Oh, all right, then.' Maudie glared at Frank. 'I'll ask him, if you're going to make a fuss about it. Anyway, Richard never stays grumpy for long.

'Come here, you two,' she told Maisie and Beth, who were sharing the task of peeling a mountain of potatoes. Maudie hustled them off into a corner of the room.

'Now, what you have to—' Maudie stopped abruptly, and looked over the girls' heads at Frank. 'Don't you go listening, Pa,' she said, her eyes narrowing.

'No, I won't take any notice,' Frank said.

He made a great show of talking to Lucy, but it was impossible not to catch a few words of what Maudie was telling the girls so earnestly: 'She's expecting, you know,' 'Not till September,' 'Even bigger soon,' 'Makes her sore in her...' The last word of that phrase was delivered in a voice too low for Frank to hear.

'And on top of all that, she's got this thing wrong with her blood,' Maudie finished in a louder voice. 'Richard says she needs to rest, so that's what we've all got to make her do. Pa, you'll have to help too.'

'Mmm? What was that?' Frank asked, feigning a sudden realisation that Maudie was speaking.

'You'll have to help with getting Ma to rest. She's pretty smart, Ma is, so we'll have to be even smarter. You girls are going to have to be one step ahead of her, and you'll have to keep it up all day.'

Maisie was directing a blank look at Maudie. 'What's she on about?' she asked Beth.

'I don't know,' Beth said. 'What do you mean, Maudie?'

'You've got to stop Ma trying to do so much work. She thinks she's got to organise you two all the time because you're hopeless—'

'We are not hopeless!' Beth protested.

'Well, Ma thinks you are. Anyway, you know what she's like— she's always got to be bossing everyone around.

'It's just a matter of being organised,' Maudie went on. 'You'll start first thing in the morning. What happens when you get up, Pa?'

'Your ma gets up the same time I do, and she comes out to get breakfast on. It's worse in the summer, with me getting up so early.'

'Yes, well, we don't need to worry about that,' Maudie said briskly. 'Ma'll be right again by next summer. Now, you two,' she told Beth and Maisie, 'it's time you started getting breakfast on by yourselves.'

'We help her with it,' Beth pointed out. 'She wakes us up when she comes out of a morning.'

'Helping her with it's not enough,' Maudie said. 'You should be doing it by yourselves.'

'But she won't let us,' Beth said.

'Don't give her the option. You know what time her and Pa get up— you need to get up about half an hour before that. Maybe a whole hour until you get into the way of it. Get everything on the go, then take a cup of tea into Ma before she's even got out of bed. That'll make sure she stays there.'

'She'll go crook,' Beth said. 'She'll say what were we doing, getting up so early.'

'Tell her you couldn't sleep,' said Maudie. 'Say you woke up early and you couldn't get back to sleep, so you thought you might as well get up.'

'I suppose…' Beth said doubtfully.

'We'll have to get up really early,' Maisie said, pulling a face at the notion.

'But you can take turns,' Maudie said. 'You won't have to get up that early every day. So that's not a problem, is it?

'Then there's all the other jobs that need doing,' she went on before the girls had a chance to respond. 'You mustn't just wait around for Ma to tell you what to do next. You know what jobs get done what days, just get on and do them.'

'But she *likes* telling us what to do,' Beth protested.

'No, she doesn't. Well, she does when she's all right, but just now while she's not the best it only makes her grumpier, trying to think out what to tell you all the time. No, the thing to do is to start doing a job before Ma even has the chance to think of telling you.' She fixed them both with a hard stare. 'And you've *got* to make a proper job of things.'

'We do,' Beth said.

'And she's *so* fussy,' Maisie put in. 'If you leave just a tiny spot on the floor when you do the scrubbing, she goes on and on.'

'There's nothing wrong with being fussy,' Maudie said self-righteously. 'I'm fussy myself about scrubbing.'

'Oh, yes, it's easy for you to be fussy,' Beth said, stung into a rare show of temper by her sister's superior tone. 'Easy to be fussy when you

434

don't have to do it yourself.'

Maudie held Beth's eyes, a sombre expression on her face. 'Don't you want Ma to get better?'

Beth's lower lip trembled. 'Of course I do. I want it more than anything.'

'Me, too,' Maisie put in.

'Then it's up to you two to look after her. That's not asking much, is it?'

The girls shook their heads.

'Right, you can start now,' said Maudie. 'Maisie, you carry on with those spuds, but I want you to show me how you do the floor, Beth. You can do that corner over there. Then when you've finished the vegies I'll get you both to—'

'Are you going to help us?' Beth interrupted.

'No,' Maudie said. 'I'm going to watch you two do the jobs and see where you need to be doing them better.'

'While you just sit and do nothing?'

'Oh, I'm going to write out a list of the jobs for you, so you won't have to remember what needs doing every day. Get me a pencil and some paper, Beth.'

'But that's not fair,' Beth said. 'You just sitting there watching us. Why don't you help?'

Maudie's calm seemed unshakeable. 'What's the point of that? I can't be here every day, can I? The best thing I can do for you two—and for Ma—is see that you know what to do to make things easy for her. That's sense, isn't it? Isn't that sense, Pa?' she added, making a claim on the authority he could offer.

Frank only hesitated for a moment before answering; any vague affront to Beth's and Maisie's dignity faded into insignificance against the hope that Maudie was holding out. 'It sounds pretty good to me. Don't be too rough with them, though, love,' he added in an attempt at mediation. 'You don't need to go ordering them around so much.'

'That's all right, then,' said Maudie. 'Come on, you girls, get on with it.'

Beth and Maisie muttered under their breaths in a half-hearted fashion, but Maudie had judged them accurately: they were both willing to put up with a good deal of bossing from Maudie as long as they thought it would help them look after Lizzie.

'Now, Pa, it's your job to see she goes to bed early,' Maudie told Frank. 'If you start going to bed a bit earlier, she won't want to sit up by herself. So you make sure you do that. You won't forget, will you?'

'I think I can manage that, love.' Frank waited till Beth and Maisie were paying them no attention, then spoke to Maudie in a low voice. 'I don't know if you should've been telling the girls all that stuff, you know,' he said. 'You were talking about the baby and all, weren't you? I don't know what your ma would have to say about that.'

'She won't know unless someone tells her, and no one will.'

'I suppose so, but... well, they're a bit young for all that, aren't they? Well, I know Maisie's older than you, but she's not married.'

'Richard says ignorance does more harm than knowledge ever could,' Maudie said, reciting it like a lesson carefully memorised. 'I think that's quite right, don't you? Anyway,' she relented, leaning closer to whisper in Frank's ear, 'I didn't tell them much. Nothing that'd frighten them off.'

Maudie drew up her list of tasks for the girls, and when she judged they were due for a rest she went over the list with them in great detail. She seemed satisfied with their understanding by the time Rosie came home from school and Kate got up from her afternoon sleep.

Maudie was not foolish enough to try the appeal to their better nature that had worked so well with Beth and Maisie. She told the two little girls what jobs they should be doing, told them that they had to do whatever Beth and Maisie said, and announced that she would watch them do the dusting and the other tasks that were delegated to them. When she had finished speaking, she folded her arms and waited for the protests.

'You can't tell us what to do!' Rosie said immediately. 'We don't have to do what you say.'

'Oh, yes you do,' Maudie said calmly.

'No, we don't. We don't, eh, Kate?'

'No,' Kate agreed, always eager to follow her sister's lead.

'Yes, you do,' Maudie repeated. 'Because if you don't...'

She put a hand on each girl's shoulder, drew them close, and spoke in a low voice. Kate gave a frightened squeak; Rosie's eyes grew wide, but she managed to maintain her mutinous air.

'He wouldn't,' she said. 'Richard wouldn't do that.'

'He would if I told him to,' Maudie said.

Rosie turned to a higher authority. 'Pa, Maudie says if we don't do what she says she'll make Richard give us horrible medicines.'

'And needles,' Kate put in, her voice high with fear. 'Big needles.'

'Well, if you're going to be naughty, I'll tell Richard you're sick,' Maudie said in a coolly reasonable voice. 'I'll tell him you need medicine, you see. Nasty, nasty medicine—and injections, too. So you'd better do what I say.'

'Don't let her, Papa,' Kate pleaded.

Frank tried to harden his heart against their pleas, with only partial success. 'Don't frighten them, Maudie.' He paused, and chewed reflectively at his lip. 'But you'd better do what your sister says, you two,' he told the little girls. 'She knows what's best.'

'And if you don't...' Maudie left the threat hanging unspoken, then she swept Rosie and Kate out of the room so that she could check their dusting skills.

Frank was in the room when Lizzie woke from her unexpected afternoon nap.

'How do you feel, love?' he asked softly. 'Did you have a good sleep?'

Lizzie frowned in confusion. 'Fancy me going to sleep like that. I don't know what came over me.'

'Well, there's nothing wrong with having a lie-down. I wouldn't mind one myself sometimes of an afternoon.' He studied Lizzie's face, noting with pleasure how the signs of tension had drained from it. 'You look good, Lizzie. Course, you always do look good.'

'You talk a lot of rot,' Lizzie scoffed. She heaved herself up against the pillows, brushing aside Frank's attempt to help. 'I'll get up in a minute. See what those girls are up to. Is Maudie still here?'

'No, Richard came and got her about half an hour ago. It was good to see her, eh?'

'Mmm,' said Lizzie. 'She said she'll come out again soon.'

'That'll be good. I bet you liked seeing Lucy, too.'

'I suppose so,' Lizzie conceded. 'She's not a bad baby. I gave Maudie a bit of good advice—that girl had no idea about a few things.'

Frank sent out a silent message of gratitude to his daughter for her uncharacteristic meekness in having allowed herself to be lectured in such a way. 'It's good if you can help her.'

'She's not going to have her christened till my baby's born. We might get the two of them done together. Fancy her calling her that.'

'What, Lucy? It's quite a nice name, isn't it?'

'It's all right. I mean the other one.' Lizzie's mouth curved into a self-satisfied smile. 'Didn't she tell you? She's called her Lucy Elizabeth.'

Frank looked up at what he took for a sound from the direction of the bedroom, then slumped back in his chair when he realised the noise had come from outside.

'It's pretty quiet up there,' he said, indicating the passage with a tilt of his head. 'Seems like ages since the nurse got here.'

'It's not as long as all that,' Richard said. He pulled out his watch and checked the time. 'Scarcely two hours.' He closed the watch and put it away, then patted Frank's arm. 'I'm sure it seems much longer to you, though.'

'Yes, it does.' Frank stared at the passage, willing some noise to come out of it. 'You know, I hate hearing her yell out when the pains take her—when she does that, I think it's the worst thing in the world. Then this part starts—the quiet bit, when she's under the chloroform and you can't hear anything. This is the worst bit. At least when she's yelling out I know she's alive.'

'Now, you mustn't let yourself think that sort of thing,' Richard said. 'I'm quite sure the nurse would've called me if there was any problem. I did impress on her that she was to do so if she was in the least bit worried.'

'I know, I'm being stupid about it,' Frank said. 'Trouble is, I always have been when it's anything to do with Lizzie. You'd think I'd be used to it by now, after seven of them, but...' He shrugged.

'So it doesn't get any easier?'

Frank shook his head. 'Not really. This time seems just about as bad as it did with Maudie. Almost worse, in a way, with Lizzie being so crook all through it. I don't know what I would've done if Maudie hadn't got the girls looking after her like she did.' He looked longingly at the door again. 'I just wish it was all over and Lizzie was all right.'

Richard made a noise indicative of sympathy, encouragement and understanding all at the same time. Frank realised with a vague feeling of guilt what dismal company he was being to his son-in-law.

He and Richard had had it prearranged between them for many weeks that Richard would come out when the nurse did, though Frank had been careful to keep their plan a secret from Lizzie. Maudie was on the farm, too, though not within hearing distance; neither Frank nor Richard had been foolish enough to try and stop her from coming. She had spent the time since her arrival setting the girls largely unnecessary tasks that had the virtue of keeping them out of the house.

'I'm really grateful to have you here,' Frank said. 'I'm sure this nurse knows what she's doing—it's a nuisance we had to use a new one this time, but it couldn't be helped—but it's good to know you're right here just in case anything... well, you know.'

'I know, Frank. And I hope I'll have nothing more important to do than keep you company while we wait.'

The passage door opened, and they both looked up. The nurse stood in the doorway, her face showing the marks of a wearying two hours.

'I nearly called you just now, Doctor,' she said, and that admission told Frank that things had not gone smoothly; the nurse had made her disapproval of Richard's presence obvious as soon as she had arrived, a few minutes after Richard's own arrival. 'It was touch and go right at the end. But I managed on my own.'

'How is she?' Frank asked urgently. 'How's Lizzie?'

'She's as well as can be expected,' the nurse said. 'She lost a fair amount of blood, and I had to give her a lot of chloroform, so she's not going to be sensible for a good while.'

'But she's all right, isn't she?' Frank pressed.

'She will be, after she's had a good rest. She'll be as well as ever.' The nurse's expression softened at the sight of the relief flooding Frank's face. 'Aren't you going to ask about the baby?' she said, allowing herself a slight smile.

'Eh?' With an effort, Frank forced his attention to extend beyond Lizzie's well-being. 'Oh, yes, how's the baby?'

'You've a fine son, Mr Kelly. And what a size he is! I'd wager that child's ten pounds if he's an ounce. No wonder we had a struggle to get him out. Why, I'd—Mr Kelly, what are you doing?' she said as Frank pushed past her to go up the passage.

'Going to see Lizzie, of course.'

'Oh, no, you can't go in there—I haven't cleaned her up. I would've done that before, it was just with you seeming so anxious I thought I'd better let you know as soon as all was well. She's not in a fit state for you to see her yet.'

'Then I'll just have to see her dirty,' Frank said.

When he stepped into the bedroom, he saw why the nurse had been reluctant to let him in. Lizzie was lying on several layers of torn sheets, all of them stained with her blood, and her thighs were dark with it. Her head tossed from side to side on the pillow. She was mumbling meaningless sounds, but there was no sign of consciousness.

'Look what I've done to you,' Frank murmured. He squatted beside the bed and stroked a damp wisp of hair from Lizzie's forehead. 'No more babies, Lizzie,' he said to the oblivious figure on the bed. 'I don't care what you try next time. No more babies.'

The nurse swept into the room, carrying a basin of water. 'I'll be getting on with my work now, Mr Kelly, *if* you don't mind.' She arranged the sheet so that Frank could no longer see those stained thighs. 'That doctor says he's coming in to take a look at Mrs Kelly as soon as I've got her decent, though I'm sure I don't know why he'd be doing such a thing. Your son's in the cradle if you care to look at him,' she added pointedly. 'I did manage to get him cleaned up before I came out to you.'

Frank took her hint and stepped over to the cradle. A red, wrinkled creature lay there, waving his fists around and regarding the world with an air of resentment. Perhaps he looked bigger than the other babies had; it was hard for Frank to remember such details. He certainly looked uglier, with his head squashed by his rough passage into the world.

Frank bent low over the cradle to study his new son more closely. 'You've been a lot of bother, boy,' he told him softly. 'You'd better be a comfort to your ma once you're old enough to take notice of people.'

He pulled a chair closer to the cradle and sat down, keeping out of the nurse's way while wishing she would hurry up and leave him alone with Lizzie. He passed the time watching the baby and sneaking occasional glances over his shoulder at Lizzie when he thought the nurse was not watching.

'He's a fine boy,' said a voice from close behind him, and Frank looked up, startled.

'I didn't hear you come in, Richard. Yes, I suppose he is. I hope Lizzie'll be pleased with him, after what she's been through. How do you think she is?'

Richard caught the nurse's eye; her mouth set in a disapproving line as she smoothed the sheet over Lizzie and stepped back from the bed clutching her basin, the water now stained with red.

'There's no more bleeding—none to worry about, anyway,' she said. 'You've no need to be disturbing her private parts.'

'And no foreign matter coming out with the blood?' Richard asked. The nurse shook her head emphatically. 'Then I shan't disturb her.' Richard studied Lizzie's face, felt her pulse and put a hand against her forehead.

'Her breathing's steady, and there's no sign of infection,' he told Frank. 'I think you can let yourself stop worrying.' He smiled at Frank's expression of relief. 'And I rather think you'd like some privacy,' he said, ushering the nurse out of the room.

Frank nodded, though there was no one to take any notice of the gesture. He moved the chair close to the bedside, sat down and took Lizzie's hand in both of his, then settled himself to wait patiently for her to wake.

440

26

'What do you think we should call him?' Lizzie asked.

Frank smiled, enjoying the sight of her obvious pleasure in the plump baby suckling at her breast. It was pleasant to steal an occasional half hour from his work to sit in the bedroom with Lizzie and the new baby, though he often felt that he was the loser in the battle for a share of Lizzie's attention.

After her earlier pregnancies, Lizzie had always been eager to be up and about again, resenting the ten days or more of bed rest that the nurses always urged. But this time she seemed quite content to stay in bed and fuss over her baby, taking only a distant interest in the running of the household. Frank had not expected ever to see Lizzie cede her authority to the girls, even temporarily, and it was this ready abdication that more than anything else told him just how much the birth had drained her.

'You've taken a while to get around to thinking about that, haven't you? I was beginning to think the policeman would be on to me for not registering the little fellow.'

'What rot! He's only two weeks old.'

'I know. You're usually a bit faster with the names, that's all.'

'I don't think I am,' Lizzie said, and Frank did not press the point. He had detected an almost superstitious reluctance on her part to name this child, a reaction unlike anything he had seen in Lizzie before. He suspected she had been so frightened of losing the child who had cost her so much in the bearing that she had not dared tempt fate by giving him a name. It was a relief to know she had got over that fear.

'I'd sort of thought...' Frank said. 'Well, I just... you haven't got any names picked out, have you?'

'No. I didn't get around to thinking of any, somehow.'

Frank nodded wisely. He had a suspicion that Lizzie had been hoping for another girl, for no better reason than to compare her own baby daughter with Maudie's. For that very reason, Frank was glad the new baby was a boy. Though the acquiring of a fourth son had set his mind working on the task of seeing that all his sons would be properly set up in life.

Still, he reflected, two weeks old was a little early to be worrying about how this child would provide for a wife and children. The baby's more immediate need was for a name.

He leaned over to kiss Lizzie on the forehead, careful to avoid squashing the child. 'I'd sort of like to call him after Ben.'

'You'd *what?*' Lizzie gave such a start that the baby hiccuped, lost the nipple, and screwed up his face in a threatened yell until Lizzie guided the questing mouth back onto her breast. 'It's all right, sweetie, your silly father just gave me a shock,' she soothed. 'What do you want to do that for, Frank? Ben, of all people! He's never done us any favours, that's for sure. When I think of what he did to you, going off with all that money and you having to—'

'Ben's dead, Lizzie.' Frank's voice sounded unnaturally flat in his own ears. 'He's dead.'

'Dead?' Lizzie echoed stupidly. 'But you never said… when? When did he die? What happened?'

Frank leaned back against the bed head, his hands tucked behind his head. 'I don't know exactly when he died—that's the worst part about it, I suppose. My own brother dead, and me not knowing. But it was about two months ago that I heard—around the end of July.'

'That long ago? Why didn't you tell me before?'

'I didn't want to upset you, love. You had enough on your plate back then, with this fellow giving you all that trouble.'

'He wasn't much trouble,' Lizzie said, but her protest was half-hearted. Lizzie was no longer bothering to pretend that her pregnancy had been anything but unpleasant. 'I'm over all that now, anyway. But fancy you having to keep quiet about it all that time,' she said, her voice trembling. 'I hate to think of you keeping something like that to yourself.' Her eyes brimmed with tears.

Frank put an arm around her. Tears seemed to come far too readily to Lizzie since the baby's arrival; a weepy wife was a new experience for Frank, and not a phenomenon he felt entirely comfortable with. It was just one of the marks the harrowing pregnancy and birth had left on Lizzie. But it meant she needed him more than he was used to, and that brought a kind of pleasure in itself.

'Don't feel bad, love. I had a few talks with Richard—you know, things I remembered from when me and Ben were little, that sort of thing. Maudie was good about it, too. And I told Beth—I didn't exactly mean to, but she caught on that something was up. I knew I could trust her not to let on to you. She's a good kid, Beth is. She's good to talk to about things.'

Lizzie sniffed. Frank held his handkerchief to her nose and she blew noisily into it. 'Chuck that in the wash, Frank, it smells a bit. But what happened to Ben? How did you find out?'

'I got a letter. There was a little parcel came in the mail, all nicely wrapped up, and a letter in with it. I didn't know the writing, but as soon as I opened the parcel I knew something had happened to Ben.'

He took his arm from around Lizzie's shoulders and crossed the room to fetch a small object from the chest of drawers. 'This was in it.'

Lizzie peered at his outstretched hand. 'What a nice watch. It looks quite old.'

'It was Pa's. Ben got it when Pa died, and he took it with him when he went. Now it's come to me.'

He put the watch on the bedside table before lying down beside Lizzie again. 'Ben ended up somewhere down South—some place I'd never heard of. He got a job on one of those big sheep stations they have down there. A shepherd, he was.' He gave a snort. 'That would've suited Ben, eh? Nothing to talk to but sheep. No people to get on his nerves.'

'No women, you mean,' Lizzie corrected.

'Well, Ben didn't like talking to men much, either. He liked things quiet.' Frank lapsed into silence as he thought over what the letter had said.

'Must've been quiet up in the mountains, even for Ben. It took them a while to catch on that he was missing. The letter I got, the boss's wife wrote it. I suppose the fellow thought women are better at that sort of thing.

'Ben had told someone that he came from Ruatane, and that he had a brother. That's how they knew to send word to me. You know Ben, he wouldn't have said much more than that, and he'd only have said that much after a few drinks.

'He'd been up there in the mountains with the sheep all summer, she said. They bring them down in the winter, before the snow comes. Ben's lot seemed a bit late coming, then by the time July came in they thought he might be in a bit of bother, so they went up looking for him.'

'And they found him dead,' Lizzie finished for him.

Frank nodded. He had to swallow a lump in his throat before he could go on. 'They took him down to the big house and had a doctor out to see what had done it. Something wrong with his chest, the doctor said—he thought it hadn't happened all that long ago, according to this woman. And no one to tell him to take to his bed when he felt poorly, I suppose.'

'He could've stayed here, you know,' Lizzie said. 'I'd've looked after him.'

'I know, love. It wouldn't have suited Ben, though. He wasn't any good at getting on with people.'

'I bet the kids would've brought him out of himself. You can't be shy with kids around.'

'That's true enough.' Frank stroked the baby's cheek, musing on how quickly the ugly, wrinkled creature had been transformed into this plump cherub. 'Ben never got the chance to find that out. And he's never going to have kids of his own.'

'You're soft, you know that, Frank? It was Ben's idea to go wandering off, no one made him. He probably could've talked someone into marrying him, there's always women who're a bit desperate.'

The baby had lost interest in suckling for the moment. Lizzie tucked her breasts back into her nightdress and cuddled him against her, studying the little face turned up to hers. 'Benjamin, I suppose his proper name was?'

'I suppose it was. Yes, that's right, I remember Ma calling him Benjamin once in a blue moon.'

'That's quite nice, really. Benjamin. Benjy.' She jiggled the baby gently. 'Benjy?' she said, raising the pitch of her voice, and the baby's eyes widened slightly at the sound. 'Yes, you like that, don't you, sweetie?'

The little mouth started working again. Lizzie pulled out a full breast and offered it to the baby. 'All right, we'll call him Benjamin.'

'Thanks, Lizzie. Ben would've liked that. It's good to think I can do something for him. I mean, I've got everything, really, and Ben ended up with nothing.'

'Now, don't you go getting silly over it. You did plenty for Ben—not that he gave you any say in it, helping himself to his share of the money like that, and you with a family to provide for. Well, you had me, anyway. And we started having the kids pretty quickly. You've no reason to feel guilty.'

'I know, love.' Frank squeezed her hand, taking an odd sort of pleasure in being scolded by her. There was a time when Lizzie would have verbally flayed him for such foolishness, but her scoldings were noticeably half-hearted these days.

Much of the vigour had gone out of Lizzie with the bearing of this child, and Frank sensed that it would never be fully restored. It troubled him to think she might never be quite the same again, but far more powerful than any vague yearning for the old Lizzie was his overwhelming relief that he had not lost her.

He lifted her hand and kissed it. 'I'm lucky, you know, Lizzie.'

'You're soft, Frank.' But she made no move to disengage her hand from his.

*

'There's milk in the jug over here, see?' Amy said. 'The scones are under that cloth—there's biscuits in the tins, too, if he wants something else. Be sure and break them into little pieces for him, though, he can't manage otherwise. Oh, and there's—'

'I can find the stuff, Ma,' David interrupted. 'It's time you were going. Hey, don't go putting the cups out, I can do that.'

'It'll save you bothering. Now, it'd be good if you could talk your father into sitting in the parlour for a while, that sometimes brightens him up a bit, but if he gets tired you be sure and take him back to bed. He gets those awful headaches if he overdoes it. And see he doesn't get cold, he doesn't seem to notice until he's really shivering. And make sure—'

'Ma, you've already told me all that. Come on, get a move on. You don't want to be late for the party, eh?'

Amy sat down at the table. 'I shouldn't be going at all,' she fretted. 'I don't know why I let you talk me into it. Oh, I don't think I can.'

'Now, don't start all that again,' David said. 'You've got to go, Aunt Lizzie's expecting you. And it's pretty special, isn't it, with them having both the babies christened. Even Pa said you're to go.'

Amy could not resist a smile at that gentle thrust. 'I never thought I'd see you and your father siding against me, Dave.'

'Well, he can see you're due for an outing. And if you don't get a move on they'll all have gone home by the time you get there! Come on, Ma.' He took hold of her unresisting hand and tugged her upright.

It was a very special occasion, Amy had to keep reminding herself. Nothing less momentous than the joint christening could have persuaded her to abandon tending Charlie, even for the hour or so she expected to be away. Now that David had got into the habit of sitting with his father for an hour every evening, giving Amy the chance to tidy the kitchen and make the bread without interruption, she could see that Charlie had learned not to be frightened of his son.

But that did not stop her feeling guilty and anxious. 'Remember to keep him warm,' she reminded David again as he helped her on with her cloak. 'And make sure the tea cools down a bit before you give him a cup, or he'll scald his mouth. You know you have to hold the cup for him, don't you? And—'

'Ma!' David interrupted. 'I *know*. I know all that. And if you say one more word, I'm going to pick you up and carry you outside and dump you on the ground. Hurry *up*.'

Amy obediently went down the steps, but she paused at the base. 'But you must—no, listen a minute,' she said when David raised a warning finger. 'I'm going, really I am. But I've got to say this one thing first. If your father's taken poorly, you must send for me. Run over to Uncle John's, there'll be someone home. Will you promise me you'll do that, Davie? I don't think I can go unless you do.'

'He'll be all right. Oh, don't get in a state over it. I promise. If Pa gets sick I'll send for you. He won't, though.'

Amy smiled. 'No, I don't think he will. You're very good with him.' She ran back up the steps, planted a kiss of gratitude on his cheek, then hurried down and began her walk before David had the chance to scold her again over her tardiness.

The christening ceremony began so quickly after Amy's arrival that she was guiltily aware it must have been delayed for her sake. But the feeling of guilt was soon lost in the pleasure of being surrounded by so many people that she loved. Even Mrs Coulson was there; she smiled warmly at Amy from her place near Arthur and Edie.

Apart from a brief, startled squeal from Lucy when water was poured over her forehead, the two babies behaved perfectly, to the conspicuous relief of the minister. He was an elderly bachelor who had only recently arrived in the district, and whom Amy had never seen before, and his discomfort at having to cope with not one but two babies was obvious. She was not surprised when he made his excuses as soon as his task was over, and escaped from the house before Lizzie could ply him with food and drink.

Amy was a little disappointed when John and Harry and their families left soon after the minister, though she knew the reason well enough. Neither of her older brothers would willingly stay in the same room as Susannah for any longer than politeness demanded.

But there was another guest whom Amy was delighted to see, and who seemed in no rush to leave. As soon as Amy arrived, Sarah beckoned her over to the place she had saved at her side. Sarah had come out with Susannah and Thomas, as Susannah was eager to tell everyone.

Sarah seemed in a strange mood, Amy found soon after sitting down beside her. She was clearly tense, and several times she began a sentence only to break off abruptly. Amy wished she could probe the reason for Sarah's mood, but the number of people crammed into the parlour meant she could do no more than talk quietly about innocuous subjects.

Amy saw Susannah looking rather hopefully in Arthur's direction when John and Harry made their departures; Susannah was clearly under no illusion about Arthur's feelings towards her. But Arthur did no more than answer Susannah's look with a grim stare before he turned his attention back to the rest of the company.

This was a rare outing for Arthur and Edie; in fact it was the first time they had left the farm since the previous summer. Arthur was close to seventy now, and had condescended to use a stick to get about ever since a fall the previous autumn had left one leg somewhat unsteady. But he wore his age proudly, his shoulders unbowed by the years that had slowed his movements.

Amy was reminded painfully of her father as she studied Arthur. He should have had the same peaceful old age his brother was enjoying, she thought wistfully. Instead, his last years had been soured by strife and pain; Susannah's incessant complaints, and Jack's sense of guilt over Amy's fate.

But Arthur shared his house with three females who, in their different ways, devoted much of their time to looking after his comfort. Edie tended to fuss about rather vaguely, full of good intentions but more often than not forgetting what she had meant to do within a minute or two of having voiced the thought. She would announce plaintively that Arthur liked the other sort of jam better, or Arthur needed a warmer jacket brought to him, then look about as if expecting the desired item to materialise of its own free will.

It was Lily who made sure that both Arthur and Edie were well cared for. In Lily a kind heart and a strong feeling of gratitude were mixed with sound good sense, and her parents-in-law reaped the benefits. Amy noticed that Lily's attention never left the elderly pair for more than a few minutes, and today Lily was including Mrs Coulson in her solicitous care. It was Lily who placed rugs over their laps to see that they were kept warm, and Lily who arranged a footstool under Arthur's feet. She then assigned her daughter to stay close to Arthur, Edie and the nurse, and to fetch them anything they wanted. Ten-year-old Emma was a quiet, solemn girl who clearly took her responsibility seriously.

Amy could see that Arthur enjoyed the attention, though he grumbled unconvincingly that there was 'too much fussing about'. He made much of little Lucy, who sat on his lap gurgling and cooing, looking suitably cherubic in her long gown trimmed with a mass of white lace and ribbons, and he did not even object when the little girl took hold of his beard and gave it a firm tug.

'Strong little thing, isn't she?' Arthur remarked as he disengaged his beard from Lucy's fist. 'She's a fine child, this one. She's my great-granddaughter, you know,' he announced to the room in general. 'That's something out of the usual, having a great-grandchild.'

'And a new grandson,' Lizzie put in sharply, ever alert for any imagined slight to one of her children. 'You've got a new grandson, too.'

'I know that,' Arthur said. 'He's a fine enough little chap, too. But I've more grandchildren than I can shake a stick at—I've got...' He frowned as he attempted the calculation, then admitted defeat. 'How many grandchildren have I got, Edie?'

'Eleven,' Edie said promptly. She might be vague about many things, but Edie could effortlessly call to mind the names of all her grandchildren. 'Maudie's the oldest, and Benjy's the youngest.'

'Eleven of them,' Arthur echoed. 'There's no sense making a fuss over another one. But a great-grandchild, now that's something. It's not every man has a great-grandchild.'

'I've got one, too,' Edie said, smiling contentedly.

'Well, of course you have,' Arthur said. 'If I've got one, so have you.'

'But it's nice, isn't it?' Edie said, her smile not faltering. 'It's just nice.'

Arthur gave an exaggerated sigh. 'You say some silly things at times, Edie.' He reached out to squeeze her hand.

The footstool shifted a little with his movement, and the vigilant Lily hurried over to straighten it. 'Is that better, Father?' she asked. 'Your leg isn't hurting you, is it?'

'No, no, I haven't had a twinge all day,' Arthur said. 'It's just about right now, this leg of mine. I'll be down at the cow shed again before long, see what sort of a job you've been making of things, boy.'

This last was directed at Bill, who was watching his father with a mixture of exasperation and amusement. 'Don't be in too much of a rush, Pa,' he said mildly. 'I can just about manage to keep the other fellows in line by myself. And don't forget I've got Arfie helping now.' Amy saw him catch Lily's eye for a moment; Lily answered his grin with a small smile of her own.

'Mmm, that's true enough,' Arthur said. 'He's a great milker, that one. I've never seen a boy get through the cows like he does. Still, that doesn't mean I don't need to start keeping an eye on the rest of you fellows again.'

'You want to take care of yourself,' Bill persisted. 'There's no sense overdoing it. I remember John and Harry saying how they used to wish Uncle Jack would lie in of a morning, not go wearing himself out milking every day.'

Arthur's face twisted into a scowl, but it was not directed at Bill. Amy followed his gaze as it crossed the room to settle on Susannah.

'It wasn't milking that killed Jack,' he said, echoing Amy's own thoughts.

Susannah had not caught his words, but she seemed to sense his attention. She looked up sharply and met Arthur's baleful glare with a resentful one of her own.

They might have held each other's eyes for an uncomfortable length of time if Maudie, blithely unaware of the hostility crackling across the room, had not come between the two of them.

'Now, Grandpa, you can't have Lucy all to yourself,' she said to Arthur. 'There's other people want to give her a cuddle too, you know.'

She scooped Lucy up into her arms, then looked around the room speculatively. Her eyes soon settled on Sarah, and a look of sympathy spread over her face. How sad, her expression said as clearly as if she had spoken. Here was a woman who had no husband and no paragon of a child to exult in.

Generous in her awareness of her blessed state, Maudie went over to Sarah. 'I bet you'd love to hold Lucy, Miss Millish.' Before Sarah had a chance to deny any such desire, the baby was on her lap. 'There, that's nice, isn't it?' Maudie said, beaming at the sight.

Sarah sat rigid, staring in some dread at the creature that had descended on her. 'What do I do with it?' she asked.

Maudie laughed. 'Cuddle her, of course! Here, I'll show you.' She took hold of Sarah's hand and drew her arm around Lucy. 'Put your arm behind her back like this—that's right, sit her up properly or she'll think you're going to give her a feed.' She took a step backwards and studied them in satisfaction. 'Isn't that nice? Have a good, long hold of her, you don't get the chance much.'

Maudie moved about the room, glancing back from time to time to enjoy the sight of Lucy on her reluctant perch. 'Lucy's such a good baby,' Amy heard her say. 'She'll go to anybody.'

Lizzie obviously took this as a slight on her own baby. 'Benjy's too little to get passed around like a parcel,' she said, clutching the baby closer. 'I don't want him getting upset or anything.'

She glared at Maudie as if daring the girl to argue. But Maudie said nothing, merely raised her eyebrows and smiled knowingly.

'Yes, Lizzie's pretty careful of the little fellow,' Frank said. 'She doesn't even let me hold him most of the time.' He gave Lizzie a grin.

'I do!' Lizzie protested. 'Don't go telling stories, Frank. I'm just careful with him, that's all.'

She hesitated, then, 'You can have a hold of him if you like,' she said, holding the baby out towards Amy.

Amy took the offer for what it was: a sign of Lizzie's love and trust. 'I'd love to, Lizzie.' She took the baby and nestled him into the curve of her arm.

Benjy had been lulled by warmth and the hum of voices around him. He looked mildly surprised at being shifted from one lap to another, but seemed content with his new situation. He stared up at Amy with apparent interest.

The baby was warm against her, and the milky smell of him was heady. He was a plump, fair-haired child, big for his age and with an air of robustness that hampered his mother's efforts to treat him as a tiny, delicate creature. But when Amy closed her eyes and relied on smell and touch alone, the warmth and scent of him brought a feeling of drowsy pleasure.

'There's something about a baby, isn't there?' she murmured, more to herself than anyone else.

She opened her eyes and saw the solicitous look on Lizzie's face. 'Is Benjy all right?' Lizzie asked. 'He's not used to other people. He's not getting upset, is he?'

'He's a lovely, lovely baby, Lizzie,' Amy said. But he was not her baby, despite the tricks memory was playing on her. 'You're lucky to have him. You'd better take him back now, though. We don't want him to get upset, do we?' She replaced him in Lizzie's ready arms and planted a soft kiss on his cheek.

'I've finished with this one, too, thank you,' Sarah said plaintively, trying to catch Maudie's eye. But she would have had to shout to get Maudie's attention away from the conversation she was engrossed in with Lily. Sarah sighed, and bounced Lucy on her lap in a half-hearted way.

Lucy, who had been studying Sarah with an increasingly suspicious gaze for some time, began to squirm.

'I wish she wouldn't wriggle like that,' Sarah said. 'I'm scared I'll drop her.'

Lucy squirmed all the more, and screwed up her face ominously.

'Oh dear,' Sarah said. 'I think she's going to cry.'

Richard glanced over at them, and came to Sarah's rescue before Amy had the chance to take the baby. 'Here, let me,' he said, relieving Sarah of her unwanted burden. 'I've hardly had the chance to hold my daughter all day, with so many other people wanting the pleasure.'

As soon as she realised she was back in familiar arms, Lucy settled again. She giggled in delight as Richard bounced her gently, then she nestled comfortably into the crook of his arm.

'I must say it's a relief to see I haven't done her any lasting harm,' Sarah said. 'She was beginning to look quite odd, with her face all red like that.'

'She could tell you weren't confident with her,' Amy said. 'That's why she got nervous.'

'What a very sensible child,' Sarah remarked, stretching her arm gingerly. 'However do parents cope with having their arms go numb all the time?'

'Oh, yes, she's very clever,' Maudie said, drawn back to their group by the praise of her daughter. 'She's very forward at things. She can just about sit up already, and she can hold a little doll all by herself.'

'Benjy's a lot younger than her,' Lizzie put in quickly. 'He'll be doing those things soon enough.'

'Well, of course he will,' Maudie said, enjoying the chance to be condescending to her mother. 'Honestly, Ma's silly as anything over Benjy,' she confided to those close to her. 'You wouldn't think she'd had eight babies. Lucy *is* very clever, though,' she added, quietly but with certainty. 'Isn't she, Richard?'

'I'm hardly unbiased, dear. But as far as I'm concerned, she's the cleverest child the world has ever seen. Aren't you, my darling?' He tickled Lucy; the baby laughed and waved her arms about.

'Then I hope you'll have her properly educated, Doctor Townsend,' said Sarah. 'It would hardly be right to waste her abilities, would it?'

'Oh, I don't think we need to worry about that just yet,' Richard said, but Sarah was prepared to press the point.

'It does no harm to think ahead. Your daughter might want to study. You'll need to see that she's properly prepared to do so.'

'We're going to send her to school, Miss Millish,' Maudie said, clearly puzzled by Sarah's comments. 'You've got to send kids to school, anyway.'

'I think Miss Millish is thinking of education beyond what Ruatane might be able to offer, darling,' Richard said. 'I do appreciate your concern, Miss Millish,' he added, carefully polite but unable to hide his amusement.

'But why would she want to do that?' Maudie said, still puzzled. 'I mean, she's not going to have to *work* or anything.' She said the word as though it were something rather shocking.

'No, she won't,' Richard agreed. 'I do expect to be able to provide for my daughter, Miss Millish. She won't be put in a position where she has to support herself by her own efforts.'

Sarah stared hard at Richard. 'I've heard that there are men— professional men like yourself, Doctor Townsend—who don't actually *have* to work themselves. Who have adequate private means, but choose to work for some other reason. Would you have any views on such a matter?'

Richard's expression told Amy that he had not missed the allusion to himself. He still appeared to be searching for a reply when Sarah answered the question for him.

'I rather suspect that the reason might be a desire to feel useful. Would you agree?'

'I think that's a fair assessment,' Richard said guardedly.

Sarah pounced. 'And why shouldn't your daughter feel the same way? Why shouldn't she have a desire to be useful?'

'Lucy will be useful to her mother, of course. I would hope that she'll find that rewarding.'

Sarah regarded him steadily. 'If you had a son, Doctor Townsend, and he wished to be a doctor, what would your feelings be?'

'Well, naturally I'd be pleased. And of course I'd help him in any way I could, though I hope I'd try not to push my own desires beyond what the boy wanted for himself.'

'And what if your daughter happens to want the same?'

'Be a doctor?' Maudie said, clearly shocked. 'What, go poking around in people's insides? What an awful idea! Ooh, I'd never let Lucy do anything like that. You wouldn't want her to do that would you, Richard?'

Richard hesitated before replying. 'I think… I think I would have to give the matter proper thought if the occasion arose.' He hesitated again, for longer this time, then said, 'I'd try not to stand in the way of something Lucy really wanted, as long as I was convinced it was truly the best for her.'

'Give her the opportunity, Doctor Townsend,' Sarah said. 'Give her a proper education. Fit her to make up her own mind in a sensible way.'

'I take your point, Miss Millish,' Richard said. 'Thank you for your interest.'

'I *think*,' Maudie said, still bristling, 'I *think* we know what's best for Lucy.' She took Lucy from Richard and flounced off in a rustle of petticoats, giving Sarah the barest of nods as she went.

Richard went after her and put a hand on her arm. As Amy and Sarah watched, they spoke quietly together. Maudie gave a slight toss of her head, then glanced back at Sarah and her gaze softened. She looked down at the baby in her arms and whispered something to Richard.

'She's feeling sorry for the "old maid",' Sarah remarked drily. She sank back in her chair, apparently a little deflated after the confrontation. 'I suppose I've caused offence now. I'm rather good at that.'

'I don't think you really caused offence,' Amy said.

'Oh, yes I did. Don't look so anxious, Mrs Stewart, I've no intention of feeling guilty over it. Doctor Townsend was being patronising, and that's something I won't stand for. The fact that I'm a woman doesn't mean I'm incapable of talking sense.'

'I'm sure Richard didn't think that,' Amy said. 'I expect he just hadn't thought about education for girls.'

'He was being patronising,' Sarah insisted. 'My father was the finest man I've ever known, and from the time he realised that I had a decent brain I don't recall his ever being patronising to me. If I never had to suffer it from Father, I've no intention of tolerating it from any other man.'

Amy hesitated, reluctant to argue with Sarah but anxious to be fair. 'I don't think Richard meant any harm. He's very nice, really he is. I like Richard.'

Sarah smiled at her, her face softening. 'I suspect you like most people, Mrs Stewart. You don't seem very good at disliking. Anyway,' she said, suddenly serious again, 'I didn't come here to waste my time arguing with Doctor Townsend. I came to talk with you.' She looked about her, frowning. 'Though there's precious little chance of privacy, is there? Do you think we'd be noticed if we slipped off for a walk?'

Amy glanced up at the mantel clock. 'No, I can't, I really should be leaving. I said I'd only be an hour.'

'No!' Sarah said, startling Amy with her fervour. 'No, you can't go yet! Not when we haven't talked. I don't know when I'll have the chance again. I mightn't ever—'

She broke off, noticing Amy's discomfort at the attention Sarah's raised voice was attracting. 'And now I'm making a fool of myself, and upsetting you into the bargain,' she said more quietly. 'But I have to talk to you, Mrs Stewart.'

'We've been talking, haven't we?' Amy said, puzzled by Sarah's mood. 'Sarah, I'm sorry, but I really do have to go. It's not fair on Dave to leave him looking after his father by himself too long.'

'I hardly see that it would hurt him to take some share of the burden.'

'Oh, he does. Dave's a big help to me. I don't know how I ever managed without him.'

Sarah's mouth set in a narrow line. 'Yes, your precious David.'

'And you got him back for me,' Amy said, feeling a warm rush of gratitude at the memory.

'I don't need reminding of the fact,' Sarah murmured.

Amy moved around the room making her farewells. Sarah hovered near her, and Amy introduced her to Mrs Coulson.

To Amy's surprise, the nurse seemed inclined to be rather cool towards Sarah. 'You're part of Mrs Susannah Leith's family, are you?' Mrs Coulson said, her voice tight. 'I can see a certain resemblance.'

'No, not at all,' Amy answered for Sarah. 'It's just that Sarah came out with Susannah and Tom. Sarah's Lily's cousin, you see.'

Mrs Coulson looked a little confused, and Amy could see that the nurse was struggling to remember just who Lily was. 'So she's part of your family, dear?' she asked uncertainly.

'Well, yes, she is in a way,' Amy said, anxious not to confuse the nurse further.

Mrs Coulson studied Sarah, then turned to Amy and smiled. 'That's lovely, dear. I'm so pleased.' She tilted her face to receive Amy's kiss. It gave Amy a start to realise that Mrs Coulson seemed to be getting muddled in her memories, but her old nurse seemed cheerful enough.

Beth made her up a small parcel of christening cake to take home for David and Charlie, and Lizzie dispatched Danny to catch a horse to take Amy home on.

'I'd come and see you off, but I think Benjy wants a feed,' Lizzie said as they stood just outside the parlour door. They hugged as well as they could with the baby between them, then Lizzie took herself off into the bedroom with the mildly fractious Benjy.

Sarah had followed Amy to the parlour doorway. She came out onto the verandah and down the steps with her. 'How stupid of me,' she fretted. 'I could take you myself if I'd only had the sense to ride out. Whatever possessed me to come with Mrs Leith?'

'It's quite a long ride,' Amy said. 'It was a good idea to get a lift with Susannah.'

'I won't pretend I enjoy Mrs Leith's company, though I suspect she intends to dine out on me for some time. I heard her talking to the minister before he escaped—"Miss Millish is one of *the* Millishes, you know,"' she said, affecting a mincing tone. '"Such a distinguished family, and such a charming girl. We're quite friends already." If only she knew,' Sarah murmured. 'But it suited me to come out with her and Thomas—at least I thought it did at the time. Why does your uncle dislike her so much?' she asked. 'And what did he mean by what he said about what killed your father?'

'She poisoned him,' Amy said fiercely. 'That's what killed Pa.'

'She—I beg your pardon? I don't particularly like Mrs Leith, but... murder?'

Amy calmed herself with an effort. 'I didn't mean it like that. She didn't put something in his food or anything. She just... oh, I can't really explain it properly, Sarah. They didn't get on very well, and Susannah made Pa's life a misery. I shouldn't be telling you all this, either.'

'It's most interesting,' Sarah said. 'And did she—'

'Don't, Sarah, please,' Amy interrupted. 'I shouldn't have said what I did, and I don't want to say anything else. If it comes to that, I did my share of upsetting Pa.'

'Did you?' Sarah fixed her with a keen stare. 'As much as Mrs Leith did?'

Amy dropped her gaze to the ground. 'I hope not,' she murmured.

'And now I'm being nosy again. I'm good at that, as Cousin Bill delights in telling me. And today I seem to be particularly good at upsetting you. Amy, I don't want to waste our time together.' Sarah did not seem to notice that she had forgotten to address Amy correctly. 'Not when it might be the last chance we have.'

She took Amy's hand almost timidly. 'I'm going away. I'm going back to Auckland.'

'But... you've gone home for a trip before,' Amy said, confused by Sarah's intensity. 'You'll be back, won't you?'

'I don't know. Not for some time, anyway, if I do come back at all. I've resigned from the school. I'm coming of age soon, you see. I need to devote some time to settling my affairs, now that I'll be fully responsible for managing the estate. It's all been rather self-indulgent, coming down here.'

It seemed an odd thing to say, but Amy did not press her to explain. 'I hope you will come back, Sarah. I'll miss you.'

'Perhaps I will.' Sarah managed a half smile. 'I don't know if I can bear to stay away. We can dream about it, can't we?'

A hard knot formed in the pit of Amy's stomach. 'Don't say that. I don't dream about things.'

'Why not? You have to have dreams, or why would you bother going on with life? I once read somewhere that it's dreams that raise us above the animals.'

'Dreams cause trouble,' Amy said, shuddering a little at dark memories. She had had dreams of going to wonderful places and doing exciting work. Malcolm had had dreams of glorious battles. 'They make you want things you can't have, and that makes you do things you shouldn't.'

'Who's to say you can't have those things?' Sarah gazed intently at Amy. 'Perhaps it's just a matter of wanting them enough.'

She shook her head. 'I have a dream of you coming to stay in my

455

house. And here you are fretting to get back to them after an hour away. Some dreams are more of a challenge than others, aren't they?'

Amy saw Danny approaching them, leading a horse by the reins. 'I've got to go,' she said. 'Will you come and see me before you go away?'

'No,' Sarah said. 'Not with *him* there. I can't bear to see you with him. Oh, I wish I'd come out by myself today! And to think of not seeing you again! Mrs Stewart, will you write to me? It would be something.'

'I don't know what I'd find to tell you, I never do anything very interesting. But I'd like that, Sarah.'

'Tell me everything you do. Don't go worrying about whether it's interesting or not, I want it all. Try and make it as if I was still here.'

Sarah reached into a pocket in the seam of her skirt and withdrew a small card. 'It's one of my visiting cards—see, it has my address on it. You will write, won't you? Promise me you will?'

'I promise. I'll try and write every week.'

'Oh, I wish…' Sarah suddenly clutched at Amy's shoulders, leaned down and kissed her. Amy realised with a start that Sarah was holding back tears with difficulty.

'Sarah, I—' she began awkwardly. But Danny was there and waiting, and Sarah turned towards the house, one hand across her mouth as she walked away.

27

October – December 1905

David had heard the horse approaching, and he was already on the back doorstep pulling on his boots when Amy came up to the house.

'Good timing, Ma. I was just thinking it was about time to get the cows in.'

'How did you get on with your father?' Amy asked breathlessly. 'Is he all right?'

'He's fine,' David assured her. 'We got on pretty good. It's a bit hard talking to him sometimes—you know how he gets, talking sense for a bit then wandering off back into the old days. He seems pretty sensible today, except he kept asking where you were. He'd forgotten you'd gone out. I took him out on the verandah for a bit, while it was warm.'

'That was a good idea. He hasn't been getting much fresh air lately, I've been worried he might take a chill. Did you have to help him with anything?'

David knew what she meant without her having to elaborate. 'Yes, he asked me for a hand. That's when I took him out on the verandah.'

'Didn't you use the chamber pot?'

'No, I thought it'd be easier to do it out there. I just gave him a hand with… you know, getting everything out.'

'I never thought of doing that,' Amy said in surprise. 'I don't know if I could.'

'You used to help me when I was a little fellow,' David reminded her, looking mildly embarrassed at the admission. 'Pa didn't seem too worried. I sort of made a joke of it, you know? I said we could have a contest, see who could get furthest. I told him me and Mal used to do that.' David frowned. 'He went a bit quiet when I said that. I'd forgotten how he's silly about not wanting anyone to talk about Mal.

'He said a funny thing after that, though,' David went on. 'He told me to get the lawyer to come out and see him. Why does he want me to do that?'

Amy was taken aback. 'I don't know, Dave. I suppose you'd better do it, though. Don't go into town specially, wait until you're going in anyway.' She silently resolved to speak to the lawyer before Charlie did, to warn him of Charlie's possible confusion.

Amy went through to the parlour, where David had settled Charlie. 'How are you feeling?' she asked. 'Not too tired?'

'You've been gone a long while,' he said, frowning at her.

Well, perhaps an hour seemed a long time to Charlie, Amy reflected. She sat on the floor by his chair and reached under his nightshirt to massage the muscles of his calves, inclined to cramp from lack of use. 'I know. I won't be going out like that again, it was a bit special today. Has Dave been looking after you all right?'

'He's not been too bad. He's not a bad boy, that Dave,' Charlie allowed, and from him it was high praise. 'You been to Kelly's place, have you? What'd you go there for?'

'They had a christening today,' Amy told him yet again. 'It was a special one—they had two babies done.'

'Whose bairns?'

'Well, Benjy's Lizzie and Frank's new baby. He's six weeks old now, he's a lovely baby.'

'Kelly's bairn?' Charlie said. 'How many's that?'

'Eight of them now. I don't think they'll have any more, though, Lizzie had a bit of bother having Benjy.' Seeing how much of a shock the news was to Charlie, she tried to make light of it. 'Poor old Frank, fancy having to get used to all those broken nights again. I'm glad we don't have to put up with new babies all the time.'

But Charlie was not listening. 'He's got a pile of sons, that Kelly. Didn't know he'd got another one. Lucky bugger.'

There was no comfort Amy could offer to that sense of loss. She took refuge in trying to distract him from his bleak thoughts. 'Maudie got Lucy done, too. That was the other baby.'

'Who's Maudie? Who's Lucy?' Charlie said irritably. 'Don't know who you're on about.'

'Maudie's Lizzie and Frank's oldest. Do you remember her?'

Charlie frowned in thought. 'She was born the time of the earthquake. When the mountain blew up.'

'That's right. Fancy you remembering all that—I'd just about forgotten, myself.'

'She's a bairn of her own now?'

'Yes. Lucy's nearly six months old, I think. Oh, she's a lovely baby, Maudie's proud as anything of her.'

Charlie was quiet for some time. 'The boy was older than her,' he said.

Amy had hardly dared hope that Charlie would ever allow himself to speak of Malcolm again. She held her breath for a moment, startled, then spoke gently. 'Yes, he was. Mal was seven months older than Maudie. He'd have been twenty this year.'

'Twenty. Just about a man.'

And instead he was dead. Amy took Charlie's unresponsive hand in her own and held it, but she sensed that it would upset him too much to talk about Malcolm any more just now. She would raise the subject again soon, she promised herself. For too long Charlie had pretended he had forgotten Malcolm.

That evening she took the photograph of Charlie, herself and the boys from her bedroom and put it back on the mantelpiece where it belonged.

Amy hoped that as the weather grew warmer Charlie might become a little stronger. She began taking him out to the verandah most days, sure that sun and fresh air would do him good.

She had hoped, too, that a brighter outlook than the four walls of his room might cheer him. But he seemed to grow quieter rather than livelier, often sitting staring out over the edge of the verandah for hours on end without saying a word.

He hardly seemed to notice whether Amy was there or not when he was in one of these moods. When she came out with his lunch one day in December, he showed no sign that he had heard her approach. She came up slowly, anxious not to startle him. As she moved in front of him, she was troubled to see that his face was wet with tears.

He had seen her now, and it was too late to slip away quietly. She put the tray with his lunch down on the little table beside him and sat on a stool next to him.

'What's wrong, Charlie?' she asked. 'Don't you feel well?'

He rubbed his hand across his eyes in a clumsy attempt to clear away the tears. 'Useless. That's what I am. Bloody useless.'

Amy took a handkerchief from her apron pocket and wiped his eyes. 'No, you're not. Dave needs you to tell him what to do on the farm. He asks you things all the time, you know he does.'

'Don't know whether he's making a decent job of it or not. Can't get out there to keep an eye on him. Can't get out on my farm.'

He looked past her to the pasture stretching away in the distance. The sea was a silver-spattered pool of blue at the end of the valley, but Charlie's gaze did not go beyond the boundaries of his land. 'Can't get out on my farm,' he echoed. 'Might as well be dead.'

'Don't say that,' Amy soothed. 'You mustn't fret about things.' She stopped, aware of how inadequate a word 'fret' was for what Charlie was feeling. He wasn't fretting over his land; he was mourning the loss of it. Amy could not bear to watch his suffering without doing her best to ease it.

She sat beside him in silence, pondering the details of how she might manage it, before she made the suggestion. 'How would you like to go on a picnic?' she asked, careful to make her voice bright. 'We could have one tomorrow, the three of us. I'll make a nice lunch with all the things you like, and Dave can show you what he got done over the winter. You can see the new calves, too. It'll be nice, won't it?'

His eyes opened wide, then his face crumpled. 'I can't. My leg won't work.'

But Amy had seen his look of wonder as, just for a moment, he had let himself believe he could go walking over his land once again. 'Yes, you can. You can walk a little way if I help you. Take your stick, and you can lean on me. We don't need to go very far. Please, Charlie,' she urged gently. 'Please.'

Charlie made a rumbling noise of disgust. 'Ah, if it'll put a stop to your nagging I might as well. Now shut up about it for five minutes, can't you? I want my lunch.'

'All right,' Amy said, turning her face aside to hide a smile as she leant over to pick up his tray. Charlie's show of grumpiness was the best sign she could have hoped for. It told her that the idea of the picnic had roused him more than anything else could have.

'I've got pies and sandwiches in that one, and cakes and scones in the other basket,' Amy told David. 'Did I put the boiled eggs in? Yes, there they are. Be careful of the scones specially, they've got jam on them. Let's see, two bottles of lemonade should be enough, and I've put in some beer for your father.' She looked around the kitchen. 'Have I forgotten anything?'

'You've got enough to feed half a dozen of us, it should be enough,' David said. 'Aw, heck, then there's all these rugs and things to carry!' He rolled his eyes in pretended horror.

'Oh, stop complaining! You'll hardly even notice it, a big, strong boy like you,' Amy said with a laugh. 'Anyway, it's worth it if it cheers your father up,' she added, suddenly serious again.

Charlie's eyes were brighter than Amy could remember having seen them in years as they set off. He grasped his stick in his good hand, the other arm around Amy's shoulders, and took his first few cautious steps.

They had begun well enough, but not many minutes passed before Amy had to ask herself if she had done the right thing. Charlie was leaning on her more and more, and his steps became more hesitant.

They reached a steeper part of the paddock. Charlie stumbled, and would have fallen if Amy had not been taking so much of his weight. His near fall frightened him, and he leaned more heavily than ever on her. When he missed his footing again, he trembled so violently that they had to stop and wait for him to calm a little.

Amy chose a path as carefully as she could with the distraction of being hardly able to breathe from Charlie's convulsive grip, but a few steps further on they struck a rough patch of pasture. Charlie's foot twisted under him, and before she could take a firmer hold he had fallen to the ground, dragging her with him.

David dropped his burdens and helped the two of them up to a sitting position. Amy was only slightly winded, but Charlie sat hunched on the ground, refusing to take the hand David held out to help him stand.

'I can't do it,' he said miserably. 'I can't walk.'

Amy checked him over for injuries. 'I don't think you've hurt yourself. You just got a fright, Charlie. Sit here and rest for a minute, then we'll try again.'

Charlie shrank away from her touch. 'I can't,' he repeated. 'Just leave me be for a bit. Then you can give me a hand getting back to the house.'

Amy felt tears pricking her eyes at the dull misery in his voice. She had to persuade him into carrying on with this outing, but she had no idea how; not when he was so frightened.

She looked up at David with a mute appeal for help. His eyes met hers, then flicked to his father and back again.

'Can you carry this stuff, Ma?' he asked, glancing at the baskets and rugs.

'I think so. What are you—'

Before she had the chance to finish, David had bent down and scooped Charlie up in his arms as easily as if he had been a child. 'This'll be better,' he said matter-of-factly. 'Now, where are we having this picnic, Ma?'

Charlie was so startled at this treatment that for a few moments he could not speak at all. He recovered his voice and spluttered his outrage.

'What the hell do you think you're doing? Put me down, you bloody fool.'

'I don't know, we can't let all that stuff Ma's cooked go to waste,' David said, unperturbed. 'We're going down to the creek aren't we, Ma?'

'I thought we'd set it out where those trees come down close to the bank,' Amy said, hastily gathering up the things David had dropped. 'Can you manage that far, Dave?'

'No trouble,' David said. He adjusted his load slightly, then set off down the hill, ignoring Charlie's protests.

Amy had chosen the closest spot to the house that could provide both water and shade. David lowered Charlie carefully to his feet and supported him with one arm around his waist while Amy began setting out their picnic.

As soon as she had spread a rug they sat Charlie down on it. He seemed so weary that he was barely able to sit upright. Amy pressed close to him so that she could take a share of his weight.

Before offering him any food she waited until he had recovered his strength a little, watching him anxiously as his chest heaved. The months of forced inactivity had left him even weaker than she had realised.

Feeding Charlie was a slow business, with every bit of food having to be broken into smaller pieces so that he could chew it, though eating outdoors had the advantage that dropped crumbs did not matter. Amy found she had ample time to eat her own share while she waited for Charlie to manage each mouthful.

Charlie was tired again by the time he had eaten and she had cleared out his mouth for him. She persuaded him to lie back with his head in her lap, and she and David talked quietly while Charlie lay resting.

He dozed fitfully for a while, then Amy saw that his eyes were open and he was listening to their voices.

'Do you remember us having picnics years ago?' she asked. 'I used to bring Mal down when he was little, so he could see you.'

'No,' Charlie said after a moment's frowning concentration.

'Well, I suppose I didn't do it very often. It might only have been the once, now I come to think of it.'

'I don't remember that, Ma,' David put in.

'Of course you don't, Dave, it was before you were born.'

'You were carrying him,' Charlie said suddenly. 'You brought the boy down with you, and you said you were carrying another one.'

David looked away, grinning at Amy's embarrassment. 'No wonder I don't remember, eh?'

'So you do remember, then, Charlie?'

'Aye. It's come back now.'

Amy studied him for signs that the reminder of Malcolm might have upset him, but he looked pensive rather than distressed. He said nothing for some time, but a little later, when Amy and David next lapsed into silence, he looked up at David and said, 'You can tell your brother he can come home if he likes.'

Amy caught her breath and sent David a silent plea for understanding, but he seemed to sense the right response. 'I'll tell him that next time I'm talking to him,' he said.

'Tell him to hurry up about it,' Charlie added.

'I'll do that, Pa.'

Charlie nodded almost imperceptibly. His eyes closed, and he dozed briefly.

When he woke again, David talked to him about the work he had been doing on the farm. He pointed out the paddock where the young calves were grazing; then, seeing the look of frustration on his father's face at not being able to see them properly, David guided Charlie's uncertain steps the short distance to the calves.

They gave Charlie time to rest again before Amy started packing up the remains of their picnic. On the way back up to the house Charlie submitted to being carried with slightly better grace than he had coming down, mustering what dignity he could given his position.

The outing had left him so exhausted that Amy put him straight to bed when they got back to the house, but his eyes were almost feverishly bright from the excitement of the day. Amy slipped into his room to see how he was whenever she had a free moment that afternoon. Every time she came in Charlie began talking about what he had seen, and what David had told him about the farm.

By dinner-time he had regained enough energy to be restless, so eager to talk about the farm that Amy had trouble getting him to concentrate on eating his dinner. She smiled to herself at the sight of Charlie sitting up in bed bright-eyed and moving his good arm about excitedly. It was incongruous to see those eyes suddenly so alive in the shrunken face. The face was that of a frail old man, but the eyes were Malcolm's.

David took her place that evening for his usual stint at Charlie's bedside. When Amy went in to settle Charlie for the night, she saw a troubled look on David's face.

'Ma, he thinks… you know what he was saying before…' David said in a low voice as he passed her in the doorway. He shrugged helplessly. 'I didn't want to spoil it for him.'

Charlie still seemed bright. 'That's a good lot of calves we got this year,' he told Amy as she took her seat beside the bed. 'Should be plenty of pasture for them, too.'

Amy took up her sewing and stitched away, nodding and smiling and making an occasional vague murmur. Charlie was simply enjoying the chance to talk about the farm. He needed an audience, but not a particularly vocal one.

'I'll get them to clear that bit of scrub over behind the big hill,' Charlie said. 'I never got on to that bit.'

'Get who, Charlie?'

'The young fellows. They can start it when the boy gets home.'

Amy bent low over her stitching to hide her expression. 'Charlie, Mal isn't…' But there was no kind way to remind him. Better that Charlie take some pleasure from his fancy than for her to force cruel reality back on him. 'That's a good idea,' she murmured.

He talked away, sometimes to Amy but much of the time apparently to himself. As the room darkened, Amy lit the lamp and continued with her sewing. When her eyes grew tired, she put the work away in her basket and dimmed the light a little.

Charlie's speech gradually grew more slurred, and there were longer gaps between each word. Even when he had lapsed into silence, Amy sat on beside him, wanting to be sure he was asleep before she left.

She put out the lamp and waited in the darkness, listening to the sound of his breathing. She waited so long that she dozed briefly, then woke and waited a little longer. At last she dared creep from the room, but before she had reached the door she heard him stir.

At first Amy thought she must have disturbed him, despite her careful silence. But Charlie had not woken. He was dreaming; tossing about restlessly, and mumbling words she could not make out.

No, it was more than a dream, Amy realised when she had crept close to the bed. The distress in his voice was clear. Charlie was having a nightmare.

And the nightmare had words in it; words she could make no sense of. Charlie was talking rapidly, his voice more distressed by the moment, but it was in a language that Amy did not understand.

The words fractured into sobs, then resolved again into that mysterious language. And in the midst of what seemed a string of gibberish, Amy heard a word she understood.

'Mam-mee,' Charlie sobbed. 'Mam-mee.'

It could mean nothing else. The voice wailing for his mother might have been Malcolm's or David's when they were tiny, crying out for Amy to stop it hurting. She would have crawled over broken glass to have reached that voice.

She sat on the bed and took hold of him, forcing him to stop his restless tossing. 'I'm here,' she soothed. 'I'm here.'

Charlie clung to her, fear lending him strength. He babbled a little more, then Amy felt the rigidity leave his body as he woke and slowly grasped the reality of his surroundings.

She relaxed her hold a little. 'Are you all right? Do you want me to light the lamp?'

Charlie swallowed noisily. 'Suit yourself,' he said, his voice hoarse.

Amy groped around for the matches and lit a candle. Charlie's face looked grey in the dim light, the streaks of tears silvery trails that disappeared into his beard. He stared at her from red-rimmed eyes.

'I could warm you some milk if you like,' Amy said. 'It might help you get back to sleep.'

He made no reply. He watched her in silence for a few moments, then said in an unnaturally flat voice, 'The boy's dead.'

'Yes, he is,' Amy said quietly. 'Is that what you were dreaming about?'

Charlie shook his head and turned away from her gaze.

'Do you want to talk about the bad dream?'

He moved his head on the pillow to look at her again. 'Was I talking a load of nonsense?'

'I couldn't understand the words,' Amy said, grateful that she could answer him truthfully while sparing him humiliation. 'I think it was another language.'

Charlie looked startled, then pensive. 'I thought I'd lost the Gaelic. Must still be in there somewhere.'

Locked away with memories of his mother. Amy could guess what he had been dreaming, and why he had woken from the nightmare with the knowledge of Malcolm's death suddenly clear. Losing his mother and losing Malcolm had intertwined, the two griefs melding into one pain.

She lit the lamp and put out the candle. 'See if you can get back to sleep. I'll stay here till you feel better.'

But Charlie showed no sign of falling asleep. He shook his head when she again offered warm milk, and made no answer when she asked if he wanted anything else. He lay against the pillows staring up at the dim ceiling.

'I'm cold,' he complained after a long silence.

That was something she could help him with, though the night seemed warm to Amy. She hurried to fetch a blanket from her bed and spread it carefully over him.

'Is that better?'

'What did you go rushing off like that for?' he asked, fixing her with a resentful stare.

'Just to get you a blanket. I wasn't gone long.'

She saw him shiver, and she tucked the blanket in more snugly. 'I get awful lonely at night,' he said in a low voice. 'I wake up in the night and there's no one there.'

'I'm here, Charlie. I'm here.'

'But you go off. I wake up and you've gone off.'

Amy stroked his forehead. 'I'll stay here all night, then.' She turned the lamp down low and tried to make herself a little comfortable on the hard chair.

'Amy?' The word sounded clearly in the silent room, though his voice was faint. It struck Amy that Charlie had taken to using her name even when there was no one else to hear them, instead of the abusive words he had been accustomed to fling at her. 'I'm still cold.'

She frowned in concern, sure that two blankets should be more than enough on so mild a night. 'Do you want another blanket? I could get my bedspread.'

'No. Don't want blankets.' He looked at her with a sort of longing in his face, and Amy realised what he was too frightened to ask.

'Do you want me to get in bed with you?' The words were out before she could call them back.

Charlie nodded without looking at her, then sneaked a glance. 'I wouldn't give you any bother. Don't think I could even if I wanted to,' he added miserably.

Amy studied him, memories etching their way through old channels of almost-forgotten pain. She had long ago made the decision never to share his bed again, though it had meant defying Charlie in all his frightening strength.

But that strength was long gone. Charlie was the frail creature lying in his bed, old and sick and crying for his mother. To hold fast to her decision would be cruelly selfish.

'All right. I'll go and get my nightie, then.'

'No!' he said in distress. 'Don't go away!'

He was frightened she would not come back, Amy knew. 'But Charlie, I've got to…'

She admitted defeat when his face crumpled in threatened tears. 'I suppose I don't have to, really.'

She took off her dress and camisole, unlaced her corset, then sat down to take off her stockings, aware of Charlie's eyes on her all through the exercise. She stood up again to undo her outer petticoat, then folded the garments and placed them on the chair, pleased at the knowledge that her chemise and under petticoat covered her as decently as a nightdress would have.

Charlie's face was a picture of disappointment when she looked over at him. 'You got any legs under there?'

Amy hesitated for a moment, then took off her remaining petticoat, leaving her legs bare from where her drawers ended just above her knees.

Charlie stared avidly at her. 'You'd just about raise a dead man, you would.' She saw signs of his hand's surreptitious motions under the covers. 'Just about,' he murmured.

He watched as she took down her hair, as if fascinated by every movement. When all the pins were out, Amy began plaiting her hair as well as she could without being able to brush it first, but she stopped when the look of disappointment returned to Charlie's face.

'Can't you leave it long?' he asked. 'Long like a girl's?'

It would be thick with knots in the morning, but it was hard for her to deny him anything he wanted. She shook her hair loose so that it fell in a mass of waves to her waist, turning around slowly as she did so that Charlie would get a clear view of her.

She sensed his nervousness when she climbed into bed beside him, and felt it matched by her own. She fought down her shyness, telling herself this was no different from the way she had comforted David when he was a small boy by taking him into her bed.

Charlie startled her by yanking on her arm as roughly as his weakness allowed.

'What do you want, Charlie?'

'Want you to move over a bit.'

She smiled into the dimness. 'I'm not like a cow that you have to shove, you know. You could try asking me.'

'I didn't think of that.'

She reached over to put out the lamp, then pressed close to him. 'That's nice, isn't it?'

'Aye.' For a little while he lay without moving. Then she felt his hand creep up her thigh and over her belly. It hovered uncertainly before daring to press one of her breasts through her chemise.

She felt him tremble, though whether at his own boldness or for fear she would push his hand away she was unsure. 'Not much of it, is there?' she said, trying to make light of the moment. 'I've never had much of a bosom, except when I was feeding the children.'

'You're just right,' Charlie said. 'A woman shouldn't look like a cow in milk.'

It was not the most graceful of compliments, but none the less sincere for that. 'Thank you,' Amy murmured.

Emboldened by his success, Charlie explored her breasts with his fingers, though when he tried to slide his hand under her chemise Amy gently guided it back on top of the fabric. 'I've got things sorted out for when I'm gone,' he told her.

'Don't talk like that, Charlie. You'll feel better soon.' She stroked his hand where it lay nestled between her breasts. 'Look how lively you are tonight.'

But Charlie was having none of it. 'I'm no bloody use around here any more. Can't do a decent day's work.'

'You've done your share. You're having a rest these days, that's all. You've earned a rest.'

'What about you? You could do with a rest, too.'

'Well, I've got Dave to do the heavy things for me. Dave and I are much younger than you, we don't get so tired.'

'When will you get your rest?' he persisted.

Amy laughed softly. 'Oh, by the time I'm your age I expect I'll have a nice little daughter-in-law to boss around. I'll just sit about all day and tell her what to do.' She smiled at the unlikely notion.

'That'll be fair enough. See that you do. When I'm gone—' he began again.

'Charlie, please don't talk like that.'

'Shut up and listen, woman. I'll be gone before long, and I know full well there'll be no weeping for me. I've got things sorted out with the lawyer fellow. I had him out... I don't know. Back in the spring, it might have been.'

'It was in October,' Amy said. 'I remember.'

'I forgot about having him out here. It all got muddled in my head for a spell. Well, he's drawn it all up in lawyer talk. I'll not have the government taking my farm when I'm gone. I had to get the lawyer to change what he wrote out for me years back. It was all going to the boy in those days.'

Amy heard the catch in his voice. 'Don't talk if it upsets you, Charlie.'

Charlie cleared his throat noisily and went on. 'Dave'll get the farm. That's all written out in the proper words so the government can't take it. Hope he looks after it properly,' he said in a low voice.

'He will. Dave loves the land nearly as much as you do, you know. He takes after you in that.'

'He'd better make a decent job of it. Anyway, he'll get the place when I'm gone. But you can carry on living here.'

'Of course I will,' Amy said, puzzled. 'Where else would I go?'

'You can carry on here,' Charlie repeated. 'I got the lawyer to write it out proper. Dave can't kick you off the place.'

He meant it as a gift, and Amy tried to sound suitably grateful. 'Thank you, Charlie,' she said carefully. 'Thank you for thinking about me like that. But Dave wouldn't do that, you know. I'm sure he wouldn't send me away.'

'Well, some blokes can be bloody stupid about appreciating their women,' Charlie said gruffly. 'I'll not give him the chance to muck things up for himself. You can stay here as long as you like, unless...' He trailed away, cleared his throat again and said, 'Unless you get wed. I expect you'll get wed again.'

'No, I won't,' Amy said.

'You could get another husband. You're still a fine looking woman.' His voice told her how much he hated the very thought of it.

'I don't want another husband. I've never wanted another man since we got married. I've told you that lots of times, haven't I?' She could not repress a shudder as she thought of the last time she had tried to tell him. With her body screaming from the pain of his blows, she had tried to make him believe she had not been flaunting herself in front of other men.

'You never wanted me.'

Amy could find no kind answer to so undeniable an accusation, so she said nothing. She pressed more closely against him and squeezed his hand in hers, hoping to calm him.

But Charlie went on, his voice cracking slightly. 'I remember you lying there. Lying in my bed and crying for the other fellow.'

'No!' Amy said, shocked at the idea. 'No, I didn't!'

'Aye, you did. I'd hear you bawling. It was like he was in the bed between you and me. I couldn't shove him out of the way to get at you. I could get hold of you and mount you, but it was him you were crying for.'

'Charlie, I wasn't—I swear I wasn't. Not for him.' *I haven't even thought about him in years.* 'I'd stopped crying for him months and months before we got married.'

She heard the disbelief in his voice. 'What were you bawling all the time for, then?'

They were memories she would sooner have buried, but he had to be answered. 'Because I was scared, mostly. Especially just at first.'

'What did you have to be scared about? You knew what was to happen to you.'

'But I hardly knew you. Just because... just because a girl's been with a man doesn't mean she's anybody's. I had to get used to you.'

Hanging between them in the darkness was her urge to be fully honest, despite her reluctance to speak of things that had brought such pain.

'And I was crying for... Charlie, do you remember you made me promise not to talk about something? It was the first night we were married. You said I was never to talk about it, and I promised I wouldn't. Do you release me from that?'

'Don't know what you're on about.'

469

'But do you release me from it?' Amy persisted. 'Can I talk about it?'

He shrugged, a small movement of his shoulders. 'Say whatever you want.'

'I was crying for…' She had to stop and take a deep breath before she could be sure her voice was under some sort of control. 'I was crying for my baby. The one I gave away. I missed her.' *I still do.*

'You had a girl child?' he said slowly, as if working through a puzzle. 'I never thought of you having a girl.'

'Women do sometimes, you know.' Her attempt to make her voice light sounded feeble in her own ears.

'But you always had boys.'

'I always had boys with you. You seem to father boys all the time.'

That pleased him, as she had known it would. She felt a small wave of energy pass through his body. 'That's true enough,' he said, sounding quite puffed up at the notion.

He was silent for a while, pondering the idea further. 'A girl. You could… you could've maybe kept a girl.'

'Don't,' Amy said quickly. 'Don't say that.'

'I didn't want another man's son under my roof. I didn't want another man's son inheriting my farm. A girl wouldn't have mattered the same.'

'Don't say that. It's like losing her all over again.' A dry sob racked her. She held herself rigid, clinging desperately to shreds of self-control. 'It wouldn't have worked out,' Amy said when she could trust herself to speak. 'You wouldn't have loved her like one of your own.'

'Don't know what you're on about. I'd've done right by the girl.'

'It's for the best. It was the best for her.' Even after so many years of telling herself, the words sounded hollow.

He soon lost interest in the idea of her little girl. 'Three of them in a row you had. The little one died. He was too small. All boys, they were. Only three of them, though.'

'How many did you want, Charlie?'

She felt him shrug. 'About six of them. Seven, maybe. Aye, seven sons would've been a fine thing.'

'Seven!' Amy could not hold back a laugh. 'Where would we have put them all?'

'I was going to build on to the place when you'd had a few more. I drew it out once on a bit of paper, how I was going to build on. Wonder where I put that bit of paper,' he mused. 'Haven't seen it for a while.'

'I could never have had all those babies. I'm not made for childbearing like that. You should've married a big, strong girl like Lizzie.'

'I took what I could get,' Charlie said brusquely.

Amy smiled. 'Well, I suppose we all do that in the end, don't we?'

She sensed that he had made himself uncomfortable by his own words. 'I didn't mean... I never saw a woman I wanted more than you.' He clutched convulsively at her, making Amy gasp at the sudden grip on her breast. 'I used to see you going past my gate. Or out in the paddocks playing. Some days I'd hang around by the boundary and hope you'd come by. There were nights I couldn't sleep for wanting you.'

Amy was too stunned for sensible speech by the notion of Charlie in such a state over her. 'I... I never knew you were... I...' She trailed off helplessly.

'I remember one time—it was the haymaking, I think. You were out in the fields with that cousin of yours, the one Kelly wed. You and her were dancing round in the field holding hands. You had a yellow dress on, and a bonnet with green ribbons. You were dancing around so fast your bonnet came off so as it was just hanging by the ribbons.'

He took a lock of her hair and twined his fingers through it. 'Your hair was flying out around your head, and you were laughing and laughing. Like you'd die of being happy. I thought I'd never seen a lovelier thing. And I wanted you. I wanted you!'

His hand jerked, and Amy gave a small cry at the pain in her scalp. She disengaged her hair from his fingers, her hand trembling so much that she could barely control it. 'Charlie, I was... I remember that bonnet,' she said in a quavering voice. 'That was before Granny died. I must have been... I don't know, eleven maybe. No older than that.'

'I don't know how old you were. I just know I wanted you.'

No wonder I was frightened of you when I was little. Even as a child, she had sensed that there was something to fear in those brooding stares of his.

'I knew I couldn't have you. It didn't matter the same when no one else had you either. I could... I could think about having you.'

Dream about me, he means. Charlie used to daydream about me. Never for a moment had Amy suspected she had been the subject of anyone's dreams; least of all Charlie's.

'I knew he was going to get you as soon as I saw you hanging around with him.' He made a noise of disgust. 'Him with his pretty face and fancy ways. He was going to take you off to Auckland. I couldn't have you.' His voice cracked, and his hand clutched at Amy's.

'But you did,' she whispered, her mind still reeling from what he had told her. 'You got me after all.'

'You weren't virgin.' The old, familiar note of accusation was in his voice.

471

'No. You knew I wasn't when you asked for me. But I wasn't a whore, either. A girl doesn't have to be one or the other.'

'I stopped going to the whores, you know.' It was almost an apology.

'I know.' *I'd've had to take him in and do his buttons for him if he was still going there*. She had to repress a laugh that had a hint of hysteria about it at the grotesque image.

'I stopped when I still had the use of my legs,' he said, as if he knew what she was thinking. 'It was years back.'

Around the time Malcolm had died, Amy suspected. That had been when Charlie had begun turning into an old man.

'They were none of them like you, those whores. I never wanted them like I did you.'

'Please don't talk about whores any more. I don't want to hear about them.'

'I wanted you for years,' he said broodingly. 'Years and years. I didn't have you for long.'

'Twenty years, Charlie. We've been married twenty years.'

'I didn't have you as a wife for long. You stopped being a wife to me. Suppose you think I was too hard on you.'

Trading accusations now would be pointlessly cruel. 'You did what you thought best.'

'That was the end of the bairns, once you left my bed.'

Amy shook her head, forgetting for a moment that he could not see her. 'I don't know, I think maybe I couldn't carry babies any more, anyway. I think something might have gone wrong with my insides when I had Alexander. Remember how I lost all those babies afterwards?'

'I kicked the last one out of you,' Charlie said, his voice unnaturally thick.

'There's no need to upset yourself thinking about that. Maybe I would've lost it anyway, like the other ones.'

'Suppose you think I was too hard on the boy, too.'

Amy paused, choosing her words carefully. 'You always tried to be a good father. You worked hard.'

'I drove my son away,' he said, his voice raw. 'Drove him away to go and get himself killed.'

'You loved him, Charlie. I think Mal must've known that at the end. I don't think you can love a person as much as you did Mal without them knowing it.'

He was quiet for some time. 'I drove you away, too. I drove you away so you wouldn't be a wife to me.'

She knew he was weeping, although he was managing to do it while barely making a sound. 'I think there's more to being a wife than sharing a bed,' she said softly. 'Anyway, I'm here now.' And she would be there from now on, she promised silently; as determined never again to let him sleep alone as she had once been determined never again to share his bed.

She rolled over to lie facing him, and guided his arm around her. 'We're a bit slow, you and me.'

'What do you mean?'

'Well, here we are, married twenty years and this is our first proper cuddle! We're a silly pair.' She raised her head from the pillow until her face was close to where she judged his must be. And for the first time in twenty years of marriage, she pressed her lips to his in a willing kiss.

Charlie was soon asleep, worn out with emotion and warmed by the closeness of her body. Amy did no more than doze, alert in an instant and ready to hold him close and comfort him when he woke up whimpering.

He did not wake again. When the room began to lighten with the first hint of sunrise and Amy heard David walking out to the back door with what he fondly imagined to be a catlike tread, she slipped out of bed and began pulling on her clothes, with no sign that Charlie had heard her.

When she had her petticoats on she paused to stand over the bed and look down at him, peaceful as a child. So peaceful that Amy frowned, leaning closer.

She had never seen Charlie looking like that. Every line had been smoothed away; every mark of bitterness and cruelty had faded. It was as if his face had been melted like old, damaged wax and re-cast into an image of peace.

'Charlie?' she whispered, knowing there would be no answer. There was no sign of movement from the covers over his chest, and when she retrieved his wrist there was no pulse.

She placed his hand on his chest, pulled her dress on over what underwear she was wearing and went to call David.

He was still on the porch, pulling on his boots while Biff waited beside him. 'I think he's gone, Davie,' she told him. 'Your father's passed away.'

David did not seem startled by the news. 'I thought he must've been in a bad way, he was getting so muddled about things yesterday.'

Amy shook her head. 'No, he was sensible before the end. He remembered everything—about Mal, and you, and... well, everything.'

David stood up and put his arm around her. 'Don't you worry, I'll look after everything,' he said solemnly. 'I'll see to whatever needs doing.' Then he ruined the effect by chewing at his lower lip and casting an anxious look at Amy. 'Ma, do you… do you know what needs doing?'

Amy smiled faintly. 'I think so. We need to get a doctor, so you'd better go in and see Richard.'

'But I thought you said he was dead.'

'He is, Davie. But a doctor has to sign a certificate to say how he died. Go around to the minister's after that, I'll need to talk to him about the funeral. Oh, and the carpenter, go and see him, too, if you feel able. He'll have to come out and measure your father up. I'll get you something to eat before you go, though, it's too early for you to be bothering Richard.'

'What about the milking?'

'Go over to your Uncle John's after you've had a bite to eat. Tell them what's happened, and they can do your milking this morning.'

'You'd better come over there with me,' David said, but Amy shook her head. 'You've got to, Ma—I can't leave you here by yourself with him.'

'He's not going to hurt me, is he? Don't argue, Davie, I'm not going anywhere just now. It wouldn't be respectful, leaving him on his own.'

'Ma, you should…' David shrugged and admitted defeat. 'No use arguing with you,' he muttered.

When David had had a hurried breakfast and set off next door, Amy returned to the bedroom and took her familiar seat by Charlie's side. He still looked peacefully asleep; as if he might wake any moment and smile at her.

We could have made a go of it, Charlie. Not been all lovey-dovey or anything, but we could have got on all right. If only you hadn't been so angry all the time. If only you hadn't made me so frightened.

'What a waste,' she whispered aloud, and felt her eyes brimming. She put her hand up to her face and pulled her fingers away wet with tears.

'There, you see?' she told him, holding her hand close to his unseeing face. 'No weeping for you, you said. You were wrong about that, too, Charlie. You always were wrong about me.'

She brushed her wet fingers against his cheek, offering the tears as a final gift.

28

April 1906

Frank double-checked the last total in his quarterly accounts (he had never quite learned to trust his own arithmetic), replaced the pen in its inkstand and leaned back in his chair, regarding the results with quiet satisfaction.

'How does it look, Pa?' Joey asked. Over the last year Frank had encouraged his oldest son to take more interest in the farm accounts, painfully aware of how difficult he had found the task when he had first begun to keep good records of his income and expenses.

'Pretty good. We got plenty of heifers last year, and good prices for them, too. Here, take a look.'

He pushed the accounts book across the table to Joey and sat back again, mulling over some plans that were not yet sufficiently formed for him to share them with anyone but Lizzie. Frank was fully aware that he had four sons to provide for, and that the farm, successful though he had made it, would not support four families if his sons turned out to be as fruitful as he and Lizzie had.

'Yep, things are looking pretty good,' he told Joey. 'That's not to say I couldn't be doing better, mind you. I've got a few ideas to try out this year.'

'I guess maybe you never really finish, eh?'

'No, I guess you don't. But you know what? Sometimes you put things off for years and years, thinking you'll do them when you've got everything straight. There comes a time when you need to stop for a bit, look at what you've got and make sure you're not taking it for granted.'

'You do?' Joey said, his face showing how obtuse he had found his father's last speech.

Frank grinned at him. 'Yes, you do. Don't go thinking your old man's going soft in the head, Joey. One of these days you'll know what I'm talking about. That ink dry yet?'

Joey dabbed cautiously at the page. 'Seems to be.'

'Give it here, then. Better not leave it lying around or Benjy'll end up chewing it like he does everything else. Don't know how he manages to do that when he can't even crawl yet.' He shook his head over the mystery. 'I think I'll go into town tomorrow,' he said as he put the accounts book away.

'Can I come?'

'Not this time, Joe. I've got some private business to do. Something I've let get a bit overdue.'

Frank got back home in the middle of the afternoon after his visit to town the next day, to find Beth and Maisie working in the kitchen.

'Where's your ma?' he asked.

Beth raised her eyes heavenwards. 'Playing with Benjy in the parlour.'

'She's *always* playing with Benjy,' Maisie put in.

'We hardly ever see her out here of an afternoon,' Beth added.

Frank grinned at their exaggerated expressions of long-suffering. 'Well, it's a good thing you two know what you're doing, isn't it? Leave those spuds for a bit, they're not going anywhere. I got you something in town.'

'What? What?' they chorused, hovering around him as excited as five-year-olds.

'There you go, one each,' he said, drawing two carefully folded pieces of fabric from his jacket pocket. 'Silk scarves, they tell me these are. They should be good ones, Mrs Nichol said they're the latest thing from Auckland.'

'They're lovely, Pa,' Beth said, throwing her arms around his neck and planting a kiss on his cheek. Maisie would not be so demonstrative, but she thanked him with her eyes. 'Why are we getting a present, though?'

'Just for being good girls and helping your ma. Anyway, it feels like a good day for presents.'

He went into the passage, leaving the girls trying on their scarves and adjusting each other's. Lizzie was sitting on the sofa where a patch of afternoon sunlight made it cosy, and, just as the girls had said, she was playing with Benjy.

She looked up at Frank's entrance and smiled. 'Here's Papa, Benjy. Say hello to Papa. Mind you don't squash him, Frank,' she said when Frank sat down beside her.

'Give him here.' Frank lifted Benjy onto his own lap, sat him up and fixed him with a stern gaze. 'Now listen, son. I can see that you and me are going to have some fallings out in a few years.'

'Don't say that!'

'Well, he's got to learn,' Frank said, maintaining his stern expression with difficulty. He wagged his finger at Benjy. 'You needn't think I'm going to let you get between me and your ma when I fancy a cuddle.'

Benjy stared at the finger as if fascinated, then reached out and took hold of it. He looked up at Frank and chortled in delight at his accomplishment.

476

Frank sighed, then gave in and laughed. 'You know, I used to think Maudie was the one who took after you the most, love,' he said to Lizzie. 'I'm beginning to think it's this fellow.

'Don't go trying your tricks with me, boy,' he said, disengaging his finger. 'How about you hop out of the way for a minute?'

Ignoring Lizzie's protests, he lowered the baby to the floor, propping him up against the sofa. Benjy seemed quite satisfied with his new position, playing with his feet through his knitted booties in between gazing around the room from this fresh perspective.

'My turn now,' Frank told Lizzie. He slipped an arm around her and squeezed, enjoying the milky smell of her and the smooth feel of her dress against his hand. 'Maudie sends her love. She said they'll be out on Sunday.'

'That'll be nice.'

'Lucy was awake while I was there, I had a cuddle of her. She's talking away like nobody's business these days—not so as you can understand her, but she's making plenty of noise.' He smiled at the memory of the little girl on his lap. 'Maudie reckoned she said "Grandpa" today. Didn't really sound like that to me, but I suppose Maudie can understand her better.'

Lizzie snorted. 'Maudie thinks that child's a prodigy. I wouldn't be surprised if Benjy talks about the same time Lucy does, he's very forward with things. Aren't you, sweetie?' she cooed to the little boy. 'First babies are usually slower with talking, anyway.'

Frank grinned at her. 'You and Maudie are as bad as each other. Well, I reckon Lucy and Benjy are both pretty good. I went to see the bank manager today.'

'Why'd you do that?'

'Just a few things I've been thinking over, with the young fellows growing up and all. You know I told you how I heard down at the factory that old man Carr's thinking of selling his place?'

'Well, I suppose he's got to, since he had that falling out with Tilly's husband. He's too old to run the place by himself, especially with his bad leg, and Martha's not likely to get married now.'

'No, she's left it a bit late,' Frank said. 'Anyway, I'd been thinking I might go and have a yarn with Carr. I thought I'd better talk to Mr Callaghan first, though, see what he thought of the idea.'

'You'd have to borrow a lot of money, wouldn't you?'

'I expect so. I'll get you to help me figure it out later, when the little fellow's asleep. Funny, isn't it? The better off I get, the more money I seem to borrow.' He shrugged. 'I guess it's just the way it works.'

'Well, you know what you're doing when it comes to farming,' Lizzie said.

'And I've got you to tell me when I'm being stupid. I'm in no rush about this farm thing, though, we'll see how it works out. Hey, I saw Mrs Nichol today, she's running the produce part of the Show. She said I was to tell you to be sure and get your preserves into town in time if you want to enter them.'

'Oh, I don't think I'll bother this year,' Lizzie said. 'It's not worth it when I'm not even going to the Show.'

'You're sure you don't want to come?'

Lizzie shook her head. 'I don't want to take Benjy into a crush like that, it might upset him. Anyway, you get people with diseases and things at shows. No, you can take the other kids in.'

'I saw Dave at the factory this morning, I told him to come to the Show with us,' said Frank. 'He's going to help me and the boys with getting the cows in to town.'

'Dave's a good boy,' Lizzie said. 'And he's very good to his mother.'

'Mmm.' Frank studied Lizzie's face, smiling as he did so.

'What are you looking at me like that for?' she asked.

'Just thinking what a beauty you are, and what a lucky man I am.'

'Oh, don't talk rot. Move over a bit so I can pick Benjy up, I think he wants to get on my lap again.'

'Benjy can wait a minute,' Frank said. 'He's had you all afternoon.' One arm still firmly around Lizzie so that she could not lean down to pick up Benjy, he reached into his jacket pocket with the other hand. 'I got you a present today.'

'Did you?' Lizzie's eyes lit up in a smile. 'That was nice. What did you do that for?'

'Because you're the best wife in the world, and I know when I'm well off.' He placed the long, slim box wrapped in tissue paper in Lizzie's outstretched hand.

Lizzie laughed at his solemn expression. 'And what made you realise that all of a sudden? You're silly sometimes, Frank.'

He shook his head. 'It wasn't sudden. I've been wanting to do this for... I don't know, fifteen years or more. Since Beth was a little thing. And it's your birthday this month, anyway.'

'People don't usually get special presents just for being thirty-nine,' Lizzie said, still amused. 'And wrapped up so nice and all.'

'Open it, then,' Frank said, impatient to see her response.

Lizzie carefully undid the tissue paper, folded it and placed it on a side table. 'I can use that again,' she said, thriftily pleased. 'What a pretty box this is.'

She lifted the lid of the box and gasped at the sight. 'P-pearls?' she said in a faint voice. 'A whole necklace of them?' She tore her eyes away from the necklace with difficulty. 'Frank, how much did this—'

'Never you mind,' Frank said, placing a finger on her lips to silence her. 'A hundred necklaces wouldn't be worth what you are. Anyway, what's the use of having money if I can't do what I want with it?' He smiled at the look of wonder on Lizzie's face. 'Do you like it?'

'Like it?' Lizzie echoed faintly. 'It's… it's the most beautiful thing I've ever seen.'

'It should suit you, then. Are you going to try it on?'

Lizzie ran her fingers delicately over the pearls. 'Not now. I'll have to wait till I've got a nice dress on.'

'Try it on now,' Frank insisted. He lifted the necklace from its box and held it up.

'I can't,' Lizzie protested. 'I've just got this old dress on, and I've got a bit of baby sick down the front.'

'Try it on,' Frank repeated. 'Here, I'll do it up for you. Turn around.'

Lizzie obediently twisted around to let Frank fasten the diamond clasp at the back of her neck, then turned to face him again. 'How does it look?' she asked, her voice almost shy.

Frank studied the sight. A shaft of sunlight fell across Lizzie's chest, the pearls answering the light with a luminous glow. The creamy skin of Lizzie's face had the same translucent glow in the warm light, and her eyes were sparkling.

A sudden tugging at his trouser leg distracted Frank for a moment. He looked down to see Benjy clutching at the cloth and gazing at him with a plea in his face. Frank scooped him up and nestled him into the crook of his arm.

The baby snuggled against him as Frank turned his attention back to Lizzie. He reached out to brush the pearls, already warmed by Lizzie's body, then raised his hand to brush her soft cheek. 'Perfect. Just perfect.'

The morning was mild enough for Amy to sit on the verandah after she had done the breakfast dishes and indulge in the luxury of reading a book.

She had so much time to call her own these days that she sometimes felt a little guilty over it. 'You've done your share, Ma, you're due for a rest,' David always told her, unaware that he was echoing his father's opinion. It still seemed strange to have no one to look after but David and herself. Not since early childhood had she had such light demands made on her.

An unexpected movement caught her attention. Amy shaded her eyes and stared down the track. It was a rider approaching, she soon realised; and her next realisation was that it was an odd piece of riding.

Not that any lack of skill was being shown by the rider; quite the reverse. Whoever was coming up to the cottage must be an accomplished rider to be keeping their seat given the strange pace they were forcing their horse into. The horse would suddenly burst into a fast canter, then as suddenly come back to a walk so slow that it was more of an amble. A few steps on and the rapid canter would begin again.

The horse had reverted to that dawdling walk by the time the rider was close enough for Amy to see that her visitor was a woman. She went around to the back of the house in time to see the rider pull up.

'Sarah!' Amy exclaimed. 'I didn't know you were coming! Oh, it's lovely to see you! Here, let me help.'

She held the reins while Sarah dismounted, then tethered the horse to the nearest fence. 'I can hardly believe it.' Amy put her arms around Sarah's waist and planted a kiss on her cheek, having to stand on tiptoe to reach.

For a moment Sarah held herself so stiffly that Amy was afraid she had given offence, then she abruptly put her own arms around Amy's shoulders and clutched at her. 'I can hardly believe it myself,' she murmured as she released Amy.

'When did you get here? I didn't hear you were coming, didn't Lily know? Where are you staying?'

Sarah smiled faintly and held up her hand to fend off the flow of questions. 'Let me catch up, Mrs Stewart. I got in late yesterday afternoon. No, Lily didn't know I was coming. No one knows I'm here except you, in fact. I'm staying at one of the hotels.'

'A hotel? There's no need for you to stay in a place like that,' Amy said, startled. 'You could… you could stay here,' she offered shyly. 'We've got the room now. I know it's not flash like you're used to, but it'd be lovely if you could.'

Sarah shook her head. 'Thank you. It's very kind of you to offer. But I don't think so. Whatever happens.'

'Just as you please, then,' Amy said, trying not to feel hurt. 'How long do you think you'll be in Ruatane?'

'I… I don't quite know,' Sarah said, looking away as if reluctant to meet Amy's eyes. 'It rather depends on you.'

It seemed an odd thing to say; in fact Sarah seemed to be in as strange a mood as she had the last time Amy had seen her. But she was too full of the unexpected pleasure of Sarah's company to be dwelling on her manner.

'I'll get a halter so we can let your horse out in the paddock,' Amy said. 'You're not going off in a hurry, I hope?'

'Will I be a dreadful nuisance? Would you rather I went immediately?'

Amy looked at her in surprise. 'But Sarah, I just asked you to stay here instead of at the hotel, didn't I? Of course I don't want you to go.'

'Oh. So you did,' Sarah said tensely. 'I'm sorry, I'm not quite thinking straight. So it's not an inconvenient time for me to descend on you?'

'Not a bit of it—I hope you'll stay all day. But let's turn this horse out, then you won't have to worry about leaving it tied up.'

She fetched a halter from the shed, glancing under the horse's body as she came back. 'A mare. She's a pretty one. Whose is she?'

'I'm not quite sure. I told the people at the hotel I wanted to hire a mount, and they produced this one.'

'It's probably one of Mr Winskill's. Would you run the stirrup up while I do the halter, Sarah?'

Sarah frowned. 'I don't think I know how. I suppose I could try.'

'No, I'll do it,' Amy said. She ran up the stirrup, undid the girth and pulled off the horse's saddle, then turned the animal out into the paddock. 'I'm sorry, I thought you'd know how to handle the tack, with you being a good rider.'

'I must confess that at the end of a ride I always used to put the reins in the stable boy's hand and go off about my business. It never occurred to me to wonder what he did with the horse after I'd finished.'

'Well, I don't suppose there was any point, if you had someone to do it for you.' Amy looped her arm through Sarah's. 'Come inside and I'll make us a cup of tea.

'What a shame you've missed Dave,' Amy said as she led Sarah into the kitchen. 'He's gone to the show today, I shouldn't think he'll be back till just in time for milking.'

Sarah gave an odd little laugh. 'As it happens, I went to a good deal of trouble to miss Dave. Though I must say you helped there.'

'I don't know what you mean, Sarah.'

'You told me about this show in one of your letters. You said Dave would be going with Mr Kelly, but you didn't expect to go yourself.'

'So I did.' Amy frowned at Sarah, puzzled. 'Do you mean… did you come down all the way from Auckland specially to see me? And you wanted to be sure Dave wouldn't be home?'

Sarah hesitated before speaking. 'Let's just say I wanted to be certain of having some undisturbed time with you. Having Dave hovering around expecting you to wait on him was not what I had in mind.'

'Dave doesn't expect me to wait on him,' Amy said, as close to scolding as she dared. 'He's the most easy-going boy you could ever meet. I think… I think you'd like him if you got to know him properly.'

'Perhaps,' Sarah said. 'I'm prepared to admit that I may not have been entirely fair towards Dave. Not entirely sensible, anyway.'

She smiled slightly. 'Actually, I have seen him today, though I made sure he didn't see me. I paid a brief visit to the show this morning, just to be certain that Dave hadn't decided to play truant. Fortunately he does rather stand out in a crowd.'

'Doesn't he just,' Amy said proudly. 'The kettle shouldn't be too long boiling,' she said as she buttered some scones. 'We'll take everything through to the parlour when it's ready. Sit down, why don't you?'

'What? Oh, yes, thank you,' Sarah said distractedly. But she made no move to sit; instead she prowled around the kitchen, peering at shelves, looking out the window, and studying things as mundane as the bench and the range.

'Are you all right?' Amy asked, studying the younger woman's restlessness with some concern. 'Are you quite comfortable?' She wondered how she could politely point out the direction of the privy.

'Yes, thank you,' Sarah said, running her fingers over a dent in one of the walls. Amy was grateful that Sarah was unlikely to guess it had been made by Charlie's fist.

'I mean, I know it's a long ride out from town,' Amy said.

'Yes, it is quite a long way.' Sarah straightened and faced Amy. 'I hoped it would give me the opportunity to put my thoughts in order. I'm afraid it failed badly.'

'Well, if you need anything, just ask,' Amy said. It was the best she could do.

'Come into the parlour,' she said when she had put the teapot on a tray along with cups and saucers and a plate of scones. 'It's nicer in there.'

She led the way into the next room, and put the tray down on a small table. 'You've seen our parlour once before, haven't you?' she said, remembering Sarah's brief visit, when she had caught Charlie in his nightshirt and Amy in a layer of stinking mud.

'Have I? Oh, yes, so I have. I must say I didn't take much notice of the room at the time.' Sarah stared around the small parlour. 'This is your… main room?'

Amy had a suspicion that Sarah had been about to say 'best' room. 'Yes, it is. I suppose it seems small to you, but there's only Dave and me to fit in it. This is where I keep my... oh, wait a minute.'

She hurried out to the verandah and came back into the room clutching her volume of Byron. 'I was reading this one! I left it out there when you came, I forgot about it with the surprise of seeing you. Isn't that funny, that I should be reading it just when you arrived? I love it, Sarah. I've read it over and over.'

Sarah caught her in a searching gaze. 'Including the third canto?'

'I've read all of it,' Amy said. 'What's specially in that part?'

'Never mind.' Sarah turned away. Amy had the odd impression that she had failed to understand something she should have.

'This is where I keep my books,' Amy said, pointing to the middle of the mantelpiece where the books stood in a small row. She had brought them out of her room since Charlie's death, and they now had pride of place in the parlour. She slipped the volume of poetry amongst them and ran her finger softly along the jackets of the books, taking pleasure in the feel of the leather.

Sarah studied the collection, her face twisted in a way that suggested she was unsure whether to laugh or cry. 'These are all the books you have?'

Amy nodded proudly.

'I'd have sent you dozens if I'd known,' Sarah murmured.

'But I've got lots already. People think I'm silly with all my books.'

'Do they? I don't think you're silly, Amy.'

She looked along the mantelpiece from the books, to the family photograph that stood close by them.

'Is this you?' she asked, lifting the brass frame to examine the picture.

'Yes, that's Mr Stewart and me and the boys.'

Sarah peered more closely at the photograph. 'That's a boy? Don't tell me it's Dave?'

Amy smiled at the picture of the plump child in her arms. 'Yes, it is. Wasn't he pretty? Much too pretty for a boy. Such curls he had.'

'You look so young,' Sarah said pensively.

'Let's see, Davie wasn't quite two then, so I must have been twenty.'

'And this is your other son? The one who died in the war?'

'Yes, that's Mal.' The thoughts that ran through her head at the memory of Malcolm were too complex even to attempt to voice. 'My poor Mal.'

'He doesn't look a bit like you.' Sarah studied the photograph, frowning in concentration as she looked at the tiny faces. 'Did he have dark hair, too?'

'No, red. Flaming red hair, Mal had.'

Sarah broke the silence that fell between them while Amy was lost in her own musings. 'Do you have any other photographs? I'm very fond of them.'

'I've got one of Mama,' Amy said, delighted at the excuse to show off her treasure. 'It's in my room, I'll get it.'

'Is your room off the kitchen?' Sarah asked when Amy returned. 'I'd somehow assumed the main bedroom was off the parlour in these cottages.'

'It is. That's Dave's room now.'

Sarah's face hardened. 'Do you mean to tell me he evicted you from your bedroom when his father died?'

'No, not a bit of it,' Amy said, stung to David's defence. 'Dave wanted me to have that room, but I made him take it. This is his farm now, it's only right that he has the big bedroom. Anyway, I like my own little room better than that one.'

She grasped at the chance to change the subject. 'Look at my picture. This is Mama, here.'

Sarah studied the photograph. 'Oh, yes,' she said softly. She raised her eyes to look at Amy. 'She was very lovely.'

She returned her attention to the picture. 'Do you remember her?'

'A tiny bit. I was only little when she died, but I do remember her, only just.'

'You're lucky,' Sarah said. 'Are you in this one?'

'Yes, I'm the baby Mama's holding.'

Sarah smiled. 'I can't say I recognised you.'

'And this is Pa, and these are John and Harry.'

But Sarah seemed only mildly interested in the others; her attention kept returning to Amy and her mother. 'It's a lovely photograph,' she said, handing it back to Amy at last.

'Yes, isn't it?' Amy placed the photograph on the mantelpiece, beside the one of her with Charlie and the children, then sat down and began pouring the tea. 'Now, you must tell me everything you've been doing lately.'

'Is that a polite reminder of what a poor correspondent I've been?'

'Well… I haven't heard from you for a little while,' Amy said carefully. She had written to Sarah, telling her of Charlie's death, as soon as the fuss of funeral arrangements and the stream of visitors in the days after the service had given her an opportunity. Sarah had written a reply so short that it had come close to being curt. Since then Amy had had a few brief notes, but even those had ceased to arrive over the past month or so. 'I know you're busy, though.'

Sarah put her cup down on its saucer, stood up, and paced across the room and back with rapid strides. 'If you knew the letters I've started and never finished—or the ones I've hurled into the fire, or torn up and thrown in the waste paper basket,' she said bleakly.

'You don't need to worry like that,' Amy said, startled. 'Just write about any old thing, I love hearing from you.'

'I wanted to get it *right!*' Sarah said, turning a wild-eyed face to Amy. She saw Amy's anxious expression, and her shoulders slumped a little. 'You'll be wishing you'd gone into that show, rather than be faced with me in such a mood.'

'No, I'd have missed you if I'd done that! I'd have been awfully disappointed.' Amy reached out a hand for Sarah's, but Sarah's face was turned away.

'I don't like going to things like that just now, not while I'm in mourning,' Amy went on, filling up the awkward silence. 'People don't want to see me all in black when they're having a nice time. Anyway, it wouldn't seem quite respectful so soon after Mr Stewart died.'

'Such deceptions we're forced into by social pressures,' Sarah said in a low voice.

'What do you mean?'

'The thought of you in black. Thank heavens you're not wearing it today.'

'Oh, it's not practical around the house,' Amy said, brushing an imaginary crease out of her blue flowered cotton dress. 'I wore it at home for the first three months, but now I only wear proper mourning clothes when I go out.'

'But it's such a lie, isn't it? Mourning, for goodness sake! You're not mourning him!'

'Sarah, don't talk like that, please!' Amy said, deeply shocked. 'It's not respectful.'

'But you're not!' Sarah protested. 'How could you possibly be mourning a dreadful man like that? You must have *detested* him,' she said, practically spitting the word. 'A coarse, brutish creature like that.'

Amy took a deep breath, and steeled herself to be stern. 'That strikes me as a very strange way to speak to a widow, Miss Millish.' Sarah looked up sharply at being addressed in such a manner, but Amy made herself go on in the same stiff tone. 'I'm afraid if you keep speaking like that I'll have to ask you to leave.'

'No!' Sarah's face was suddenly ravaged with fear. 'Don't send me away, please don't.' She alarmed Amy by dropping to her knees in front of her. 'If you send me away now, I'll never, ever have the courage to come back again.'

Amy reached out to stroke Sarah's hair. 'I don't want to send you away. But I can't let you talk about Mr Stewart like that.'

She struggled for the right words to express her thoughts. 'We had our problems, him and I. But all he had in the world was Dave and me. I did my best to look after him before he died, and now he's gone I do my best to treat his memory with respect. I wouldn't even allow Dave to speak of his father like that, so I can't let anyone else, can I?'

Sarah's mouth softened into something close to a smile. 'I suppose you wouldn't be what you are if you acted any differently.'

Amy gave a little shrug. 'I don't know. This is just how I am.' She smiled at Sarah's awkward posture. 'Sit down, why don't you? Your tea must be getting cold.'

'What? Oh, yes,' Sarah said, regarding her neglected cup in vague surprise. She sat down and took a quick sip from the cup, then stood again and resumed her pacing.

'Goodness me, you are fidgety,' Amy said, mildly amused. 'You'll be tiring yourself out, rushing around like that.'

Sarah stopped her movement to stare at Amy. 'And you're like a deep pool of stillness in the middle of a storm. No matter how the world buffets you, you take it serenely.'

She paced again, stopping from time to time to study the photographs on the mantelpiece or to stare out the window, then resuming her rapid movement. 'I'm always like this when I'm trying to make up my mind to something. Or when I'm trapped inside by the weather just when I feel like being outside and active.' She smiled pensively. 'Mother used to scold me for it—she said it was dreadfully unladylike, stalking about the room like a man. Poor Mother, I always was something of a mystery to her.'

'She must have been very proud of you.'

'I don't know. But I do know she was very loving.' She turned on her heel and crossed the room again.

'Really, Sarah, I've never seen anyone as restless as you!' Amy had the slight impression as she said it that she had once seen someone, long ago. But she could not quite call the memory to mind, though she was vaguely troubled by it. 'You're sure you're comfortable?'

'I'm as comfortable as the situation allows.' Sarah stopped pacing, turned and faced Amy.

'Amy, I'm… oh, God, how do I do this?' she said, her voice shaking. 'It's not covered in any of the books of etiquette that Mother used to delight in giving me.'

'Whatever's wrong?' Amy asked, concerned at the sight of Sarah's troubled face. 'What is it you want to do?'

'I...' Sarah crossed rapidly to Amy and sat on the floor at her feet. Amy thought with relief of the good sweeping she had given the floor the previous day. 'I want to return something to you. Something I think you must have lost a long time ago.'

Sarah twisted away and reached under her collar to undo a fine, gold chain, then slipped her hand down the front of her bodice and took hold of the chain, still facing away from Amy.

She turned back to Amy with something clutched in her hand. 'I wore this on a velvet ribbon for years, but the velvet got so worn that I was afraid I'd lose it. I still have the ribbon at home. This is yours, Amy.'

She stretched out her hand, and Amy automatically held out her own to take it. Something small but surprisingly heavy slipped onto her palm. Amy stared down at a gold brooch in the shape of the letter 'A'.

For a moment she gazed at the brooch in confusion, wondering why it looked so familiar. Then memory leapt the twenty-one years since she had last seen this brooch lying in her hand. A tiny, dark-haired baby had been nuzzling at her breast, and Amy had held out the brooch to the woman who was to take her daughter away.

Amy's heart gave a great, convulsive leap as it started beating again. The brooch was threatening to slip from her hand; she clenched her fingers over it so tightly that she felt the edges dig into her palm.

'Ann,' she whispered. 'You're Ann.' She stared at the face so close to hers and wondered how she could not have known before.

'Yes,' Sarah said, her voice barely audible. 'I hope I'm not too much of a disappointment.'

'You're... you're perfect.'

'Oh, no I'm not.'

'You *are*,' Amy insisted. 'You're just what I've longed and longed for you to be. Look at you! You're pretty, and you're clever, and you've had all sorts of education. You can do anything you want to, and you've got a beautiful house and lovely things. Everything I wanted for you and I knew I'd never be able to give you. That's why I gave you away, Ann... Sarah. But...' She shook her head in a futile attempt to stop it spinning. 'But how...?' So many questions were tumbling over themselves that she could not think how to start asking any of them.

Sarah smiled at her. 'Unlike you, I haven't just had a rather dramatic shock. Sit quietly and drink your tea, and I'll tell you the whole story as well as I'm able.'

She took her own chair and settled her hands in her lap. 'Shall I start with how I found you? Or do you want me to go further back?'

'Can you start with when you were a baby?' Amy said faintly, her mind still reeling from the effort of trying to match the tiny baby with the assured young woman who sat beside her.

Sarah gave a little laugh. 'I can't remember quite that far back, but I'll do my best.

'I think I was about six years old when I first found out that you existed. I remember coming home one day absolutely beside myself because a child at school had told me that Mother wasn't really my mother. Of course I blurted it all out to her, full of righteous indignation, and expecting her to tell me what a lie it was.'

'What did she tell you?' Amy whispered.

'She did it very nicely. She sat me on her lap and said of course she was my mother.

'But I'd had another mother first, she told me. When I was very small another lady was my mother. But while I was still a little baby my first mother got very sick, and she knew she wouldn't be able to look after me properly. So she went to see a lady who looked after children, and she asked the lady to find me a new mother.

'This lady knew that Mother and Father wanted a little girl exactly like me, so when my first mother died she gave me to them to look after.'

'But I didn't…'

'No, I'm very aware of that. It made it easier for Mother to explain it in that way, I suppose. And it satisfied me at the time. She gave me the brooch and the ribbon that day, too—she told me they'd belonged to my first mother. And she told me your name had been Amy. I was allowed to wear the brooch sometimes as a special treat, but most of the time Mother kept it tucked away safely.'

Amy became aware of the brooch still clutched in her hand. 'It's yours, Sarah. It belongs to you.'

'You're quite sure?'

'Yes. I wanted you to have it, and I still do. It was the only thing I had to give you.' She put the brooch in Sarah's hand and closed her fingers over it. The storm of emotions that had buffeted her since Sarah's revelation abruptly overwhelmed her. She buried her face in her hands and sobbed.

Sarah put an arm around her shoulders. 'You gave me a wonderful home.'

'That's what I wanted,' Amy said through her sobs. 'I wanted to keep you, too. It nearly killed me to give you away.'

She fumbled at her sleeve for a handkerchief, failed to find one and sniffed noisily.

'Have mine,' Sarah said, pushing a lace-edged handkerchief into Amy's hand.

Amy blew her nose and felt a little recovered. 'But your name doesn't begin with A. Not the name they gave you.'

'I still have the names you gave me. Sarah Ann Elizabeth, my name is. That's what I was baptised as. Quite a mouthful, isn't it? I nearly had Amy tacked on the end of it, Mother told me much later, but Father drew the line at that. He said sentiment was all very well, but I'd never learn four names off by heart.' She smiled fondly at the memory. ' "My silly, sentimental Helen," he used to call Mother. "And of course I wouldn't have you any other way." '

'They must have been very kind.'

'The kindest parents one could wish for a child. Mother meant her little deception kindly, but she must have regretted not having been quite honest fairly soon. She was hearing me my prayers that evening, and I'd got up to "God bless Maurice in Heaven"—he was my brother, he died when I was only three.'

'I'm sorry,' Amy said quietly.

'Oh, I hardly remember him. He was a great big boy of thirteen, and he was at school in the daytime, so I don't think I can have seen much of him. I remember wearing a black arm band for a long time, and Mother cried a lot at first and she never wore bright colours again, but I forgot him quite quickly. He was the only child Mother and Father ever had of their own.

'Well, as I say, I did my "God bless Maurice in Heaven", and then I said to Mother, "Shouldn't I say 'God bless Mama in Heaven', too?" Goodness knows how she felt when I said that, but she could hardly say no. So for years and years I prayed for you every night.'

'I did for you, too,' Amy whispered.

'Not as if I was dead, I hope. Mother's story satisfied me for years. Then when I was thirteen... well, I went through a dreadful stage. Mother could do nothing right. I used to argue with her more or less on principle. Were you ever like that?'

'I don't know,' Amy said. 'I suppose... well, I was twelve when Granny died, so I'd been busy looking after her when she was sick, then I had Pa and the boys to do for. And I was helping at the school for a while, too. I didn't really have time to fall out with people. I was nearly thirteen when Susannah came, though, I used to have lots of rows with her.'

'Looking back, I don't think Mother was usually at fault. Having met you both, I doubt if I could say the same of Mrs Leith. Well, one day I'd been arguing with Mother about… oh, I don't even know what it was about. Something ridiculous. I got myself worked up into quite a state, and I suddenly flung at her, "You never understand what I want. I wish my real mother hadn't died." '

'The poor woman!' Amy said, shocked.

'Yes. I don't tell the story with any pride in my own actions. Mother went quite white, and she left the room without saying a word. We hardly spoke to each other the rest of the day—I was far too stubborn to apologise, though I knew I shouldn't have said such a thing. But that evening, when I'd gone up to my room, Mother came in and sat on the edge of the bed, very stiff and quite unlike herself.

' "I'm only going to speak of this once," she told me. "Your mother didn't die." I was too stunned to say a word, I think I just lay there and gaped at her like an idiot.

' "She was a very young girl, not much older than you are now, and she'd been dreadfully wronged by a man. She couldn't look after a child on her own, so she gave you up to me.

' "I've always been grateful to that little girl," she said. Then she leaned down and gave me a kiss.' Amy saw that Sarah's eyes were brimming with tears. 'That tells you a good deal about Mother. I'd been hideous to her that day, and she could still treat me so.'

'I wanted you to have a mother like that,' Amy said through her own tears. 'I wanted people who'd be kind to you.'

'I never raised the subject with her again, and I'd like to think I was less horrid to her from then on. I suppose I'd begun to grow up at last.

'But I didn't stop thinking about you, and wondering what you were like. When Father died I was helping Mother go through his papers, and I came across my birth certificate. I hid it away from Mother, but I used to pull it out and study it. Your name on my certificate, the names you gave me, and your brooch. That was all I had of you.'

'Your birth certificate?' Amy abruptly realised the implication. 'It had a blank where your father's name should have been, didn't it? It looked as though I didn't even know who he was. That's not true,' she said urgently. 'I did know who he was.'

'I know,' said Sarah. 'Even if I'd wondered before, I'd be sure of it now that I know you.'

'But didn't you hate me when you saw that big blank space?' Amy asked, almost fearful of the answer. 'I was always frightened you'd hate me.'

Sarah shook her head. 'Remember how Mother had spoken of you.

Thanks to her, I always thought of you as a poor, frightened little girl. How could I hate you?

'I didn't start searching for you till after Mother died. It wouldn't have felt right to, I think she'd have been hurt if I had. When I did start, I was surprised at how easy it was. I had your name, and your age, from my birth certificate. So I sent away for yours.' She smiled at Amy. 'That's when I found out you'd given me your mother's name.

'I had to look up Ruatane on a map. But there was something about the name that rang a bell. Then I was going through Mother's old address book one day, and I found Lily's address.'

She laughed at the memory. 'There it was, staring up at me from the page. "Mrs William Leith (née Lily Radford), Ruatane." What could I do but take that as a sign that fate was on my side? There was my cousin Lily—and of course she has turned out to be a sort of cousin after all, although we're not related by blood—in the town that I was looking for, and what's more having married into your family. I had to assume that all Leiths in a place the size of Ruatane were likely to be related.

'Of course I had to follow things through after a sign like that. I only remembered Lily vaguely, she's so much older than I am, but I was prepared to impose on the relationship. It was easy enough to get a position at the school, they always struggle to find enough teachers in these country areas.

'Getting here was the easy part. Then I had to find out which of the horde of women Lily seemed to be related to was you, and then… well, that was hardest of all. Then I had to find out how to tell you. I soon realised that it wouldn't be easy while *he* was alive, and I certainly didn't want to get you into trouble. And somehow there was never the right moment.' She smiled wryly. 'The right moment. It's taken me till now to find it.'

Amy stared at her, hardly daring to believe it all. 'I wish you could have met Pa.'

'Really? I might have had trouble being polite to him. After all, he made you give me up.'

'No, it wasn't like that. Pa was always kind to me. He only wanted the best for me.'

'The best! Marrying that brute of a man! To think of you, buffeted about like that. Packed off to such a man. Oh, the injustice of it! A woman like you.'

'I'm not a saint, Sarah,' Amy said, uneasy at such praise. 'Don't make me out to be one.'

'You're a martyr, then. A martyr to other people's ideas of propriety.'

Amy shook her head in confusion. 'I was trying to make up for things. I gave you away, and I married Charlie. It was to make things right for everyone. To make up for the wrong things I'd done.'

She hesitated, then asked the question to which she dreaded the answer. 'Do you want to know who your father was?'

'Do you want to tell me?'

'No,' Amy admitted. 'But... but if you ask me, I think I've got to tell you. You've the right to know.'

'I'm not going to ask. Oh, I won't pretend I don't have a little normal human curiosity about who he was. He must have been tall, I do know that,' she said, smiling at her tiny mother. 'But... how shall I put this? For one thing, he obviously took little enough interest in my existence, since you had to give me up, so I try to repay his indifference. And for another, I've never in any way felt the lack of a father.

'Mother was a lovely, lovely woman and I loved her dearly. But we struggled to make sense of one another, and not with any great success. She couldn't understand why I had such a passion for learning, and even less this desire of mine to become a teacher. "But there's no need, Sarah," she'd say. "Your father's provided for your future, you don't need to think of such things." But it wasn't enough for me to sit around the house counting my blessings and arranging flowers, or spending my evenings at fashionable parties. I had to *do* things, I had to *try* things. I wanted the world to be bigger than that. Do you understand what I mean?' she asked, a plea in her face.

'Yes,' Amy whispered. 'Oh, yes.'

'Father did understand. Not about my wanting to be a teacher, but about wanting to learn. I don't think Father took much notice of me when I was tiny. He got me for Mother as a sort of toy—I don't mean that to sound nasty, but he knew she longed for a little girl, so he got me for her.

'I think it must have come as a terrible blow to him when Maurice died. It took him some time to realise that the little creature with all those silly ribbons and laces and curls was actually a human being, with some sort of brain. But I adored him, always, and I was always begging to go with him when he went out.'

She smiled at the memory. 'He did used to take me about with him, too. Even to business meetings sometimes, when they weren't particularly formal. Goodness knows what those other men thought. I remember every now and then Mother would say, "Couldn't you spend a little time with me this morning, Sarah?" And of course I'd stay home that day, and for a few days there'd be no outings with Father. Only for a few days, though.

'Father didn't pay much attention to my education at first. He was quite happy for me to go to the genteel little school Mother chose for me, run—I'm sorry, *conducted*—by an elderly gentlewoman of reduced means. I learned to read and write, and how to do acceptable embroidery—though I was always too impatient to be very good at needlework—but very little else.

'When I finished there, Mother arranged for me to go to one of those ridiculous schools for young ladies. The sort that turns out girls who excel in a particular type of silliness. I put up with it for one dreadful year. Then I made such a fuss about not wanting to go back, and Father knew that I had a few brains despite the best efforts of the elderly gentlewoman and the teachers at the school for young ladies, so he insisted that I go to a real school.

'It was a girl's school, but it actually aimed to educate its pupils. Mother was shocked by the whole idea, especially when she found that I'd be expected to take examinations there, but I was terribly pleased with myself.'

Sarah smiled wryly. 'My pride took a well-deserved fall when I found that, thanks to the year at the elegant school, I wasn't up to the academic level of most of the other girls, especially in mathematics. So Father got me a tutor, and that shocked Mother even more. A *male* tutor! Mother used to sit in the room with us all the time the tutor was there, stitching away at her embroidery and watching us disapprovingly.

'I did catch up. Actually, I did quite well, and Father seemed delighted. When I was old enough to discuss such things sensibly, he explained that he wanted me to be able to look after my business interests properly. By the time I was fifteen, Father's heart had begun to give him trouble, and he knew he might not be there to see me into adulthood.

'We discussed the issue quite rationally, considering how much I hated the idea of losing him. He did suggest marriage to a sensible man—I'm not sure if he had anyone in particular in mind—but I left him in no doubt as to my feelings on that score. He said that if I didn't want a husband found for me, then a decent education was the alternative. That way I could look after my own interests, and I'd be less likely to fall into the clutches of a scoundrel. Father did make me promise him that I'd never marry a fool or a scoundrel, no matter how pretty a face he had. It hasn't been a difficult promise to keep.

'Mother was shocked at how long my education went on. She used to get quite distressed about it, especially when she'd been taking tea with some of her more foolish friends. She said I'd strain my brain, and

493

become ill with it.' Sarah shook her head, smiling. 'I don't think I did.'

'You're perfect,' Amy whispered. 'Just perfect.' She held out her arms, and Sarah slipped into them.

Much later, Sarah raised her head from Amy's lap.

'I'm going to leave now,' she said softly.

'No!' Amy clung convulsively to her.

'Yes, I am.' She disentangled herself from Amy's embrace and stood up. 'I've given you a lot to think about, and I want you to have some peace to take it all in.'

'Will you come back?'

'Oh, yes.' Sarah smiled. 'You'll have trouble keeping me away from now on.'

She looked down at Amy, her brow creased in thought. 'I'm not sure what to call you. I can't bear to say "Mrs Stewart" any longer, though I suppose I'll have to in front of other people. May I call you Amy when it's just the two of us?'

'If you want.'

'I don't think I can call you Mother, you see. That's what I called Mother, and it somehow belongs to her.'

'Of course,' Amy said gravely. 'It wouldn't be right.' *Say it*, she cried out silently.

'Mother must have been older than you are now when I was born, I think. I only remember her with grey hair. You're too young to be called Mother.'

She smiled down at Amy. 'I wonder…' she said, her head tilted to one side. 'Yes, that seems right. For special times like today, at least.' Her smile broadened as she knelt down to Amy again. 'Mama,' she said softly.

It took some time for Sarah to disengage from the fresh embrace, but she managed at last. 'You'll have Dave coming home if we don't get a move on, and I want you to have some time to yourself before then. I really must go.'

Amy was still clinging to her arm as Sarah was about to mount the horse. 'I never said goodbye to you, Ann,' she whispered.

Sarah smiled and kissed her again. 'Now you're never going to have to.'

Amy wandered aimlessly around the garden in front of the cottage, the sliver of moon barely giving enough light for her to make out the shapes of the trees. She ran her hands over their rough trunks and seemed to feel the life throbbing through them.

The night was mild, and the darkness seemed full of soft voices. Night birds were calling from the bush. Amy wondered how she could ever have thought the low hooting of a morepork had a mournful sound. There were spirits out there in the gentle darkness; the easy spirits of those she had loved and who had loved her. Even some benign vestige of Charlie might be there, reluctant to abandon his precious land. Amy felt warmed through to the centre of her being.

'Thank you,' she whispered to the warm night and to the heavens above it.

A light appeared on the verandah, startlingly bright to her dark-adjusted eyes.

'Ma? Are you out there?'

'Yes, Dave, I'm here,' she called back.

David closed the door on the light streaming from the parlour and came down the steps, finding Amy by the direction of her voice. 'Are you all right, Ma? What are you doing wandering around in the dark?'

'I'm just enjoying the night and the stars and everything. Isn't it lovely tonight? Did you ever see such stars? I'd forgotten how beautiful they can be.'

She saw his mouth curve into a grin. He put an arm around her. 'You're a funny little thing sometimes, you know, Ma.'

Amy gazed up at him. 'How did I ever come to have such tall children?'

David's body felt delicious against hers as he shrugged. 'Tall father, I suppose.' He looked down at Amy, frowning slightly. 'Are you sure you're all right? I mean, coming out here in the dark by yourself and everything. You've been funny all evening, come to that. You're not upset about anything?'

'Upset?' Amy laughed aloud in sheer delight. She stood on tiptoe to fling her arms around his neck and kiss him. 'Davie,' she said as she released his lips, 'what on earth have I got to be unhappy about?'

Author's Note

The Waituhi Valley and Ruatane will not be found on any map of the Bay of Plenty. They are my own inventions, though their descriptions are coloured by places that were familiar to me in childhood. The characters and their stories are likewise my own creation; any resemblance to real people is coincidental.

The broader setting of *Promises to Keep*, however, is the real New Zealand of the period. Events referred to are actual, historical ones; from such major events as the Tarawera eruption, the baby farming scandal and the extension of the suffrage to women through to relatively local events such as the great Bay of Plenty floods of 1892.

I have attempted to be true to the period covered. The coastal steamers named, for instance, are among the ships that served the Bay of Plenty during those years, and the details of family life and farm work are as authentic as I could make them.

An area where I have compromised between strict historical accuracy and avoiding confusion for the reader is in the size of families. The average family size during the period of the book was six surviving children, so Frank and Lizzie's eight would have been respectable rather than remarkable. An affectionate couple like Arthur and Edie would be more likely to have had six or seven children than their four. But families of this size for all the families in Amy's generation would have led to a plethora of names and frustration for the reader. For the same reason, I have minimised the naming of children after parents and grandparents that the Victorians so delighted in.

The almost total absence of Maori from the book may puzzle some readers. During the period covered by this work, Maori and Pakeha were comparatively isolated from each other; certainly in parts of the Bay of Plenty, where large tracts of land had been confiscated so recently, Maori and Pakeha typically did not worship together, nor were their children educated together. Seeing a Maori would have been no novelty for Amy; exchanging more than a word or two with one certainly would.

The ease with which Sarah was able to access her own original birth certificate and to trace Amy might surprise New Zealanders brought up during the period of closed adoptions. Such strict secrecy about adoptions is, in fact, quite a modern phenomenon, dating from 1955. Even the policy of issuing new birth certificates for adopted children, carrying the names of the adoptive parents instead of the birth parents, did not begin until 1915.

Several Maori words appear, mostly as placenames and names of plants. For readers interested in the correct pronunciation of these words, a pronunciation guide can be found at:

www.maori.org.nz/kotereo/

My heartfelt thanks go to my husband for his never-failing support and encouragement during the long process of writing this novel. He was my inspiration for the very finest aspects of Frank's character.

Shayne Parkinson

Printed in Great Britain
by Amazon